W9-CXL-752

THE NOSY NEIGHBOR

Also by Fern Michaels

Pretty Woman
Family Blessings
The Real Deal
Crown Jewel
Trading Places
Late Bloomer
No Place Like Home
The Delta Ladies
Wild Honey

FERN MICHAELS

THE NOSY NEIGHBOR

DOUBLEDAY LARGE PRINT HOME LIBRARY EDITION

POCKET BOOKS

New York   London   Toronto   Sydney

This Large Print Edition, prepared especially for Doubleday Large Print Home Library, contains the complete, unabridged text of the original Publisher's Edition.

An *Original* Publication of POCKET BOOKS

 POCKET BOOKS, a division of Simon & Schuster, Inc.
1230 Avenue of the Americas, New York, NY 10020

ISBN: 0-7394-5499-4

Front cover illustration by Alan Ayers

Manufactured in the United States of America

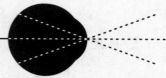

This Large Print Book carries the
Seal of Approval of N.A.V.H.

THE NOSY NEIGHBOR

Prologue

Lucy Baker stared across the room at the twelve empty jury seats. She wanted to scream with frustration. What was taking them so long? The judge said the jury had signaled they had a verdict, but that was forty-five minutes ago. She dropped her hand to her side and crossed her fingers. *Please, God, let the verdict be guilty. Please, please, please.*

She tugged at the hem of her skirt. Lucy's brother Steven—sitting second chair on this case—leaned over and smiled confidently. His expression clearly said, don't sweat it, our client is going to walk out of this courtroom a free man. We did our job, and our bank account is now five hundred thousand dollars more robust.

Her brother was right—Justin Riley was going to walk because she had put up a superb defense. Unparalleled and unequaled, according to the press. That same press had followed her career and dubbed her Lucky Lucy along the way. What it all meant was she'd never lost a case. Yet. A guilty verdict was wishful thinking on her part. Nonetheless, she started to pray, saying the words she'd learned so long ago in catechism class and now had all but forgotten. Today, for some reason, she feared that God wasn't listening to her heartfelt plea. Why was that?

She felt rather than saw her client jerk to attention. Her brother followed suit. The judge was about to enter the courtroom.

The bailiff walked to the front of the judge's high desk and said, "All rise. The Honorable Sidney Blake presiding."

A hush fell over the courtroom but not before someone coughed. Papers rattled, feet shuffled on the hard wooden floor. Someone else cleared their throat as the jury filed in and took the same seats they'd sat in for the past three weeks.

The judge banged his gavel. Lucy sat up straighter in her chair. This was the moment when her blood always ran cold.

The moment.

The judge turned to face the jury. "Ladies

and gentlemen of the jury, have you reached a verdict?"

"We have, Your Honor." The foreman of the jury, a retired schoolteacher named Abner Scribner, stood and handed a folded sheet of paper to the bailiff, who in turn handed it to the judge. Lucy watched as the judge unfolded the sheet of paper, read the contents, and folded the paper to return it to the bailiff, who then passed it back to Abner Scribner.

"Will the defendant please rise."

Justin Riley rose to his full six-foot-four-inch height. He was trembling. The thought pleased Lucy. Lucy stood, then moved to the side to take her place alongside her client, with Steven on his opposite side. *Please, God, let this scumbag be found guilty. Please, please, please.*

Abner Scribner cleared his throat and focused his attention on Justin Riley. "We find the defendant, Justin Riley . . . not guilty."

The courtroom erupted in joyous outcries. Justin's courtroom fan club, his parents, the media, his brothers and sisters, all shouted with glee. Lucy felt herself being squeezed, then pummeled on her arms by Justin's fists. Thank God it was Steven who was hugging her. "I have to get out of here!" she hissed into her brother's ear. "Now!"

"But—"

"You deal with the press," she interrupted, not wanting to hear anything he had to say. "I'm going to the office, then I'm going home. I never want to see Justin Riley again as long as I live, and no, I am not going to any celebratory gathering, so don't even ask."

Lucy motioned to the bailiff, and whispered, "Can you get me out of here and to my car before they attack me?" The bailiff, an older, kindly gentleman, smiled and nodded. Lucy tugged at the jacket of her charcoal gray Armani suit, knowing hundreds of eyes were following her exit.

Lucy faltered once when she heard Lorraine Sumpter, the victim's grandmother, shout, "I hope you rot in hell, Lucy Baker!" Lucy didn't look back. There was no need. She could see Annie Sumpter's grandmother behind closed eyes. She even dreamed about the little old lady. Now, she would probably have nightmares about Annie's grandmother.

It was six-thirty when Lucy rode the elevator to her suite of offices on the eighteenth floor. The lighting in the hallway was dim. Like she cared. She fit the key into the lock, opened the door, and walked inside. One long arm reached out to shove the dead bolt home. She dropped her briefcase on the floor. Angrily, she kicked it across the reception area before she slid out of her shoes. Her shoulders slumped as she walked down the long hallway to her private office. There, with the door closed, she could cry. She could scream and yell and vent to her heart's content. If she wanted to. *To what end?* she asked herself.

Lucy sat down in her ergonomic chair, which was surprisingly comfortable, and looked around at the luxurious office. Everything was tony, high-end, and shrieked of billable hours. That was what the law was all about—billable hours.

Lucy was off the chair a moment later, padding through the meadow of sea-green carpeting that hugged her ankles, to the minifridge, where she withdrew a bottle of wine. She carried it and a Baccarat wineglass reserved for clients back to her desk. It took her a full five minutes to work the corkscrew. She poured till the wine sloshed over onto her desk. Two gulps, and it was gone. She poured again. Two more gulps. Her eyes teared up when she poured the third glass. Big mistake. She hadn't eaten today because she'd been a basket case, knowing the verdict was coming in.

"I can't do this anymore."

"I don't *want* to do this anymore."

Tears rolled down her cheeks as the telephone console on her desk lit up, every line, including her private line, blinking. *They can blink from now till the end of time, for all I care.*

Lucy brought the wineglass to her lips and sipped. Tears kept running down her cheeks. Bitter tears of victory. She blinked away her tears to see her brother standing in the doorway, a look of something she couldn't define in his expression. Wariness, fear, anger? Whatever it was, she didn't care about that either.

Steven's voice sounded jittery when he asked, "Are you all right?"

Lucy eyed her handsome brother and was reminded of Justin Riley. They were both tall, preppy, handsome, the type of man women drooled over. Both of them knew how to take advantage of that particular characteristic. She continued to watch

as Steven shuffled his feet. He didn't, however, cross the threshold. No one ever entered Lucy's private office unless invited.

"Do I look like I'm all right, Steven?" Even
she was surprised at how slurred her words
sounded.

"You look . . . drunk."

"That's because I *am* drunk. If I'm drunk,
I have to look like I'm drunk." To prove her
point, she reached for the bottle and upended it.

"I think you've had enough, Lucy. Come
on, I'll drive you home."

Lucy looked around the office again. She
had to squint to bring the room into focus.
The rich mahogany paneling, the custom-
made cherrywood desk, the wine-colored
Naugahyde furniture, the custom book-
shelves with the leather-bound law books,
the thick carpeting, the lavish drapes, all
courtesy of billable hours. "I don't want to
do this anymore, Steven."

"You always say that after a verdict, Lucy.
Go home and sleep it off. Things will look
different tomorrow." His voice was pleading—he was worried. Yes, his sister always
said she wanted to quit practicing law after
a verdict, but she had never gotten drunk

after a verdict. Even he knew that this time was different. He wished he had the guts to step into her office.

"It wasn't till closing arguments that I knew that bastard was guilty. Afterward I accused him of being guilty, and do you know what he said, Steven?"

"No. What did he say, Lucy?" Steven asked, knowing he wasn't going to like the answer.

"He didn't answer. He laughed at me instead. His eyes said it all. The State's case was circumstantial. Justin Riley is a pedophile and a murderer. I don't care how good-looking, or how preppy he and his rich, influential family are. He is what he is. And I got him off. Me and you. Do you hear me, Steven? We sold ourselves to the Rileys for five hundred thousand dollars. And you know what else? The Rileys paid us in full— their account is current."

"The jury said he was innocent," Steven reminded her. "We did our jobs. We gave him the best defense possible, and we got lucky. That's what defense lawyers do. The law says justice was served. Mr. Riley Senior said he's giving us a bonus of a hundred thousand. That's not shabby, Lucy. We followed the letter of the law. We did what we were hired to do."

"Steven, read my lips. The guy killed that little girl. I know it, and you know it. He is now walking free to do it again because we did such a damn good job. I haven't been able to sleep since he laughed at me. I can barely eat. I wasn't absolutely sure until that precise moment. I saw it in his eyes. Do you want to know something else? His sister and his mother believe he did it, too. His sister Sally told me the things he used to do to her when she was little. And to her little friends. Don't take that bonus. That's an order, Steven."

"All right, Lucy, I won't take the bonus. But it's a mistake not to take it because we earned every damn dime of it."

Lucy brushed at her hair to get the spiky bangs off her forehead. Fashionable hairdo or not, it was annoying her. She couldn't remember the last time she had been so tired, so drunk. She slugged from the bottle, and, when nothing came out, she said, "Ooops, gotta get another bottle. Don't even think about telling me I can't, Steven. Go home. I'm going to sleep here on the sofa tonight. I have a lot of thinking to do."

"You can't possibly think with your snoot in a bottle. Come on, Lucy, let me take you home. We can get some coffee and talk all night if you like." Home was a brownstone on East Forty-ninth Street that he and Lucy had inherited from their parents. The bottom floor was rented out to two doctors for enough money to pay the taxes and utility bills. Lucy lived on the second floor, Steven on the third. It worked for all concerned.

"I'm talked out, little brother. Didn't you hear what I said? I don't want to do this anymore. I've had it with the criminal justice system. I need to get a life. I'm sick and tired of working ninety hours a week so some jerk can go out there and mutilate a little girl because of some sick—Go home, Steven, and leave me alone."

"They're just about ready to announce your appointment to the bench. Are you giving that up, too?" Steven asked uneasily.

Lucy yanked at the cork, and both cork and corkscrew flew across the room. "Wow, did you see *that*? The answer is yes. I told you to go home."

"All right, I'm going."

" 'Night, Steven!" she bellowed.

When she finally managed to weave her

way back to the ergonomic desk chair, Lucy could see that the telephone console was still lit up. The blinking red light indicated there was voice mail on her private line. Only four people had her private number. Steven, the mayor, her housekeeper, and Jonathan St. Clair. She pressed the button to hear the message.

"Lucy, it's Jon. I just flew in this afternoon and heard about the verdict on the news. I was calling to invite you to dinner, but I guess you're out with your colleagues celebrating. Congratulations. They said you were the best of the best, honey." His carefully modulated voice turned intimate, and Lucy had to strain to hear the words. "I could have told them how really wonderful you are, but they didn't ask me. I'll call you in the morning. Sweet dreams, my darling."

Lucy eyed the newly opened wine bottle with a jaundiced eye. Did she really want to drink more wine? Of course she did. She tilted the bottle and watched the wine splash into the glass and over her desk. She sat down and propped her feet on the desk.

Jonathan. Jonathan with the infectious smile and crinkly eyes. Jonathan with the wicked sense of humor. Jonathan the consummate lover. She'd known Jonathan for a year, having met him on the tennis court at the City Raquet Club. One thing had led to another, and they'd ended up a couple. She thought she loved him. He said he loved her. Sometimes she found that hard to believe. She flipped the pages of her day planner to confirm what she already knew. In the year she'd known him, she'd been with Jonathan a total of twenty-two times. Either she was tied up in a court case or he was traveling on business. There had been one, wild, delicious four-day weekend where they'd both professed their love. Then she hadn't seen him for a solid month. Phone calls and e-mails were not the most satisfying kind of interpersonal communication for a woman going on thirty-eight whose biological clock was ticking. And yet their relationship worked for both of them.

Lucy slurped from the wineglass. She felt like crying all over again because she knew she was drunk and had just missed out on spending an evening with the man she adored. Talk about stupid, bad luck. Hers was running at an all-time high. As she made her way to the couch, wineglass in hand, she couldn't help but wonder if her parents were spinning in their graves over her decision to abandon the practice of law.

Both her parents had been attorneys. Her mother had been in family law, her father in corporate law. They'd built the firm. Then, nine years after her mother died, her father had retired to roam the world and she and Steven had taken over. At the height of his retirement while he was exploring the Amazon, he'd contracted a jungle disease she couldn't even pronounce and died within two weeks. Baker, Baker, Wong, and Lickenstein was one of the most prestigious firms in the city. There never had been a Wong or a Lickenstein. Her father had thought it was more impressive to have four names on their letterhead when he started the firm. Lucy couldn't ever remember a client asking for Wong or Lickenstein. What she did know for sure was that with her and Steven at the helm, the firm had one of the best criminal practices going.

Lucy moved over to the couch and plopped down. In the morning she was going to have the Queen Mother of all hangovers. She reached for the pillow one of her first clients had crocheted for her. It was tacky, with its gaudy colors and equally tacky fringe hanging from the corners, but she loved it. A moment later she was sound asleep.

1

Six Months Later

Lucy Baker shoved her tennis racquet into its case, waved to her tennis partner, and proceeded to jog across the high school field to the track where she would run her daily five miles. A roll of thunder caused her to pick up her feet and sprint. When she reached the track, she tossed her canvas bag onto the bleachers and took off running.

Tennis, and a five-mile run every day regardless of the weather, had became a routine for her in the six months since she'd stopped practicing law.

Lucy kept one eye on the threatening thunderclouds overhead and the other on the track. She picked up her speed, not wanting to get caught in a thunderstorm. Off in the distance she could hear hard, rolling thunder, which seemed to be getting closer. One more lap to go. If she pushed it into high gear, she could pass the other runners, who looked like they were dragging. It was always this way on the last lap, she thought smugly.

She loved passing the muscle boys, shouting out words of encouragement. They were slugs compared to her. In all fairness, not that they needed to know, she'd run track in high school as well as college. She'd hurdled, too. Best on her team. She had the medals to prove it. Of course, they were locked away in one of her trunks. One didn't show off medals. At least *she* didn't. It was enough for her that she'd earned them, had them, and could look at them anytime she wanted to. Sometimes she needed to remind herself that at one time she'd been the best of the best.

Her coaches had said she was good enough to go to the Olympics. She had thought so, too. But life got in the way, and she'd had to bow out. She didn't have any regrets. Taking care of her mother during the last two years of her life had been more important than bringing home the gold.

Lucy whizzed past the bleachers at the south end of the track. She couldn't help but notice two men in dark suits, their arms crossed over their chests. She wondered which one of the guys on the track they were waiting for.

Sweat dripped down Lucy's face, soaking the tank top she was wearing. Her muscular arms glistened. She was hurting. She'd pushed too hard, too fast on her last lap. "No pain, no gain," she muttered over and over as she flew down the track. She saw the bleachers beckoning her. For one wild moment she thought she was at the wrong end of the track when she saw the two men approaching the north side bleachers. They must have run at her own speed to get there at the exact moment she came to a stop, bent over, with the palms of her sweaty hands on her knees as she took deep breaths. They looked as if they were in great physical shape under their dark suits. She wondered again who they were waiting for.

When her breathing was almost normal, she walked over to the end of the bleachers away from the men and did leg stretches. Out of the corner of her eye, she could see them approaching her. Lucy looked around to see if anyone was paying attention. Her heart kicked up a beat. This was suburbia, nothing happened in suburbia.

Lucy was about to reach up to the second row of seats for her gym bag when one of the men handed it to her. "Lucy Baker?"

"Yes. I'm Lucy Baker." She waited. They could have passed for twins. Frick and Frack. Yin and Yang.

"Special Agent Harry Conover. This is my partner, Larry Smith."

"What does that mean? Special agents of what?" She could feel an itch settle between her shoulder blades.

"We're from the Federal Bureau of Investigation." Two badges were suddenly shoved under her nose. Lucy backed up a half step and reached for the men's credentials. She read them carefully before she handed them back. She waited, her heart thumping inside her chest.

"We'd like to talk to you for a minute."

Lucy looked up at the darkening sky. She could still hear the thunder, now directly overhead. It sounded more ominous for some reason. "Why? I haven't done anything wrong. I pay my taxes on time and never cheat. I never even got a parking ticket. It's going to pour in another minute. Like I said, why?"

"We could sit in our car and talk."

Lucy snorted. "I-don't-think-so!" No sooner were the words out of her mouth than the sky opened up. Within seconds she was soaked to the skin. "As you can see, I'm already drenched. If you want to get those nice suits all wet, oh, well," she said with false bravado. Why did the FBI want to talk to her?

The agent named Harry said, "We'd like to talk to you about your fiancé."

Lucy gaped at the two men. "Jonathan? Why? Oh, God, did something happen to him?"

"Not yet," Larry said. "We'd like you to tell us about your relationship with Mr. St. Clair."

Lucy relaxed. The rain was coming down harder. Before long it would be like a waterfall. "I'm going to marry him. We're engaged." She waved her ring finger to show off her three-carat diamond.

"We already know you're getting married next year, on Valentine's Day. You have your gown. Let's see, you purchased it at Bethany's Bridal Shoppe. They're doing the alterations as we speak. The invitations have been ordered. You're holding the reception at the Ritz-Carlton. I believe there are 250 guests expected. Dinner is a choice of lobster or filet mignon. The salad is an arugula medley. Vegetables are baby carrots, peas from the Emerald Isle, potato-apple fritters, and flaky croissants. Dessert is wedding cake. Cristal champagne will flow endlessly," Agent Smith said, his expression as flat as his tone.

Lucy didn't like what she was hearing. There was nothing like an FBI check to put the fear of God into a person. There was shock as well as fear in her eyes as she backed up one step, then another. They followed her.

"A pretty pricey wedding for a girl who graduated at the top of her law school class, quit a thriving criminal law practice, and now makes popcorn balls and sells them through a catalog."

Well, they had one thing wrong. She wasn't the one who made or sold the popcorn balls. Lucy eyeballed the two agents. "I make an honest living, and I pay my taxes. Listen, I have to go home. It was nice talking with you gentlemen. If you want to talk to Jonathan, call him or go to his apartment. He doesn't leave for work till around nine-thirty when he's in town." She knew for a fact that Jonathan wasn't in town. Let them spin their wheels.

The agent named Larry wiped the rain from his forehead. "If we wanted to talk to Mr. St. Clair, we would have gone to see him. We know his habits as well as we know yours. Agent Conover and I would like to talk to you."

"What do you want to talk about? If it's about Jonathan's business, I'm afraid I can't help you. I don't know anything about it."

It was raining harder now. Since she was already soaked clear through to her skin, what did it matter? "Furthermore, I don't have to talk to you. The last time I checked, this was still a free country. Now, if you'll excuse me, I have to go home."

"Miss Baker." It was Agent Conover talking now. "It's imperative you not tell Mr. St. Clair about our meeting this morning. By the way, Jonathan St. Clair is not your fiancé's real name."

Lucy whirled around. "What are you talking about? Of course it's his real name. Jonathan is Jonathan. You must have him mixed up with someone else." Overhead, thunder boomed, followed by a streak of jagged lightning ripping across the gray sky.

"If you talk to your fiancé, it will jeopardize the case we're working on. We can take you into custody if we want to. In order to avoid that, we're asking you to cooperate with us."

Take me into custody. Jonathan isn't Jonathan. I'm having a nightmare, and I'll wake up any second now. She pinched herself. She felt the pain.

"All right, I won't say anything to Jonathan. Now can I go?"

"We'll know if you break your promise, Miss Baker. Do you know what obstructing justice means?" Agent Conover asked. "Of course you do; you're a lawyer."

"Of course."

"We'll talk again, Miss Baker."

"No, Agent Smith, we will not talk again because there is no need for us to talk. I cannot help you with whatever it is you're doing or investigating. I told you I would not say anything to Jonathan, and I won't. That's the end of it."

"Where was your fiancé born, Miss Baker?"

"Winchester, Virginia, but then you probably already know that."

Both agents threw their hands up in the air. They looked like they were catching rain by the handful. "You see, wrong again. Your fiancé was born in Akron, Ohio. Do you want to know his real name?"

His real name. They were making Jonathan sound like some kind of criminal. Lucy could feel her shoulders start to slump. Her voice could barely be heard over the rumbling thunder. "What is it?"

"Leo Banks. His friends used to call him Lucky Leo. Does that ring any bells for you, Miss Baker?" Agent Smith asked.

Lucy looked at both agents. She hoped they would freeze in the rain, just the way she was freezing. They'd just invaded her life and turned it upside down. She thought about the thousands of seed pearls that were being sewn on her wedding gown. The FBI agents had made a mistake. Of course, this was all a mistake.

"I never heard the name before. I'm telling you, you have the wrong person. Jonathan is not this . . . this Leo Banks person. I would know. I saw a picture of the house he grew up in. The house is in Winchester,

Virginia. I know the street and house number, but I can't think of it right this minute."

"Were you ever there, Miss Baker?"

This was all wrong. This shouldn't be happening. But it was. "No, I've never been there." Both agents raised their eyebrows.

She sounded desperate when she said, "Jonathan is incredibly busy. We just couldn't find the time to get down there. Winchester is a bit of a drive."

"The house in Winchester belongs to one of Leo's friends."

It's all a bunch of lies. It has to be all lies.

"Did you ever meet your fiancé's parents?"

"How could I meet them? They live in Spain. If we couldn't find the time to go to Winchester, Virginia, how could we find the time to go to Spain, or Chile, where his sister lives? He has no brothers, just one sister. I'm leaving now."

"How convenient. We'll talk again, Miss Baker," Agent Conover said.

Lucy ignored both men as she jogged off, her feet squishing inside her sodden sneakers. She needed to go home, where it was warm and toasty, so she could think. Hot, black coffee was a must. What had just transpired was too preposterous for words.

"One more thing, Miss Baker," Agent Smith called out. "Be careful, your life could be in danger."

Lucy raised her right hand and gave the agent a single-digit salute. She wondered if he saw it through the pouring rain. She'd heard his words, though. Until that moment, she'd never been colder in her life. Or more frightened.

Twelve minutes later, Lucy bolted up the front steps, body-slammed the front door, barreled through, and headed straight for the downstairs shower, where she stepped in—clothes and all—to let the steaming water wash over her. She shook from head to toe. The stink of her own fear clogged her nostrils until she thought she was going to choke to death.

Lucy reached for the shampoo bottle and poured some over her long, tawny hair. The same hair Jonathan liked to run his fingers through after they made wonderful, satisfying love. Jonathan.

No, not Jonathan St. Clair. Leo Banks from Akron, Ohio.

It had to be a lie. Otherwise, the relationship she thought was so wonderful was all a lie. It couldn't be! Not now, when the seed pearls were being hand-sewn onto her wedding gown.

She knew a thing or two about the FBI. Actually, she knew more than she wanted to know. Dogs with bones. They never gave up. They always got their man.

Lucy was finally warm, so she kicked off her sneakers and peeled off her clothes. She continued to stand under the needlelike spray, knowing she was going to need at least half a jar of body lotion for her skin once she toweled dry. Did she really care? Maybe she needed to care because Jonathan said her skin was like silk and satin all rolled into one. Yes, she needed to care.

Instead of drying herself off with a towel, she reached for a thick, thirsty robe that Jonathan had bought for her at the Ritz-Carlton when they'd vacationed on Amelia Island.

Even though the heat blasted from the registers and the steam was still fogging up the bathroom, Lucy shivered.

In the kitchen, she did everything automatically. She filled the coffeepot, plugged in the toaster, took bread out of the wooden bread drawer, reached for the jam, which was nestled behind a quart container of orange juice. She poured. She softened the butter in the microwave and reached for the vitamin bottle. The beginning of a new day. Something she always looked forward to.

Rain beat against the kitchen window. Lucy brought her clenched fist up to her lips to stifle a cry that was about to erupt from her soul.

Two men. Awful words. And her world as she knew it was changed. How could that be?

Lucy poured coffee, buttered her toast, then spread the strawberry jam on it. She carried both the coffee and the plate to the table, along with a napkin. She eyed the glass of orange juice but didn't move to pick it up. She knew she wasn't going to eat the toast either. How could she? It would stick in her throat like wet straw and strangle her. Instead, she gulped at the coffee, burning her tongue and throat. She'd forgotten the cream and sugar. She detested black coffee, but Jonathan loved his black, the stronger the better.

She needed to think. Instead, she let her

gaze slide past the kitchen doorway to the dining room, where a pile of wedding invitations waited to be addressed and stamped. She'd started writing them out two days ago. She knew in her gut she would never mail them. Not now. Probably not ever.

Tears puddled in her eyes and rolled down her cheeks. She made no move to wipe them away. She continued to sip at the scalding coffee as she sniffed and sniffled.

The FBI agents had been wrong. She didn't make popcorn balls, nor did she sell them. She did, however, work three hours a day for Nellie Ebersole, a delightful elderly lady, who supplemented her income doing just that. All she did was process orders on the computer because the old lady had bad eyesight and didn't want to learn the intricacies of the computer. It was something to do to fill the hours of her days until she decided what new direction she wanted to take in her life.

She'd moved here to Edison, New Jersey, almost six months ago, exactly two weeks after Justin Riley walked out of the courtroom a free man. She'd rented the house she was living in for a month, then purchased it, bought new furniture, and settled down to vegetate. Sadie, her golden retriever, loved the huge backyard, and was happily digging a tunnel to the next yard so she could visit Clueless Cooper, a hundred-pound golden Lab. Coop, as he was known in the neighborhood, was tunneling on his side of the fence, too. Sooner or later they were going to meet somewhere underground. She hoped the meeting would be everything Sadie wanted it to be.

Lucy groaned when she saw Sadie run up to the deck and slam against the sliding door. She was covered in mud. She inched the door open and squeezed through. Damn, the temperature must have dropped twenty degrees since she'd gotten home. "You know the drill, Sadie," Lucy said as she slid back the cover of the hot tub. The retriever hopped onto the bench and into the tub, where she splashed around until she was clean, then hopped out. She shook off the excess water as Lucy shocked the hot tub with chemicals, turned on the jets, and replaced the cover.

She was almost to the door when she heard someone shouting. She cocked her head to peer around the corner to see a dark-haired man dressed in a business suit jumping up and down by the fence. "Hey, you! You with the dog! Do you think you can keep that mutt of yours inside when my dog is outside?"

Clueless Cooper's owner. He hadn't come over and introduced himself or welcomed her to the neighborhood in the six months she'd lived here. He only yelled at her from the other side of the fence about her dog. A couple of times during the summer she'd caught him peering nosily into her backyard. What a jerk! "Why don't you try keeping your mutt inside when *my* dog is outside? What do you expect me to do, stand by the door all day and watch to see if your dog is outside? Get real, mister," Lucy snarled. Like she needed a confrontation with her nosy neighbor today of all days.

"You're going to be a hard-ass about this, aren't you? I can tell by the sound of your voice you're a troublemaker," the man on the other side of the fence challenged.

Lucy chewed her lower lip to keep from laughing. She offered up a parting salvo before entering the house. "Try sitting on a pointy stick for a while, you . . . you . . . lawyer." She knew he was a lawyer, a commercial litigator with a firm in New York because Nellie Ebersole had told her all about the neighbors. She'd referred to Coop's owner as a delectable hunk of beefcake who couldn't seem to hang on to a woman. Crazy hours, crazy dog, she'd theorized. She'd gone on to say that if the neighbors didn't take pity on him, he'd starve to death and that he stank up the neighborhood when he tried to grill. The summary on one Wylie Wilson by the neighbors was that he was as clueless as his dog, a shark in the courtroom, and one handsome fortysomething dude. Just what Lucy needed.

Sadie bellied across the carpet in the family room, her eyes soulful as she looked up at her mistress as though to say, you take the fun out of everything. Lucy tried to ignore her as she padded barefoot into the kitchen to pour more coffee. She was scanning her grocery list when Sadie reared up and raced to the sliding glass doors, her bark so shrill the hair on the back of Lucy's neck stood on end.

There on her deck was Clueless Cooper, covered in mud from head to toe. Obviously, he'd finished the tunnel from his side of the yard. A second later the door slid open, thanks to Sadie's paw on the latch, and Coop was in the house. All one hundred pounds of him. Lucy watched in horror as the huge dog hopped on the beige sofa, then onto the matching chair, before he hopped down and rolled over and over on the beige carpet. Lucy shrieked and shouted to no avail. The dogs raced through the house leaving a trail of mud that was going to take her all day to clean up.

"Damn!" she said succinctly, just as the doorbell rang.

Lucy knew who it was even before she opened the door. He looked sheepish, she had to give him that. He looked good, too, and he smelled . . . sexy. "I hope you brought your work clothes, because I'm not cleaning up after your dog," she shouted, to be heard over the sound of the dogs' barking.

"Listen . . ."

"No, you listen. Your dog tunneled over here. That makes you culpable. He is your dog. He's trying to make out with my dog, which is an exercise in futility because Sadie has been fixed."

"Cooper's fixed, too. I'm sorry. I'm running late this morning. I didn't know about the tunnel. I guess he's been digging it for some time. It's usually dark when I get home. I guess I should have seen it, but I didn't. What do you want me to do? I have to be in court by ten o'clock, and I just missed the train." He whistled sharply for his dog, who ignored him completely.

"Sadie!" Lucy bellowed. The retriever ignored her, too. Angrily, she stomped her way down the hall to the last room on the right, where she stared in horror at the bedroom she'd spent weeks decorating. The champagne satin comforter was streaked with mud, the matching chair was so dirty it looked like it had come from the garbage dump. Both dogs sat up straight, their rumps on her satiny pillows. Sadie had the good sense to slide off the bed and wiggle under it, knowing full well Lucy couldn't reach her. Cooper stared defiantly at his owner and his hostess.

"I'll make this up to you, I swear I will," Wylie said, his voice desperate-sounding. "Look, I'm going to have to drive to the city. I really have to go, or the judge is going to fry my ass. When I get home tonight, I'll come over here and help you clean up. I'll pay for any and all damages."

"You expect me to leave all this till sometime tonight when you get home. In your dreams, mister!"

"Yeah. Yeah, I do. I don't have any other options right now." Wylie had his hand inside Coop's collar and was dragging him off the bed. Lucy took a small amount of pleasure in seeing some of the mud rub off on her neighbor's pant leg. She grinned as he cursed under his breath. At the door he turned, and sniped, "That remark about the pointy stick was uncalled for." The moment the door closed behind her neighbor, Lucy shouted for Sadie, who continued to ignore her.

If nothing else, Sadie and Cooper's romp had driven the ugly thoughts concerning Jonathan and the FBI agents from Lucy's mind.

An hour later, Clueless Cooper was back on the deck demanding to be let into the house. Wylie Wilson must have a doggie door. It was cold, and it was still raining. A heavy sigh escaped Lucy's lips when she let herself out onto the deck. She moved the cover of the hot tub, and said, "Get in; then you can come in the house." Clueless Cooper, whom she now knew for certain to be as clueless as his owner, jumped in, paddled around, then hopped out. He looked up at her with puppy-dog eyes that melted her anger. "Okay, come on. You can keep Sadie company." The house shook as Coop beelined through the rooms in search of his friend.

Jurisprudence was never this interesting, she thought as she leafed through the yellow pages to call Disaster Master Cleaning Service. She was told they could accommodate her in three hours for the sum of four hundred dollars. She was no fool; she snapped up the offer and clicked off the phone. Wylie Wilson was going to be four hundred dollars poorer by this evening.

Lucy stared down at the emerald-cut diamond on her finger. Tears burned her eyes as she wondered if there would ever be a matching band on that finger. The FBI was wrong. They had to be wrong. Jonathan was Jonathan, not that Leo Banks or that Lucky Leo person. It was all some big misunderstanding. It had to be. It just had to be.

2

Lucy's thoughts turned dark as she found herself staring down at the emerald-cut diamond on her ring finger. Suddenly, she saw the gaudiness of it, the look-at-me statement it seemed to be making. The moment Jonathan had placed it on her finger she'd been reminded of the square solar lights that lined her driveway. She'd always wanted a marquise diamond, but Jonathan had wanted to surprise her and had picked out the ring himself. The thickness of the gold band plus the heaviness of the stone weighed down her hand. Suddenly, it didn't feel right. She slipped it off her finger. Where to put it? Finally, she dropped it into the toe of one of her sweat socks and rolled it and its mate into a ball. Jonathan had made a point of telling her he'd insured the ring. She wondered if it was true.

Five minutes later she was dressed in a navy blue sweat suit and sneakers. She rummaged in the vanity drawer for a rubber band for her ponytail. For some reason she was having a hard time getting warm. She was almost to the door of her bedroom when she realized how quiet the house was. Tiptoeing down the hall, she looked into the guest bedroom to see both dogs asleep side by side on the queen-size bed. *Even animals need friends,* she thought.

Carrying a cup of coffee, she walked through the family room, where she tried not to stare at the muddy furniture, and turned the corner and walked up the steps to the room over the garage that she used as an office.

The frog, or as the Realtor called it, the finished room over the garage, was a room of built-ins. Built-in desk, built-in book-shelves, built-in entertainment center, and built-in storage. The bathroom was small, with a toilet, tiny sink, and an equally tiny built-in shower. Sometimes she came up with Sadie just to sit and veg out with the TV. Maybe it was just to say she used all the rooms in the big house. Sadie loved running up and down the steps. Sometimes she would hide her toys and chew bones under the comfortable sofa.

Lucy sat down and hugged her knees to her chest. She really needed to think about what the FBI agents had said to her. Really think about it. She was a lawyer, so that had to mean she was smart enough to figure out what was going on where her fiancé was concerned.

For starters, how much did she *really* know about Jonathan St. Clair other than she'd turned her heart over to him. Jonathan, with the wicked sense of humor; Jonathan, with the laughing eyes and crinkly smile. Jonathan, who was never shy about telling her how much he loved her. He'd spun a tale for her about how wonderful and rich their lives would be once they got married. He'd said he planned on cutting back on his traveling so he could be home more because he wanted to be a hands-on husband and father. Four children, he'd said with a wicked grin. And he wanted them all to look like her.

Was it Jonathan St. Clair or Leo Banks who had made all those promises? She wished she knew. She also wished there was a way to call her fiancé, not to tell him what the agents had said, but just to hear his voice.

Her thoughts drifted to the last time she'd been with Jonathan. It was such a wonderful three-day getaway at a little inn on the Chesapeake that was private and secluded. Three whole days, half of which were spent in bed, the other half walking along the shore, holding hands, staring at one another as they both whispered promises they swore they would never break. He was the consumate lover, gentle, kind, considerate, passionate. A satisfying lover.

Jonathan was a true romantic, something that had surprised her in the beginning. He loved giving her silly little gifts, then stunning her with a diamond bracelet that almost blinded her. She pretended to love the bracelet, which she did, but she loved the snow globe more.

Once he'd surprised her by scattering rose petals on the sheets when they made love. The scent of the roses and the loving words he'd whispered had been a heady mix as he caressed her in all the right places. Over and over, he'd professed his love, promising that life together was going to be wonderful. She'd believed him.

Then, of course, there was the wine. Very, very good, expensive wine. Way too much wine. Now that she thought about it, those trysts were always a little blurry in her memory. Maybe the romance and the sex were colored by the wine, and she was too stupid to know the difference. Her brother said she was one of the smartest people he knew. She assumed he meant professionally. She was convinced now that where men were concerned she really was stupid.

When it had been time for him to leave the last time he'd visited, she'd cried. She never cried. Well, hardly ever. All that expensive fine wine had been the culprit. Jonathan had cupped her face in his big hands as he'd whispered more endearing words, then kissed away her tears. He'd called her ten minutes later just to say he loved her and to make her laugh, which she did. Knowing how alone she was feeling, he'd continued to call her every ten minutes for the next few hours until he boarded his flight.

"Bastard!" was all she could think of to say. And now this . . . whatever this was.

In all the time she'd known him, he'd never once given her his travel itinerary. His home base, such as it was, was a small one-bedroom apartment on East Seventy-ninth Street. She knew she could call the number at the apartment, leave a message, and sooner or later, most often days later, Jonathan would return her call. At least that's always the way it had been. For some reason, she knew things weren't ever going to be the same again.

Jonathan was in Guatemala. At least that's where he said he was going two weeks ago. He'd promised to be home for Thanksgiving, which was a week away.

Jonathan did not have a key to this house, and she didn't have a key to his apartment. *Now, where did that thought come from?* she wondered. She'd never been to the apartment. There was no need really. When she'd met him, she'd been living in the city at the brownstone on Forty-ninth Street, right around the corner from the United Nations Building. He'd always preferred to go to her place, claiming it was bigger and more comfortable than his apartment. Now, she felt an urgency actually to *see* where her fiancé lived.

If the Disaster Master people arrived on time, she could leave them to do their work while she loaded the dogs into her sports utility vehicle and drove into the city to

Jonathan's apartment, pick the lock, and be back by dinnertime. Early in her career she'd represented a client named William Fogerty also known as Three-Fingered Willie who had been accused of multiple burglaries. She'd gotten him off. To show his thanks at her skilled representation, he'd spent hours showing her "the tricks of the trade," which she'd actually enjoyed learning. When Willie said he was confident she could pick any lock as well as he could, she'd felt pleased. Willie had been so happy with his acquittal, he'd given her her very own lock picking kit. She'd doubled over laughing, knowing she'd only have occasion to use it when she accidentally locked herself out of her own home, but still, she'd kept it, and now she was glad she had brought it with her to New Jersey. *If* she believed what the federal agents had told her. Well, there was only one way to find out.

Jonathan brokered business deals and received a commission for his efforts. He'd intimated that he was a multimillionaire. He looked the part, dressed the part, and acted the part. She had to admit she didn't know what kind of deals he brokered, and when she had inquired, he'd wagged his finger playfully under her nose and said his business was the same as hers, confidential and client-privileged. She'd never asked again, but she had discussed it with her brother. Between the two of them they'd finally decided Jonathan was the man who brought the money boys together. A sheik in Saudi Arabia who wanted to buy some high-end real estate in New York without anyone being the wiser. Or, as Steven put it, anyone who wanted to conclude a high-stakes business deal without the facts leaking out to the opposition called on Jonathan St. Claire. And for his efforts, Jonathan was rewarded with a percentage of the deal.

What could Jonathan possibly have done to make the FBI place him and, as a consequence, her, under their microscope? And why would her own life be in danger? Did the agents think she knew something damaging about Jonathan?

Lucy finished the coffee in her cup. She herself was a free agent. Again. Nellie Ebersole, the popcorn lady, was leaving for Fort Myers, Florida, over the weekend, where she would reside until the end of March. That meant Lucy was out of her part-time job until the first of April. By April 1, she would be back from her honeymoon in Greece and be ready to settle down to being Mrs. Jonathan St. Clair. She shivered when she thought that the first day of April was April Fool's Day. Tomorrow night was the going-away potluck supper for Nellie that the neighbors were throwing. Her contribution was to be Swedish meatballs. She wondered what Clueless Cooper's owner would bring.

If she wanted to, she could drive to Jonathan's apartment in New York and take a look around. She could also drive to Winchester, Virginia, tomorrow. If she left at dawn, she could scout out the area and make the return trip home on the same day. How hard could it be to locate the house Jonathan said he grew up in? She could take the picture with her since it was in her album. She supposed she could fly to Spain if she had to. Checking out Jonathan's parents shouldn't be that difficult. She could go to the American embassy and ask for help. Or, maybe she could call the embassy for the information she needed.

Why am I thinking like this? "I have to prove them wrong," she muttered. "I know they have Jonathan mixed up with someone else."

Lucy bounced off the sofa and walked over to the window. The rain had turned to sleet. It was a horrible day for horrible thoughts.

I would know, Lucy thought, *if my fiancé was some kind of criminal. I don't know any such thing. Why am I so willing to take the word of two FBI agents? Because . . . because . . .*

There *were* a few things. One slight disagreement she'd had with Jonathan a few months before Jason Riley had walked out of the courtroom a free man. Jonathan had been in town for five days. He'd begged her to take the case of a friend of his. She'd turned him down flat. He'd been perturbed but had tried not to show it. She couldn't even remember what the case was about. Another time he'd said he could get her all the business she wanted. High billables on each and every case. She'd told him she had all the business she could handle, and she didn't ever want to mix business with pleasure. He'd said he understood, but things had changed after that. Subtly, but still they'd changed.

Then, a few weeks later, she'd told Jonathan that despite how unusual it was for a criminal defense lawyer to be considered for a judgeship position on the state supreme court, she was up for one. His attitude had changed again. He'd been practically euphoric at the news.

But then had come the Justin Riley case and her decision to stop practicing law. When she had told Jonathan, he'd called her stupid, though he'd apologized immediately.

Damn, did her decision to stop practicing law have something to do with what was going on? How could it? Her career or lack thereof didn't affect Jonathan. Or did it?

Lucy was staring intently at the bust of Blackstone sitting on her desk when the phone shrilled to life. She almost jumped out of her skin. Should she answer it? What if it was the FBI agents? Maybe it was Nellie Ebersole or her brother, Steven. She reached for the phone and said hello cautiously.

The voice on the other end of the phone sounded just as cautious. "This is Wylie Wilson, your next-door neighbor. I called Nellie, and she gave me your number. I'm calling to apologize again and to tell you I will help you clean your house. And, I'll pay for any damage."

Relief washed through Lucy. "Okay. The Disaster Master people will be here shortly. They said it would cost four hundred dollars. If they can't clean my satin bed comforter, I'll buy a new one and give you that bill, too. I think you should know your dog is here again."

"What?" the lawyer squawked.

"I said your dog is here. Obviously, you must have a doggie door or else you left your back door open. He came through the tunnel. I made him jump in the hot tub to clean up, and he's sleeping right now in my guest room. Hello. Are you there?"

"I'm sorry. I should have thought about the doggie door. I was in such a rush this morning I wasn't thinking clearly. Listen, I'll find a way to make all this up to you. I promise. Coop really is a good dog. His problem is he's lonely. I think he lives for the times you let your dog out. He pines by the door and waits. It's sad."

"You're breaking my heart. Stop it. Let's not make a habit of this, okay? Don't worry

about your dog while he's here. Is there anything else?" she asked coolly.

"Well, there is one other thing. When you
pick up whatever it is you're taking to
Nellie's potluck supper, could you pick me
up some seasoned wings? That's what I'm
supposed to bring. I'll pay you, of course."

"Do you think I'm some kind of maid service put on this earth for your conven-
ience?" Lucy squawked indignantly. "I'm
cooking my contribution. You are supposed
to cook it, not buy it. The neighbors say no
one eats the store-bought stuff."

"Oh. I guess I won't be attending then. I
won't have time to make anything. Can you
feed Coop? I didn't have time this morning.
He loves meat loaf. He has a stomach condition, and it's the only thing he can eat. I
have to go now. I'll see you later. Thanks
again for watching Coop."

"You expect me to make your dog a meat
loaf?" Lucy asked incredulously as she
stared at the buzzing receiver in her hand.
She replaced the phone just as the stairs
started to shake with Sadie and Coop
bounding up the steps. The frog was new
territory for the Lab, and he had to smell
every inch of it, his tail, like a weapon,

swishing furiously. Sadie sat back on her haunches, her eyes adoring as she watched her new friend frolic in the space that was originally hers.

Lucy snapped her fingers, and said, "Sit!" Coop looked around. Since his new best friend was already sitting, he took the command to heart and sat. He waited for approval, and Lucy was lavish in her praise. He licked her hand, whined softly, and lay down at her feet. Sadie followed suit.

Lucy dropped to her knees and tussled with the two dogs, who barked and rolled over and over, then on top of one another. They jumped on her, sat on her, tugged the rubber band out of her ponytail, and stretched out for a nap. Giggling, Lucy went downstairs to make fresh coffee.

Maybe she should leave the dogs in the frog when she drove into the city. She could leave dry dog food and water, lock the door so they wouldn't bother the cleaning crew and the cleaning crew wouldn't bother them. It was doable.

All she had to do was wait for the Disaster Master people.

Ahead of schedule by an hour, the crew arrived with a ton of cleaning equipment.

Lucy spent ten solid minutes explaining what she wanted done, locked up the dogs, gave instructions to the bonded crew on how to lock up, and left the house for the forty-five-minute drive into Manhattan.

It was twelve-forty-five when she parked the car in her brother's spot at his building and then took a cab to Seventy-ninth Street. It was going to be tricky. Jonathan had told her once it wasn't a doorman building, but there was an elevator operator. And he was on duty. He glowered at her as she stepped in, and said smartly, "Seventeenth floor please."

Lucy hoped the operator didn't wait to see if whoever she was visiting was home. He didn't. Sighing with relief, she walked around the short hallways until she spotted Jonathan's door. A business card was taped to the front door. Three locks. Customary and not out of the ordinary for New York City. Not a problem. She could pick a lock with the best of them, thanks to her old client, Three-Fingered Willie.

The moment all three locks snapped free, she opened the door and stepped inside, carefully locking the door behind her. She'd expected to see lavish furnishings because

Jonathan loved fine things. For some reason she thought an interior decorator would have done the job. Her jaw dropped when she looked around the living room. A chair and a floor lamp were the only furnishings. A phone and an answering machine sat on the floor. There was no blinking red light, so that had to mean there were no messages.

There were no towels, no carpets, and no soap in the bathroom. The room she surmised to be the bedroom had a chair and a table with a small lamp on it. The only thing in the closet was a windbreaker that smelled like Jonathan and a pair of running shoes sans shoelaces.

In the kitchen, she opened the cabinets. Blank space stared back at her. The refrigerator that was plugged in and running held two bottles of Evian water and a tray of ice cubes. Nothing else.

Had Jonathan moved and forgotten to tell her? Had Jonathan ever lived here? Was this just an address for business cards? What? When she sat down on the chair, a puff of dust swirled upward. She stood immediately. Did *anyone* live here? Unlikely.

Now what? she asked herself, looking around.

If she hadn't leaned up against the wall by the door, she probably never would have seen the small mailbox key hanging on a nail at the side of the door. She recognized it because she'd had one just like it when she'd lived on Forty-ninth Street.

Lucy felt light-headed at the mere thought of going near Jonathan's mailbox. Tampering with the United States mail was a federal offense. She wanted to cry at what she was thinking and feeling.

She'd been a criminal defense attorney long enough to know she'd screwed up by running here to Jonathan's apartment just hours after her meeting with the federal agents. She knew without a doubt that someone, probably Frick and Frack, had followed her into the city. How could she have been so stupid? She'd just given them another reason to suspect her. Of what, she didn't know. They probably thought she was either tearing up stuff, burning it, or trying to hide it. That's exactly what she would think if she was in their place. There was a lot to be said for suspicious minds.

Lucy looked longingly at the mailbox key but knew she wasn't going to touch it. Touch it. What had she touched? Doorknobs, the cabinet doors, and the refrigerator handle. That was it. With a tissue from her purse, she wiped everything she'd touched, then let herself out of the apartment. She relocked the door with the aid of one of Willie's picks, walked over to the elevator, and pressed the button.

She was back home in her own house at three-thirty. The house sparkled. The crew was worth every cent she'd paid them. By three-forty-five she had her hands deep into a meat loaf mixture. Clueless Cooper's owner was paying for this meat loaf, too.

Damn you, Jonathan, what are you involved in? A fat tear rolled down her cheek.

The phone rang, but she didn't answer it because her hands were full of egg, bread crumbs, and hamburger meat. Whoever it was would call back.

Five minutes later, Lucy covered the roasting pan and slid it into the oven. She looked around and knew that the dogs had to go out, but the yard was too muddy, which meant she would have to walk them. She found an extra leash of Sadie's, put on her coat, and left the house, the dogs literally dragging her. The slush on the road had turned into a sheet of sheer ice. She picked her way carefully, the dogs now walking just as gingerly. As she struggled along behind them, she couldn't remember when she'd had a more miserable day.

When they had gone about a half mile, Lucy announced, "Okay, guys, come on, time to head home." The words were no sooner out of her mouth when her feet went out from under her, and she was on the ground. She felt a sharp pain in her foot and ankle, an even sharper pain behind her right ear. Stunned by the fall, she stared around groggily at the dogs. She'd let go of the leashes when she fell.

She saw it then, the wire from the utility pole skittering across the road like a skinny snake. A live wire. Her heart pounded in her chest when she saw the high wind whip the wire in her direction.

She struggled to get up, rolling over so she could get to her knees when she felt Coop put all his hundred pounds against her back to steady her, and yet the wire swiped her rubber boot. She felt the electrical shock from her foot all the way to her head. With Coop's help she rolled over again, out of reach of the wire. Sadie yipped her approval until Lucy was on her feet. The golden Lab stared up at her. *This dog loves me,* Lucy thought crazily. What was even more weird, she realized she actually liked, maybe even loved, Clueless Cooper. She was glad now that she'd made a meat loaf for him.

Steadying herself on one foot, her vision blurry, Lucy bent down to hug the wet dog, who whined his approval. *I'm alive,* she thought. *I wasn't electrocuted.*

Their leashes dragging on the road, the two dogs separated and walked alongside Lucy until they were back at the house. Inside, she hopped around as she found towels to dry off the dogs and herself. She was exhausted by the time she built a fire, which blazed within seconds. The dogs immediately lay down by the hearth and went to sleep.

Lucy poured herself a glass of wine, kicked off her shoes, and settled down on the sofa. She tried not to think about the pain in her ankle or the weird feeling inside her head. She gingerly touched the peanut-sized bump behind her ear. The aspirin she'd downed would take some of the edge off the pain. When she was a kid, she'd fallen off her bike and sprained her ankle. To her mind, the pain and the swelling looked the same. She could move her foot, so that had to mean nothing was broken. Later she'd soak it, and the next day an Ace bandage would help. *I'm living under a black cloud,* she thought as she finished the wine in her glass. She poured a second glass.

This is nice, she thought. *Sitting here all cozy and warm while bad weather beats against the house. The two dogs close by, dinner roasting in the oven. What could be better?* A man maybe, someone to hold her hand, to curl up against. Jonathan? Jonathan wasn't a warm and fuzzy kind of guy. He was passionate, though.

She thought about her neighbor and wondered what kind of guy he was. He had to be at the very least her own age, possibly a few years older. Since it was obvious he lived alone with Coop, he had to be a bachelor. Maybe he was divorced. Maybe he was engaged. Did she care?

Lucy closed her eyes and was asleep within seconds. She didn't wake until the timer on the stove buzzed. She rubbed the sleep from her eyes as she hobbled to the kitchen to remove the meat loaf from the oven. It smelled good. While the meat loaf cooled, she slid some frozen peas and carrots into the microwave oven, along with two scrubbed baking potatoes. She debated making a salad but scratched the idea when her ankle started to throb in tune with the throbbing inside her head.

The front doorbell rang just as Lucy finished mixing the peas and carrots into the meat loaf for both dogs. She looked at the clock—7:10. It must be her neighbor. She called loud enough over the barking dogs for him to come in. "I'm in the kitchen," she shouted. The dogs barked louder.

Wylie appeared in the kitchen doorway, a check in his hand. "Smells good," he said hopefully.

Lucy called the dogs and set the bowls on the floor. "Help yourself. I made some baked potatoes in the microwave. They won't be crusty, though. No salad either. I sprained my ankle," she said, holding out her swollen ankle, "while I was walking the dogs. I gave my head a good clout, too. I also got clipped by a live wire. Coop saved the day, though. He helped me get up on my feet. The stuff is in the vegetable bin if you want to make a salad. I guess that means I'm inviting you to dinner. What exactly is wrong with Coop that he can only eat meat loaf?"

"It's a long story. Coop was really sick for a long time and was slowly starving to death when I found him during a really bad storm. God only knows how long he was out there on his own. I took him to that vet on Oak Tree Road. He had to have some stomach surgery, and even when he came home it was still touch-and-go. I started to feed him little bits with my fingers, and he started to eat again. I appreciate your taking care of him and making him the meat loaf. I usually do it on Sunday. I make a whole batch of it, but I ran out this week. He won't eat the deli kind if I buy it. He just wants mine. Looks like he likes yours, too. I'll make the salad, and thanks for inviting me."

"You'll have to walk them after they eat. The yard is too muddy to let them out. Do you always talk so much?"

"It's the lawyer in me. You remind me of someone. Did we ever meet?"

Lucy stared at the tall man cutting up her lettuce. She wanted to say, if I had met you, I would remember you. And then she did re-member meeting him years earlier when he was a prosecutor. She'd gone up against him and won. She hated lying to her neighbor, but lie she did. "I don't think so." What was the point in telling him she'd looked different back then in her designer, high-powered court suits, fashionable flaming red hairdo, exquisite makeup. Today her hair was back to its natural tawny color. The high-powered suits had been replaced with jeans and sweat suits. She looked exactly like what she was, a suburbanite.

"Maybe you have a twin out there somewhere. Everything looks nice and clean. I guess you were satisfied, huh?"

"Yes, they did a good job, and, no, you don't owe me any more money." He was good-looking. Dark brown hair and brown eyes. Five o'clock shadow, but that was okay. Good suit, so well made it fit him perfectly. She looked down at his Brooks Brothers loafers. A nice shine. His tie, loose at the neck, was nice, too. Obviously, he knew how to dress. To her eye, he looked like a runner or a jogger. On the other hand, maybe he simply worked out at a gym in the city on his lunch hour the way her brother did. Whatever he did in the way of exercise put him in good physical shape. She felt disloyal to Jonathan just thinking about Wylie.

Lucy rubbed at her throbbing temples as she struggled to keep up with her end of the conversation. "How is it that you know how to make meat loaf? I realize it isn't rocket science, but most men would opt for steak or chicken or go with takeout. That's what my brother does. Of course, he doesn't have a dog."

"I was married for ten years awhile back. My ex-wife had no expertise in the culinary department. I realized if I didn't want to starve, I would have to learn to cook. She was a lawyer climbing up the ladder. When she got where she wanted to go, on my back, she divorced me. She turned around, married a newscaster, and lives in Scarsdale. She now has a cook, a housekeeper, a gardener, and a chauffeur. Guess that was more than you wanted to know. Couldn't think of any other way to let you know I'm available. If you were looking that is." His expression was sheepish yet hopeful.

"Oh," was all Lucy could think of to say.

"Yeah, oh. I wouldn't marry a lawyer again if they paid me my weight in gold."

"Oh," Lucy said again.

Wylie chopped a skinny cucumber and dumped it into the bowl. His movements were deft as he cored and sliced a tomato. He tossed the salad, uncapped a bottle of blue cheese dressing, and placed everything in the middle of the table. "Do you think I should walk the dogs now, or should we eat first? Do you mind if I take off my jacket and tie?"

"No, I don't mind. I think you should walk them now. I'll set the table."

"No, don't do that. Wait till I get back. You need to stay off your foot. I'll make you a good foot bath after dinner. You probably should see a doctor. If you hit your head, you might have a concussion."

When Wylie returned he was wearing jeans and a heavy sweatshirt. Obviously, he had stopped at his own house to change. He looked even better in casual clothes. Nice thighs under the jeans.

Lucy enjoyed dinner despite her throbbing ankle and head. She let Wylie do most of the talking.

"So, what are you, independently wealthy or what? The neighbors say you're home all the time and only work a few hours a day for Nellie. Great old gal, isn't she? I miss her in the winter." He peered at her across the table as he waited for her reply.

"I have a . . . nest egg. I live frugally," Lucy said by way of explanation. "I got burned out and moved here to the burbs. End of story." All she could think about was Wylie saying he would never marry a lawyer again.

"Where's that eye-popping ring you were sporting this morning? Are you engaged? You don't strike me as a person who would wear something that ostentatious. Costume jewelry, huh?" Wylie said, pleased with himself at his assessment of Lucy's engagement ring.

Lucy shrugged as she sipped at her coffee, relieved that Wylie was satisfied with his own answer.

An hour later, Lucy marveled at her spotless kitchen. "You do good work," she said, laughter ringing in her voice.

"My mother's upbringing. She taught us to clean up after ourselves and always to offer to help out. Otherwise, she said, no one will invite you back. There were nine of us, so we had to learn how to do our own laundry, make beds, clean, and cook. You should see the hospital corners on my sheets. So, do you think you'll invite me back?"

"There is that possibility. My mother always said we should be neighborly."

"Mothers are great people. If you can make your way into the living room, I'll build up your fire and fix that foot bath I mentioned. By morning, you'll be right as rain, a little tender, but you'll be able to get around. A bucket will do."

Lucy explained where everything was and made her way into the living room, where both dogs were sitting on the sofa. They waited to see if they had to get off. When Lucy sat down, they relaxed, their heads on their paws, the picture of contentment.

Lucy sat up to put her bare foot into the steaming bucket of water. "Ohhh, that feels good. What's in it?"

"Just you never mind what's in it. It's an old secret family remedy my mother came up with for all us kids. We were forever breaking or spraining something. I should be going. I have to be in court early tomorrow morning. I can't afford to have the judge chew my ass out again. Thanks for dinner and thanks for taking Coop. I'll be sure to block the doggie door so he doesn't do an encore."

Sadie slinked off the sofa and tried to be invisible, as did Coop. Lucy knew exactly what they were doing and where they were going. Sadie was going to show Clueless Cooper her hiding place under the bed, where no human had gone before.

"C'mon, Coop, let's go. Time to go home."

"You're too late. They've gone to ground. Coop wants to stay with Sadie. Right now, I can guarantee they are both under my bed. They won't come out either. It's okay, he can stay the night," Lucy said generously. Suddenly she realized she liked this new neighbor of hers. And she really liked his dog, too.

"What about tomorrow?"

"I'm not going anywhere, so it's okay if he stays. I have one more pound of hamburger meat, but after that you'll have to take him home. By the way, you better pick up something for me so *you* can take it to the party tomorrow night. I'll call Nellie and explain what happened. Press the button on the lock, and the door will lock itself on your way out."

Wylie looked dubious. "Are you sure?"

"I'm sure. He really isn't any trouble. I kind of like him. It's obvious he likes Sadie, and if Sadie is happy, I'm happy."

"You are a nice lady, Lucy Baker." He pronounced her last name, Bay-cur. "Did I tell you I was available? My hairline is not receding like most men's my age. I work out, know how to cook and clean house. I come from sturdy stock, and my cholesterol is normal."

Lucy blinked. In one breath she knew more about Wylie than she knew about Jonathan. "I will store all that other information aside for a time when I might need it." In spite of herself, Lucy burst out laughing. *Bay-cur.* "How did you know my last name?"

"Rachel at Number 12 told me who you were when you moved in. Seems she knows the Realtor who sold you your house. She said your name was Lucy Bay-cur, and I remembered it."

Lucy didn't bother to correct the way he pronounced her last name once she realized seventy-five-year-old Rachel Muller with her German accent was the one who'd told him her name. That was another reason why Wylie didn't connect her to the ace criminal defense attorney she'd once been.

" 'Night, Lucy."

" 'Night, Wylie."

The moment the door closed and locked behind Wylie, both dogs thundered down the hall and leapt onto the couch. Lucy laughed again.

A fitting end to an awful day.

3

Two things happened simultaneously the next morning when Lucy woke up on the couch with the two dogs. The phone rang, and the doorbell rang. She struggled to a sitting position and reached for the phone. She said hello as she hobbled to the front door, thinking it was Wylie who'd come to walk the dogs. It wasn't Wylie, but he *was* walking up the driveway. Frick and Frack stood in front of her. She sighed, then her heart took an extra beat when she recognized Jonathan's voice coming from the phone that was pressed to her ear. "Can you possibly call me back in a few minutes? I sprained my ankle, and my neighbor is here to walk the dogs, Sadie and his own. Yes, ten minutes is fine," Lucy said as she ushered the men into the foyer and watched as Wylie loped up the driveway and into the house. Both dogs barked a boisterous greeting.

Lucy swiveled on one foot to reach for the dog leads hanging on the coatrack by the front door. Wylie's eyes were full of questions as he gazed at the two men, who stepped aside to permit the dogs to take center stage. His expression clearly said most people don't get visitors at six o'clock in the morning. When he realized Lucy wasn't going to introduce him, he fastened the leashes onto the dogs' collars so he could lead the pair down the driveway.

"Looks like a nice guy," one of the agents said.

Lucy eyed the two gray suits, hoping the fear she was experiencing didn't show on her face. "He's my neighbor. I sprained my ankle yesterday. As you can see, he came over to walk the dogs. Isn't it a little early for a visit from the FBI? What do you want?"

"We stopped by the tennis court and track, but you weren't there. We thought something might have happened to you."

"Something did happen to me. I slipped on a patch of ice yesterday and sprained my ankle. I also gave my head a good crack." She fingered the bump on her head and winced. "I repeat, what do you want?"

Instead of answering her question, the

second agent said, "Was that Mr. Banks on the phone?"

"I don't think that's any of your business, Agent Conover. Why are you here? I told you yesterday I don't know anything about Jonathan's business. If I don't know anything, how can I possibly help you?"

Lucy wondered how two men could wear identical blank expressions.

"Then why did you go to his apartment yesterday? Did you leave him a note or a warning? That's another way of saying we don't believe you."

Pretend outrage rang in Lucy's voice. "You followed me!"

"Why did you go there?" Agent Conover asked a second time. "You said you had never been to Mr. Banks's apartment, but all of a sudden, after we spoke, you suddenly wanted to visit your fiancé's apartment. I guess you were a little surprised to see that it was empty."

Conover had her there, and she knew it. Lucy motioned to the two agents to follow her into the kitchen. She nodded as she watched the water drip through the coffeepot. She turned on one foot and reached into the cabinet for a cup. One cup. There was no way she was going to offer these two a cup of coffee. She tried unobtrusively to sneak a look at the clock on the range to see how much time she had before Jonathan called back. A precious few minutes. "Since you know the apartment is virtually empty, I hope you had a search warrant when *you* entered."

The agents ignored her comment. "We have it on good authority that Mr. Banks will be joining you for Thanksgiving. That's six days from now. We were going to ask you to come into our office in Manhattan, but seeing as how you're slightly incapacitated, we can have our superiors come here. We need to talk, Miss Baker. We want you to help us."

The words sounded so ominous that Lucy felt herself cringe. What exactly did they mean by *help*?

"How many times do I have to tell you, I don't know anything about Jonathan or his business. Yes, I was upset yesterday after we spoke. I didn't believe what you said about my fiancé. That's why I went to his apartment. In case you don't already know, I picked the lock. I don't know why there isn't any furniture other than a few chairs and tables. Maybe Jonathan doesn't like the area, or maybe he can't break his lease. He's only in the city a few days at a time. Perhaps he likes staying at a hotel where everything is done for him. I simply don't know. There's nothing I can do to help you because I don't know anything. What right do you have to come here and turn my life upside down this way?"

Agent Conover looked pointedly at his watch. "We'll call you to set up an appointment. Be sure to answer your phone, Miss Baker."

The moment Lucy opened the door to usher the two men out, Wylie and the dogs blasted through. She would have slammed and locked the door if not for Wylie and the dogs. Wylie unhooked the two leashes and hung them on the peg on the coatrack. Lucy thanked him and waited to see what he was going to do. Instead of leaving, he followed the dogs to the kitchen. She groaned as she locked the door behind the two agents.

In the kitchen, Lucy watched as Wylie handed out chews to the two dogs, who trotted off to the living room. It irritated her that her neighbor was making himself so at home.

"Talk about your steely-eyed whoever and whatever they are. Those guys looked like CIA wannabes to me. Are you okay, Lucy? You look worried. Is something wrong?"

Lucy brushed at the hair that was falling over her forehead, aware suddenly of how she looked and what she was wearing—a faded plum-colored sweat suit. The phone rang at that precise moment. Answer it, not answer it? Lucy opted for the latter.

"It's just my brother. He calls every morning before he goes to work. That old sibling thing. With eight brothers and sisters I'm sure you understand what I'm talking about." She hated the sound of desperation ringing in her voice.

"Well, sort of. No one calls to check on me except my mother, and she only calls on Sunday afternoon. Two o'clock sharp, and woe is me if I'm not there to answer. Can I have a cup to go? Listen, I'll be home early to walk the dogs. Please don't even try going out. The roads are sheets of ice."

Lucy grimaced. "Okay, *Dad.*"

Wylie laughed as he made his way to the front door, coffee cup in hand. He waved, then shouted, "Take good care of my dog."

"Don't forget to pick up some stuff for Nellie's party." They sounded like an old married couple, Lucy thought.

Back in the kitchen, Lucy looked at the small four-cup coffeepot and decided to make another pot. When the phone rang, she sucked in her breath, and, with as much enthusiasm as she could muster, said, "Hello!" It was Agent Conover calling to say the meeting would be at three o'clock that afternoon.

Wonderful, one more thing to worry about! The phone rang a second time just as she poured fresh coffee into her cup. This time it was Jonathan with an edge to his voice. Another time, another place, and the hardness might have bothered her. "Where are you, Jonathan?" she asked, not sounding completely friendly herself. The question surprised him. She could tell by the gap in the conversation.

"Buenos Aires. Why?"

"Just curious. I thought you were in Guatemala. Sometimes you remind me of a phantom. You're here, you're not here; then you're there, and you're not there. Whatever will you do when you don't travel as much?"

"Spend all my time with you. You sound

different this morning. I tried calling you a few minutes ago, but there was no answer." To Lucy's ears, the statement sounded accusatory. Normally, she'd fall all over herself with an explanation as to why she hadn't answered the phone. Just then she didn't feel like acting normal. She was also feeling a smidgen of guilt about Wylie. "I sprained my ankle yesterday, Jonathan, as I told you. My neighbor came to walk the dogs, and I had to be hospitable because tonight is Nellie's going-away party. Are you in a hurry or something? It seems to me you're always in a hurry when you call me." She knew he would be able to detect the anger she was feeling in her voice. She didn't care.

"No, I'm not in a hurry. It just wasn't like you not to answer the phone. I like knowing you're sitting there waiting for me to call. I'm looking forward to seeing you. Are we eating in or going out for Thanksgiving dinner?"

"I'll leave that up to you, Jonathan, but tell me now if you want me to cook, so I can order the turkey from the butcher. Are you going to be staying here or at your apartment?"

"With you. I'll stop by to pick up my mail

and repack my suitcase. I'm heading off to Madrid when I leave on the Sunday after Thanksgiving."

Lucy knew a lie when she heard it. Almost to a man, every client she'd ever had lied at some point. Even her brother lied sometimes. She wondered if Wylie was a liar, too. More likely than not, Jonathan would get a phone call the day after Thanksgiving and off he'd go. It was his pattern. "You're only staying for a few days! When will you be back?"

"For Christmas. For ten whole days. Let's try to get away for a few days? How does four days in Aruba sound? Or we could go back to Amelia Island and get in some golf."

"Sounds wonderful," Lucy said. She wondered when he was going to ask her about her ankle or the bump on her head. Did she tell him about cracking her head? She couldn't remember, and in the end, what difference did it make? He wasn't going to ask her how she was, that was the bottom line.

"Lucy, I have a client who could really use your services. I'd take it as a personal favor if you'd come out of your self-imposed retirement to represent him. It's a million in legal fees easy. I want to talk about it when I get there for Thanksgiving."

They'd had this conversation so many times, Lucy had lost count. She wasn't in the mood to go three more rounds with Jonathan, not with the FBI spying on her. They were probably listening to her phone conversation at that very moment.

Jonathan took her silence to mean he'd finally worn her down. "Any more news on your appointment to the bench?"

Actually, there was news, but she wasn't about to share it with Jonathan. She'd been dropped from the list of possible candidates. "No, not really. Why do you ask?"

"Because I'd like to see you wearing a black robe. Preferably with nothing on under it." He chuckled at his own wit. "Seriously, you earned it, Lucy. I don't want to see you do something you'll regret later on. Besides, I think it will be a real hoot to introduce you as, my wife, the judge." He laughed then. His laugh wasn't half as nice as Wylie's laugh, Lucy decided. She felt disloyal all over again.

Lucy thought about all the seed pearls for her gown and the wedding invitations on her dining room table.

"I'm being paged, Lucy. I have to go. I'll see you on Wednesday. Let's eat in. Just you and me. Promise you'll dream about me."

"Oh, I'll dream about you, all right, Jonathan. Have a safe trip home," Lucy said curtly.

"I love you."

This was where she was supposed to return the sentiment. She couldn't force the words past her lips. She pressed the button to disconnect the call. In doing so, she hoped this wasn't one of those things she'd come to regret later on.

It wasn't until she showered and washed her hair that she started to feel strange. The bump on her head seemed to be smaller than it was the night before, the size of a peanut. She wondered if she might have a concussion. When her head hit the road it had been almost incidental compared to the pain in her ankle. She wondered if the electric current that ran up her side had anything to do with the ferocious headache pounding behind her eyes. She'd been more concerned with her ankle than the dull, throbbing headache that had just blossomed into a full-blown, mind-bending headache. Lucy washed down a handful of aspirin and crawled into bed. Maybe if she slept for a few hours in her own bed, the headache would let up.

When she woke, it was noon. Lucy's ankle felt better, but she still had a dull pounding inside her head. She lay quietly for a few moments, trying to identify the sounds she was hearing. The television must be on. If not, someone was in her house chattering up a storm. She made her way to the bathroom to swallow more aspirin, then headed for the kitchen, where she ate a bowl of cereal. She shrugged when she realized the television wasn't on.

Lucy let the rambunctious dogs out into the backyard, satisfied that the ground was frozen and they wouldn't return full of mud. Five minutes later they scampered back in and immediately ran down the hall to the guest room, where Sadie kept all her junk. Lucy headed for the couch, walking gingerly to avoid putting pressure on her ankle. She called Nellie to explain the situation and express her regrets about not being able to attend the going-away party.

Lucy realized she had nothing to do until three o'clock, when the FBI agents would arrive.

She finally admitted to herself that she was bored. The law had been her life. Maybe she needed to think about going back to the firm and taking on only those cases where she was convinced her client was innocent. As if that were even possible.

Lucy leaned her head against the back of the sofa. Her ears were starting to hurt. She wondered what that meant. Maybe she was coming down with a bug of some kind. It was almost three o'clock. Time for her visitors. If she didn't help the agents, they could charge her with obstructing justice. When they got done with her, she'd never practice law again. *Oh, God, Jonathan, how could you put me in such a position?*

To pass the time, Lucy made herself a grilled cheese sandwich with a small green salad. She barely tasted what she was eating because her brain was going ten miles a minute as she tried to figure out what was going to happen to her life. Her thoughts were so scattered she felt like a kaleidoscope was inside her brain. In brilliant color.

She had to keep blinking her eyes to ward off the blurriness.

After she tidied up the kitchen, Lucy made her way to the living room to wait for Frick and Frack's "superiors" to show up. Before she sat down, she threw some logs on the smoldering embers and watched the fire spring to life. She felt just like the fire, like her body was crackling with something . . . *electricity.* To prove her point, she ran the palm of her hand up and down her arm and heard the little snicks that told her she was right. Again, she wondered what it meant.

Precisely at one minute to three, both Coop and Sadie raced to the door. A second later the bell rang. Lucy calmed the dogs as she dragged her injured foot across the carpet. At one point, she thought she saw sparks on the carpet. *I must need glasses,* she thought as she opened the door. Coop reared back and howled. Sadie barked her disapproval. Neither dog moved, but both of them tucked their tails between their legs. A clear sign to anyone who knew dogs that meant don't mess with me or anyone close to me.

The two men and one woman stopped in

their tracks as they eyed the two golden dogs. "Stay," Lucy said to Sadie. She knew Clueless Cooper would do whatever Sadie did. She motioned for the trio to follow her into the living room.

Lucy offered them nothing more than a place to sit. "Let's skip the small talk and cut to the chase. I told your two agents I know nothing about my fiancé's affairs. I don't see how I can possibly help you. What is it you want from me? Just so you know, I am not one bit happy with what is going on. Until yesterday, I had a nice life, and you and your agents are turning it inside out."

The agents stared at her, obviously paying little if any attention to what she was saying. "Allow me to introduce myself," the tallest of the three said. "I'm Agent Harry Mason, this is Special Agent Sylvia Connors, and the man on my left is Agent Thomas Lawrence. Fine animals you have here. Very protective, I see. That's a good thing when a woman lives alone."

Lucy nodded. She wasn't giving up anything, even if it was the mating habits of dogs. She stared across at the agents with unblinking intensity, wishing Mason would get on with it so she could take a nap. She blinked, then rubbed her eyes. For just a second the room was fuzzy, slightly distorted. *Concussion.* The thought made her heart race.

"Miss Baker, Agent Conover's report indicates he's explained our suspicions concerning Leo Banks. You, of course, know Leo Banks as Jonathan St. Clair. I'd like you to look at these photographs and tell me if the man you know as Jonathan St. Clair is the man in the photographs."

Lucy reached for the eight-by-ten black-and-white glossy prints of her fiancé. How handsome he was. She nodded. "Yes, that's my fiancé."

"Now, I want you to look at these pictures. This is Leo Banks at his high school graduation, his college graduation, random pictures taken over the past three years by one of our agents. Do you agree they are pictures of one and the same man?"

Lucy sucked in her breath. There was no denying the likeness. She nodded again, biting down on her lip so she wouldn't cry. As hard as she tried, she couldn't help but stare across the room at the dining room table. The female agent followed her gaze and looked at her with pity in her eyes. Lucy felt faint with the realization that the agents hadn't lied to her.

Anger at her circumstances rippled through her. "A lot of people change their names for a variety of reasons. That doesn't necessarily make them criminals. What is it you *think* Jonathan has done?"

"Do you want the long or the short version, Miss Baker?" Lawrence asked coolly.

Lucy brought her hands up to massage her temples. "I want you to tell me everything," she whispered.

Lucy almost jumped out of her skin when the reply came firm, hard, and cold. "Murder, drug dealing, money laundering. None of which we can nail him with. The list is very long. Your boyfriend is a very arrogant, respected, sophisticated businessman. He has his fingers in a lot of different pies. His legitimate enterprises are a front for a very sophisticated money-laundering operation that no government has been able to penetrate until now. In the last five years we suspect he's moved three billion, that's billion with a *b,* through his legitimate businesses.

"Where did you get the money to buy that ten-million-dollar house in the Watchung

Mountains, Miss Baker?" Agent Mason demanded.

All Lucy could do was gape at the agent. "What ten-million-dollar house? I've never been anywhere near the Watchung Mountains in my life. This house you're sitting in right now is the only property I own." Before she could blink, a property deed was thrust under her nose.

Lucy skimmed the contents. Her throat constricted, making it difficult to swallow. "This isn't mine. There must be some mistake. It's not mine," she said again, this time more forcefully. "I don't care what that deed says."

Agent Lawrence stared at Lucy with a jaundiced eye. "Mr. Banks leased that property for a number of years. It's his home base. It's where he goes when he's here in the States. A little over a year ago, he bought the property outright and transferred the deed into your name. Without a doubt, it is a valuable piece of real estate. The security system alone is worth hundreds of thousands of dollars. The whole place is loaded with motion sensors, laser trip wires, and tremor plates. Terrorists and drug dealers use devices like that. Now, to our way of thinking, if you're a normal person who just safeguards his privacy, that's one thing, but systems like the ones installed on that property make us wonder what Mr. Banks is hiding. Or what you're hiding since the property is in your name. In addition, there are a half dozen very-high-end vehicles parked in the six-car garage. Six-car garage," the agent repeated sourly. "They're all in your name, too. A Bentley, a Mercedes, a Porsche, a Rolls-Royce, a Lamborghini, and a 1965 restored Mustang convertible. Not to mention the fleet of cigarette boats he has stashed in Florida. They're in your name, too. Those cigarette boats raise your net worth considerably."

"I don't care. They aren't mine. I don't even know what a cigarette boat is. I think I heard the term once when I watched *Miami Vice* on television, but that's all I know. I didn't know about the cars until this moment. I drive a BMW. I make payments every month. It's a leased vehicle, for God's sake. I'm telling you the truth." Lucy cringed at the desperation in her voice. Fear, unlike anything she'd ever experienced, rushed through her.

"What about these?" Special Agent Connors asked. Lucy watched in horror as brokerage statement after brokerage statement slid out of the manila folder Connors had been holding. Goldman Sachs, Prudential, Merrill Lynch, Smith Barney, Charles Schwab, and a few more she couldn't read because they were upside down. "Your name is on every single one of these accounts. The account total in case you're interested, is 21 million dollars. These statements make you a very wealthy lady, Miss Baker."

A scream built in Lucy's throat. "They aren't mine! I can't even begin to comprehend 21 million dollars. Check the signature. I never opened any of those accounts. It's all a big mistake. You can check my income statements. What are you people trying to do to me?"

Another sheaf of papers fell out of the manila envelope. An amended tax return—bearing her signature. Agent Lawrence ignored her stunned expression when he said coldly, "We're trying to get you to help us. Do we have your attention now?"

Lucy clenched her teeth. "Yes, you have my attention. I want a lawyer."

Special Agent Connors snorted. "You are

a lawyer, Miss Baker. All we're doing is asking you questions. If you want to lawyer up,
that's going to make us think you might not
be telling the truth. You don't want to mess
with an OOJ charge, now do you?"

Lucy felt light-headed. No one wanted to
mess with obstruction of justice charges. At
least no one with even minimal intelligence.
She shook her head so hard she thought
she was going to pass out from the pain.

"Good." Special Agent Connors smiled.

"By the way," Mason continued, "Mr.
Banks, who began using the name Jonathan St. Clair a good many years ago, is
the beneficiary on all those brokerage accounts. The real Jonathan St. Clair, by the
way, died as a child, before children got social security numbers. So it was simple for
Banks to steal his identity and get seemingly legitimate documents in the St. Clair
name. He's also the beneficiary on all the
life insurance policies in your name. Twenty-
five million that we know of. We don't know
for certain, but we suspect he has a quit-
claim deed, signed by you turning the
house over to him for the sum of ten dollars, all ready to go on the house in the
Watchung Mountains in case . . ."

"In case of what?" Lucy snapped. "I only have a fifty-thousand-dollar life policy. I make quarterly payments. It's a whole life policy. Prudential Insurance. You're crazy, you're all crazy!" Lucy snapped again. Although it didn't seem possible for her head to pound harder, it was. *I'm going to explode right here in front of these people,* she thought.

"Your untimely demise."

It was a nightmare, pure and simple. Things like this didn't happen to people like her. They happened to other people. The sick feeling in the pit of her stomach was working its way up to her throat. The pounding inside her head was unbearable. She was going to wake up any minute and realize she was having a terrible dream. She pinched the inside of her arm but felt the pain. She was wide-awake, and this was no nightmare. *Your untimely demise.* She shuddered at the words, and a chill washed over her.

Lucy's eyes snapped open. The three agents were staring at her with pity in their eyes. Agent Lawrence pointed to the pile of papers and the photographs on the coffee table. "We can make this all go away if you agree to help us."

Lucy snorted. It was blackmail pure and simple. Her legal brain kicked in. "I want to see that in writing. My brother can handle the legal work. It's that, or it's no deal. You do not have my legal signature on any of those documents. Those are forgeries and you damn well know it. Yes, you can drag me down, but in the end, I'll win because I didn't do anything wrong." Brave words that meant squat. She knew it, and the agents knew it.

The agents stood as one. "You look tired, Miss Baker," the third agent said quietly. "We'll be in touch. Soon. Don't get up. We can see ourselves out."

A sob caught in Lucy's throat. "Take your junk with you," she said, pointing to the pile of papers and photographs.

"They're for you, Miss Baker. We want you to study them so when we contact you again, you'll appreciate what a precarious position your fiancé has placed you in. We want you to think about what has happened and what can still happen. We'll be in touch," Agent Lawrence said, just before the door closed behind him.

Lucy cried then because she didn't know what else to do. In the whole of her thirty-eight years, she'd never been so miserable. Lucy thought about Jonathan's quick little visits, the weekend getaways, the little gifts he'd given her, the way he'd whispered in her ear, the way he'd kissed her. There had been no bells, no whistles, no breathtaking moments. She'd always been contented after sex, though. Her blood didn't sing when she was around him. Did she love him? She thought she did. She liked him, or at least she had. Now, she couldn't abide hearing his name mentioned. And yet she was going to marry him. Why was that? Because her clock was ticking, because her friends were all married. Because there wasn't a line of men outside her door begging for her hand in marriage. Because it was time to get married. Well, she didn't have to worry about that any longer. She wasn't getting married to Jonathan or anyone else!

Her head pounding, her ankle throbbing, she hobbled into the dining room, every expletive she'd ever heard in her life spewing from her lips. With a sweep of her arm, she sent the pile of wedding invitations flying across the table and onto the carpet. The dogs twirled and pranced as they tried to catch the swirling invitations. When Lucy saw that there were four invitations left on the table she was like a maniac as she ripped and tore at them.

Both dogs, uncertain if this was a fun thing or not, jumped back into the fray, romping on the cream-colored invitations, then chewing at them.

Satisfied that the invitations were ruined, Lucy pivoted around on her good foot and hopped her way back to the living room, where she collapsed on the sofa. She was suddenly chilled to the bone, more proof that she was probably coming down with a bug of some sort. She reached for the colorful afghan Nellie Ebersole had made her for her birthday and snuggled under it.

The dream, when it came, was springtime in the Watchung Mountains. She was hosting a gala soirée to celebrate her appointment to the bench. Off in the distance, as she brought her champagne flute to her lips, she could see a man dressed in camouflage fatigues pointing a high-powered rifle directly at her. She screamed when the flute shattered in her hand.

Did the marksman miss?

Was it a warning?

Lucy opened one eye. "Sadie! Don't bark in my ear like that. Oh, God, now what?" She rolled off the couch and hopped her way to the door. Expecting to see the federal agents demanding to be let in, she was stunned to see Wylie, his arms full of packages. Takeout for Nellie's party. "What time is it?" she mumbled.

"Almost six o'clock. The party was canceled. Seems like everyone on the street has the flu or something like the flu. We're going to have to eat all this stuff ourselves. You look like you have it, too. Do you?"

Lucy did her best to focus on her neighbor, but her vision was too blurry. He was so cheerful, she wanted to slap him. "I think I'm catching something; but worse than that, I think I might have a concussion. I must have hit my head harder than I thought. If that's not what it is, then that electric charge did something to my body. My vision is all blurry. It clears up, then the blurriness comes back. My ears hurt, and I have a killer headache."

"Do you want me to take you to the doctor? There's a good one right down the road. He's a GP, and everyone on the street goes to him. He'll make a house call if you need it. Do you want me to call him?"

The concern in her neighbor's voice pleased Lucy as she hobbled to the kitchen. Her voice was apologetic when she said, "I think I'll wait till morning, and if I don't feel better, I'll make an appointment. Is he open on Saturday?"

"Yeah, he has hours from eight to noon on Saturday."

"By the way, I didn't make a meat loaf for Coop. I think there's enough left from yesterday if you mix it with something."

"If you want, I can take the dogs to my house, or I can stay here and take care of them. I can make us some dinner and a meat loaf for Cooper. I can fetch and carry for you, too. Are you running a fever?"

"I don't know. Probably. I had chills a while ago. Yes, please stay. I'd appreciate it, Wylie. I'm sorry I never made an effort to introduce myself after I moved in. I guess life just got in the way. I like your dog. I really do."

Wylie jerked at his tie and tossed it over a kitchen chair. His suit coat followed. "I like making myself at home. I'll borrow your slicker to walk the dogs," he said, pointing to the coatrack by the back door. "When I get back, I'll make you some hot tea. Do you have any cognac? My mother swears by hot tea and cognac. Makes you sweat. Go back on the couch and don't do anything. I'll replenish the fire. You can thank me some other time." Wylie grinned as he bustled about.

Even as bad as she felt, Lucy took a moment to marvel at how sexy her neighbor looked in his white dress shirt, the collar open, the sleeves rolled up to his elbows. She admitted she had a *thing* about white dress shirts on certain men. Men like Wylie. Jonathan in the same attire did nothing for her. How weird was *that*? She pushed the thought away. She had enough on her plate just then without thinking about a sexy neighbor she'd met only the day before.

Grateful for the help and attention, Lucy tottered back to the living room and the sofa that beckoned. She leaned her head back and closed her eyes. She heard the door open and close before she drifted off to sleep . . . again.

On his return, dressed in jeans and a fleecy sweatshirt that said GEORGETOWN on the back, Wylie set to work in the kitchen.

He worked swiftly and cleaned up after himself as he mixed up the meat loaf, slid it into the oven, and removed the contents from the take-out restaurant onto plates. While he worked, he talked to the dogs, who watched him intently. "I'm probably a better cook than I am a lawyer." He looked down at Coop and felt a pang of something he couldn't identify. His dog was in love with another dog and her owner. Where did that leave him in the mix? Standing on the sidelines, that's where.

As he waited for the water for Lucy's tea to boil, he set about adding kindling and logs to the dying fire in the living room. When he was finished, he dusted his hands and walked over to the sofa where Lucy was sleeping. He put his hand on her forehead the way his mother would have. She didn't seem overly warm to him.

He stood back to watch her. When she was asleep, she looked vulnerable, and so very pretty. He was almost certain he'd met her someplace, somewhere before, but he couldn't recall where or when.

He bent over the coffee table to shuffle the papers and photos back into the manila folder lying on the floor. If there was one thing Wiley hated, it was a mess. He wasn't being nosy, he really wasn't but he'd never seen so many brokerage accounts in one person's name in his life. Nor had he ever seen so many zeros. He barely looked at the arrogant-looking, elegantly dressed man in the photos. He was about to replace everything in the folder when he thought better of it. He left the papers and photos just the way they were and headed for the dining room where he saw the litter on the floor.

Wylie gaped at the chewed-up invitations, knowing instinctively that Coop had had his teeth in the shredded mess. He sighed heavily as he picked up everything and placed it on the dining room table. He wondered what *this* was going to cost him.

His shoulders slumped as he walked back to the kitchen, where he made the tea and drank it himself. His lovely neighbor was getting married. Just his dumb luck. Damn, he really liked Lucy. He'd even dreamed about her last night, and he'd almost killed himself getting to her house that afternoon.

"Story of my life," he muttered to the snoozing dogs.

4

Lucy woke at eight o'clock, when she felt a cold wet nose nudge her chin. Through sleep-filled eyes, she did her best to focus on Sadie and her surroundings. She felt groggy and cranky at being disturbed. When she opened her eyes wider, she saw her neighbor sitting across from her. He looked like he belonged in the chocolate-colored chair. He even looked like he belonged to the room. She wondered how that could be. "It's eight o'clock," she mumbled, looking down at the watch on her wrist.

"Yep, it's eight o'clock," Wylie said cheerfully. "Are you hungry? I was starved, so I ate when I fed the dogs. I kept yours warm. How do you feel?"

Lucy massaged her temples. "Don't ask. Did anyone call?"

"Your phone rang four times, but I didn't answer it. I assumed you had voice mail, and it would pick up your messages. So"—

he clapped his hands—"do you want dinner or not?"

"I'm not really hungry, Wylie. Maybe later. Thanks for taking over. I feel so . . . so awful. I feel like there's a Chinese fire drill going on inside my head. It's like a hundred voices all talking at once, and yet nothing is clear. It's starting to scare me." Tears of frustration puddled in Lucy's eyes.

Wylie was off the chair and on his knees by the couch in a heartbeat. Papers crunched beneath his knees—the brokerage statements.

"Hey, it's all right. I'll take you to the doctor in the morning unless you want me to phone now for a house call. If it's really bad, I can scoot you over to Emergency at Kennedy. Do you still have the headache?"

"Actually, no. But my head is . . . busy. I'm hearing stuff. My God, maybe I'm having a nervous breakdown." She shook her head, hoping to clear it of the noise. "I can wait till morning."

Wylie inched upward so that he was sitting on the coffee table. "You are not having a nervous breakdown. However, you might have a concussion. You were fine before the fall, weren't you?"

Lucy nodded, her gaze going to the dining room, where she'd destroyed her wedding invitations. *Maybe she's one of those people who have telekinetic powers.* A moment later, she said, "I am not one of those people with telekinetic powers, Wylie, so get that idea out of your head. I can't even predict rain when there are storm clouds overhead."

Wylie's jaw dropped. "What are you talking about?"

"You just said I must be one of those people who have telekinetic powers."

"No, I didn't. I didn't say a word."

"I heard you, Wylie." *I should scoop her up right now and take her to the hospital.* "I'm not going to the hospital, either, so get that out of your head, too. Oh, my God, your lips aren't moving!" Lucy burrowed deeper into the corner of the sofa. Her voice was full of panic when she said, "I just read your mind, didn't I?" A scream built in her throat. "I did, didn't I?"

Wylie stood up and moved back to the chair he'd been sitting on earlier. He had to say something. "Yes," he croaked.

. . . statements . . . too many zeros . . . married. "I'm not getting married. You saw

the brokerage statements. Were you snooping? You were thinking other things, but they aren't coming across clearly. You moved away. Oh, God, oh God, oh God! There's something wrong with my brain. Maybe it was that electric wire. I don't want to read your mind. Don't think. Please, don't think. Make your mind blank. I didn't hit my head that hard. That wire touched my shoe, but I wiggled away. I did feel a shock run up the side of my body, but then Coop boosted me up, and I got out of there. That live wire was dancing all over the road." She was babbling, and she knew it. "You aren't thinking, are you?"

Don't think, Wylie. How was that possible? A person had to think. He lied, and said, "No, I'm not thinking." Wylie struggled for a diversion because this was beyond bizarre. "Listen, Coop got into your invitations and chewed them up. I'll pay for them. I'm sorry about the bank statements. I was trying to tidy up, but I thought you might think I was snooping. I wasn't. I left everything the way it was. I did clean up the invitations though." He was babbling just as she was. "Listen, I have to think. If I don't think, I'll go nuts."

"Maybe you should go home. Coop didn't do anything. I'm the one who ripped up those invitations." She *heard* fragments of his thoughts again. *Klutz . . . this is scary. . . . maybe a CAT scan or an MRI.* "Are you scared because of me or because you're a klutz? Or am I the klutz? You're right, I need to see a doctor about my head." Lucy's voice was full of panic when she said, "You don't think this is fatal, do you?"

Wylie rubbed at the stubble on his chin. He suddenly felt like Clueless Cooper. "No, of course not. Just a little glitch of some kind. I'm sure there's a pill or shot for it. Maybe a shrink . . ." He knew it was the wrong thing to say the minute the words shot out of his mouth.

"You are crazier than I feel right now if you think that! Even I know there's no pill for something like this. If I go to a shrink, they'll lock me up and throw away the key. I'll be a freak. Promise me you won't tell anyone, Wylie. I need to think. Really think. Go out to the kitchen and let me see if I can . . . read . . . *hear* your mind at a distance. Promise first."

"Well sure. Whom would I tell? Maybe

you're just stressed. Sometimes it helps if you talk about things that are bothering you." He didn't mean to look at the dining room table, but he did. "The ring is gone from your finger. You did say you weren't getting married, so I have to assume something went awry. Maybe that's what's stressing you out."

"You're a lawyer, right? I want to retain you. Here," Lucy said, fishing in the purse that was on the table behind the sofa. "Here's five bucks for my retainer. Everything is now privileged, and you can't talk to anyone about me. Correct?"

"Well, yeah. Okay, you're my client." Wylie pocketed the five dollars. "I'm not going to like this, am I?" he said as he made his way to the kitchen.

"No," Lucy whispered, "you are not going to like this at all. Think!" she shouted.

"All right, I'm thinking!" Wylie bellowed from the kitchen. "Can you hear me?"

"I can hear your voice but I can't *hear* your thoughts," Lucy shouted again. "Keep thinking."

Ten minutes later, Lucy called a halt to the experiment. "Obviously, in order for me to *hear* you, you have to be reasonably close."

As she hugged her knees to her chest, both dogs pressed against her sides. "I'm scared, Wylie. I don't think I've ever been this scared before. I don't know what to do."

"I have an idea, Lucy. I'll warm up some dinner for you, make you a cup of tea, and we can talk. I have all night. Since tomorrow is Saturday, I don't have to go into the city. I'll help in whatever way I can." All thoughts of the legal brief he had intended to work on during the weekend flew right out of his mind.

Lucy took a moment to reflect on what she was doing. Who was this man she was literally trusting with her life? A neighbor whose dog had moved in with her so it could be with her dog. A neighbor she had only seen once or twice and had never even spoken to until a day ago. Maybe she really was crazy and needed a shrink. *No,* she told herself, *Wylie is okay. He's warm, compassionate, and he loves animals. Putting my trust in Wylie is not a mistake.* Childishly, she crossed her fingers.

Lucy walked out of Kennedy Hospital on Saturday afternoon with Wylie at her side.

Surprisingly, her head was quiet. The CAT scan, the MRI, and all the other tests she'd undergone had showed no abnormalities. As Dr. Schlesinger put it, "You're golden!"

Wylie cupped Lucy's elbow in his hand. "I don't know about you, but I sure feel relieved. You must be exhausted. Why don't you wait here while I get the car. It's still pretty icy, and this light snow is masking the ice patches."

"Okay, Wylie. I really appreciate your coming with me today. I owe you."

Wylie yanked at the baseball cap on his head. He turned the brim to the back before he loped off to the parking lot.

Lucy stepped under the overhang as a family of four exited the building. She strained to pick up their thoughts as they discussed the new baby they'd just seen. Nothing came back to her. She frowned. Maybe she could only *hear* thoughts if the person was stressed, excited, or angry. Maybe she herself had to be stressed, excited, or angry. She'd certainly felt that way last night. She was calm now that a team of doctors couldn't find anything wrong with her after five hours of testing. Maybe the whole thing was some kind of crazy fluke. She was glad she hadn't told any of the doctors about the Chinese fire drill going on inside her head. She was relieved also because she wouldn't have to seek out a shrink and bare her soul.

Wylie pulled alongside the curb in his Land Rover, reached across, and opened the door for her. The heater was blasting warm air. Lucy buckled up and leaned her head back against the headrest. "Are you thinking, Wylie? Because if you are, I can't *hear* you."

Wylie grinned. "That's a relief. Listen, how do you feel about going out for some Chinese? While you were being tested, I did all my Saturday errands, made Coop his meat loaf, fed the dogs, picked up my dry cleaning, and did my week's grocery shopping. I even washed some clothes. My evening is free."

"Chinese is good, but let's take it home. The weather's pretty ugly. I'd rather sit by a fire and eat. I miss the dogs."

"That's doable. You sure you're feeling okay?"

"Pretty much so. My head isn't a war

zone at the moment. What if it comes back? How am I going to deal with that?"

Wylie stopped for a traffic light at the corner of Grove and Oak Tree Road. "I don't know, Lucy. I think you should try and figure out why this happened to you. Stress does some really strange things to people. If you want to talk about it, I'm a good listener. You paid me a retainer, so you might as well get your money's worth."

Lucy laughed. "You have a point. Do you want me to call and order the food?"

"Good idea. Get some of everything. Do you like Chinese beer?"

Lucy looked across at Wylie. "I love Chinese beer. Do you?"

"Yeah, and Japanese beer, too. I like eating hibachi food with a good bottle of Sapporo. How about we go tomorrow night? Little Tokyo has the best." Wylie waited, holding his breath, for her answer. If she said yes, that meant they had a date. If she said no, that would mean she was still hung up on the guy who gave her the headlamp for a ring. A ring she no longer wore.

Lucy weighed the question. She thought about the federal agents, about Jonathan and what was going on in her life. She adored Japanese food. "I'd love to go to Little Tokyo with you, Wylie."

Well hot damn! She must like me, he thought.

She must like me. Lucy turned to look at Wylie. "Why wouldn't I like you after all you've done for me?"

Wylie slammed his foot on the brake and turned into the parking lot of the grammar school on Oak Tree Road. After the Rover came to a complete stop, he turned to look at her. "I didn't say anything, Lucy. You just read my mind. *Again."*

Lucy stared at Wylie as she struggled to digest his words. Her head wasn't hurting. She felt fine. Even the pain behind her eyes and ears was gone. "Are you sure you didn't say anything?"

Wylie yanked at his cap. "I'm positive. I was thinking how great it was and that maybe you liked me after all. I was excited."

Lucy tilted her head for a better look at her companion. "Maybe that's part of the answer. You were excited. Are you thinking now?"

"Yes, of course."

"Well, if you are, I don't have a clue as to what you're thinking. This is crazy!" Lucy dropped her head into her hands and started to cry.

Wylie looked across at Lucy, uncertain what to do. If there was one thing in the world he hated, it was seeing a woman cry. For a moment he was tempted to lie and say he'd spoken aloud just so she would stop crying. "Listen, Lucy, we're going to figure this out. I have a friend who's on staff at Duke University. He studies parapsychology and stuff of that nature. I can call him. It won't hurt to ask questions. I'm thinking this is just a temporary kind of thing, something you're going to have to live with till it . . . till it goes away. You said yourself you were feeling better, your head is clear, nothing hurts. You did have all those tests. Physically, you're okay."

Lucy raised her head and wiped her eyes with the back of her hand. "Okay," she murmured. "Are you still thinking?"

"Yes. My brain is going a mile a minute. Can you hear me?"

Lucy shook her head. "Okay, I was going to call the restaurant. We can talk about this later."

"Sounds like a plan to me." Wylie jammed

the baseball cap back on his head. "Make sure you get some hot mustard."

By ten o'clock the kitchen was clean, Wylie had walked the dogs, replenished the fire, and poured a fresh glass of beer for both himself and Lucy. He carried a tray loaded with munchies to snack on.

This was what he liked, what he had hungered for when he was married to Allison. It hadn't happened because Allison wasn't into home, hearth, dogs, and Chinese out of a carton. The only time she'd ever curled up on the sofa was when she had the flu. She didn't like a fire because it bothered her cat-green contact lenses. She didn't like beer because it bloated her. Chinese and Japanese food made her sleepy. The only time she came alive was when she went shopping or they dined at a five-star restaurant.

"Do you want me to go home, Lucy? I don't mind sleeping here on the couch. I don't think you should be alone."

"No, Wylie, please stay, but you don't have to sleep on the couch. I have a spare bedroom. I don't think I want to be alone."

Wylie heaved a sigh of relief as Coop

bounded onto his lap. He did everything but purr so Wylie would rub his belly. His owner obliged.

Sadie snorted her jealousy and started to paw the carpet. She let loose with an ear-splitting bark. Coop leaped off Wylie's lap and raced down the hall after his girlfriend. Lucy laughed. "Dogs are so funny some-times."

Wylie stretched out his long legs, his eyes on the dancing flames that were so mes-merizing. He risked a glance at Lucy, who was staring at him intently. He wanted to say something, but the words stuck in his throat. The decision was taken out of his hands when the phone rang. He could see the panic in Lucy's face when she debated if she should answer the phone.

"I always get nervous when the phone rings after nine o'clock," Wylie volunteered.

"Yeah, me, too." Lucy picked up the phone, her greeting strained and cautious.

She listened to Special Agent Connors ask how she was feeling before she agreed to a meeting at noon on Monday. "Fine," was Lucy's comment before she hung up the phone. She was jittery. That meeting, she knew, would be where the rubber met the road.

"Is something wrong?" Wylie asked. "What? You look scared to death. Tell me. Listen, I have a gun. I'm not a great shot, but I can shoot. I have a permit, too. What? Talk to me, Lucy."

Lucy debated for all of five seconds. "Okay, come over here," she said, pointing to the sofa. Wylie needed no prompting. He walked over and sat beside her.

Lucy pointed to the stack of brokerage statements. "Those are just the beginning." She talked nonstop for twenty minutes, ending the conversation by pointing to the shredded remains of the wedding invitations on the dining room table. "I'm going to sell my gown on eBay!"

Wylie stared at his neighbor. "That's . . . that's spook stuff."

"No, spooks are what they call CIA agents. FBI agents are just cold, steely-eyed people with no hearts. They believe I know all about this. I swear to God, I don't know a thing. They're ruining my life. Remember that man in Atlanta who they thought had something to do with the bombing at the Olympics? They ruined his life. That's what they're going to do to me."

"Only if you let them. You said that's not your signature on the brokerage accounts. That will hold up in a court of law. As your lawyer, I know how to get down and dirty if you want me to."

Lucy pressed her knuckles against her eyes so she wouldn't cry. "Wylie, the signature on those papers is mine. I've been racking my brain, trying to figure out how all this happened, and now I remember. They have me dead to rights. That's why they were so smug when I kept saying my signature was forged."

Lucy lowered her head, her eyes full of shame. "About a year ago, Jonathan and I were celebrating some big deal he'd put together. I don't even know what the deal was, just that it was big, and he'd made a bundle of money. We were at my place in New York and had had several bottles of wine. The truth is, I was pretty tipsy. I thought Jonathan was, too. Out of the blue, he opened his briefcase and pulled out all these papers and asked me to sign them. Most of them were blank, you know, the last page on a stapled document. He said his attorneys were putting my name on some of his holdings so if anything happened to him, I'd benefit. He cited how things happened with airlines after 9-11, and he wanted to make sure I was taken care of. I signed everything he put in front of me. I never gave it another thought until those agents showed up. I was going to marry the man, so why wouldn't I sign the papers? I wasn't thinking like a lawyer at the time," Lucy said defensively. "It is my signature on every single piece of paper, and it is my word against Jonathan's. I feel so incredibly stupid. I knew better, and I still did it. I guess he had me bewitched."

"That's not good, but then you already know that. What exactly does the FBI want you to do?"

"That's just it, I don't know. They're coming back on Monday at noon. I guess you need to be here since you're my lawyer now. Like I said, I just kept telling them I didn't know anything. I don't, not really. They want me to help them. With the FBI hounding me and what's going on in my head, I don't know if I'm coming or going.

"Jonathan duped me, Wylie! It wasn't like I was desperate to find a man, to get married. I wasn't. He came along, a nice guy, he knew how to flatter me and treat me as if I were special, and I fell for it. Dammit, he isn't even who he says he is, and he's coming here on Wednesday. That's only four days away. How am I supposed to act? What am I supposed to say?"

Wylie stared at Lucy, a helpless look on his face. "I guess the agents will tell you what to do and what to say. I can make a pest of myself if that will help."

"There's one other thing, Wylie. I probably should have told you earlier, but I didn't know you. I don't mean that I know you now . . . this isn't coming out right. Look, I didn't exactly lie. I just didn't . . . what I didn't do was . . . you *do* know me. You prosecuted a case in which I was the defendant's attorney. I'm Lucille Baker, not Baycur. Rachel Muller has a strong accent and pronounces my name wrong. Please, don't hold that against me. I moved here to New Jersey because I was burned out. I needed to fall back and regroup. People as a rule have a very jaded opinion of lawyers. I didn't want anyone to know what I did. We can talk it to death, but I would prefer not to."

Wylie slapped at his forehead. "I knew I knew you. You look different. Didn't you have very short red hair back then? Man, you were hell on wheels in that courtroom. I almost didn't mind losing to you. I did, but it was a pleasure watching you strut yourself. You just walked away, eh? Just like that."

"Yes, just like that. And now this. You aren't angry with me, are you?"

"Nah. I understand. I have six sisters. I know how women think and act. Are you giving up the law altogether? What's your feeling now about the guy you were going to marry?" He hoped his voice sounded casual.

"No, I'm not giving up the law. I was just thinking the other day about how bored I was. I'll probably go back to the office after the first of the year. If I'm not in jail, that is. As for Jonathan . . . I don't know how I feel about him—aside from angry. It's over, that's for sure. Will I pine away for him? I doubt it. I thought I was in love with him. Maybe I was in love with the idea of love."

Her voice was so pitiful-sounding, Wylie grinned. He knew all about that. His mother was forever telling him stories about his sisters and the bums they were going out with.

Fear of becoming old maids, she'd said. He needed to say something to wipe away the awful look on his neighbor's face. "I don't think that's necessarily a bad thing, Lucy. How much do you think you can get for your gown on eBay? I have a bunch of junk I'm thinking of selling," Wylie added, his curiosity aroused.

Lucy burst out laughing. Wylie joined in at his own expense.

She's free. Maybe that means I have a shot. Been a long time since I met anyone I like half as much. We have a lot in common, we're both lawyers, even though I said I would never again marry a lawyer. She loves my dog. That might be a plus. Lucy lowered her gaze to her lap. There was no way she wanted Wylie to know she was hearing his thoughts. Especially thoughts like these.

"You aren't reading my mind, are you?" Wylie asked uneasily.

Lucy shook her head. "I think I'm going to go to bed. Tomorrow I'm going to drive to Rutgers and use their library. I want to read up on what's going on inside my head. You're welcome to come along."

"Well, sure. Good night, Lucy. I can make

us eggs Benedict in the morning to earn my keep if that's okay with you."

"It's very okay with me. I love eggs Benedict."

"Oooh, it's so beautiful," Lucy gasped as she walked over to the sliding doors to let the dogs out into the yard. "I can't believe it snowed five inches during the night. Before Thanksgiving no less. It looks just like a winter wonderland. The dogs are having so much fun." She watched as both dogs raced the length, then the width of the yard, barking and yelping at the strange phenomenon.

Wylie chuckled at Lucy's exuberant tone as he, too, looked out the kitchen window at the cavorting dogs. He looked up when Lucy entered the kitchen. She looked surprised at what she was seeing. "I borrowed your apron since I'm a sloppy cook. I went home earlier to shower and shave and to turn up my heat. I've been up since five o'clock. Did you sleep well?"

Lucy sat down at the table. Wylie looked so at home in the kitchen. *Her* kitchen. Jonathan had an aversion to kitchens. She couldn't ever remember if he'd set foot in the kitchen of her brownstone when she'd lived in New York. Most times she'd brought him a cup of coffee or a drink. She'd never cooked for him, though. Thanksgiving would be the first time.

"I hope this tastes as good as it looks," Lucy said, unfolding her napkin. "I feel like I'm taking advantage of you, Wylie. But, to answer your question, I slept soundly."

Wylie raked his fingers through his unruly hair. He squinted at his neighbor, a suspicious look on his face. "You are not taking advantage of me. I'm glad I can help. I haven't had this much excitement since I broke my ankle. That was six years ago. You aren't reading my mind, are you?"

"No, I'm not. I wish I could explain how it works, Wylie. Right now I can hear a jumble of voices. There's nothing clear, nothing distinct. Once in a while a clear word will surface, but it has no meaning. I guess right now it's because all the neighbors are outside shoveling snow and talking to one another. Are you thinking now?"

"Yes. I was wondering if you want me to call my friend at Duke. You didn't answer me when I asked you yesterday. Are we still on for the Rutgers library?"

"I am if you are. You have four-wheel drive, right? Let's see what we come up with at the library, if anything, before you call him."

Lucy was clearing the table when the phone rang. She looked at Wylie, who was on his way out to clear her driveway with his snowblower, and he looked at her. He shrugged. Lucy saw him wince when she said, "Oh, Jonathan, I wasn't expecting your call."

Wylie's face darkened as he used his index finger to offer up a salute.

"Lucy, are you there?" Jonathan's voice was sharp. "Did you hear a word I said?"

"No, Jonathan, I did not hear what you said," Lucy responded coolly. "We had a snowstorm last night, and your voice keeps fading in and out. Wet wires, I assume." Her voice was even cooler when she said, "What did you say?"

"I said, I'm not going to be able to join you for Thanksgiving after all. I called to apologize."

The relief Lucy felt was immeasurable. "Perhaps that's a good thing, Jonathan. I think I'm coming down with the flu. It seems everyone in the neighborhood has it. My brother will probably come here and bring dinner with him. Is there anything else?"

"You sound like you're trying to get rid of me."

The chuckle on the other end of the phone didn't sound sincere to Lucy's ears.

"No, no, Jonathan. I know how busy you are. I was looking forward to seeing you," she lied. She wondered if her tongue would fall out. When she was a kid her mother had scared the daylights out of her and Steven. She'd told them their tongues would fall out if they told a lie or even a little fib. Lucy remembered walking around with a mirror in her pocket to make sure her tongue was still there.

"I really miss you. I hate this traveling. I can't wait till we get married so I can cut back. Eat an extra slice of turkey for me, sweetheart. I have to run now. I love you, darling."

Lucy didn't bother to respond. Instead, she pressed her finger down to break the connection. There was no way in hell she was going to tell Jonathan St. Clair she loved him. No way in hell. Right now, right this very minute, she hated the suave, sophisticated man she was supposed to marry. The most she could say about him was that he was decent in bed. Not great but okay. She didn't know how she knew, but she knew that Wylie would be spectacular between the sheets. Her body grew warm at the thought. She chastised herself immediately. She'd just met the man, for heaven's sake, and here she was thinking about how he'd perform in bed. Better not to think about things like that. Her life was messed up enough at the moment without adding Wylie to the mix.

The ride down Route 27 with Wylie driving his Land Rover was mostly spent talking about the weather, snowplows, and the newscast predicting even more snow later in the day. "Not to worry, Lucy, this baby can handle anything," Wylie said confidently referring to his Rover. "I hope we're still on for Japanese this evening." He took his eyes off the road for a minute to look across at his companion. She looked wonderful this morning, dressed in a sky-blue winter jacket with matching wool slacks. A snow-white wool hat covered her hair. He liked the way little tendrils escaped by her ears.

"I'm looking forward to it. So, you really like driving a truck like this?"

"Absolutely. The gas mileage isn't that great, but I wouldn't give it up for anything. It's five years old. My friend, the one I was telling you about who works at Duke, has the big Range Rover. Of course he needs it, with four kids. He loves to go four-wheeling with his family. Jake is my best friend. We've known each other since our college days, when we were in the same fraternity. Do you have a best friend?"

"Not really. I was pretty much a book-worm, and beyond the necessities for pro-fessional contacts, I'm not a joiner. You know how it is with the law. If you're a lawyer, you're married to the profession. There isn't much time for a social life. Tell me about your friend. How did he get into parapsychology?"

"I'm not really sure. I can give you the ver-sion he hands out to most people. Seems he and his mother both have what he calls extrasensory perception. When we shared an apartment when I was at Georgetown Law, he was forever cautioning me about doing or not doing things. He was usually on the money. The guy is a pure whiz. He's got his doctorate and an MBA.

"His wife was Miss North Carolina in the Miss America pageant ten years ago. She was the first runner-up. Nice lady. She's always trying to fix me up with one of her friends," Wylie said hoping to get a reaction from Lucy. When nothing was forthcoming, he said, "I know you'll like him. The truth is, it's impossible not to like Jake," and focused on the snowy road ahead of them.

Five minutes later, they arrived at the library. "Let's split up. We'll hit the stacks, you take one shelf, and I'll take another. We can make notes and check stuff on the Net when we get home."

"Sounds good." Lucy hopped out of the truck and immediately went down on her fanny. Wylie bent down to pick her up and ended up right next to her. He laughed uproariously at their predicament. With their faces just inches apart, vapor from their mouths colliding, Wylie leaned slightly forward, intending to kiss her. Alarmed at how much she wanted that to happen, Lucy moved away from him, and the moment was quickly lost.

Finally, they both managed to get to their feet and into the library. Both of them were huffing and puffing as they shook the fine snow from their jackets. Neither one mentioned how close they'd come to locking their lips together.

"This is a daunting task," Lucy mumbled an hour later. "I've got a list a yard long. We can try the Internet later. Most of what I found are just case studies of people who suddenly get a feeling that something is happening to a loved one and come to find out that whatever it was actually happened. There seem to be thousands of those that are documented. I haven't found one instance where anyone *hears* another person's thoughts."

"Are you hearing anything now?" Wylie asked as he perused his own list.

"Background voices, but they sound far off. Are you thinking, because if you are, I'm not picking up on it?"

I'm thinking I wanted to kiss you till your teeth rattled, Wylie thought. He watched Lucy's eyes to see if she was picking up on his thoughts. It didn't appear so. "I found a book titled *The Frontier of the Mind.* I think you are receiving some sort of transmissible signal, for want of a better word, from someone else's brain. Like mine, when you *hear* me. I think we will just *borrow* this book and return it later. I'll stick it inside my jacket. Tell me if anyone is looking. We'll bring it back or send it FedEx with a donation. Tell me when the coast is clear."

Lucy's eyes scanned the massive library. "Do it now," she whispered.

"Done! Okay, let's get out of here," Wylie said in a jittery voice.

"You go out to the car, Wylie. I want to walk around here for a while to see if I . . . *hear* anything. Until now, you're the only person I've been around aside from the FBI agents. I want to see if . . . if I have the same unusual ability here as at home."

"Okay," Wylie said as he walked quickly out of the library, the "borrowed" book under his jacket. He knew he'd never make a good thief. His heart was pounding so fast he thought he was going to pass out.

Lucy waited until the door closed behind Wylie before she made her way into the library's main reading room. She walked slowly as she tried to *hear* things. Libraries were normally quiet to begin with, so this was probably an exercise in futility, she told herself as she walked around the seating area. She was nervous, her hands twitching as she concentrated on two students sitting together at a table. She almost tripped on the blue carpet when she *heard* one of the two students' thoughts. *Man, how can I study after last night? She was so hot I thought I was going to go up in smoke.* Lucy clapped her hands over her ears as she pressed forward.

As she meandered around, she heard words, some clear, some muffled. She heard a reference to a washing machine, a thought about a grade that was unacceptable. A whole jumble of words suddenly seemed to come from all directions. The Chinese fire drill again. She turned and rushed to the front of the library. As she passed the librarian, she heard the librarian arguing with herself about whether to tell her husband she was pregnant or wait another month. Lucy wanted to tell her to tell him now but she didn't. Instead, she slammed through the doors and saw Wylie waiting in front of the building. He took her hand and guided her across the parking area to the Land Rover. After she helped him clear the snow from the front and back windshields, she hopped into the truck, buckled up and proceeded to tell him what she'd *heard*. When he laughed, Lucy grimaced. "I bet I could get a job in a circus with this . . . new talent of mine."

Wylie laughed again but he reached over to pat her hand. It felt so comforting. Lucy relaxed immediately.

"Jake can interpret all this for us. I don't understand it any more than you do. He's a real force in his own field, so let's leave it to the experts. You feeling okay?" Wylie asked anxiously.

"Yes, I feel fine. My head is quiet now. When we were clearing the snow away, I had the feeling that the snow was buffering my thoughts. Does that make sense?"

Wylie shrugged. "Listen, Lucy, I don't want you to get upset, but I called Jake last night after you went to sleep. I really called him just to talk. He volunteered to come here. I swear to you, I didn't ask him. He'll be here tomorrow. And, he's staying through Thanksgiving. His wife and kids went to Minnesota because his mother-in-law broke her hip and Jane wants to be with her mother. I couldn't say no. If you don't want to talk to him, that's okay. He's going to be staying with me. I'm just trying to help, Lucy."

Lucy smiled. "I know that, Wylie. It's okay. The feds are coming back tomorrow. Up till now it's been a mind game with them. Tomorrow they're going to bring out their big guns. It might be a good thing if your friend is here. You can both sit in on the meeting."

"With this new . . . ah . . . power of yours, you are now the eight-hundred-pound gorilla. Think about that, Lucy."

5

Lucy woke up to a quiet white world. As she looked out at the yard, which was covered in a blinding pristine whiteness, she remembered that Wylie had taken the dogs when he'd left last night so they could play in the snow.

She wondered if the FBI agents would still come today. Were they like the mailmen, undeterred by sleet, snow, or rain? Thinking about them set her stomach to roiling with fear again. *How could I have been so utterly stupid where Jonathan was concerned?* Because when you were working eighty hours a week having a fiancé in absentia suited you just fine.

Twenty minutes later, Lucy was in the kitchen, whipping up pancake batter and frying bacon, while coffee dripped into the pot. She almost jumped out of her skin when she heard a *thwamp, thwamp* sound at the sliding glass doors. She burst out laughing when she went to the door to see Coop and Sadie, covered in snow from head to foot. Obviously, they'd tunneled from yard to yard and come up through the snow. They barreled through the house to the front door just as the doorbell rang.

"It's a holiday!" Wylie bellowed as he stepped out of his Timberlands. "Hmmm, smells good. I could eat a horse. Or, whatever it is you're making."

Lucy laughed again. "Pancakes, bacon, coffee, juice." This was nice. Good-looking guy, his dog, her dog, her cooking in the kitchen. A roaring fire in the fireplace. Snowbound. The stuff dreams were made of. In this case a nightmare if she carried the thought any further.

"How'd you sleep?" Wylie asked as he made himself at home in the kitchen by setting the table, getting out napkins and silver. "I slept like a log," he volunteered.

"I did, too. I woke up, and it was so quiet. I missed the dogs, though. I can't believe they made it through the tunnel and then up through all that snow."

"Sadie wanted to get home, and Coop was right behind her. They're in love." He guffawed.

Wylie looked really good this morning, in a yellow sweater and jeans that fit him like a second skin. Nice buns and great thighs. Lucy felt like she was sizing up a chicken at the market.

"How's the head?" he asked.

"Quiet. I was thinking when I woke up that maybe this whole thing is just some temporary fluke."

Wylie stared at her. "Lucy, I just don't know. Weather permitting, Jake should be here soon. I checked the airport, and flights are coming in. I hope he can make it from the airport. He told me not to pick him up, that he would rent a car."

Lucy placed a stack of buttermilk pancakes in front of Wylie, then fixed two plates for the dogs.

Wylie looked across the table, wondering if Lucy was tuned in to his thoughts. He didn't ask. It didn't matter to him if she knew he was worried about the FBI's visit. He knew enough about the way the bureau worked to realize that there was no way in hell Lucy was going to get away from them unless she did what they wanted.

While Lucy cleared the table, he watched her and liked what he was seeing. Hell, he liked everything about her. Today she was wearing a long-sleeved pink shirt, open at the throat, and jeans that hugged her slim hips. Nice shape, 110 pounds, he judged. Nice blond hair, too, although today she wore it pinned on top of her head in a knot secured by tortoiseshell combs. He knew his mother would like Lucy. His dad would dote on her.

Wylie's cell phone chirped. He rummaged in his pocket and flipped it on. "Where are you, buddy?" he asked when he recognized Jake's voice. "You're standing in my driveway! Hot damn. Come next door, and we'll cook you some breakfast.

"It's Jake. He's here! I don't believe that guy! He eats like a truck driver, just so you know. Guess that's him knocking on the door."

Coop and Sadie made it to the door before Wylie. Both dogs barked happily, but they reared back when they heard a bark coming from the bag hanging on Jake's shoulder.

"I had to bring Lulu. My mother-in-law is allergic to dogs." Jake shrugged as he lowered the canvas carry-on to the floor and unzipped it.

Coop and Sadie skidded backward when a five-pound Yorkshire terrier dressed in a pink sweater with matching bow in her hair pranced out of the bag and started to yip and yap as she sniffed and pawed at her new surroundings.

Lucy stifled a laugh as she extended her hand. "Lucy Baker," she said.

"Jake Parsons. This little stick of dynamite is Lulu. My four-year-old twins named her. They also like to dress her up. Cheaper than buying Barbie clothes. She's trained," he added as an afterthought.

Lucy eyed the studly-looking shrink with the sparkling eyes behind the trench glasses. He looked like a movie star with curly, dark hair.

"How are the roads?" Wylie asked, leading his friend toward the kitchen.

"Horrendous. Don't go out unless you have to. As I was leaving the airport they announced they were closing it. And LaGuardia and Kennedy, too." He bent down to scoop Lulu into his arms.

Lucy started to whip up more pancake batter, while Wylie meticulously placed bacon into the fry pan. This movie star type couldn't possibly help her. What could this hunk who traveled with a miniature dog do for her? She turned around to see the Yorkie squirming to be put down on the floor. "If you're worried about the dogs hurting her, don't." She looked up to see both dogs in the doorway. Both looked like they were poised for flight.

"Coop thinks Miss Lulu is a wind-up toy. Watch," Wylie said as he took Lulu out of Jake's arms and set her down on the floor. She yapped immediately, the pink bow in her hair jiggling with excitement. Clueless Cooper advanced tentatively into the kitchen, then stopped in his tracks while Sadie hung back, her tail tucked between her legs.

Miss Lulu did a little dance, her tiny feet skittering this way and that, all the while yapping her head off.

"Nah, they aren't going to hurt her. Coop will figure out she's real when she nips his feet." Wylie grinned.

The trio watched as Coop bounded over to the yapping dog, bent down to sniff her, then circled her, his weaponlike tail swishing furiously. A second later, he had the pink sweater bunched in his teeth and was trotting off with his prize. Miss Lulu looked

around, undecided if she was being rescued or captured. She let out a joyful bark
as Coop romped down the hall.

Lucy shrugged. "I think it's a good thing.
That little gal looks to me like she can hold
her own."

"That's the problem. I'd hate to see her
hurt Coop." Jake guffawed as he snatched
a strip of bacon off the plate. "She can be a
dynamo when she sets her mind to it."

Wylie hooted with laughter. Lucy turned
to hide her smirk. Sadie did not like other female dogs, especially bossy female dogs.
She might also be jealous if Coop paid too
much attention to the little fur ball. Something else to worry about.

Lucy sipped at her coffee while Jake ate
his breakfast. The two men talked about the
weather, North Carolina, and the dogs. She
tried to shift her mind into neutral to see if
she could read either man's mind. Nothing
was coming through. She finally gave up
and started to think about Jonathan. Maybe
the reason Jonathan had canceled his trip
was because he knew the FBI was onto
him. Maybe he would go back to one of the
third-world companies he did business with
and never be heard from again. Or, maybe

he was busy plotting her death, as the FBI had implied. She shivered inside the pink shirt she was wearing.

The minute Jake Parsons finished his second cup of coffee, Lucy cleared the table and turned the dishwasher on.

"That was very good, Lucy. I enjoyed every bit of it. It's refreshing to find a young woman who actually cooks as opposed to ordering in. Now," he said, placing a tape recorder in the middle of the table, "let's get started. I want you to start at whatever you perceive to be the beginning. I only know what Wylie has told me. For now, let's make the starting point the day you decided to give up practicing law."

Lucy looked down at the tape recorder self-consciously. She was nervous, the words tumbling from her lips in her haste to get them out. From time to time she looked across at Jake Parsons to see his reaction, but his facial expression was totally blank. Wylie simply leaned back in his chair and sipped at his coffee, never taking his eyes off Lucy.

Thirty minutes later, Lucy threw her hands in the air, and said, "That's it. The three agents are due today. I imagine they'll be calling soon. The weather may have slowed them down a bit." She looked at the two men, waiting for them to speak.

"Do you want us here when the feds come?" Jake asked.

"Yes. I think I need witnesses. I'm not hearing anything from either of you," Lucy said sourly. She fixed her gaze on Jake, and said, "Maybe it all went away, and I'm back to normal."

"All things are possible. I never close the door to anything. When you do that, you miss all the good stuff."

"Can you tell me if this is a long-term thing, short-term, a fluke? What?" Lucy asked. "Do you know of anyone else who . . . who can read people's minds?"

"No, not personally. As far as I know, there are no documented cases like yours either. However, I have heard of several cases from others in my field. Three, to be exact. All three refused, quite adamantly, to continue with testing, saying they didn't want to be written up, turned into freaks or sideshows. I also know all three are being monitored, but it will never show up in black-and-white. Anxiety, fear, adrenaline rushes, all three can contribute to what you are experiencing, Lucy. In time, you can probably use your new ability to your advantage once you learn how to control it.

"I know you want me to explain how something like this could happen. All I can do is try. There have been many, many papers written on ESP, extrasensory perception, and even professors and researchers at prestigious universities like Duke and Harvard have been persuaded that human beings can actually read the thoughts of others. The evidence presented has been hard as well as statistical." Jake massaged his temples as he tried to figure out how best to explain Lucy's condition in layman's terms. "In the 1930s at Duke University, before my time, there was this researcher named Joseph Banks Rhine, who is considered the father of serious scientific research into the paranormal. He had a colleague named Carl Zener, and they did the first systematic study on the subject of extrasensory perception. It was a colorful card study. He used bright colors and geometric symbols. The subjects he worked with were receiving information from something besides the known five senses when they viewed the cards, so he said it was a sixth sense.

"Rhine defined this sixth sense as ESP. Then he subdivided it into four basic abilities. Telepathy. Clairvoyance. Precognition. And psychokinesis."

It sounded ominous to Wylie. "Which one does Lucy have?" he asked carefully.

"In my opinion, Lucy is telepathic. That's the ability to tune in to the thoughts of others, or sometimes, inject your own thoughts into another's mind. I don't think she has the ability to do the latter.

"Clairvoyance is the power to see things that aren't available to you by the five senses and aren't known by other people.

"Precognition is the skill of looking into the future and seeing events before they take place. Sometimes through the subconscious or when you're dreaming or even daydreaming.

"Psychokinesis is the ability to use the power of the mind to influence matter; moving objects by thought is an example."

"That's pretty scary stuff," Wylie said.

"To you, maybe. I deal with it day in and day out. There aren't that many believers out there," Jake said. "There are, however, a robust number of people with at least one of the four abilities I just told you about. However, our numbers are growing daily, by that, I mean believers. There was even a television show about a man who got a newspaper a day ahead telling him what was going to occur.

"Ordinary people can develop ESP with no logical explanation. It simply happens. One day they wake up and can read someone else's thoughts. I've read some of those case histories, and I've kept an open mind. Still do. They were not cases like yours, however, where trauma was involved. Some small part of your brain was altered when you got that electrical shock would be my best guess. You aren't going to die or anything like that," Jake added hastily. "In time, if your ESP doesn't fade, you'll learn to live with it the way the others do.

"The cases I've mentioned aren't listed by name but by number for anonymity. I remember one in particular had to do with a person who dealt with magnetic fields day in and day out. He gave up his profession and is now a landscape painter. None of the cases were subjected to the traumas that you were is what I'm saying."

Lucy's shoulders slumped. "So what you're really saying is you can't help me."

"That's pretty much it unless you want to become a case history. Even then, I don't think I can help you. You can speak with a psychiatrist or a neurosurgeon if you like. Most people tend to shy away from doing that because, like you, they've been tested medically and given a clean bill of health. If you want to go that route, it's entirely up to you. Like I said, eventually you'll be able to control what you want to *hear* and not *hear.* You'll try not to subject yourself to undue anxiety. Life will go on, Lucy. You haven't been able to hear either one of us since we sat down here, right?" Lucy nodded. "Things are quiet, no one is upset, we're just talking normally. You're fine.

"Right now I see the federales as your immediate problem."

As if on cue the phone rang. Lucy jerked to attention. Was it the feds or Jonathan? She didn't know which she feared more.

When the phone rang for the seventh time, Jake asked, "Aren't you going to answer it?"

Lucy grabbed the phone. A moment later she growled into it, "One-thirty is fine, Mr.

Lawrence. Of course I'll be here." Lucy hung up the phone and looked across at the two men. "It was Agent Lawrence. They'll be here at one-thirty."

"If I might, I'd like to make a suggestion," Jake said. He reached for the recorder and removed the small cassette to replace it with a fresh one. "Tape the agents while they're here. Meet with them in your family room so you can keep the recorder between the cushions. This is way too serious for you not to have proof of what's been said and by whom. I don't think it will be to your advantage for us to stay here for the meeting. I think the agents and Lucy will be more relaxed, more open with each other if we aren't hovering. Those guys get pissy when you tread on their turf. They know we're here as backup, and that's a good thing. The tape recorder will do the rest. Do you agree, Wylie?"

"What are you saying, Jake? Hell no, it is not a good idea. No, no, no, we are not going to leave Lucy here with those agents."

"Get real, Wylie. They are not going to harm Lucy. All they're going to do is talk to her, question her. Everything will be recorded. Will you please trust me on this?"

"Are you sure, Jake? I mean *really* sure? I don't like leaving Lucy alone, period."

"I think your little lady can handle things. She does have this new ability to *hear* things. She also has a cell phone and a killer dog to protect her. She doesn't need either one of us."

Wylie looked like he still wasn't convinced, but he gave in at the mention of the killer dog. "Okay, I'm going to go home now so I can mix up some meat loaf for Coop. I gotta settle Jake in, Lucy. We'll be back for lunch if you invite us. Noon is good for us."

Some nice hot soup with crusty bread would be a really good lunch, especially on a day like this. Lucy whirled around. "I'm not excited. I'm relatively calm. Both of you appear to be calm. So, how come I know you would like some nice hot soup with crusty bread?"

Jake turned, his jaw slack. "I was just thinking . . . I don't have the answer, Lucy. I wish I did. The only thing I can think of is you got upset when Agent Lawrence called you just now. You look . . . *twitchy.* Are you feeling nervous?"

"Yes, I am. I dread meeting and talking with them because I know they think I'm lying. If they can't get Jonathan . . . Leo, whatever his name is, they're going to get me."

"When the roads clear a little more, maybe we should check out that multimillion-dollar house the FBI says you own. There might be something in the house that will help us figure out exactly what is going on," Wylie said.

Lucy nodded.

Wylie whistled for Coop, who came on the run, Sadie and Miss Lulu alongside. All three skidded to a stop as they tried to figure out if they were going out, staying, or what. Coop galloped to the door when he saw Wylie slip into his jacket. Miss Lulu pawed her owner's leg to be picked up, while Sadie hugged Lucy's leg.

At the last second, after Jake marched ahead of him, Wylie turned, his face a mixture of emotions. He leaned forward, smacked Lucy on the lips, and squeezed her arms. "Call if you need me!" He kissed her again when Jake bellowed for him to hurry up.

When the door closed behind her guests, Lucy felt a little dazed, but in a good way. Smiling, she took Sadie into the kitchen and offered her a treat. Sadie turned her head, walked over to the sliding door leading to the deck, and lay down, her head between her paws.

Ten minutes later, as Lucy was emptying the dishwasher, she heard Sadie slam herself against the sliding door, her bark loud and shrill. She went into the family room in time to see Coop bound through the snow with Miss Lulu's pink sweater clutched between his teeth, Miss Lulu attached to the sweater. Miss Lulu looked happy as a lark, her pink bow bouncing every which way.

"Guess your boyfriend can't stand to be without you, Sadie," Lucy said as she opened the door. Sadie almost turned herself inside out as she romped and barked with her buddy. Miss Lulu sat on the sidelines watching, her dark eyes sad and forlorn. This time Sadie was the one who nuzzled the little dog until she had a firm hold on the pink sweater. A second later, Miss Lulu perky as ever, went along for the ride. All three dogs trotted through the room, then down the hall to Sadie's lair.

If only life were that simple, Lucy thought as she sat down at the table. Was it a good idea to go to the mansion in the Watchung

Mountains? If there was as much security as the agents said there was, how would she ever get in? Since she was the owner, according to the FBI, she could call the police, give them some story about losing the code or something to that effect so they wouldn't investigate and arrest her when she set off the alarm. *Where there's a will there's a way,* she thought grimly.

Lucy pondered the more immediate problem that was Jonathan. How could she have been so stupid where he was concerned? Why wasn't her heart broken? Why wasn't she feeling anything other than fear?

Her gaze swept to the portable phone on the kitchen counter. She should have called Steven days ago. Her brother, razor-sharp, might have some ideas on how to deal with the feds. If she told him, he'd worry about her and become a pest. Steven had always felt the need to play the role of big brother even though he was her little brother. Wylie was a good stand-in. Why cause Steven grief?

Steven had never liked Jonathan. The truth was, Steven had never liked anyone she dated more than three times. He'd said Jonathan was a phony. At the time she'd thought of it as a "guy thing" and didn't pay attention. Another time, Steven had said Jonathan was a gutter fighter. Just feelings I have, he'd explained. Well, how right he was. Maybe the reason she'd never told him what was going on was because she didn't want to hear him say, I told you so.

Lucy bolted out of her comfortable chair when the phone shrilled behind her. Sucking in her breath she reached for it, her greeting cautious. "Steven!" she said in relief when she heard her brother's voice.

"I'm just calling to check on you," a deep voice said. "How's the weather in Jersey?"

"Pretty much the same as in New York, little brother. Did you open the office?"

"I'm here but that's about it. Listen, sis, I'm calling to ask if you mind if I don't make it for Thanksgiving. A couple of the guys want to go skiing. Your fiancé isn't one of my favorite people as you know. You two won't miss me at all."

"Actually, Jonathan can't make it, so I'm having dinner with a neighbor. It's fine, Steven, don't give it another thought. Don't go breaking your legs. I'd make a lousy nurse, and you'd make a worse patient."

"I'll be careful. I'll call you when I get back. Give Sadie a hug for me."

"Will do. 'Bye, Steven."

Lucy walked back into the living room to get the manila folder lying on the coffee table. Earlier she'd been too panicked to go through the material the agents had left her. Now, though, she needed to look at everything carefully, using her legal brain, not the paranoid brain she'd used thus far.

At twenty minutes to twelve, Lucy stuffed the deeds, the copies of insurance policies, the brokerage statements, her tax forms, and the titles to boats and cars back into the envelope. She closed it securely. She hoped she never had to look at it again.

How in the hell could anyone with a brain believe she was capable of money laundering? How? Angry beyond words, Lucy stomped her way to the family room. On the count of three she was going to toss the whole mess into the fire. Suddenly, she was angrier than she'd ever been in her life. In the end she dropped the envelope behind the wide-screen television set. Since the monster set sat catercorner, it was doubtful anyone would look behind it to the tangled mess of wires from the VCR, the cables, and the new DVD player she'd installed just last week. She didn't know why she felt the need to hide the envelope.

Her eye fell on the stolen library book, *The Frontier of the Mind.* Unfortunately, both Wylie and she had closed the book in disgust, with Wylie saying, "Between us, we have two fine, legal minds, and neither one of us can make sense of this brain stuff. You know what I think, Lucy? I think you got it, and you're stuck with it." And she was . . . stuck with it.

Back in the kitchen, Lucy picked up the phone to call her neighbor. Her message was short and curt, "I'm making lunch now."

Lucy's anger stayed with her as she banged pots and pans and slammed the refrigerator door. Anger was better than tears, she thought, as she slapped cheese between slices of bread.

The dogs didn't bother to investigate when Wylie and Jake came through the front door.

Lucy forced a smile as she opened soup cans. She turned back to the business at hand and strained to see if she could *hear* either man's thoughts. Her head felt clogged up the way it did when she had a sinus infection. *She's never going to agree to go to Watchung. She's too pissed. I never saw such a rigid back. She's no match for those FBI stooges. She won't know what hit her by the time they get done with her. If I ever get my hands on that schmuck who set her up like this, I'll strangle him.* The words were crystal clear, but she couldn't tell which man she should attribute the thoughts to. Possibly both of them. It must be Wylie, she decided. She felt pleased that he cared enough to want to strangle Jonathan. Not that he would. Still, the thought was nice.

My mother always served those little white soda crackers with tomato soup. Tomato soup isn't the same unless you have those little crackers. Lucy reached up into the cabinet for a package of the crackers Wylie was thinking about. She turned and plopped them in the middle of the table. He looked at her in awe. She nodded.

Jake stared up at her. "If you can harness that anger you're feeling right now, you just might be able to figure out what the agents have in mind. That's another way of saying work yourself into a frenzy before they get here. Can you do that?"

Lucy threw her hands up in the air. "I don't know. This is all new to me. I tried the other day to . . . to do it, but it didn't work. I was upset, but I wasn't angry at the time. All I can do is play it by ear and hope for the best. You're right about something else, too. They might *look* like the Three Stooges, but they aren't that stupid."

Jake toyed with the silverware in front of him. "You read my mind. I am totally amazed. This is the first direct contact I've had with a person who could actually do it. Reading case histories is not the same thing." Subdued excitement rang in his voice, and it did not go unnoticed by Lucy. She felt herself shivering at the realization that she'd become a freak.

"By the way, we were watching the Weather Channel at Wylie's. The worst of the storm is over, and the roads have been sanded and salted. We can make a try for that house in the mountains after the agents leave if you're up for it. The bad news is there is another worse storm riding on the tail of this one. They've been using the word *blizzard* a lot."

Lucy ladled soup into bright yellow cups. "I'm up for anything at this point" she said curtly.

6

Jonathan St. Clair eyed his expensive crocodile luggage with a jaundiced eye. He was getting damn sick and tired of packing and repacking his pricey luggage. He was also damn sick and tired of airplanes and hotel rooms. It didn't matter if the airplane was his own private Gulfstream V or that the rooms were suites in five-star hotels. The truth was he was damn sick and tired of just about everything in his life. And today he hated Chile in particular.

Stepping back, cutting back, whatever you wanted to call it, wasn't working for him. He told himself the bottom line was his own greed, but that wasn't really true. What he was experiencing, and what he refused to acknowledge, was panic. With Congress's passage of the Patriot Act, he was now on the FBI's radar screen, and he wasn't just a little blip. He knew he was a very big blip, which meant that travel back to the States was a gamble. He wasn't sure he was ready to take that particular gamble. Not yet, anyway. The bottom line was he wanted out of the business that was driving him ragged. When you were the best in your field, and people were comfortable with the results you got for them, why would they want to see you retire? They didn't. Instead, they offered to pay you more and more until you couldn't refuse the high-seven-figure commissions. It was that simple. Besides, you couldn't spend money in a federal prison.

A threat was a threat no matter how nicely worded it was. He'd been in the business far too long not to recognize the subtle threats that his clients tossed his way after they upped his percentages to obscene amounts of money. More than he could ever spend in his lifetime.

Those same clients had their lifestyles in place, their money secured, their very lives shielded by layers and layers of protection while he was front and center as he scrambled twenty-four hours a day to make sure he kept both feet two steps ahead of the law. They were just waiting for him to make a mistake, and in his present frame of mind, it was just a matter of time before he slipped.

He knew he had been on the FBI's radar screen for some time, knew it was just a matter of time before they made a move on him. He'd tried to warn his greedy clients, but they'd refused to listen. Because they refused to listen, he'd canceled his trip to the States. If his situation didn't improve quickly, he would probably have to cancel his Christmas trip, too.

He realized that he was sweating even though the air-conditioning was turned to the coolest setting. Now he was going to have to change his shirt again. He thought he could smell his own fear as he ripped at the shirt he was wearing, a simple, fine linen, round-necked shirt that cost four hundred dollars. He was addicted to fine, costly things. It was the reason he worked on the wrong side of the law.

His diamond-studded Rolex watch told him he had just enough time to change his shirt, repack his bag, attach the manacled briefcase that his clients demanded he use to his wrist, and go downstairs to wait for the chauffeured car that would take him to the airport and his Gulfstream.

He was an attractive man, one men envied and women fawned over. Tall and lean, with sharp-chiseled features, penetrating gray eyes that could turn steely as flint, perfect ruler-straight teeth, and a crop of slightly wavy hair that was all his own. He tipped the scales at 180 and was perfectly proportioned for his six-foot height. He wore a year-round bronzed tan that flirted with his graying temples. More than one person told him he could have posed for *Town & Country* or *GQ,* a compliment so pleasing to him that he traded on it when necessary.

Jonathan gazed at his reflection in the mirror as his mind continued to race. Satisfied that he looked his impeccable self, he snapped the cuff onto his wrist, picked up his case, and started for the door. There was no time to wait for a bellhop. He'd cut it a shade too close this time around. He wondered why that was. Maybe because he was jittery, his nerves twanging for some reason. He'd been fine until the last few phone calls to Lucy. His stomach had protested by tightening up after their conversations because he'd heard something in his fiancée's voice he'd never heard before. That was when he'd started to feel uneasy, and the feeling remained with him.

As he rode down in the elevator, Jonathan thought about his fiancée. It wasn't like Lucy to be so careless that she'd fall and sprain her ankle. She was a runner, a true athlete. She was like a gazelle in motion. No, it was unlike Lucy to fall. Her voice had been so cool. On second thought, *cool* was the wrong word. The right word was *strained.* Now why would Lucy's voice be strained? Unless . . . unless someone was around asking questions or somehow she had gotten some notion of the real reason he'd had her sign all those papers a year ago. He needed to call Lucy again to see if he was being paranoid or his survival instincts were on the money.

Jonathan stepped out of the elevator into the marble-and-tile lobby of the hotel. His gaze raked the interior of the lobby until he found the chauffeur standing near the wide double doors. He held up his hand. Within seconds the driver had his bag in his hand and was striding toward a luxurious Mercedes-Benz. A Mercedes-Benz and an experienced chauffeur were always at Jonathan's disposal.

Outside, Chile's humidity slapped Jonathan in the face. Perspiration beaded on his brow as he stepped into the icy-cold air-conditioning of the car. His destination, Zurich, Switzerland, for a nine-hour stay, then on to Mexico, where he would meet with his new client, back to Zurich for six hours, then on to Cairo. Within a week he'd probably have pneumonia. He constantly amazed himself at how he managed to stay hale and hearty with all the traveling from one intense climate to another. Hot to cold. Cold to hot. A good way to get sick. Maybe it was all the airtime or the rich food or . . . something else, but the past week he'd felt unlike himself. Almost as if a bug were creeping up on him in slow motion. He'd been popping aspirin by the handful to ward off whatever it was. Like aspirin could ward off fear.

Five minutes later, his baggage was stowed, his briefcase on his lap. He leaned back and closed his eyes for the 25-km ride from Santiago to Rudahauel, where the Gulfstream was waiting for him. His mind wandered back to his fiancée.

There was no way in hell she could know *anything*. His organization had so many firewalls installed that even he had trouble sometimes understanding the scope of his many operations. He definitely needed to call Lucy again just to satisfy himself that their relationship was on firm ground and it was only his imagination working overtime. The minute the Gulfstream reached its cruising altitude, he would call Lucy, regardless of the time difference.

Fifty minutes later the Gulfstream reached its cruising altitude. Jonathan undid his seat belt and motioned to the lone steward that he'd like a drink and a sandwich. While he drank and chewed his way through roast beef with mustard on fresh-baked bread, he thought about his fiancée and their upcoming wedding. Being married would make him more human in his clients' eyes. He also knew if he wasn't careful, being married could be dangerous. For Lucy more so than himself. Disgruntled, aggressive clients tended to get nasty and from time to time threatened to take out that nastiness on family members. Jonathan shrugged. Life was full of nasty surprises. Getting married probably wasn't one of his better decisions, but once he'd made up his mind, all his future plans quickly fell into place. The fact that Lucy was a top-notch attorney was a plus he couldn't deny. It wasn't written in stone that he had to be in love to get married. He needed Lucy, needed her respectability, her background. And for a while he'd have a woman in his bed. When it was time for her to go, she would go. It was that simple. Would he shed any tears when that happened? Perhaps in public.

Jonathan shook his head to clear his thoughts, but somehow Lucy stayed right there with him. What really surprised him about Lucy was as smart as she was, she hadn't picked up on anything. He chuckled to himself. Maybe when the lovebug bites a woman she doesn't think about anything else.

At best, life with sweet Lucy would be boring, but that was what he needed. For a while, at least. But there was no way in hell he was going to live in that saltbox of a house she had bought in Edison, New Jersey. He'd go out of his mind in twenty-four hours if he had to live in a two-thousand-square-foot house. If the timing was right, and if things progressed the way he wanted them to, he might give serious thought to opening the house in Watchung.

Jonathan thought about his parents, who'd lived in a small house much like the one Lucy now lived in. His father had worked his whole life in the Firestone rubber factory in Akron. His parents had struggled to pay their mortgage, make car payments, meet other household expenses, while still trying to donate 10 percent of their salary to the church. The first chance he got, he moved them to the other side of the world, where they lived in the lap of luxury. He was a good son. He called regularly and tried to visit at least once every two months for a few days.

His fiancée had simple tastes: she wasn't into designer clothing, jewelry, or fancy cars. She considered it all a waste of money, preferring to sock her money into a pension fund.

The dog was going to have to go, though. He would never live in a house that had a dog. That might pose a problem, with Lucy being such a dog lover. He could take care of that.

He'd told Lucy he wanted children, but he had lied. He'd been stunned when she said children were not in her immediate plans. That had clinched the engagement. It didn't hurt that Lucy was a lawyer, one of the best in Manhattan, according to his sources—sources who knew about such things. Her brother Steven was almost as good as Lucy in the courtroom. He remembered how angry he'd been when Lucy had said she was chucking the law. He'd called her stupid that day, and she hadn't really gotten angry. He was going to need her legal expertise at some point. How she could turn down representing some of his clients on the shady side of the law for big bucks boggled his mind. Her knowledge of the law was one of the reasons he'd chosen her. The day he'd met her on the tennis court had been planned in great detail, and she'd never even suspected. Maybe he gave her too much credit for being smart. Maybe his original assessment that she was stupid was spot on.

Jonathan could feel his stomach muscles start to tighten up. Something, somewhere, was amiss. Had he made a mistake? More to the point, had one of his clients made a mistake that could lead back to him? In the twenty years since he'd started JSC Enterprises, he had never before been fearful. He could feel the fear, smell it; it was starting to choke him.

Jonathan unlocked the cuff on his wrist, massaged it gently, then opened his brief-case on the tray in front of him. He withdrew a digitally encrypted satellite phone and speed-dialed Lucy's home number. He lis-tened to the phone ring eight times before her voice mail clicked on. His brows knitted together as he tried to imagine where she was and what she was doing. If she had the flu, she might be sleeping. He grimaced at the thought. The phone was a lifeline to Lucy just the way it was to him. If she was there, she would have answered the phone. It was a long flight, he could always call later.

Jonathan pulled out his laptop, flexed his fingers. While he was by no means a bean counter or number cruncher, he did know what his assets were, down to the penny. He smiled as a blizzard of numbers raced across the screen. It would take him a life-time to spend all the money he'd accumu-lated even if he spent a million dollars a day. He might be exaggerating but if so, it wasn't by much.

He hoped he lived long enough to spend it all.

Lucy sat in front of the fire hugging her knees, tears dripping down her cheeks. She needed to get a grip on her life, figure out what she was going to do and stop relying on other people, well-meaning or not, to help her. When the agents arrived, she needed to act like the lawyer she was instead of this wishy-washy person she'd turned into in less than a week. A sob escaped her throat. A second later, the three dogs were circling her, Lulu leaping into her lap. Sadie pressed against her side, Coop's big paws circled her neck. They whined, their bodies shaking at the strange sounds coming from her mouth. She spread her arms to encircle all three dogs, then laughed as she wiped at her eyes on the sleeve of her shirt. "I'm okay. Just a bad moment there. The bridal shop called to tell me my wedding gown is ready for my final fitting. If you stop and think about it, that's pretty damn funny from where I'm sitting."

Fear was for other people, not a savvy, high-priced lawyer like her. In the blink of an eye, she disengaged herself from the dogs and went up the steps, landing with a painful thump on her tender ankle. She ignored the pain as she limped into her bedroom, stripped down, and decked herself out in a long, paisley skirt with a delicious thigh-high slit up the side. She stepped into suede boots, mindful of her ankle, and donned a pumpkin-colored cashmere sweater. A lustrous set of pearls found their way to her neck, as did matching earrings.

In the bathroom she undid the ponytail and brushed her hair till it framed her face like a nimbus. Reaching for the atomizer, she spritzed the air and stood under the fragrant spray. *Now* she was ready for the federal agents.

The dogs followed her down the steps just as the doorbell rang. Lucy made one stop at the sofa to turn on the small cassette player, then placed it between the cushions where she planned to sit.

Through the beveled glass at the side of the front door, Lucy could see the same trio who had grilled her on Friday. They looked like they were freezing. Good.

Lucy glanced at her reflection in the mirror hanging in the foyer. She smacked her lips and wiggled them to distribute her lipstick evenly. She did her best to feather her eyebrows with her pinkie finger, fluffed her hair, and smoothed down her skirt. A wasted minute. She opened the door, her expression cold and hostile as she motioned the agents inside. The dogs sniffed and growled, but they didn't bark. They did follow her to the living room and took up positions at her feet, their eyes wary, their ears flat against their heads. Even Lulu's perky pink bow seemed to wilt.

Her eyes still cold and angry, Lucy crossed her arms over her chest. In body language it meant, take your best shot, but you aren't getting anything out of me because I don't know anything. She waited, staring first at one agent, then the other, and on to the third. The same way she stared at prosecution witnesses in the courtroom. Most of the time it unnerved people.

And then her head started to buzz. She could feel a distinct ringing in her ears, too. The sound was the same as when her brother Steven turned on his electric razor. She cautioned herself not to panic as she took long, relaxing breaths. She was partially successful. *My anger or theirs?* she wondered.

Then it hit her in a jumble of thoughts. The Chinese fire drill was back but in low gear. She could have been in Madison Square Garden or Shea Stadium, listening to a hundred people all talking at once. *Concentrate,* she told herself. *Don't think, make your mind blank. Listen.* It was hopeless, nothing was coming through, and she suddenly felt stupid because she didn't know what her expression was giving away.

To calm her twanging nerves, Lucy stood up and walked behind the sofa, where she had a good look at all three agents from higher ground. She liked to stand when she interviewed witnesses or cross-examined them. Those seated were always at a disadvantage. The person standing was the power person. "Well?" she said coldly.

There it is, she thought with elation. *Maybe changing position has something to do with it.* She felt like laughing out loud. *No prairie flower . . . she's had time to think . . . hard as nails . . . no backup . . . classy skirt . . . cost more than I make in a month . . . she's not going to cave . . . she looks like she knows something we don't. . . . dogs . . . not killer dogs . . . not guard dogs . . . where's the neighbor . . . I'm never going to get warm again . . . hit her hard . . . right between the eyes . . . no wiggle room . . . give her just enough rope . . . throw out a carrot . . . offer a deal . . . maybe she isn't as dumb as she looks. I wish I was on some warm island somewhere.*

Lucy started to tingle all over. She could hear them thinking, but she couldn't pin down which thoughts belonged to whom. She waited, feeling almost giddy at what she was *hearing.*

"How would you like to cut a deal, Miss Baker?" Agent Lawrence asked.

The chaotic transmissions—that was how she thought of what she was experiencing—suddenly stopped. She felt normal again. It might be a good time to throw all three of the agents for a loop. "I really am smarter than I look, Agent Lawrence. Throwing a carrot my way isn't going to get me to tell you something I don't know. You could toss me twenty miles of rope, and it isn't going to make a difference. I'm a lawyer, and I know my rights. As a lawyer, I am always open to negotiations. What's the deal?" she snapped.

Special Agent Connors reared back in her chair as Coop rose to his feet and growled. It pleased her that all three agents looked stunned. Why shouldn't they? She'd just read their minds. In another minute they'd chalk it up to coincidence.

It wasn't true what they said about male FBI agents being good-looking and manly, not to mention virile. Nor was it true about female FBI agents being beautiful the way they were portrayed in the movies. Agent Mason, who was packing twenty extra pounds around his middle, looked up at Lucy. "We want you to help us set a trap for your boyfriend."

"And I would do so because . . ."

"You would do this because you are a responsible citizen and because we have you boxed into a corner. It's the only way you'll get off the hook." *She'll go for it, I know she will.*

Lucy's head was back in play again. Yahooo. Her voice rang with angry confidence when she said, "You really think I'll go for a deal like that?" The agent looked at her, his eyes popping wide. "I'm off the hook anyway because I didn't do anything wrong. I don't scare easy, Mr. Mason. The burden of proof is on you. I can account for my time, my money, my savings, and anything else you want accounted for during the last ten years, way before I ever met Jonathan St. Clair. You know it, and I know it. We both know you can turn this into a messy circus, but in the end I'll come out whole. Now if you want my help, spell it out, put it in writing, and maybe we can deal. That's my offer. Take it or leave it."

Special Agent Connors stood up to move closer to the fire. She must have been the one who was thinking she'd never get warm again. "We're prepared to consider it," she said. Lulu ran over to where she was standing, sniffed her boots, and barked. "Shoo, go away," Connors said, waving her hands. Lulu continued to sniff and snarl.

"We want you to tell us everything you know about Leo Banks, no matter how insignificant you may think it is. Start from the moment you met him."

This is where she'll trip herself up. She has no clue what we know and don't know. Lucy took a moment to puzzle over what she was feeling. The fire drill and Shea

Stadium were gone. Her head was quiet, and her ears weren't ringing. She was reading and hearing their minds. She was actually calm, shooting down everyone's theory about anxiety and anger. "It's not all that interesting, Agent Mason. If you're hoping I'll trip myself up, think again. Know Your Enemy 101. You're probably thinking I have no clue as to what you know and don't know. Just like you don't know what I know and don't know." Lucy smiled. The FBI agent looked spooked. Good.

Special Agent Connors moved back to her chair, Lulu dogging her every step. The little dog positioned herself at her feet and stared up at the woman with bright eyes, defying her to move again. If she did, the fuzzy boots would go right out from under her. Terriers had a bad habit of sinking their teeth into something and never letting go. It looked to Lucy like Special Agent Connors knew all about terriers.

I hate dogs, especially little ones. This one looks like a rat dressed up for Halloween. Yuk. Lucy almost laughed out loud. She should ignore Special Agent Connors's thoughts, then thought otherwise. "I see you hate dogs, especially little dogs that look like rats dressed up for Halloween. Dogs know when people don't like them. Did you know that?"

Special Agent Connors looked away, a strange look on her face. *Either I'm crazy, or she's crazy, and she's reading my mind.* She turned back to face Lucy, who was smiling. There was no way the lawyer was responding to this thought.

"Yes, I have heard that said about small dogs," Special Agent Connors said. "When I was a child I was bitten rather badly. I've been afraid of dogs ever since," she volunteered.

Lucy turned her attention to the two male agents, her eyebrows raised. She flipped her hand backward as though to say, let's get on with it.

"Tell us about Leo Banks."

"There's nothing much to tell you. I met him about eighteen months ago on the tennis court. He liked me, I liked him. It worked for us because he understood my working eighty hours a week. He traveled constantly. I was lucky if I saw him once a month. He called regularly. He was always a gentleman with me. He was thoughtful, sent me gifts, said all the things a woman wants to hear.

We got engaged, were going to get married last year but postponed it. We were supposed to get married in February. That isn't going to happen now. I know nothing about his business except what he told me. He said he brokered business deals between different parties. He was the go-between. That is the sum total of what I know." Lucy's face was devoid of any kind of expression, but she felt alert and wary.

"Okay for now. Maybe something else will come to you later on," Agent Lawrence said.

Agent Mason stood up and took his turn standing next to the fireplace. "Your boyfriend, Leo Banks, popped up on our radar screen two years ago while we were investigating another case that he was involved in. A key player so to speak. Until that time, he was *under* our radar screen. It's not easy for our agents in third-world countries, as you can imagine. Since that time, we've been tracking him. I see no harm in telling you that the man is like a phoenix, he keeps rising out of the ashes. He's here, he's there, he's everywhere. You can do that when you have the network he has. He also has a Gulfstream that ferries him around at a moment's notice. Our people have to fly commercial. We managed to lose him quite a few times, and the bureau is not proud of that. We aren't sure if he's the main man or the main man's right hand. It is what it is.

"Mr. Banks treads on thin ice sometimes. He's as slick as they come, and one almost has to think he leads a charmed life. About six months ago he managed to swindle a Colombian drug dealer who was trying to put together a deal in Florida to gain some legitimacy and got away with his skin intact. We have the dealer in custody minus his money. He told us all he knows, which of his cronies pay Banks megamillions to set up legal businesses." The agent fixed his gaze on Lucy, and said, "The man is a pro at laundering money. Now he's on a hit list with the Colombians. That's a serious hit list. One simply doesn't screw around with those thugs.

"If scenarios like that aren't enough to keep you awake at night, here's another one. He killed one of his clients at point-blank range when the man refused to pay a higher percentage of the deal they were working on. Banks has a bad habit of agreeing to a deal and then, at the eleventh hour,

raising the stakes. You're probably wondering how we know this. The man took a long
time to die, and he talked. Deathbed con-
fessions are something we pay attention to.
Then there was Adam Ligar. Banks killed
him, too, but that was a long time ago. I
have more stories like these two, but you
look a little ill, Miss Baker, so I'll save them
for another time."

Not only did Lucy look ill, she felt ill. My
God, she was going to marry the man they
were talking about. Lucy's mind raced. "If
you're so convinced he's doing what you
say, why don't you just arrest him? What are
you waiting for?"

"The right moment. We need an airtight
case. Going off half-cocked gets you
nowhere. And the man never asked you to
sign a prenuptial agreement?" Connors
lifted her eyebrows to show what she
thought of that question.

"No. We talked about it. Jonathan said
nothing would sour a marriage like a
prenup. I was surprised, but he said he
waited this long in life to get married, and it
would be for a lifetime, and he wanted to
share. I don't need his money. I had a career, I have my own portfolio, a pension

fund, a stake in a lucrative law practice, and an inheritance from my parents. On my own, I could be comfortable for the rest of my life."

All three agents stared at Lucy, knowing they would be working the rest of their lives until it was time to collect their retirement. Lucy thought she saw resentment in Special Agent Connors's face.

Agent Lawrence chewed on his lower lip before he spoke. "Your fiancé is not a broker. A broker is a legitimate businessman. Leo Banks is a *facilitator.*" The term sounded obscene coming out of his mouth. "If someone wants something delivered or spirited out of the country, they call Leo Banks. Sometimes that *something* turns out to be a *person* or *persons.* Leo is known for getting the job done. In fact, Leo offers up a personal guarantee or he doesn't take that robust seven-figure commission you mentioned. Being a lawyer, you should know the first rule is, *follow the money.* That's what led us to you, Miss Baker. To our knowledge Banks has about fifteen different aliases with passports to match. He's also a master at disguising himself. A little spirit gum, a little latex, different clothes, and he's a different man. Three months ago he flew into Heathrow Airport dressed as a rabbi. Sad to say, we were a little slow to figure that out. Are you following me, Miss Baker?"

Lucy was following him all right, but she was more concerned at the moment with her head going quiet on her. Nothing was coming through. She wondered what would happen if she told them she could *hear* their thoughts. They were waiting for her to say something. She grappled in her mind for something to say. "You . . . you're making Jonathan sound like . . . like James Bond, Hannibal Lecter, and Jack the Ripper."

Agent Lawrence grimaced. "He's got all the same hardware as Bond. Why does one man need six cigarette boats? Do you know anything about cigarette boats, Miss Baker?" Lucy shook her head.

"Let me bring you up to speed, then," Agent Lawrence said. "They're long and low, usually black-hulled. Very sleek. The low profile makes it almost impossible to pick them up on radar. Now, if the water conditions are right, and if the engine compartment is insulated properly and the exhausts baffled, it wouldn't be detected by infrared sensors. Those babies can do eighty knots with no sweat. A boat like that can outrun anything on the water. It's the boat of choice for drug runners and some arms runners, too. And you have six of them in your name." Lucy started to feel sick to her stomach at the agent's words.

"Why does Leo Banks need a fleet of cars? Why does he use digitally encrypted satellite phones? His laptop is encrypted, and he has enough firewalls installed to drive any encryption specialist to the brink of insanity. None of the above makes our job easier." He asked again, "Are you following me, Miss Baker?"

Lucy nodded, her heart pumping furiously. God in Heaven, who was this man she'd promised to marry?

Special Agent Connors picked up the conversation. "That brings us to the house in Watchung that has your name on the deed. We're a little concerned with the elaborate security attached to that property. Do you know anything about alarm systems, Miss Baker?"

Lucy licked at her dry lips. "I have an alarm system here in the house, but it's standard. Keypad, panic button, all the doors and windows are armed. I put it on when I go to bed at night. My own personal feeling is a dog is the best security in the world. The only reason I have an alarm system at all is to make my brother feel better. He insisted I have it installed. So, to answer your question, no, I know nothing about sophisticated alarm systems. I also know nothing about the house in Watchung. I told you that already." She tried to clear her mind, strained to pick up a word, but nothing was coming through.

Connors acted like she hadn't heard Lucy's words. "I believe Agent Lawrence informed you the other day of the house's unusual security system complete with laser trip wires and tremor plates. But did he mention our experts tell us they suspect there are pressure pads in the house that would activate, and trigger alarms, as well as release an incapacitating gas? This is warfare type of security. Now, our question to you is, why would a person need that kind of security if, as you say, he is a legitimate broker and does business ethically and aboveboard?"

All Lucy could do was shake her head. "What is it you want me to do?" she whispered miserably.

"Help us to get our hands on Mr. Banks. When do you expect to see him again?"

Lucy could feel her stomach start to churn. "Jonathan was supposed to come for Thanksgiving, but he called the other day and said he couldn't make it. He is coming for Christmas for ten days. I haven't talked to him since. And, no, I did not tell him about any of our conversations. If I agree to help you, are you going to make . . ."

"Your immediate problem go away?" Agent Lawrence said. "We'll discuss the matter with our superiors at Justice and get back to you. Tomorrow. This might be a good time for you to explain why you defended José Rafael and Manuel Aroya. Both men are associates of Leo Banks."

"What?" Lucy sputtered.

Mason's face showed disbelief. "You didn't know?"

"No! No, I did not know." Lucy hated herself for saying it, but she said it anyway. "I guess that's why Jonathan was so upset when I said I was giving up the law after Aroya's trial. Then I changed my mind and kept on working. Up until the acquittal came in, I thought he was innocent. Then he looked at me with this . . . this . . . smug look, and I knew he was guilty as hell. I was sick to my stomach. I knew right then I couldn't do it anymore. Steven talked me into staying on. Jonathan was very upset. Then, after my last case, I finally made up my mind to hang it all up. Jonathan has been nagging me ever since to go back to the firm. I swear to you, I didn't know those men knew Jonathan. All either one said to me at the initial consultation was that they had heard I was the best of the best and they needed the best. They had the money to pay my fees, and I don't come cheap. Later on, Jonathan said he *knew of* José Rafael, and Aroya, but did not know either of them personally, and had followed the case in the papers. I had no reason not to believe him then."

"They, as in Leo Banks and his people, would have put the squeeze on you if you'd been appointed to the bench. The house, the brokerage accounts, the cigarette boats, all of that would have been used to blackmail you," Agent Lawrence said quietly.

Lucy fought down the bile that was rising in her throat. At the same time she strained to *hear* their thoughts, but to no avail. She looked down at the hands on her watch. How long was the tape in the cassette player? An hour on each side or was it a thirty-minute-sided tape? Would it make a sound when it clicked off? She didn't know.

She had to get rid of the agents now. "I don't think we have anything else to discuss. I'll wait for you to get back to me tomorrow. What that means is this meeting is over." To make her point, Lucy started for the door, the dogs following her.

The moment the door closed behind the federal agents, Lucy locked it and slumped against it. She was definitely in the tall grass now, and the view ahead was not to her liking.

7

The two men sat in Wylie's kitchen staring at one another. Wylie spoke first. "What do you think, Jake?" He didn't realize he was holding his breath until it exploded out of his mouth like a gunshot.

"What I think, old buddy, is you have the hots for your neighbor, and you can't see straight." The parapsychologist shrugged. "Listen, I wouldn't stake my reputation on it, but I think Lucy's condition will fade in time. Right now she's on a high unlike anything she's ever experienced. Plus, she's a woman, and women tend to get emotional, even women lawyers. Now, if her present condition isn't what's bothering you, I bet you're worried about the man in her life who is responsible for all this. Right or wrong?"

Wylie ran his fingers through his hair before he got up to make a pot of coffee. "The bastard set her up," he barked. "Yeah, I like her. I like her a lot, as a matter of fact. You don't think she loves him, do you, Jake?"

"Nah. You know what I think, Wylie. I think she was *relieved* that this happened. That's my own ESP at work. You got anything to munch on?" the handsome parapsychologist asked.

Wylie reached up to the top of the refrigerator and tossed Jake a bag of corn chips. He poured two cups of coffee and set them on the table.

"Coffee and corn chips don't go together, Wylie. Don't you have any Coke or Pepsi?"

"No. The weather's been too bad to go to the store. Just drink the damn coffee already, Jake."

"Testy, aren't we." Jake grinned. "You know, for a guy, this is a cozy, comfortable kitchen," Jake said, changing the subject in the hopes of driving away the intense look on his friend's face.

"My mother decorated the kitchen. She pretty much did the whole house after my ex cleaned me out," Wylie said, waving his arms at the green-and-yellow balloon-type curtains, the matching yellow crockery, and the green plants, one in the corner by the bay window, one hanging over the sink, and one in the corner of the counter. All looked lush and green, with no yellowing leaves. "Mom said I have no decorating sense. She calls me every Sunday to make sure I water and feed the plants. It's easier to follow through than it is to try and explain why they die. Been there, done that. Actually, Jake, I take great pride in my plants," Wylie said defensively.

"Well, good for you. If there was ever a guy who should be married, it's you. You really like Lucy, huh?"

Wylie rolled his eyes. He gulped at the scalding coffee in his cup, his eyes watering. "They should be leaving by now, don't you think?"

Jake fished in the bag for a fistful of chips. He popped them in his mouth, one at a time, and crunched down. "You could check to see if their car is still there. That would be one way to find out."

"Wiseass," Wylie muttered as he sprinted to the living room window.

"You're right, they're leaving," he shouted. "Should we be discreet and wait like two minutes or barrel over there right now?"

Jake shook his head. If his friend wasn't

in love, he was about to fall head over heels for his neighbor. "Whatever floats your boat, Wylie."

"I think we should wait ten minutes, or so. I don't want to seem . . . you know, pushy. Yeah, ten minutes is good. What should we do while we're waiting, Jake?"

Jake's face scrunched up in a grin. "When was the last time you got laid, Wylie?"

Wylie pretended horror. "Is that what you think this is all about, sex? Well, it isn't. It's about helping, understanding, being there, my dog loves her, and then maybe sex. Not in that order. Shut the hell up, Jake. Why'd you ask me that anyway? It's none of your damn business."

"We *are* prickly. Relax, Wylie."

"Easy for you to say, Jake. You aren't personally involved!" Wylie huffed.

As soon as the FBI agents left, the phone rang. Lucy was on her way to the kitchen in search of the brandy bottle. If there was ever a time in her life when she needed a drink, this was it. She didn't hurry to answer the phone, thinking it was Wylie. She took a healthy swig straight from the bottle. Her eyes burning, she carried the bottle to the family room and answered on the speaker-phone. Her greeting was flat when she said, "Hello."

"Good afternoon, darling," Jonathan St. Clair said cheerfully, his voice coming through the speakerphone loud and clear.

Lucy looked at the bottle she was hold-ing, then at the phone on the table. She felt like pitching both into the fireplace. "Jonathan, I wasn't expecting your call." What an incredibly stupid thing to say.

"I've been thinking about you and missing you. I'm just so sorry I won't be there for Thanksgiving. I just wanted you to know it's tearing me apart. I promise to make it up to you over Christmas, though. I never break a promise, you know that. How are you, dar-ling?"

Once the question would have thrilled her. Now, it scared the hell out of her. An ac-tress she wasn't, but she tried. "Well, Jonathan, I'm sad that you won't be here. I do miss you, and I'm looking forward to spending the holidays with you. Should I wait to pick out the Christmas tree till you get here, or should I get it, put it up, and then, when you get here, we'll decorate it?" Lucy felt sickened at the artificial lilt in her voice and wondered if Jonathan was picking up on it. He was not stupid, as she knew very well.

"I'm not one for tromping through fields to pick out a tree. I can, however, see myself putting the star on top." The chuckle in his voice sounded forced to Lucy's ears.

Lucy swigged from the brandy bottle. "Actually, Jonathan, I was planning on getting the tree from the Sunoco station where I get my gas. They deliver and set it up for a small fee." She was feeling light-headed. Now, she wished she'd eaten more instead of picking at her food earlier. Drinking on an empty stomach was not a good idea.

"Do you miss me?"

"Of course. Do you miss me?" Lucy asked, in return, hoping that her voice did not give away just how much she did *not* miss him.

"More than you know. By the way, I'm on a plane headed for Switzerland. Would you like me to send you some Swiss chocolate? I know you have a sweet tooth."

"That would be wonderful, Jonathan. You always think of me, don't you?" Lucy took another swig from the bottle. *You're a weasel Jonathan St. Clair/Leo Banks or whoever you are. Like I would really eat anything you sent me.*

"Are you ready to go back to work, honey?"

Lucy looked at the brandy bottle in her hand with narrowed eyes. "Not really." A devil perched itself on her shoulder. "I'm going to sell my interest in the firm to Steven. I want to be a full-time wife. I am going to take such good care of you, Jonathan," she said sweetly. "I'm going to cook, and bake, and iron, and all that stuff. I'm going to plant a garden. I might extend the deck a little farther and put in a swimming pool. Life in the *burbs!* Doesn't that sound wonderful, Jonathan?"

"It wasn't exactly what I had in mind, darling. We'll talk about it when I get there," Jonathan replied, his voice dropping to somewhere near the subzero level.

Ignoring the coldness in his tone, Lucy continued. "Jonathan, what is it exactly that you do? I know you broker deals, but what kind of deal are you working on now?" As she waited for his response, Lucy took another belt out of the brandy bottle. There wasn't much left. "Jonathan, are you still there?"

"I'm still here, Lucy. Why do you ask? Maybe I should ask why you want to know. You made a point of saying you could never discuss your cases with me, and I told you I can't discuss my clients. I sign a confidentiality agreement before I begin to work for a client. In my business, it's a necessity. You know how that works, don't you?"

Lucy opted to ignore the question. "My gown is finished," Lucy blurted. "The dogs chewed up the wedding invitations. Everything seems to be going wrong. The roof is leaking," she lied. "I'm thinking we should postpone the wedding until June. Maybe the dogs chewing up the invitations is an omen of some kind."

The silence on the other end of the phone was palpable. Now that she had Jonathan's attention, Lucy rolled on. "And, the IRS sent me a notice," she lied still again. "They want to talk to me January 17 at 9 A.M. I am not looking forward to talking with them. I'm always meticulous about preparing my tax forms." The silence on the other end of the phone sizzled. She wondered if she'd gone too far. Lucy felt the need to prod him once again. "What do you think, Jonathan?"

"Routine, darling. I told you to get rid of that dog. Pay extra and order new invitations. Money talks, sweetheart. We are not postponing our wedding. You are mine, and I intend to claim you. Don't even think about it. I have to hang up because we're starting to make our descent now. I'll call you in a day or so. I love you." *Sure you do, you weasel. Well, guess what, I don't love you. Another thing, there is not going to be a wedding in February or June because if I have anything to do about it, you'll be in prison by then. So there, Jonathan St. Clair, aka Leo Banks.*

Lucy was prevented from making a reply because she was draining the last of the brandy in the bottle. She clicked the cordless phone to the OFF position and sat down on the sofa. She was tipsy if not outright drunk, and she knew it. She was also scared out of her ever-loving wits. In all the time she'd known Jonathan, she'd never, ever heard him use the tone of voice she'd just heard humming over the wire.

The dogs thundered down the hallway and around the corner to the front door. She could barely hear the bell with all the barking going on. The door was locked. That meant she had to get up and open it. It had to be Wylie and his friend, the parapsychologist.

When she opened the door both men stared at her glassy eyes. It was Coop who nudged her toward the sofa in the family room. Lucy stared around at the room as though wondering how she got there. She rubbed at Coop's silky back.

"Coffee! I think we could all use some strong, black coffee," Wylie said enthusiastically as he pantomimed behind Lucy's back, urging Jake to get Lucy to talk. In her condition he had no idea what would be forthcoming.

Jake propped his elbows on his knees and leveled his gaze on Lucy. "So, how did it go? Are they going to let you off the hook or what? Did you *hear* anything that will help the situation?"

Lucy fumbled for the cassette recorder, digging between the cushions on the sofa. Jake reached across to take the recorder, his bright blue eyes twinkling at Lucy's condition.

"It's still on, the tape is almost full. Let's

see what we have here," Jake said, as he pressed the REWIND button. Lucy leaned back and listened to herself and the FBI agents. When Wylie handed her a huge mug of black coffee, she reached for it with both hands.

Wylie positioned himself on the sofa next to Lucy but not too close. Coop leaped up and wiggled next to him. Lucy and he reached out to stroke the big dog's head at the same time. A jolt of electricity whipped through Wylie at Lucy's touch. Neither one moved. Sadie sat up on her haunches and barked, Lulu yapping at the top of her lungs. A second later, both dogs were on the sofa, and the highly charged moment was gone.

"I guess you didn't remember to turn off the recorder before the phone call, huh?" Jake said.

"No, I guess I forgot. I was pretty wired at that point. Then Jonathan or . . . whatever the hell his name is, called. That's when I finished the brandy." Lucy propped the coffee cup between her knees as she waved her arms in the air. "I lied all over the place to . . . to that man. When I hung up, I was scared. I never heard such a cold tone in his voice before. Do you think I tipped him off?"

Wylie eyeballed the parapsychologist sitting across from him. He shook his head imperceptibly. Jake nodded. "I suppose anything is possible," Jake said. "Since I don't know the man, I don't want to be rash and say yes. Did you *hear* anything significant when you met with the FBI agents?"

"Yes and no. Nothing that's going to help me. I really tried there at the end to *hear* something, but nothing came through. We have to wait till tomorrow for them to get back to me. Do you think my phone is tapped? If it is, they heard my conversation with Jonathan. Are we going to go up to Watchung or not?" Lucy asked, changing the subject.

"Are you up to it?" Wylie asked, concerned. Lucy looked at him and smiled, her eyes lighting up. Wylie thought it the most endearing smile in the world.

Again, Wylie forced himself to look away and locked his gaze with Jake's. He shrugged.

"I'm up to it. The brandy will start to wear off soon. The coffee will help. By the time we get there I should be fine. I'm not a drinker. I hardly ever drink. Well, sometimes, a glass of wine or a beer, but I don't *guzzle*.

What about the roads? If we're going, we should go now." She was babbling but didn't know how to stop. Then she heard the click of the recorder again and her own voice as she spoke to Jonathan. Lucy felt herself cringe, and was aware of how still both men had become. Even the dogs didn't move, sensing something was suddenly different.

Lucy threw her hands in the air. "So, I forgot to turn the damn thing off. You can hear Jonathan since I put him on speakerphone. Easier to drink my brandy that way. Are you picking up the change in his voice?" Both men nodded. It was a relief when Jake switched the recorder off. No one said anything.

Wylie jumped up first. "If we're going, let's go." To Lucy's ears, his voice sounded brusque and cold. It bothered her. She didn't like the look she was seeing on Jake's face either.

"Wait just a damn minute, you two. It was a stupid phone call. I was trying to act normal, not to raise any suspicion where Jonathan is concerned. Not that it's any of your business, but I was playacting. And drinking at the same time to make it easier.

Read my lips. I do not love Jonathan St. Clair or whatever his real name is. I don't think I ever did. Now, you can run with that in whatever direction you want. I'm also not hearing any of your thoughts. I can be ready in five minutes. I take it the dogs are staying here."

Properly chastised, both men nodded.

"I'm suddenly thinking this is not such a good idea, Jake. If we're going to the house that Lucy allegedly owns, are we going with the intention of breaking and entering? Or, are we doing a simple drive-by? There's a good eight inches of snow out there, and there might be more in Watchung. What's that snow going to do to all that warfare security those agents said was in place? I think we need to fall back and regroup."

Jake slapped at his forehead and cursed under his breath. "Sometimes I am stupid. Wylie, do you remember Mitch Logan?" Wylie frowned but nodded. "He's a Navy SEAL. Remember how he was regaling us with stories at our ten-year reunion?" Wylie nodded again, wondering where Jake was going with all this. "Well, according to the alumni newsletter, he's out of the SEALs now because of a severe back injury. He put together a security company somewhere outside of Washington, DC—Fairfax, Virginia, I think. I'm thinking we should call him and ask him to help us out here. If anyone can help us, it's him. The guy has some big government contracts, so he must be good."

"How do you know all this?" Wylie asked.

"I *read* the newsletters unlike you, who throws them away."

Wylie looked offended. "I don't throw them away. I let them pile up, and eventually I read them. Good idea. You got his number?"

"Not with me. I'm sure you have it at home. Go look. The guy's a fraternity brother. We're supposed to stick together. I'm up for a daylight drive-by and maybe a talk with some of the neighbors."

Five minutes later, Wylie returned with his alumni telephone list. Mitch Logan's name was in the middle of the list along with the name of his security firm, Millennium Security.

Wylie unzipped his jacket just as Lucy made her way into the den. Her eyes were full of questions as she watched Jake punch out a number on his cell phone.

Wylie drew her aside and explained what was going on. "You look as relieved as I feel," he said quietly.

Lucy took off her sky-blue jacket and tossed it over the back of the chair. She sighed. "I am relieved we're not going up to Watchung today. I know in my gut if we went there, the FBI would know it within seconds. All this snow would only hinder us anyway."

"How's the head?" Wylie asked, to have something to say.

"I have a dull headache, but I attribute that to the brandy. I took some aspirin. Nellie kept wanting to fix me up with you. She kept saying how nice you were, and I should check you out before I got married," Lucy blurted.

Wylie blinked in surprise. "Nellie was always on my case about introducing you to me. It just never worked out. It took two dogs for us to meet. I guess I owe Coop big-time. Maybe I'll upgrade his meat loaf from ground chuck to ground round." Lucy burst out laughing. Wylie thought it a wonderful sound. He thought everything about the woman standing next to him was wonderful. "Did you mean what you said about that guy you were going to marry?"

Lucy nodded just as Jake clicked his cell phone shut. "Okay," he said, "we're in business. Mitch is going to leave now and drive here. He said he should arrive around eight. First thing in the morning, we'll head up to the mountains. He said he has all kinds of equipment that will locate and disarm any kind of security. I think it's safe to say we're in good hands. At least for the moment.

"I did my part, so you two can make dinner. I'm going to your house, Wylie, and take a shower and a nap. I also want to call my wife. I'll leave Lulu here. You guys okay with that?" Wylie and Lucy nodded.

Spending the balance of the afternoon with Wylie was not an unpleasant thought, Lucy decided as she made her way into the kitchen, Wylie behind her.

Lucy opened the freezer and looked at the contents. She reached for a pot roast that was frozen solid. It wouldn't make any difference if it was frozen or not as long as she cooked it in a pressure cooker. As she unwrapped the freezer paper, she fixed her gaze on her neighbor. "Are you sorry you got caught up in my mess, Wylie?"

Wylie jammed his hands into the pockets of his jeans. "No. I just feel helpless because there isn't anything I can do except be your friend and help out with the dogs. Are you okay, Lucy?"

Lucy rummaged in the bottom of one of the cabinets for the pressure cooker. "No, I'm not all right. I feel like some kind of freak. What if this thing in my head never goes away? What if . . . what if . . . Jonathan really does come for Christmas? How am I going to handle that? He's going to want . . . *you know,*" she said, throwing her arms in the air. "They want me to trap him. I don't exactly have a problem with that depending on how long it takes to put everything into motion. It's the between time that is bothering me. And, all those insurance policies. I'm worth more dead than I am alive. The truth is, I'm scared out of my wits."

Wylie felt like his heart was being ripped out of his chest. "Listen, throw that meat in the pot and let's go out and play in the snow. I haven't done that in years, and I bet you haven't either." Seeing Lucy's frown of indecision, he took charge of the meat. He snapped the lid on the pot with the air of a professional. "Now, let's get dressed and have some fun."

Lucy laughed as Wylie escorted her to the coatrack. She was dressed within seconds and out the door in minutes. Then tried to run in the deep snow but kept falling. "Snow angels! Snow angels!" Lucy laughed.

Wylie dived into the snow in the front yard and started to move his hands and legs. "My God! The last time I did this I was six years old!" Lucy followed suit, laughing and giggling. "The trick is," Wylie shouted, "to get up without disturbing the angel imprint."

In the end it was impossible not to disturb the imprint, the snow was just too deep.

"Let's build a snowman. A big one. I think the snow is wet enough to roll the balls." They huffed and puffed as she rolled a giant ball for the base. Breathless with the exertion, Lucy found herself leaning against Wylie. She was so close she could smell his aftershave, feel his warm breath on her cheek. She knew in that instant she was committed to this man forever and ever. She *heard* it then. *God, how I love this woman. I feel like slinging her over my shoulder and carrying her off to my lair.*

Lucy leaned even closer. "Guess what,

Wylie, you don't have to put me over your shoulder. I'll go with you willingly. So there!" She took off running but didn't get far because Wylie tackled her. They both went facedown in the snow. Their arms around each other, they rolled down the front lawn. When they reached the road, Wylie smacked his cold lips on hers so fast she saw stars. A long time later she said, "I'd tell you to do that again, but right now I feel like I'm on fire. Can we do it again later?"

"Does the Pope pray? Well, yeah. I'm available twenty-four/seven!"

"I'll write that down," Lucy giggled as she struggled to her feet. "I guess you know Jake is watching us from the front window."

Wylie laughed. "Those parapsychologists are a curious lot."

Together they trudged through the snow to the front door. "I have hot chocolate, kiddies," Jake said, as he held out two steaming cups.

Back in the kitchen, their wet clothes in the dryer, Wylie harked back to Lucy's confession about being scared out of her wits.

"Coop and I could move in with you. We could say my heat went out or something like that. Hell, if you need bodies to fill up the house, I can have a few of my friends move in, too. Nothing like having to step over a bunch of bodies everywhere to quell . . . *you know.* I'll do the vegetables while you braise the meat," he said, changing the subject abruptly.

"Okay," Lucy said agreeably. "You have to go back to work tomorrow, don't you?"

"Yes, I do. Jake will be here, though. I'll try to make it an early day. I have two paralegals and a partner who can cover for me. I don't have to be in court, so that's a plus. It will work out, Lucy."

Lucy adjusted the flame on the burner as the roast sizzled in the hot oil. "Do you ever get burned out, Wylie? Do you ever question yourself, the system, your clients?"

"Every damn day," Wylie said cheerfully. "My second choice after law was forestry. I think I would have made a hell of a forest ranger. Did you have a second choice?"

"Not really. I didn't really know what I wanted to be. My brother always wanted to be a lawyer. Our parents were lawyers, so I guess it was natural. For a little window of time, when I was first in college, I wanted to be this one-of-a-kind athlete. I was a distance runner, and I qualified for the Olympic trials, but then my mother got sick, and I had to bow out. Only after my mother died did I go to law school. I'm still not sure why. Maybe it was because I wanted to prove myself in the same arena my mother operated in. It's hard to give up a dream, but you know what they say, everything happens for a reason. What would have been your game plan if you had become a ranger and found yourself face-to-face with a grizzly?"

Wylie threw back his head and guffawed. "To run like hell!"

He was *so* cute. Lucy laughed out loud.

Wylie rinsed the carrots, onions, celery, and potatoes he'd peeled, then put them in a large yellow bowl. "You remind me of a girl I used to know my first year in college. Her name was Angie and she was homecoming queen. Typical blond, blue-eyed nymph. Every single guy on campus wanted her. I had the inside track, though, because I had a car. It was a bucket of bolts, and it didn't run. The guys in the dorm and I worked on it every spare minute we had. Among ourselves, we christened it the Sex Machine. It was a convertible and strictly for picking up chicks. Back then our hormones were raging. I paid fifty bucks for it from some shyster, and he overcharged me by forty-nine bucks. It had some good tires on it, though. We painted it robin's-egg blue. To match Angie's eyes. Let me tell you, that was one spiffy-looking vehicle."

Lucy's eyes twinkled. "Is this a sad story?"

Wylie shrugged. "The day of her maiden voyage, I called Angie and said I'd come by her dorm to pick her up. I think every student on the floor was outside when I picked her up. It was a perfect spring day, not a cloud in the sky. Everyone ooohed and aaahed when she climbed in. Do you know what she said to me?"

"I don't have a clue," Lucy said.

"Well, what would you have said?"

"This *is* a sad story. I guess I would have said, 'Where are we going?' "

"Nope. She said . . . she said, 'Put the top up! I don't want to mess up my hair!' "

Lucy pretended horror, her hands going to her lips. "No!"

"Yes! The Sex Machine didn't have a top. Well, it did, but it was in tatters, and it didn't work. It was a convertible! When I told her it didn't work, she got out of the car and left me sitting there. I couldn't even drive away because the damn car wouldn't start. The guys had to push it back to the garage off campus where we kept it. That was the end of my inside track with Angie Motolo. I was suicidal for a whole day."

Lucy clamped the top onto the cooker and set the pressure gauge. She dusted her hands dramatically. "That is a sad story. What happened to Angie Motolo?"

"She married the trombone player in the school band and is now a hostess on one of those shopping channels. I called in one night to buy some socket wrenches and they put me on the air with her. Usually the hostesses get chatty with the customers, so I told her who I was. She said she didn't remember me or the robin's-egg blue convertible. They hustled me off the air real quick. Her loss." Wylie grinned.

Lucy burst out laughing and couldn't stop. Wylie clapped her on the back, but she kept on laughing and choking. Later, he couldn't clearly remember how it happened, but he was kissing her, and she was kissing him back.

With gusto.

A long time later, Wylie held her at arm's

length and looked into her eyes. "Tell me it was okay to do that."

Her head reeling, Lucy said, "It was okay for you to do that. I'm not engaged any longer," she said, wiggling her ring finger. "And to think you live next door and we never met."

"Yeah, that's mind-bending all right. My mind is going in all directions here, Lucy Baker," Wylie said hoarsely.

"So is mine, Wylie," Lucy gasped.

"Why don't we try doing that again and see what happens?"

"I think that's a very good idea, Wylie." Lucy moved closer, her eyes glazed.

"Ahhh," was all Wylie could say, before he found warm, moist lips covering his own.

8

It was a quarter to eight when Lucy flipped on the outside light and opened the door to admit the biggest man she'd ever seen in her entire life, ex–Navy SEAL Mitch Logan. Lucy smiled, Mitch smiled, and the dogs went ballistic as they tried to climb all over him, sensing a friend. Wylie whistled, and the dogs calmed almost immediately, except for Lulu, who was crawling up Mitch's pant leg. With hands as big as ham hocks, the big man scooped her up and rubbed his cheek against her little head. He tweaked the bow on top of her head before he grinned from ear to ear. "She's a girl, right?"

"That she is, and she's been leading these two," Lucy said, pointing to the re-triever and the lab, "around by their noses. Come in, come in, it's cold out there," she said shutting the door. "Dinner's ready. We were just waiting for you to arrive. I'm Lucy Baker," she said, extending her hand.

Lucy watched as the men acted like college freshmen as they slapped one another on the back, hugged, said it was way too long between visits. She listened to the male banter and suddenly felt like everything in her life was going to be all right. She hoped she wasn't wrong.

Lucy finished setting the table while Mitch washed up, the dogs right beside him. "The dogs love Mitch because they know he likes animals," Jake said. "He has a whole team of K-9 dogs he uses in his business. They're in demand, big-time."

This is nice, Lucy thought as she placed bowls on the table. She stood back to look at the mound of food she'd prepared—the six-pound roast, sliced to perfection, garlic mashed potatoes, fresh string beans with slivers of julienne carrots, mushroom gravy, yeast rolls, soft golden butter, and a large garden salad. A small bowl of mango chutney garnished the platter next to the meat. The blackberry cobbler would be just cool enough when it was time for dessert.

"No business while we're eating," Jake said. "We don't want to insult Lucy with shop talk after she slaved over this wonderful repast all afternoon."

It was a dinner Lucy enjoyed, dealing mostly with the three men's college antics. The blue convertible, however, was the main topic of conversation. Lucy felt a tad jealous of the faceless Angie Motolo as the guys ribbed Wylie, who soaked it all up with a wide grin. While they joked back and forth, Lucy struggled and strained to see if any of their thoughts would come through. She lowered her hands to her lap and crossed her fingers. Maybe *it* was finally gone.

Jake took charge the moment he finished his cobbler and accepted a refill in his coffee cup. Lucy cleared the table, but she listened intently as the men talked. She could feel Mitch Logan's eyes on her. She knew he was taking her measure and wondered if she was coming up short or not. And then she heard him. *She looks frazzled. What the hell kind of guy is she mixed up with?* She was so stunned, she dropped a handful of silverware. All three men stared at her.

Flustered, Lucy bent down to pick up the silverware. "I am frazzled. The truth is I am scared out of my wits. I don't know what kind of man Jonathan or Leo Banks is. I'm learning real fast, though. Let's just say somehow, some way, he managed to be- witch me, okay?" This last she said angrily. She was damn sick and tired of defending herself.

The big man held up his hand. "Whoa, there, Miss Lucy. I want you to back up a moment and think about what you just said. The word *scared* is not in my vocabulary, and I want you to erase it from yours. From here on in, I want you spittin' mad. Not scared, mad. That . . . ah . . . that little thing in your head can be used to your advan- tage. Don't be frightened of it. I think some- body," he said, pointing upward, "wants you to have that particular ability right now at this point in time. Otherwise, you wouldn't be experiencing what you're experiencing. That's how you have to look at it for now. You're alive, you're young, you're healthy, and we're going to make this all come out right. And, no, it does not spook me that you can read my mind. I'd like some more coffee please."

"Well, when you put it like that, I guess you have a point," Lucy acquiesced as she reached for the coffeepot. It *was* going to be all right. She could feel it in her bones.

Jake slid the minirecorder into the middle of the table and turned it on. Mitch Logan listened intently as the FBI agents talked about the security at the house in Watchung. When Jake turned the recorder off, three sets of eyes stared at Mitch Logan.

"I think I can handle this. I know exactly what they're talking about. Mr. Whatever-his-name-is must have some pretty powerful friends to install that kind of security. The last time I saw anything even remotely resembling what the agents were talking about was in a drug lord's compound in El Salvador. I was a SEAL then. Makes you wonder what that guy has stashed in his house."

"What about all the snow?" Wylie asked.

"Snow, rain, sand, makes no difference. I have everything I'll need in the back of my truck. If you don't mind, I'd like to call a guy I know who lives in Sparta, right here in New Jersey. He retired from Delta Force and works for me from time to time. I'd like him to meet us at the house. I checked the map before I left, and he's sixty minutes away.

That okay with you guys?" Everyone nodded. "Good, then it's a go. He's waiting for
my call. Now, if it's okay with all of you, I'd
like to turn in. I get up at four, and it's been
a long day."

Five minutes later, Lucy was holding the
door open for her guests. "Do you feel better now?" Wylie whispered.

"A lot better. I'd really feel wonderful
if Jonathan wasn't coming for Christmas.
Good night, Wylie. I'll see you in the morning."

"You don't mind keeping all the dogs,
do you?"

"Not at all." She knew Wylie wanted to
kiss her. She wanted him to kiss her, too,
but Jake and Mitch were waiting. "Tomorrow's another day," she said, and smiled.

The house seemed exceptionally quiet
when she closed and locked the door behind her guests. She immediately armed the
security system. Someone like Jonathan
could probably disarm the system in a
heartbeat. *Someone like Jonathan.* How
weird the thought was. Lucy gave herself a
mental shake to drive it away. Well, she had
a backup. If Sadie couldn't shred an in-
truder's skin down to the bone, Coop would

use his brute force, knock him down, and sit on him while Lulu chewed him to pieces. The thought was so amusing, Lucy burst out laughing.

She was still laughing when she entered her bedroom to see all three dogs sound asleep on her bed. There was barely enough room for her from the looks of things.

Lucy brushed her teeth and fixed her hair into a ponytail before she went back downstairs to check the dying fire and turn off the lights. She stood for a moment watching the last of the flames in the huge fireplace, wondering what was going to happen to her nice, quiet life now that Wylie was in the mix. A river of heat raged through her body when she remembered how she'd returned his kiss. She'd never kissed Jonathan like that. She'd never felt anything like what she'd felt with Wylie when she was with Jonathan.

Lucy sat down and hugged her knees, the warmth from the fireplace embracing her. She wondered what the men next door were doing. Were they talking about her? Probably. She thought about Mitch Logan in his red-and-black plaid lumberjack flannel shirt. From the tip of his military buzz cut to the tips of his toes, he looked every bit as fearful and as awesome as Jake said he was. And, he wasn't the least bit concerned that she could read his mind. *Amazing,* she thought.

She needed a game plan where Jonathan was concerned. In a courtroom, she could hold her own with the best of them. When it came to affairs of the heart she was a dud, and she knew it. Was Jonathan planning on killing her, as the agents implied? The man had used her. And she had allowed it, which didn't say much for her. She hated thinking about her ex-fiancé. Thoughts about his handsome good looks, his lean, muscled body, and the times they'd made love had become hateful memories. She cringed, shame enveloping her when she thought about the things she'd done with that lean, muscled body. Things Jonathan would expect when he arrived for Christmas. "Like hell!" she snarled.

Lucy knew deep down that Jonathan had picked up on something in her voice. She knew him well enough to be aware of the little nuances in his voice. She wished now that she had said something to Wylie or

Jake about how afraid of the man she was. On the other hand, maybe they knew. No, men were dense about things like that. The dogs would have to be her security, her balance, her protectors. Better not to think of such things. Better to get up and go to bed.

Lucy's hand was on the newel post as she prepared to head up to the second floor when the phone rang. She shrugged as she made her way back to the kitchen, where she'd left her cordless. "Hello," she said cheerfully, thinking it was Wylie on the other end of the phone. To her dismay, she heard Jonathan's rich chuckle reverberating in her ear.

"Oh, darling, I'm glad I caught you. I thought you might have turned in already. I think I had too much wine at dinner, and for some reason I can't seem to compute the time difference. How are you? Do you miss me?"

How can I miss a low-down skunk? "You're right, Jonathan, I was halfway up the stairs, on my way to bed, when the phone rang." *Too much wine, my foot.* Jonathan never, ever lost control. He only drank more wine than he should when he knew he was in bed and would get at least five hours of sleep. Usually after making love. Maybe he was with some other woman. The thought pleased her. *He's worried about the IRS,* she thought. *That's the reason for this call.* "I'm fine, Jonathan, how are you? Of course I miss you. I'm counting the days till you get here. Where are you, Jonathan?"

"I'm still in Zurich. I'll be heading for Cairo shortly. You've been on my mind, darling. All I've been doing is thinking about you instead of business. I know you're worried about your IRS meeting. I'm sure it's some minor nitpicking item they're homing in on."

Lucy sucked in her breath. *You bastard.* "Actually, I put it out of my mind, Jonathan. The one thing I don't do, and have never done, is mess around with my tax records. As a lawyer, I'm trained to keep impeccable records. My brother and I check each other's returns to make sure neither one of us inadvertently forgets to put something in. I was just antsy seeing the letter. It will be fine. I don't want you worrying about me, Jonathan. They did not indicate that this was an audit. Let's not waste our time talking about those pests at the IRS. Let's talk about *us.* Tell me what you're doing and when can I expect to see you?" *Never* would be the appropriate response to her question.

Jonathan's laughter didn't sound genuine. Lucy found herself shivering. She cradled the phone on her neck and shoulder so she could hug her arms against her chest. *Just hang up already, Jonathan. I hate talking to you. I hate you. You're making my skin crawl.* Still, she had to play the game so she could return to her nice, normal life. And, the only way she could do that was to help the FBI trap the man she'd promised to marry.

"You sound like you miss me, Lucy. I'm doing my best to clear the decks, darling. If all goes well, I might be able to finagle a few extra days to make it a full two weeks instead of ten days. What do you think of that?"

Lucy wished she could tell him exactly what she thought of that statement. Her mind raced. Two weeks was fourteen days. That would mean he would arrive on her doorstep somewhere around the . . . what? The seventeenth or the eighteenth of December, give or take a day either way, as-

suming he would leave to go back to whatever rock he lived under on January 2.

Lucy struggled to work enthusiasm and
excitement into her voice. "Fourteen whole
days! Jonathan, this will be a first for
you . . . *us,*" she purred. "As soon as this
pesky snow starts to melt, I'm going to go
shopping for a whole new wardrobe."

Jonathan chuckled again. It sounded just
as forced as before. "You know what they
say, less is more." Lucy felt light-headed at
the insinuation. "Do you know what else,
darling? I was sitting here thinking I'd like to
take you dancing. I want to feel you next to
me, your body pressed tight against mine
as we glide across the floor with other people watching us, knowing we're going to
make love when the night is over. I'm getting hard just thinking about it."

Lucy blinked at the sound of the words
and the meaning. She wanted to gag.
"Hmmm," was all she could get past her
tight lips. Let him think whatever he wanted
to think.

"Does that mean we're on the same
wavelength?" Not bothering to wait for her
response, he said, "Of course it does. When
you go shopping, be sure to pick up some

dancing slippers and a slinky, sexy dress. Get a red one. I love you in red."

He must be thinking about someone else. She didn't own anything, even underwear or pajamas, that were red. Red, in her opinion, was a harlot color. Did Jonathan know that? Her arm, wrist, and hand ached the way she had the receiver pressed to her ear. *Why isn't he hanging up?* She couldn't take one more minute of this.

A stifled yelp escaped her lips. "Oh, my goodness, Sadie just threw up. I have to hang up now, Jonathan." Just as she was about to end the call, she heard him mutter something that sounded like, "On the rug?"

Jonathan snapped the cell phone shut, his eyes speculative as he stared out the window of his hotel room. It would be dawn in a few minutes. A new day. He felt the pulse in his wrist. Too fast. Way too fast. He needed to calm down and think about the conversation he'd just had with his fiancée. Really think.

Jonathan moved then, across the elaborate suite of rooms to the room service tray that had arrived just as his call to Lucy went through. There was nothing like a jolt of pure Colombian coffee to jump-start the morning. Just what he needed, caffeine. He gulped at the hot, dark brew.

Jonathan licked at lips that felt dry. Lucy was suspicious. Of what? The IRS letter? There was no way she could know about the brokerage accounts or the house in Watchung or the amended tax returns. Or could she? She had to know or suspect something. Why else did she sound so . . . so *wary* when he called her, like she was choosing her words, thinking, weighing what she was going to say. Damn, the feds had probably paid her a visit.

As always, when Jonathan was under pressure, he sat down at the ornate desk and turned on his laptop. Blizzards of files and numbers raced across the screen. His holdings. His security. The totally different life he was about to embark on come the new year. A life he'd prepared for with his own sweat, blood, and yes, even a few tears. With the money he'd secreted around the world, he could take his place among the rich and famous, with Lucy at his side.

He'd chosen Lucy from a hundred other women because she knew the law and had credibility. After they were married, he'd suggest some of the famous salons in Paris.

Perhaps a little plastic surgery. A haute couture wardrobe, and she would be worthy of holding on to his arm. Her French was so-so, and he would insist she become fluent.

Why was he having all these thoughts when the very real possibility that he would have to kill Lucy banged around inside his head?

If his instincts were right, and they'd never failed him before, maybe he should cut his losses where Lucy was concerned and sever his relationship with the lawyer. Damn, if the *federales* were onto him, he was going to have to do some clever shape-shifting in order to enter the good old US of A.

It was getting lighter outside the windows. Jonathan walked over, opened the draperies, and stared down at the city. Damn, it was snowing again. He hated the cold. He really did. The French Riviera was the place to be at this time of year. Any time of the year for that matter.

Jonathan flipped open his encrypted cell phone and proceeded to punch in a number he knew from memory. His voice firm and cool, he canceled his proposed meeting in Cairo, saying urgent business demanded he return to the United States. The promise of a rescheduled meeting and a discount calmed the voice on the other end of the line.

Jonathan's next call was to Swissair. Better to fly commercial than have his pilot bring the Gulfstream to Lucerne. He thought then about his latest acquisition, a Bell Jet Ranger helicopter. He couldn't wait to play with that particular new toy. Payment for a job well-done. He smiled, but the smile didn't reach his eyes. His immediate business taken care of, he could concentrate all his efforts on what he was going to do about Lucy Baker.

If there was one thing in life that Jonathan St. Clair, aka Leo Banks, hated, it was a switch in plans that had been synchronized down to the last sync. That's when things went wrong, ordinary, little things that brought men like him to their knees.

Well, that wasn't going to happen to him. He'd worked too long, too hard, to secure the good life that was about to become his.

Jonathan poured the last of the coffee

from the silver pot. As Jonathan gazed out on the swirling snow, he pictured Lucy in his mind and wondered if he would miss her if his instincts were on target.

9

Lucy rolled over to feel little puffs of breath on her neck. She opened one eye, then the other. Lulu was curled into a tight ball on her shoulder, half under the covers and half out. The little pink bow jiggled each time she exhaled. Lucy smiled as she reached out to stroke the tiny head. Lulu immediately bounded up, ready to play. Coop and Sadie were on the bed an instant later. All of them tussled for a minute or two before Lucy swung her legs over the side of the bed.

"Okay, troops, time to go out and do your thing. Oh, oh," she said, padding down the carpeted steps. "Looks like it snowed during the night." Two minutes later, Lucy eyeballed the mountain of snow on top of the hot tub. At least another six inches must have fallen. That had to mean Wylie wouldn't be heading for Manhattan. The thought pleased her.

Lucy unlocked and slid the sliding glass door to the side. Coop bounded through, his bark high and shrill. Sadie was right behind him, nipping at his tail as they raced to the back of the yard. Lulu stuck one tiny little paw into the snow on the deck, then backed inside, the pink bow jiggling furiously. "Okay, little one, let me get yesterday's paper." Not trusting the Yorkie, Lucy scooped her up and carried her to the family room, where she grabbed the sports section of the paper. She spread the paper and Lulu piddled, then ran to the door to watch her new best friends cavorting in the snow.

In the kitchen, Lucy made coffee. What would all this new snow mean to the guys' trip to Watchung? For some reason she didn't think it would make a difference to Mitch Logan. Jake, however, looked like a creature of comfort. Wylie would be game for anything if he didn't go into work. That left her. Well, she had a ski suit and rubber boots, so that meant she was up to the trek if the men thought it advisable.

Mitch had said he drove up in a truck, so he was prepared. Wylie's Land Rover had four-wheel drive. By the time the coffee dripped all the way, Lucy had herself convinced the trip would go on schedule.

Was the trip a good idea or a bad one? She simply didn't know. What she did know was that she wanted this whole mess to be over and done with.

The phone rang just as Lucy added cream to her coffee. Her voice was wary when she uttered a greeting.

"Luce, it's Steven. I'm just calling to tell you the city is shut down pretty tight. No one was expecting this much snow. I'm not even going to attempt to go to the office. I think I'm going to hang out at home, drink a few beers, and watch some videos. How are things with you, sis?"

"Same old, same old. Sadie loves the snow. She's out there right now having a grand old time. I just got up as a matter of fact. Anything new?"

"Lucy, why don't you just come out and ask me if I'm seeing anyone new. Actually, I am. Her name is Belle Andrews. She's a lawyer at Justice. Long legs. Looks good in a bikini, and she likes me. Oh, did I mention she can cook? She can. She thinks I'm handsome, and she likes to run her fingers through my curly hair. Did I leave anything out?"

Lucy laughed. "Does she have any outstanding marks on that beautiful body?"

"A real strawberry mark by her belly button. Is that more than you wanted to know? Hey, anything on Jonathan? How are the wedding plans going?"

Lucy sucked in her breath. "The wedding is off, Steven. I'm going to tell Jonathan when he arrives for Christmas. It's not something I'm comfortable saying over the telephone."

Steven whooped his pleasure. "Glad you're seeing the light of day, Lucy. That guy was all wrong for you. I, for one, am relieved. Guess that means you have to go on the prowl again."

Lucy's voice turned indignant. "I have never, nor will I, go on the prowl. There is this really nice guy next door. All I have to do is walk up to the fence, and I can see and talk to him. You'd like him, Steven. Maybe we can get together. I can meet all of you in the city, and we can do dinner one night if this freaky weather ever clears up. I can't wait to meet the ravishing Belle."

"Okay, sounds like a plan. This neighbor of yours, does he have a name?"

"Of course he has a name but you don't need to know it. I don't want you running any checks on him. He is what he is, a nice guy, a lawyer. I'll call you next week, okay?"

"You got it, sis. Why don't you go out and play in the snow with Sadie?"

Lucy laughed again. "Great idea. I did that yesterday. Maybe I'll do it again today. See ya, Steven."

Lucy wished she was a kid again, when life was simple. In those days she ate, played, ate, played until she was exhausted, then slept. There were no worries, no angst, no betrayals unless you counted the time Janet Williams told Bill Kelly she called him stinky because he needed deodorant. She'd made snow angels with Betty Lou Saylan, had ice-skated on Desty's pond with Betty Lou. She should call Betty Lou, who now lived in a little town in Virginia. And, she would, just as soon as her life returned to normal. Maybe she'd even take a drive to see her. Old friendships were the best even when they were reduced to semiannual phone calls and the extra special Hallmark Christmas card along with a "family" letter describing the year's activities. Yes, she would get in touch with Betty Lou.

It was nine-thirty when Lucy showered, dressed, and made her bed, which the dogs immediately messed up by playing tug-of-war with the comforter. Wylie should have called by now to announce their plans. Was the trip on or off? Lucy stared at her reflection in the stainless-steel Sub-Zero refrigerator while she waited for a fresh pot of coffee to brew. She was dressed for a day in the snowy mountains. She'd layered her clothing underneath the plum-colored, fleece-lined sweat suit. Warm cashmere leggings covered her legs. At the moment she was wearing slippers, but if the trip was on, she'd change into her rubber boots. Knowing her hair was going to get mussed up inside the hood of her parka, she'd simply piled it on top of her hair with tortoise-shell combs to hold it in place. If Wylie did not call soon, she would have to start peeling off her carefully assembled cocoon of clothing.

Outside, the thermometer on the deck

said it was a freezing twenty-nine degrees. Just thinking about the cold made Lucy shiver. With nothing else to do while she waited for Wylie and his friends, Lucy emptied the dishwasher and folded the towels in the dryer. She hated emptying the dishwasher, but it was something to do. Maybe she should call Wylie's house. Then again, maybe she shouldn't.

She couldn't help thinking about Jonathan's phone call the night before. She wished she knew if her telephone was bugged. Did the federal agents listen in on her calls? Would they ask if she'd heard from Jonathan? Did she dare lie? To what end? She shook her head wearily. Maybe she needed to switch mental gears and think about Thanksgiving. For a moment, she couldn't remember how many days she had to get a turkey.

Lucy was jolted from her thoughts when all three dogs let loose with earsplitting barks as they raced in tandem to the front door. She sighed in relief as she made her way through the dining room to the front door. When she opened it, Wylie announced that they had come for breakfast.

"In that case, I hope you brought it," Lucy

said curtly. "I can offer toast and jam, but that's about it."

"We'll take it," Jake said happily. "I'm also up for heated leftovers."

Mitch took his seat at the table and stared up at Lucy. "Are you up for our trip to the mountain, Miss Lucy?" The giant of a man was always so formal and so polite. A smile tugged at the corners of her mouth. She loved the way "Miss Lucy" sounded rolling off his tongue. She was almost positive he'd had a Southern upbringing. Later, she would ask.

Lucy nodded. "With the new snow, I wasn't sure if we were going or not." She pointed to the sweat suit she was wearing. "I'm ready to go." She dropped bread into the four-slice toaster that she had retrieved from its home in the cabinet and poured coffee. She rinsed the empty pot and made a second. "By the way, Jonathan called again last night just as I was locking up. Maybe it's just me, but I think he knows something is going on."

"Something *is* going on. We're going to find out what the man is up to and why the feds are on your case. We spent the last hour loading all my gear in Wylie's cargo hold. We can't take my truck because there's only room for one passenger," Mitch said as he rolled up the sleeves of his thick, woolen shirt. Today, the colors were blue and black. His wide-wale corduroys matched the blue in the lumberjack shirt. He wore the same buff-colored Timberland boots Jake and Wylie had on. To Lucy's eyes he still looked as big as a grizzly bear. He also looked like her savior. She hoped she was right.

As the three men gulped and munched, Lucy elaborated further on Jonathan's phone call. The trio said nothing, only nodding from time to time until she wound down at last.

It was finally time to go. Lucy let the dogs out one last time, cleared the table, and slipped into her ski jacket. She was as ready as she would ever be.

Wylie drove, Lucy in the passenger seat. Mitch and Jake in the backseat. It took them twenty minutes to make their way out of the development to Park Avenue, which had been plowed and sanded. Still, driving was treacherous, four-wheel drive or not. Another hour was spent trying to reach

Route 22, which would take them to Watchung and Jonathan St. Clair's house.

The men talked about football and cars as Lucy stewed and fretted in the front seat, wondering what they would find when they arrived at the house that had her name on the deed.

They used up another thirty-five minutes on the highway by driving past the property because the driveway hadn't been plowed. Wylie drove until he found an exit and turned around. This time they all looked for the marker, hoping the Land Rover would make it up the steep, twisting driveway to the very top of a hill.

"The snow's making the driveway look bigger and longer than it is," Mitch said. "I think you can get as far as those electronic gates, Wylie. We pile out, and I do my thing. Let's see what this baby can do." The engine of the Land Rover whined and strained as it fought its way through the deep snow. Twice, the four-by-four bucked, then stalled, slipping backward.

"Miss Lucy, come around to this side and drive. The three of us will push you up to the crest. Low gear." Lucy felt like cheering when the Land Rover came to a halt on level ground near the fortresslike gates.

Hands on hips, Mitch looked around. He pulled his navy wool hat down over his ears. "Impressive," was all he said.

"Makes you kind of wonder what's behind those awesome-looking gates," Jake said.

Awesome was definitely the right word, Lucy thought. Iron spikes, ten inches tall, stood up from the iron grille of the fence and gates. Thick shards of glass were embedded in the concrete between the spikes. Put there, Lucy assumed, in case anyone was foolish or daring enough to climb over the fence. She risked a glance at Wylie, whose face was totally unreadable. Lucy felt sick to her stomach. What *was* he thinking? She strained to pick up his thoughts, but nothing came through. She crossed her fingers inside her warm mittens that he wasn't thinking she was part of whatever was going on at this house.

"Let's get to it, gentlemen," Mitch said, opening the cargo hold to remove his equipment. "Let's see how serious this dude is about his privacy."

Lucy watched as the trio hauled out mysterious-looking gadgets and equipment.

What they were for, she had no idea. James Bond would probably know. Shivering, hugging her arms to her chest, she watched as the three men plowed through the snow with their futuristic-looking tools.

"The windows of the house are multiple-pane glass. They have a Mylar film inside. To you guys that means anyone outside the house with a laser listening device wouldn't be able to hear a thing inside. I'm thinking this is a safe house of some kind." Mitch swung a long tool and pointed it toward the Tudor-style house. "The walls of the house are lined with copper. That's so nothing can be picked up from monitoring devices on the outside. I saw something like this in Venezuela. This is drug lord surveillance," he said, sweeping the grounds with something that looked like a metal detector. "This guy must have some big bucks. The security he's got here is worthy of the White House or Colombia. The Colombians never stint on security and back it up with trained commandos. Now why does a guy who brokers business deals need something like this in his backyard?" Mitch asked. He didn't expect a response. Instead, he walked through the grounds in the deep snow, pushing first one gadget, then an-other, and yet others until green lights glowed coolly on the equipment all of them carried.

"Okay. The green lights tell me I've lo-cated all the sensors. Now all I have to do is disarm them. I want you all to stand in the driveway behind the car in case one of these little beauties decides to go off. Boom!" he said playfully.

Thirty-five minutes later, Mitch looked at the green buttons that were slowly turning from yellow to red. "Red is the safe zone," he said cheerfully. "Relax, guys, I know what I'm doing. I did it for fifteen years, and I have citations saying I'm the best of the best. This is puppy-dog stuff. The real test is going to be disarming the gate and the next round of embedded security. Then comes the house." Wylie and Jake looked skeptical.

Mitch was in back of the Land Rover, stowing his gear and replacing it with differ-ent tools and gadgets. Everything glowed and vibrated. "What is all that stuff?" Lucy asked, in a hushed whisper.

"Tools of the trade, Miss Lucy. We live in a different world today and need such things. These things," he said, motioning to the packed cargo hold, "are all government issue. Updated equipment we used when I was a SEAL and Drew was with Delta Force. Oh, oh, looks like we have company. I'm thinking it's my buddy, but just to be on the safe side, don't move. Don't even blink." Mitch's hand, she noticed, was inside the blue-and-black lumberjack shirt. *Shoulder holster,* she thought. *This is all just a bad dream.* She pinched herself to make sure. It was all too real she decided when she felt the pain in her arm where she'd pinched herself.

No one moved when they heard a car door slam shut. All of them relaxed when a voice called out. "Yo, Mitch, you up there? It's me, Drew."

Mitch's gloved hand fell to his side as he maneuvered his way to the driveway. Lucy saw a tall man wearing a backpack coming up the driveway. A suntanned man who looked like Charles Atlas, the bodybuilder. He was handsome, probably in his late thirties, possibly his early forties, with a buzz cut like Mitch's. He wore jeans, probably over long underwear, boots, a long-sleeved shirt, and a hunter green down vest. When he removed his sunglasses, Lucy saw he had bright, summer blue eyes.

Introductions were made, hands shaken, then Lucy was outside of the loop as the men traded gear, poked and probed each other's tools, and talked in low voices. The minutes crawled by. Lucy climbed into the Land Rover and turned on the engine. The heat kicked on almost immediately. She sighed with relief. She leaned back and stared out the window at the house the feds said belonged to her. Why did Jonathan need all this security?

Then she heard it. If she had been standing next to the men outside the truck, the words couldn't have been any clearer. She was hearing Mitch's thoughts.

And then Wiley's thoughts. She was sure they were Wiley's thoughts. *She can't be involved in this. There's no way. She's scared out of her wits. Hell, I'm scared out of my wits, and I don't even know the stupid guy.*

Then the newcomer, a man who didn't even know her. *There's something weird going on here. The word* trap *comes to mind. This is New Jersey, for God's sake. Stuff like this doesn't happen around here. No stake-*

outs. Where the hell are the feds when you need them?

Jake's thoughts were different. *A nice juicy cheeseburger, with onion rings on the side. Maybe a double malt. French fries with loads of ketchup when this is over.*

Lucy sighed. If, and it was a big if, Jonathan was responsible for this security, this house, and everything the feds said, what did the word *safe* really mean? If Jonathan had the kind of money they alluded to, he would be able to find her anywhere.

Minutes crawled by. Minutes that turned into an hour. The sun that had been bright just minutes ago was gone, the day turning gray and ominous. Lucy rolled down the window. The air felt heavy with the threat of more snow to come. She shrugged as she watched the gray overcast sweep across the sky. The weather was just as freaky as what was happening to her. She wiggled around in her seat to see what the four men were doing. Mitch and Drew both had cell phones to their ears. That told her they were stymied. They must be calling other experts, hoping for clues as to how to disarm the sophisticated systems in place. Wylie and Jake looked like they were frozen to the ground. Jake's nose was as red as a cherry. Wylie ran in place to keep warm. She knew they were chilled to the bone.

Wylie looked in her direction, saw the rolled-down window, and ran over. He leaned into the warm car, little puffs of steam escaping from between his lips.

"What's wrong?" Lucy asked.

"Mitch said he hasn't seen anything like this before. Drew agreed. They said this stuff is updated practically on a daily basis. I think they're checking with members of their old units. Drew said he knows a spook at the CIA who might be able to help. This gadgetry is way beyond anything I've ever heard about." Wylie shook his head and walked back to join the men.

Lucy cracked the driver's-side window before she settled down to snooze. That was when she heard the sounds on the windshield. Snow was silent. This was hard-driving sleet slamming against the wind-shield. Sleet meant the roads would freeze up. Suddenly she felt frightened and didn't know why.

What *were* they doing out there? Just seconds ago she was thinking about taking a nap. Suddenly she was too angry and frightened to sleep. Her adrenaline pumping, Lucy hopped out of the truck, her head down to avoid the stinging sleet as she slogged her way over to the men by the gate. "Why don't we just climb over the damn thing?" she shouted to be heard over the wind and sleet.

"That's exactly what we're getting ready to do, Miss Lucy," Mitch shouted back. "We're betting the guts of this security gate are on the other side, inside that stone gatehouse, and the owner has a special encrypted card that he just flashes when he wants to go in and out of this gate. It's obvious we don't have one of those particular cards, so we're going to blow the system. Wylie is going over first and will blow it. I want you to stand back."

Card. Lucy's memory stirred. "Wait a minute. What kind of card are you talking about?"

"You know the kind you swipe through a lock or show it faceup to a small screen. Sometimes they go by eyes or thumbprints for ID. It's okay, we know what we're doing, Miss Lucy."

"Wait. Please wait. I think I might have the

card. Jonathan gave me a card several months ago. Early in the summer. He said it was for international shopping, you know, for when we went to Europe. Okay, okay, so I was stupid. To me it was just a weird-looking credit card," she said defensively at the skeptical looks on the men's faces. "I put it in my wallet and forgot about it till just now. You can make whatever you want out of that. If you give me a minute, I'll get it for you."

Minutes later, when Lucy handed over the card, Mitch looked at it, then at her. His gaze was so intense, Lucy felt like he had nailed her to the ground. He handed it to Drew Warner, who walked up to the gate and simply waved the card in front of the monitor. The gates slid open with barely a sound. Lucy felt queasy and light-headed as she followed the men through the gate.

Wylie reached for her hand. He bent over, and shouted into her ear, "Smile, it adds to your face value. Look, we're inside, and that's all that matters."

Lucy nodded as she watched Drew and Mitch roam the property inside the gate. Even through the stinging sleet, she could see small dots of green, yellow, and red on the equipment they carried. Wylie led her to an overhang by a small round-arched back door. The narrow eave deflected some of the sleet. Jake joined them a few minutes later.

There, close to the house, Lucy found she didn't have to shout at the top of her lungs to be heard. "I swear, I forgot about the card, I actually believed it was what Jonathan said it was, an international credit card. Since I never had one, how could I know if it was real or not? I was taking everything Jonathan said back then at face value. The card did say GLOBAL on the front of it. It looked like a damn credit card, Wylie." If she hadn't been so cold, she would have burst into tears of frustration. *Why is this happening to me?*

"If he tried to keep this house secret, why would he have given the card to you?" Jake asked. "How were you supposed to get into the house? All it does is open the gate."

"I don't know, Jake," Lucy wailed at the outright suspicion in his voice. "I don't know anything about how or what Jonathan did. You have to believe me."

Jake took off his gloves and blew on his

fingers. "No offense, Lucy, but your fiancé must have thought you were really stupid."

"Yes, I guess he really did," Lucy snapped. "And, I just proved to everyone how really stupid I am. He bamboozled me, okay. I take full responsibility for my own stupidity, but I am not involved in anything he did or said."

Wylie put his arm around her shoulder and pulled her close. "We're going to figure this all out, Lucy. Don't go off the deep end now."

The trio remained under the narrow overhang shivering, their teeth rattling with cold for another forty minutes—at which point Mitch and Drew returned their gear to the truck and brought back different equipment. Another forty minutes passed as they explored for trip wires, then deactivated the alarm system and locks.

At last they were all inside the garage. Mitch fumbled for a light switch. All of them reared back at the huge black Chevy Suburban sitting squarely in the middle of the six-car garage. For some reason it looked obscene to Lucy. Obscene *and* frightening. Lucy wondered about the other six cars the FBI agents had mentioned. Nothing had been said about anything as prosaic as a Chevy Suburban.

Another twenty-five minutes passed while Drew checked out the Suburban and Mitch worked the keypad outside a door that led into the main body of the house. Eventually they were inside the house, all of them standing in the kitchen. Jake pressed a wall switch, and the gray room sprang to light. Outside, sleet hammered against the windows, sounding like nails being shot from a nail gun. Wylie looked around for a thermostat and turned it up to ninety degrees. Immediately a warm rush of air spewed from the baseboard grates.

Lucy looked around the huge kitchen. This was not a kitchen Martha Stewart would love. While state-of-the-art, there was nothing warm and cozy about the room. The word *institutional* came to mind. Every appliance was Sub-Zero, and stainless steel. Even the sink. The floor was dove gray granite. The hanging pot rack over the center island was loaded down with shiny stainless-steel pots and pans. *Never used,* Lucy thought as she looked up at the contraption. She could see the glue marks on the pots where the price stickers had once been. Out of curiosity, she opened the refrigerator. It was empty. She opened the freezer, and it was full. She reached for a package of frozen ground coffee and a container of half-and-half. "I'll make some coffee," she said curtly. "We all need to warm up."

Mitch nodded as he walked away, Drew Warner on his heels. Jake and Wylie stayed with Lucy in the kitchen. Her voice was a whisper when she said, "I don't think anyone lives here or has ever lived here." Lucy pointed to the glue marks on the pots hanging overhead. The tears she'd been holding in check escaped and rolled down her cheeks. "What *is* this place?"

Wylie grimaced. Jake looked at the pots. "I don't know, Lucy. Mitch said he thought it was a safe house. What that means exactly, I don't know. It's getting warmer; let's check out the rest of the place. C'mon, it's going to be all right. We have professionals helping us now. Right, Jake?"

"Absolutely," Jake said as he removed his topcoat and muffler. "Actually, it's getting downright toasty in here."

A short hallway led them to an immense room that seemed to be, aside from the kitchen, the entire first floor. Lucy blinked. It was a round room. Lucy was reminded of a soccer ball. How could a square house have a round room? And it was white, so white it was dazzling.

A round white brick fireplace sat squarely in the middle of the room, the venting hood going all the way up to the ceiling and probably through the roof. Lucy couldn't remember if she'd seen a chimney when she was outside or not. She tried to calculate the size of the pit and finally likened it to two circular hot tubs. Six huge cherry logs with strips of kindling laid between them were ready to be ignited. A circle of deep, white, velvet couches surrounded the strange-looking fireplace. No matter where you sat, you would have a view of the fire. There were no tables, no plants, no pictures on the wall—no knickknacks of any kind. The floor was hardwood, probably oak, and strangely enough it wasn't the least bit dusty. She wondered if the house was hermetically sealed. The thought sent chills up and down her arms.

The wraparound windows were cloaked in heavy white brocade shot through with silver thread, the only concession to color.

Was silver a color? *Is there a silver color in a Crayola box?* she thought inanely. She decided silver wasn't a color. And the world would go on with the knowledge Lucy Baker deemed silver not to be a color. She must be losing her mind.

Lucy peered down into the pit and frowned. For some reason she didn't expect to see ashes. But there they were. Someone had been there, and that someone, at some point, had built a fire. A few of the bricks on the bottom were scorched and black. Little piles of ash rested under the neat pile of wood.

"It smells like . . . wallpaper paste," Jake said thoughtfully. "Maybe it's a paint smell. Maybe just a new house smell. What do you think, Mitch?"

"I think it's a paint smell combined with the fact the house has been closed up. This is definitely either a safe house or a stopping-off place for people on the run. I'm going to check out the rest of the house. Don't open those drapes," he cautioned.

"Check this out, Mitch!" Drew called from the front foyer, which was out of sight of the round room. They all ran through the arched doorway to a small foyer littered with mail.

"The guy has one of those chutes like banks use at their drive-throughs. When the mail gets to here, the cylinder just opens, dumps the mail, and returns to the mailbox, probably someplace at the bottom of the driveway. I must have missed it on our way in. There's nothing here but catalogs and junk mail. Everything is addressed to 'Lucille Baker' or 'Resident.' "

If Wylie hadn't been holding on to Lucy's arm, she would have fallen. To prove what Drew was saying, Lucy stooped down and picked up a Crate and Barrel catalog. Sure enough, her name was on the label. She started to feel sick all over again.

"It's just a catalog, Lucy. It doesn't mean anything," Wylie said.

"Like hell it doesn't mean anything. This junk says I live here. Me—Lucy Baker—I get mail at this address. No wonder the feds are on my back. God, how I hate that man for doing this to me!"

Wylie shrugged. "Have it your way, Lucy. To me, it means nothing. There's not one piece of personal mail, not one bill of any kind. That says a lot in my book."

Her eyes hard, her voice grim, Lucy said, "Try telling that to the feds the next time they show up. Hell, they're probably watching and spying on us right now."

"Now what?" Jake asked.

Mitch fixed his gaze on Jake. "Drew and I are going to investigate the upstairs and the attic while you guys pour us that coffee. It should be ready by now."

Five minutes later, just as Lucy was starting to pour coffee into the cups, Mitch called them upstairs. They ran, jostling one another in their haste to see what Mitch had found.

"What?" they said in unison at the doorway to a small room, no more than eight-by-ten in size.

Drew looked at them with a strange expression on his face. "I saw a room like this in Somalia that belonged to some badassed dudes."

"Yeah, and what's that supposed to mean?" Wylie asked, his voice on the shaky side.

His eyes hard as flints, Drew looked from one to the other.

"It's called a dead room."

10

"And a dead room would be . . . what?" Wylie growled. "We're just ordinary people here in case you haven't noticed. There doesn't appear to be anyone dead in this room, so I have to assume it means something else entirely."

Lucy's jaw dropped as she gazed around the small room. Something lumpy with the look of Styrofoam had been sprayed onto the walls and ceiling. The door was padded with strange-looking quilted material that resembled shiny plastic. The floor was intertwined wire-and-rubber matting. A scary-looking room in her opinion. As she tried to absorb what she was seeing, she could hear Mitch and Drew explaining to Jake and Wylie what they were analyzing on the computer table. Since she didn't understand the high-tech talk, she only heard snatches that left her even more clueless than before. Underwater parabolic eavesdroppers, fish-eye camera, microphones, a video console for the fish-eye camera, hard laser microphones. What she finally deduced from their conversation was that the room enabled whoever was in it to have conversations that were truly secure.

"What's that?" Lucy asked, pointing to the center of the table.

"I'm glad you asked," Mitch grimaced. "They're the latest in technology. The mikes and headphones enable people to talk on the phones face-to-face, have conference calls secure in the knowledge that whatever they say stays safe in this room. That's why it's called a dead room."

"Why would someone need something like that?" Jake asked.

"I don't have any answers, Jake. You could try asking the feds or the guy himself. There isn't anything more we can do here. So, let's check out the basement, drink our coffee, and head for home. The big question is, do you want all this stuff we dismantled activated or what?"

"No!"

"Okay, Miss Lucy, you're the boss. We will lock the door and reset the house alarm, though. You don't want strange people crawling around in here. You have the card to the gate so if you want to come back, you can just swipe it. I'll write down the code to the alarm system. You can come and go as you please. A word of warning, Miss Lucy. Somewhere, someplace, the person who installed all this hardware is going to know it's been compromised. They probably knew the minute we started dismantling the system. And before you can ask, the people who did this are experts. Your guy probably brought them in from other countries. It's not the kind of security you want your neighbors or your local security people to know about."

Drew fixed his gaze on Lucy and Wylie. "You might want to give some serious thought to relocating or else have the feds give you some kind of protection. From the looks of things, there's been some serious stuff happening here. It's anyone's guess if it is still going on. The federal agents were right when they told you it was dangerous, and you could get killed. Think about it."

Like I can think about anything else. Lucy nodded.

Mitch shrugged, his eyes worried. "Let's

have that coffee before we head back to your house."

"I'll take mine to go. I've got some pretty steep roads to travel. I'll be lucky to make it home by midnight," Drew said.

In the kitchen, Lucy poured a mug of coffee for Drew. "Thanks."

"Be careful," Drew said, as he shook hands all around before heading out the door with his coffee. He called over his shoulder. "Call me if you need me."

Mitch gulped at his black coffee. "Drew is right, Miss Lucy. You stumbled onto something that could get you killed. My suggestion to you is get in touch with the *feebs,* lay it out, bring them back here if necessary, and clean your skirts. Do that as soon as you can. Then relocate."

As Lucy sipped at the scalding coffee, she strained to *hear* the men's thoughts. Under the circumstances, she expected to hear a jumble, but nothing was coming through. Her shoulders slumped.

Wylie turned the thermostat to sixty-five before he placed his empty coffee cup in the sink.

Mitch set the alarm in the garage, and then they exited. The garage door closed with a loud bang. The little group, their heads down, ran as fast as they could through the deep snow and stinging sleet to the car outside the gates. Breathless, they piled into the vehicle. Wiley turned the key in the ignition and pushed the heater as high as it would go. Then he hopped out and scraped the ice from the front and back windshields. From his pocket he withdrew an aerosol can of deicer and sprayed both windshields. The wipers slid smoothly across the windshield as he slipped the SUV into reverse. They literally slid down the driveway and out to the main road.

What would normally have been a thirty-five-minute ride took them almost three hours before they pulled into Wylie's driveway. Wylie's head slumped down on the steering wheel the moment he turned off the ignition. "I need a drink!" he mumbled. "Hell, I need two drinks! I don't ever remember driving in road conditions like this in my whole life."

"Relax, you got us home safe and sound," Jake said cheerfully. "I'll personally make your drink."

"Good, because I have to make a meat

loaf for Coop. Lucy, are you coming in or are you going home?" Wylie asked.

Meat loaf. The dogs. A drink. She was back in the world of normalcy. Safe and sane. There were no dead rooms in Wylie's house or in hers either. There were no security gates or things that would blow up if you stepped on them, no trip wires, no mail chutes here in this quiet neighborhood. "I'll go home and bring the dogs over. My larder is bare, so we'll have to raid yours. Have my drink ready when I get there," Lucy said, as she hopped out of the SUV.

The dogs knew she was home. She could hear them barking all the way in Wylie's yard. When she reached her own driveway she was surprised to see footprints in the snow. Someone must have been by earlier. Who? One of the kids from one of the side streets wanting to shovel her driveway? She shrugged as she fitted the key into the three locks on her front door, glad that she'd added the mega lock at the top of the door that went into the molding. As she swung the door open, she was greeted by three clamoring dogs.

Inside, she raced through the house, her gaze going every which way as she looked for accidents or a sign that someone was or had been in the house. She didn't see anything, so that meant the dogs were just barking because they really needed to go out. She turned on the floodlights on the deck as her hand went to the lock on the sliding glass door. There were footprints in the snow all over the deck. She started to shake as she bent down to take the dowel out of the sliding track. Even if someone had a key to the slider, the dowel wouldn't allow them to open the door. Whoever had been in her yard must have climbed over the fence or else was tall enough to reach up, over, then down to the latch on the other side of the fence. Who?

The door swished open. The dogs barreled outside, even Lulu, who immediately piddled on the deck. The moment she was finished, the Yorkie started to sniff at the indentations just the way the others were doing. Who? Who had been in the backyard? Not some youngster wanting to shovel the driveway. Who?

Coop looked up and threw back his head and howled. Lucy jumped at the sound. Sadie moved across the deck to the fence gate. Her nose in the snow, she walked back and forth, but she didn't bark. Did that mean she'd picked up the scent of someone she knew? *Who?*

"Who? Who? Who?" She sounded like an owl. She called to the dogs. They all bounded into the house. Lucy waited to see if they'd sniff out anything unusual. They didn't. That meant no one was in the house. Who in their right mind would enter a house where a dog like Coop barked? *Who?*

Jonathan, that's who.

Lucy felt an adrenaline rush at the thought. She looked down at her watch. It was quarter to eight. Time enough for Jonathan to have gotten there from wherever he'd been when he had called last night. Lucy could feel her insides start to clench up at the implications of what she was thinking.

Quicker than lightning, she ran around the downstairs rooms, turning off all the lights. In the kitchen she snapped off the nightlight over the stove. Total darkness washed over her. Sadie growled at the strange goings-on. Lulu yelped to be picked up, and Lucy obliged. Coop started to prowl, sniffing at the track of the sliding glass doors.

Lucy crept over to the little alcove off the

kitchen where the pantry was located. No windows, no doors where a person could be seen. She started to shake. Hot tears of anger and frustration burned her eyes. *Weaklings and sissies cower in fear,* she told herself. *Top-notch lawyers with brains are trained to stand up to just about anything. Yeah, well, today was over the top. He's playing with my head, that's what he's doing. I know it because I know Jonathan. I should call the FBI right now and tell them what we found.*

"Maybe I should call the feds," Lucy muttered. "But if I don't know if I should trust them, what's the point?" She thought about how nasty they'd been to her, how cold and uncaring. "The hell with it," she muttered again. She backtracked in her thoughts. If she told them she thought the footprints belonged to Jonathan, they'd probably laugh their heads off. They'd say she was just trying to wiggle out from under their scrutiny. She smacked her hands together. That thought alone convinced her it was not in her best interests to call the agents. Lucy dropped to her knees, Lulu clutched tight against her chest. "Listen up, you two," she said to Coop and Sadie. "We're going to

Wylie's house. Straight across the yard." Her voice was so jittery and shaky that the dogs actually paid attention to what she was saying. Lulu licked at her chin.

She was still wearing her jacket. She slipped into her rubber boots, scuffling along as she herded the dogs to the front door. Key in hand, she took one last look around before opening the door to let Coop and Sadie out, then locked it. There were wings on her feet as she crossed the yard to Wylie's house. She didn't bother to knock, just let herself in. Wylie was watching her from the foyer when she turned around and snapped the dead bolt.

Lucy was breathless from the run in the deep snow across the yard. "Someone was in my backyard. They must have been by the front door, too. Coop pitched a fit, but not Sadie, so that means the scent she picked up was someone she knew. Lulu picked up on it, too. I'd appreciate it if you'd close your blinds, Wylie," Lucy said. She could have saved her breath because Wylie was already closing the vertical blinds. Mitch meandered into the foyer, Jake behind him. Both had beer bottles in their hands.

Wylie explained Lucy's nervousness as she kicked off her boots and shed her jacket.

Mitch was the first to speak. "When it snows like this, people have a tendency to look out their windows from time to time to see if it's still snowing, how deep it's getting. Call some of your neighbors and see if they saw anyone at your house, Miss Lucy."

Lucy hung up her ski jacket. "After being in that house, I think I'm spooking myself. I suppose it could have been a youngster wanting to shovel the driveway."

Mitch swigged from his near-empty bottle. "If that's the case, then the kid would have knocked on other doors in the neighborhood. It won't hurt to call around, Miss Lucy."

"While you're doing that, Lucy, I've got to finish the meat loaf for Coop. By the way, that's what we're having for dinner, with baked potatoes and canned corn. I have some cabbage if anyone wants to make coleslaw or fried cabbage. Then I have to go across the street to feed Rachel Muller's cat and change the litter box. I almost forgot I was supposed to do that. She's liable to call me tonight to ask how the cat is. It won't take me long."

Curiosity ringing in her voice, Lucy asked, "Where's Rachel? I thought I saw her this morning."

"She went to Delaware to spend Thanksgiving with her sister. Her brother was picking her up just as we were leaving. I've had a key to her house forever. She used to take the cat, but he's old now and doesn't travel well. On nice days she used to walk Coop while I was at work."

"Lulu is going to be mighty upset if you come home smelling of cat," Jake warned. "We might as well have something besides corn. I'll do the coleslaw."

They were chatting about mundane matters, hoping to wipe away the look of anxiety on Lucy's face.

"I think I'll have a beer. Jonathan could have been on a plane when he called me last night. If he was, he could very well be here. Maybe I should call one of the agents. I think I figured it out. Jonathan is trying to play with my head so I'll go off the deep end," Lucy said as she marched into the kitchen. "Jonathan knows I haven't made any real friends since I moved here. Aside from Nellie, that is. He also knows Nellie goes south for the winter, and so he figures I'm here alone. I'm sure that's what he's doing. When I walked away from my law practice, he said a *stable* person wouldn't do something like that. When I said I didn't want to be a judge and was going to turn down the offer, he made a really big deal about it, saying I was losing it, that I wasn't *stable,* that I was teetering on the edge. Believe it or not, I laughed in his face." Lucy gulped at the beer she was holding.

"And, Miss Lucy, he would do this . . . why?"

Lucy watched as Wylie pulled on his jacket and boots and made his way to the front door, Rachel Muller's key in his hand. An ordinary, kind thing to do for a neighbor. Jake was chopping cabbage, and Mitch was pacing the kitchen. The dogs were tussling in the family room with a long, coiled, braided rope. Everything just then seemed normal.

"Why?" Lucy shrugged. "An unstable person, someone teetering on the edge, wouldn't make a good impression on the FBI now, would she? They're crawling all over me, trying to wear me down. They think I'm lying about the brokerage accounts and the house in Watchung. Remember what you were thinking when I came up with that card that opened the gate? I saw all of your faces. You were thinking, how convenient it was that all of a sudden I remembered I had it. You know you all thought I might be mixed up in whatever Jonathan has going on. I'm not," Lucy said wearily as she sat down next to Mitch.

Mitch locked his gaze on her. "And you think he's here now because of the footprints you saw in the snow."

Lucy nodded. "Yes."

"Call around the neighborhood and see what you can find out. Want another beer?"

"Yes, thank you, I would like another beer."

Wylie blew into the house like a wild gust of wind, his arms loaded with groceries. His eyes were watering, and his cheeks were red from the stinging snow. "Rachel left all this stuff on the table for me along with a note. She won't be back till next Saturday. We are going to have a feast, lady and gentlemen. The cat is doing nicely, thank you."

Jake was the only one who seemed interested in the array of food.

"I saw Rudy clearing his driveway," Wylie continued, "so I asked him if anyone had been around asking to shovel driveways, and he said no. He said he was watching television in between blowing out his driveway. As a matter of fact, he said other than us and Rachel leaving, no one has been on the street all day. What he said was, there were no strange cars on the street."

A look of disgust washed over Lucy's face. "A kid wanting to shovel snow wouldn't arrive in a car. Nor would Jonathan if he was up to something and being sneaky about it. He could very easily have come in from the back, off Frances Road. He could have parked on Richard Road and walked up this street. We haven't been plowed out. Maybe he didn't want to get stuck. I'm telling you, it was Jonathan. Where's your phone book, Wylie?"

Wylie bent down to open one of the kitchen cabinets. He handed her the white pages. "We've eliminated three already, Nellie, Rachel, and Rudy. That leaves Carol, Joan, the new people on the corner, the Hendersons, and Tom and Alice."

They watched as Lucy dialed her neighbors, one by one. The conversations were short and succinct. No one had offered to shovel their driveways. No one had seen anyone around her house all day.

"Then who was at my house?" Lucy demanded when she hung up from the last call. "Did he just drop from the sky?"

Jake scooped his chopped cabbage into a bowl. "This could turn out to be one of those little mysteries in life that is never explained or solved. You're here, you're safe, the dogs are safe, and that's all that matters. We won't let anything happen to you, Lucy."

"What's the game plan, guys?" Mitch asked. "I'm going to be heading home in the morning. But I can always come back if you need me. If you just want to ask me something, call or e-mail me. I'm going to write up a report for you. You can hand it over to the *feebs* or you can just keep it. Your call. My firm does work for a bunch of different government agencies, and our credibility is above reproach. I think I'll start on the report right now, Wylie, if you show me where your computer is. After dinner, I'm going straight to bed. The plows will be working overtime tonight, but by five or so, the roads should be in good shape. I've got a business to run, and I hate being away more than a day or so. Did I mention that my bill will be in the mail?"

When Wylie and Mitch left the kitchen, Lucy plopped her elbows on the table, dropping her head into the palms of her hands. "I think I'm scared, Jake. I thought I knew Jonathan, but I don't know *this* Jonathan. My God, I was going to marry the man. I don't know what he's capable of. I wouldn't make a good spy. I guess I gave myself away a hundred different ways when I spoke to him. The one thing I do know about Jonathan is he is not a stupid man. Then there's this . . . this thing going on inside my head. I'm staying here tonight. I don't care if I have to sleep on the floor."

Jake sat down across from Lucy. "Fear is a healthy emotion, Lucy. I would probably be worried about you if you tried to blow all this off as inconsequential. My personal opinion is you have to open up to the feds. Don't hold anything back, or it will jump up and bite you. Truth always wins out in the end."

"No, Jake, truth does not always win out in the end. I'm a lawyer, I should know. If I had a nickel for every dishonest client who said they were telling the truth, I'd be rich. God, I'm tired. How about you?"

"I can't remember when I had as much fresh air as I've had today. I think I'm going to go to bed after dinner, too."

Lucy leaned across the table. "Jake, after seeing that house, what do you think Jonathan is up to?"

"Jeez, Lucy, I don't know. Like Drew said, the guy's a badass dude. He must be one hell of an actor for you to have been so bewitched."

"I swear to you, Jake, it never occurred to me that my ex-fiancé was anything other than what he professed to be. Maybe I was too busy with work and wrapped up in my own world to pick up the clues. Fool me once, shame on you; fool me twice, shame on me. He knows I'm onto him. I just wish I knew what all that stuff at the house means."

"If you put my feet to the fire and I had to venture a guess, I'd say your old friend Jonathan is bringing illegal people into this country, and that house is a stopover. A place that is safe and secure until they get to their final destination, wherever that might be. Money laundering is a billion-dollar business. Then there are the drugs. I think you can just about take your pick or go with all three."

"Aside from all that first-class security, there's something about that house that bothers me. I can't quite put my finger on it," Lucy said, frowning.

Jake nodded sympathetically.

Ninety minutes later, the kitchen was cleaned, the leftovers—of which there weren't many—were wrapped and stored in the refrigerator. Mitch and Jake both headed off to bed, saying good night.

Wylie turned to Lucy and put his hands on his hips. "It's just you and me, Lucy. I'm as tired as those guys, but I'm wired, too. Let's put another log on the fire, have a snort of brandy, then we can go to sleep. You can have my bed, I'll take the couch."

"No, Wylie. I'm not taking your bed. I sleep on my own couch fairly often. I'll just curl up with the dogs here by the fire. I'll be fine."

Wylie added two logs to the fire. Sparks showered upward. Lucy was reminded of the Fourth of July sparklers she and Steven used to wave around when they were kids.

While Wylie poured brandy into two balloon glasses, Lucy wiggled her fanny back and forth, the warmth from the fire racing up and down her back. How good it felt.

Glasses in hand, Wylie led her to the couch. They sat down next to each other, each of them more than a little aware of the other. Lucy strained to *hear* Wylie's thoughts. She almost fell off the couch when she *heard . . . what now, Romeo? Do I put my arm around her shoulder, do I kiss her? Maybe I should ask first. She'd laugh her head off if she knew I haven't been with a woman in over a year. What the hell is she thinking? Is she waiting for me to make a move?*

Lucy watched as Wylie gulped at the fiery liquid in his glass. When she saw his eyes start to water, she set her glass aside, moved to the right, throwing her right leg over his and yanking him toward her, all at the same time. "I think you need to kiss me *right now.*" The command came out in a sexy, throaty growl.

Wylie obliged. Talk about wishful thinking.

When they finally came up for air a long time later, the three dogs were on their haunches staring at them intently. Lucy burst out laughing.

Wylie stared at Lucy. "I liked that. Yeah, I did. I mean, I really did. You're a great kisser. I haven't been kissed like that in oh . . ."

"A little over a year." Lucy giggled.

Wylie pretended outrage. "You read my mind. That's dirty pool."

Lucy laughed again. "I was getting impatient. You couldn't make up your mind. You know us lawyers, we have to make snap decisions. By the way, I liked it, too. Want to do it again?"

"Are you one of those women who likes to toy with a man's affections? I don't want to have my heart broken."

"You're serious, aren't you? That wasn't a fun question, was it?"

Wylie jumped up and walked over to the fireplace. He poked at logs that didn't need to be poked. He turned around, his eyes bright. "I was serious. I think I started to have feelings for you that first day I met you. Coop loves you, so that endeared you to me right off. I don't want to catch you on the rebound, Lucy. Been there, done that. I'm thinking if you aren't ready or if you don't share my feelings, then we should sit on separate chairs. Or . . . or something."

Lucy bounded off the couch, causing the dogs to move backward. "Do you think I just go around kissing guys who have nice dogs? Huh? Well, do you? Listen, there's a lot going on in my little world right now. The fact that I allowed myself to kiss you, and make no mistake, I kissed you, should be all the proof you need that I . . . that I . . . care about you."

She was right next to him, her body a hairbreadth away from his. She could smell the brandy on his breath. He opened his arms, and she stepped into them. She felt the hardness of him as she laid her head against his chest. Nothing had ever felt this right, this good. A sigh of pure happiness escaped her lips.

Wylie swayed dizzily, his gaze going to Coop, who seemed to be drooling in anticipation. His mouth worked silently. She likes meat loaf. The huge dog stared at his master a moment before he lay down, stretched out, his head dropping onto his paws. Wylie almost swooned. That was Coop's seal of approval.

"Want to go for it right here, or are you one of those women who needs a bed?" Damn, was that growling voice his?

"A bearskin rug would be nice."

"Uh-huh?" His eyes almost bugging out of his head, Wylie couldn't believe what he was seeing. A sweatshirt flying across the room, sweatpants dropping to the floor.

Lucy laughed as she unhooked her bra. "You better hurry or you won't be able to catch up."

Speed. She wanted speed. "Watch this!"

Lucy watched.

11

The man standing at the twentieth-floor window of the Woodbridge Hilton Hotel that was a mere seven minutes by car to Lucy's house bore absolutely no resemblance to the man known as Jonathan St. Clair. His identification, international driver's license, credit cards, and passport said his name was Spiros Andreadis, a Greek national. His credentials said he worked for a Swiss clock company. Thanks to shoe lifts, Spiros Andreadis was two inches taller than Jonathan St. Clair. His eyes were a startling blue opposed to Jonathan's hazel and now stood out sharply against his olive complexion. Spiros's hair was coal black and matched his mustache. Jonathan St. Clair sported sandy-colored hair, and his upper lip was clean-shaven.

The Greek's clothing, shoes, and all items in his possession shrieked that they were *not* made in America. His luggage, one bag, was sturdy, battered cowhide and bore travel stamps from all over the world.

His shoulders stiff, his stance angry, Jonathan whirled away from the window. It was late, he should go to bed. The only problem was that he was too angry to go to bed. He'd spent close to two hours tramping through a virtual blizzard to reach Lucy after a dozen phone calls to her home and cell went unanswered, only to find she wasn't home. He was further irritated that he didn't have a key to her house. Lucy's explanation for why she wouldn't give him a key was simple, "Jonathan, I'm always home, why do you need a key?" What Lucy didn't know was he *did* have a key. Three visits ago, he'd been so miffed at her refusal to give him a key, he'd waited till she finished her fourth glass of wine and fell asleep, at which point he took the key from the peg by the back door and pressed it into some melted candle wax. The next day he'd gone to a drugstore and within ten minutes he had a bright, shiny key in his hand. For all the good it did him. Who knew Lucy would add a new lock, the kind that went into the molding at the top of the doorframe. She'd never stuck dowels in the sliding doors before, either. At least he didn't think she had. Right now he was too angry to think straight.

If she had been home and opened the door, he would have killed her. "Always pay attention to your gut warnings," he muttered.

The last thing he'd expected when he walked off the plane was snow. He'd left tons of snow, ice, and cold in Zurich. He'd expected temperatures in the high thirties. It was, after all, only November. He also hadn't expected the phone call he'd received as he was going through customs. The moment he'd heard the voice on the other end of the line he knew what had happened. "The property was compromised several hours ago." His eyes murderous, Jonathan, aka Spiros Andreadis, snapped the encrypted cell phone shut and jammed it in his pocket. His instincts were on the money. The only question was, who had compromised the house and property in Watchung, Lucy or the FBI?

His original intention had been to go to the apartment he maintained in Manhattan. His second thought was to check into a New York hotel. Furious after the phone call, he'd rented a car and headed through the storm to New Jersey. It was a damn good thing he hadn't gone to the house in Watchung, which had been his third choice.

He had to fall back and regroup, something he'd never had to do in his line of business. It was not a pleasant thought.

He was back at the window, his expression still murderous. *Just how the hell much snow is out there anyway?* According to the Weather Channel and the desk clerk, it was going to snow through the night. He supposed he should feel lucky because, according to the clerk, all the airports were shut down. With the airports closed, anyone following him would be stuck at one airport or another. By the same token, he wouldn't be able to leave if the airports didn't open up soon. "Lucky, my ass," he muttered.

Jonathan flipped open his cell phone again and dialed Lucy's number. When her voice mail came on, he hung up. It was after midnight: where was she? He rang the number again and again, hanging up each time after the seventh ring. If she was sound asleep, the steady ringing should alert her or, at the very least, rouse the damn dog who slept on her bed.

The startling blue eyes narrowed. *Maybe she isn't home. Where do people go in the middle of a snowstorm? Nowhere, that's where.*

Jonathan continued to watch the falling snow. He wondered how the rental Lexus would do in all this snow. What he really needed was a powerful SUV, but the rental agency said none were available. He'd never driven a Lexus before that day. He didn't even know if it had front-wheel drive. What if he got stuck in the snow? Maybe it would be better to wait till morning. He could pass the time by ordering drinks from room service and dialing Lucy's number. *Where the hell is the woman I'm supposed to be marrying?*

Angry beyond words, Jonathan hooked his foot under one of the chairs in the hotel room and dragged it closer to the window. He sat down and stretched out his legs so they rested on top of the heating unit.

He'd made a mistake, and that mistake's name was Lucille Baker. Down through history, he'd been told, women were men's downfall. Sex, according to history, was the reason nothing went right in the world. A sound of pure misery escaped Jonathan's

lips. Sex had nothing to do with his predicament. He didn't love Lucy Baker. She was
just someone to use to help him set up his
retirement and a new life. His original plan
had been to get rid of her a year or so into
the marriage. A divorce if she behaved herself and wouldn't come back to haunt him.
A nice clean kill à la Adam Ligar if she
stepped out of line.

Where had it all gone wrong? He knew
that *he* hadn't made a mistake because he
was a perfectionist and an expert at covering his ass, so it had to be on Lucy's end.
Left to her own devices she would never,
ever, have stumbled onto his affairs. Somehow or other he'd come up on either the
CIA's, or the FBI's radar screen. He'd gone
to extraordinary lengths to protect himself
once he knew they were onto him. Knowing
how the government agencies worked, they
had probably paid Lucy a visit and threatened all kinds of things. That would surely
account for the change in her attitude. Lucy
was no actress; he'd picked up on her nervous tone immediately. She was probably
scared out of her wits. Then there was that
little tidbit about the Internal Revenue Ser-

vice appointment. He'd seen through that immediately, too.

Jonathan's feet hit the floor with a thud. He got up, called room service, and ordered a bottle of Chivas Regal and a bucket of ice. He then dialed Lucy's number again from his encrypted cell phone. Again he hung up on the seventh ring.

He started to pace because he was furious and needed to do something to control his anger. He was angry because he knew Lucy was hiding out. It really infuriated him that she thought she was smarter than he was. He had to find her, and he had to find her soon. He closed his eyes—envisioning a net descending over him. Well, that wasn't going to happen. He continued his frantic pacing until there was a knock on the door. He accepted the tray and handed the waiter a fifty-dollar bill. "Keep the change."

Three drinks later, the edge was off his panic, his breathing had returned to normal, and he was beginning to feel drowsy. He was back on the chair watching the snow slap against the windows as he tried to plot out the coming hours.

Twenty minutes later, he sat up straight as the thought hit him like a thunderbolt. Nellie!

The old lady Lucy worked for part-time. She went to Florida for the winter. Lucy had said there was a going-away dinner for her not too long ago. That meant Nellie's house was empty. All he had to do was break in and watch and wait for Lucy to return home. Satisfied with his plan, Jonathan walked over to the king-size bed and pulled down the covers. His last conscious thought before sleep overtook him was, *Get in my way and you get what you deserve.*

The dream was always the same, and that night it was no different. Usually it came just before he was due to wake up, enabling him to remember the details clearly . . .

He was a vagrant, a bum in filthy clothes with rags tied around shoes that he'd stolen from someone else. He needed the rags because the shoes he was wearing were too big. He dragged his feet as he picked through garbage Dumpsters for aluminum cans and anything else he could sell or barter. He wanted to cry that he'd been reduced to picking through garbage to survive. Until a year ago, Leo Banks had had a good life, a nice apartment, a car, a pension plan, and a small amount of money in a savings account. Small because he liked fine things and didn't deny himself. He knew the value of savings and set aside what he could so that he could still enjoy a good life. He was, after all, only twenty-five, with a goal of retiring at forty. He had plenty of time to save for retirement. To him, the savings account was more of an emergency fund.

In his dream, he wondered what happened to the $2800.

He was whistling as he rode the elevator to the seventeenth floor. He smiled and waved at the receptionist who, for some reason, was ignoring him on that fine spring morning. It didn't matter. Then he noticed that no one else was greeting him or giving him high fives. Puzzled, he walked down the hall to his office and stopped short when he saw two men in dark suits waiting for him. He could feel his stomach start to flip-flop as he saw one of the men pull a set of handcuffs out of his pocket. His face draining of all color, he listened to the charges of embezzlement, then he was read his rights as he was led away, protesting that he hadn't done anything wrong. The conversation on the ride to police headquarters consisted of two words from the men: "Shut up."

He walked up a pair of dirty steps, careful not to get his new suit dirty by brushing against the walls. His handcuffs were removed before he was shoved into a room and told to sit and wait.

It was some kind of crazy mistake. He hadn't embezzled any money from anyone. Obviously, he needed a lawyer. If ever there was a time to use his emergency fund, this was it. He hoped his $2800 was enough to cover the up-front money all lawyers charged when they agreed to take on a client.

As he stewed and fretted, he heard a commotion outside the room. He likened the sounds to what he imagined a bomb scare would sound like. Walking to the door, he opened it to see cops, detectives, and office personnel running in all directions. He didn't stop to think but moved with lightning speed. It took him only a second to slide out the door and cross the room to the dirty steps and dingy walls. He never looked back.

He half ran and half walked down the street till he found a long narrow alley that led to other darker, smellier alleys until he came to where a group of homeless people lived. The little community of vagrants stared at him, but no one stopped or questioned him. He found a wooden lettuce crate oozing rotted lettuce and sat down. He hugged his arms around his chest as he struggled to get his emotions in check. He tried to figure out what had happened to bring him there. He sat for hours, his new neighbors watching him. When he started to cry, a toothless old woman came over and started to croon to him. He cried harder as he sobbed out his story. The old woman motioned to the others, who gathered close with offers of scraps of food and some water. One old man even offered half a cigarette.

"We won't tell," someone said. Frightened out of his wits he listened as his new best friends told him where he could get free food and a free bed for the night. Days, his friends said, were spent scavenging for things to sell and barter. The old lady told him to take off his fancy clothes and brought him a pile of rags to put on. She said she would wrap up his clothes and shoes, and put them away. He was so numb that he agreed.

Days later when he came out of his stupor, he tested out his disguise by walking past the police station with a few of his new friends and generally hanging out until the two detectives who had arrested him showed up. He walked right past them, deliberately jostling them. Both looked right through him with no sign of recognition.

Safe.

This, then, was his new life. He knew if he tried to use his ATM card, he'd be picked up within minutes. He also knew he would never be able to go back to his apartment. His new car would be repossessed. He couldn't risk calling any of his friends because they wouldn't want to get involved. That he knew as surely as he knew he had to keep breathing in order to stay alive.

Days passed, then weeks, and finally months. Almost a year to the day of his arrest, he looked into the backpack he'd found in someone's trash can, and counted out his money. He had $647 dollars and a gun that was fully loaded. The gun was stolen, too. It was payback time. He'd had a whole year to figure out who set him up for the embezzlement charge—his manager's son-in-law. With that knowledge under his belt, he spent three whole months with the help of his homeless friends tracking Adam Ligar and his every movement until he had his routine down pat.

"Dolly!" he called to the old woman. "It's time to get my suit cleaned and my shoes polished. D day!" The old crone cackled as she hurried off to get the suit and take it to the cleaners. An old man named Billy hauled out some rags and polished Jonathan's shoes by spitting on them. It was a perfect shine.

He cleaned up at a gas station and tied his hair back into a ponytail. His beard was on the scruffy side, but it would do.

It was time.

The meeting with Adam Ligar was at a steakhouse called the Barb Wire. He'd called earlier, arranged the appointment by saying he was interested in hiring a new broker and business manager and only had a few hours but a ton of money to invest. Ligar couldn't agree fast enough.

He'd chosen the Barb Wire because it was a dim and noisy bar where no one paid attention to anyone else. He kept reminding himself he was the one with the gun. Besides, he'd been a broker in training and could walk the walk and talk the talk. Which was exactly what he was going to do.

Leo looked at the slick little weasel sitting across from him. "Tell me how you'll invest my $750,000 if I decide to go with your firm."

Dollar signs flashed in Ligar's eyes. "You look familiar, do I know you?"

Leo shrugged. "I do a lot of business with a lot of people. Anything is possible." The weasel frowned.

"This place is just too crowded and noisy. Let's take a walk up to the park. It's a nice night. We can talk as we go along. If I like what you have to say, I'll hand over a check on our way back," Leo said.

"This certainly is a weird way of doing business, but okay. Every day is a learning experience," the weasel said. He shrugged as much as to say, what the hell. "I have some good municipal bonds, a couple of triple A's, and a good up-and-coming high-tech stock called Sotech."

"That's a dog. You'll have to do better than that. Give me something that's going to make me some money. I want to retire at an early age."

"Where'd you get the seven-fifty? You transferring from another house?"

"No. It's an inheritance, and I don't want to lose it. My *real* portfolio is at Merrill Lynch."

"You know what, you remind me of a guy who used to work at our firm. He was arrested for embezzling money out of dormant accounts."

Leo laughed. "What happened to him?"

Ligar shrugged. "Don't know. Police lost him after they arrested him. Hasn't been seen since."

It was Leo's turn to shrug. "So, is that it, a few triple A's and a few munis?"

"If you can give me a few more days, I might be able to come up with something. You have to admit this is pretty short notice."

Leo looked up at the dark sky. Stars twinkled overhead. He was happy to see that the park was almost empty. Mothers were home with the kids; the old people were safe in their houses. A few runners and joggers and a stray bum were the only people he could see, and they were off in the distance. Perfect.

"Let's sit down for a minute. I want to

think about something," Leo said, pointing to a park bench far enough off the path that no joggers or runners would bother them or, for that matter, even notice them, but close to a pay phone.

The weasel was antsy. "This park isn't as safe as it looks. People get mugged and killed here on a weekly basis."

"Uh-huh. Okay, Adam, hand it over."

"Hand what over?" the broker squeaked, fear rattling his voice.

"Your wallet. I mean business. The cops never got me after I escaped, as you well know. I was innocent. You lousy creep, you set me up. You're the one who embezzled the money. You were always logging on to my computer and my files. Stealing from the family is a no-no. C'mon, I don't have all day." The gun flashed in the sliver of moonlight that slid out from its cloud cover.

"You son of a bitch! I knew you looked familiar. Put that stupid gun away, Leo, before it goes off. I didn't set you up."

"I don't think so. Oh, yeah, you set me up. I've had a whole year to do nothing but think. Give me your wallet and the keys to that fancy Mercedes. Do it now, Adam, or I'll blow your damn head off."

"Listen, Leo, let's talk about this. We can work something out." He sounded like a whiny little kid who had dropped his ice cream in the dirt.

Leo clicked off the safety. It sounded exceptionally loud. He loved it that his old colleague was whining and begging. The gun was all-powerful.

"Okay, okay."

Leo eyed the little pile of personal effects, which included Adam's passport, on the bench. You got an ATM card, Adam?"

"Doesn't everyone?"

"I don't. Thanks to you. What's the pin number? Don't even think about lying to me." Adam rattled it off. Leo made a mental note of it.

"Now, we're going over to that pay phone, where you'll call your wife and tell her something came up and you're going out of town for a few days. Tell her you'll call her later. Make up one of those lies you're so good at. What's your home number?"

"It's 207-2323." Adam's voice was even shakier by then, all sound of belligerence gone. Eyes wary, he watched Leo dial his home number. "What are you going to do? C'mon, Banks, let's make a deal here."

"Like that's really going to happen. Stop whining. It's not manly. Say what I told you to say."

To make his point, Leo jabbed the gun into Adam's side as he started to talk. "Dorothy, something's come up, and I have to go to the Caymans. I think I'll be gone for three days or so. I'll call when I know more. Everything's fine. It's a guy who has a boat-load of money he wants to invest. I sort of fell into it. You gotta strike while the iron's hot in this business. That's what your father told me when he hired me. Yeah, I love you, too."

"Does Dorothy know about you hopping the blonde in payroll and that waitress at Starbucks?" Leo asked as he forced the hapless broker to return to the park bench.

Adam was openly sweating in the cool spring evening. "You know she doesn't. What do you want, Banks? Look, if it's money, my wife has plenty. I can get it for you. Leo, if you shoot me, you'll go to jail for the rest of your life."

"I want everything you've got. Everything you stole from me. What I don't want is your wife's money. How much money is in your wallet?"

"About five hundred dollars."

"How much in the account with the ATM card?"

"Maybe forty-four hundred."

"How much can you take in one day?"

"Two thousand."

"What's the limit on your credit cards?"

"They're all maxed out except the Citi card. My limit is $7500. My wife likes to shop." Sniveling, he wiped his nose on the sleeve of his jacket. His eyes were wet and pleading.

Backing away from the man who had changed his life, Leo Banks digested the information before squeezing the trigger and shooting Adam Ligar smack between the eyes. He looked around to see if anyone was within eyesight or earshot. No one. Being careful not to get any blood on his clothes, Leo took five minutes to roll Adam off the bench and into a deep grove of shrubbery, where he removed Adam's jacket and shoes. He whipped off the broker's Rolex and stuffed it in his pocket. Let the police think Ligar was just another homeless man until they made a proper ID. Leo laughed all the way back to the Barb

Wire, where he picked up Adam's Mercedes and drove off.

Leo spent the next two hours driving from one ATM machine to the next, taking out as much money as he could. When he hit the magic number of $2000, the maximum Adam's bank allowed in one twenty-four-hour period, he tossed the ATM card in the nearest trash can. His next stop was an all-night drugstore, where he bought packages of underwear, socks, and shaving gear.

He registered at the Algonquin, where he showered, shaved, and ordered the biggest steak on the hotel's menu. In the morning, he shopped until the stores called a halt and said his card was overdrawn. It was fair. The charges equaled out to the amount in his 401k. Then he found a less-than-scrupulous car dealership and sold Adam's fancy Mercedes for seven thousand dollars, well under its twenty-thousand-dollar value. A bonus from Adam to him for the year he'd lived the life of a homeless bum. He left the dealership with a smile on his face as he trotted over to Citibank and cashed the check.

Then he visited the establishment of an "entrepreneur" he had come across in his year on the streets and had a photograph taken and carefully substituted for Adam Ligar's photograph on Ligar's passport. Then, to cover his tracks somewhat, he took a cab to Kennedy, where he took the shuttle to Washington. He had a cabbie take him to the nearest travel agency, where he booked a flight to London for later that day. At six-fifteen, Leo Banks boarded his flight.

When he set foot on British soil he became Jonathan St. Clair, Spiros Andreadis, Nathan Willowby, Dunston Craig, and a host of other identities.

12

Lucy woke slowly, savoring the warmth of the cocoon she was wrapped in. She sighed happily as she remembered where she was and what had transpired earlier. She reveled now in the warmth coming from the body next to her. A smile started to build on her lips. "Hmmm," she murmured. "You feel *soooo* good." She waited for a reply and when none was forthcoming, she frowned. Maybe Wylie was a sound sleeper. A *real* sound sleeper. She wiggled her leg, then her thigh and hip.

"Woof!"

Lucy bolted upright, her face registering a hundred different emotions all at the same time. "Coop! Sadie! Lulu!" And then, "Wylieeee!"

He came on the run, spatula in hand. She could tell he'd already showered because his hair was still wet, and he was dressed in jeans that hugged his lean frame and a muscle shirt that was tattered around the sleeves. NOTRE DAME was stenciled across the front. He even had shoes on, while she was buck-ass naked with three dogs curled alongside of her on top of the blanket. The fire was blazing, she could feel the heat.

"There's nothing like the body warmth of a dog," Wylie said happily. A sappy grin plastered itself on his face. Seeing the look of chagrin on Lucy's face, he started to babble. "I had to get up early to make sure Mitch got off okay. I helped him put chains on his tires. That was a workout in itself. You know how I like to run every morning. Well, if you don't know, I do. Since this snow I haven't been able to run, and that makes me feel like I'm cheating my body. Why are you letting me babble like this?" He waved the spatula in the air as Coop tried to jump up to get a lick.

Lucy enjoyed his sudden discomfort. "Did . . . did Mitch see me sleeping here?" Lucy asked as she finally got her tongue in working order.

"Uh-huh. Jake saw you here, too, when he came downstairs. I don't know this for a pure fact, but I don't think they know I was sleeping there, too, by you, alongside of you." He shook his head again, the spatula doing double time, as was Coop. "What I mean is I don't think they have any idea we had sex. I can't be sure, but I don't think so."

"I'm naked under this blanket, Wylie."

Wylie hopped from one foot to the other. "Yeah, I know." He lowered the spatula, and Coop grabbed it. The three dogs raced down the hall.

"Don't make my eggs with that spatula," Lucy said as she struggled to wrap the blanket around her. "I'm going to take a shower now. What time is breakfast?" she asked coldly.

"Okay, I see that you're ticked off at me. Whatever it is I did, I'm sorry. Are you mad that Jake's here? Listen, I can tell him in no uncertain terms that we did not have sex last night. I'll do that if it's what you want. Why would he even care, assuming he does know? He's married, he can have all the sex he wants."

Lucy shot him an evil grin as she got to her feet. She stormed off, muttering that men loved to brag about their sexual conquests.

"Not me. I'm not one of those men who brag about my sexual conquests."

"Liar!" Jake said as he entered the room, demanding to know when breakfast was being served. "Morning, Lucy, did you sleep well?"

"Shut up, Jake!" Lucy snarled as she made her way up the steps, the blanket trailing behind her.

"So you two had sex last night, huh? How was it? Was it everything you thought it would be?" Jake asked gleefully.

"Shut up, Jake, and it's none of your business if I had sex last night or not, and where the hell were you when it was time to put the chains on Mitch's truck? You were sleeping, that's where you were, because I could hear you snoring all night long. If I was doing that, how could I be having sex? Breakfast is right now. Don't you ever think about anything but food?"

"Prickly this morning, aren't we?" Jake smirked.

In the kitchen, Wylie turned to look at his friend, his face full of menace. "If you say one word, even intimate that you think we had sex, I am going to kick your ass out in the snow and let you freeze to death. Lucy is a sensitive person, and right now she's going through a difficult time. Women don't like it when men discuss what goes on between them. It's supposed to be a secret."

Jake stared at Wylie with keen interest. "You certainly are knowledgeable when it comes to women. You led me to believe you were a lost cause. You are an interesting case, Wylie. I might even decide to study you someday. C'mon, c'mon, I'm starving here. Four eggs and a load of that nice pink ham. I'll make the toast."

Upstairs, Lucy listened at the heating vent in the bathroom through which Wylie's and Jake's voices carried clearly. For the first time in days she giggled. With happiness. When was Jake leaving? She wished it was right then, so she could drag Wylie back to bed. Their night had been the most satisfying sex she'd ever had in her life. Wild, crazy, and wonderful.

As Lucy washed her hair, her womanly wiles surfaced. Maybe she could entice Wylie to go down to Nellie's house or over to Rachel Muller's house. Jake liked to take naps. A sterling idea. After all, there wasn't really anything else to do on a day like this but watch television or read a book. Television, book, sex. Only a fool would choose the first two.

Life was suddenly looking good, but the smile left her face and her mood darkened. How could she be thinking about sex when her life was in danger? Maybe she was losing her mind. Or, more likely, she'd already lost it. Shower over, her hair wrapped in a turban, Lucy wrapped a towel around her body as she padded to the window to look outside. All she could see was a blanket of whiteness. It had to be the blizzard of the century. Maybe two centuries. One thing for certain, Wylie wouldn't be going to the city. Probably not for the rest of the week. She crossed her fingers that the power wouldn't go out.

Lucy dressed in the same clothes she'd worn the day before. Later, she'd go to her own house for fresh clothes.

Brushing out her wet hair, she strained to hear Jake and Wylie talking in the kitchen. She cautioned herself that eavesdroppers never heard anything good about themselves. She shrugged when she heard both men grousing about the snowstorm. Wylie's terminology was extremely colorful, while

Jake fretted that they might run out of food before the storm blew itself out.

As Lucy descended the stairs she tried to come up with a casual plan to pretend she hadn't slept with Wylie the night before. Never having been in a situation quite like this where a guest was in residence the *morning after,* she was unprepared as to how to handle it. She was in for some ribbing, she could almost guarantee it. *Alleged* sex. Uh-huh. Always fall back on legalities.

She needn't have worried. Jake did little more than nod because he was too busy eating and watching the weather report on the counter television. Wylie looked like a professional chef as he stirred, whipped, and flipped. A huge smile on his face, the kind men wear after a night of *alleged* rousing sex, he motioned her to sit down. She scowled.

"They're calling this a blizzard," Jake said, between mouthfuls of food. "Yesterday they said this was the worst storm in fifty years." He pointed to the kitchen window with his fork to make his point. "This morning they're saying it's the worst storm in a century. I sure hope you guys have good, solid roofs on your houses. There's gotta be at least a foot of snow on your house, Lucy. Yours, too, Wylie. Yep, this is definitely a blizzard."

Wylie slid a plate across the table to Lucy. The scrambled eggs looked light and fluffy. The ham was pink and succulent. The toast was just the right color, and the butter was soft. Perfect!

"Sooner or later the power is going to go out. We've been lucky so far. How are you fixed for wood, Wylie?" Lucy asked.

"I have a good-sized stack on the deck," Wylie said, sitting down across from Lucy. "Everything is shut down, the airports, the turnpike, the parkway. Even the post office and banks, and, of course, the schools. I think we're looking at the rest of the week here. When it stops, it's going to take days to dig out. It's a bit of a reprieve for you, Lucy, as far as the feds go. I wish you'd call the FBI and tell them we suspect Jonathan was here yesterday. I know, I know, the foot-prints are gone. You need to document everything. Call and even if they pooh-pooh it away, it will make me feel better. Tomorrow is Thanksgiving. It's kind of sad when you think about it. Thanksgiving is when families are supposed to be together. I bet a lot of people whose travel plans fell through with the weather will be eating weenies and whatever is in their freezers. We're the lucky ones, Lucy, we're together with the dogs, and Jake is here. Personally, I'd like to see our table filled with friends and family, but if this is all we get, I'll take it."

Lucy nodded solemnly, pleased at how Wylie viewed the holiday she always considered so special.

"Now, Friday is normally part of that holiday, then the Christmas season kicks in. Marooned until next Monday. Woohoo! When are you leaving, Jake?" This all was said so happily, Lucy had to stifle the laugh that was bubbling up in her throat.

Lucy almost choked on the ham in her mouth. She could hardly wait to hear Jake's answer.

"Well, it's like this. The airports are going to be backed up for days. I think I'll rent a car and drive back as soon as the roads open. Have I worn out my welcome already?"

Wylie didn't look the least bit embarrassed. "Of course not. Stay as long as you like. I was just curious. So, gang, what should we do today?"

Jake pondered the question, his dark eyebrows knitting until they met in the center of his forehead. "I'm going to go online and see if I can find out a little more about Lucy's predicament. I want to e-mail some colleagues. You know, just in case your power goes out. I hate wasting time. Not to worry, I'll be out of your way. How about you guys?"

"I'm going to work out for a while. I've been thinking about taking out the snowblower to clear Rachel's driveway." Wylie turned to look at Lucy. "Nellie has that big deep freezer in her garage. What do you think the chances are there might be a turkey in there or at least a very big chicken?"

"A very good chance. Nellie belongs to a food service that delivers sides of beef all cut up and packaged, plus all kinds of food. I think Rachel may belong to it, too. Nellie loves to cook and feeds half the neighborhood. You know that. You've been one of her recipients many times. When Rachel Muller was sick this past spring, Nellie cooked for her and her husband for two full weeks because Gerhard can't even boil water."

"Good! I'll use the snowblower on Nellie's driveway, too. See," Wylie said, waving his fork in the air, "now we have a plan. Jake, you clean up, I'm going to work out. How about you, Lucy?"

"What kind of equipment do you have in your workout room?"

"A treadmill, a cycle, a rowing machine, weight bench, a universal. Want to join me?"

"I'll take the treadmill. My ankle feels good enough now. If I start out slow, it should be okay. Lead the way," Lucy said, tossing her napkin on the table.

Wylie's workout room was just that, a workout room. Aside from the carpeted floor and the exercise equipment, a television sitting on a bracketed shelf attached to the wall, and a pile of books and legal pads in the corner, there was nothing else in the room, not even a chair.

Wylie turned on the television with a remote. Martha Stewart was preparing a wild rice/chestnut dressing for the turkey she was about to cook.

Lucy climbed on the treadmill, hooked on the heart monitor, set the grade, and began by warming up. She walked, then jogged before she broke into a run at 4.5.

Forty minutes later, she looked down at the distance button and saw that she had already gone four miles. Her normal routine was a ten-mile run. When the numbers changed to read five miles, she felt the first twinge in her ankle. She slowed a little, but the twinge turned into a sharp pain. She stumbled and was about to yank out the safety key when Wylie caught her; otherwise, she would have fallen. "What's wrong?"

"I think I overdid it. I should have quit at four miles. If you have an Ace bandage, I might be able to nip this in the bud."

Wylie raced off and returned with an elastic foot brace. Lucy sat down on the treadmill while Wylie pulled off her Nike. She pulled on the foot brace, stood up with Wylie's help, and tried putting pressure on her foot. She nodded. "It feels okay. I'll just give it a rest while you work out, or I can make some coffee."

Wylie smiled. "Stay, I like the company. You sure you're okay?"

"I'm okay. Listen, I'm sorry about my surly attitude earlier."

"Yeah, me too. I don't want you to feel embarrassed. We're all adults here."

Lucy nodded. "While I was taking a shower I was thinking we could either go to Rachel's or Lucy's house and . . . and . . ."

Wylie almost dropped the hundred-pound weight he was holding, onto his foot. His eyes took on a glazed look as sweat dripped down the front of the muscle shirt. "And . . ." he prodded.

Laughter bubbled up in Lucy's throat. "And . . . we could look for a turkey in their respective freezers."

"You're a smart-ass, Lucy Baker," Wylie said as he placed the weight on the end of the bar. "That's not what you were thinking at all, and you know it. You know you want to ravage and plunder this finely muscled, sinewy body of mine. Admit it!"

This time Lucy let the laughter escape her lips. "And you're a mind reader too. Keep pumping that iron. I like my men *hard.* Hey, what *are* those books over there in the corner? Are you researching something?"

"I'm working on my thesis. You aren't the only one who is fed up with the legal profession. I want to teach, not practice law. By this time next year, if all goes well, I'll be teaching political science somewhere."

"That's wonderful, Wylie. You never said a word, why?"

"You never asked. I'm not one of those guys who runs around yelling, hey, look at me, I'm going for my doctorate. Actually, I'm kind of shy."

Lucy laughed again. "Yeah, right. You weren't shy last night."

Wylie could feel his ears turn pink. "Correct me if I'm wrong here, but who was it who was gasping, hoo hoo hoo! You weren't exactly a shrinking violet. Hell, you were the whole damn bouquet."

Lucy grinned. She was loving this. The mornings after with Jonathan had always been so . . . stiff and cold. "That's a compliment, right?"

Wylie leered at her. "Damn straight it was a compliment. The best I can give. It was a great night, Lucy. I'd like to do it again. I could just kick myself that I never allowed Nellie to introduce us. Look at all the time we wasted."

"Everything happens for a reason, Wylie. Back then, it probably wouldn't have worked. Think of all the fun we can have *making up* for lost time."

Wylie groaned as he replaced the weights and rolled over onto his stomach. He propped his chin in his hands to stare up at Lucy. "This isn't fun and games with me, Lucy. I care about you. I really do. There's some baggage we have to clear away first before we can have a serious relationship. Just so you know, I get a little *schizy* about rebound relationships. I don't want to be the interim boyfriend. My parents are gonna love you."

Tears pricked at Lucy's eyes. She didn't trust herself to say anything. She reached out to him. Wylie took her in his arms and held her close. There was nothing sexual in the embrace, just warm comfort and a new bonding. "I think we belong together," Wylie whispered in her ear. Lucy nodded.

"When should I get the ring?" Wylie laughed, breaking the moment.

"The minute this snow stops and the stores reopen. Just a little one, Wylie, a carat," she teased.

"You got it," he teased back. "Okay, let's fortify ourselves with some coffee before we head down to Nellie's house. God, would you look at that snow!"

"You look at it. I'd rather look at your handsome puss," Lucy said as she pushed him down the hallway to the kitchen.

Once the coffee was ready and they sat down at the kitchen table, Wylie turned serious. "We really didn't talk much about yesterday. How are you feeling about all that?"

Lucy knew Wylie wasn't referring to their night in front of the fire. "I don't know what to think. I think Mitch and his friend were as befuddled as I am. Why in the world does Jonathan need so much security? What *is* this all about? Do you think Jonathan was bringing people illegally into the country or bringing in drugs, and that's why he needed a safe house? I am never going to understand this, Wylie."

"If you want my opinion, and it's just my opinion, I think it's all about money. The amounts of money the feds told you about are not chicken feed. Always follow the money. I think this is about *very large sums of money.* Money laundering. I'd stake my bank account on it. Think about it, Lucy. He moves money, different amounts each time, say from England to France, to maybe

Latvia, three places total. Normal transactions. No one is going to pay attention to three transactions. It's done twenty-four/seven. Then maybe on to the Channel Islands or maybe the Marshall Islands. Multiply that by say fifty transactions, different locations, different amounts, and you come up with *kazillions* of dollars. All he needs is one man in the wire transfer room on his payroll, and your guy is golden. God alone knows what his cut is. I bet he has safe houses all over the globe. That house in Watchung is just one of many. If he smells trouble, he's gone. I bet you 'Jonathan' has dozens of identities. You following me?"

"Yes. Yes, I am. You could be right, Wylie. It makes sense. He wouldn't want to give up his citizenship, but if he did, and he married me, he would always be able to come back here if he wanted to. Assuming no one was on his trail. Yes, I think you're right. The last thing he ever expected was for me to catch on. I wouldn't have, either, if those agents hadn't come up to me that day when I was running. In a million years I never would have believed any of this. Never. I feel so stupid," Lucy said vehemently.

Wylie's voice was soothing when he said,

"There's no need for you to feel stupid, Lucy. The guy's a slick con. He worked overtime to cover everything up. It doesn't matter how you were alerted, you were, and now the playing field has shifted."

Lucy ran her hands through her still-damp hair. "For God's sake, Wylie, I'm a lawyer. I should have picked up on something. Now that I think back, there were all kinds of clues. I was blind. The worst thing is, I don't think I was ever in love with him, and yet I was going to marry him. I *think* I was going to marry him. Maybe I wasn't," she dithered. "I sure put off addressing those wedding invitations long enough. I am almost one hundred percent convinced I would not have gone through with it." There, she'd said the words aloud, and she meant them.

Wylie's chest puffed out. He smiled. "I don't think you would have gone through with it either. You know why. You told me the guy doesn't like dogs. You'd never get rid of Sadie, would you?"

"No more than you would get rid of Coop. You know what, Wylie, you're really a nice guy. I like you a lot. Bushels in fact. And, you make decent coffee, too. Your meat loaf ain't half-bad either."

Wylie's chest puffed out even farther. He couldn't wait to take this young woman home to meet his family. This was *the one.* He could feel it from the top of his head right down to his toes. At last he'd found the sock to mate to his shoe. His mother always said for every old shoe there's an old sock. It wasn't a very romantic saying, but he finally knew what she meant. He didn't know how he knew, but he knew that Lucy Baker would love him, warts and all, just as he would love her.

Wylie and Lucy both beamed when Jake entered the kitchen. "Are we doing lunch?" His voice was hopeful as his gaze roamed the neat, tidy kitchen.

"No, we're doing coffee. Wylie and I are going over to Rachel's and Nellie's houses to see what we can scrounge up. If you pick all the meat off that ham bone, I can make some split pea or bean soup for supper, or I can make us some pot pies. You decide while we go on the hunt for Thanksgiving dinner. I feel like a Pilgrim, don't you, Wylie?"

Wylie threw back his head and laughed until tears rolled down his cheeks. Lucy and Wylie dressed as warmly as they could, layering sweatshirts and parkas. The boots were the last to go on. Lucy fingered the keys to her house in the pocket of her jacket before she pulled on fuzzy, pink mittens. Adjusting the scarf around her neck and over the lower part of her face, she said, "Okay, I'm ready. I want to go to my house to get some clean clothes first. Rachel's house is closest to mine, so let's hit it after my house. If we find enough food, we might not have to go to Nellie's."

Wylie nodded as he opened the door. Snow and cold air *swooshed* into the foyer. It took both of them to pull the heavy oak door shut behind them.

It was ten-thirty when the couple exited the house.

"I'll go first," Wylie said. Step into the footprints I leave. It will be easier. Jeez, this snow is up to my thighs."

It took them thirty minutes to fight their way through the snow and wind across the wide expanse of yard to Lucy's house. Both of them were exhausted when Lucy fitted the key into the lock with numb hands. The moment they were inside, Wylie stomped his feet before kicking off his boots to dump the snow out of them. His wool socks were cold and wet. So were Lucy's.

"I have socks," Lucy said. "Dry out our boots while I get my clothes and the socks. Check my thermostat, Wylie, and set the faucet in the laundry room sink to drip. I don't want my pipes to freeze up."

"My feet are like ice," Lucy said when she returned with the socks. Let's put them in the dryer so they're warm when we put them on." The clothes in her hand went into a plastic bag she tied around her waist.

"We're crazy, you know that, right?" Wylie said five minutes later as he pulled on a pair of Lucy's socks. "I hope you have spares because the same thing is going to happen when we get to Rachel's house and then, if necessary, Nellie's."

"You're right. Wait here." Lucy ran back upstairs and returned with a bundle of rolled-up socks. She added them to the plastic bag.

"Okay, heat's fine, water's dripping. Let's go."

Lucy opened the door, the arctic chill, driving snow, and the fierce wind drove her backward. Wylie stiff-armed her as they fought together to close the door and lock it.

"Same drill, Lucy, walk in my footprints. I'm going in a straight line, catercorner to Rachel's house. Stay close," Wylie shouted, to be heard over the ferocious wind.

Easier said than done, Lucy thought as she struggled to step into the indentations Wylie made in the snow. The problem was, he had long-legged strides, and by the time she was ready to plop her left foot down, she fell down instead. Wylie picked her up seven times before they made it across the street to Rachel Muller's house. Both of them were breathing like racehorses when Wylie finally made it to the overhang of the walk-through door leading into the garage. Inside, they both fell to their knees, struggling to breathe normally.

"This is crazy, Wylie. Why can't we just eat hot dogs tomorrow? Thanksgiving is about giving thanks, not about food. God, I wish I was sunning my butt in Florida or some tropical paradise."

Wylie groaned. "C'mon, we have to get in the house. I'll turn the heat up to warm us. We'll change socks and dry out our boots before we head out again."

Lucy started to laugh then and couldn't stop as Wylie led her into the kitchen.

"What's so funny?" Wylie demanded as he cranked up the thermostat.

"Remember when I told you I thought we could come here or Nellie's house and make out away from Jake? Boy, was that ever wishful thinking."

Wylie flopped down on one of the kitchen chairs. He was still breathing hard as he struggled to get out of his ski jacket. "If you told me right now you wanted to hit the sheets, I'd have to tell you no can do."

"Don't give it another thought. I don't have the strength to take off my clothes. This is so damn crazy. Tell me again why we're here."

"Because nobody eats hot dogs on Thanksgiving. I'm trying to be a good host here, Lucy, even if we're stealing food from our beloved neighbors. Ask yourself if you want to see Jake waste away to nothing. Then there's Coop. He'll go ballistic if he doesn't get his meat loaf. I live for that dog."

"Ahhh." Lucy sighed. "It's getting warmer. Tell you what, Wylie. Find a towel, and I'll rub your feet if you rub mine. Then we'll put on warm socks."

"Okay, but I can't get up. It took us twenty minutes to cross the street, but I've had four-hour workouts that didn't leave me this drained. You must be exhausted. I'd come over there and sit with you, but I can't move."

"Stay where you are. I am beyond exhausted. Let's just sit here. Don't talk. Dream. Do anything but move or talk. Whatever you do, don't go to sleep."

"Okay."

Then Lucy broke her own order. "We don't even know if Rachel has a turkey or a chicken in her freezer. What if this was for nothing, Wylie?"

"I'll kill myself. If there is one, let's not go to Nellie's house, okay? God, I hate snow, this snow in particular. Hey, I'm starting to sweat."

"Shut up, Wylie. I told you not to talk. If you keep talking, you won't have to kill yourself, I'll kill you."

"Oooh, I love it when you talk like that." Wylie slid off the chair and rolled over to where Lucy was sitting. "If we get married, do you think we'll fight? Will we ever go to bed angry with each other? How many kids do you want? We should get a cat, too, and maybe a bird. A real menagerie."

"Yeah, okay. You sure do talk a lot."

"That's why I am going to make an outstanding teacher. Come on, Lucy, we can't stay here. Let's get this show on the road. I want to go home and take a nap."

"Wuss," Lucy said, staggering to her feet. She peeled off her jacket, tossed it on the floor, and ripped off her cold, wet socks. She tossed dry socks from her sack at Wylie and told him to empty out their boots.

Together, they checked Rachel Muller's deep freezer in the garage. "Oooh, tell me this isn't the mother lode," Wylie said, moving freezer packages. "And she labels everything, too, with the date."

Lucy watched as Wylie withdrew two ten-pound capons and set them on the floor. Five packages of ground sirloin came out next. "What else do you want? She has a ton of frozen vegetables, even sugared sweet potatoes with marshmallows. Told you this was the mother lode," he said as he piled up packages of frozen vegetables.

Lucy looked at the pile of food. "We can eat off the chickens for a day or so with leftovers. The ground sirloin is for Coop. Let's take a pork loin. We can always come back if we run out. Take some bread and those Sara Lee cakes. It might take a while for delivery trucks to make it to the supermarkets. We'll be okay because we still haven't explored Nellie's freezer. God, I am so glad we don't have to trudge all the way down there. I don't think I could make it."

Wylie pointed to the pile of food on the floor. Frozen food was heavy. "How are we going to get this home?"

"I guess we have to bag it and tie it around our necks or our waists. Hey, look, there's a sled hanging on the wall. Rachel's grandson comes to visit, so I guess the sled is for him."

"Nah, we don't have anything to tie it on with. Besides, it will be more trouble to pull the sled than it will be to drag the sacks. We'll double some garbage bags and just drag them behind us. Unless you have a better idea."

"Nope. Let's do it."

"It should be easier going home since we made tracks coming here."

"Yeah, well, those tracks are probably full of snow by now," Lucy grumbled.

Back inside Rachel's house, Lucy dressed,

rummaged for plastic sacks for the food as Wylie turned the thermostat down to seventy and let the faucet in the kitchen sink drip. Within ten minutes they were ready for the trek home, with each of them dragging one of the sacks of food.

"You're right, Lucy, I feel like a damn Pilgrim on the hunt. I'd beat my chest, but I'm too damn tired."

Lucy knew Wylie was talking, but his voice was carried away on the wind. Her head down, she concentrated on stepping into the tracks he made. She lost track of time and was so exhausted she bumped into him when he came to an abrupt stop. She was colder than she'd ever been in her life. She couldn't feel her feet inside the high rubber boots. All she knew was they were full of snow. "What's wrong?" she managed to gasp.

"I don't know how to tell you this, but I overshot my house. We're at Nellie's house."

"Nellie's house!" Lucy screamed. "Nellie's house!" she screamed again.

"Lucy, I can't see in front of my face. Yeah, Nellie's house. It looks like we're in her driveway. I know it's her house because

I can see that metal sun sculpture she has nailed to the garage door under the overhang. You know what else. Someone is here because there are footprints going around to the back."

"Who cares? It's probably Nellie's grandson. More than likely he got stranded at the train station and made it here. He lives in South Plainfield. Let's go, Wylie. Get your bearings and move. I can't believe we're at Nellie's house. Weren't you a Boy Scout?"

"No, I wasn't a Boy Scout. I was too busy mowing lawns, shoveling snow, and delivering papers. God, I hate snow—or did I say that already! I feel like a damn packhorse," Wylie said as he turned around and moved across the virgin snow toward his own house. Lucy followed him blindly.

If it hadn't been snowing so heavily, or if the wind hadn't suddenly ratcheted up, one or the other of them might have seen the curtain on the upstairs bedroom window move as a man peered out of it.

13

At seven o'clock that morning Jonathan St. Clair let his gaze sweep the hotel room he'd been staying in. He grimaced at the cowhide suitcase, thinking of the cheap European clothes inside. He fumbled around inside until his fingers touched the canvas fanny pack that held numerous passports, matching IDs, and a stack of CD-Rs. The laptop glared up at him. Take it or not take it. Better to leave it, but first he had to dismantle it, just in case he wasn't able to return to the hotel.

Working with an economy of motion, Jonathan ripped out the motherboard and stuffed it into his fanny pack. Now, he was ready to go.

Just minutes ago, he'd used the laptop to access MapQuest to get directions to Lucy's house. But instead of listing Lucy's address, he'd substituted the words, Golden Acres Shopping Center. He copied down the information, then deleted the request.

Jonathan walked back over to the window. Suddenly, he felt nervous, uneasy. He didn't like the feeling. Not at all. He felt bile rising in his throat, the heavy breakfast threatening to erupt. Was he losing his edge? "Three strikes and you're out," he muttered.

Never a serene person, he realized he was fast coming up on strike three.

First it was Lucy and her strange behavior. The second was his decision to put his business on hold and fly to the States. Third was this unprecedented snowstorm and the house in Watchung that was compromised. Maybe he was on strike four and too stupid to recognize it. He shivered with the draft coming in around the windows. So much for hermetically sealed windows.

Jonathan shivered, not with cold but a mixture of fear and apprehension.

According to MapQuest, it was a little over four miles to the shopping center near to where Lucy lived. Knock off a quarter of a mile, and it was still almost four miles. Would he survive in the weather outside? Not unless he had a pair of boots. He shivered again as he imagined being brought down for lack of a pair of storm boots. Well, that wasn't going to happen.

His heavy wool coat over his arm, Jonathan marched to the door and thrust it open. He half expected to see the maids working in the hallway, but it was empty. That meant no one would be getting clean sheets.

The elevator was full when he stepped in and rode to the lobby. He wasn't surprised to see the milling crowds of people, some sleeping on the leather furniture or in the wooden chairs in the lobby restaurant. He took his time as he meandered around looking at people's feet, then at his own. Most of the men were wearing either Brooks Brothers tasseled loafers or wing tips like he was wearing.

Jonathan walked to the back entrance, hoping to see a door labeled MAINTENANCE. When he found it, he knocked softly and opened the door. The room was empty. Seeing no boots, he backed off and walked toward the glass doors that led out to the snow-filled parking lot, where hundreds of cars were parked every which way, all covered with mountains of snow. He didn't know if it was his imagination or not, but it looked like the snow was abating somewhat.

He saw the maintenance workers then. Some with shovels, some with snowblowers. All were fighting a losing battle. All the men he could see wore high, rubber boots. Now, all he had to do was get a pair of those boots. Eventually, one or more of them would take a break, come indoors, and go to the maintenance room, where he would be waiting.

Jonathan backtracked and boldly walked toward the maintenance room, where he opened the door and walked inside as though he belonged there. As far as he could tell, no one paid him any attention. He held his breath to see if anyone followed him into the room demanding to know what he was doing. His sigh was mighty when nothing happened. He looked at his watch—7:30.

He waited.

It was nine o'clock when the door finally opened and two weary men stepped into the room. Jonathan watched from his position behind a tall metal cabinet as both men shed their plastic outerwear, winter clothing,

and heavy, rubber boots. The taller of the
two men rummaged in a bag on the floor
and brought out a huge Thermos of coffee.
He poured for both of them. Neither man
said a word as they gulped at the hot drink.
When they finished their coffee, the same
man reached again into the canvas bag and
brought out an ordinary-looking kitchen
timer. Jonathan could hear the clicks on the
timer as the man turned it on. He waited five
minutes, then another five minutes before
he stepped out from behind the metal cabinet. Both men were sound asleep, both
snoring loudly. Cautiously, he removed both
men's boots, stepped into one pair, folding
down the others and stuffing them into
the canvas bag along with his wing tips.
He looked back at the men. Neither had
moved. He was almost to the door when he
remembered he needed a hat. He ran back
and snatched a wool cap off the table. His
nose wrinkled at the cheap scent that
wafted past his nose as he drew the hat
down as far as it would go over his ears.

Three minutes later he was outside, trying
to make his way to the driveway that led to
the road. He had memorized the MapQuest
directions and knew exactly where he was

going. All he needed was to get to his destination.

By the time Jonathan worked his way to the front of the hotel and the downward-sloping driveway, he was already exhausted. The boots were impossibly heavy, and, before he knew what was happening, he was on his rear end, sliding down the partially cleared drive. When he finally used the heels of the boots to bring himself to a skidding stop, snow had ballooned up and around him, going up his sleeves and down his boots. Overhead, the stinging flakes beat against his face as it covered him better than any blanket. He looked over his shoulder and saw the handles of the green canvas bag at the top of the driveway. He had no conscious memory of dropping the bag. It looked, from what he could see, like it was in a drift. If the snow continued the way it was, it would be covered completely in another hour. It would be sheer torture to try and make his way back to the top of the driveway. So he would lose his wing tips. He made the decision to leave the bag.

Somehow, Jonathan managed to get to his feet. As far as the eye could see, there was nothing but a vast wasteland of snow.

There was no sign of humanity, no cars, no trucks, no sign of life. He knew, as he climbed over a steep snowdrift, that to his right was the Metro train station. All he had to do was make it to the traffic light, cross over, and he would be on Wood Avenue. A steep hill if he chose to go that way. Or, he could make a left on Route 27 and walk to the town of Metuchen, where he would then follow Central Avenue to Edison. There he would make another left on Park Avenue and take that directly to the development where Lucy lived.

His head down, Jonathan trudged on, opting to take Route 27 in the hope snowplows had been through earlier.

Time lost all meaning as Jonathan urged his body and his feet to cooperate.

He talked to himself when the images of warm waterfalls and tropical breezes failed to help him. He cursed and vented, his lips blue with cold.

It was eleven-thirty by his watch when he came to an intersection.

Jonathan had yet to see a human being or a vehicle. He kept slogging forward, past Saint Joe's School for Boys on the left, private homes on the right. He trudged up a small hill and saw a huge sign that said CHARLIE BROWN'S RESTAURANT.

The scarf around his neck was full of ice and bone cold on his neck. He knew he was in trouble when he started to feel light-headed. Would he die out there?

He heard the sound, saw dim yellow lights through the swirling snow, and knew instantly that it was a snowplow. He didn't stop but kept moving. The plow turned right. There was supposed to be a traffic light, but it was out. It had to be Park Avenue.

Jonathan turned and followed the plow. It was easier going. Maybe he wouldn't die after all. Still, it took him another twenty minutes to trudge to the gas station on the corner of Stephenville Parkway and Park Avenue. He walked the half block, falling twice, face-first into the snow. He managed to get to his feet knowing he was close to Nellie's house. Just a little farther. He literally staggered to the corner of David Court and turned right. He fell again, got up, and fell back down. He rolled and rolled, over and over, until he came to the first house on David Court. Using the last of his strength, he struggled to his feet, forged his way up the driveway and around to the side door of the garage. With his elbow, he smashed one of the small panes of glass, slid his hand inside, and undid the lock. He literally fell through the open door.

The boots were the first thing to come off before he entered the kitchen. He felt drunk when he lurched his way to the thermostat to turn it up. When he went back to the garage to close and lock the door he thought he heard voices. *I must be delirious.*

Back inside Nellie's house, he looked around. Other than the furnishings, the house had the exact same layout as Lucy's. He started to shed his clothes as he made his way to the first-floor bathroom, where he turned on the shower. Thank God there was hot water. His body burned and tingled as he stood under the steaming spray. Maybe he should use cold water, tepid water. Like hell.

He still wasn't sure if he was going to die or not. He told himself at that point he didn't even care. All he wanted was to be warm again.

When the hot water ran cold, Jonathan stepped from the shower and put on Nellie's flannel bathrobe, hanging on the back of the

door. He shuffled out of the steamy bathroom in search of liquor. He found a bottle
of cognac and a bottle of apricot brandy in
one of the kitchen cabinets. He couldn't get
the bottle to his lips fast enough. When his
throat and stomach protested, he capped
the bottle.

The house was cozy warm as he made
his way to the second floor, the brandy bottle clutched tightly in his hand. He'd read
somewhere that old people liked to use
electric blankets. He hoped Nellie was one
of those people. She was. He turned the
blanket to high before he pulled down the
covers. While he waited for the bed to warm
up, he rummaged in Nellie's drawers and
found a pair of flannel pajamas. Nellie must
be fat, he decided as he climbed into them.
One leg into the pajama bottom, he jerked
to awareness and hobbled to the bedroom
window when he heard what he thought
was Lucy's voice. And then another voice
carried on the wind. A man's voice. Lucy
and a man, literally outside this house. A
devilish smile ripped across his face. He
yanked at the pajama bottom as he made
his way to the bed. "Glad to know where I
can find you, Lucy. See you later . . ."

Jonathan fell into the bed. He had the presence of mind to turn off the blanket before he pulled the covers up to his chin. His last conscious thought was that he wasn't going to die after all. The watch on his wrist said the time was 1:12.

Jake and the dogs were waiting in the foyer when Lucy opened the door. Wind and snow spiraled through. Coop reared up and started to howl. Sadie followed suit. Lulu danced around in a circle, yapping and growling.

"We must look like something from another planet," Wylie said. "It's us!" he said to the howling dogs as he dropped his sack of food. The moment he ripped off his dark hat, the dogs stopped their racket.

"You look . . . frozen," Jake said.

"Guess what, Jake, we *are* frozen. You're in charge of this food," Wylie said, pointing to the sacks of food that were dripping melted snow onto the floor. "Lucy and I are going to get into some warm clothes and sit by the fire. I don't know when I've ever been this exhausted."

Lucy just shook her head as she stepped

out of her boots and weaved her way to the steps. "I'm going to take a warm bath. I'd appreciate it, Jake, if you'd make a blazing fire. I'm going to wrap myself in a blanket and take a nap."

"Me, too," Wylie said. "You're in charge, Jake."

"Hey, Lucy, the FBI called. They want you to call them back. The agent said it was urgent. I left the number by the phone in the family room. And, before you can ask, they said they got Wylie's number from the phone book. I guess they assumed you would be here. Those guys don't miss a trick. I didn't confirm or deny but said if I saw you, I'd give you the message."

Lucy's response was to raise her middle finger high over her head. Jake chuckled as he picked up the sacks of food, a happy smile on his face. He wasn't going to starve after all.

It was seven o'clock, and time to wake up his hosts, when Jake set the table. The timer for the oven pinged, confirming his intention. Ah, his Bisquick biscuits were done. They were a rich golden color. Perfect. The pot on top of the stove held chili, the only thing he really knew how to cook. He hoped he hadn't made it too hot. He himself loved hot, the hotter the better. Who was he kidding? He loved food, anything that was chewable. He'd chopped onions and grated cheese to sprinkle on top of the robust meal. He'd even baked the pie he'd found pushed back behind bags of soup bones in the freezer. The expiration date on the box said the pie had expired six months ago. He ignored the date and cooked it anyway. Pie was pie, and it was frozen, so how could it be bad?

He'd played housekeeper all afternoon while his hosts slept. He'd replenished the fire three or four times, cleaned the hallway, set the capons in cold water in the laundry room sink to thaw, put everything else away, then watched the snow fall outside.

Jake walked over to the sliding glass doors, where he turned on the deck lights. Damn, it was still snowing. Perhaps not as heavily, but it was still coming down.

He went into the family room, where he bent down to wake up his hosts. "Rise and shine, boys and girls, dinner is ready. It's seven-thirty, and it is still snowing. Chop-

chop. I slaved all afternoon in the kitchen, and I don't want it to get cold."

Lucy stretched inside the quilt she was wrapped in. She felt blissfully warm and contented. "Seven-thirty at night!"

"Uh-huh. You've been asleep for over five hours. It's supposed to snow through the night and finally stop by midmorning tomorrow."

"What did you cook, Jake? Hey, I thought you didn't know how to cook," Wylie grumbled as he kicked his quilt aside.

Jake flapped his arms to get them to move. "My one and only specialty, red-hot chili. We have biscuits and pie and, of course, fresh coffee. Let's go, let's go. I'm starving."

Lucy was on her hands and knees trying to get upright. Every muscle and bone in her body protested. Jake reached out a hand to pull her to her feet. She winced in pain as she limped her way to the downstairs bathroom.

Jake braced his feet solidly on the floor before he held out his hand to Wylie.

"Son of a bitch," Wylie seethed. "I hurt, Jake."

"Stop whining and get your ass upstairs and cleaned up. Work the kinks out."

Wylie eyed the stairway and knew he couldn't make his legs go up them. "I'll just wait for Lucy to come out. So the FBI called . . ."

"Yeah, and they sounded . . . pissed that neither you nor Lucy was here. They did say it was urgent, Wylie. I think Lucy should call them after dinner."

"Yeah, well, that's Lucy's decision," Wylie said as he staggered, with Jake's help, toward the downstairs bathroom. His eyes shut, he leaned wearily against the wall and waited for Lucy to come out.

Lucy pushed her chair away from the table. "That was really good, Jake. I ate way too much. Where did you learn to make biscuits?"

"I followed the directions on the box. It wasn't like I had anything else to do. You guys were wiped out, and I didn't know how long you'd sleep. How about some pie?"

Lucy shook her head, as Wylie said, "A small piece and some more coffee. Lucy's right, Jake. The chili was hot and delicious. Thanks for taking over."

Jake bustled about the kitchen but talked as he worked. "Lucy, are you going to call that guy at the FBI?"

"In the morning. What could he possibly have to tell me that's urgent? The morning is time enough, and besides, it's almost ten o'clock. They're just guessing that I'm here. Somebody probably alerted them that we were in Watchung. Like that's urgent. I've read enough novels about the FBI to know everything they do or say is urgent with them. I told you before, I don't trust them. I think I just overreacted yesterday. There's no way Jonathan could get here in this storm. If I had to take a wild guess as to the 'urgent' call, I'd say they probably have information that he's on a flight here or his flight is grounded. I'll start to worry when there's something more for me to sink my teeth into." Lucy grinned suddenly. "Let's not forget these three killer dogs who are guarding us. As I said, morning is time enough."

"Lucy, this might be a good time for me to start testing you if you're up to it. I'd like you to develop your powers of ESP so you can call on them if you ever find yourself in a dangerous situation.

"Do you remember when I first got here, I told you both about the Pentagon's secret projects. They wanted to investigate extrasensory phenomena to see if the sheer power of the human mind could be harnessed to perform various acts of espionage. It was written up in the *New York Times* sometime during the mideighties. They spent millions of dollars, according to three different reports. I'm in the process of trying to track all this down. I don't know what it will mean other than to prove maybe you're one of those people whose mind can be harnessed. I don't think we're talking espionage here, but maybe something damn close to it. On the other hand, it could really have nothing to do with you, and your condition is just temporary, a freak occurrence that will dissipate in time."

"I don't want to be a freak of nature. I just want it to go away," Lucy said.

"No, Lucy, you don't want it to go away until this crisis is over. You and I are going to go in a quiet room, and I'm going to work with you. We'll see if we can rein your, ah, new talent, in to the point where you can control it and call upon it if you need to. I am almost certain, when your life returns to normal, your . . . talent will fade away. We should get a weather update before we start."

Wylie looked up from his pie. "Why?"

Jake shrugged.

When Coop and Sadie barreled through the laundry room and raced to the sliding doors Lucy bolted out of her chair. "You didn't close the blinds, Wiley," she admonished as she ran into the windowless laundry room.

"What the hell . . ." Wylie, too, was off his chair, running toward the sliding doors. Coop was growling and snarling as he raced back and forth, Sadie on his heels. Lulu cowered by Jake's feet, begging to be picked up. He obliged.

The little dog's trembling limbs brought Jake to attention. "Lock the damn doors, Wylie. *NOW!*" Wylie didn't have to be told twice. He slammed the latch into place and dropped the dowel standing in the corner into the track. He looked confused when he turned around to stare at Jake.

Lulu in one hand, the cordless phone in

the other along with the sticky Post-it, Jake headed for the laundry room.

Lucy cowered in the corner beside the dryer, her hands cupped over her ears. *Damn snow . . . bitch . . . ruin my life . . .* Her face was whiter than the snow that was blanketing their immediate world.

Wylie and Jake both dropped to their knees. "What? What's wrong, Lucy? Did you *hear* something?" Jake demanded.

Coop was even wilder by then, running and leaping on the back of the couch and down on the other side as he tried to paw at the vertical blinds covering the sliding glass doors. Sadie sat up on her haunches, throwing her head back and howling, an ungodly sound.

Jake took command. "Get it together, Lucy, and call the number. I'm dialing it for you. You can do this. They said it was urgent." Jake identified himself, and said, "Agent Lawrence, I have Miss Baker for you. Hold please."

Lucy dropped the phone twice before she was able to bring it to her ear. Her whole body shook from head to toe when she said, "This is Lucy Baker."

"Where are you, Miss Baker?"

"What difference does that make? What is it that is so urgent?" She let her head rest against the wall as she listened, her eyes closed. Wylie and Jake both reared back when Lucy barked, "How do you know that? If you're trying to frighten me, you are certainly succeeding! No, I haven't heard from Jonathan. I'm not home, and I don't have my cell phone with me. I suppose Jonathan might figure out I'd be someplace close to home, but that's a bit of a stretch to my mind. However, he did call the day before when the storm was just beginning. He does get weather reports, and he does watch television while he's away, so there's a good chance he knows about our weather conditions. As you said on more than one occasion, he's not stupid. It's only logical for him to think I wouldn't go far. Unless Jonathan has magical powers, how could he possibly know which house I'm in? I don't know why the dogs are barking, Agent Lawrence. How could he possibly get to me? We have four feet of snow outside. It's a blizzard. I thought you were FBI. If you knew it was Jonathan, then why didn't you pick him up? How many damn times do I have to tell you, I don't know anything about

Jonathan's activities. I don't give a damn what you think, Agent Lawrence."

Wylie sat down on the floor across from Lucy. She was getting mad. *Good,* he thought. Better she should be mad than a cowering basket case. Color was coming back to her cheeks, too. The dogs were still barking and howling.

"Yes, we did go to the house in Watchung. My friends knew some men who have expertise in security systems. They dismantled the systems and turned them off. They don't work now. You said it was my house. Why shouldn't I go there? I wanted to see what I own. There was nothing in the house except some high-tech equipment. And there was a Chevy Suburban SUV in the garage, a car you never mentioned in your catalog of fancy vehicles. It was a waste of time and energy going there. Go check it out yourself. I'll give you the code to the house alarm and there's a card for the gate. Everything else is off. Why didn't I call you? Why should I? The last time we spoke, you said, when you left, that you would be in touch. To me that means you were supposed to call me, not the other way around. Well, goddammit,

Agent Lawrence, if you are so sure of your facts, why aren't you here protecting me? I'm a taxpayer. Well, if you can't get here, how do you expect Jonathan to get here? I don't believe you, Agent Lawrence. How could Jonathan be here, and what do you mean by *here*? I'm not home, so where is here?"

The trio looked at one another. Wylie thought the phone conversation was over and reached for the phone. Lucy shook her head.

"Fine. Yes, I understand. Well, dammit, get a horse and sleigh and come and get me." Lucy pressed the button to end the call. Jake and Wylie looked at her expectantly.

"They think Jonathan is here. Like in the neighborhood or somewhere close. They said they tracked him when he left Zurich, but they lost him in New York. He's using another name and some kind of disguise. Real cloak-and-dagger stuff. They had him right up till he went through customs, and that's when they lost him. They think he's coming for me. What *are* those dogs barking at?"

Wylie locked his gaze with hers. "Either

someone is out there moving around, or some kind of animal is invading Coop's turf. I don't know, Lucy."

"I *heard* him. I know it was him. If I *heard* him, that has to mean Agent Lawrence is right, and he's close. My God, he might be in the backyard."

"What did you hear, Lucy?" Jake asked.

"I heard the words *damn snow,* the word *bitch,* and then the words *ruin my life.* Maybe it was Dick Palmer, the guy who lives across the street. He's always fighting with Marion. He talks like that. He's always calling Marion a bitch and saying she ruined his life. I think that's how they communicate. You know, by fighting with one another. Everyone on the street knows what a miserable person he is. He hates being home. I don't know why those two stay married. It could have been Dick. It could have been Jonathan, too. I don't know. Nothing else is coming through. I'm trying, but there's nothing there. If Agent Lawrence is right, we're sitting ducks."

"The guy would have to be Superman to get through that snow. Look what it did to us, and we only crossed the yard. How could he get here from New York? Everything is shut down tight. The airports are closed. The train station is closed. For sure there are no cabs out and about. The police are citing people who try to go on the roads. I heard that on the five o'clock news," Wylie almost shouted.

"Look, I do not know how he got here, but he could be here, and you two know it. Explain those tracks at my house. Well?"

Wylie threw his hands in the air. "I have a gun. I'm not much of a shot, but if push comes to shove, I know how to take off the safety and I know I could plug someone if he broke into my house. I have two baseball bats, too. Think about it, Lucy, the guy can't have a weapon. He could never get one through the airports. Not even a knife. Yeah, I suppose he could have bought one in New York, but how likely is that?"

"I have a gun, too, at my house. Jonathan knows I have it. Maybe it was he who left those footprints, and he was trying to get it. To kill me with my own gun. Oh, God! Why is this happening to me? I didn't ruin his damn life, he ruined it himself. Did you close all the blinds, Wylie?"

"Yeah. Listen. How's this for an idea? Let's all go to Rachel's house."

"Why? He doesn't know where you live, Wylie. He doesn't know anything about you other than that you are a neighbor whose dog I was watching. You could live in any one of the twelve houses on the block. Why go to Rachel's house?"

Wylie shrugged. "It was a thought. You know, confusion, throw the guy a curve, that kind of thing. I guess you're right. If he doesn't know where I live, there's no point to moving out. I'm going upstairs to get the gun, though. Do you want me to go to your house and get yours?"

Before Lucy could respond, Jake said, "Yeah, Wylie, get her gun. Bring yours down here. I know how to shoot. Actually, I'm a fair marksman."

"Okay, where's the gun, Lucy? Is it loaded?"

"Of course it's loaded. Why have a gun if you don't keep it loaded? It's not like I have children living in my house. It's in my night table drawer. The table on the right side of the bed. There are a few extra clips, too, so bring those. Are you sure you don't mind going out again?"

"Hell, yes, I mind, but I'm going to do it anyway. In case nobody noticed, the dogs are quiet now. It was probably only a stray animal, maybe a possum or a squirrel, whose weird scent set them off. Sit tight, I'll be back."

Lucy wondered if Wylie really believed what he was saying or if he said the words for her benefit. She made no move to leave the corner of the laundry room. Sadie trotted into the room and sat down on her lap. Coop sat alongside them both. She stroked their silky heads as Jake followed Wylie out to the foyer.

"My gun is in the top dresser drawer under my socks. I'm going to take it with me," Wylie said as he donned his ski jacket and hat.

"Don't shoot yourself in the foot, Wylie. How long should I give you before I go out looking for you?" Jake asked.

"Forty minutes," Wylie responded grimly. "Not a minute longer."

"Gotcha."

14

The moment Jake slammed and locked the front door behind Wylie, Lucy started to pace, her eyes glued to the watch on her wrist. Jake noticed that she carefully avoided walking past any of the windows in case her shadow could be seen from outside. At least, that's what he surmised.

Lucy circled the dining room, the kitchen, and then the foyer. "Do you think Jonathan is here, Jake?"

"Yes," he said. There was no point in kidding himself or Lucy. "Yes, I do," he said again.

Lucy twisted the watch on her wrist as though by moving it back and forth, the time would go faster. "You know what, Jake? I do, too."

"Well, there's three of us and one of him. We have two guns. I want you to think about something else, Lucy. Remember how difficult it was and how cold and exhausted you and Wylie were, and all you did was walk back and forth across the yards. If he's here, he's on foot. The police are citing people and giving them five-hundred-dollar tickets if they're caught out on the roads with a vehicle. Your guy doesn't sound like the mountaineer type. You gave me the impression he's a bit of a dandy. Don't go giving him too much credit, Lucy."

"Then why were the dogs going nuts like that? Who made those footprints at my house? He's here. Hey, with all we now know, he could have weaseled himself into someone's house by saying he was stranded. No one would turn him away in this weather. He'd flash wads of money to make it harder to turn him away. Jonathan loves money and assumes everyone else does, too."

Jake brought his arm up to see the numerals on his watch. "Wylie should be on his way back by now. Come on, Lucy, nothing is going to happen to my buddy. You like him, don't you?"

"Yes, I do, Jake. I like him a lot. I just wish I hadn't gotten him involved—you, too—in this mess. I feel like such a fool. I am really having a hard time accepting how stupid I was where Jonathan is concerned."

Jake walked to the window and parted the vertical blinds to peep out. "The bad news is, it's still snowing, but the good news is I see Wylie. He's near that little grove of cedars that separates your property from his. Don't be so hard on yourself, Lucy. At one time or another, most of us have done things we wished we hadn't. You found out in time, and we're going to make it right."

"Why does he feel he has to kill me, Jake?"

"We don't know for sure that he does want to harm you. That was a statement the FBI threw out to scare you. We don't know if it's true or not. If it is, my guess would be he thinks you're onto him and will try to trap him for the authorities. He wants to keep his good life. A stretch in the slammer doesn't fit in with his game plan. That's the best I can come up with."

Lucy threw herself into Wylie's arms the moment the door opened. She looked up at him and gave a shaky laugh. "You have icicles on your eyebrows. What took you so long? I was so worried." Lucy jabbered, as

Wylie took off his jacket and sat down on the small bench across from the front door. She struggled to pull off his boots.

Jake trotted off and returned with clean socks and the bottoms to a pair of flannel pajamas. Lucy backed off and watched as Wylie dropped his pants and shed his wet socks. He wasn't a boxer man. It pleased her. She took a full minute to appreciate his hard, muscled thighs. She grinned wickedly when he caught her eye.

"Don't even think about it," he groaned.

"Okay," Lucy said agreeably.

Wylie reached over to his jacket, took Lucy's gun out of his pocket, and handed it to her. Then he took out his own. "I'm going to bed," Jake said, looking at the guns. "I'll be upstairs if that makes a difference. Are you guys going to sleep down here?"

"Yes," they said in unison, as Wylie reached for the gun in Lucy's hand and made sure the safety was on both hers and his before he returned the .22 to Lucy.

Lucy led Wylie to the sofa in front of the fire and handed him the quilt he'd used earlier that day. After adding a log to the fire, she sat down next to him. Wylie wrapped the quilt around them both. The guns on the coffee table glared up at them. Wylie reached down and opened a copy of *Time* magazine, which he spread on top of the guns before he cuddled next to Lucy. Within seconds, the dogs were on the couch with them, burrowing in the quilt for comfortable positions.

"Go to sleep, Wylie, you look exhausted. I've got the guns and the dogs, and I'll wake you if anything goes awry. The phone is here, too, and Jake is upstairs. I'd give up everything in the world that I hold dear if I could go back and avoid getting you involved in my problems."

Lucy smiled when she heard Wylie's light snoring. She stroked Coop's head. "He's a real okay guy, this master of yours," she whispered to the dog. She leaned back into the softness of the couch and stared into the fire.

As Lucy stroked Wylie's dark hair, aware of how wonderful he felt next to her, she thought that maybe some good would come of all this intrigue and angst she was going through. Meeting Wylie and falling for him, and she was falling for him, was the icing on the ugly cake named Jonathan St. Clair.

She had an analytical mind, at least where the law was concerned. Maybe she should think about this whole mess as though a client had dumped it in her lap. She nodded to herself. *Go back to the beginning. Way back.*

Lucy knew she was ordinary, not spectacularly beautiful, but she wasn't ugly either, nor did she have the best figure in the world. She knew how to apply makeup, fix her hair, and cover what she perceived as her flaws. What was it that had attracted Jonathan to her? Her capabilities, her professional success, her personality, what? She'd been flattered, that much she did remember, when he'd singled her out. Flattered by his attentions because he was so handsome, so virile, she'd thrown caution to the winds and plunged into an affair with him.

It had taken some juggling, what with working eighty-hour weeks and staying true to her clients, as well as maintaining her legal winning streak. It didn't hurt that Jonathan traveled and was away more than he was in New York. When he did return, their get-togethers were that much more intense. More often than not they spent the two or three days in bed, only getting up to eat or have some wine.

She realized that what she had loved was the sex, not necessarily the man. But the magnificent engagement ring and his marriage proposal had helped to convince her that marriage to Jonathan would be fine. When the passion and sex were gone, what would their marriage be like? How many times had she asked herself that question? She hated the word *divorce*. But there it was. When she'd expressed these thoughts to her fiancé, he'd pooh-poohed them away, saying their love for each other would last a lifetime. Then he'd pour her more wine and, like a fool, she'd guzzle it, and they'd hop in the sack.

She'd had doubts from the beginning, she just hadn't acted on them. She'd been so happy to have a sexy man in her life who had appeared to want to commit himself to her.

What had they talked about? Had there ever been any meaningful, profound discussions? None that she could recall. Somehow or other, Jonathan had always managed to relegate any serious discussion to another time.

What a fool she'd been.

Red flags should have gone up when she asked him *exactly* what he did, and he evaded the question, simply saying he brokered business deals and received a commission for his efforts plus a generous expense account. There were never any precise details or even little anecdotes. He'd gone on to say she shouldn't worry her pretty little head about such things. He would take care of her in the style she deserved.

Her brother Steven hadn't liked Jonathan. She should have paid more attention to that, too, but she hadn't.

Then there was the sudden deluge of clients—less-than-savory characters—right after Jonathan came into her life. Clients who didn't balk at her outrageous fees and always offered a bonus when the acquittal verdict came in. Steven always chortled at their robust incomes. Now that she thought about it, Jonathan always seemed to phone her the evenings the verdicts came in. At first she hadn't paid much attention, but when Steven had commented, "your boyfriend acts like he knows these guys," she'd started to pay attention until she came to the same conclusion herself.

Bad actress that she was, she'd tried to pry something out of Jonathan, and all he'd done was look at her with cold, narrowed eyes. "What are you trying to say, Lucy?" was enough for her. She'd never brought up the subject again. She'd cut back, though, refusing to take on more cases or dumping them on Steven. When one prospective client pitched a fit right in the office when she turned him down, she knew for certain he was a referral from Jonathan. She'd never said a word to Jonathan, waiting for him to work his way around it. He did, and she'd looked him right in the eye and said she was too busy to take on any new clients no matter what they were willing to pay. Eventually, Steven came around to her way of thinking and refused to take cases they both thought were suspect. Of course, she could prove none of this. And that's why she hadn't told all this to the FBI agents when they'd asked about José Rafael and Manuel Aroya. For all she knew the people she'd turned away could have read or heard about her impressive winning record in the courtroom.

Maybe that's where she made her first mistake. Maybe her first mistake wasn't when she told Jonathan about the "upcoming IRS interview." Then again, maybe it was when she told Jonathan she was leaving the firm and turning down the judgeship.

Whatever it was, it no longer mattered. As Steven was fond of saying, the fat was in the fire.

Knowing and understanding all that, why did Jonathan want to kill her? Assuming, of course, that what the FBI agents said was true. Why didn't he just fade away, call off the wedding, and drop off the face of the earth? Surely he wasn't madly, passionately in love with her. No, it had to be more than that. Maybe he thought she knew something she didn't realize she knew. Like signing those documents the night he got her drunk? He was too cocky, too arrogant to believe the authorities were on his trail. Or was he?

He'd canceled the Thanksgiving trip, then moved up his Christmas trip. Now, if the FBI was correct, he'd changed his plans again and was back in the States. Figuratively, if not literally, in her backyard. She thought about the ruckus the dogs had made earlier.

Maybe he *was* in the backyard. Maybe he had tried to get into her house.

Lucy's eyes snapped open. She hoped to God that she was safe here in Wiley's house. She didn't want any harm to come to him, Jake, or the dogs. She didn't want to die either. She wanted to have a relationship with Wiley and maybe, just maybe, marry him and have children, a little girl to dress up in a bonnet and starched pinafore, and black patent Mary Janes. Did they still make pinafores for little girls? A little girl she could push on a swing attached to the big apple tree in the backyard, a little girl she could teach to ride a bike and to play hopscotch. A little girl who would run to her shouting, "Mommy, Mommy!" A little girl to kneel with at the side of her bed to say her nightly prayer. A little girl who smelled like warm sunshine and fresh flowers. A little girl to love, to hug, to squeeze, and to kiss. A little boy to deck out in sneakers and blue jeans, a little boy who looked like his daddy. A little boy who skinned his knees and waited for that kiss and the Band-Aid that would make it all go away. A little boy who would throw his arms around her neck, and say, "I love you, Mommy, a bushel and a peck and a hug around the neck." A little boy with a red wagon filled with treasures. It would be the first thing she bought him. Every little boy needed a bright red wagon. Tears blurred in her eyes. Would she ever come out of this whole?

There were so many things she still wanted to do. She wanted to go to the seashore and paint pictures. She wanted to hang new wallpaper in her kitchen and paint the woodwork. She'd always wanted to swim with the dolphins. She wanted to go to the cemetery to visit her parents' graves.

She wanted to run the New York Marathon, too. Someday. Building a small front porch onto her house was another thing she wanted to do. She hated the stoop, hated the small overhang. She wanted a front porch so she could sit on it in nice weather in the evenings. Preferably with someone like a husband and that little boy and girl she wanted so desperately. Strange how until meeting Wylie she had never wanted children. Had she somehow realized that Jonathan was not the type to be a father? If that wasn't to be, then with Sadie and perhaps a neighbor stopping by just to chat with over a cup of coffee.

She wanted to belong to the neighborhood like Nellie, Rachel, and Wylie belonged. The neighbors counted on each other. She wanted them to count on her, too, just the way she wanted to be able to count on them. Plus a whole host of other things. Things she hadn't thought about until the FBI agents warned her of her own mortality. Now, suddenly, those things seemed like the most important things in the world.

"I hate you, Jonathan St. Clair. I damn well hate your miserable guts."

"Amen to that," Wylie said groggily. He sat up and rubbed the sleep from his eyes. His voice turned anxious when he asked, "Did something happen, Lucy?"

"No, Wylie, nothing happened. I was sitting here trying to figure out where I messed up. You know what I think. I think he picked me. Picked me, Wylie. I really think he thought he could mold me into whatever scheme I was to play a part in. I didn't play the game right, though. Somehow or other I screwed up and threw his plans into a tailspin. Now, if we could just figure out what those plans are, maybe we could make this all go away and get on with our lives. How do you feel, Wylie?"

"Like I was kicked by a mule a few times. Is it still snowing?"

"Yes. It's not supposed to stop until mid-morning tomorrow, Thanksgiving Day. Are you hungry? I think there's some pie left if Jake didn't finish it off before he went to bed."

"No. This is nice, sitting here with you and the dogs. I don't want to move. I can't believe I fell asleep, though."

Lucy cuddled closer. Wylie clasped her hand under the covers. "When this is over, Lucy, and it will be over, are you and I . . . what I mean is . . . ah, hell, you know what I'm trying to say here."

Lucy smiled in the glow from the fire. "Yes, but only if you swear on Coop that you're over Angie Motolo."

Wylie threw back his head and laughed so loud, Coop reared up and barked. "Lady, you drive a hell of a bargain. I swear on Coop that I will never think about Angie Motolo again. But," he said, holding up his hand, "what do we do when we run across her at my class reunion?"

"I'll think about that when the time

comes. How's that going to work with us living next door to each other? I don't want to give up my house. I'm psyched to build a front porch."

"I love front porches. I grew up with one. We used to sit out there on the floor on rainy days and play Monopoly and other board games. We had a swing. Are you going to have a swing?"

To Lucy's ears it sounded like the most important question in the world. "Yep, and I'm going to paint it Dartmouth green to go with my shutters."

"Will you be happy hanging out with a stuffy college professor?"

Lucy pretended to think. "Will you be happy hanging out with a smart-mouth lawyer who, in legal circles, is considered the best of the best?"

"Oh, yeahhhh," Wylie drawled. "What happens if I get a teaching job out of state?"

"Like a good, dutiful wife, I'll go where my husband goes."

"You're saying you'll marry me. I'm supposed to ask you first. Did I miss something here?"

For the first time in her life, Lucy was flustered. "But you said . . . I thought . . . are you saying you don't want to marry me?"

In the blink of an eye, Wylie was out of the covers and down on one knee on the floor. He reached for her hand. "I was kidding. Will you . . ."

Coop was off the couch, and on his hind legs, his front paws wrapped around Wylie's neck. He grabbed for the big dog and finished what he was going to say. "Will you marry me? This big *galoot* goes with the deal, and you have to promise to help me make his meat loaf every day. Swear to me on Sadie, or I withdraw my proposal."

Lucy eyed the man kneeling in front of her. She could read the anxiety in his eyes. She knew he was serious about Coop. "I accept your proposal and the restrictions. I will always cater to Coop's needs. How could you even think otherwise? I've come to love that dog. Are we going to have a prenup? I like them for other people but not for myself."

"That's how I feel. Jeez, we're a pair, aren't we? Wait a minute. What about the dogs?"

"What about them? Sadie is mine and

Coop is yours. There's no problem that I can see."

"Yeah, yeah, there's a problem. I want them to be *ours.*"

Wylie's tone was light, almost teasing, but Lucy now knew him well enough to know the dogs were an important issue. "Okay, I like that. His and hers sound cold and calculating. I like them being ours. We can change their papers if you want."

"Coop doesn't have papers. I told you I found him. I hope that doesn't make a difference. I wouldn't trade Coop for all the pedigrees in the world."

"Okay. Boy, I'm glad that's settled. Hey, want a beer?"

"Well, sure, if you're going to fetch it. Bring some rawhides for these guys. I'm going to use the last of the wood to build up the fire. From here on in, we'll have to start busting up the furniture if we want a fire. I have a couple of boxes of those starter logs, but they don't throw off any heat."

"I'm not that much of a pioneer, Wylie. Just crank up the heat," she called over her shoulder as she made her way into the dark kitchen, the dogs right behind her.

Lucy found the rawhide chews in a yellow

Happy Face cookie jar. She jammed them into the pocket of her sweatpants before uncapping two bottles of Michelob. Bottles in hand, she was about to leave the dark kitchen when she saw Coop start to slink on his belly, growling deep in his throat. Sadie followed suit while Lulu danced around in circles whining and whimpering.

Lucy froze in her tracks. Her eyes on the dogs, she called out, "Wylie, I think you better come out here."

"Don't tell me we're out of beer," Wylie exclaimed. He looked from Lucy to the dogs, who were slinking from one sliding glass door to the other before he ran back into the den, where he picked up both guns. He hoped he had the guts to use the lethal weapon in his hand if need be. In the kitchen, he took both bottles of beer from Lucy's hands and set them on the table.

"I'm not sure, but I think I saw pinpoints of light between the blinds. Like someone waving a flashlight around. Don't turn on any lights, Wylie. The dogs aren't barking and howling. What's that mean?" Lucy asked fearfully.

"I don't know. Coop is very territorial. If someone invaded his yard, he'd go ballistic the way he did before." He stood close to Lucy, who was trembling. "Look, the lights are out, no one can see in. The doors are locked. We have two guns. *TWO!* If you're thinking I should go out there in the snow, think again. It wouldn't do us any good. Inside, now, that's a different story. This is my turf. We have the dogs and these weapons. I want you to go to the front window, Lucy, and look out to make sure it's still snowing. You can tell by the streetlight across the street. I don't want to risk turning on the deck lights to alert anyone. You know, just in case. What I don't like right now is that Coop's tail is down between his legs. So is Sadie's. The fur ball has a cropped tail, so who knows about her. For sure you don't mess with a dog when his tail drops down. Move, Lucy!"

In the end, Wylie had to nudge her. She did move then, running to the window. She was back in an instant. In a shaky voice, she said, "It's still snowing. I couldn't even see Rachel's house through the snow. What are we going to do, Wylie?"

"Nothing, Lucy. We're going to sit here and wait. This might be a good time for you to go off by yourself, maybe the laundry

room, and try to see if you can *hear* anything. Really try, Lucy. Nothing is going to
happen. I promise." Wylie patted her shoulder the way her father used to do when she
was a little girl. The pat meant things would
be all right.

Lucy licked at her dry lips. Her head
bobbed up and down as she walked toward
the laundry room. She wished she could explain to Wylie, to make him understand that
she couldn't *turn on* what she heard. Still, if
it made Wylie feel better, she would do it.

Lucy hated herself for cowering in the
corner like some dimwit.

Warm air gushed from the vent under the
laundry room sink and warmed Lucy's legs.
She tried to make her mind go blank, to
think about nothing but the mounds of
snow outside the house. She envisioned
deep, snow tracks, flashlights, falling snow.
She did her best to conjure up a picture of
Jonathan, with Coop and Sadie chasing him
through the snow. Some of the tension
eased in her shoulders with the vision.
Nothing was coming through. She kept
trying. Finally, she said, "I give up." She
stomped her way to the kitchen in frustration.

Lucy was calm now, even embarrassed at the way she'd fallen apart. *I really have to get a handle on this,* she thought. *I cannot let that man invade my life like this. If I do, I'll be a drooling idiot and no good to anyone.*

Sadie nipped at Lucy's arm to remind her of the rawhide chews she had in her pocket. She smiled.

Lucy was surprised to find Jake sitting with Wylie at the kitchen table. They'd turned on a light.

"Lucy, you said there was something that bothered you about the house in Watchung. What bothered you? Sit there, dammit and don't say another word until you know what it is. That's a damn order, Lucy. I'm through wasting time here," Jake said forcefully. He pounded the kitchen table to make his point.

Lucy dutifully, and meekly, sat down at the table and let her mind have free rein. Jake and Wylie watched her intently, like two precocious squirrels whose gazes were fixed on a pile of nuts.

Twenty minutes later, Lucy bounded off the chair. "I can't think with you two watching me. I don't know what it is. Listen, I was cold, angry, and worried about the storm.

All that security blew my mind. It was probably nothing. Why don't we just go in the den and watch a video or something?"

"Why don't we *not* do something like that. I have an idea," Jake said. "Let's do a word association test. Maybe something will jog your memory. Are you up for it, Lucy?"

Lucy looked upward at Wylie, who nodded in agreement. "Okay," she said.

"Good. Let me get a pad and pen, and I'll be right back."

"I'm just agreeing to this to humor Jake. My brain is tired, Wylie. I don't have any clues; there's nothing hidden in my head. God, I just want this to be over. And, by the way, I have cabin fever. I need to go outside. I need fresh air. I feel like I'm in a damn tomb."

"We all feel that way, Lucy. Try not to think about it. Before you know it, the roads will be plowed, and we'll be able to get in our cars and get out and about."

Lucy snorted. "Assuming we can find said cars. What makes you think they'll even start up. In Buffalo, during that storm in '77, the engines were nothing but blocks of ice."

"So we'll use our blow-dryers to melt the ice. You're whining, Lucy."

"I know, Wylie, and I hate myself for it. I can't seem to help it."

"Then you need to try harder," Jake said, sitting down across from Lucy. "Now here's how we're going to do this. I say a word, and you respond immediately. Don't stop to think. Blurt out the first thing that comes to your mind. For instance, I'm going to say one word now. You respond. Stove."

"Cook," Lucy said smartly.

"It might help if you lean back in the chair and close your eyes."

Lucy did as instructed. "All right, I'm ready."

"Alarm."

"Two, six, eight, nine. It's the code to my alarm system," Lucy said.

"House"

"Cozy."

"Snow."

"Danger," Lucy said.

"Dogs."

"Unconditional love," Lucy responded.

"Jonathan."

"Evil," Lucy shot back.

"Stainless steel."

"Institutions."

"Security gates."

"Secrets," Lucy said.

"Dead room."

"Mortuary."

"Round."

"Square."

"White."

"Virginal," Lucy quipped.

"Evil."

"Jonathan."

"Fear."

"Hide."

"Fireplace."

"Fire, logs, flames. I know that's three, but they popped into my head," Lucy said.

"Square."

"Round. White. Dirty."

"Dirty."

"Jonathan's fireplace. That's it. That's what bothered me. Who in their right mind would have a white fireplace? Certainly no one I know. There were ashes in it, and a few of the white bricks were dirty. No, no, that's wrong. Those bricks had smudges on them. There was no soot inside the hood. I clearly remember looking up inside it. Most fireplaces have a trapdoor on the floor where you just open it up and brush the ashes through it. I have a huge barrel in the crawl space under the house. That's where my ashes go. It has to be a barrel or a drum of some kind because oftentimes the embers are hot, and you don't want a fire under the house."

"She's right, Jake. I have a barrel under mine, too. I empty it out every spring."

"So, what are you trying to say, Lucy?"

"We were supposed to think that the fireplace was used. If we thought about it at all. I think we were supposed to be confused, or anyone else who entered that house, for that matter, at the round room. We all commented on it, don't you remember? Not only was it round, it was startling white. The fireplace or the fire pit, whatever you want to call it, was the focal point. But, once you saw it, recognized it for what it is, you didn't give it a second thought because your mind went to the roundness and the startling white. I remember someone saying we needed sunglasses. Am I crazy here?"

Jake tapped the pen in his hand on the tabletop. Wylie scratched his head, his expression perplexed.

"Well, will someone say something?" Lucy said.

"What you're thinking is, something is hidden underneath, is that it? My own trap-door in my fireplace at home is on hinges. There's not a lot of room to sift the ashes through either side of it. I have to pry it open with the fire tongs and brush the ashes through. It's a messy job."

"Ours are the same way. That doesn't have to mean Jonathan St. Clair's is the same. It could be a flat steel plate with a ring to lift off. Just like a lid. What do we think is in there?" Wylie asked.

Two blank faces stared at him.

"Are you thinking money, records, drugs, an arms cache, what?" Wylie persisted.

The blank faces continued to stare at him.

"Maybe all of the above. Nah, this is about money. If this guy is as global as I think he is, he has to have a home base somewhere. Maybe that house is his home base and, as such, it's where he keeps his stash, whatever his stash is," Jake said.

Lucy spoke for the first time. "Do you want to know what I think?"

"Hell, yes," Wylie exploded.

"This is just my opinion, but I think

Jonathan would never hide anything that could aid and comfort him. He'd keep it on his person. I'm talking about his bank records. Anything that could be hidden is on a computer. He carried it with him all the time. Sometimes, when he was in Europe, he would chain it to his wrist. He told me that himself. I think whatever is hidden, if I'm right, and it's there, is a record of the people he did business with. For want of a better term, his bargaining chip, if things ever went awry. A way for him to cut a deal. I think it was Agent Lawrence who, in one of our very first conversations, said we were talking about billions of dollars. That's billions with a *b*. In my head, that translates to drugs. What do you think? Am I off the wall here, or does this all make sense to either one of you?"

"Honey," Wylie said, bending over to hug her, "I think you nailed it."

Lucy grinned from ear to ear. "We have to call the agents and tell them. Not that they can do anything right this moment, but they can call it in and have other agents look into it.

"Okay, having said all that, Jonathan just wants to kill me because . . ."

"You upset the little world he created for himself. It's a vengeance mentality thing with him. You have to pay for disrupting his world. It's that simple. A little while ago you said to keep it simple."

Lucy looked from one to the other. She suddenly felt nauseated. When Jake left, Lucy realized that the session was over. She looked at Wylie, a devilish glint in her eyes.

"You know what, Wylie, your dog is the only dog I know who has his own room. He's got two beds, boxes of toys, and he sleeps with you."

A grin stretched across Wylie's face. "It's called devotion. Now that he has new friends, I'm just someone who makes him meat loaf. I admit, I was a little jealous at first."

"Really! Me, too. Sadie was always glued to me. I guess it's a good thing. Hey, you want to mess around?"

Wylie's eyes almost bugged out of his head. "You mean like . . . *mess around*?"

"Uh-huh. Me, you, together. If you're too tired . . ."

"Tired! Who, me? I'm the guy who just had a nap. No sirree, I'm not the least bit tired. I'm up for . . . what I mean is I'm, ah, yeah, I'm *up."*

Lucy wiggled her eyebrows as she led Wylie over to the fire. "If you're sure you're really, you know, *up,* then let's get to it. Before the fire burns down."

Wylie was already pulling off his shirt. "I thought you were worried about Jake being in the house."

"Jake who?" Lucy purred.

Wylie's sweatpants dropped to the floor. "Yeah, Jake who?" His voice was so hoarse, he had a hard time believing the words came out of his mouth. "I'm ready," he said, diving onto the pile of quilts Lucy dragged over from the couch. "Let's do that *thing* we did the last time."

"Did you like *that*?" Lucy purred.

"Oh, man, did I ever. Hurry up, it's cold."

Then she was on top of him, his head clasped in both her hands. She kissed him until his ears turned beet red. Wylie groaned, convinced that kissing Lucy was one of life's greatest pleasures. He was stunned when she pulled away and stared down at him. "You ready, big guy?"

"Yeahhhh," Wylie said exuberantly.

"Then, let's do it. Remember now," Lucy

said, breathing little kisses all over his face, "no screaming, no yelling, no kicking on the floor."

"I'm not making a promise *like that*!"

"Me either."

15

Special Agent Sylvia Connors stared out of the eighteenth-floor window of the Hyatt Hotel in New Brunswick, where she and her two fellow agents had been staying since the onset of the worst storm in a century. In the whole of her career, she'd never felt this hopeless.

She was cranky, out of sorts, and was rapidly becoming angry at her colleagues' callous attitude toward Lucy Baker. Attribute it to her background, training, expertise, whatever, she knew Lucy Baker had told them the truth. Mason and Lawrence thought otherwise.

Sylvia clenched her teeth as she picked up her conversation with her colleagues. "She's in grave danger. I'm telling you, she's Banks's victim. You two know squat about women."

"Get off it, Connors. She's in this up to her eyeballs. Did you really expect her to admit to anything? She's a lawyer, for God's sake. She loves that word *allegedly.* She was marrying the guy. We went along with you when you demanded a handwriting expert to verify her signature. The proof came back positive. It's her damn signature. She's in it right down to her toes, so cut us some slack here."

"There are all kinds of ways to coerce a signature out of someone. Trickery is something Banks probably excels at. She probably thought she was signing something else the way a lot of people do when their intended or their spouse asks them to. I've done it, and don't tell me you haven't either. Your wife says, sign the tax form, and you sign it because she's the one who took everything to the accountant, then picked it up because you were too damn busy, and all she wants is the refund, and the sooner the better."

"Then that makes her a lousy lawyer in my opinion," Agent Lawrence said, speaking for the first time.

Sylvia eyed her two weary colleagues, knowing she looked as awful and as tired as they did. The three of them had been wearing the same clothes for almost three days.

The storm had caught them all unawares, and they'd been lucky to secure the suite of rooms, with Lawrence sleeping on the sofa, Mason on a rollaway, the bed falling to her. For that she was grateful.

They'd been sniping at one another for the past twenty-four hours, ever since the call came through alerting them to Banks's arrival at Kennedy Airport and the fact that he had disappeared. Mason punched his fist into the pillow he'd been sleeping on. His face was full of anger. "Tomorrow is Thanksgiving," Mason said. "My wife is going to have a fit when I don't make it home. We have a thirty-pound bird and are expecting twenty-two people."

Sylvia Connors sniffed. "I think your wife and kids will be eating that bird by themselves. There are no open roads. And just to keep the record straight, we have a woman's life at stake here, and showing up for a turkey dinner seems kind of insignificant compared to that. I think Lucy Baker would agree."

Agent Mason had the grace to look embarrassed.

Agent Lawrence frowned as he clicked on his cell phone. "It's dead," he said, disgust ringing in his voice. "And the charger is in the car, probably frozen. Mason's went out last night. How's yours, Connors?"

"The battery is low, but it's still working. If I'm lucky, ten, maybe eight minutes of airtime. For now, we use the hotel phones."

Lawrence walked over to the window. His voice was almost a whisper, when he said, "It looks like the end of the world out there. What's that saying, 'not fit for man or beast'?"

"I assume the beast you're referring to is Leo Banks. No sane person would be out in that . . . that . . . *stuff.* When this case is wrapped up, I'm putting in for a transfer to San Diego. They have almost perfect weather," Mason said.

"Why are you so certain Baker is clean on this deal, Sylvia?" Agent Lawrence asked.

Senior to her two partners, Sylvia locked her gaze on Mason first, then Lawrence. "No cold, hard facts if that's what you mean. I agree that everything points to her as being his partner, but it's more than that. I saw the way her eyes kept going to that pile of wedding invitations. We destroyed her world. We barged in there and ripped it up one side and down the other. She had no clue. And, do you remember Conover telling us she was wearing this sparkler on her ring finger that was as big as a headlight? When we saw her, she wasn't wearing it. That means she took it off because of what she was told about her fiancé. I'll bet you lunch at Burger King that she hasn't put it back on, either. See, that's what you have to understand about women. Unless she can be certain we have the wrong man, unless we can prove without a doubt to her that the guy she was planning on marrying is not a global crook, that ring is never going to see the light of day again.

"In addition, an engagement ring is a commitment. Lucy Baker is no longer committed. The commitment ceased the day Conover and his partner talked to her. Bottom line, she's telling us the truth, and we have to protect her."

Both agents stared at Sylvia, aware of her past record and her climb up the ranks. She had more citations than the two of them put together, and that's why she was the leader of their team. Both men shrugged. It was as much as she was going to get from either one of them.

"Assuming you're right," Mason said

grudgingly, "how the hell did he get here from New York. Everything is shut down tight. Where is he holed up?"

Connors ran her fingers through her thick hair. She realized she needed a haircut. "If I knew that, I'd tell you. I'm assuming a hotel or motel somewhere. There are a hundred or so from Newark down to Edison. The only thing that gives me even the littlest bit of comfort is that Lucy Baker is at Wylie Wilson's house. There's another man there, too, some academic. And, let's not forget the dogs. Dogs are a powerful deterrent to someone with evil intentions."

"We're powerless to do more than we're doing, which is nothing," Lawrence grumbled. "The switchboard here at the hotel is swamped. I've been trying for hours to get an outside line. There's no way to check the hotels and motels. If we knew which hotel or motel he was staying at, we might be able to figure out how he could get to Baker's house from there. We're five to seven miles away. He could be less than a mile away. If he's desperate, he might take a chance on foot. Tell me what you want me to do, Connors, and if I can do it, I will. If you're right, I don't want to see her harmed

or killed. I'd like a notch in my belt by appre-
hending him. Hell, who wouldn't?"

Sylvia Connors looked down at her Fer-
ragamo shoes, then over at the other
agents' feet. Both wore tasseled loafers.
Their clothing was winter clothing but not
blizzard attire. There was nowhere they
could pick up suitable outerwear, not at that
point in time. Three raging cases of pneumonia coming up.

"The weather report said the snow was to
stop around midmorning. I have an idea.
Mason, I want you to go down to the desk,
ask for the manager, tell him when the
snowplow comes through, we want to be
on it. See if you can make arrangements for
the driver to drop us off at a spot where the
Edison plows can pick us up. They have to
pay attention to the request, we're FBI. If
necessary, we'll commandeer the plow."

Lawrence looked across at Sylvia, a new
respect showing in his gaze. "Good idea.
Guess that's why they pay you the big
bucks."

Sylvia Connors snorted. Overworked and
underpaid was more like it. "It's the only
thing I can think of. Just keep trying for outside lines and check the hotels and motels.

Check the ones closest to where Baker lives. Better yet, go down to the manager's office and, unless there is some kind of emergency, take over the phones. I don't think they'll give you any trouble. If they do, come and get me. Since it's my turn at the shower, I'll be doing that while you do what you have to do." *God, I hope there's some hot water,* Sylvia thought as she made her way to the bathroom.

Inside, after she locked the door, she sat down on the edge of the tub and dropped her head into her hands. She was worried witless about Lucy Baker. And, right then, there was nothing she could do about it. Not until the storm abated. She hoped that wouldn't be too late.

She'd tried hard during the initial meetings with the lawyer to be cool and professional, almost to the point of not caring. It was a facade, though, because her stomach had churned, her heart had pounded, and her head throbbed. Because . . . once, light-years ago, she'd been in a similar situation.

During her senior year at Northwestern University, she'd worked at a bank part-time as a teller. Within a month of starting work, she'd met Daniel Westport, a suave, preppy young man going for his master's. So, he'd said. Like everything else he'd told her, it was a lie. His name wasn't even Daniel Westport, and he wasn't a student. The truth was, he'd said a lot of things. Things she'd loved hearing. His only flaw as she saw it back then was his obsession with the banking profession. He'd ply her with wine until her tongue loosened, and she'd answer all his questions without a second thought.

Until the day the bank was robbed while she was working. The three robbers wore ski masks. Everything had been synchronized down to the last sync. They knew where all the security buttons were, knew the backgrounds of the employees, knew where the vault was. In short, they knew everything because she'd told him, albeit unwittingly, never suspecting a thing. What she'd never been able to put behind her was the senseless killing of the guard by the front door, an older man due to retire in less than six months.

Until the police showed up at her apartment and started asking questions, she'd been just like Lucy Baker, she didn't know anything, didn't suspect a thing, never knew her fiancé had a past, or that he'd changed his name. She'd been in love.

She left her job at the bank and started to waitress at a cocktail lounge. The tips were better, and she wasn't home in the evenings. As hard as she tried, she couldn't regain the old feeling she'd had with Daniel. He sensed it, and he also sensed her aversion to being touched by him. She did her best to break it off, even moved from her apartment to one with two other young women.

Daniel had started to stalk her. She bought a gun, enrolled in martial arts classes, but she was still fearful. The day she couldn't take it anymore she went to the police and told them she suspected Daniel was the brains behind the robbery, but that she didn't know if he was the one who killed the guard or not. She didn't stint on what she considered her involvement either.

Two attempts on her life later, she'd cut and run, Daniel on her trail. One of the detectives, a fatherly man, had been watching over her, on his own time, unbeknownst to her until that fateful day. Five more minutes and she would have been dead, a victim of a random shooting. That fatherly detective with honed instincts had fired off a shot and killed Daniel. Now when she thought about it, she didn't know who was more stunned, the detective or herself. She learned later that it was the first time the detective had ever fired his gun. He'd called her girlie when he put his arms around her. Even now, she remembered how he'd trembled and yet he'd tried to calm her down, turning her face away from the man he'd killed who had been intent on ending her life.

Five minutes.

Every year, from that day on, no matter where she was, no matter what she was involved in, she flew back home and took Detective Janson to dinner on December 17.

Not only did she owe her life to Detective Donald Janson, she owed her career to him as well. He was the one who persuaded her to apply to the FBI when she graduated from Northwestern third in her class. Every time there was an award ceremony, he was in the front row, cheering her on. As an orphan, it meant the world to her.

Right that instant, she'd give anything to have enough minutes on her cell phone to call him. She'd tried earlier to get through the switchboard, but was unsuccessful. She just wanted to talk over the case with him, to see if he had any insights she might have missed.

Donald Janson was the one who taught her to go by her gut instincts. That's half of all investigative work. Screw the manual, screw procedure, go with your gut instinct. Later, you can worry about the manual and procedure.

It wasn't that she ignored the manual and procedure. She stayed true, playing by the rules but always with a clear understanding that if her gut instinct reared up, that's what she paid attention to.

It was in high gear now. She knew that Lucy Baker was *that* close to having her life snuffed out.

"Not if I can help it," she muttered as she stepped under the shower. The water wasn't hot, it wasn't warm, but it wasn't freezing cold either. She hoped she could work up a lather with the hotel shampoo.

The only thing that consoled Special Agent Sylvia Connors, even a little bit, as she stood under the shower was, if she couldn't get to Lucy Baker, neither could Leo Banks. "Wherever you are, Leo Banks,

I'm coming after you, so watch out," she murmured to the cool spray beating on her body. "I'll find you, too. You can count on it."

Spiros Andreadis, aka Jonathan St. Clair, aka Leo Banks, prowled through Nellie Ebersole's house searching for clothing. He'd slept for five hours and woke when it was dark. His body ached from head to toe. The medicine cabinet held a variety of headache tablets. He gulped three Advils and washed them down with ice-cold water. He didn't feel one bit better. On top of his aches and pains, he had a thundering headache.

Hoping food would ease the pounding in his head, he rummaged till he found a pound cake in the freezer and a package of freeze-dried coffee. He devoured the whole cake, which he spread with strawberry jam that he found in a kitchen cabinet, and consumed the contents of the four-cup coffeepot. An apple pie was thawing on the kitchen counter. For later.

Nellie Ebersole was a neat, tidy person, he would give her that. Everything appeared to be geometrically aligned. The hall closet held an array of winter clothing, two long coats, three short coats, a lined raincoat, four umbrellas hanging on special hooks. On the floor, next to a rack holding clogs and rubber boots, was a basket that held neatly folded scarves, wool hats, leather gloves, and wool gloves. He could wear the hat and scarf, but the gloves and boots were too small for him. The top shelf held boxes of catalogs for her popcorn ball business. He took a minute to admire the bright colors before he shut the door. He moved on to the guest bedroom and struck pay dirt. The scent of mothballs was strong. It became overpowering when he opened the closet door to see what he surmised was Nellie's deceased husband's clothes. He tried to breathe through his mouth while he rummaged. The man must have been big, tall like himself but with a huge waist. *Okay, that's why leather makers manufactured belts.* Lucky for him Nellie hadn't been able to part with her husband's belongings. Maybe knowing they were there gave her comfort. *Now, where in the hell did that thought come from?* he wondered.

There were shoes, ankle-high boots,

sneakers, sandals, slippers, and a pair of dark green knee-high Wellingtons. He knew just by looking at them that they would fit. He smacked his hands together in glee.

The dresser drawers gave up everything he needed, warm, wool socks, underwear, and tee shirts. One drawer held nothing but thermal underwear. Jonathan's fist shot into the air.

A smaller drawer held a box of cigars and three packs of cigarettes, one pack opened. Obviously, the faceless, nameless Mr. Ebersole had been a smoker. He wondered when the man had died. How stale was the tobacco? Like he cared? When he made his next pot of coffee he'd either smoke the cigarettes or the cigars. Whatever he was in the mood for at the time. Not that that mattered either.

Because he was a thorough person, Jonathan kept opening and closing drawers. He poked and prodded at the deceased man's belongings. He couldn't believe his luck when he moved a thick argyle-patterned sweater to see a gun along with the paperwork that meant Nellie's husband came by the gun legally. A box of clips sat next to the gun. *Everybody has guns these days,* he thought smugly. *What is this world coming to?* The gun felt comfortable in his hand. Familiar and comfortable.

Jonathan kept searching but found nothing else that interested him. He looked around at the house he was inhabiting. It was all so . . . so *middle-class.*

Jonathan took a full minute to wonder if it would bother him to wear a dead man's clothes. He decided it wasn't going to bother him at all, just as it wasn't going to bother him to use the man's gun to kill someone. It wouldn't bother him to use his smokes either.

He continued rummaging through the small house for other things that might benefit him. He walked back down the steps to a small room off the dining room that Nellie obviously used as an office for her popcorn ball business. Everything in the room was neat and tidy, as well as colorful. The deep wine-colored chair was ergonomic as well as comfortable. The file cabinets lining the room were every color of the rainbow. Above the file cabinets hung framed pictures of popcorn balls wrapped in brilliant-colored cellophane. Cheerful, he decided. *Old people must like bright colors.* He himself was a beige/navy blue kind of person. Conservative.

Because he had nothing else to do at the moment, Jonathan riffled through Nellie's files. His eyebrows shot upward a few times when he saw what a lucrative little business the old lady ran from her home. No overhead. She contracted out the making of the popcorn, contracted out the wrapping and shipping, paid Lucy a small salary, and still banked—after taxes—over a hundred thousand a year. He looked at her income tax records and saw that she also collected $1400 a month in social security benefits plus six hundred a month from her husband's pension and another $1600 a month from her own pension fund.

Nellie Ebersole was solvent.

Jonathan was about to pick up the phone to dial Lucy's number when the cell phone in the breast pocket of the pajamas started to vibrate. He opted not to answer it. Instead, he followed through with his intention to dial Lucy's number. He let it ring seven times before he hung up. He then dialed her cell phone number and listened when a metallic voice said the person he was trying to call was either out of roaming range or the phone was turned off. "You can't avoid me forever, darling Lucy," he said softly as he turned on Nellie's computer.

A Mickey Mouse clock on the wall over the computer said it was eight-thirty. No time for fun and games. He had to get down to business. He bustled then, going upstairs to change into Nellie's husband's clothes. He was back downstairs in minutes, fully clothed, and out in the garage.

Goddamn snow! Was it ever going to stop?

Even though he had tucked the heavy corduroy trousers down over the Wellies, he could feel snow inside them. Snow stung and beat at him as he struggled to cross the yard to the house that sat between Nellie's and Lucy's houses. He tried to remember if Lucy had ever told him who lived in the middle house. When he couldn't remember, he decided she had never told him.

As he forced his body to move, he felt like he was swimming against the tide, caught in a pool of Jell-O. His already tired body started to protest again. He was at the edge of Nellie's property. He knew it was the edge because he was prevented from going farther by a chain-link fence as high as his waist. If he wanted to get on the other side of the fence, he had to lean over and fall into the snow. With the height and weight of the snow, it was the same as stepping over a log, or so he thought. He ordered his mind to comply and did his best to step over the fence. He fell facedown, snow going up the arms of the heavy jacket and down under its collar. He was exhausted when he finally managed to get to his feet. He froze in his tracks when he heard fierce barking from the dark house looming ahead of him. He didn't like dogs because he didn't trust them. What he was hearing was a deep, belly bark that made his nerves tingle.

The night was dark, and yet it was light, with the sea of white snow. For a moment he thought that he might be seen if someone looked out through the windows. He retreated and fell back over the fence. *Big mistake.*

Never panic. He needed to keep going, barking dog or not. When it dawned on him that he could barely see the nearest house through the swirling snow, he realized that he couldn't be seen. Why had he panicked?

When no answer surfaced, he went back over the fence and moved on, taking care to stay far enough away from the house so he wouldn't be seen. Now he could hear a chorus of barking dogs. More than one? Two? Maybe three? Would the owner let the dogs outside? Unlikely. He kept going, but he was trembling. He didn't like the feeling. He still kept going.

A long time later, he knew he had crossed the yard and was standing next to Lucy's wooden fence. All he had to do was lean over it, and he would be on the other side. Just like the chain-link fence. He bellied over, picked himself up, and crossed the yard to Lucy's deck. There were no tracks anywhere other than his own. That meant Lucy wasn't home. Sadie, her big dog, would have made a path of some kind. He was looking at virgin snow. He eyed the mountain of snow on top of the hot tub. He struggled with the door, but it was locked. He squinted to see if he could see between the slats of the vertical blinds. The house was pitch-black, with nothing to be seen except the glowing red dot on the alarm system. Wherever Lucy had gone, she'd armed the system before she left. So, he wasn't going to be able to get his hands on her gun. If there was one thing he didn't need right then, it was a nervous female with a gun. The thought infuriated him as he turned around and headed back the way he came.

The trip back was easier because he could walk in his tracks. He could still hear the barking dogs. Plural. Maybe Lucy was in that house. Her and Sadie. She'd said something about watching a neighbor's dog. One dog, not plural. Her dog and the neighbor's dog made for plural. That would certainly account for the loud barking. The really odd thing was, whoever lived in the house hadn't turned on the outside light to see if anything was out there to cause the dogs to bark. Strange.

Numb with cold, Jonathan stood perfectly still to see if any other lights would come on in the house. None did. Maybe whoever was inside *was* hiding. From him. Lucy and the neighbor. It wasn't a far-fetched thought. In fact, it made so much sense he started to tremble again. This time with rage.

Back in Nellie's house, Jonathan shed his wet clothes and boots, leaving a trail as he made his way to the bathroom for a hot shower. He stopped once, half-naked, to pick up his encrypted cell phone. He needed to charge it. Thank God he'd had the presence of mind to stick the small charger in his pocket before he left the Hilton. It still had enough juice to make a few short phone calls. Namely Lucy.

Under the steaming spray, a thought came to Jonathan. It was so simple he didn't know why it took a sojourn in the snow to think of it. Nellie kept files. Nellie, according to what Lucy had told him, was the matriarch of the street. That had to mean she would probably have all the homeowners along with their telephone numbers in a file someplace on her computer. All he had to do was find the file, and he could start calling on the neighbors, asking for Lucy. Damn, maybe he wasn't losing his edge after all. He knew he wouldn't have one bit of trouble accessing Nellie's files since he'd accessed them earlier. Lucy had laughed when she told him how computer illiterate Nellie was. They'd laughed again over Nellie's choice of password, which was popcorn.

Simple minds, simple solutions. He

thought about all the firewalls and security he had on his own system. Understanding high tech was the only way to go, especially in his line of work.

Jonathan padded down to the guest room, stepping over the wet clothes he'd left behind to help himself to more of Mr. Ebersole's warm, dry clothing. As before, the smell of mothballs was overpowering.

Then he was in the kitchen making fresh coffee and heating the apple pie in the microwave oven. He ate all of the pie except for one slice that he saved for later. He carried his third cup of coffee into Nellie's small office. He leaned back on the ergonomic chair, propped his feet up on the desk like he belonged. He fired up one of the cigars he'd confiscated. A cloud of blue-gray smoke sailed upward as he puffed on the cigar to make it draw. It was no Havana, but it would do.

Jonathan puffed contentedly as the tenseness left his body, and he became more relaxed. The Mickey Mouse clock told him it was shortly after ten. The whole night loomed ahead of him.

A half hour later, Jonathan's feet hit the

floor. It was time to meet the neighbors on David Court.

It was so easy it was almost laughable. The file was named simply, Neighborhood. Every person was listed, along with their address and phone number, and cell phone number if they had one. Thoughtful Nellie had even added a brief summary of each person, age and size. He surmised Nellie was a gift giver.

Within seconds, Jonathan whittled the list to Lucy's neighbor. One Wylie Wilson, attorney-at-law. Age thirty-nine, divorced, six-foot-three. Dog's name is Clueless Cooper. A golden Lab. Ninety-five pounds of animal, he read. He copied down the phone number and turned off the computer. Then a terrible thought struck him.

His fingerprints were all over Nellie Ebersole's house.

16

The pier glass said she looked beautiful. More important, she felt beautiful. The women, Nellie, Rachel, Wylie's sisters and mother, oohed and aahed as Nellie positioned the white veil on Lucy's head. The best part was, she felt like a bride. And she would be, in thirty minutes. Maybe thirty-five minutes if the minister was slow. Happiness sparkled in Lucy's eyes as she twirled around one last time for the benefit of everyone.

"Something old, something new, something borrowed, something blue. You have all those things, don't you?" Rachel Muller asked fretfully.

"I have everything, Rachel. A blue garter, my mother's pearl earrings, the diamond pendant, Wylie's wedding gift to me, and I borrowed an ankle bracelet from Wylie's sister. I'm good to go."

Wylie's mother, who wore a perpetual

smile, cupped Lucy's face in both her tiny hands. "I know it's a little early, but I wanted to be the first to welcome you into our family." Her voice dropped to a mere whisper that only Lucy could hear. "My son loves you so much he aches with the feeling. A mother knows these things. Be as good to him as I know he will be to you."

Lucy choked up. Not trusting herself to speak, she bobbed her head up and down. She looked deep into her almost-mother-in-law's eyes. Esther Wilson smiled from ear to ear; so did Lucy. She was going to love belonging to this large, lusty family. She was already friends with the six sisters. She'd never been happier.

"Time to go," Nellie said. "The limo is here. The girls will hold your train until you get down the steps, then we'll pin it up. The judge got here a few minutes ago." The judge Nellie was referring to was Judge Logan Applebaum, and he was giving away the bride. It seemed fitting since Lucy's first job out of law school was clerking for him. Steven was the best man, and Wylie's sister Iris was her maid of honor.

It was going to be a small church wedding at St. Helena's on Grove Avenue, the reception a little larger. Family, neighbors, and a host of good friends. After the ceremony, the bride and groom would come back to the house, as the reception was in the backyard. Wylie had taken the fence down between his house, her house, and Nellie's house to accommodate the tents and assorted tables and chairs. Nellie and Wylie's sisters and mother had prepared all the food. Wylie's father and brothers had seen to the rainbow of flowers that were everywhere. They had also installed a portable dance floor and hired a DJ for later. After the reception, Lucy and Wylie were going to honeymoon in Hawaii for two full weeks.

The ride to the church was short. Lucy had to take deep breaths three different times to calm her jittery nerves. She had one foot out of the limo when she heard the bell. She didn't know they rang the church bells for weddings. How nice, she thought as she made her way across the concrete apron that led to the front door.

Inside, Lucy took a deep breath, the sound of the bells louder there. She reached for the judge's arm and took another deep breath. The moment the organist struck the first chord, she would walk through the door. The bells were louder now. The organist was right on cue. The doors opened just as the bell gave one last, loud peal. She gaped as she stared at the two people blocking the doorway.

Angie Motolo and Jonathan St. Clair!

Lucy woke, struggled with the quilt that was covering her. Half-asleep, her fist lashed out. "Your phone's ringing! How dare you invite Angie Motolo to our wedding! How dare you, Wylie! Didn't you hear me, your phone's ringing."

Wylie struggled to come out of his deep sleep, befuddled at why Lucy was shouting. "What the hell . . ."

"When a phone rings in the middle of the night it's usually bad news. Aren't you going to answer it? We can talk about Angie Motolo later, and don't think for one minute I'm going to forget about it either," Lucy babbled sleepily.

"Huh?" Wylie mumbled and growled under his breath as he struggled to reach the portable phone on the coffee table where he'd left it before they fell asleep. The room was dark except for the red, glowing embers of the dying fire. He groped for the phone in the darkness and finally found it.

Lucy scrunched herself into a tight ball to keep warm. She tried not to listen to Wylie's end of the conversation which was really nothing more than a few grunts of surprise. She was startled when he held out the phone to her. Without thinking, she reached for it, her eyes full of questions. "I think it's the feds," Wylie hissed.

"In the middle of the night?" She knew before she heard the voice on the other end of the phone that it wasn't the federal agents on the other end of the line. "This is Lucy Baker," she said in her sleep-filled voice.

"Darling, how are you? I've been listening and watching the news of your storm. You must be overwhelmed. I had a devil of a time getting through to you. Your home phone and cell don't seem to be working. So, I put my own agile brain to work and asked myself what I would do if I was in your position, and I decided I would probably gather all the neighbors under one roof, pool resources, and food for safety reasons. Tell me I guessed right, darling?"

There was no time for finesse, this was

Jonathan on the phone. In the middle of the night. Raging anger raced through her. "Where are you calling me from, Jonathan? How did you know I was here and where did you get this number?" Wylie bounded up off their nest of quilts. Under other circumstances, Lucy might have laughed. Instead, fire and anger spewed from her eyes.

"I'm in Cairo. I told you where I was going, don't you remember? Even halfway around the world, we still get stateside news. I became so alarmed at the storm news, I started calling the weather bureaus. As I understand it, there is no transportation, there are eight to nine feet of snow up the East Coast, snow is to the rooftops and the National Guard is being called in. The different bureaus used the word *paralyzed* repeatedly. I think that's what scared me. That's why I became so alarmed. Are you sure you're okay?"

"I'm fine, Jonathan. How considerate of you to worry about me. In a few hours I'll be preparing a Thanksgiving dinner with a little help from my neighbors. You didn't tell me how you got this number. It's the middle of the night, Jonathan."

"I called Information, and explained the

reasons I needed everyone's number on the street. The young lady was most helpful. People do tend to pull together when disasters like this occur. You sound terribly grumpy, darling, so I'm going to hang up and let you get back to sleep now that I know you are with friends and neighbors. I just wanted you to know even though I'm half a world away, I'm checking on you because I love you. Take good care of yourself and all your neighbors. I'll see you soon, darling."

"How soon is soon, Jonathan?" Lucy asked flatly.

Lucy heard the chuckle and cringed. "Sooner than you think, my darling. Sweet dreams."

Lucy stared at the pinging phone. She was stunned to see that her hand was steady when she handed the phone back to Wylie. "He said he was in Cairo. He sounded like he was in the next room. He knows I'm here in your house. That call was a warning. He wants me to sweat. I'm telling you, Wylie, he thinks I betrayed him, and he's coming after me. He knows more about this storm than you and I know. He said the National Guard is being called in, and he said we had four or five feet of snow. How in the hell could he know that?"

Wylie shivered as he reached for his clothes. "Look, I don't know about you, but I'm done sleeping for the night. I'll make us some coffee and turn the heat up. I want to hear the news, too. I want you to think about every single word that man said to you and I want you to repeat it. Then we're calling those agents. No more *futzing* around."

Lucy reached for her own clothes and pulled them on. Minutes later, she joined Wylie in the kitchen. The coffee was already dripping into the pot when Wylie held out his arms to her. She stepped into them. He cradled her head against his chest as he stroked her hair. "It's going to be okay, Lucy. There's no way he can get to you. The man is playing with your head."

"He's here, Wylie, I know it. The rest was all lies. I know he's here. The dogs know he's here. I don't know exactly where he is, but he's somewhere close by. And, you're right, he's trying to mess with my head. I'm going to call the agents now. I don't care if I do wake them up. What did I do with that number, do you know?"

Wylie trotted into the den to return with a slip of paper in his hand. Lucy drew a deep breath before she picked up the phone to dial the number from the slip of paper. She was stunned to hear Agent Lawrence say, "Our battery is low, please call the Hyatt in New Brunswick if you want to talk to Agents Lawrence, Connors, or Mason. Ask for extension 1702."

Lucy blinked and held out the phone to Wylie. "The agent said their battery is low. They're at the Hyatt in New Brunswick, extension 1702. Where's your phone book, Wylie?"

Wylie opened one of the kitchen cabinets and pulled out the thick book. Lucy flipped pages until she found the hotel listings. She punched in the numbers and was not surprised to hear a busy signal. She held out the phone so Wylie could hear the busy signal.

"Just keep hitting the redial. Sooner or later you'll get through. I hope," he muttered. "Damn, it's still snowing. It's up past the kitchen window now. I'm starting to feel like I'm sealed in a tomb."

Lucy raked her already messy hair with

her left hand as her right hand kept hitting the redial. "Please don't say that."

"Okay, I won't say that. Let's get the weather." He turned on the television set and sat down with his coffee. He stared at the small screen, his heart pumping furiously. Instead of things getting better, they appeared to be getting worse. Now, the anchor was comparing this storm to the Blizzard of '77, which hit Buffalo, New York, killing twenty-nine people over a three-day period. His heart gave a little jump of fear when the television station started showing footage from that particular storm and making comparisons. "It's the drifts," he said inanely.

Lucy nodded as her thumb kept hitting the redial. "At least they're still saying the snow will stop by midmorning. That's only six or seven hours away. Thank God, your heat is still on. If it goes out, then we will have to burn your furniture. Those starter logs of yours aren't going to help us one little bit."

Wylie stretched out his legs. "If I had my choice of picking someone to be marooned with, I'd pick you, Lucy." He leaned across the table, and whispered, "I guess you know I've fallen in love with you." He waited, not realizing he was holding his breath. Wasn't she going to say anything? Had he just made a fool of himself?

Lucy licked at her dry lips. "I was having this . . . wonderful dream when the phone rang. In my dream I thought the sound was the sound of church bells. I was marrying you in my dream. Nellie and Rachel helped me with my wedding gown. Your mother and your sisters were there. Your mother wanted me to assure her that I would be as good to you as you would be to me. She told me in my dream that you loved me so much you ached with the feeling. She said a mother knows these things. I told her yes, I would be good to you."

Wylie just stared at her.

"Then we went inside the church and the bells were still ringing. When the organist started 'The Wedding March,' the doors opened and . . . and . . ."

"And, what? What, Lucy?"

Lucy doubled over laughing. "There was Angie Motolo and Jonathan blocking my way into the church. I slugged them both!"

"Jesus."

"Yeah. Then I stepped over them," she

fibbed. "Then I woke up. I guess the bell I was hearing in my dream was the phone ringing. Oh, my God, the phone is actually ringing. Extension 1702. This is FBI business, put me through immediately," Lucy said in her best courtroom voice, a voice that clearly said, I'm in charge.

"Special Agent Connors speaking."

"This is Lucy Baker, Special Agent Connors. I'm sorry for calling you at this hour but you did say I could get in touch with you at any hour of the night or day. Jonathan St. Clair just called me. He *said* he was in Cairo, but I think that's a lie. Earlier in the evening, the dogs went wild trying to get outside. I think it's safe to say no animal was lurking out there. Possibly a two-legged animal, but not a four-legged one. Then, a few hours later they were sniffing and snorting again, but they didn't bark and howl. I think he's close by, and the dogs are picking up his scent. I want you to know right now, right up front, that I have a gun."

"Can you see any footprints outside?" Connors asked.

"Visibility is zero. The snow is three-quarters of the way up the sliding doors. We can't see beyond. It's just a wall of snow.

The point I'm trying to make here is, he's playing with my head. He found out I'm here at Wylie Wilson's house. He was warning me that he could get to me."

"That's exactly what he's doing, Miss Baker."

"Is there anything we can do or should do?"

"Not right now. What's the closest motel or hotel to your house?"

"There's nothing that's right around the corner if that's what you mean. The closest would be five miles in any direction. It's a guess, but I don't think it's more than that."

"There are no available vehicles to be found," Connors said, "and the authorities are arresting anyone stupid enough to venture outdoors. We're hoping to commandeer one of the snowplows or possibly a snowmobile as soon as the snow stops. We will do everything in our power to get to you. Sit tight. Is there anything else you want to tell me?"

"Like what, Special Agent Connors?"

"You must be thinking about this nonstop. I'm assuming you've gone over your relationship with this man a thousand different times. Maybe you remember something that didn't seem important to you earlier, but which, when added to the mix, helps to make sense of the whole. Anything like that."

"No. I'd tell you if there was. Are you saying you finally believe me?"

"Miss Baker, I believed you from the beginning. We had to see which way you'd go. Women in love do strange things."

"Well, I'm not in love. With Jonathan," she added hastily when she saw the stricken look on Wiley's face. "Wait a minute. Actually, Special Agent Connors, there is something I think you should know. Hear me out here. That house in Watchung . . . it's stark white and round. It's pretty hard to get past all that whiteness and the roundness. I think all that was deliberate so no one would think about anything other than those two things. I remember looking at the fireplace and thinking how odd it was that it was white. It looked like it had been used, but the more I thought about it, the more I convinced myself it was just scattered ash. There's a trapdoor on the floor that you open and brush the ash through as opposed to shoveling it out. I have the same thing here in my own house. I think that's where Jonathan hid whatever he's hiding. I'm trying to help here. It's up to you to check it out."

"Okay, we'll check it out as soon as we can. In the meantime, we'll do our best to get to you as soon as possible. Don't do anything rash. Just be aware."

"All right. We'll save some dinner for you and your partners."

"That would be nice. The hotel here is just about out of food. We're going to try and get some additional cell phones. I'll call you with the number if we're successful. There is every possibility we'll be cut off from one another for a while. I don't want you to panic."

"I won't panic, Special Agent Connors. I told you, I have a gun, and the dogs. If you can't get here, Jonathan can't get here."

"We'll be in touch, Miss Baker."

Lucy handed Wylie the phone. "You heard my end of the conversation. Their cell phones are dead, but they're going to try to get others. The good news is they're going to commandeer a snowplow as soon as they can. If we're lucky, they might be able to get to us late in the afternoon."

Wylie reached across the table for Lucy's

hand. "It's been a long time since I've been up at this hour. I'm going to be forty in a few months. Those days of partying and staying up late are long gone. Just so you know, I've become a creature of comfort and habit."

Lucy smiled as she scooted her chair closer to Wylie's. "I was never a party person. Maybe I take myself too seriously. At least my brother thinks so. Guess what, it's not a bad thing. At least I don't think it is. Did I tell you in my dream we were going to Hawaii for two weeks on our honeymoon?"

"No kidding! Can we afford Hawaii?"

Lucy giggled. "I didn't get that far in my dream. I guess so." Her voice turned fretful when she said, "Who is going to take care of the dogs?"

"My mom and dad will come and stay at my house. They love Coop, and Mom doesn't mind mixing up meat loaf every day. Not a problem. So, we're getting married. When?"

When indeed. "When I get a new wedding gown. When this thing in my head goes away. When this is all over. I think the big question is where we are going to live. I want to make sure we do it right, Wylie. Do you understand that?"

Wylie squeezed her hand. "Perfectly. In my off moments, I've been thinking of selling my half of the firm to my partner and devoting all my time to my thesis. If I do that, I think I could be done by August or September. That's not too long to wait, is it?"

Lucy looked up at Wylie. She loved this man, really, truly loved him. And yet she'd only known him a short while. She felt like she'd known him forever. She laughed out loud when Wylie said, "I feel like I've known you forever."

"Now who is reading whose mind. I was thinking the exact same thing just this minute. I'm so very happy, Wylie. I don't have the words to tell you. They say everything happens for a reason, and I guess you were the reason. The Jonathan thing. I'm not going to lie to you, I'm petrified at what that man can do. Yet, I'm happy. Explain that please."

Wylie looked befuddled, his hands rubbing at his bristly cheeks and chin. "We were meant for each other. That old shoe and old sock thing my mother always talks about. The whys, the hows, the whats simply don't matter."

Lucy leaned her head on Wylie's shoulder. He put his arm around her. "It's three-thirty in the morning in case you're interested."

Laughter gurgled in Lucy's throat. "I'm not interested. It's nice sitting here with you in the kitchen."

"When I was growing up, our kitchen was always the busiest room in the house. All of us kids did our homework at the kitchen table, and let me tell you, that took some juggling, especially with our milk and homemade cookies. We played board games on the same table. Mom was always cooking or baking. We had a picnic table and benches for a table because there were so many of us. The dog's bed was in the kitchen by the vent. The cat slept next to him. All the neighbor kids, all our friends, hung out at our house. Mom always made everyone feel welcome. She fed all of us and our friends. Stuff cooked in one pot to make it stretch. Was it like that for you?"

Lucy shook her head. "Not in the least. Remember, my parents were lawyers. We had a series of housekeepers. Summers, Steven and I were sent to camp. We had all these after-school activities to keep us busy. There was no time for neighborhood friends or playing outside. My only outlet was the track team. After college I was invited to the Olympic trials, but I had to decline when my mother got sick. I spent two years nursing her. Steven was younger, and we were pretty close. We became really close when we were teens. As to food at mealtime, my parents were rarely home at dinnertime. Usually it was just Steven and me. We used to have a Sunday supper where our parents would ask us for a summary of our week. Then we were dismissed. We weren't a warm and fuzzy family. And, we weren't allowed to have pets. Steven had a goldfish named Burt, but it died, and he never wanted another one. He used to talk to Burt for hours.

"We had to say, yes, ma'am, and yes, sir, to our parents. My parents never called me Lucy, it was always Lucille. Steven is the one who started calling me Lucy."

Wylie digested all this, his heart sad. "Didn't you have aunts and uncles or grandparents to pick up the slack?"

Lucy shook her head. "We did, but they were just like my parents. I wish you could have seen what our Christmases were like. The family came to the house on Christmas Eve, each of them brought us one present. Usually it was something we didn't want, need, or that was either too big or too small. Even as kids we knew they weren't interested in us. The really funny thing is, the wrapping looked like it cost more than the actual present. My mother dressed us up like we were going to be photographed for some magazine ad. We had to stand by the piano no one knew how to play and sing a carol. Steven could never remember the words, so I had to do most of the singing. I hated every minute of it. We didn't get to sit at the table with the grown-ups. We ate in the kitchen with bibs on so we wouldn't mess up our fancy clothes. Then we were dismissed.

"Every damn year, Steven and I would huddle upstairs and stay awake all night to see if, when we were younger, Santa would leave gifts. Then, as we got older, if our parents would leave gifts under this enormous fancy tree."

Wylie sucked in his breath. He hated what he was hearing. Hated that the woman sitting next to him, the woman he loved, had experienced even one moment of childhood angst. His voice was gruff, bordering on harsh. "And did they?"

"There were always presents but never what either one of us wanted or asked for. We were never greedy. We'd each ask for one thing. It never happened. We got books, usually leather-bound classics, scarves, gloves. I think I was thirteen when I found out the housekeeper did the Christmas shopping as well as the wrapping. I almost think that was worse than finding out there was no Santa Claus. After a while, neither of us bothered, and we did our best to sleep through Christmas. Then when we went to college, we didn't bother going home for the holidays. We'd go off together somewhere, just the two of us, and make our own Christmas. Steven is just a year younger than I am, did you know that?"

"Jesus. Well, I knew your brother was younger but I didn't know it was just by a year. That's a good thing, Lucy. You could relate to one another growing up with no distance between you."

Lucy got up and walked over to the coffeepot. She reached for Wylie's cup. "I've been having these chaotic thoughts the past couple of days. I guess that happens when someone is out to harm you, especially when that someone was a person you planned on marrying. You, Wylie, are the only person I ever discussed my life with, aside from Steven. So, as long as I'm telling you all about me, I might as well tell you the rest. My guilt. For years I've said I was okay giving up my dream of going to the Olympics and competing to take care of my mother. After a while, I think I even started to believe it. The truth is, I resented it. I didn't want to do it. In fact, I hated doing it. But a daughter is supposed to do those things, so I did them.

"My mother was incredibly demanding during those two years. She absolutely refused to have a nurse, someone she considered a stranger, taking care of her. She had no idea what a stranger I was to her. She had no idea at all. She wore me down, beat me down, almost to the ground. Steven went off on her once for the way she treated me, and she looked right through him and didn't even respond. He'd come to the house to give me a break for a night out. He was going to sit with her, but she would have none of it. As sick as she was, she ranted and raved. Steven just left the room and closed the door and forcefully pushed me out the door. I went to the park and just sat for hours."

Wylie wanted to stop her, but he knew Lucy had to get it all out. All he could do was listen.

Lucy walked over to the table and set the cup down with a steady hand. She remained standing, her gaze far away as she continued on. "I paid for that little outing. Big-time. That's when I started going to a shrink. Flash forward, he told me it was okay for me not to like my mother. Once I accepted that, I hired a nurse and a relief nurse. I did the things I was supposed to do and no more. When my mother died, I knew in my heart I had done everything humanly possible to make her comfortable. I didn't have to shower her with love because I had no love to give. I didn't grieve, nor did Steven. We were just relieved.

"Do you know what both my parents' goals in life were, Wylie?"

"No, Lucy, what was it?"

"They wanted to be judges. They wanted those black robes. They wanted the bench and the gavel. That's what their whole lives were about. Do you believe that?"

Wylie shrugged. "Is that why you turned down the appointment? Did you consider it sacrilegious or something?"

Lucy looked around, a vague expression on her face. "Or something. Well, that's my story. Pretty sad, huh?"

"Nah. Stuff like that happens more than you know. People have a hard time opening up and spilling their guts. What they don't understand is when they do that, the healing process begins. If you don't get it out, it festers like a boil that needs lancing. I'm proud of you, Lucy. Steven, too, though I don't know him.

"Listen, we're going to have a wonderful life. I promise. We're going to live in a college town that has sidewalks and big, old trees. We'll go to rallies, cheer on the school's team, interact with other professors and teachers. We'll help students get their start. You and I can sit in front of the fire and discuss our days. We can take turns cooking and walking the dogs. We'll rake leaves and burn them, and plant flowers. I love the smell of burning leaves. We'll pick pumpkins and put them on the front steps with candles inside. We used to do that at our house. Kids will drop by for extra help, we'll invite them in, and they'll become our friends and we'll mentor them. We'll have a big open house at Christmas with a grab bag so everyone gets a gift. We'll go out to some field and cut down the biggest tree there is. We'll lug it home on the truck and invite the kids to help decorate. Lots of kids don't go home for the holidays, like you and Steven and a lot of the foreign students. Home and hearth stuff, making a difference. It won't be an exciting roller-coaster kind of life, but it will be filled with love and contentment. That's how I see it anyway. It's what I want. I hope you do, too, Lucy."

"I do. My God, you have no idea how much I want that, crave it. It's what I need. Do you think we'll have fights?"

"Hell yes. Think about how sweet the making up will be."

Lucy laughed. "Do you have any idea how good you are for me? What's that saying, 'you're the wind beneath my wings'? Together we'll soar. So there."

Wylie kissed her, a long, lingering kiss that spoke of endless tomorrows, a kiss that she returned with just as much passion and promise.

"I love you, Lucy Baker," Wylie whispered in her ear.

"I love you, Wylie Wilson," Lucy whispered in return.

17

The three federal agents stared at the television screen in their room, their eyes wary and questioning. It was seven o'clock, and the light outside was blinding. Beyond the window, the world was a sea of white snow. Visibility, according to the commentator, had not improved. Still, they were predicting an end to the snow by midmorning. Just three hours away. Sylvia Connors didn't believe it for a minute. Neither did the others.

"This is only the second storm to be labeled a national disaster." The commentator on the television news station droned on, citing similarities to the first national disaster in Buffalo in 1977. It was obvious the man was tired, he had dark circles under his eyes and was dressed in the same clothing he'd been wearing for the past three days. "The army is being called in to augment the National Guard. Sad to say, ladies and gentlemen, there are going to be a lot of

Thanksgiving tables with empty chairs this year."

The three agents turned away and walked to the window as the anchor rattled on about how the snow, when it was finally removed, would have to be dumped in the Raritan River. A plea, he said, was going out to everyone who owned a snowmobile or four-wheel drive, to stand ready to donate them for rescue efforts. Everyone was urged to stay tuned after still another warning to stay indoors.

Agent Mason started to pace. "That guy used the word *paralyzed* six times in two minutes. How many times has he said twenty-nine people died in 1977? How many times did he say visibility has been zero for the past thirty-six hours, and how many times has he said wind gusts range from thirty to forty to sixty miles an hour at times? A hundred!" he said, answering himself. "How can that guy," he asked, jerking his head in the direction of the television, "possibly know or even estimate the damage at $200 million at this point in time? Sometimes I hate the media. They run with something and don't know when to stop."

"What do you think of Lucy Baker's

phone call in the middle of the night?" Sylvia asked carefully. She was fed up with talking about the snow and the storm.

"Cairo, my ass," Lawrence said succinctly. "We have proof he came into this country with phony papers. The guy is trying to scare her. I'm having some real trouble with the fact that he's even here at all. We never should have lost him. The guy's a pro, which means he's smarter than our guys. Why didn't he just cut his losses and lose himself abroad? What's here that he's risking getting caught?"

Mason nibbled on a hangnail that had been plaguing him for days. His hands were dry and chapped, his cuticles ragged. "The guy fits the profile of a person obsessed with himself. He's cocky and arrogant. He's in danger of losing it all, whatever 'it all' turns out to be. This he knows. He's blaming Lucy Baker for what's going on. So he has to eliminate her so he can go back to his own world. This guy is so arrogant, so self-absorbed, he doesn't think there's a chance in hell he'll get caught. I also think it's safe to say this storm is causing him some fretful moments. How is he going to

get away? The exit is almost more important than the arrival and the mission."

"And . . ." Sylvia said.

Mason threw his hands in the air. "There
is no *and*. That's it."

"Desperate men do desperate things.
He'll find a way. That's the first thing guys
like that plan—not the mission but the escape," Lawrence said. "Look how long it's
taken us to get this far. Three years. Like
you said, the guy's a pro."

"So are we," Sylvia snapped.

"In a fair fight or race, the good guys usually win in the end. Unless the unknown
comes into play. Then the playing field
opens up wide. All you have to do is look
outside. That's the unknown, the unexpected. It works more to his advantage than
ours." Disgust registered on Lawrence's
face. "Damn, I hate snow!"

Sylvia squeezed her eyes shut as she
saw pictures of Lucy Baker, Wylie Wilson,
and their houseguest, dead on the floor in
Wilson's house. The picture was so horrendous, she bolted for the bathroom, but it
didn't erase the vision or the knowledge of
all the other murders Leo Banks had committed. Her shoulders drooped. Lucy and

her friends were sitting ducks, and there was nothing she could do about it. Nothing. She squared her shoulders and walked back into the suite's living room. "How much longer before that snowplow gets here?"

"They said eight o'clock. It was iffy. When it gets here it gets here," Mason snapped irritably. He wasn't looking forward to braving the elements.

"Go back downstairs and see if you can find out anything. Find all three of us some boots and some heavier outerwear. Explain to the manager we'll reimburse everyone when this is over. Tell them to give me an outside line immediately and to keep it open. Don't look at me like that, Mason, do it!" Sylvia said, just as irritably.

When the door closed behind Mason, Sylvia looked over at Lawrence. "What do you think, Tom?"

Lawrence scratched at his head as he shrugged. "I don't know. Everything is getting jerked around by this damn storm. For whatever it's worth, I think he's close by, and I think he's made an attempt already but the storm foiled it. He knows where she is, even if she's with other people, so that makes his job easier. Where he is, I have no idea, but wherever he is, he has access to a phone, and yeah, he's trying to scare her. The guy she's with, Wilson, he's no lightweight either. Those two dogs would make me take a step backward. And, you said, she has a gun. The visiting guy doesn't appear to be any kind of threat, but you never know. You wanna run with this or what?"

Sylvia snorted. "Run where? Lucy said she thinks he's got something hidden under the fireplace. Any ideas?"

Lawrence's face registered despair, as well as disgust. "Nope. None. It's got to be something pretty awesome to warrant the kind of security he has installed there."

Connors's eyes narrowed. "Not so awesome if Wylie Wilson's friends dismantled it. I'm talking about the system, not what's inside."

"I think our pal was just trying to cover himself from the locals. They wouldn't know what to make of it. Goes with the profile. He's cocky, never thinking anyone other than the locals would home in on him. Maybe money, maybe drugs. And, Baker said there was only an SUV in the garage, a car we didn't even have in our inventory.

What happened to the other vehicles? I think people went there and got them, his pals. Do I know why? No, I don't. What other explanation could there be for the other vehicles? One is left for St. Clair himself. Admit it, Connors, we're operating blind here. Half our case is assumptions. The guy is like quicksilver."

A scream ripped from Sylvia Connors's throat. In the blink of an eye, Lawrence had his gun in his hand as he pivoted to the right and to the left. "Jesus Christ, *what?*" he roared.

"Look, it's stopped snowing!"

Lawrence mopped at his forehead as he replaced his gun in his shoulder holster. "Christ, Connors, you almost gave me heart failure."

Connors looked sheepish. "Sorry, Tom. It really has stopped. Look for yourself. In your life, have you ever seen this much snow?"

Lawrence continued to mop at his forehead. "No, and I hope I never have to see this much snow again. Where the hell is Mason?"

As if in answer to his question, Agent Mason opened the door and dragged a hotel dolly into the room. On it were assorted jackets and parkas with hoods, a pile of gloves, scarves, and what looked like a small mountain of boots. "The plow is due in thirty minutes, the outside line is clear, and we owe a fortune for this gear. And, lady and gentleman, it has stopped snowing. They're singing in the bar downstairs. The booze is flowing, and it's all free. They ran out of food late last night, in case anyone is interested. There must be seven hundred people milling about. Everyone who made it on the train this far plus all the regular guests. It's a zoo down there."

Connors listened with half an ear as she dialed Wylie Wilson's house. "Mr. Wilson," she said, when she heard his voice, "this is Special Agent Connors. We're told that a plow should be here in about thirty minutes. That's not carved in stone, however. The good news is it has stopped snowing. I have no idea how long it will take us to get to your house but we wanted to tell you we're on our way. Hold a second, Mr. Wilson.

"Mason, did you get us some cell phones?"

Agent Mason offered up a snappy salute.

"Yes, ma'am, Special Agent Connors, ma'am. I managed to snag three Nokias. They belong to the manager, the assistant manager, and the reservations clerk. They put a sticky on the side with the number on it, and they've been charged, so we're good to go. We either have to return them or pay for them." Mason handed one of the phones to Sylvia.

"Mr. Wilson, write down these cell phone numbers as I read them off to you. Please, repeat them back to me. Good. You'll see us when you see us.

"Then I guess we should avail ourselves of some of this outerwear and head downstairs to wait for the plow. Does anyone know the temperature?"

Mason slipped his arms into a shearling-style jacket. "According to the television in the bar, it's around twenty-seven degrees. That's pretty damn cold if you want my opinion."

"Mine, too," Lawrence and Connors said in unison.

18

Less than three hundred feet from where Jonathan St. Clair sat smoking, Lucy rubbed oil on the capons she was getting ready to put into the oven. She used a heavy hand with the ground pepper.

Thanksgiving.

Lucy was washing her hands in the kitchen sink when she heard the thought. *Crash and burn, baby . . . This is a hiccup . . .* "Wylieeeee!"

It was Jake, his sandy hair standing on end, who responded to her call. "What's wrong? I passed Wylie in the hall upstairs. He was heading for the shower. You're white as this kitchen counter. Did something happen?"

Lucy told him what she'd *heard.* "Do you think that means he's close by, Jake?"

"There's no way of knowing, Lucy," Jake said quietly as he poured himself a cup of coffee. The tests done on people that I read about were all in one location. Same medical building, same house, close proximity, that kind of thing. However, there are documented cases where a subject picked up on things a hundred miles away. I think there are six cases like that. My guess, and that's what it is, a guess, would be he's close."

Lucy's head bobbed up and down. "That's my guess, too. I feel him, Jake. I really do. He's close by. I can't explain how I know, I just know. The agents are on the way. Listen to the news, it's almost scary. No, that's wrong, it *is* scary. I wish there was something I could do, but this storm . . ."

"I hear you. You know, Lucy, I woke around five-thirty. My bed was so warm and toasty I didn't want to get up, so I just lay there thinking. I think my brain was going a mile a minute. I tried to dissect this whole thing, to put it into some kind of chronological order so it would make sense. I kept coming back to the same things every time. What would the man gain by marrying you? Why did he put the house and the brokerage accounts in your name, and why did he buy all that insurance? More important, how did he pull it all off? How did he get around the physical you should have taken for the insurance company? Why did he put that house in Watchung in your name? It's coming up to the first of the year, and in January, people start thinking about filing their income tax statements. How was he going to get away with that? Where do those brokerage statements go? And the paperwork pertaining to the house. I think all that stuff goes to the apartment you said he has in New York. I bet you a dollar he has someone pick up his mail once a week or something like that. Whoever picks it up is probably paid very well and knows how to keep their mouth shut. That person probably mails it to a drop box or someplace out of the country. It's so . . . detailed. Most crooks try to keep things simple, so they don't make mistakes."

Lucy made an unladylike sound in her throat. "It's pretty much like that in the law, too. Keep it simple, stupid. The more you plot, the more you scheme, the greater likelihood you're going to get caught and prosecuted for your efforts because, somewhere along the way, it gets hairy, and you make a mistake. Nothing about Jonathan was simple. He thrives on details. It's like a challenge to him.

"Do you want to know what I think, Jake? I think he was going to marry me and then . . . and then he was going to . . . kill me. Everything would then go to him legally. I also think he has setups like this all around the world. Jonathan is a global person, as the FBI pointed out. That's just another way of saying, he'd scratch me off his list and move on to another part of the world if this end of his venture went awry. He never thought I would find out what was going on."

"What's going on?" Wylie said, entering the kitchen, the dogs trailing behind him.

Lucy looked up at him and smiled. Her heart thumped in her chest at what she was feeling for this man towering over her. He'd shaved and was wearing jeans and a hunter green sweatshirt with DARTMOUTH on the back. Wylie loved collecting sweatshirts from different universities. They were his casual wardrobe, all old, all faded, but comfortable.

"We were discussing Jonathan, but we didn't come up with anything concrete. We're just guessing, at least I am. Gut feelings, that kind of thing. Maybe if and when the agents get here, they'll have some input. He's close by, Wylie. I can *smell* him."

"It's entirely possible," Jake said, "that he actually made it here and is in someone's house holding them hostage. Don't look at me like that. How else do you explain the dogs' strange behavior? He could have been prowling the neighborhood. Hell, you couldn't see your hand in front of your face when it was snowing. He could have tried to get into Lucy's house that first day. Anything, where that man is concerned, is a possibility."

"You two think about it while I get my clothes out of the dryer and take a shower. Wylie, turn the oven on in ten minutes," Lucy instructed.

"Yes, ma'am," Wylie said, saluting smartly before he blew her a smacking kiss that Lucy returned with the same gusto. Jake pretended to be embarrassed, to the delight of both of them.

Under the steaming shower, Lucy's thoughts turned somber. If Jonathan managed somehow to get to her, she'd never know what it would be like to be married to Wylie. She'd never have that little girl and boy, never get to meet his students, never see her brother Steven again. *If.* Like hell.

As the shower rained down on her, Lucy relaxed as she tried to get to that place in her head where she could *hear* a thought. *Lucy to Jonathan, Lucy to Jonathan,* she thought inanely. There was a buzzing sound in her ears and a *thrumming* sound in her head. She stopped rubbing shampoo into her hair and leaned back against the tile shower to take advantage of the moment. Then she *heard* it. *Harvey. Talk about stupid, dumb luck. Damn cold. Just wait it out. No crash and burn for you, buddy. So close. So very close. Return to fight another day. Wait it out. Relax. I'm going to get you, Lucy. I know you know I'm looking for you. I'll find you, too. Spend your days looking over your shoulder. You're the one who is going to crash and burn. Not me, never me.*

And then it was all gone, the buzzing in her ears, the *thrumming* sound inside her head. Gone. Lucy shivered against the cold tile. She immediately scooted under the hot spray and rinsed the shampoo from her hair. Her mind raced as she finished her shower and dressed in the Liz Claiborne plum-colored sweat suit she'd taken from the dryer. Her head was soaking wet, but she didn't bother to use Wylie's blow-dryer. Instead, she ran a brush through her hair, fluffed it with her fingers, and left the bathroom, but not before she hung up her wet towels and gathered up her dirty clothes to throw in Wylie's washer. When this was all over, she was going to burn these sweat suits and buy bright yellow ones. Maybe a pumpkin-colored one, too. She needed color in her life. Rich, vibrant colors.

Downstairs she took a deep breath and held her audience captive as she repeated what she'd *heard* in the shower.

Her voice jittery, Lucy asked, "Do you think it means what I think it means? That wherever he is, he's leaving because he's afraid he's going to get caught. Wasn't there a movie about a rabbit named Harvey or something?"

Both men stared at Lucy as though she'd lost her mind. Wylie shrugged. "What would a rabbit named Harvey have to do with anything?"

Lucy threw her hands in the air as she inched closer to Wylie. "He's leaving wherever he is, but he's coming back to fight another day. He wants me to crash and burn.

Isn't that what pilots say when they fly those super airplanes? Wall Streeters and lawyers have been saying it for years. Jonathan is, among other things, a movie buff. He always prided himself on seeing first-run movies no matter what part of the world he was in. I don't know if it means anything or not. Probably not."

"Where the hell is he?" Jake suddenly boomed. Lucy and Wylie reared backward to gape at him.

Jake cursed under his breath as he waved his empty coffee cup about. "We should have figured this all out by now. Why haven't we?"

"Because Jonathan, or whatever his name is, has had lots of time to plan all this. We just fell into it. He knows what he's doing, and we don't. It's that simple," Wylie said.

"Well, we should know. We aren't stupid, for God's sake. The guy's a scumbag, a con, and he's starting to piss me off. Big-time. Now, let's sit down here and talk."

Jonathan St. Clair looked at his appearance in the foyer mirror. No one would think he was anything other than a shuffling old man who had lost his bearings and was looking for warmth.

Dressed in Nellie's husband's oversize clothing with a little padding here and there really did make him look like an old man. He was also wearing one of Nellie's gray wigs he'd found in a drawer that he'd hacked and cut. He still sported the mustache he'd had earlier. The gray watch cap he pulled on his head held the wig in place, allowing just enough gray hair to show at the sides.

Jonathan felt confident that none of the neighbors who were busy with their snowblowers and shovels would pay any attention to him if he shuffled along with a destination in mind.

His plan was to go to the door, ring the bell, and push his way inside, gun in hand. Whatever happened after that was unknown. Hopefully, he would walk away leaving three dead people and as many dogs behind. He'd then clear the snow off the Rover with the four-wheel drive and capable of getting through this snow that was sitting in the driveway, at which point he'd get in, hot-wire it if he couldn't find the keys, and drive away slick as you please. He wasn't

sure yet about his getaway. He rather
thought he'd make his way to the Metro
Park train station, switch up license plates
from a stranded car or, if the trains were
running, take the next train to New York,
where he could lose himself. He could book
a room in a small hotel, work out a disguise
that would pass muster, and board the first
flight he could get to wherever it was going.
He had enough bogus identities to take him
around the world. He'd made a clean getaway after he killed Adam Ligar, so there
was no reason to think he wouldn't get
away with it this time, too.

Jonathan hated the thought that he had
to cut his losses where the house in
Watchung was concerned. All those beautiful, sparkling diamonds, all those bearer
bonds, all those bars of gold he'd secreted
under the fireplace. Sometimes, you just
had to cut your losses and walk away. He
consoled himself with the fact that he had
other stashes in other places. Still, Lucy had
to pay for this particular loss.

He wondered what she was doing, right
now, this very minute. Was she cooking
Thanksgiving dinner? Was she laughing and
talking with the man she was with, Wylie?

Were they drinking good wine or that swill
Lucy bought in the supermarket? Like he
really cared what she was doing. Just a few
more minutes and everyone in that cracker
box of a house would be toast. Jonathan
opened the garage door and looked around.
He waited a few minutes, his ears tuned
to any kind of activity. Minutes ago he'd
heard a snowblower. Two men and a boy
had been shoveling and shouting to one
another. Now there was only silence. He
moved then, slowly, the rubber boots that
were too big almost coming off his feet in
the deep snow. He used his knees to propel
himself forward just as he heard a garage
door open. Ah, the man with the snowblower was finished and going back into the
garage. From what he could see, he had the
road all to himself. Even so, it was slow going as he made his way to the house next
door.

Wylie was blue with cold when he
stomped his way into the small foyer. He
was also covered with snow. Coop and
Sadie had to be rubbed down with towels.
Both dogs were shaking as Lucy led them

to the fire where Lulu was prancing and yip-
ping her delight that her new best friends
were back in the fold.

"I cleared a narrow path to the road for
the agents if they manage to get here. A few
of your neighbors were doing the same
thing. I'm going upstairs to take a hot
shower! Hey, where's Jake?"

"In the study talking to his wife. Do you
want me to make you a cup of hot tea?"

Wylie, who was halfway up the stairs,
turned and called down, "I'm going to stand
under the shower till it runs cold. Wait till I
come down. Are the dogs okay?"

"They'll be fine as soon as they warm up,"
Lucy shouted, wondering if Wylie heard her.
She shrugged as she made her way to the
kitchen. She looked around. What was she
doing before Wylie came in? Taking the
garbage out to the garage, that's what she
had been doing. She made a mental note to
buy a trash compacter.

The bag was too heavy to carry, so she
dragged it to the garage. The moment she
opened the door she got a whiff of old
garbage. She looked down at the five trash
bags. She knew without a doubt the smell
would invade the house if she didn't remove

it. Since Wylie had shoveled a path to the road she could drag the bags down the path and dump them at the side of the road. If nothing else, the contents would freeze and kill the odor.

Lucy walked back into the house for her parka. First, though, she checked on the dogs. They were all sleeping side by side. Jake was still on the phone, and she could hear the water running upstairs. Wylie was as good as his word, using up all the hot water. She peeked into the oven. Everything was roasting nicely.

Lucy made her way to the garage, where she dragged all of the trash bags to the front door. Before she opened the door she tied the strings to the parka hood, put on boots and mittens. Using her feet she shoved the bags out the door and then closed it. The cold air was sharper than razor wire, the wind and swirling snow almost blinding her as she dragged the bags to the end of the shoveled path. Maybe, she thought, this wasn't such a good idea after all.

Huffing and puffing, Lucy was pushing and sliding the third bag to the end of the shoveled path when she saw the old man who seemed to be waving to her. Who was he? Did he need help? Maybe he was visiting someone on the street? He looked like he was in distress. She shouted, "What's wrong?" just as the man approached the end of the path that Wylie had shoveled.

Two things happened instantaneously. She heard Coop's and Sadie's shrill barks, and she tripped over the garbage bags just as the man's hand reached out to grab her.

The voice was menacing when he said, "Pick up your feet and move, goddammit! Into the house. I have a gun, and I'll use it."

"Jonathan!" Lucy gasped in horror.

"In the flesh! Unless you want to die right here, move!"

Oh, God! Oh, God! Why hadn't she *heard* him? Instead of moving, she took a deep breath and screamed Wylie's name. A second later she felt Jonathan's hand clamp over her mouth. Scared out of her wits at Jonathan's intentions she allowed herself to be dragged up the path to the front door. She could hear Coop body-slamming the door. Where was Wylie? Was Jake still on the phone? The dogs' shrill barking should have alerted both men by now. In her struggle, Lucy looked over her shoulder. She

couldn't see a soul. She knew anyone looking out their window would think the old
man was helping her or vice versa.

They were almost to the door when it
blew open. Wylie in a bathrobe, water dripping from his head and face stood transfixed. Jake appeared out of nowhere.

Jonathan released his hold on Lucy and
pushed her through the door. She literally
slid across the wet tile floor.

Jake bent down to help Lucy to her feet,
never taking his eyes off the man who had
burst through the door. Seeing the gun in
Jonathan's hand, he said, "Whoa! Whoa!
Take it easy."

One hand in Coop's collar, the other in
Sadie's collar, Wylie did his best to restrain
both animals. Lucy knew Wylie was keeping
the dogs from attacking Jonathan who
wouldn't think twice about shooting them.
That left Lulu, who danced and pranced and
yipped but well out of Jonathan's way, the
crazy pink polka-dotted bow jiggling furiously. Jake bent down to pick up the yapping dog. He whispered something to the
quivering little dog and she quieted immediately.

"Back up, all of you. Into the den. That

goes for the dogs, too. If any of you make a move, I'll shoot! Better yet, put those damn dogs in the garage. Do it now!" Jonathan shouted louder than necessary. "The rat goes in there, too," he said, waving the gun in Lulu's direction. He stepped back to make sure neither man nor dog got too close. Then, the gun steady in his hand, he shrugged out of the heavy oversize jacket and let it drop to the floor. The gun never wavered. His stance was steady and firm. Even from where she was standing, Lucy could see how his eyes were glittering. Right then she wanted to kill him with her bare hands.

No one argued with Jonathan's order.

Lucy bit down on her lip as she tried to harness her new ability. Concentrate, she told herself. Shift into neutral. This isn't happening. It's all a bad dream. She heard it then but it wasn't Jonathan. It sounded like . . . it sounded like Agent Connors. *Almost there . . . c'mon, c'mon, move this damn thing . . . the house . . . barking . . .* What did that mean, almost there? Did there mean here? This house? The dogs were barking. Were the agents close enough to hear the dogs? She heard the faint sound of the snowplow then and almost fainted. If so, that meant three agents with guns.

"Don't do it, Wylie! Don't lock the dogs up. Your days, Jonathan, of telling me what to do are over. If you're going to do it, do it *now!*" Lucy snarled, hoping to divert his attention so either Wylie or Jake could tackle him.

Wylie had his hand on the knob of the door to the garage when Lulu leaped out of Jake's arms. The Yorkie was a five-pound dynamo as she flew back to the den and attacked Jonathan from the rear, leaping up to latch on to the back of his pants, which were far too big. Her teeth in the material, she tugged and tugged until his trousers started to slip down toward his knees. Off-balance now, he was taken by surprise and was whirling and twirling trying to shake off the tenacious little dog. Lulu held on for dear life but was losing the polka-dotted bow she was so proud of.

"Get this goddamn dog off me!" Jonathan roared, just as Coop jerked free of Wylie's hold.

One hundred pounds of solid dog moved at the speed of light, but the retriever didn't go for Jonathan's throat; he went to his back and ripped Lulu from her precarious perch. Wylie moved even faster and kicked the gun out of Jonathan's hand. Jake picked it up as the two men squared off, the dogs howling and barking. Both men were at a disadvantage, Wylie in a robe and Jonathan with his sagging trousers. Lucy squeezed her eyes shut, then opened them in time to see Wylie sitting on Jonathan's chest while Jake held the gun pointed directly at Jonathan's head.

Lulu, furious at being left out of all the excitement, marched over to the prone man and bit his ear. Lucy bent down and picked her up. "We have to tie him up. With wire. With something he can't get out of. Let's put him in the garage so he can freeze. Do it quick, Wylie, I can't stand looking at him." She was half-crying, half-sobbing. God, where were those agents?

Jonathan struggled, but Wylie held his position. "You twitch again, you son of a bitch, and you're dead!" Jonathan ignored him as he tried to buck Wylie off his chest. Wylie's clenched fist smashed dead center in his Adam's apple. "The wire's on the shelf in the garage, Lucy. Get it."

"Okay. I see it. There's a whole spool, enough to wrap him up like a mummy."

"Coop, sit on this guy. If he moves, rip out what's left of his throat."

Coop sat.

Five minutes later, Leo Banks, alias Jonathan St. Clair, was trussed and ready to go in the garage. "Wylie, can he talk?" Lucy asked.

"I doubt it. Why?"

"Why? I want to know the why of it all. I deserve to know why he did this to me."

"Because he could, Lucy. The important thing is he didn't get away with it. I crushed his larynx. He should be in a hospital, but we aren't going to worry about that right now. The FBI can deal with him if they ever get here. It's okay, Lucy, we got him. You're never going to have to worry about this guy again." Wylie opened the door and pushed Banks through. Then he took a second strand of wire and looped it through the garage door handle. He looked at the others and grinned. "If he so much as jiggles, he's going to go up and down like a yo-yo." He slammed the door shut and smacked his hands together. "Damn, I do good work! You can put that gun away now, Jake."

"Why didn't I *hear* him, Jake? I *heard* the agents. Why? Do you think it's gone, my talent or whatever we're calling it?"

"I don't know, Lucy, but I seriously doubt it. My guess would be that St. Clair simply wasn't thinking. He was operating by rote if that makes sense. He was simply doing what he thought he had to do and wasn't thinking about it. Time will tell."

"I hate it that *that man* is in your garage. I heard those agents a little while ago. Where are they?"

The doorbell rang at that exact moment. Jake answered it. The agents blew into the house, guns drawn. They looked around, puzzled expressions on their faces. "Thank God you're all right. The damn plow stopped dead at the corner. It took us a good fifteen minutes to trudge our way up here," Agent Connors said. "Listen up, we have a plan."

Lucy started to laugh and couldn't stop. "C'mere, Agent Connors," she said leading the woman to the door leading to the garage. She flipped on the light switch. "Allow me to introduce Leo Banks." Lucy stepped aside so the other two agents could see their quarry. "He's all yours."

Lucy left the men to explain the situation to the FBI agents. She returned to the kitchen and her Thanksgiving dinner. She thought about setting the table in the dining room but decided on the kitchen. For some strange reason people were always more comfortable eating in the kitchen.

As she was stirring the gravy the Chinese fire drill inside her head returned. Lucy stopped what she was doing and turned up the volume on the television set sitting on the counter so the sound would drown out her thoughts.

Suddenly, her kitchen was full of people. Good people, all of them. Dinner was ready to be served but not just yet. She stared at the trio of agents. There had been a point in time when she'd considered them her enemy. Now she viewed them as her saviors. Not that she was discounting Wylie's and Jake's efforts. Three wise men. No, two wise men and one very wise, compassionate woman. She suddenly felt safer than she'd felt in days. "Can I get you some coffee and brandy? You're just in time for dinner. You have no idea, no idea at all of how glad we are to see you."

"Yes, Miss Baker, I'll take a brandy and a

cup of hot coffee," Sylvia said. "I was terribly worried about you three," she said simply. "I'm on duty, but at this point in time I don't much care. I have never been so cold in my whole life. Something smells wonderful. We all have a lot to be thankful for on this day."

Lucy didn't trust herself to speak, so she just nodded.

And then it was time to say grace and get down to the serious business of eating dinner. They all bowed their heads as Lucy said grace. The familiar words warmed her heart. She looked around her table. Everyone was smiling. Really smiling. Her thoughts totally clear, she waited for the bowl of mashed potatoes to be passed to her.

She felt Wiley's knee touch hers under the table. She grinned from ear to ear. *Now,* everything was perfect.

A long time later, a group of new agents appeared via snowplow and carted Leo Banks away. The agents all shook hands. Sylvia Connors wrapped her arms around Lucy and whispered, "The guy's a hunk. Don't you dare let him get away. If you invite me to your wedding, I'll be sure to come."

I knew she was aces. These other

clods . . . just men . . . They don't know the first thing about women . . . I hope she's happy . . . The dogs are super. Makes me want to get one.

So she still had her talent. That was okay. She'd learn to work around it. Lucy nodded at the agent in agreement.

Lucy and Wylie, their arms around each other's waists, stood watching until the agents were down at the end of the street before they closed the door.

"I thought they'd never leave," Wylie said reaching for her.

"Hmmm, let's do what we do best, Wylie."

"And what might that be, Lucy Baker?"

Lucy crooked her finger before she reached for his shirt collar to drag him behind her to the stairs. "You talk too much, Wylie Wilson. Actions are better than words."

"Lucy Baker, you are a woman after my own heart," Wylie bellowed as he galloped up the steps behind her.

Epilogue

Lucy stared at her reflection in the pier glass, remembering the dream she'd had months earlier. She looked like a bride, and she felt like a bride. She crossed her fingers that nothing would go awry, not today or any other day. *Please,* she prayed silently, *let me be happy. Please.*

"You look beautiful, Lucy," Wylie's mother, Esther, said warmly as she kissed her almost-new-daughter-in-law's cheek. She brought her ear closer to Lucy's ear, and whispered, "Please be as good to my son as I know he'll be to you. My son loves you so much he aches with the feeling." Lucy's eyes widened in surprise, and Esther laughed. "Wylie told me about your dream, and he told me to say that to you." She hugged Lucy, careful not to disturb the satin gown or the veil hanging to Lucy's shoulders.

They were every bit as wonderful as Wylie

said they were. The sisters were petite versions of Wylie, each with Wylie's sense of humor. She had loved them on sight. And they seemed to love her in return. She felt a moment of sadness that they would be moving away, but Wylie said one of the advantages of having a large family was that someone was always visiting. The brothers, both tall and good-looking like Wylie, were replicas of his handsome father, which meant she would have beautiful children.

Lucy looked around at Rachel Muller, Nellie, and the other neighbors gathered in her bedroom, along with the female side of Wylie's family. "I wish I had the words to tell you how happy I am."

Wylie's mother laughed. "You don't need any words, dear. It shows on your face. Welcome to the family. I want lots of grandchildren, remember that."

Lucy flushed a rosy red. Then she grinned. "I'll keep it in mind."

"I'm glad you decided on a backyard wedding. The flowers are in bloom, and we decorated everything. It's more intimate if you know what I mean. And the dogs can attend. Wylie took the fences down last week, so we have three yards for the overflow. It's perfect, Lucy, and the weatherman cooperated." Nellie looked at Esther and the sisters, and asked, "We really do have enough food, right?"

"More than enough, and I even made a meat loaf for Coop. All they have to do is say, I do, then we can party up a storm. I heard the DJ warming up a little while ago," Esther said happily.

Steven opened the bedroom door and stared at his sister. "Jeez, you look . . . great! The minister is ready. Wylie's about to collapse, and the guests are assembled, all 150 of them. It's time, Lucy."

Lucy rushed over to her brother. "I'm glad you're giving me away, Steven. I'm glad you're my brother. We need to say nice things to each other more often."

"Okay."

"Your neighbor, Mrs. Henderson, has her little organ all ready to play 'The Wedding March.' You ready, Lucy? Everyone is ready. Can we do it now? I'm nervous, can you tell?"

"I never would have guessed." Lucy smiled as the women moved past her to go downstairs to take their seats. She reached for the basket of flowers that Nellie had arranged from her garden when she looked down to see Lulu decked out in a jeweled collar and matching ribbon in her hair. She tried to claw her way up Lucy's gown. The hell with protocol. She reached down for the little dog and plopped her in the middle of the basket of flowers. "Okay, little brother, I'm ready. Are you sure Wylie is okay?"

"Hell no, he's not okay. He's in a stupor. Coop won't leave his side. Someone tied a blue ribbon around his neck, and he does not like it one little bit."

"Who? The dog or Wylie?"

Steven laughed. "I hear our cue. Just be happy, Lucy. That's all I want for you."

Lulu yipped as Lucy started down the steps and continued to yip right up to the moment the bride took her place in front of the minister, at which point she settled down in the middle of the flower basket and went to sleep.

Lucy looked through her veil at Wylie, her heart swelling with love. This was forever and ever.

Ten minutes later, the minister said, "I now pronounce you husband and wife. You may now kiss the bride!" Wylie obliged with gusto. "I love you, Mrs. Wilson!"

"I love you, Mr. Wilson."

Mrs. Henderson hit the keyboard with the same amount of gusto, and everyone shouted their congratulations as the happy couple made their way outside to mingle with their guests.

"I think everyone is here that we invited," Wylie said happily. "It's nice to have friends like this."

"I didn't see the agents. Did they make it?"

"Yes, Mason and Lawrence brought their wives, and Connors got some tall dude who looks like he climbs mountains for a living. Oh, look, here they come."

Introductions were made, and everyone kissed the bride. The men shook hands.

Sylvia Connors drew Lucy to the side and handed her a small flat gift wrapped in shiny white paper and topped with a huge silver bow. Her eyes sparkled when she said, "I wonder if you'd mind opening this now, Lucy."

Lucy reached for the package, and said, "Is that your guy? He sure is big! Is he the one?"

Special Agent Connors flushed and nodded. "Yes, he's the one. He belongs to our hiking club. His name is Sven. He's Norwegian. Will you hurry up already and open the present."

The shiny white paper and silver bow fell to the ground as Lucy gaped at the picture she was holding. "Oh, my God! Oh, my God! Wylieeee! Look, it's . . . it's Jonathan."

The picture wasn't all that good but the message was clear. Leo Banks wearing handcuffs and a baggy, orange suit glared at the camera at his arraignment.

"One of my colleagues took the picture. I wanted you to start off your new life knowing the man who caused you such grief will be locked up for the rest of his natural life. Have a good life, Lucy."

Tears gathered in Lucy's eyes as she hugged the agent. "Thank you." She handed the picture back to the agent along with the wrapping.

"Not to worry, I bought you some eight-hundred-thread-count sheets. This," she said indicating the picture, "isn't your wedding present." The agent laughed as she walked away with her new beau.

"Wow!" was all Wylie could say.

If I wasn't married, and if Wylie hadn't got-

ten there first, I'd snatch her up in a heart-beat.

Lucy stopped in her tracks and looked around. Jake was grinning from ear to ear. Lucy flushed and winked. Jake laughed out loud, then moved away, his beautiful wife clutching his arm. He knew she'd just read his mind.

"What's so funny?" Wylie asked.

"Nothing. Hey, who's that little cutie over there with the four kids? Is she a relative you forgot to tell me about?"

Wylie looked everywhere but at the cutie and at Lucy. Finally, when Lucy pinched his arm, he said, "Oh . . . she's . . ."

"Angie Motolo?"

"Ah . . . yeah, yeah. My mother said I should invite her."

"I'm glad you did, Wylie. Even if she did break your heart. It mended, and now I have it."

Wylie beamed. "Yeah, my mother said something like that. God, I love you!"

"I love you more!" Lucy said.

"Jeez, our first fight."

Coop reared back and howled. Sadie did the same thing. Lulu leaped out of the flower basket and they raced off.

"There goes our family," Wylie said happily. "Ooops, I forgot to tell you, Lulu is staying with us for the summer. Jake and his wife are going to Denmark for some kind of special something or other. That little girl is ours till they get back."

"Perfect. Just perfect," Lucy said, as she linked arms with her brand-new husband. Stars in their eyes, they strolled off to greet all their guests.

MOTHERLESS BROOKLYN

ALSO BY JONATHAN LETHEM

Girl in Landscape

As She Climbed Across the Table

Gun, with Occasional Music

Amnesia Moon

The Wall of the Sky, the Wall of the Eye (stories)

MOTHERLESS BROOKLYN

JONATHAN LETHEM

DOUBLEDAY
NEW YORK LONDON TORONTO SYDNEY AUCKLAND

PUBLISHED BY DOUBLEDAY
a division of Random House, Inc.
1540 Broadway, New York, New York 10036

DOUBLEDAY and the portrayal of an anchor with a dolphin are
trademarks of Doubleday, a division of Random House, Inc.

This novel is a work of fiction. Names, characters, places, and incidents either are
the product of the author's imagination or are used fictitiously. Any resemblance
to actual persons, living or dead, events, or locales is entirely coincidental.

Book design by Brian Mulligan

Library of Congress Cataloging-in-Publication Data

Lethem, Jonathan.
Motherless Brooklyn / by Jonathan Lethem.
p.   cm.
I. Title.
PS3562.E8544M68   1999
813'.54–dc21   99-18194
                    CIP

ISBN 0-385-49183-2

Printed in the United States of America

October 1999

First Edition

10 9 8 7 6 5 4 3 2 1

For my Father

WALKS INTO

Context is everything. Dress me up and see. I'm a carnival barker, an auctioneer, a downtown performance artist, a speaker in tongues, a senator drunk on filibuster. *I've got Tourette's.* My mouth won't quit, though mostly I whisper or subvocalize like I'm reading aloud, my Adam's apple bobbing, jaw muscle beating like a miniature heart under my cheek, the noise suppressed, the words escaping silently, mere ghosts of themselves, husks empty of breath and tone. (If I were a Dick Tracy villain, I'd have to be Mumbles.) In this diminished form the words rush out of the cornucopia of my brain to course over the surface of the world, tickling reality like fingers on piano keys. Caressing, nudging. They're an invisible army on a peacekeeping mission, a peaceable horde. They mean no harm. They placate, interpret, massage. Everywhere they're smoothing down imperfections, putting hairs in place, putting ducks in a row, replacing divots. Counting and polishing the silver. Patting old ladies gently on the behind, eliciting a giggle. Only—here's the rub—when they find too much perfection, when the surface is already buffed smooth, the ducks already orderly, the old ladies complacent, then my little army rebels, breaks into the stores. Reality needs a prick here and there, the carpet needs a flaw. My words begin plucking at threads nervously, seeking purchase, a weak point, a vulnerable ear. That's when it comes, the urge to shout in the church, the nursery, the crowded movie house. It's an itch at first. Inconsequential. But that itch is soon a torrent behind a straining dam. Noah's flood. That itch is my whole life. Here it comes now. Cover your ears. Build an ark.

"Eat me!" I scream.

*   *   *

"Maufishful," said Gilbert Coney in response to my outburst, not even turning his head. I could barely make out the words—"My mouth is full"—both truthful and a joke, lame. Accustomed to my verbal ticcing, he didn't usually bother to comment. Now he nudged the bag of White Castles in my direction on the car seat, crinkling the paper. "Stuffinyahole."

Coney didn't rate any special consideration from me. "Eatmeeatmeeatme," I shrieked again, letting off more of the pressure in my head. Then I was able to concentrate. I helped myself to one of the tiny burgers. Unwrapping it, I lifted the top of the bun to examine the grid of holes in the patty, the slime of glistening cubed onions. This was another compulsion. I always had to look inside a White Castle, to appreciate the contrast of machine-tooled burger and nubbin of fried goo. Kaos and Control. Then I did more or less as Gilbert had suggested—pushed it into my mouth whole. The ancient slogan *Buy 'em by the sack* humming deep in my head, jaw working to grind the slider into swallowable chunks, I turned back to stare out the window at the house.

Food really mellows me out.

We were putting a stakeout on 109 East Eighty-fourth Street, a lone town house pinned between giant doorman apartment buildings, in and out of the foyers of which bicycle deliverymen with bags of hot Chinese flitted like tired moths in the fading November light. It was dinner hour in Yorktown. Gilbert Coney and I had done our part to join the feast, detouring up into Spanish Harlem for the burgers. There's only one White Castle left in Manhattan, on East 103rd. It's not as good as some of the suburban outlets. You can't watch them prepare your order anymore, and to tell the truth I've begun to wonder if they're microwaving the buns instead of steaming them. Alas. Taking our boodle of thusly compromised sliders and fries back downtown, we double-parked in front of the target address until a spot opened up. It only took a couple of minutes, though by that time the doormen on either side had made us—made us as out-of-place and nosy anyway. We were driving the Lincoln, which didn't have the "T"-series license plates or stickers or anything else to identify it as a Car Service vehicle. And we were large men, me and Gilbert. They probably thought we were cops. It didn't matter. We chowed and watched.

Not that we knew what we were doing there. Minna had sent us without saying why, which was usual enough, even if the address wasn't. Minna Agency errands mostly stuck us in Brooklyn, rarely far from Court Street, in fact. Carroll Gardens and Cobble Hill together made a crisscrossed game board of Frank Minna's alliances and enmities, and me and Gil Coney and the other Agency Men were the markers—like Monopoly pieces, I sometimes thought, tin automobiles or terriers (not top hats, surely)—to be moved around that game board. Here on the Upper East Side we were off our customary map, *Automobile* and *Terrier* in Candyland—or maybe in the study with Colonel Mustard.

"What's that sign?" said Coney. He pointed with his glistening chin at the town house doorway. I looked.

" 'Yorkville Zendo,' " I read off the bronze plaque on the door, and my fevered brain processed the words and settled with interest on the odd one. "Eat me Zendo!" I muttered through clenched teeth.

Gilbert took it, rightly, as my way of puzzling over the unfamiliarity. "Yeah, what's that *Zendo*? What's that?"

"Maybe like Zen," I said.

"I don't know from that."

"Zen like Buddhism," I said. "Zen master, you know."

"Zen master?"

"You know, like kung-fu master."

"Hrrph," said Coney.

And so after this brief turn at investigation we settled back into our complacent chewing. Of course after any talk my brain was busy with at least some low-level version of echolalia salad: *Don't know from Zendo, Ken-like Zung Fu, Feng Shui master, Fungo bastard, Zen masturbation, Eat me!* But it didn't require voicing, not now, not with White Castles to unscrew, inspect and devour. I was on my third. I fit it into my mouth, then glanced up at the doorway of One-oh-nine, jerking my head as if the building had been sneaking up on me. Coney and the other Minna Agency operatives loved doing stakeouts with me, since my compulsiveness forced me to eyeball the site or mark in question every thirty seconds or so, thereby saving them the trouble of swiveling their necks. A similar logic explained my popularity at wiretap parties—give me a key list of trigger words to listen for in a conversation and I'd think about nothing else, nearly jumping out of my clothes at hearing the slightest hint of one, while the same task invariably drew anyone else toward blissful sleep.

While I chewed on number three and monitored the uneventful Yorkville Zendo entrance my hands busily frisked the paper sack of Castles, counting to be sure I had three remaining. We'd purchased a bag of twelve, and not only did Coney know I had to have my six, he also knew he was pleasing me, tickling my Touretter's obsessive-

compulsive instincts, by matching my number with his own. Gilbert
Coney was a big lug with a heart of gold, I guess. Or maybe he was
just trainable. My tics and obsessions kept the other Minna Men
amused, but also wore them out, made them weirdly compliant and
complicit.

A woman turned from the sidewalk onto the stoop of the town
house and went up to the door. Short dark hair, squarish glasses, that
was all I saw before her back was to us. She wore a pea coat. Sworls of
black hair at her neck, under the boyish haircut. Twenty-five maybe,
or maybe eighteen.

"She's going in," said Coney.

"Look, she's got a key," I said.

"What's Frank want us to do?"

"Just watch. Take a note. What time is it?"

Coney crumpled another Castle wrapper and pointed at the glove
compartment. "You take a note. It's six forty-five."

I popped the compartment—the click-release of the plastic latch
was a delicious hollow sound, which I knew I'd want to repeat, at
least approximately—and found the small notebook inside. GIRL, I
wrote, then crossed it out. WOMAN, HAIR, GLASSES, KEY. 6:45. The
notes were to myself, since I only had to be able to report verbally to
Minna. If that. For all we knew, he might want us out here to scare
someone, or to wait for some delivery. I left the notebook beside the
Castles on the seat between us and slapped the compartment door
shut again, then delivered six redundant slaps to the same spot to
ventilate my brain's pressure by reproducing the hollow thump I'd
liked. Six was a lucky number tonight, six burgers, six forty-five. So
six slaps.

*   *   *

For me, counting and touching things and repeating words are all the
same activity. Tourette's is just one big lifetime of tag, really. The

world (or my brain—same thing) appoints me *it*, again and again. So I
tag back.

Can *it* do otherwise? If you've ever been *it* you know the answer.

*   *   *

"Boys" came the voice from the street side of the car, startling me and
and Coney both.

"Frank," I said.

It was Minna. He had his trench-coat collar up against the breeze,
not quite cloaking his unshaven Robert-Ryan-in-*Wild-Bunch* grimace.
He ducked down to the level of my window, as if he didn't want to be
seen from the Yorkville Zendo. Squeaky cabs rocking-horsed past
over the pothole in the street behind him. I rolled down the window,
then reached out compulsively and touched his left shoulder, a regular gesture he'd not bothered to acknowledge for—how long? Say, fifteen years now, since when I'd first begun manifesting the urge as a
thirteen-year-old and reached out for his then twenty-five-year-old
street punk's bomber-jacketed shoulder. Fifteen years of taps and
touches—if Frank Minna were a statue instead of flesh and blood I've
have buffed that spot to a high shine, the way leagues of tourists burnish the noses and toes of bronze martyrs in Italian churches.

"What you doing here?" said Coney. He knew it had to be important to not only get Minna up here, but on his own steam, when he
could have had us swing by to pick him up somewhere. Something
complicated was going on, and—surprise!—we stooges were out of
the loop again.

I whispered inaudibly through narrowed lips, *Stakeout, snakeout,
ambush Zendo.*

The Lords of Snakebush.

"Gimme a smoke," said Minna. Coney leaned over me with a pack
of Malls, one tapped out an inch or so for the boss to pluck. Minna

put it in his mouth and lit it himself, pursing his brow in concentration, sheltering the lighter in the frame of his collar. He drew in, then gusted smoke into our airspace. "Okay, listen," he said, as though we weren't already hanging on his words.

Minna Men to the bone.

"I'm going in," he said, narrowing his eyes at the Zendo. "They'll buzz me. I'll swing the door wide. I want you"—he nodded at Coney—"to grab the door, get inside, just inside, and wait there, at the bottom of the stairs."

"What if they come meet you?" said Coney.

"Worry about that if it happens," said Minna curtly.

"Okay, but what if—"

Minna waved him off before he could finish. Really Coney was groping for comprehension of his role, but it wasn't forthcoming.

"Lionel—" started Minna.

*   *   *

Lionel, my name. Frank and the Minna Men pronounced it to rhyme with *vinyl*. Lionel Essrog. *Line-all.*

Liable Guesscog.

Final Escrow.

Ironic Pissclam.

And so on.

My own name was the original verbal taffy, by now stretched to filament-thin threads that lay all over the floor of my echo-chamber skull. Slack, the flavor all chewed out of it.

*   *   *

"Here." Minna dropped a radio monitor and headphones in my lap, then patted his rib pocket. "I'm wired. I'll be coming over that thing live. Listen close. If I say, uh, 'Not if my life depended on it,' you get out of the car and knock on the door here, Gilbert lets you in, two of you rush upstairs and find me quick, okay?"

Eat me, dickweed was almost dislodged from my mouth in the excitement, but I breathed in sharply and swallowed the words, said nothing instead.

"We're not carrying," said Coney.

"What?" said Minna.

"A piece, I don't have a piece."

"What's with *piece*? Say *gun*, Gilbert."

"No gun, Frank."

"That's what I count on. That's how I sleep at night, you have to know. You with no gun. I wouldn't want you chuckleheads coming up a stairway behind me with a hairpin, with a harmonica, let alone a gun. I've got a gun. You just show up."

"Sorry, Frank."

"With an unlit cigar, with a fucking Buffalo chicken wing."

"Sorry, Frank."

"Just listen. If you hear me say, uh, 'First I gotta use the bathroom,' that means we're coming out. You get Gilbert, get back in the car, get ready to follow. You got it?"

Get, get, get, GOT! said my brain. *Duck, duck, duck, GOOSE!*

"Life depended, rush the Zendo," was what I said aloud. "Use the bathroom, start the car."

"Genius, Freakshow," said Minna. He pinched my cheek, then tossed his cigarette behind him into the street, where it tumbled, sparks scattering. His eyes were far away.

Coney got out of the car, and I scooted over to the driver's seat. Minna thumped the hood once, as if patting a dog on its head after saying *stay*, then slipped past the front bumper, put his finger up to slow Coney, crossed the pavement to the door of One-oh-nine, and hit the doorbell under the Zendo sign. Coney leaned against the car, waiting. I put on the headphones, got a clear sound of Minna's shoe scraping pavement over the wire so I knew it was working. When I looked up I saw the doorman from the big place to the right watching us, but he wasn't doing anything apart from watching.

I heard the buzzer sound, live and over the wire both. Minna went in, sweeping the door wide. Coney skipped over, grabbed the door, and disappeared inside, too.

Footsteps upstairs, no voices yet. Now suddenly I dwelled in two worlds, eyes and quivering body in the driver's seat of the Lincoln, watching from my parking spot the orderly street life of the Upper East Side, dog-walkers, deliverymen, girls and boys dressed as grown-ups in business suits shivering their way into gimmicky bars as the nightlife got under way, while my ears built a soundscape from the indoor echoes of Minna's movement up the stair, still nobody meeting him but he seemed to know where he was, shoe leather chafing on wood, stairs squeaking, then a hesitation, a rustle of clothing perhaps, then two wooden clunks, and the footsteps resumed more quietly. Minna had taken off his shoes.

Ringing the doorbell, then sneaking in? It didn't follow. But what in this sequence did follow? I palmed another Castle out of the paper sack—six burgers to restore order in a senseless world.

"Frank," came a voice over the wire.

"I came," said Minna wearily. *"But I shouldn't have to. You should clear up crap on your end."*

"I appreciate that," went the other voice. *"But things have gotten complicated."*

"They know about the contract for the building," said Minna.

"No, I don't think so." The voice was weirdly calm, placating. Did I recognize it? Perhaps not that so much as the rhythm of Minna's replies—this was someone he knew well, but who?

"Come inside, let's talk," said the voice.

"What about?" said Minna. *"What do we have to talk about?"*

"Listen to yourself, Frank."

"I came here to listen to myself? I can do that at home."

"But do you, in fact?" I could hear a smile in the voice. *"Not as often, or as deeply as you might, I suspect."*

"Where's Ullman?" said Minna. *"You got him here?"*

"Ullman's downtown. You'll go to him."

"Fuck."

"Patience."

"You say patience, I say fuck."

"Characteristic, I suppose."

"Yeah. So let's call the whole thing off."

More muffled footsteps, a door closing. A clunk, possibly a bottle and glass, a poured drink. Wine. I wouldn't have minded a beverage myself. I chewed on a Castle instead and gazed out the windshield, brain going *Characteristic autistic mystic my tic dipstick dickweek* and then I thought to take another note, flipped open the notebook and under WOMAN, HAIR, GLASSES wrote ULLMAN DOWNTOWN, thought Dull Man Out of Town. When I swallowed the burger, my jaw and throat tightened, and I braced for an unavoidable copralalic tic—out loud, though no one was there to hear it. "Eat shit, Bailey!"

Bailey was a name embedded in my Tourette's brain, though I couldn't say why. I'd never known a Bailey. Maybe Bailey was everyman, like George Bailey in *It's a Wonderful Life.* My imaginary listener, he had to bear the brunt of a majority of my solitary swearing—some part of me required a target, apparently. If a Touretter curses in the woods and there's nobody to hear does he make a sound? Bailey seemed to be my solution to that conundrum.

"Your face betrays you, Frank. You'd like to murder someone."

"You'd do fine for a start."

"You shouldn't blame me, Frank, if you've lost control of her."

"It's your fault if she misses her Rama-lama-ding-dong. You're the one who filled her head with that crap."

"Here, try this." (Offering a drink?)

"Not on an empty stomach."

"Alas. I forget how you suffer, Frank."

"Aw, go fuck yourself."

"Eat shit, Bailey!" The tics were always worst when I was nervous, stress kindling my Tourette's. And something in this scenario was making me nervous. The conversation I overheard was too knowing, the references all polished and opaque, as though years of dealings lay underneath every word.

Also, where was the short-dark-haired girl? In the room with Minna and his supercilious conversational partner, silent? Or somewhere else entirely? My inability to visualize the interior space of One-oh-nine was agitating. Was the girl the "she" they were discussing? It seemed unlikely.

And what was *her Rama-lama-ding-dong?* I didn't have the luxury of worrying about it. I pushed away a host of tics and tried not to dwell on things I didn't understand.

I glanced at the door. Presumably Coney was still behind it. I wanted to hear *not if my life depended on it* so we could rush the stairs.

I was startled by a knock on the driver's window. It was the doorman who'd been watching. He gestured for me to roll down the window. I shook my head, he nodded his. Finally I complied, pulling the headphones off one ear so I could listen.

"What?" I said, triply distracted—the power window had seduced my magpie mind and now demanded purposeless raising and lowering. I tried to keep it subtle.

"Your friend, he wants you," said the doorman, gesturing back toward his building.

"What?" This was thoroughly confusing. I craned my neck to see past him, but there was nobody visible in the doorway of his building. Meanwhile, Minna was saying something over the wire. But not *bathroom* or *depended on it.*

"Your friend," the doorman repeated in his clumsy Eastern European accent, maybe Polish or Czech. "He asks for you." He grinned, enjoying my bewilderment. I felt myself knitting my brow exaggeratedly, a tic, and wanted to tell him to wipe the grin off his face: Everything he was seeing was not to his credit.

"What friend?" I said. Minna and Coney were both inside—I would have noticed if the Zendo door had budged.

"He said if you're waiting, he's ready," said the doorman, nodding, gesturing again. "Wants to talk."

Now Minna was saying something about "... *make a mess on the marble floor...*"

"I think you've got the wrong guy," I said to the doorman. *"Dickweed!"* I winced, waved him off, tried to focus on the voices coming over the headphones.

"Hey, hey," the doorman said. He held up his hands. "I'm just bringing you a message, friend."

I zipped down the power window again, finally pried my fingers away. "No problem," I said, and suppressed another *dickweed* into a high, chihuahuaesque barking sound, something like *yipke!* "But I can't leave the car. Tell my *friend* if he wants to talk to come out and talk to me here. Okay, *friend?*" It seemed to me I had too many friends all of a sudden, and I didn't know any of their names. I repeated my impulsive flapping motion with my hand, an expedient tic-and-gesture combo, trying to nudge this buffoon back to his doorway.

"No, no. He said come in."

"... *break an arm...*" I thought I heard Minna say.

"Get his name, then," I said, desperate. "Come back and tell me his name."

"He wants to talk to you."

"Okay, *eatmedoorman,* tell him I'll be right there." I powered up the window in his face. He tapped again, and I ignored him.

"... *first let me use your toilet...*"

I opened the car door and pushed the doorman out of the way, went to the Zendo door and knocked, six times, hard. "Coney," I hissed. "Get out here."

Over the headset I heard Minna shut the bathroom door behind him, begin running water. *"Hope you heard that, Freakshow,"* he whispered into his microphone, addressing me directly. *"We're getting in a car. Don't lose us. Play it cool."*

Coney popped out of the door.

"He's coming out," I said, pulling the headphones down around my neck.

"Okay," said Coney, eyes wide. We were in the thick of the action, for once.

"You drive," I said, touching my fingertip to his nose. He flinched me away like a fly. We hustled into the car, and Coney revved the engine. I threw the bag of cooling Castles and paper wreckage into the backseat. The idiot doorman had vanished into his building. I put him out of my mind for the moment.

We sat facing forward, our car shrouded in its own steam, waiting, vibrating. My brain went *Follow that car! Hollywood star! When you wish upon a cigar!* My jaw worked, chewing the words back down, keeping silent. Gilbert's hands gripped the wheel, mine drummed quietly in my lap, tiny hummingbird motions.

This was what passed for playing it cool around here.

"I don't see him," said Coney.

"Just wait. He'll come out, with some other guys probably." *Probably, gobbledy.* I lifted one of the headphones to my right ear. No voices, nothing but clunking sounds, maybe the stairs.

"What if they get into a car behind us?" said Coney.

"It's a one-way street," I said, annoyed, but glancing backward at this cue to survey the parked cars behind us. "Just let them pass."

"Hey," said Coney.

They'd appeared, slipping out the door and rushing ahead of us on the sidewalk while I'd turned: Minna and another man, a giant in a black coat. The other man was seven feet tall if he was an inch, with shoulders that looked as though football pads or angel wings were hidden under his coat. Or perhaps the petite short-haired girl was curled under there, clutching the tall man's shoulders like a human backpack.

Was this giant the man who'd spoken so insinuatingly? Minna hurried
ahead of the giant, as if he were motivated to give us the slip instead of
dragging his heels to keep us in the game. Why? A gun in his back?
The giant's hands were hidden in his pockets. For some reason I envisioned them gripping loaves of bread or large chunks of salami, snacks
hidden in the coat to feed a giant in winter, comfort food.

Or maybe this fantasy was merely my own self-comfort: a loaf of
bread couldn't be a gun, which allotted Minna the only firearm in the
scenario.

We watched stupidly as they crossed between two parked cars and
slid into the backseat of a black K-car that had rolled up from behind
us in the street, then immediately took off. Overanxious as we were,
Coney and I had at some level timed our reactions to allow for their
starting a parked car, and now they were getting away. "Go!" I said.

Coney swerved to pull the Lincoln out of our spot, batted bumpers,
hard enough to dent. Of course we were locked in. He backed, more gently thumped the rear end, then found an arc sufficient to free us from the
space, but not before a cab had rocketed past us to block the way. The
K-car tucked around the corner up ahead, onto Second Avenue. "Go!"

"Look," said Coney, pointing at the cab. "I'm going. Keep your
eyes up."

"Eyes up?" I said. "Eyes out. *Chin* up." Correcting him was an involuntary response to stress.

"Yeah, that too."

"Eyes open, eyes on the road, ears glued to the radio—" I suddenly
had to list every workable possibility. That was how irritating *eyes up*
had been.

"Yeah, and trap buttoned," said Coney. He got us right on the tail
of the cab, better than nothing since it was moving fast. "What about
gluing your ears to Frank while you're at it?"

I raised the headphones. Nothing but an overlay of traffic sounds
to substitute for the ones I'd blotted out. Coney followed the cab onto
Second Avenue, where the K-car obligingly waited in a thicket of

cabs and other traffic for the light to change. We were back in the game, a notion exhilarating and yet pathetic by definition, since we'd lost them in the space of a block.

We merged left to pull around the first cab and into position behind another in the same lane as the car containing Minna and the giant. I watch the timed stoplights a half mile ahead turn red. Now there, I thought, was a job for someone with obsessive-compulsive symptoms—traffic management. Then our light turned green and we lurched all together, a floating quilt of black- and dun-colored private cars and the bright-orange cabs, through the intersection.

"Get closer," I said, pulling the phones from my ears again. Then an awesome tic wrenched its way out of my chest: *"Eat me Mister Dicky-weed!"*

This got even Gilbert's attention. "Mister Dicky-weed?" As the lights turned green in sequence for us the cabs threaded audaciously back and forth, seeking advantage, but the truth was the lights were timed for twenty-five-mile-an-hour traffic, and there wasn't any advantage to be gained. The still-unseen driver of the K-car was as impatient as a cabbie, and moved up to the front of the pack, but the timed lights kept us all honest, at least until they turned a corner. We remained stuck a car back. This was a chase Coney could handle, so far.

I was another story.

"Sinister mystery weed," I said, trying to find words that would ease the compulsion. It was as if my brain were inspired, trying to generate a really original new tic. Tourette's muse was with me. Rotten timing. Stress generally aggravated tics, but when I was engaged in a task the concentration kept me tic-free. I should have done the driving, I now realized. This chase was all stress and no place for it to go.

"Disturbed visitor week. Sisturbed."

"Yeah, I'm getting a little *sisturbed* myself," said Coney absently as he jockeyed for an open spot in the lane to the right.

"Fister—" I sputtered.

"Spare me," groused Coney as he got us directly behind the K-car at last. I leaned forward to make out what I could of the interior. Three heads. Minna and the giant in the backseat, and a driver. Minna was facing straight ahead, and so was the giant. I picked up the headphones to check, but I'd guessed right: no talk. Somebody knew what they were doing and where they were going, and that somebody wasn't even remotely us.

At Fifty-ninth Street we hit the end of the cycle of green lights, as well as the usual unpleasantness around the entrance to the Queensborough bridge. The pack slowed, resigning itself to the wait through another red. Coney sagged back so we wouldn't be too obvious pulling in behind them for the wait, and another cab slipped in ahead of us. Then the K-car shot off through the fresh red, barely missing the surge of traffic coming across Fifty-eighth.

"Shit!"

"Shit!"

Coney and I both almost bounced out of our skins. We were wedged in, unable to follow and brave the stream of crosstown traffic if we'd wanted to try. It felt like a straitjacket. It felt like our fate overtaking us, Minna's losers, failing him again. Fuckups fucking up because that's what fuckups do. But the K-car hit another mass of vehicular stuff parked in front of the next red and stayed in sight a block ahead. The traffic was broken into chunks. We'd gotten lucky for a minute, but a minute only.

I watched, frantic. Their red, our red, my eyes flicked back and forth. I heard Coney's breath, and my own, like horses at the gate— our adrenalinated bodies imagined they could make up the difference of the block. If we weren't careful, at the sight of the light changing we'd pound our two foreheads through the windshield.

Our red did change, but so did theirs, and, infuriatingly, their vehicular mass surged forward while ours crawled. That mass was our hope— they were at the tail end of theirs, and if it stayed densely enough packed, they wouldn't get too far away. We were almost at the front of ours. I slapped the glove-compartment door six times. Coney accelerated impulsively and tapped the cab in front of us, but not hard. We veered to the side and I saw a silver scrape in the yellow paint of the cab's bumper. "Fuck it, keep going," I said. The cabbie seemed to have the same idea anyway. We all screeched across Fifty-ninth, a madcap rodeo of cabs and cars, racing to defy the immutable law of timed stop-lights. Our bunch splayed and caught up with the rear end of their splaying bunch and the two blended, like video spaceships on some antic screen. The K-car aggressively threaded lanes. We threaded after them, making no attempt to disguise our pursuit now. Blocks flew past.

"Turning!" I shouted. "Get over!" I gripped the door handle as Coney, getting fully into the spirit of things, bent topological probability in mov-ing us across three crowded lanes full of shrieking bald rubber and cring-ing chrome. Now my tics were quieted—stress was one thing, animal fear another. As when an airplane lands shakily, and all on board concen-trate every gram of their will to stabilize the craft, the task of imagining I controlled things I didn't (in this case wheel, traffic, Coney, gravity, fric-tion, etc.), imagining it with every fiber of my being—that was engage-ment enough for me at the moment. My Tourette's was overwhelmed.

"Thirty-sixth," said Coney as we rattled down the side street.

"What's that mean?"

"I dunno. Something."

"Midtown Tunnel. Queens."

There was something comforting about this. The giant and his driver were moving onto our turf, more or less. The boroughs. Not quite Brooklyn, but it would do. We bumped along with the thicken-ing traffic into the two dense lanes of the tunnel, the K-car safely tied up two cars ahead of us, its windows now black and glossy with reflections from the strips of lighting that laced the stained tile artery. I relaxed a bit, quit holding my breath, and squeaked out a teeth-clenched, Joker-grimacing *eat me* just because I could.

"Toll," said Coney.

"What?"

"There's a toll. On the Queens side."

I started digging in my pockets. "How much?"

"Three-fifty, I think."

I'd just put it together, miraculously, three bills, a quarter, a dime and three nickels, when the tunnel finished and the two lanes branched out to meet the six or seven toll booths. I balled the fare and held it out to Coney in a fist. "Don't get stuck behind them," I said. "Get a fast lane. Cut someone off."

"Yeah." Coney squinted through the windshield, trying to work an angle. As he edged to the right the K-car suddenly cut out of the flow, moving to the far left.

We both stared for a moment.

"Whuzzat?" said Coney.

"E-Z Pass," I said. "They've got an E-Z Pass."

The K-car slid into the empty E-Z Pass lane, and right through the booth. Meanwhile Coney had landed us third in line for EXACT CHANGE OR TOKEN.

"Follow them!" I said.

"I'm trying," said Coney, plainly dazed by this turn of events.

"Get over to the left!" I said. "Go through!"

"We don't got an E-Z Pass." Coney grinned painfully, displaying his special talent for rapid reversion to a childlike state.

"I don't care!"

"But we—"

I started to pry at the wheel in Coney's hands, to try and push us to the left, but it was too late by now. The spot before us opened, and Coney eased the car into place, then rolled down his window. I plopped the fare into his open palm, and he passed it over.

Pulling out of the tunnel to the right, we were suddenly in Queens, facing a tangle of indifferent streets: Vernon Boulevard, Jackson Avenue, Fifty-second Avenue. Et cetera.

The K-car was gone.

"Pull over," I said.

Chagrined, Coney parked us on Jackson. It was perfectly dark now, though it was only seven. The lights of the Empire State and the Chrysler loomed across the river. Cars whirred past us out of the tunnel, toward the entrance to the Long Island Expressway, mocking us in their easy purposefulness. With Minna lost, we were nobodies, nowhere.

"*Eatmepass!*" I said.

"They could of just been losing us," said Coney.

"I'd say they were, yes."

"No, listen," he said feebly. "Maybe they turned around and went back to Manhattan. Maybe we could catch them—"

"Shhh." I listened to the earphones. "If Frank sees we're off his tail, he might say something."

But there was nothing to hear. The sounds of driving. Minna and the giant were sitting in perfect silence. Now I couldn't believe that the man in the Zendo was the same as the giant—that garrulous, pretentious voice I'd heard couldn't have shut up this long, it seemed to me. It was surprising enough that Minna wasn't chattering, making fun of something, pointing out landmarks. Was he scared? Afraid to let on he was miked? Did he think we were still with him? Why did he want us with him anyway?

I didn't know anything.

I made six oinking sounds.

We sat waiting.

More.

"*That's the way of a big Polish lug, I guess,*" said Minna. "*Always gotta stay within sniffing distance of a pierogi.*"

Then: "*Urrhhf.*" Like the giant had smashed him in the stomach.

"Where's Polish?" I asked Coney, lifting away one earphone.

"Wha?"

"Where around here's Polish? *Eat me pierogi lug!*"

"I dunno. It's all Polish to me."

"Sunnyside? Woodside? Come on, Gilbert. Work with me. He's somewhere Polish."

"Where'd the Pope visit?" mused Coney. It sounded like the start of a joke, but I knew Coney. He couldn't remember jokes. "That's Polish, right? What's it, uh, Greenpoint?"

"Greenpoint's Brooklyn, Gilbert," I said, before thinking. "We're in Queens." Then we both turned our heads like cartoon mice spotting a cat. The Pulaski Bridge. We were a few yards from the creek separating Queens and Brooklyn, specifically Greenpoint.

It was something to do anyway. "Go," I said.

"Keep listening," said Coney. "We can't just drive around Greenpoint."

We soared across the little bridge, into the mouth of Brooklyn.

"Which way, Lionel?" said Coney, as if he thought Minna were feeding me a constant stream of instructions. I shrugged, palms up toward the roof of the Lincoln. The gesture ticcified instantly, and I repeated it, shrug, palms flapped open, grimace. Coney ignored me, scanning the streets below for a sign of the K-car, driving as slow as he could down the Brooklyn side of the Pulaski's slope.

Then I heard something. Car doors opening, slamming, the scuff of footsteps. Minna and the giant had reached their destination. I froze in mid-tic, concentrating.

"Harry Brainum Jr.," said Minna in his mockingest tone. *"I guess we're gonna stop in for a quick installation, huh?"*

Nothing from the giant. More steps.

Who was Harry Brainum Jr.?

Meanwhile we came off the lit bridge, where the notion of a borough laid out for us, comprehensive, had been briefly indulgeable. Down instead onto McGuinness Boulevard, where at street level the dark industrial buildings were featureless and discouraging. Brooklyn is one big place, and this wasn't our end of it.

"You know—if you can't beat 'em, Brainum, right?" Minna went on in his needling voice. In the background I heard a car horn—they weren't indoors yet. Just standing on the street somewhere, tantalizingly close.

Then I heard a thud, another exhalation. Minna had taken a second blow.

Then Minna again: *"Hey, hey—"* Some kind of struggle I couldn't make out.

"Fucking—" said Minna, and then I heard him get hit again, lose his wind in a long, mournful sigh.

The scary thing about the giant was that he didn't talk, didn't even breathe heavy enough for me to hear.

"Harry Brainum Jr.," I said to Coney. Then, afraid it sounded like a tic to him, I added, "Name mean anything to you, Gilbert?"

"Sorry?" he said slowly.

"Harry Brainum Jr.," I repeated, furious with impatience. There were times when I felt like a bolt of static electricity communing with figures that moved through a sea of molasses.

"Sure," he said, jerking his thumb in the direction of his window. "We just passed it."

"What? Passed what?"

"It's like a tool company or something. Big sign."

My breath caught. Minna was talking to us, guiding us. "Turn around."

"What, back to Queens?"

"No, Brainum, wherever you saw that," I said, wanting to strangle him. Or at least find his fast-forward button and push it. "They're out of the car. Make a U-turn."

"It's just a block or two."

"Well, go, then. *Brain me, Junior!*"

Coney made the turn, and right away there it was. HARRY BRAINUM JR. INC. STEEL SHEETS., in giant circus-poster letters on the brick wall of a two-story plant that took up a whole block of McGuinness, just short of the bridge.

*   *   *

Seeing BRAINUM on the wall set off a whole clown parade of associations. I remembered mishearing *Ringling Bros. Barnum & Bailey Circus* as a child. Barnamum Bailey. Like Osmium, Cardamom, Brainium, Barnamum, Where'smymom: the periodic table of elements, the heavy metals. Barnamum Bailey might also be George and Eat Me Bailey's older brother. Or were they all the same guy? Not now, I begged my Tourette's self. Think about it later.

*   *   *

"Drive around the block," I said to Coney. "He's here somewhere."

"Quit shouting," he said. "I can hear you."

"Shut up so I can hear," I said.

"That's all I said."

"What?" I lifted an earphone.

"That's all I said. Shut up."

"Okay! Shut up! Drive! Eat me!"

"Fucking freakball."

The block behind BRAINUM was dark and seemingly empty. The few parked cars didn't include the K-car. The windowless brick warehouse was laced with fire escapes, wrought-iron cages that ran the length of the second floor and ended in a crumpled, unsafe-looking ladder. On the side street a smallish, graffitied Dumpster was tucked halfway into the shadow of double doorway. The doors behind were strapped with long exterior hinges, like a meat locker. One lid of the Dumpster was shut, the other open to allow some fluorescent bulbs sticking up. Street rubbish packed around the wheels made me think it hadn't moved in a while, so I didn't worry about the doors behind it. The other entrance was a roll-up gate on a truck-size loading dock, right out on the brightly lit boulevard. I figured I would have heard the gate sing if it had been raised.

The four stacks of the Newtown Creek Sewage Treatment Plant towered at the end of the street, underlit like ancient pylons in a gladiator movie. Fly an inflatable pig over and you'd have the sleeve of

Pink Floyd's *Animals* album. Beneath its shadow we crept in the Lincoln around all four corners of the block, seeing nothing.

"Damn it," I said.

"You don't hear him?"

"Street noise. Hey, hit the horn."

"Why?"

"Do it."

I concentrated on the earphones. Coney honked the Lincoln's horn. Sure enough, it came through.

"Stop the car." I was in a panic now. I got out onto the sidewalk, slammed the door. "Circle slow," I said. "Keep an eye on me."

"What's the deal, Lionel?"

"He's here."

I paced the sidewalk, trying to feel the pulse of the blackened building, to take the measure of the desolate block. It was a place made out of leftover chunks of disappointment, unemployment and regret. I didn't want to be here, didn't want Minna to be here. Coney paced me in the Lincoln, staring dumbly out the driver's window. I listened to the phones until I heard the approach of my own steps. My own heart beating made a polyrhythm, almost as loud. Then I found it. Minna's wire had been torn from his shirt and lay tangled in a little heap on the curb of the side street, at the other end of the block from the Dumpster. I picked it up and pushed it into my pants pocket, then ripped the headphones off my neck. Feeling the grimness of the street close around me I began to half-run down the sidewalk toward the Dumpster, though I had to stop once and mimic my own retrieval of the wire: hurriedly kneel at the edge of the sidewalk, grab, stuff, remove phantom headphones, feel a duplicate thrill of panic at the discovery, resume jogging. It was cold now. The wind punched me and my nose oozed in response. I wiped it on my sleeve as I came up to the Dumpster.

"You jerks," Minna moaned from inside.

I touched the rim of the Dumpster and my hand came away wet with blood. I pushed open the second lid, balanced it against the doorway. Minna was curled fetally in the garbage, his arms crossed around his stomach, sleeves covered in red.

"Jesus, Frank."

"Wanna get me out of here?" He coughed, burbled, rolled his eyes at me. "Wanna give me a hand? I mean, no sooner than the muse strikes. Or possibly you ought to get out your brushes and canvas. I've never been in an oil painting."

"Sorry, Frank." I reached in just as Coney came up behind me and looked inside.

"Oh, shit," he said.

"Help me," I said to Coney. Together we pulled Minna up from the bottom of the Dumpster. Minna stayed curled around his wounded middle. We drew him over the lip and held him, together, out on the dark empty sidewalk, cradling him absurdly, our knees buckled toward one another's, our shoulders pitched, like he was a giant baby Jesus in a bloody trench coat and we were each one of the Madonna's tender arms. Minna groaned and chuckled, eyes squeezed shut, as we moved him to the backseat of the Lincoln. His blood made my fingers tacky on the door handle.

"Nearest hospital," I breathed as we got into the front.

"I don't know around here," said Coney, whispering, too.

"Brooklyn Hospital," said Minna from the back, surprisingly loud. "Take the BQE, straight up McGuinness. Brooklyn Hospital's right off DeKalb. You boiled cabbageheads."

We held our breath and stared forward until Coney got us going the right way, then I turned and looked in the back. Minna's eyes were half open and his unshaven chin was wrinkled like he was thinking hard or sulking or trying not to cry. He saw me looking and winked. I barked twice—"yipke, yipke"—and winked back involuntarily.

"Fuck happened, Frank?" said Coney without taking his eyes off the road. We bumped and rattled over the Brooklyn-Queens Express-

way, rottenest surface in the boroughs. Like the G train, the BQE suffered from low self-esteem, never going into citadel Manhattan, never
tasting the glory. And it was choked with forty- or fifty-wheel trucks,
day and night.

"I'm dropping my wallet and watch back here," said Minna, ignoring the question. "And my beeper. Don't want them stolen at the hospital. Remember they're back here."

"Yeah, but what the fuck happened, Frank?"

"Leave you my gun but it's gone," said Minna. I watched him
shuck off the watch, silver smeared with red.

"They took your gun? Frank, what happened?"

"Knife," said Minna. "No biggie."

"You're gonna be all right?" Coney was asking and willing it at
once.

"Oh, yeah. Great."

"Sorry, Frank."

"Who?" I said. "Who did this?"

Minna smiled. "You know what I want out of you, Freakshow? Tell
me a joke. You got one you been saving, you must."

Minna and I had been in a joke-telling contest since I was thirteen
years old, primarily because he liked to see me try to get through
without ticcing. It was rare that I could.

"Let me think," I said.

"It'll hurt him if he laughs," said Coney to me. "Say one he knows
already. Or one that ain't funny."

"Since when do I laugh?" said Minna. "Let him tell it. Couldn't hurt
worse than your driving."

"Okay," I said. "Guy walks into a bar." I was watching blood pool
on the backseat, at the same time trying to keep Minna from tracking
my eyes.

"That's the ticket," rasped Minna. "Best jokes start the same fucking way, don't they, Gilbert? The guy, the bar."

"I guess," said Coney.

"Funny already," said Minna. "We're already in the black here."

"So guy walks into a bar," I said again. "With an octopus. Says to the bartender 'I'll bet a hundred dollars this octopus can play any instrument in the place.'"

"Guy's got an octopus. You like that, Gilbert?"

"Eh."

"So the bartender points at the piano in the corner says, 'Go ahead.' Guy puts the octopus on the piano stool—*Pianoctamus! Pianoctamum Bailey!*— octopus flips up the lid, plays a few scales, then lays out a little étude on the piano."

"Getting fancy," said Minna. "Showing off a little."

I didn't ask him to specify, since if I had he'd surely have said he meant me and the octopus both, for the *étude*.

"So guys says 'Pay up,' bartender says 'Wait a minute,' pulls out a guitar. Guy gives the octopus the guitar, octopus tightens up the E-string, closes its eyes, plays a sweet little fandango on the guitar." Pressure building up, I tagged Coney on the shoulder six times. He ignored me, driving hard, outracing trucks. "Guy says 'Pay up,' bartender says 'Hold on, I think I've got something else around here,' pulls a clarinet out of the back room. Octopus looks the thing over a couple of times, tightens the reed."

"He's milking it," said Minna, again meaning us both.

"Well, the octopus isn't good exactly, but he manages to squeak out a few bars on the clarinet. He isn't going to win any awards, but he plays the thing. *Clarinet Milk! Eat Me!* Guy says 'Pay up,' the bartender says 'Just wait one minute,' goes in the back rummages around finally comes out with a bagpipes. Plops the bagpipes up on the bar. Guy brings the octopus over, plops the octopus up next to the bagpipes. *Octapipes!*" I paused to measure my wits, not wanting to tic out the punch line. Then I started again, afraid of losing the thread, of losing Minna. His eyes kept closing and opening again and I wanted them open. "Octopus looks the bagpipes over, reaches out lifts one pipe lets it drop. Lifts another lets it drop. Backs up, squints at the bagpipes.

Guy gets nervous, comes over to the bar says to the octopus—
Accupush! Reactapus!—says to the octopush, *fuckit,* says *gonnafuckit*—
says 'What's the matter? Can't you play it?' And the octopus says 'Play
it? If I can figure out how to get its pajamas off, I'm gonna fuck it!'"

Minna's eyes had been closed through the windup and he didn't
open them now. "You finished?" he said.

I didn't speak. We circled the ramp off the BQE, onto DeKalb
Avenue.

"Where's the hospital?" said Minna, eyes still shut.

"We're almost there," said Coney.

"I need help," said Minna. "I'm dying back here."

"You're not dying," I said.

"Before we get in the emergency room, you want to tell us who did
this to you, Frank?" said Coney.

Minna didn't say anything.

"They stab you in the gut and throw you in the fucking garbage,
Frank. You wanna tell us who?"

"Go up the ambulance ramp," said Minna. "I need help back here. I
don't wanna wait in some goddamn walk-in emergency room. I need
immediate help."

"We can't drive up the ambulance ramp, Frank."

"What, you think you need an *E-Z Pass,* you stale meat loaf? Do
what I said."

I gritted my teeth while my brain went, *Guy walks into the ambulance ramp stabs you in the goddamn emergency gut says I need an immediate stab in the garbage in the goddamn walk-in ambulance says just a
minute looks in the back says I think I've got a stab in the goddamn walk-in
immediate ambuloaf ambulamp octoloaf oafulope.*

"*Oafulope!*" I screamed, tears in my eyes.

"Yeah," said Minna, and now he laughed, then moaned. "A whole
fucking herd of 'em."

"Someone ought to put you both out of your misery," muttered
Coney as we hit the ambulance ramp behind Brooklyn Hospital,

driving against the DO NOT ENTER signs, wheels squealing around a pitched curve to a spot alongside double swinging doors marked with yellow stencil EMS ONLY. Coney stopped. A Rastafarian in the costume of a private security guard was on us right away, tapping at Coney's window. He had bundled dreadlocks pushing sideways out of his hat, chiba eyes, a stick where a gun should be, and an embroidered patch on his chest indicating his first name, Albert. Like a janitor's uniform, or a mechanic's. The jacket was too big for his broomstick frame.

Coney opened the door instead of rolling down the glass.

"Get this car out of here!" said Albert.

"Take a look in the back," said Coney.

"Don't care, mon. This for ambulances only. Get back in the car."

"Tonight we're an ambulance, Albert," I said. "Get a stretcher for our friend."

Minna looked terrible. Drained, literally, and when we got him out of the car you could see what of. The blood smelled like a thunderstorm coming, like ozone. Two college students dressed as doctors in green outfits with rubber-band sleeves took him away from us just inside the doors and laid him onto a rolling steel cart. Minna's shirt was shreds, his middle a slush of itself, of himself. Coney went out and moved the car to quiet the security guard pulling on his arm while I followed Minna's stretcher inside, against the weak protests of the college students. I moved along keeping my eyes on his face and tapping his shoulder intermittently as though we were standing talking, in the Agency office perhaps, or just strolling down Court Street with two slices of pizza. Once they had Minna parked in a semiprivate zone in the emergency room, the students left me alone and concentrated on getting a line for blood into his arm.

His eyes opened. "Where's Coney?" he said. His voice was like a withered balloon. If you didn't know its shape when it was full of air it wouldn't have sounded like anything at all.

"They might not let him back here," I said. "I'm not supposed to be here myself."

"Huhhr."

"Coney—*Eatme, yipke!*—Coney kind of had a point," I said. "You might want to tell us who, while we're, you know, waiting around here."

The students were working on his middle, peeling away cloth with long scissors. I turned my eyes away.

Minna smiled again. "I've got one for you," he said. I leaned in to hear him. "Thought of it in the car. Octopus and Reactopus are sitting on a bench, a fence. Octopus falls off, who's left?"

"Reactopus," I said softly. "Frank, who did this?"

"You know that Jewish joke you told me? The one about the Jewish lady goes to Tibet, wants to see the High Lama?"

"Sure."

"That's a good one. What's the name of that lama? You know, at the end, the punch line."

"You mean Irving?"

"Yeah, right. Irving." I could barely hear him now. "That's who." His eyes closed.

"You're saying it was someone named—*Dick! Weed!*— Irving who did this to you? Is that the name of the big guy in the car? Irving?"

Minna whispered something that sounded like "remember." The others in the room were making noise, barking out instructions to one another in their smug, technical dialect.

"Remember what?"

No answer.

"The name Irving? Or something else?"

Minna hadn't heard me. A nurse pulled open his mouth and he didn't protest, didn't move at all.

"Excuse me."

It was a doctor. He was short, olive-skinned, stubbled, Indian or Pakistani, I guessed. He looked into my eyes. "You have to go now."

"I can't do that," I said. I reached out and tagged his shoulder.

He didn't flinch. "What's your name?" he asked gently. Now I saw in his worn expression several thousand nights like this one.

"Lionel." I gulped away an impulse to scream my last name.

"Tourette's?"

"Yessrog."

"Lionel, we're going to do some emergency surgery here. You must go wait outside." He nodded his head quickly to point the way. "They'll be needing you to handle some papers for your friend."

I stood stupefied, looking at Minna, wanting to tell him another joke, or hear one of his. *Guy walks into—*

A nurse was fitting a hinged plastic tube, like a giant Pez dispenser, into Minna's mouth.

I walked out the way I'd come in and found the triage nurse. Thinking *arbitrage, sabotage,* I told her I was with Minna and she said she'd already spoken to Coney. She'd call out when she needed us, until then have a seat.

Coney sat crossed-legged and cross-armed with his chin clamped up angrily against the rest of his face, corduroy coat still buttoned, filling half of a kind of love seat with a narrow shelfload of splayed dingy magazines attached to it. I went and filled the other half. The waiting area was jammed with the sort of egalitarian cross-section only genuine misery can provide: Hispanics and blacks and Russians and various indeterminate, red-eyed teenage girls with children you prayed were siblings; junkie veterans petitioning for painkillers they wouldn't get; a tired housewife comforting her brother as he carped in an unceasing stream about his blocked digestion, the bowel movement he hadn't enjoyed for weeks; a terrified lover denied attendance, as I'd been, glaring viciously at the unimpressible triage nurse and the mute doors behind her; others guarded, defiant, daring you to puzzle at their distress, to guess on behalf of whom, themselves or another, they shared with you this miserable portion of their otherwise fine, pure and invulnerable lives.

I sat still for perhaps a minute and a half, tormented images of our chase and the Brainum Building and Minna's wounds strobing in my skull, tics roiling in my throat.

"Walksinto," I shouted.

A few people looked up, confused by my bit of ventriloquism. Had the nurse spoken? Could it have been a last name? Their own, perhaps, mispronounced?

"Don't start now," said Coney under his breath.

"Guywalks, walksinto, guywalksinto," I said back to him helplessly.

"What, you telling a joke now?"

Very much in the grip, I modified the words into a growling sound, along the lines of *"whrywhroffsinko,"*—but the effort resulted in a side-tic: rapid eye blinks.

"Maybe you ought to stand outside, you know, like for a cigarette?" Poor dim Coney was just as much on edge as I was, obviously.

"Walks walks!"

Some stared, others looked away, bored. I'd been identified by the crowd as some sort of patient: spirit or animal possession, verbal epileptic seizure, whatever. I would presumably be given drugs and sent home. I wasn't damaged or ailing enough to be interesting here, only distracting, and slightly reprehensible in a way that made them feel better about their own disorders, so my oddness was quickly and blithely incorporated into the atmosphere.

With one exception: Albert, who'd been nursing a grudge since our jaunt up the ambulance ramp and now stood inside to get away from the cold, perhaps also to keep a bloodshot eye on us. I'd given him his angle, since, unlike the others in the waiting room, he knew I wasn't the patient in my party. He stepped over from where he'd been blowing on his hands and sulking in the doorway and pointed at me. "Yo, mon," he said. "You can't be like that in here."

"Be like what?" I said, twisting my neck and croaking *"Sothis-guysays!"* as an urgent follow-up, voice rising shrilly, like a comedian who can't get his audience's attention.

"Can't be doing *that* shit," he said. "Gotta take it else*where*." He grinned at his own verbal flourish, openly pleased to provide this contrast to my lack of control.

"Mind your own business," said Coney.

"Piece! Of! String!" I said, recalling another joke I hadn't told Minna, also set in a bar. My heart sank. I wanted to barge in and begin reciting it to his doctors, to his white intubed face. *"String! Walks! In!"*

"What's the matter with you, mon?"

"WEDON'TSERVESTRING!"

I was in trouble now. My Tourette's brain had shackled itself to the string joke like an ecological terrorist to a tree-crushing bulldozer. If I didn't find a way out I might download the whole joke one grunted or shrieked syllable after another. Looking for the escape hatch I began counting ceiling tiles and beating a rhythm on my knees as I counted. I saw I'd reattracted the room's collective attention, too. *This guy might be interesting after all.*

Free Human Freakshow.

"He's gotta condition," said Coney to the guard. "So lay off."

"Well, tell the mon he best stand up and walk his condition out of here," said the guard. "Or I be calling in the armada, you understand?"

"You must be mistaken," I said, in a calm voice now. "I'm not a piece of string." The bargain had been struck, at a level beyond my control. The joke would be told. I was only a device for telling it.

"We stand up we're gonna lay a condition on *your* ass, Albert," said Coney. "You unnerstand that?"

Albert didn't speak. The whole room was watching, tuned to Channel Brooklyn.

"You gotta cigarette for us, Albert?" said Coney.

"Can't smoke in here, mon," said Albert softly.

"Now, that's a good, sensible rule," said Coney. " 'Cause you got all these people in here that's concerned about their *health*."

Coney was occasionally a master of the intimidating non sequitur. He certainly had Albert stymied now.

"I'm a *frayed knot*," I whispered. I began to want to grab at the nightstick in Albert's holster—an old, familiar impulse to reach for things dangling from belts, like the bunches of keys worn by the teachers at St. Vincent's Home for Boys. It seemed like a particularly rotten idea right now.

"Afraid of what?" said Albert, confused, though understanding the joke's pun, in a faint way.

"Afrayedknot!" I repeated obligingly, then added, "Eatmestringjoke!" Albert glared, unsure what he'd been called, or how badly to be insulted.

"Mr. Coney," called the triage nurse, breaking the stalemate. Coney and I both stood at once, still pathetically overcompensating for losing Minna in the chase. The short doctor had come out of the private room. He stood behind the triage nurse and nodded us over. As we brushed past Albert I indulged in a brief surreptitious fondling of his nightstick.

Half a fag, that's what Minna used to call me.

"Ah, are either of you a relative of Mr. Minna's?" The doctor's accent rendered this as *misdemeanors.*

"Yes and no," said Coney before I could answer. "We're his immediates, so to speak."

"Ah, I see," said the doctor, though of course he didn't. "Will you step this way with me—" He led us out of the waiting area, to another of the half-secluded rooms like the one where they'd wheeled Minna.

"T'mafrayed," I said under my breath.

"I'm sorry," said the doctor, standing oddly close to us, examining our eyes. "There was little we could do."

"That's okay, then," said Coney, not hearing it right. "I'm sure whatever you can do is fine, since Frank didn't need so much in the first place—"

"T'mafrayedknot." I felt myself nearly choke, not on unspoken words for once but on rising gorge, White Castle–flavored bile. I swallowed it back so hard my ears popped. My whole face felt flushed with a mist of acids.

"Ahem. We were unable to revive misdemeanor."

"Wait a minute," said Coney. "You're saying unable to revive?"

"Yes, that's right. Loss of blood was the cause. I am sorry."

"Unable to revive!" shouted Coney. "He was re*vived* when we brought him in here! What kind of a place is this? He didn't need to be revived, just patched up a little—"

I began to need to touch the doctor, to deliver small taps on either shoulder, in a pattern that was absolutely symmetrical. He stood for it, not pushing me away. I tugged his collar straight, matching the line to his salmon-colored T-shirt underneath, so that the same margin showed at either side of his neck.

Coney stood in deflated silence now, absorbing pain. We all stood waiting until I finally finished tucking and pinching the doctor's collar into place.

"Sometimes there is nothing we can do," said the doctor, eyes flicking to the floor now.

"Let me see him," said Coney.

"That isn't possible—"

"This place is full of crap," said Coney. "Let me see him."

"There is a question of evidence," said the doctor wearily. "I'm sure you understand. The examiners will also wish to speak with you."

I'd already seen police passing through from the hospital coffee shop, into some part of the emergency room. Whether those particular police were there to detain us or not, it was clear the law wouldn't be long in arriving.

"We ought to go, Gilbert," I told Coney. "Probably we ought to go right now."

Coney was inert.

"Problyreallyoughttogo," I said semicompulsively, panic rising through my sorrow.

"You misunderstand," said the doctor. "We'll ask you to wait, please. This man will show you where to go—" He nodded at something behind us. I whipped around, my lizard instincts shocked at having allowed someone to sneak up on me.

It was Albert. The Thin Rastafarian Line between us and departure.

His appearance seemed to trigger comprehension in Coney: The security guard was a cartoon reminder of the real existence of police.

"Outta the way," said Coney.

"We don't serve string!" I explained.

Albert didn't look any more convinced of his official status than we were. At moments like this I was reminded of the figure we Minna Men cut, oversize, undereducated, vibrant with hostility even with tear streaks all over our beefy faces. And me with my utterances, lunges, and taps, my symptoms, those extra factors Minna adored throwing into the mix.

Frank Minna, unrevived, empty of blood in the next room.

Albert held his palms open, his body more or less pleading as he said, "You better wait, mon."

"Nah," said Coney. "Maybe another time." Coney and I both leaned in Albert's direction, really only shifting our weight, and he jumped backward, spreading his hands over the spot he'd vacated as if to say *It was someone else standing there just now, not I.*

"But this is a thing upon which we must insist," said the doctor.

"You really don't wanna insist," said Coney, turning on him furiously. "You ain't got the insistence required, you know what I mean?"

"I'm not sure I do," said the doctor quietly.

"Well, just chew it over," said Coney. "There's no big hurry. C'mon, Lionel."

MOTHERLESS BROOKLYN

I grew up in the library of St. Vincent's Home for Boys, in the part of downtown Brooklyn no developer yet wishes to claim for some upscale, renovated neighborhood; not quite Brooklyn Heights, nor Cobble Hill, not even Boerum Hill. The Home is essentially set on the off-ramp to the Brooklyn Bridge, but out of sight of Manhattan or the bridge itself, on eight lanes of traffic lined with faceless, monolithic civil courts, which, gray and distant though they seemed, some of us Boys had seen the insides of, by Brooklyn's central sorting annex for the post office, a building that hummed and blinked all through the night, its gates groaning open to admit trucks bearing mountains of those mysterious items called letters, by the Burton Trade School for Automechanics, where hardened students attempting to set their lives dully straight spilled out twice a day for sandwich-and-beer breaks, overwhelming the cramped bodega next door, intimidating passersby and thrilling us Boys in their morose thuggish glory, by a desolate strip of park benches beneath a granite bust of Lafayette, indicating his point of entry into the Battle of Brooklyn, by a car lot surrounded by a high fence topped with wide curls of barbed wire and wind-whipped fluorescent flags, and by a redbrick Quaker Meetinghouse that had presumably been there when the rest was farmland. In short, this jumble of stuff at the clotted entrance to the ancient, battered borough was officially Nowhere, a place strenuously ignored in passing through to Somewhere Else. Until rescued by Frank Minna I lived, as I said, in the library.

*   *   *

I set out to read every book in that tomblike library, every miserable dead donation ever indexed and forgotten there—a mark of my profound fear and boredom at St. Vincent's and as well an early sign of my Tourettic compulsions for counting, processing, and inspection. Huddled there in the windowsill, turning dry pages and watching dust motes pinball through beams of sunlight, I sought signs of my odd dawning self in Theodore Dreiser, Kenneth Roberts, J. B. Priestley, and back issues of *Popular Mechanics* and failed, couldn't find the language of myself, as I failed to in watching television, those endless reruns of *Bewitched* and *I Dream of Jeannie* and *I Love Lucy* and *Gilligan* and *Brady Bunch* by which we nerdish unathletic Boys pounded our way through countless afternoons, leaning in close to the screen to study the antics of the women—women! exotic as letters, as phone calls, as forests, all things we orphans were denied—and the coping of their husbands, but I didn't find myself there, Desi Arnaz and Dick York and Larry Hagman, those harried earthbound astronauts, weren't showing me what I needed to see, weren't helping me find the language. I was closer on Saturday mornings, Daffy Duck especially gave me something, if I could bear to imagine growing up a dynamited, beak-shattered duck. Art Carney on *The Honeymooners* gave me something too, something in the way he jerked his neck, when we were allowed to stay up late enough to see him. But it was Minna who brought me the language, Minna and Court Street that let me speak.

*   *   *

We four were selected that day because we were four of the five white boys at St. Vincent's, and the fifth was Steven Grossman, fat as his name. If Steven had been thinner, Mr. Kassel would have left me in the stacks. As it was I was undersold goods, a twitcher and nose-picker retrieved from the library instead of the schoolyard, probably a retard of some type, certainly a regrettable, inferior offering. Mr. Kassel was a teacher at St. Vincent's who knew Frank Minna from the neighborhood, and his invitation to Minna to borrow us for the afternoon was a first glimpse of the glittering halo of favors and favoritism that extended around Minna—"knowing somebody" as a life condition. Minna was our exact reverse, we who knew no one and benefited nothing from it when we did.

Minna had asked for white boys to suit his clients' presumed prejudice—and his own certain ones. Perhaps Minna already had his fantasy of reclamation in mind, too. I can't know. He certainly didn't show it in the way he treated us that first day, a sweltering August weekday afternoon after classes, streets like black chewing gum, slow-creeping cars like badly projected science-class slides in the haze, as he opened the rear of his dented, graffitied van, about the size of those midnight mail trucks, and told us to get inside, then slammed and padlocked the doors without explanation, without asking our names. We four gaped at one another, giddy and astonished at this escape from our doldrums, not knowing what it meant, not really needing to know. The others, Tony, Gilbert and Danny, were willing to be grouped with me, to pretend I fit with them, if that was what it took to be plucked up by the outside world and seated in the dark on a dirty steel truck bed vibrating its way to somewhere that wasn't St. Vincent's. Of course I was vibrating too, vibrating before Minna rounded us up, vibrating inside always and straining to keep it from showing. I didn't kiss the other three boys, but I wanted to. Instead I made a kissing, chirping sound, like a bird's peep, over and over: "Chrip, chrip, chrip."

*   *   *

Tony told me to shut the fuck up, but his heart wasn't in it, not this day, in the midst of life's unfolding mystery. For Tony, especially, this was his destiny coming to find him. He saw more in Minna from the first because he'd prepared himself to see it. Tony Vermonte was famous at St. Vincent's for the confidence he exuded, confidence that a mistake had been made, that he didn't belong in the Home. He was Italian, better than the rest of us, who didn't know what we were (what's an Essrog?). His father was either a mobster or a cop—Tony saw no contradiction in this, so we didn't either. The Italians would return for him, in one guise or another, and that was what he'd taken Minna for.

Tony was famous for other things as well. He was older than the rest of us there in Minna's truck, fifteen to my and Gilbert's thirteen and Danny Fantl's fourteen (older St. Vincent's Boys attended high school elsewhere, and were rarely seen, but Tony had contrived to be left back), an age that made him infinitely dashing and worldly, even if he hadn't also lived outside the Home for a time and then come back. As it was, Tony was our God of Experience, all cigarettes and implication. Two years before, a Quaker family, attendees of the Meeting across the street, had taken Tony in, intending to give him a permanent home. He'd announced his contempt for them even as he packed his clothes. They weren't Italian. Still, he lived with them for a few months, perhaps happily, though he wouldn't have said so. They installed him at Brooklyn Friends, a private school only a few blocks away, and on his way home most afternoons he'd come and hang on the St. Vincent's fence and tell stories of the private-school girls he'd felt up and sometimes penetrated, the faggy private-school boys who swam and played soccer but were easily humiliated at basketball, not otherwise Tony's specialty. Then one day his foster parents found prodigious black-haired Tony in bed with one girl too many: their own sixteen-year-old daughter. Or so the story went; there was only one source. Anyway, he was reinstalled at St. Vincent's the next day, where he fell easily into his old routine of beating up and befriending me and Steven Grossman each on alternating days, so that we were never in favor simultaneously and could trust one another as little as we trusted Tony.

Tony was our Sneering Star, and certainly the one of us who caught Minna's attention soonest, the one that fired our future boss's imagination, made him envision the future Minna Men inside us, aching to be cultivated. Perhaps Tony, with his will for his Italian res-cue, even collaborated in the vision that became The Minna Agency, the strength of his yearning prompting Minna to certain aspirations, to the notion of having Men to command in the first place.

*   *   *

Minna was barely a man then himself, of course, though he seemed one to us. He was twenty-five that summer, gangly except for a tiny potbelly in his pocket-T, and still devoted to combing his hair into a smooth pompadour, a Carroll Gardens hairstyle that stood com-pletely outside that year of 1979, projecting instead from some mias-mic Frank Sinatra moment that extended like a bead of amber or a cinematographer's filter to enclose Frank Minna and everything that mattered to him.

*   *   *

Besides me and Tony in the back of Minna's van there was Gilbert Coney and Danny Fantl. Gilbert then was Tony's right hand, a stocky, sullen boy just passing for tough—he would have beamed at you for calling him a thug. Gilbert was awfully tough on Steven Grossman, whose fatness, I suspect, provided an uncomfortable mirror, but he was tolerant of me. We even had a couple of odd secrets. On a Home for Boys visit to the Museum of Natural History in Manhattan, two years before, Gilbert and I had split from the group and without discussion returned to a room dominated by a enormous plastic blue whale suspended from the ceiling, which had been the focus of the official visit. But underneath the whale was a double gallery of murky, mysterious dioramas of undersea life, lit and arranged so you had to press close to the glass to find the wonders tucked deep in the corners. In one a sperm whale fought a giant squid. In another a killer whale pierced a floor of ice. Gilbert and I wandered hypnotized from window to window. When a class of third- or fourth-graders were led away we found we had the giant hall to ourselves, and that even when we spoke our voices were smothered by the unearthly quiet of the museum. Gilbert showed me his discovery: A munchkin-size brass door beside the penguin diorama had been left unlocked. When he opened it we saw that it led both behind and into the penguin scene.

"Get in, Essrog," said Gilbert.

If I'd not wanted to it would have been bullying, but I wanted to desperately. Every minute the hall remained empty was precious. The lip of the doorway was knee-high. I clambered in and opened the flap in the ocean-blue-painted boards that made the side wall of the diorama, then slipped into the picture. The ocean floor was a long, smooth bowl of painted plaster, and I scooted down the grade on my bended knees, looking out at a flabbergasted Gilbert on the other side of the glass. Swimming penguins were mounted on rods extending straight from the far wall, and others were suspended in the plastic waves of ocean surface that now made up a low ceiling over my head. I caressed the nearest penguin, one mounted low, shown diving in pursuit of a delectable fish, patted its head, stroked its gullet as though helping it swallow a dry pill. Gilbert guffawed, thinking I was performing comedy for him, when in fact I'd been overwhelmed by a tender, touchy impulse toward the stiff, poignant penguin. Now it became imperative that I touch *all* the penguins, all I could, anyway—some were inaccessible to me, on the other side of the barrier of the ocean's surface, standing on ice floes. Shuffling on my knees I made the rounds, affectionately tagging each swimming bird before I made my escape back through the brass door. Gilbert was impressed, I could tell. I was now a kid who'd do anything, do crazy things. He was right and wrong, of course—once I'd touched the first penguin I had no choice.

Somehow this led to a series of confidences. I was crazy but also malleable, easily intimidated, which made me Gilbert's idea of a safe repository for what he regarded as his crazy feelings. Gilbert was a precocious masturbator, and looking for some triangulation between his own experiments and generic schoolyard lore. Did I do it? How often? One hand or two, held this way, or this? Close my eyes? Ever want to rub up against the mattress? I took his inquiries seriously, but I didn't really have the information he needed, not yet. My stupidity made Gilbert grouchy at first, and so he'd spend a week or two both pretending he hadn't spoken, didn't even know me, and glowering to let me know what galactic measures of pain awaited if I ratted him out. Then he'd suddenly come back, more urgent than ever. Try it, he'd say. It's not so hard. I'll watch and tell you if you do it wrong. I obeyed, as I had in the museum, but the results weren't as good. I couldn't yet treat myself with the tenderness I'd lavished on the penguins, at least not in front of Gilbert (though in fact he'd triggered my own private explorations, which were soon quite consuming). Gilbert became grouchy again, and prohibitively intimidating, and after two or three go-arounds the subject was permanently dropped. Still, the legacy of disclosure remained with us, a ghostly bond.

*   *   *

The last boy in Minna's van, Danny Fantl, was a ringer. He only looked white. Danny had assimilated to the majority population at St. Vincent's happily, effortlessly, down to his bones. In his way he commanded as much respect as Tony (and he certainly commanded Tony's respect, too) without bragging or posing, often without opening his mouth. His real language was basketball, and he was such a taut, fluid athlete that he couldn't help seeming a bit bottled up indoors, in the classroom. When he spoke it was to scoff at our enthusiasms, our displays of uncool, but distantly, as if his mind were really elsewhere plotting crossover moves, footwork. He listened to Funkadelic and Cameo and Zapp and was as quick to embrace rap as any boy at the Home, yet when music he admired actually *played,* instead of dancing he'd stand with arms crossed, scowling and pouting in time with the beat, his expressive hips frozen. Danny existed in suspension, neither black nor white, neither beating up nor beaten, beautiful but unfazed by the concept of girls, rotten at schoolwork but coasting through classes, and frequently unanchored by gravity, floating between pavement and the tangled chain-mesh of the St. Vincent's basketball hoops. Tony was tormented by his lost Italian family, adamant they would return; Danny might have coolly walked out on his parents one day when he was seven or eight and joined a pickup game that lasted until he was fourteen, to the day Minna drove up in his truck.

*　　*　　*

Tourette's teaches you what people will ignore and forget, teaches you to see the reality-knitting mechanism people employ to tuck away the intolerable, the incongruous, the disruptive—it teaches you this because you're the one lobbing the intolerable, incongruous, and disruptive their way. Once I sat on an Atlantic Avenue bus a few rows ahead of man with a belching tic—long, groaning, almost vomitous-sounding noises, the kind a fifth-grader learns to make, swallowing a bellyful of air, then forgets by high school, when charming girls becomes more vital than freaking them out. My colleague's compulsion was terribly specific: He sat at the back of the bus, and only when every head faced forward did he give out with his masterly digestive simulacra. We'd turn, shocked—there were fifteen or twenty others on the bus—and he'd look away. Then, every sixth or seventh time, he'd mix in a messy farting sound. He was a miserable-looking black man in his sixties, a drinker, an idler. Despite the peekaboo brilliance of his timing it was clear to everyone he was the source, and so the other riders hummed or coughed reprovingly, quit giving him the satisfaction of looking, and avoided one another's gaze. This was a loser's game, since not glancing back freed him to run together great uninterrupted phrases of his ripest noise. To all but me he was surely a childish jerk-off, a pathetic wino fishing for attention (maybe he understood himself this way, too—if he was undiagnosed, probably so). But it was unmistakably a compulsion, a tic—Tourette's. And it went on and on, until I'd reached my stop and, I'm sure, after.

The point is, I knew that those other passengers would barely recall it a few minutes after stepping off to their destinations. Despite how that maniacal froglike groaning filled the auditorium of the bus, the concertgoers were plainly engaged in the task of forgetting the music. Consensual reality is both fragile and elastic, and it heals like the skin of a bubble. The belching man ruptured it so quickly and completely that I could watch the wound instantly seal.

A Touretter can also be The Invisible Man.

*   *   *

Similarly, I doubt the other Boys, even the three who joined me in becoming Minna Men, directly recalled my bouts of kissing. I probably could have forced them to remember, but it would have been grudgingly. That tic was too much for us to encompass then, at St. Vincent's, as it would be now, anytime, anywhere. Besides, as my Tourette's bloomed I quickly layered the kissing behind hundreds of other behaviors, some of which, seen through the prism of Minna's rough endearments, became my trademarks, my Freakshow. So the kissing was gratefully forgotten.

By the time I was twelve, nine months or so after touching the penguins, I had begun to overflow with reaching, tapping, grabbing and kissing urges—those compulsions emerged first, while language for me was still trapped like a roiling ocean under a calm floe of ice, the way I'd been trapped in the underwater half of the penguin display, mute, beneath glass. I'd begun reaching for doorframes, kneeling to grab at skittering loosened sneaker laces (a recent fashion among the toughest boys at St. Vincent's, unfortunately for me), incessantly tapping the metal-pipe legs of the schoolroom desks and chairs in search of certain ringing tones, and worst, grabbing and kissing my fellow Boys. I grew terrified of myself then, and burrowed deeper into the library, but was forced out for classes or meals or bedtime. Then it would happen. I'd lunge at someone, surround him with my arms, and kiss his cheek or neck or forehead, whatever I hit. Then, compulsion expelled, I'd be left to explain, defend myself, or flee. I kissed Greg Toon and Edwin Torres, whose eyes I'd never dared meet. I kissed Leshawn Montrose, who'd broken Mr. Voccaro's arm with a chair. I kissed Tony Vermonte and Gilbert Coney and tried to kiss Danny Fantl. I kissed Steven Grossman, pathetically thankful he'd come along just then. I kissed my own counterparts, other sad invisible Boys working the margins at St. Vincent's, just surviving, whose names I didn't know. "It's a game!" I'd say, pleadingly. "It's a game." That was my only defense, and since the most inexplicable things in our lives were games, with their ancient embedded rituals—British Bulldog, Ringolevio, Scully and Jinx—a mythos handed down to us orphans who-knew-how, it seemed possible I might persuade them this was another one, The Kissing Game. Just as important, I might persuade myself—wasn't it something in a book I'd read, a game for fevered teenagers, perhaps Sadie Hawkins Day? Forget the absence of girls, didn't we Boys deserve the same? That was it, then, I decided—I was single-handedly dragging the underprivileged into adolescence. I knew something they didn't. "It's a game," I'd say desperately, sometimes as tears of pain ran down my face. "It's a game." Leshawn Montrose cracked my head against a porcelain water fountain, Greg Toon and Edwin Torres generously only shucked me off onto the floor. Tony Vermonte twisted my arm behind my back and forced me against a wall. "It's a game," I breathed. He released me and shook his head, full of pity. The result, oddly enough, was I was spared a few months' worth of beatings at his hands—I was too pathetic and faggy to touch, might be better avoided. Danny Fantl saw my move coming and faked me out as though I were a lead-footed defender, then vanished down a stairwell. Gilbert stood and glared, deeply unnerved due to our private history. "A game," I reassured him. "It's a game," I told poor Steven Grossman and he believed me, just long enough to try kissing our mutual tormentor Tony, perhaps hoping it was a key to overturning the current order. He was not spared.

*   *   *

Meantime, beneath that frozen shell a sea of language was reaching full boil. It became harder and harder not to notice that when a television pitchman said *to last the rest of a lifetime* my brain went *to rest the lust of a loaftomb,* that when I heard "Alfred Hitchcock," I silently replied "Altered Houseclock" or "Ilford Hotchkiss," that when I sat reading Booth Tarkington in the library now my throat and jaw worked behind my clenched lips, desperately fitting the syllables of the prose to the rhythms of "Rapper's Delight" (which was then playing every fifteen or twenty minutes out on the yard), that an invisible companion named Billy or Bailey was begging for insults I found it harder and harder to withhold.

*   *   *

The kissing cycle was mercifully brief. I found other outlets, other obsessions. The pale thirteen-year-old that Mr. Kassel pulled out of the library and offered to Minna was prone to floor-tapping, whistling, tongue-clicking, winking, rapid head turns, and wall-stroking, anything but the direct utterances for which my particular Tourette's brain most yearned. Language bubbled inside me now, the frozen sea melting, but it felt too dangerous to let out. Speech was intention, and I couldn't let anyone else or myself know how intentional my craziness felt. Pratfalls, antics—those were accidental lunacy, and more or less forgivable. Practically speaking, it was one thing to stroke Leshawn Montrose's arm, or even to kiss him, another entirely to walk up and call him Shefawn Mongoose, or Lefthand Moonprose, or Fuckyou Roseprawn. So, though I collected words, treasured them like a drooling sadistic captor, bending them, melting them down, filing off their edges, stacking them into teetering piles, before release I translated them into physical performance, manic choreography.

And I was lying low, I thought. For every tic issued I squelched dozens, or so it felt—my body was an overwound watchspring, effortlessly driving one set of hands double-time while feeling it could as easily animate an entire mansion of stopped clocks, or a vast factory mechanism, a production line like the one in *Modern Times,* which we watched that year in the basement of the Brooklyn Public Library on Fourth Avenue, a version accompanied by a pedantic voice-over lecturing us on Chaplin's genius. I took Chaplin, and Buster Keaton, whose *The General* had been similarly mutilated, as models: Obviously blazing with aggression, disruptive energies barely contained, they'd managed to keep their traps shut, and so had endlessly skirted danger and been regarded as cute. I needn't exactly strain to find a motto: silence, golden, get it? Got it. Hone your timing instead, burnish those physical routines, your idiot wall-stroking, face-making, lace-chasing, until they're funny in a flickering black-and-white way, until your enemies don policeman's or Confederate caps and begin tripping over themselves, until doe-eyed women swoon. So I kept my tongue wound in my teeth, ignored the pulsing in my cheek, the throbbing in my gullet, persistently swallowed language back like vomit. It burned as hotly.

*   *   *

We rode a mile or two before Minna's van halted, engine guttering to a stop. Then a few minutes passed before he let us out of the back, and we found ourselves in a gated warehouse yard under the shadow of the Brooklyn-Queens Expressway, in a ruined industrial zone. Red Hook, I knew later. He led us to a large truck, a detached twelve-wheel trailer with no cab in evidence, then rolled up the back to reveal a load of identical sealed cardboard crates, a hundred, two hundred, maybe more. A thrill went through me: I'd secretly count them.

"Couple you boys get up inside," said Minna distractedly. Tony and Danny had the guile to leap immediately into the truck, where they could work shaded from the sun. "You're just gonna run this stuff inside, that's all. Hand shit off, move it up to the front of the truck, get it in. Straight shot, you got it?" He pointed to the warehouse. We all nodded, and I peeped. It went unnoticed.

Minna opened the big panel doors of the warehouse and showed us where to set the crates. We started quickly, then wilted in the heat. Tony and Danny massed the crates at the lip of the truck while Gilbert and I made the first dozen runs, then the older boys conceded their advantage and began to help us drag them across the blazing yard. Minna never touched a crate; he spent the whole time in the office of the warehouse, a cluttered room full of desks, file cabinets, tacked-up notes and pornographic calendars and a stacked tower of orange traffic cones, visible to us through an interior window, smoking cigarettes and jawing on the telephone, apparently not listening for replies—every time I glanced through the window his mouth was moving. The door was closed, and he was inaudible behind the glass.

At some point another man appeared, from where I wasn't sure, and stood in the yard wiping his forehead as though he were the one laboring. Minna came out, the two stepped inside the office, the other man disappeared. We moved the last of the crates inside. Minna rolled down the gate of the truck and locked the warehouse, pointed us back to his van, but paused before shutting us into the back.

"Hot day, huh?" he said, looking at us directly for what might have been the first time.

Bathed in sweat, we nodded, afraid to speak.

"You monkeys thirsty? Because personally I'm dying out here."

Minna drove us to Smith Street, a few blocks from St. Vincent's, and pulled over in front of a bodega, then bought us beer, pop-top cans of Miller, and sat with us in the back of the van, drinking. It was my first beer.

"Names," said Minna, pointing at Tony, our obvious leader. We said our first names, starting with Tony. Minna didn't offer his own, only drained his beer and nodded. I began tapping the truck panel beside me.

Physical exertion over, astonishment at our deliverance from St. Vincent's receding, my symptoms found their opening again.

"You probably ought to know, Lionel's a freak," said Tony, his voice vibrant with self-regard.

"Yeah, well, you're all freaks, if you don't mind me pointing it out," said Minna. "No parents—or am I mixed up?"

Silence.

"Finish your beer," said Minna, tossing his can past us, into the back of the van.

And that was the end of our first job for Frank Minna.

*   *   *

But Minna rounded us up again the next week, brought us to that same desolate yard, and this time he was friendlier. The task was identical, almost to the number of boxes (242 to 260), and we performed it in the same trepidatious silence. I felt a violent hatred burning off Tony in my and Gilbert's direction, as though he thought we were in the process of screwing up his Italian rescue. Danny was of course exempt and oblivious. Still, we'd begun to function as a team—demanding physical work contained its own truths, and we explored them despite ourselves.

Over beers Minna said, "You like this work?"

One of us said *sure*.

"You know what you're doing?" Minna grinned at us, waiting. The question was confusing. "You know what kind of work this is?"

"What, moving boxes?" said Tony.

"Right, moving. Moving work. That's what you call it when you work for me. Here, look." He stood to get into his pocket, pulled out a roll of twenties and a small stack of white cards. He stared at the roll for a minute, then peeled off four twenties and handed one to each of us. It was my first twenty dollars. Then he offered us each a card. It read: L&L MOVERS. NO JOB TOO SMALL. SOME JOBS TOO LARGE. GERARD & FRANK MINNA. And a phone number.

"You're Gerard or Frank?" said Tony.

"Minna, Frank." Like *Bond, James*. He ran his hand through his hair. "So you're a moving company, get it? Doing moving work." This seemed a very important point: that we call it *moving*. I couldn't imagine what else to call it.

"Who's Gerard?" said Tony. Gilbert and I, even Danny, watched Minna carefully. Tony was questioning him on behalf of us all.

"My brother."

"Older or younger?"

"Older."

Tony thought for a minute. "Who's L and L?"

"Just the name, L and L. Two L's. Name of the company."

"Yeah, but what's it mean?"

"What do you need it to mean, Fruitloop—Living Loud? Loving Ladies? Laughing at you Losers?"

"What, it doesn't mean anything?" said Tony.

"I didn't say that, did I?"

"Least Lonely," I suggested.

"There you go," said Minna, waving his can of beer at me. "L and L Movers, Least Lonely."

Tony, Danny and Gilbert all stared at me, uncertain how I'd gained this freshet of approval.

"Liking Lionel," I heard myself say.

"Minna, that's an Italian name?" said Tony. This was on his own behalf, obviously. It was time to get to the point. The rest of us could all go fuck ourselves.

"What are you, the census?" said Minna. "Cub reporter? What's your full name, Jimmy Olsen?"

"Lois Lane," I said. Like anyone, I'd read Superman comics.

"Tony Vermonte," said Tony, ignoring me.

"Vermont-ee," repeated Minna. "That's what, like a New England thing, right? You a Red Sox fan?"

"Yankees," said Tony, confused and defensive. The Yankees were champions now, the Red Sox their hapless, eternal victims, vanquished most recently by Bucky Dent's famous home run. We'd all watched it on television.

"Luckylent," I said, remembering. "Duckybent."

Minna erupted with laughter. "Yeah, Ducky fucking Bent! That's good. Don't look now, it's Ducky Bent."

"Lexluthor," I said, reaching out to touch Minna's shoulder. He only stared at my hand, didn't move away. "Lunchylooper, Laughyluck, Loopylip—"

"All right, Loopy," said Minna. "Enough already."

"Lockystuff—" I was desperate for a way to stop. My hand went on tapping Minna's shoulder.

"Let it go," said Minna, and now he returned my shoulder taps, once, hard. "Don't tug the boat."

*   *   *

To *tugboat* was to try Minna's patience. Any time you pushed your luck, said too much, overstayed a welcome, or overestimated the usefulness of a given method or approach, you were guilty of having tugged the boat. *Tugboating* was most of all a dysfunction of wits and storytellers, and a universal one: Anybody who thought himself funny would likely tug a boat here or there. Knowing when a joke or verbal gambit was right at its limit, quitting before the boat had been tugged, that was art (and it was a given that you wanted to push it as near as possible—missing an opportunity to score a laugh was deeply lame, an act undeserving of a special name).

Years before the word *Tourette's* was familiar to any of us, Minna had me diagnosed: Terminal Tugboater.

*   *   *

Distributing eighty dollars and those four business cards was all Minna had to do to instate the four of us forever—or anyway, for as long as he liked—as the junior staff of L&L Movers. Twenty dollars and a beer remained our usual pay. Minna would gather us sporadically, on a day's notice or no notice at all—and the latter possibility became incentive, once we'd begun high school, for us to return to St. Vincent's directly after classes and lounge expectantly in the schoolyard or recreation room, pretending not to listen for the distinctive grumble of his van's motor. The jobs varied enormously. We'd load merchandise, like the cartons in the trailer, in and out of storefront-basement grates all up and down Court Street, borderline shady activity that it seemed wholesalers ought to be handling themselves, transactions sealed with a shared cigar in the back of the shop. Or we'd bustle apartmentloads of furniture in and out of brownstone walk-ups, legitimate moving jobs, it seemed to me, where fretting couples worried we weren't old or expert enough to handle their belongings—Minna would hush them, remind them of the cost of distractions: "The meter's running." (This hourly rate wasn't reflected in our pay, of course. It was twenty dollars whether we hurried or not; we hurried.) We put sofas through third-story windows with a makeshift cinch and pulley, Tony and Minna on the roof, Gilbert and Danny in the window to receive, myself on the ground with the guide ropes. A massive factory building under the Brooklyn end of the Manhattan Bridge, owned by an important but unseen friend of Minna's, had been damaged in fire, and we moved most of the inhabitants for free, as some sort of settlement or concession—the terms were obscure, but Minna was terrifically urgent about it. When a couple of college-age artists objected to our rough handling of a pile of damaged canvases the firemen had heaped on the floor, he paced and seethed at the delay; the only meter running now was Minna's own time, and his credibility with his friend-client. We woke at five one August morning to collect and set up the temporary wooden stages for the bands performing in the Atlantic Antic, a massive annual street fair, then worked again at dusk to tear the stages down, the hot avenue now heaped with a day's torn wrappers and crumpled cups, a few fevered revelers still staggering home as we knocked the pine frames apart with hammers and the heels of our shoes. Once we emptied an entire electronics showroom into Minna's truck, pulling unboxed stereos off shelves and out of window displays, disconnecting the wires from lit, blinking amplifiers, eventually even taking the phone off the desk—it would have seemed a sort of brazen burglary had Minna not been standing on the sidewalk in front, drinking beer and telling jokes with the man who'd unpadlocked the shop gates for us as we filed past with the goods. Everywhere Minna connived and cajoled and dropped names, winking at us to make us complicit, and everywhere Minna's clients stared at us Boys, some wondering if we'd palm a valuable when they weren't looking, some trying to figure the angle, perhaps hoping to catch a hint of disloyalty, an edge over Minna they'd save for when they needed it. We palmed nothing, revealed no disloyalty. Instead we stared back, tried to make them flinch. And we listened, gathered information. Minna was teaching us when he meant to, and when he didn't.

It changed us as a group. We developed a certain collective ego, a presence apart at the Home. We grew less embattled from within, more from without: nonwhite Boys sensed in our privilege a hint of their future deprivations and punished us for it. Age had begun to heighten those distinctions anyway. So Tony, Gilbert, Danny and myself smoothed out our old antipathies and circled the wagons. We stuck up for one another, at the Home and at Sarah J. Hale, our local high school, a required stop except for those few who'd qualified for some special (i.e., Manhattan) destination, Stuyvesant or Music and Art.

There at Sarah J. we St. Vincent's Boys were disguised, blended with the larger population, a pretty rough crowd despite their presumably having parents and siblings and telephones and bedroom doors with locks and a thousand other unimaginable advantages. But we knew each other, kept an eye on each other, bad pennies circulating with the good. Black or white, we policed one another like siblings, reserved special degrees of scorn for one another's social or institutional humiliations. And there we mixed with girls for the first time, about as well as chunks of road salt in ice cream, though ice cream might be a generous comparison for the brutal, strapping black girls of Sarah J., gangs of whom laid after-school ambushes for any white boy daring enough to have flirted, even made eye contact, with one inside the building. They comprised the vast majority there, and the handful of white or Latin girls survived by a method of near-total invisibility. To pierce their cone of fear and silence was to be met with incredulous glares of resentment. Our lives are led elsewhere, those looks said, and yours ought to be too. The black girls were claimed by boyfriends too sophisticated to bother with school, who rode by for them at lunch hour in cars throbbing with amplified bass lines and sometimes boasting bullet-riddled doors, and their only use for us was as a dartboard for throwing lit cigarette butts, a frequent sport. Yes, relations between the sexes were strained at Sarah J., and I doubt any of us four, even Tony, so much as copped a feel from the girls we were schooled with there. For all of us that would wait for Court Street, for the world we would come to know through Minna.

*   *   *

Minna's Court Street was the old Brooklyn, a placid ageless surface alive underneath with talk, with deals and casual insults, a neighborhood political machine with pizzeria and butcher-shop bosses and unwritten rules everywhere. All was talk except for what mattered most, which were unspoken understandings. The barbershop, where he took us for identical haircuts that cost three dollars each, except even that fee was waived for Minna—no one had to wonder why the price of a haircut hadn't gone up since 1966, nor why six old barbers were working, mostly not working, out of the same ancient storefront, where the Barbicide hadn't been changed since the product's invention (in Brooklyn, the jar bragged), where other somewhat younger men passed through constantly to argue sports and wave away offers of haircuts; the barbershop was a retirement home, a social club, and front for a backroom poker game. The barbers were taken care of because this was Brooklyn, where people looked out. Why would the prices go up, when nobody walked in who wasn't part of this conspiracy, this trust?—though if you spoke of it you'd surely meet with confused denials, or laughter and a too-hard cuff on the cheek. Another exemplary mystery was the "arcade," a giant storefront paneled with linoleum, containing three pinball machines, which were in constant use, and six or seven video games—Asteroids, Frogger, Centipede—all pretty much ignored, and a cashier, who'd change dollars to quarters and accept hundred-dollar bills folded into lists of numbers, names of horses and football teams. The curb in front of the arcade was lined with Vespas, which had been in vogue a year or two before but now sat permanently parked, without anything more than a bicycle lock for protection, a taunt to vandals. A block away, on Smith, they would have been stripped, but here they were pristine, a curbside Vespa showroom. It didn't need explaining—this was Court Street. And Court Street, where it passed through Carroll Gardens and Cobble Hill, was the only Brooklyn, really—north was Brooklyn Heights, secretly a part of Manhattan, south was the harbor, and the rest, everything east of the Gowanus Canal (the only body of water in the world, Minna would crack each and every time we drove over it, that was 90 percent guns), apart from small outposts of civilization in Park Slope and Windsor Terrace, was an unspeakable barbarian tumult.

*   *   *

Sometimes he needed just one of us. He'd appear at the Home in his Impala instead of the van, request someone specific, then spirit him away, to the bruised consternation of those left behind. Tony was in and out of Minna's graces, his ambition and pride costing him as much as he won, but he was unmistakably our leader, and Minna's right hand. He wore his private errands with Minna like Purple Hearts, but refused to report on their content to the rest of us. Danny, athletic, silent and tall, became Minna's trusted greyhound, his Mercury, sent on private deliveries and rendezvous, and given early driving lessons in a vacant Red Hook lot, as though Minna were grooming him for work as an international spy, or Kato for a new Green Hornet. Gilbert, all bullish determination, was pegged for the grunt work, sitting in double-parked cars, repairing a load of ruptured cartons with strapping tape, unfastening the legs of an oversize dresser so as to fit it through a small doorway, and repainting the van, whose graffitied exterior some of Minna's neighbors had apparently found objectionable. And I was an extra set of eyes and ears and opinions. Minna would drag me along to back rooms and offices and barbershop negotiations, then debrief me afterward. What did I think of that guy? Shitting or not? A moron or retard? A shark or a mook? Minna encouraged me to have a take on everything, and to spit it out, as though he thought my verbal disgorgings were only commentary not yet anchored to subject matter. And he adored my echolalia. He thought I was doing impressions.

Needless to say, it wasn't commentary and impressions, but my verbal Tourette's flowering at last. Like Court Street, I seethed behind the scenes with language and conspiracies, inversions of logic, sudden jerks and jabs of insult. Now Court Street and Minna had begun to draw me out. With Minna's encouragement I freed myself to ape the rhythm of his overheard dialogues, his complaints and endearments, his for-the-sake-of arguments. And Minna loved my effect on his clients and associates, the way I'd unnerve them, disrupt some schmooze with an utterance, a head jerk, a husky *Eatmebailey!* I was his special effect, a running joke embodied. They'd look up startled and he'd wave his hand knowingly, counting money, not even bothering to look at me. "Don't mind him, he can't help it," he'd say. "Kid's shot out of a cannon." Or: "He likes to get a little nutty sometimes. Forget about it." Then he'd wink at me, acknowledge our conspiracy. I was evidence of life's unpredictability and rudeness and poignancy, a scale model of his own nutty heart. In this way Minna licensed my speech, and speech, it turned out, liberated me from the overflowing disaster of my Tourettic self, turned out to be the tic that satisfied where others didn't, the scratch that briefly stilled the itch.

"You ever listen to yourself, Lionel?" Minna would say later, shaking his head. "You really are shot out of a fucking cannon."

"*Scott Out of the Canyon!* I don't know why, I just—*fuckitup!*— I just can't stop."

"You're a freak show, that's why. Human freak show, and it's free. Free to the public."

"Freefreak!" I hit him on the shoulder.

"That's what I said: a free human freak show."

*   *   *

We were introduced to Matricardi and Rockaforte at their brown-stone on Degraw Street one day in the fall, four or five months after meeting Minna. He'd gathered the four of us in the van in his usual way, without explaining our assignment, but there was a special degree of agitation about him, a jumpiness that induced a special tic-cishness in me. He first drove us into Manhattan across the Brooklyn Bridge, then underneath the bridge, to the docks near Fulton Street, and I spent the whole time imitating the nervous jerks of his head as he negotiated traffic. We parked in the middle of a concrete yard in front of one of the piers. Minna disappeared inside a small, window-less shack made of corrugated steel sheets and had us stand outside the van, where we shivered in the wind coming off the East River. I danced around the van in a fit, counting suspension cables on the bridge that soared over us like a monstrous steel limb while Tony and Danny, chilliest in their thin plaid jackets, kicked and cursed at me. Gilbert was nicely insulated in a fake down coat which, stitched into bulging sections, made him look like the Michelin Man or the Red Queen from *Alice in Wonderland*. He stood a few feet from us and methodically tossed chunks of corroded concrete into the river, as though he could earn points by cleaning the pier of rubble.

Minna emerged just as the two small yellow trucks drove up. They were Ryder Rental vans, smaller than Minna's, and identically deco-rated, one pristine, the other dingy. The drivers sat smoking cigarettes in the cabs, with the motors running. Minna unlatched the backs of the trucks, which weren't padlocked, and directed us to move the contents into his van—quick.

The first thing I laid hands on was an electric guitar, one shaped into a flying V and decorated with enameled yellow and silver flames.

A cable dangled from its socket. Other instruments, guitars and bass guitars, were in their hard black cases, but this one had been unplugged and shoved into the van in a hurry. The two trucks were full of concert gear—seven or eight guitars, keyboards, panels full of electronic switches, bundles of cable, microphones and stands, pedal effects for the floor, a drum kit that had been pushed into the truck whole instead of being disassembled, and a number of amplifiers and monitors, including six black stage amps, each half the size of a refrigerator, which alone filled the second Ryder truck and each took two of us to lift out and into Minna's van. The amplifiers and hard cases were stenciled with the band's name, which I recognized faintly. I learned later they were responsible for a minor AM hit or two, songs about roads, cars, women. I didn't grasp it then, but this was equipment enough for a small stadium show.

I wasn't sure we could fit the whole contents of the two trucks into the van but Minna only egged us to shut up and work faster. The men in the trucks never spoke or got out of the cabs, just smoked and waited. No one ever appeared from the corrugated shack. At the end there was barely room for Gilbert and me to crowd in behind the doors to ride with the band's calamitously piled equipment while Tony and Danny shared a spot up front with Minna.

We crossed the bridge back to Brooklyn like that, Gilbert and I fearing for our lives if the load shifted or toppled. After a few breathless turns and sudden stops Minna double-parked the van and freed us from the back. The destination was a brownstone in a row of brownstones on Degraw Street, red brick, stone detailing flaking to powder, genteel curtained windows. Some canny salesman had ten or twenty years before sold the entire block on defacing these hundred-year-old buildings with flimsy tin awnings over the elegant front doors; the only thing special about Matricardi and Rockaforte's house was that it lacked one of these.

"We're gonna have to take apart those drums," said Tony when he saw the doors.

"Just get it inside," said Minna. "It'll fit."

"Are there stairs?" said Gilbert.

"You'll see, you chocolate cheesepuffs," said Minna. "Just get it up the stoop already."

Inside, we saw. The brownstone which appeared so ordinary was an anomaly just through the doors. The insides—typical narrow halls and stairs, spoked banisters, high ornate ceilings—had all been stripped and gutted, replaced with a warehouse-style stairwell into the basement apartment and upstairs. The parlor floor where we stood was sealed off on the left by a clean white wall and single closed door. We ferried the equipment into the upper-floor apartment while Minna stood guarding the rear of the van. The drums went easily.

The band's equipment tucked neatly into one corner of the apartment, on wooden pallets apparently set out for that purpose. The upper floors of the building were empty apart from a few crates here and there and a single oak dining table heaped with silverware: forks, spoons in two sizes, and butter knives, hundreds of each, ornate and heavy, gleaming, bundled in disordered piles, no sense to them except that the handles all faced in one direction. I'd never seen so much silverware in one place, even in St. Vincent's institutional kitchen—anyway, those St. Vincent's forks were flat cutouts of dingy steel bent this way to make tines, that way to make a handle, barely better than the plastic "sporks" we were issued with our school lunches. These forks were little masterpieces of sculpture in comparison. I wandered away from the others and obsessed on the mountain of forks, knives and spoons, but especially those forks, as rich in their contours as tiny thumbless hands, or the paws of a silver animal.

The others shifted the last of the amplifiers up the stairs. Minna reparked the van. I stood at the table, trying to look casual. Jerking your head was good cover for jerking your head, I discovered. Nobody watched me. I pocketed one of the forks, trembling with lust and anticipation, joy in my fear, as I did it. I only just got away with it, too: Minna was back.

"The clients want to meet you," he said.

"Who's that?" said Tony.

"Just shut up when they talk, okay?" said Minna.

"Okay, but who are they?" said Tony.

"Practice shutting up now so you'll be good at it when you meet them," said Minna. "They're downstairs."

Behind that clean, seamless wall on the parlor floor lay hidden the brownstone's next surprise, a sort of double-reverse: The front room's old architecture was intact. Through the single door we stepped into a perfectly elegant, lavishly fitted brownstone parlor, with gold leaf on the ceiling's plaster scrollwork, antique chairs and desks and a marble-topped side table, a six-foot mirror-lined grandfather clock, and a vase with fresh flowers. Under our feet was an ancient carpet, layered with color, a dream map of the past. The walls were crowded with framed photographs, none more recent than the invention of color film. It was more like a museum diorama of Old Brooklyn than a contemporary room. Seated in two of the plush chairs were two old men, dressed in matching brown suits.

"So these are your boys," said the first of the two men.

"Say hello to Mr. Matricardi," said Minna.

"Yo," said Danny. Minna punched him on the arm.

"I said say hello to Mr. Matricardi."

"Hello," said Danny sulkily. Minna had never required politeness. Our jobs with him had never taken such a drab turn. We were used to sauntering with him through the neighborhood, riffing, honing our insults.

But we felt the change in Minna, the fear and tension. We would try to comply, though servility lay outside our range of skills.

The two old men sat with their legs crossed, fingers templed together, watching us closely. They were both trim in their suits, their skin white and soft wherever it showed, their faces soft, too, without being fat. The one called Mr. Matricardi had a nick in the top ridge of his large nose, a smooth indented scar like a slot in molded plastic.

"Say hello," Minna told me and Gilbert.

I thought *mister catch your body mixture bath retardy whistlecop's birthday* and didn't dare open my mouth. Instead I fondled the tines of my marvelous stolen fork, which barely fit the length of my corduroy's front pocket.

"It's okay," said Matricardi. His smile was pursed, all lips and no teeth. His thick glasses doubled the intensity of his stare. "You all work for Frank?"

What were we supposed to say?

"Sure," volunteered Tony. Matricardi was an Italian name.

"You do what he tells?"

"Sure."

The second man leaned forward. "Listen," he said. "Frank Minna is a good man."

Again we were bewildered. Were we expected to disagree?

I counted the tines in my pocket, one-two-three-four, one-two-three-four.

"Tell us what you want to do," said the second man. "Be what? What kind of work? What kind of men?" He didn't hide his teeth, which were bright yellow, like the van we'd unloaded.

"Talk to Mr. Rockaforte," urged Minna.

"They do what you tell them, Frank?" said Rockaforte to Minna. It wasn't small talk, somehow, despite the repetitions. This was an intense speculative interest. Far too much rested on Minna's reply. Matricardi and Rockaforte were like that, the few times I glimpsed them: purveyors of banal remarks with terrifying weight behind them.

"Yeah, they're good kids," said Minna. I heard the hurry in his voice. We'd overstayed our welcome already.

"Orphans," said Matricardi to Rockaforte. He was repeating something he'd been told, rehearsing its value.

"You like this house?" said Rockaforte, gesturing upward at the ceiling. He'd caught me staring at the scrollwork.

"Yes," I said carefully.

"This is his mother's parlor," said Rockaforte, nodding at Matricardi.

"Exactly as she kept it," said Matricardi proudly. "We never changed a thing."

"When Mr. Matricardi and I were children like yourselves I would come to see his family and we would sit in this room." Rockaforte smiled at Matricardi. Matricardi smiled back. "His mother believe me would rip our ears if we spilled on this carpet, even a drop. Now we sit and remember."

"Everything exactly as she kept it," said Matricardi. "She would see it and know. If she were here, bless her sweet pathetic soul."

They fell silent. Minna was silent too, though I imagined I could feel his anxiety to be out of there. I thought I heard him gulp, actually.

My throat was calm. Instead I worked at my stolen fork. It now seemed so potent a charm, I imagined that if I had it in my pocket I might never need to tic aloud again.

"So tell us," said Rockaforte. "Tell us what you're going to be. What kind of men."

"Like Frank," said Tony, confident he was speaking for us all, and right to be.

This answer made Matricardi chuckle, still toothlessly. Rockaforte waited patiently until his friend was finished. Then he asked Tony, "You want to make music?"

"What?"

"You want to make music?" His tone was sincere.

Tony shrugged. We all held our breath, waiting to understand. Minna shifted his weight, nervous, watching this encounter ramble on beyond his control.

"The belongings you moved for us today," said Rockaforte. "You recognize what those things are?"

"Sure."

"No, no," said Minna suddenly. "You can't do that."

"Please don't refuse our gift," said Rockaforte.

"No, really, we can't. With respect." I could see this was imperative for Minna. The gift, worth thousands if not tens of thousands, must absolutely be denied. I shouldn't bother to form nutty fantasies about the electric guitars and keyboards and amplifiers. Too late, though: My brain had begun to bubble with names for our band, all stolen from Minna: *You Fucking Mooks, The Chocolate Cheeseballs, Tony and the Tugboats.*

"Why, Frank?" Matricardi. "Let us bring a little joy. For orphans to make music is a good thing."

"No, please."

Jerks From Nowhere. Free Human Freakshow. I pictured these in place of the band's logo on the skin of the bass drum, and stenciled onto the amplifiers.

"Nobody else will be permitted to take pleasure in that garbage," said Rockaforte, shrugging. "We can give it to your orphans, or a fire can be created with a can of gasoline—it would be no different."

Rockaforte's tone made me understand two things. First, that the offer truly meant nothing to him, nothing at all, and so it could be turned away. They wouldn't force Minna to allow us to take the instruments.

And second, that Rockaforte's strange comparison involving a can of gasoline wasn't strange at all to him. That was now exactly what would happen to the band's equipment.

Minna heard it too, and exhaled deeply. The danger was past. But at the same moment I turned a corner in the opposite direction. My magic fork failed. I began to want to pronounce a measure of the nonsense that danced in my head. *Bucky Dent and the Stale Doughnuts—*

"Here," said Matricardi. He raised his hand, a gentle referee. "We can see it displeases, so forget." He fished in the interior pocket of his suit jacket. "But we insist on a measure of gratitude for these orphan boys who have done us such a favor."

He came out with hundred-dollar bills, four of them. He passed them to Frank and nodded at us, smiling munificently, and why not? The gesture was unmistakably the source for Frank's trick of spreading twenties everywhere, and it instantly made Frank seem somehow childish and cheap that he would bother to grease palms with anything less than a hundred.

"All right," said Minna. "That's great, you'll spoil them. They don't know what to do with it." He was able to josh now, the end in sight. "Say thanks, you peanutheads."

The other three were dazzled, I was fighting my syndrome.

"Thanks."

"Thanks."

"Thanks, Mr. Matricardi."

"Arf!"

After that Minna got us out of there, hustled us through the brownstone's odd hallway too fast even to glance back. Matricardi and Rockaforte had never moved from their chairs, just smiled at us and one another until we were gone. Minna put us all in the back of the van, where we compared hundred-dollar bills—they were fresh, and the serial numbers ran in sequence—and Tony immediately tried to persuade us he should caretake ours, that they weren't safe in the Home. We didn't bite.

Minna parked us on Smith Street, near Pacific, in front of an all-night market called Zeod's, after the Arab who ran it. We sat and waited until Minna came around the back of the van with a beer.

"You jerks know about forgetting?" he said.

"Forgetting what?"

"The names of those guys you just met. They're not good for you to go around saying."

"What should we call them?"

"Call them nothing. That's a part of my work you need to learn about. Sometimes the clients are just the clients. No names."

"Who are they?"

"They're nobody," said Minna. "That's the point. Forget you ever saw them."

"They live there?" said Gilbert.

"Nope. They just keep that place. They moved to Jersey."

"Gardenstate," I said.

"Yeah, the Garden State."

"Garden State Brickface and Stucco!" I shouted. Garden State Brickface and Stucco was a renovation firm whose crummy homemade television ads came on channels 9 and 11 during Mets and Yankees games and during reruns of *The Twilight Zone*. The weird name of the firm was already an occasional tic. Now it seemed to me that Brickface and Stucco might actually be Matricardi and Rockaforte's secret names.

"What's that?"

"Garden State Bricco and Stuckface!"

I'd made Minna laugh again. Like a lover, I loved to make Minna laugh.

"Yeah," he said. "That's good. Call them Bricco and Stuckface, you goddamn beautiful freak." He took another slug of beer.

And if memory serves we never heard him speak their real names again.

*   *   *

"Makes you think you're Italian?" said Minna one day, as we all rode together in his Impala.

"What do I look like to you?" said Tony.

"I don't know, I was thinking maybe Greek," said Minna. "I used to know this Greek guy went around knocking up the Italian girls down Union Street, until a couple their older brothers took him out under the bridge. You remind me of him, you know? Got that dusky tinge. I'd say half Greek. Or maybe Puerto Rican, or Syrian."

"Fuck you."

"Probably know all your parents, if you think about it. We're not talking the international jet set here—bunch of teen mothers, probably live in a five-mile radius, need to know the goddamn truth."

So it was, with this casual jaunt against Tony's boasts, that Minna appeared to announce what we already half suspected—that it was not only his life that was laced with structures of meaning but our own, that these master plots were transparent to him and that he held the power to reveal them, that he did know our parents and at any moment might present them to us.

Other times he taunted us, playing at knowledge or ignorance—we couldn't know which it was. He and I were alone when he said, "Essrog, Essrog. That name." He crunched up his mouth and squinted, as if trying to remember, or perhaps to read a name inscribed on the distant Manhattan skyline.

"You know an Essrog?" I said, my breath short, heart pounding. *"Edgehog!"*

"No. It's just— You ever look it up in the phone book? Can't be more than three or four Essrogs, for chrissakes. Such a weird name."

Later, at the Home, I looked. There were three.

*　　*　　*

Minna's weird views filtered down through the jokes he told and liked to hear, and those he cut short within a line or two of their telling. We learned to negotiate the labyrinth of his prejudices blind, and blindly. Hippies were dangerous and odd, also sort of sad in their utopian wrongness. ("Your parents must of been hippies," he'd tell me. "That's why you came out the superfreak you are.") Homosexual men were harmless reminders of the impulse Minna was sure lurked in all of us—and "half a fag" was more shameful than a whole one. Certain baseball players, Mets specifically (the Yankees were holy but boring, the Mets wonderfully pathetic and human), were half a fag—

Lee Mazzilli, Rusty Staub, later Gary Carter. So were most rock stars
and anyone who'd been in the armed services but not in a war. Les-
bians were wise and mysterious and deserved respect (and how could
we who relied on Minna for all our knowledge of women argue when
he himself grew baffled and reverent?) but could still be comically
stubborn or stuck up. The Arabic population of Atlantic Avenue was
as distant and unfathomable as the Indian tribes that had held our
land before Columbus. "Classic" minorities—Irish, Jews, Poles, Italians, Greeks and Puerto Ricans—were the clay of life itself, funny in
their essence, while blacks and Asians of all types were soberly
snubbed, unfunny (Puerto Ricans probably should have been in this
second class but had been elevated to "classic" status single-handedly
by *West Side Story*—and all Hispanics were "Ricans" even when they
were Dominicans, as they frequently were). But bone stupidity, mental illness, and familial or sexual anxiety—these were the bolts of electricity that made the clay walk, the animating forces that rendered
human life amusing and that flowed, once you learned to identify
them, through every personality and interaction. It was a form of
racism, not respect, that restricted blacks and Asians from ever being
stupid like a Mick or Polack. If you weren't funny, you didn't quite
exist. And it was usually better to be fully stupid, impotent, lazy,
greedy or freakish than to seek to dodge your destiny, or layer it
underneath pathetic guises of vanity or calm. So it was that I, Overt
Freak Supreme, became mascot of a worldview.

*   *   *

I called the Brooklyn directory's Essrogs one day when I was left
alone for twenty minutes in a warehouse office, waiting for Minna to
return, slowly picking out the numbers on the heavy rotary dial, trying not to obsess on the finger holes. I'd perhaps dialed a phone twice
at that point in my life.

I tried *F. Essrog and Lawrence Essrog and Murray and Annette Essrog.*

F. wasn't home. Lawrence's phone was answered by a child. I listened for a while as he said "Hello? Hello?," my vocal cords frozen, then hung up.

Murray Essrog picked up the phone. His voice was wheezy and ancient.

"Essrog?" I said, and whispered *Chestbutt* away from the phone.

"Yes. This is the Essrog residence, Murray speaking. Who's this?"

"Baileyrog," I said.

"Who?"

"Bailey."

He waited for a moment, then said, "Well, what can I do for you, Bailey?"

I hung up the phone. Then I memorized the numbers, all three of them. In the years that followed I would never once step across the line I'd drawn with Murray or the other telephone Essrogs—never show up at their homes, never accuse them of being related to a *free human freak show*, never even properly introduce myself—but I made a ritual out of dialing their numbers and hanging up after a tic or two, or listening, just long enough to hear another Essrog breathe.

*   *   *

A true story, not a joke, though it was repeated as often, tugboated relentlessly, was of the beat cop from Court Street who routinely dislodged clumps of teenagers clustered at night on stoops or in front of bars and who, if met with excuses, would cut them off with "Yeah, yeah. Tell your story *walking.*" More than anything, this somehow encapsulated my sense of Minna—his impatience, his pleasure in compression, in ordinary things made more expressive, more hilarious or vivid by their conflation. He loved talk but despised explanations. An endearment was flat unless folded into an insult. An insult was better if it was also self-deprecation, and ideally should also serve as a slice of street philosophy, or as resumption of some dormant debate. And all talk was finer on the fly, out on the pavement, between beats of action: We learned to tell our story walking.

*   *   *

Though Gerard Minna's name was printed on the L&L business card, we met him only twice, and never on a moving job. The first time was Christmas Day, 1982, at Minna's mother's apartment.

Carlotta Minna was an Old Stove. That was the Brooklyn term for it, according to Minna. She was a cook who worked in her own apartment, making plates of sautéed squid and stuffed peppers and jars of tripe soup that were purchased at her door by a constant parade of buyers, mostly neighborhood women with too much housework or single men, young and elderly, bocce players who'd take her plates to the park with them, racing bettors who'd eat her food standing up outside the OTB, barbers and butchers and contractors who'd sit on crates in the backs of their shops and wolf her cutlets, folding them with their fingers like waffles. How her prices and schedules were conveyed I never understood—perhaps telepathically. She truly worked an old stove, too, a tiny enamel four-burner crusted with ancient sauces and on which three or four pots invariably bubbled. The oven of this herculean appliance was never cool; the whole kitchen glowed with heat like a kiln. Mrs. Minna herself seemed to have been baked, her whole face dark and furrowed like the edges of an overdone calzone. We never arrived without nudging aside some buyers from her door, nor without packing off with plateloads of food, though how she could spare it was a mystery, since she never seemed to make more than she needed, never wasted a scrap. When we were in her presence Minna bubbled himself, with talk, all directed at his mother, banking cheery insults off anyone else in the apartment, delivery boys, customers, strangers (if there was such a thing to Minna then), tasting everything she had cooking and making suggestions on every dish, poking and pinching every raw ingredient or ball of unfinished dough and also his mother herself, her earlobes and chin, wiping flour off her dark arms with his open hand. She rarely—that I saw, anyway—acknowledged his attentions, or even directly acknowledged his presence. And she never once in my presence uttered so much as a single word.

That Christmas Minna had us all up to Carlotta's apartment, and for once we ate at her table, first nudging aside sauce-glazed stirring spoons and unlabeled baby-food jars of spices to clear spots for our plates. Minna stood at the stove, sampling her broth, and Carlotta hovered over us as we devoured her meatballs, running her floury fingers over the backs of our chairs, then gently touching our heads, the napes of our necks. We pretended not to notice, ashamed in front of one another and ourselves to show that we drank in her nurturance as eagerly as her meat sauce. But we drank it. It was Christmas, after all. We splashed, gobbled, kneed one another under the table. Privately, I polished the handle of my spoon, quietly aping the motions of her fingers on my nape, and fought not to twist in my seat and jump at her. I focused on my plate—eating was for me already by then a reliable balm. All the while she went on caressing, with hands that would have horrified us if we'd looked close.

Minna spotted her and said, "This is exciting for you, Ma? I got all of motherless Brooklyn up here for you. Merry Christmas."

Minna's mother only produced a sort of high, keening sigh. We stuck to the food.

"*Motherless Brooklyn,*" repeated a voice we didn't know.

It was Minna's brother, Gerard. He'd come in without our noticing. A fleshier, taller Minna. His eyes and hair were as dark, his mouth as wry, lips deep-indented at the corners. He wore a brown-and-tan leather coat, which he left buttoned, his hands pushed into the fake-patch pockets.

"So this is your little moving company," he said.

"Hey, Gerard," said Minna.

"Christmas, Frank," said Gerard Minna absently, not looking at his brother. Instead he was making short work of the four of us with his eyes, his hard gaze snapping us each in two like bolt cutters on inferior padlocks. It didn't take long before he was done with us forever—that was how it felt.

"Yeah, Christmas to you," said Minna. "Where you been?"

"Upstate," said Gerard.

"What, with Ralph and them?" I detected something new in Minna's voice, a yearning, sycophantic strain.

"More or less."

"What, just for the holidays you're gonna go talkative on me? Between you and Ma it's like the Cloisters up here."

"I brought you a present." He handed Minna a white legal envelope, stuffed fat. Minna began to tear at the end and Gerard said, in a voice low and full of ancient sibling authority, "Put it away."

Now we understood we'd all been staring. All except Carlotta, who was at her stove, piling together an improbable, cornucopic holiday plate for her older son.

"Make it to go, Mother."

Carlotta moaned again, closed her eyes.

"I'll be back," said Gerard. He stepped over and put his hands on her, much as Minna had. "I've got a few people to see today, that's all. I'll be back tonight. Enjoy your little orphan party."

He took the foil-wrapped plate and was gone.

Minna said, "What're you staring at? Eat your food!" He stuffed the white envelope into his jacket. The envelope made me think of Matricardi and Rockaforte, their pristine hundred-dollar bills. Brickface and Stucco, I corrected silently. Then Minna cuffed us, a bit too hard, the bulging gold ring on his middle finger clipping our crowns in more or less the same place his mother had fondled.

*   *   *

Minna's behavior with his mother oddly echoed what we knew of his style with women. I'd say girlfriends, but he never called them that, and we rarely saw him with the same one twice. They were Court Street girls, decorating poolrooms and movie-theater lounges, getting off work from the bakery still wearing disposable paper hats, applying lipstick without missing a chew of their gum, slanting their heavily elegant bodies through car windows and across pizza counters, staring over our heads as if we were four feet tall, and he'd apparently gone to junior high school with each and every one of them. "Sadie and me were in the sixth grade," he'd say, mussing her hair, disarranging her clothes. "This is Lisa—she used to beat up my best friend in gym." He'd angle jokes off them like a handball off a low wall, circle them with words like a banner flapping around a pole, tease their brassieres out of whack with pinching fingers, hold them by the two points of their hips and lean, as if he were trying to affect the course of a pinball in motion, risking *tilt*. They never laughed, just rolled their eyes and slapped him away, or didn't. We studied it all, soaked up their indifferent femaleness, that rare essence we yearned to take for granted. Minna had that gift, and we studied his moves, filed them away with silent, almost unconscious prayers.

"It's not that I only like women with large breasts," he told me once, years later, long after he'd traded the Court Street girls for his strange, chilly marriage. We were walking down Atlantic Avenue together, I think, and a woman passing had caused his head to turn. I'd jerked my head too, of course, my actions as exaggerated and secondhand as a marionette's. "That's a very common misunderstanding," he said, as if he were an idol and I his public, a mass audience devoted to puzzling him out. "Thing is, for me a woman has to have a certain amount of *muffling*, you know what I mean? Something between you, in the way of insulation. Otherwise, you're right up against her naked soul."

*   *   *

Wheels within wheels was another of Minna's phrases, used exclusively to sneer at our notions of coincidence or conspiracy. If we Boys ever dabbled in astonishment at, say, his running into three girls he knew from high school in a row on Court Street, two of whom he'd dated behind each other's backs, he'd bug his eyes and intone, *wheels within wheels*. No Met had ever pitched a no-hitter, but Tom Seaver and Nolan Ryan both pitched them after being traded away—*wheels within wheels*. The barber, the cheese man, and the bookie were all named Carmine—oh yeah, *wheels within wheels*, big time. You're onto something there, Sherlock.

By implication we orphans were idiots of connectivity, overly impressed by any trace of the familial in the world. We should doubt ourselves any time we imagined a network in operation. We should leave that stuff to Minna. Just as he knew the identity of our parents but would never reveal it to us, only Frank Minna was authorized to speculate on the secret systems that ran Court Street or the world. If we dared chime in, we'd surely only discovered more *wheels within wheels*. Business as usual. The regular fucking world—get used to it.

*   *   *

One day in April, five months after that Christmas meal, Minna drove up with all his windows thoroughly smashed, the van transformed into a blinding crystalline sculpture, a mirrorball on wheels, reflecting the sun. It was plainly the work of a man with a hammer or crowbar and no fear of interruption. Minna appeared not to have noticed; he ferried us out to a job without mentioning it. On our way back to the Home, as we rumbled over the cobblestones of Hoyt Street, Tony nodded at the windshield, which sagged in its frame like a beaded curtain, and said, "So what happened?"

"What happened to what?" It was a Minna game, forcing us to be literal when we'd been trained by him to talk in glances, in three-corner shots.

"Somebody fucked up your van."

Minna shrugged, excessively casual. "I parked it on that block of Pacific Street."

We didn't know what he was talking about.

"These guys around that block had this thing about how I was ugli-fying the neighborhood." A few weeks after Gilbert's paint job the van had been covered again with graffiti, vast filled-in outlines of incoher-ent ballooning font and an overlay of stringy tags. Something made Minna's van a born target, the flat battered sides like a windowless subway car, a homely public surface crying for spray paint where both private cars and bigger, glossier commercial trucks were invio-late. "They told me not to park it around there anymore. Then after I did it a couple of times more, they told me a different way."

Minna lifted both hands from the wheel to gesture his indifference. We weren't totally convinced.

"Someone's sending a message," said Tony.

"What's that?" said Minna.

"I just said it's a message," said Tony. I knew he wanted to ask about Matricardi and Rockaforte. Were they involved? Couldn't they protect Minna from having his windows smashed? We all wanted to ask about them and never would, unless Tony did it first.

"Yeah, but what are you trying to say?" said Minna.

"Fuckitmessage," I suggested impulsively.

"You know what I mean," said Tony defiantly, ignoring me.

"Yeah, maybe," said Minna. "But put it in your own words." I could feel his anger unfolding, smooth as a fresh deck of cards.

"Tellmetofuckitall!" I was like a toddler devising a tantrum to keep his parents from fighting.

But Minna wasn't distractable. "Quiet, Freakshow," he said, never taking his eyes from Tony. "Tell me what you said," he told Tony again.

"Nothing," said Tony. "Damn." He was backpedaling.

Minna pulled the van to the curb at a fire hydrant on the corner of

Bergen and Hoyt. Outside, a couple of black men sat on a stoop, drinking from a bag. They squinted at us.

"Tell me what you said," Minna insisted.

He and Tony stared at one another, and the rest of us melted back. I swallowed away a few variations.

"Just, you know, somebody's sending you a message." Tony smirked.

This clearly infuriated Minna. He and Tony suddenly spoke a private language in which *message* signified heavily. "You think you know a thing," he said.

"All I'm saying is I can see what they did to your truck, Frank." Tony scuffed his feet in the layer of tiny cubes of safety glass that had peeled away from the limp window and lay scattered on the floor of the van.

"That's not all you said, Dickweed."

That was the first I heard Minna use the term that would become lodged thereafter in my uppermost tic-echelon: *dickweed.* I didn't know whether he borrowed the nickname or invented it himself on the spot.

What it meant to me I still can't say. Perhaps it was inscribed in my vocabulary, though, by the trauma of that day: Our little organization was losing its innocence, although I couldn't have explained how or why.

"I can't help what I see," said Tony. "Somebody put a hit on your windows."

"Think you're a regular little wiseguy, don't you?"

Tony stared at him.

"You want to be Scarface?"

Tony didn't give his answer, but we knew what it was. *Scarface* had opened a month before, and Al Pacino was ascendant, a personal colossus astride Tony's world, blocking out the sky.

"See, the thing about Scarface," said Minna, "is before he got to be

Scarface he was *Scabface*. Nobody ever considers that. You have to want to be Scabface first."

For a second I thought Minna was going to hit Tony, damage his face to make the point. Tony seemed to be waiting for it too. Then Minna's fury leaked away.

"Out," he said. He waved his hand, a Caesar gesturing to the heavens through the dented roof of his refitted postal van.

"What?" said Tony. "Right here?"

"Out," he said again, equably. "Walk home, you muffin asses."

We sat gaping, though his meaning was clear enough. We weren't more than five or six blocks from the Home anyway. But we hadn't been paid, hadn't gone for beers or slices or a bag of hot, clingy zeppole. I could taste the disappointment—the flavor of powdered sugar's absence. Tony slid open the door, dislodging more glass, and we obediently filed out of the van and onto the sidewalk, into the day's glare, the suddenly formless afternoon.

Minna drove off, leaving us there to bob together awkwardly before the drinkers on the stoop. They shook their heads at us, stupid-looking white boys a block from the projects. But we were in no danger there, nor were we dangerous ourselves. There was something so primally humiliating in our ejection that Hoyt Street itself seemed to ridicule us, humble row of brownstones, sleeping bodega. We were inexcusable to ourselves. Others clotted street corners, not us, not anymore. We rode with Minna. The effect was deliberate: Minna knew the value of the gift he'd withdrawn.

"Muffin ass," I said forcefully, measuring the shape of the words in my mouth, auditioning them for tic-richness. Then I sneezed, induced by the sunlight.

Gilbert and Danny looked at me with disgust, Tony with something worse.

"Shut up," he said. There was cold fury in his teeth-clenched smile.

"Tellmetodoit, muffinass," I croaked.

"Be quiet now," warned Tony. He plucked a piece of wood from the gutter and took a step toward me.

Gilbert and Danny drifted away from us warily. I would have followed them, but Tony had me cornered against a parked car. The men on the stoop stretched back on their elbows, slurped their malt liquor thoughtfully.

"Dickweed," I said. I tried to mask it in another sneeze, which made something in my neck pop. I twitched and spoke again. *"Dickyweed! Dicketywood!"* I was trapped in a loop of self, one already too familiar, that of refining a verbal tic to free myself from its grip (not yet knowing how tenacious would be the grip of those particular syllables). Certainly I didn't mean to be replying to Tony. Yet *dickweed* was the name Minna had called him, and I was throwing it in his face.

Tony held the stick he'd found, a discarded scrap of lath with clumps of plaster stuck to it. I stared, anticipating my own pain as I'd anticipated Tony's, at Minna's hand, a minute before. Instead Tony moved close, stick at his side, and grabbed my collar.

"Open your mouth again," he said.

"Restrictaweed, detectorwood, vindictaphone," said I, prisoner of my syndrome. I grabbed Tony back, my hands exploring his collar, fingers running inside it like an anxious, fumbling lover.

Gilbert and Danny had started up Hoyt Street, in the direction of the Home. "C'mon, Tony," said Gilbert, tilting his head. Tony ignored them. He scraped his stick in the gutter, and came up with a smear of dog shit, mustard-yellow and pungent.

"Open," he said.

Now Gilbert and Danny were just slinking away, heads bowed. The street was brightly, absurdly empty. Nobody but the black men on the stoop, impassive witnesses. I jerked my head as Tony jabbed with his stick—tic as evasive maneuver—and he only managed to paint my cheek. I could smell it, though, powdered sugar's opposite made tangible, married to my face.

"Stickmebailey!" I shouted. Falling back against the car behind me, I

turned my head again, and again, twitching away, enshrining the moment in ticceography. The stain followed me, adamant, on fire. Or maybe it was my cheek that was on fire.

Our witnesses crinkled their paper bag, offered ruminative sighs.

Tony dropped his stick and turned from me. He'd disgusted himself, couldn't meet my eye. About to speak, he thought better of it, instead jogged to catch Gilbert and Danny as they shrugged away up Hoyt Street, leaving the scene.

*   *   *

We didn't see Minna again until five weeks later, Sunday morning at the Home's yard, late May. He had his brother Gerard with him; it was the second time we'd ever laid eyes on him.

None of us had seen Frank in the intervening weeks, though I know that the others, like myself, had each wandered down Court Street, nosed at a few of his usual haunts, the barbershop, the beverage outlet, the arcade. He wasn't in them. It meant nothing, it meant everything. He might never reappear, but if he turned up and didn't speak of it we wouldn't think twice. *We* didn't speak of it to one another, but a pensiveness hung over us, tinged with orphan's melancholy, our resignation to permanent injury. A part of each of us still stood astonished on the corner of Hoyt and Bergen, where we'd been ejected from Minna's van, where we'd fallen when our inadequate wings melted in the sun.

A horn honked, the Impala's, not the van's. Then the brothers got out and came to the cyclone fence and waited for us to gather. Tony and Danny were playing basketball, Gilbert perhaps ardently picking his nose on the sidelines. That's how I picture it anyway. I wasn't in the yard when they drove up. Gilbert had to come inside and pull me out of the Home library, to which I'd mostly retreated since Tony's attack, though Tony had shown no signs of repeating it. I was wedged into a windowsill seat, in sunshine laced with shadows from the barred window, when Gilbert found me there, immersed in a novel by Allen Drury.

Frank and Gerard were dressed too warmly for that morning, Frank in his bomber jacket, Gerard in his patchwork leather coat. The backseat of the Impala was loaded with shopping bags packed with Frank's clothes and a pair of old leather suitcases that surely belonged to Gerard. I don't know that Frank Minna ever owned a suitcase in his life. They stood at the fence, Frank bouncing nervously on his toes, Gerard hanging on the mesh, fingers dangling through, doing nothing to conceal his impatience with his brother, an impatience shading into disgust.

Frank smirked, raised his eyebrows, shook his head. Danny held his basketball between forearm and hip; Minna nodded at it, mimed a set shot, dropped his hand at the wrist, and made a delicate O with his mouth to signify the *swish* that would result.

Then, idiotically, he bounced a pretend pass to Gerard. His brother didn't seem to notice. Minna shook his head, then wheeled back to us and aimed two trigger fingers through the fence, and gritted his teeth for *rat-a-tat,* a little imaginary schoolyard massacre. We could only gape at him dumbly. It was as though somebody had taken Minna's voice away. And Minna was his voice—didn't he know? His eyes said yes, he did. They looked panicked, as if they'd been caged in the body of a mime.

Gerard gazed off emptily into the yard, ignoring the show. Minna made a few more faces, wincing, chuckling silently, shaking off some invisible annoyance by twitching his cheek. I fought to keep from mirroring him.

Then he cleared his throat. "I'm, ah, going out of town for a while," he said at last.

We waited for more. Minna just nodded and squinted and grinned his closemouthed grin at us as though he were acknowledging applause.

"Upstate?" said Tony.

Minna coughed in his fist. "Oh yeah. Place my brother goes. He thinks we ought to just, you know. Get a little country air."

"When are you coming back?" said Tony.

"Ah, coming back," said Minna. "You got an unknown there, Scarface. Unknown factors."

We must have gaped at him, because he added, "I wouldn't wait underwater, if that's what you had in mind."

We were in our second year of high school. That measure loomed suddenly, a door of years swinging open into what had been a future counted in afternoons. Would we know Minna whenever it was he got back? Would we know each other?

Minna wouldn't be there to tell us what to think of Minna's not being there, to give it a name.

"All right, Frank," said Gerard, turning his back to the fence. "Motherless Brooklyn appreciates your support. I think we better get on the road."

"My brother's in a hurry," said Frank. "He's seeing ghosts everywhere."

"Yeah, I'm looking right at one," said Gerard, though in fact he wasn't looking at anyone, only the car.

Minna tilted his head at us, at his brother, to say *you know*. And *sorry*.

Then he pulled a book out of his pocket, a small paperback. I don't think I'd ever seen a book in his hands before. "Here," he said to me. He dropped it on the pavement and nudged it under the fence with the toe of his shoe. "Take a look," he said. "Turns out you're not the only freak in the show."

I picked it up. *Understanding Tourette's Syndrome* was the title, first time I'd seen the word.

"Meaning to get that to you," he said. "But I've been sort of busy."

"Great," said Gerard, taking Minna by the arm. "Let's get out of here."

*   *   *

Tony had been searching every day after school, I suspect. It was three days later that he found it and led us others there, to the edge of the Brooklyn-Queens Expressway, at the end of Kane Street. The van was diminished, sagged to its rims, tires melted. The explosion had cleared the windows of their crumbled panes of safety glass, which now lay in a spilled penumbra of grains on the sidewalk and street, together with flakes of traumatized paint and smudges of ash, a photographic map of force. The panels of the truck were layered, graffiti still evident in bone-white outline, all else—Gilbert's shoddy coat of enamel and the manufacturer's ancient green—now chalky black, and delicate like sunburned skin. It was like an X ray of the van that had been before.

We circled it, strangely reverent, afraid to touch, and I thought, *Ashes, ashes*—and then I ran away, up Kane, toward Court Street, before anything could come out of my mouth.

*   *   *

Over the next two years I grew larger—neither fat nor particularly muscular, but large, bearlike, and so harder for the bantamweight Tony or anyone else to bully—and I grew stranger. With the help of Minna's book I contextualized my symptoms as Tourette's, then discovered how little context that was. My constellation of behaviors was "unique as a snowflake," oh, joy, and evolving, like some microscoped crystal in slow motion, to reveal new facets, and to spread from its place at my private core to cover my surface, my public front. The freak show was now the whole show, and my earlier, ticless self impossible anymore to recall clearly. I read in the book of the drugs that might help me, Haldol, Klonopin, and Orap, and laboriously insisted on the Home's once-weekly visiting nurse helping me achieving diagnosis and prescription, only to discover an absolute intolerance: The chemicals slowed my brain to a morose crawl, were a boot on my wheel of self. I might outsmart my symptoms, disguise or incorporate them, frame them as eccentricity or vaudeville, but I wouldn't narcotize them, not if it meant dimming the world (or my brain—same thing) to twilight.

We survived Sarah J. Hale in our different ways. Gilbert had grown, too, and grown a scowl, and he'd learned to sneer or lurch his way through difficulties. Danny coasted elegantly on his basketball skills and sophisticated musical taste, which had evolved through "Rapper's Delight" and Funkadelic to Harold Melvin and the Bluenotes and Teddy Pendergrass. If I saw him in certain company, I knew not to bother saying hello, as he was incapable of recognizing us others from deep within his cone of self-willed blackness. Tony more or less dropped out—it was hard to be officially expelled from Sarah J., so few teachers took attendance—and spent his high-school years on Court Street, hanging out at the arcade, milking acquaintanceships made through Minna for cigarettes and odd jobs and rides on the back of Vespas, and getting lucky with a series of Minna's ex-girlfriends, or so he said. For a six-month stint he was behind the counter at Queen Pizzeria, shoveling slices out of the oven and into white paper bags, taking smoking breaks under the marquee of the triple-X theater next door. I'd stop in and he'd batter me with cheap insults, un-Minna-worthy feints for the amusement of the older pizza men, then guiltily slip me a free slice, then shoo me away with more insults and maybe a slap on the head or a too-realistic fake jab to the spleen.

Me, I became a walking joke, preposterous, improbable, unseeable. My outbursts, utterances and tappings were white noise or static, irritating but tolerated, and finally boring unless they happened to provoke a response from some unsavvy adult, a new or substitute teacher. My peers, even the most unreachable and fearsome black girls, understood instinctively what the teachers and counselors at

Sarah J., hardened into a sort of paramilitary force by dire circumstance, were slow to get: My behavior wasn't teenage rebellion in any sense. And so it wasn't really of *interest* to other teenagers. I wasn't tough, provocative, stylish, self-destructive, sexy, wasn't babbling some secret countercultural tongue, wasn't testing authority, wasn't showing colors of any kind. I wasn't even one of the two or three heedless, timid, green-mohawked and leather-clad punk rockers who required constant beatings for their audacity. I was merely crazy.

*   *   *

By the time Minna returned Gilbert and I were about to graduate—no great feat, mostly a matter of showing up, staying awake, and, in Gilbert's case, of systematically recopying my completed homework in his own hand. Tony had completely stopped showing his face at Sarah J. and Danny was somewhere in between—a presence in the yard and the gym, and in the culture of the school, he'd skipped most of his third-year classes and was being "held back," though the concept was a bit abstract to him, I think. You could have told him he was being returned to kindergarten and he would have shrugged, only asked how high the hoops were placed in the yard, whether the rims could hold his weight.

Minna had Tony in the car already when he drove up outside the school. Gilbert went to the yard to pull Danny out of a three-on-three while I stood on the curb, motionless in the rush of students out of the building, briefly struck dumb. Minna got out of the car, a new Cadillac, bruise-purple. I was taller than Minna now, but that didn't lessen his sway over me, the way his presence automatically begged the question of who I was, where'd I come from, and what kind of man or freak I was turning out to be. It had everything to do with the way, five years before, I'd begun discovering myself upon Minna's jerking me out of the library and into the world, and with the way his voice had primed the pump for mine. My symptoms loved him. I reached for him—though it was May, he was wearing a trench coat—and tapped his shoulder, once, twice, let my hand fall, then raised it again and let fly a staccato burst of Tourettic caresses. Minna still hadn't spoken.

"Eatme, Minnaweed," I said under my breath.

"You're a laugh and a half, Freakshow," said Minna, his face completely grim.

Soon enough I would understand that the Minna who'd returned was not the same as the one who'd left. He'd shed his old jocularity like baby fat. He no longer saw drolleries everywhere, had lost his taste for the spectrum of human comedy. The gate of his attention was narrowed, and what came through it now was pointed and bitter. His affections were more glancing, his laugh just a wince. He was quicker to show the spur of his impatience, too, demanded less *tell your story*, more *walking*.

But at that moment his austerity seemed utterly particular: He wanted us all in the car, had something to say. It was as though he'd been away a week or two instead of two years. He's got a job for us, I felt myself think, or hope, and the years between fell instantly away.

Gilbert brought Danny. We took the backseat; Tony sat in front with Minna. Minna lit a cigarette while he steered with his elbows. We turned off Fourth Avenue, down Bergen. Toward Court Street, I thought. Minna put his lighter away and his hand came out of his trench-coat pockets with business cards.

L&L CAR SERVICE, they read. TWENTY-FOUR HOURS. And a phone number. No slogan this time, and no names.

"You mooks ever get learners' permits?" said Minna.

Nobody had.

"You know where the DMV is, up on Schermerhorn? Here." He dug out a roll, scrunched off four twenties onto the seat beside Tony, who handed them out. For Minna everything had the same price, was fixed and paid for by the quick application of twenty dollars. That hadn't changed. "I'll drop you up there. First I want you to see something."

It was a tiny storefront on Bergen, just short of Smith Street, boarded so tightly it looked like a condemned building. But I, for one, was already familiar with the inside of it. A few years earlier it had been a miniature candy store, with a single rack of comics and magazines, run by a withered Hispanic woman who'd pinioned my arm when I slipped a copy of *Heavy Metal* into my jacket and ducked for the door. Now Minna gestured at it grandly: the future home of L&L Car Service.

Minna had an arrangement with a certain Lucas, at Corvairs Driving School, on Livingston Street—we were all to receive lessons, free of charge, beginning tomorrow. The purple Caddy was the only vehicle in L&L's fleet, but others were on their way. (The car smelled poisonously new, vinyl squeaking like an Indian burn. My probing fingers investigated the backseat armrest ashtray—it contained ten neatly clipped fingernails.) In the meantime we'd be busy getting our licenses and rehabilitating the ruined storefront, fitting it with radios, office equipment, stationery, telephones, tape recorders, microphones (tape recorders? microphones?), a television and a small refrigerator. Minna had money to spend on these things, and he wanted us along to see him spend it. We might look for some suitable clothes while were at it—did we know we looked like rejects from *Welcome Back, Kotter?*—the only thing to do was drop out of Sarah J. immediately. The suggestion didn't ruffle any feathers. In a blink we'd fallen into formation, Pavlov's orphans. We listened to Minna's new tonalities, distrusting and harsh, as they warmed into something like the old, more generous music, the tune we'd missed but not forgotten. He rolled on: We ought to have a CB-radio setup, this was the twentieth fucking century, had we heard? Who knew how to work a CB? Dead silence, punctured by *"Radiobailey!"* Fine, said Minna, the Freak volunteers. Hello? Hello? We almond-studded cheeseballs were staring like we didn't know English—what exactly *had* we been doing for two years anyway, apart from researching how many times a day we could clean out our fish tanks? Silence. Spank our monkeys, rough up our suspects, *jerk off*, Minna meant—did he have to spell it out? More silence. Hello? Hey, had we ever seen *The Conversation*? Best fucking movie in the world, Gene Hackman. We knew Gene Hackman? Silence again. We knew him only from *Superman*—Lex Luthor. It didn't seem likely Minna meant *that* Gene Hackman. (*Lexluthor, textlover, lostbrother*, went my brain, plumbing up trouble—where was Gerard, the other L in L&L? Minna hadn't said his name.) Well, we ought to see it, learn a thing or two about *surveillance*. Talking all the while, he drove us up to Schermerhorn, to the Department of Motor Vehicles. I saw Danny's eyes dart to the Sarah J. boys playing basketball in the park across the street—but now we were with Minna, a million miles away. We ought to get limousine-operator's licenses, he went on. They only cost ten dollars more, the test is the same. Don't smile for the picture, you'll look like the Prom Date Killers. Did we have girlfriends? Of course not, who'd want a bunch of jerks from nowhere. By the way, the Old Stove was dead. Carlotta Minna had passed two weeks ago; Minna was just settling her affairs now. We wondered what affairs, didn't ask. Oh, and Minna had gotten married, he thought to mention now. He and his new wife were moving into Carlotta's old apartment, after first scouring the thirty-year-old sauce off the walls. We jarheads could meet Minna's bride if we got ourselves haircuts first. Was she from Brooklyn? Tony wanted to know. Not exactly; she grew up on an *island*. No, you jerks, not Manhattan or Long Island—a real island. We'd meet her. Apparently first we had to be drivers who operated cameras, tape recorders and CB radios, with suits and haircuts, with unsmiling license photos. First we had to become *Minna Men*, though no one had said those words.

But here, here was *the beauty part*. By Minna's own admission, he'd *buried the lead:* L&L Car Service—it wasn't really a car service. That was just a front. L&L was a *detective agency.*

*   *   *

The joke Minna wanted to hear in the emergency room, the joke about Irving, went like this:

A Jewish mother—Mrs. Gushman, we'll call her—walks into a travel agency. "I vant to go to Tibet," she says. "Listen lady, take my word for it, you don't want to go to Tibet. I've got a nice package tour for the Florida Keys, or maybe Hawaii—" "No," says Mrs. Gushman, "I vant to go to *Tibet.*" "Lady, are you traveling alone? Tibet is no place—" "Sell me a ticket for Tibet!" shouts Mrs. Gushman. "Okay, okay." So she goes to Tibet. Gets off the plane, says to the first person she sees, "Who's the greatest holy man in Tibet?" "Why, that would be the High Lama," comes the reply. "That's who I vant to see," says Mrs. Gushman. "Take me to the High Lama." "Oh, no, you don't understand, American Lady, the High Lama lives on top of our highest mountain in total seclusion. No one can see the High Lama." "I'm Mrs. Gushman, I've come all the vay to Tibet, and I must see the High Lama!" "Oh, but you could never—" "Which mountain? How do I get there?" So Mrs. Gushman checks into a hotel at the base of the mountain and hires sherpas to take her to the monastery at the top. All the way up they're trying to explain to her, nobody sees the High Lama—his own monks have to fast and meditate for years before they're allowed to ask the High Lama a single question. She just keeps pointing her finger and saying "I'm Mrs. Gushman, take me up the mountain!" When they get to the monastery the sherpas explain to the monks—crazy American lady, wants to see the High Lama. She says, "Tell the High Lama Mrs. Gushman is here to see him." "You don't understand, we could never—" "Just tell him!" The monks go and come back and they're shaking their heads in confusion. "We don't understand, but the High Lama says he will grant you an audience. Do you understand what an honor—" "Yes, yes," she says. "Just take me!" So they lead her in to see the High Lama. The monks are whispering and they open the door and the High Lama nods—they can leave him alone with Mrs. Gushman. And the High Lama looks at Mrs. Gushman and Mrs. Gushman says, "Irving, when are you coming home? Your father's worried!"

INTERROGATION EYES

Minna Men wear suits. Minna Men drive cars. Minna Men listen to tapped lines. Minna Men stand behind Minna, hands in their pockets, looking menacing. Minna Men carry money. Minna Men collect money. Minna Men don't ask questions. Minna Men answer phones. Minna Men pick up packages. Minna Men are clean-shaven. Minna Men follow instructions. Minna Men try to be like Minna, but Minna is dead.

*   *   *

Gilbert and I left the hospital so quickly, and drove back in such a perfect fog of numbness, that when we walked into L&L and Tony said, "Don't say it. We already heard," it was as though I were learning myself for the first time.

"Heard from who?" said Gilbert.

"Black cop, through here a few minutes ago, looking for you," said Tony. "You just missed him."

Tony and Danny stood furiously smoking cigarettes behind L&L's counter, their foreheads pasty with sweat, eyes fogged and distant, teeth grinding behind their drawn lips. They looked like somebody had worked them over and they wanted to take it out on us.

The Bergen Street office was as we'd renovated it fifteen years before: divided in two by the Formica counter, thirty-inch color television playing constantly in the "waiting area" on this side of the counter, telephones, file cabinets and computer on the rear wall, underneath a massive laminated map of Brooklyn, Minna's heavy Magic Marker numerals scrawled across each neighborhood, showing the price of an L&L ride—five bucks to the Heights, seven to Park Slope or Fort Greene, twelve to Williamsburg or Borough Park, seventeen to Bushwick. Airports or Manhattan were twenty and up.

The ashtray on the counter was full of cigarette butts that had been in Minna's fingers, the telephone log full of his handwriting from earlier in the day. The sandwich on top of the fridge wore his bite marks. We were all four of us an arrangement around a missing centerpiece, as incoherent as a verbless sentence.

"How did they find us?" I said. "We've got Frank's wallet." I opened it up and took out the bundle of Frank's business cards and slipped them into my pocket. Then I dropped it on the counter and slapped the Formica five times to finish a six-count.

Nobody minded me except myself. This was my oldest, most jaded audience. Tony shrugged and said, "Him croaking out *L and L* as his dying words? A business card in his coat? Gilbert giving out names like a fucking idiot? You tell *me* how they found us."

"What did this cop want?" said Gilbert stoically. He would deal with one problem at a time, the plodder, even if they stacked up from here to the moon.

"He said you weren't supposed to leave the hospital, that's what he said. You gave some nurse your *name*, Gilbert."

"Fuck it," said Coney. "Fuck some fucking black cop."

"Yeah, well, you can express that sentiment in person, since he's coming back. And you might want to say, 'Fuck some fucking black homicide detective,' since that's actually what you're dealing with here. Smart cop, too. You could see it in his eyes."

"Fuckicide," I thought to add.

"Who's going to tell Julia?" said Danny quietly. His mouth, his whole face, was veiled in smoke. Nobody answered.

"Well, I won't be here when he comes back," said Gilbert. "I'll be out doing his work for him, catching the motherfucker who did this. Gimme a coffin nail."

"Slow down, Sherlock," said Tony, handing him a cigarette. "I wanna know how'd it even happen in the first place? How'd the two of you even get involved? I thought you were supposed to be on a stakeout."

"Frank showed up," said Gilbert, trying to flick his depleted lighter again and again, failing to make it catch. "He went inside. Fuck. Fuck." His voice was clenched like a fist. I saw the whole stupid sequence playing behind his eyes: parked car, wire, traffic light, Brainum, the chain of banalities that somehow led to the bloody Dumpster and the hospital. The chain of banalities now immortalized by our guilt.

"Inside *where*?" said Tony, handing Gilbert a book of matches. The phone rang.

"Some kinda kung-fu place," said Gilbert. "Ask Lionel, he knows all about it—"

"Not kung fu," I started. "Meditation—"

"You're trying to say they killed him with *meditation*?" said Tony. The phone rang a second time.

"No, no, we saw who killed him—*Viable Guessfrog!*—a big Polish guy—*Barnamum Pierogi!*—I mean *really* big. We only saw him from behind."

"Which one of us is going to tell Julia?" said Danny again. The phone rang a third time.

I picked it up and said, "L and L."

"Need a car at One-eighty-eight Warren, corner of—" droned a female voice.

"No cars," I said by rote.

"You don't have any cars?"

"No cars." I gulped, ticking like a time bomb.

"How soon can you get a car?"

"Lionel Deathclam!" I shouted into the phone. That got the caller's attention, enough that she hung up. My fellow Minna Men glanced at me, jarred only slightly from their hard-boiled despair.

*   *   *

A real car service, even a small one, has a fleet of no fewer than thirty cars working in rotation, and at the very least ten on the street at any given time. Elite, our nearest rival, on Court Street, has sixty cars, three dispatchers, probably twenty-five drivers on a shift. Rusty's, on Atlantic Avenue, has eighty cars. New Relámpago, a Dominican-run service out of Williamsburg, has one hundred and sixty cars, a magisterial secret economy of private transportation hidden deep in the borough. Car services are completely dependent on phone dispatches—the drivers are forbidden by law to pick up customers on the street, lest they compete with medallioned taxicabs. So the drivers and dispatchers litter the world with business cards, slip them into apartment foyers like Chinese take-out menus, leave them stacked beside potted plants in hospital waiting rooms, palm them out with the change at the end of every ride. They sticker pay phones with their phone number, writ in phosphorescent font.

L&L had five cars, one for each of us, and we were barely ever available to drive them. We never handed out cards, were never friendly to callers, and had, five years before, removed our phone number from both the Yellow Pages and the sign over the Bergen Street storefront.

Nevertheless, our number circulated, so that one of our main activities was picking up the phone to say "no cars."

*   *   *

As I replaced the receiver Gilbert was explaining what he knew about the stakeout, doggedly. English might have been his fourth or fifth language from the sound of it, but you couldn't question his commitment. As *Bionic Dreadlog* was my likely contribution—my mourning brain had decided renaming itself was the evening's assignment—I was in no position to criticize. I stepped outside, away from the chain-smoking confusion, into the cold, light-washed night. Smith Street was alive, F train murmuring underneath, pizzeria, Korean grocer, and the Casino all streaming with customers. It could have been any night—nothing in the Smith Street scene required that Minna have died that day. I went to the car and retrieved the notebook from the glove compartment, doing my best not to glance at the bloodstained backseat. Then I thought of Minna's final ride. There was something I'd forgotten. When I steeled myself to look in the back I saw what it was: his watch and beeper. I fished them out from under the passenger seat where they'd slid and put them in my pocket.

I locked the car and rehearsed a few imaginary options. I could go back to the Yorkville Zendo by myself and have a look around. I could also seek out the homicide detective, earn his trust, pool my knowledge with him instead of the Men. I could walk down Atlantic Avenue, sit in an Arabic storefront where they knew me and wouldn't gape, and drink a tiny cup of mudlike black coffee and eat a baklava or Crow's Nest—acid, steam and sugar to poison my grief.

Or I could go back into the office. I went back into the office. Gilbert was still fumbling with the end of his account, our race up the ambulance ramp, the confusion at the hospital. He wanted Tony and Danny to know we'd done all we could do. I laid the notebook flat on the counter and with a red ballpoint circled WOMAN, GLASSES and

ULLMAN, DOWNTOWN, those crucial new players on our stage. Paper-thin and unrevealing as they might be, they had more life than Minna now.

I had other questions: The building they'd spoken of. The door-man's interference. The unnamed woman Frank lost control of, the one who missed her *Rama-lama-ding-dong*. The wiretap itself: What did Minna hope I'd hear? Why couldn't he just tell me what to listen for?

"We asked him, in the back of the car," said Gilbert. "We asked him and he wouldn't tell us. I don't know why he wouldn't tell."

"Asked him what?" said Tony.

"Asked him who killed him," said Gilbert. "I mean, before he was dead."

I remembered the name Irving, but didn't say anything.

"Somebody's definitely going to have to tell Julia," said Danny.

Gilbert grasped the significance of the notebook. He stepped over and read what I'd circled. "Who's Ullman?" said Gilbert, looking at me. "You wrote this?"

"In the car," I said. "It's the note I took in the car. 'Ullman, down-town' was where Frank was supposed to go when he got into the car. The guy in the Zendo, who sent him out—that's where he was send-ing him."

"Sent him where?" said Tony.

"Doesn't matter," I said. "He didn't go. The giant took him and killed him instead. What matters is who sent him—*Failey! Bakum! Flakely!*—the guy inside the place."

"I'm not telling Julia," said Danny. "I don't care what anyone says."

"Well, it ain't gonna be me," said Gilbert, noticing Danny at last.

"We ought to go back to the East Side—*TrickyZendo!*—and have a look around." I was panting to get to the point, and Julia didn't seem to me to be it.

"All right, all right," said Tony. "We're gonna put our fucking heads together here."

At the word *heads* I was blessed with a sudden vision: Lacking Minna, ours, put together, were as empty and tenuous as balloons. Untethered by his death, the only question was how quickly they would drift apart, how far—and whether they'd burst or just wither.

"Okay," said Tony. "Gilbert, we gotta get you out of here. You're the name they've got. So we'll get you out doing some hoofwork. You look for this Ullman guy."

"How am I supposed to do that?" Gilbert wasn't exactly a specialist in digging up leads.

"Why don't you let me help him?" I said.

"I need you for something else," said Tony. "Gilbert can find Ullman."

"Yeah," said Gilbert. "But how?"

"Maybe his name's in the book," said Tony. "It's not so common, Ullman. Or maybe in Frank's book—you got that? Frank's address book?"

Gilbert looked at me.

"Must still be in his coat," I said. "Back at the hospital." But this triggered a compulsive self-frisking anyway. I patted each of my pockets six times. Under my breath I said, *"Franksbook, forkspook, finksblood—"*

"Great," said Tony. "That's just great. Well, show some initiative for once and find the guy. That's your *job*, Gilbert, for chrissakes. Call your pal, the garbage cop—he's got access to police records, right? Find Ullman and size him up. Maybe he's your giant. He might of been a little impatient for his date with Frank."

"The guy upstairs set Frank up," I said. I was frustrated that Gilbert and his jerk friend from the Sanitation Police were getting the assignment to track Ullman. "They were in it together, the guy upstairs and the giant. He knew the giant was waiting downstairs."

"Okay, but the giant could still be this guy Ullman," said Tony irritably. "And that's what Gilbert's going to find out, okay?"

I raised my hands in surrender, then snatched an imaginary fly out of the air.

"I'll go up to the East Side myself," said Tony. "Take a look around. See if I can get into this building. Danny, you mind the store."

"Check," said Danny, stubbing out his cigarette.

"That cop's gonna come back around," said Tony. "You talk to him. Cooperate, just don't give him anything. We don't want to look like we're panicking." Implicit in this assignment was the notion of Danny's superior rapport with the *fucking black cop*.

"You make it sound like we're the suspects," I said.

"That's how this cop made it sound," said Tony. "It isn't me."

"What about me?" I said. "You want me—*Criminal Fishrug!*—to go with you? I know the place."

"No," said Tony. "You go explain to Julia."

*   *   *

Julia Minna had come back with Frank from wherever he'd gone between the dissolution of the moving company and the founding of the detective agency. She might have been the last and greatest of the Minna girls, for all we knew—she sure looked the part: tall, plush, blond by nurture, defiant around the jaw. It was easy to imagine Minna joshing with her, untucking her shirt, taking an elbow in the stomach. But by the time we got to meet her the two had initiated their long, dry stalemate. All that remained of their original passion was a faint crackle of electricity animating their insults, their drab swipes at one another. That was all that showed anyway. Julia terrified us at first, not for anything she did, but because of her cool grip on Minna, and also how tense he was around her, how ready to punish us with his words.

If Julia and Frank had still been animated, quickened with love, we might have remained in infantile awe of her, our fascination and lust still adolescent. But the chill between them was an opening. In our imaginations we became Frank and loved her, unchilled her, grew to manhood in her arms. If we were angry or disappointed with Frank

Minna we felt connected to his beautiful, angry, disappointed wife, and were thrilled. She became an idol of disillusionment. Frank had shown us what girls were, and now he'd shown us a woman. And by failing to love her, he'd left a margin for our love to grow.

In our dreams we Minna Men were all Frank Minna—that wasn't news. But now we shot a little higher: If we had Julia we would do better than Frank, and make her happy.

Or so went dreams. I suppose over the years the other Minna Men conquered their fear and awe and desire of Julia, or anyway modulated it, by finding women of their own to make happy and unhappy, to enchant and disenchant and discard.

All except me, of course.

*   *   *

In the beginning Minna had Julia installed in the office of a Court Street lawyer, in a storefront as small as L&L's. We Men used to drop in on her there with little deliveries, messages or gifts from Frank, and watch her answering phones, reading *People*, making bad coffee. Minna seemed eager to show us off to her, more eager than he was to drop in himself. Similarly, he seemed pleased to have Julia on showcase there, under glass on Court Street. We all intuitively grasped Minna's instinct for human symbols, for moving us around to mark territory, so in this one sense Julia Minna had joined the Men, was on the team. Something went wrong, however, something soured between Julia and the lawyer, and Minna dragged her back to Carlotta Minna's old second-story apartment on Baltic Street, where she'd stayed for most of fifteen years, a sulking housewife. I could never visit without thinking of Carlotta's plates of food being carried down the stairwell by Court Street's assorted mugs. The old stove itself was gone, though. Julia and Frank mostly ate out.

I went to that apartment now, and knocked on the door, rolling my knuckles to get the right sound.

"Hello, Lionel," Julia said after peering at me through the peephole. She left the door unlatched and turned her back. I ducked inside. She wore a slip, her ripe arms bared, but below it she was already in stockings and heels. The apartment was dark, except for the bedroom. I shut the door behind me and followed her in, to where a dusty suitcase lay open on the bed, surrounded by heaps of clothing. It wasn't going to be my privilege to be first with the news anywhere, apparently. In a mass of lingerie already inside the suitcase I spotted something dark and shiny, half smothered there. A pistol.

Julia rummaged in her dresser, her back still turned. I propped myself in the closet doorframe, feeling awkward.

I could make out her labored breathing as she fumbled through the drawers.

"Who told you, Julia? *Eat, eat, eat—*" I ground my teeth, trying to check the impulse.

"Who do you think? I got a call from the hospital."

"Eat, ha ha, eat—" I revved like a motor.

"You want me to eat you, Lionel?" Her tone was grimly casual. "Just come out and say it."

"Okayeatme," I said gratefully. "You're packing? I mean, I don't mean the gun." I thought of Minna reprimanding Gilbert at the car, a few hours before. *You with no gun,* he'd said. *That's how I sleep at night.* "Packing your clothes—"

"Did they tell you to come over here and comfort me?" she said sharply. "Is that what you're doing?"

She turned. I saw the redness in her eyes and the heaviness and softness of the flesh around her mouth. She groped for a pack of cigarettes that lay on the dresser, and when she put one between her grief-swollen lips I checked myself for a lighter I knew I wasn't carrying, just to make a show of it. She lit the cigarette herself, chopping at a matchbook angrily, throwing off a little curl of spark.

The scene stirred me in about twelve different ways. Somehow Frank Minna was still alive in this room, alive in Julia in her slip with her half-packed suitcase, her cigarette, her gun. The two of them were closer at this moment than they had ever been. More truly married. But she was hurrying away. I sensed that if I let her go, that essence of him that I detected would go, too.

She looked at me and flared the end of the cigarette, then blew out smoke. "You jerks killed him," she said.

Her cigarette dangled in her fingers. I fought off a weird imagining: that she'd catch her slip on fire—it did seem flammable, practically looked aflame already—and that I'd have to put her out, drench her with a glass of water. This was an uncomfortable feature of Tourette's—my brain would throw up ugly fantasies, glimpses of pain, disasters narrowly averted. It liked to flirt with such images, the way my twitchy fingers were drawn near the blades of a spinning fan. Perhaps I also craved a crisis I could master, now, after failing Minna. I wanted to protect someone, and Julia would do.

"It wasn't us, Julia," I said. "We just didn't manage to keep him alive. He was killed by a giant, a guy the size of six guys."

"That's great," she said. "That sounds great. You've got it down, Lionel. You sound just like them. I hate the way you all talk, you know that?" She went back to stuffing clothes anarchically into the suitcase.

I mimed her striking of the match, one long motion away from my body, more or less keeping my cool. In fact, I wanted to run my hands through the clothes on the bed, snap the suitcase latches open and shut, lick the vinyl.

"Jerktalk!" I said.

She ignored me. A police siren sounded out on Smith Street and Baltic, and I shuddered. If the hospital had phoned her, the police couldn't be too far behind. But the sirens stopped half a block away. Just a traffic stop, a shakedown. Any given car on any given evening on Smith Street fit a profile, some profile. The cop's red light strobed through the margin of window under the shade, to throw a glow over the bed and Julia's glossy outline.

"You can't go, Julia."

"Watch."

"We need you."

She smirked at me. "You'll manage."

"No, really, Julia. Frank put L and L in your name. We work for you now."

"Really?" said Julia, interested now, or feigning interest—she made me too nervous to tell. "All I see before me is mine? Is that what you're telling me?"

I gulped, jerked my head to the side, as though she were looking behind me.

"You think I should come down and oversee the day-to-day business of a *car service*, Lionel? Have a look at the *books*? You think that might be a good occupation for the widow?"

"We're—*Detectapush! Octaphone!*—we're a detective agency. We're going to catch whoever did this." Even as I spoke, I tried to order my thoughts according to this principle: detectives, clues, investigation. I should be gathering information. I wondered for a moment if Julia were the *her* Frank had lost control of, according to the insinuating voice on the wire at the Zendo.

Of course, that would mean she missed her *Rama-lama-ding-dong*. Whatever that was, I couldn't really picture Julia missing it.

"That's right," she said. "I forgot. I'm heir to a corrupt and inept detective agency. Get out of my way, Lionel." She set her cigarette on the edge of the dresser and pushed past me, into the closet.

Inupt and corrept, went the brain of Essrog the Idiotic. *You are corrept, sir!*

"God, look at these dresses," she said as she poked through the rack of hangers. Her voice was suddenly choked. "You see these?"

I nodded.

"They're worth more than the car service put together."

"Julia—"

"This isn't how I dress, really. This isn't how I look. I don't even like these dresses."

"How do you look?"

"You could never imagine. I can barely remember, myself. Before Frank dressed me up."

"Show me."

"Ha." She looked away. "I'm supposed to be the widow in black. You'd like that. I'd look really good. That's what Frank kept me around for, my big moment. No thanks. Tell Tony no thanks." She swept at the dresses, pushing them deeper into the closet. Then she abruptly pulled two out by the hangers and threw them onto the bed, where they spread over the suitcase like roosting butterflies. They weren't black.

"Tony?" I said. I was distracted, my eagle eye watching the ash burn longer, the glowing end of the abandoned cigarette inching toward the wood of the dresser.

"That's right, Tony. Fucking Frank Minna Junior. I'm sorry, Lionel, did you want to be Frank? Did I hurt your feelings? I'm afraid Tony has the inside track."

"That cigarette is going to burn the wood."

"Let it burn," she said.

"Is that a quote from a movie? 'Let it burn'? I feel like I remember that from some movie—*Burnamum Beatme!*"

She turned her back to me, moved again to the bed. Untangling the dresses from their hangers, she stuffed one into the suitcase, then held the other open and stepped into it, careful not to snag the heels of her shoes. I gripped the closet doorframe, stifling an impulse to bat like a kitten at the shimmery fabric as she slid the dress up around her hips and over her shoulders.

"Come here, Lionel," she said, without turning around. "Zip me up."

As I reached out, I was compelled to tap each of her shoulders twice, gently. She didn't seem to mind. Then I took hold of the zipper tab, eased it upward. As I did she took her hair in her hands, raised her arms above her head and turned, so that she rolled into my embrace. I kept hold of the tab, halfway up her back. Up close I saw how her eyes and lips looked like something barely rescued from drowning.

"Don't stop," she said.

She rested her elbows high on my shoulders and gazed up at my face while I tugged at the zipper. I held my breath.

"You know, when I met Frank I'd never shaved my armpits before. He made me shave." She spoke the words into my chest, her voice dopey now, absent-sounding. All the anger was gone.

I got the zipper to the nape of her neck and dropped my hands, then took a step back and exhaled. She still held her hair bunched above her head.

"Maybe I'll grow the hair back. What do you think, Lionel?"

I opened my mouth and what came out, soft but unmistakable, was "Doublebreasts."

"All breasts are double, Lionel. Didn't you know that?"

"That was just a tic," I said awkwardly, lowering my eyes.

"Give me your hands, Lionel."

I lifted my hands again, and she took them.

"God, they're big. You have such big hands, Lionel." Her voice was dreamy and singsong, like a child, or a grownup pretending to be a child. "I mean—the way you move them around so quickly, when you do that thing you do, all that grabbing, touching stuff. What's that called again?"

"That's a tic, too, Julia."

"I always think of your hands as small because they move so fast. But they're big."

She moved them to her breasts.

*　　*　　*

Sexual excitement stills my Tourette's brain, not by numbing me, dimming the world like Orap or Klonopin, those muffling medications, but instead by setting up a deeper attentiveness in me, a finer vibration, which gathers and encompasses my urgent chaos, enlists it in a greater cause, like a chorus of voices somehow drawing a shriek into harmony. I'm still myself and still in myself, a rare and precious combination. Yes, I like sex very much. I don't get it very often. When I do, I find I want to slow it down to a crawl, live in that place, get to meet my stilled self, give him a little time to look around. Instead I'm hurried along by the conventional urgencies, by those awkward, alcohol-fueled juxtapositions of persons that have so far provided my few glimpses of arousal's haven. But oh, if I could have just spent a week or so with my hands on Julia's breasts, then I could think straight!

*   *   *

Alas, my very first straight thought guided my hands elsewhere. I went and plucked the smoldering cigarette off the dresser, rescuing the finish, and since Julia's lips were slightly parted I stuck it there, filter end first.

"Double, see?" she said as she drew on the cigarette. She combed her hair with her fingers, then straightened her slip under her dress where I'd held her.

"What's double?"

"You know, breasts."

"You shouldn't make fun of—*Lyrical Eggdog! Logical Assnog!*—you shouldn't make fun of me, Julia."

"I'm not."

"Did something— Is there something between you and Tony?"

"I don't know. Screw Tony. I like you better, Lionel. I just never told you." She was hurt, erratic, her voice straying wildly, searching for a place to rest.

"I like you, too, Julia. There's nothing—*Screwtony! Nertscrony! Screwtsony! Tootscrewny!*—sorry. There's nothing wrong with that."

"I want you to like me, Lionel."

"You're—you're not saying there could actually be something between us?" I turned and slapped the doorframe six times, feeling my face curdle with shame, regretting the question instantly—wishing, for once, that I'd ticced instead, something obnoxious to obliterate the conversation's meaning, to smother the words I'd let myself say.

"No," she said coldly. She set the cigarette, what was left of it, back on the dresser. "You're too strange, Lionel. Much too strange. I mean, take a look in the mirror." She resumed crushing her clothes into the suitcase, more than seemed possible, like a magician stuffing a prop for a trick.

I only hoped the gun wouldn't go off. "Where are you going, Julia?" I said tiredly.

"I'm going to a place of peace, if you must know, Lionel."

"A—what?" *Prays of peach? Plays of peas? Press-e-piece?*

"You heard me. A place of peace."

Then a horn sounded outside.

"That's my car," she said. "Would you go and tell them I'll be out in a minute?"

"Okay, but—*pressure pees*—that's a strange thing to say."

"Have you ever been out of Brooklyn, Lionel?"

Breasts, underarm hair, now Brooklyn—for Julia it was all just a measure of my inexperience. "Sure," I said. "I was in Manhattan just this afternoon." I tried not to think about what I'd been doing there, or failing to do.

"New York City, Lionel. Have you ever been out of New York City?"

While I considered this question I eyed the cigarette, which had at last begun to singe the dresser top. The blackening paint stood for my defeat here. I couldn't protect anything, maybe least of all myself.

"Because if you had, you'd know that anywhere else is a place of peace. So that's where I'm going. Would you please go hold my car for me?"

*   *   *

The car service double-parked in front of the building was Legacy Pool, the furthest upscale of the Brooklyn competitors, with all-black luxury models, tinted windows, cell phones for the customers, and built-in tissue-box holders under the rear window. Julia was running in style. I waved at the driver from the stoop of her building, and he nodded at me and leaned his head back on the rest. I was trying out his neck motions, *nod, lean,* when the gravely voice appeared behind me.

"Who's the car for?"

It was the homicide detective. He'd been waiting, staking us out, slumped to one side of the doorway, huddled in his coat against the chilly November night. I made him right away—with his 10 P.M. Styrofoam cup of coffee, worn tie, ingrown beard, and interrogation eyes, he was unmistakable—but that didn't mean he had any idea who I was.

"Lady inside," I said, and tapped him once on the shoulder.

"Watch it," he said, ducking away from my touch.

"Sorry, friend. Can't help myself." I turned from him, back into the building.

The elegance of my exit was quickly thwarted, though—Julia was just then galumphing down the stairs with her overstuffed suitcase. I rushed to help her as the door eased slowly shut on its moaning hydraulic hinge. Too slowly: The cop stuck out his foot and held the door open for us.

"Excuse me," he said with a sly, exhausted authority. "You Julia Minna?"

"I was," said Julia.

"You were?"

"Yes. Isn't that funny? I was until just about an hour ago. Lionel, put my bag in the trunk."

"In a hurry?" the detective asked Julia. I watched the two of them size one another up, as though I weren't any more a factor than the waiting limo driver. *A few minutes ago,* I wanted to say, *my hands*— Instead I hoisted Julia's luggage, and waited for her to move past me to the car.

"Sort of," said Julia. "Plane to catch."

"Plane to where?" He crushed his empty Styrofoam cup and tossed it over his shoulder, off the stoop, into the neighbor's bushes. They were already decorated with trash.

"I haven't decided yet."

"She's going to a *precipice, pleasurepolice, philanthropriest*—"

"Shut up, Lionel."

The detective looked at me like I was crazy.

*   *   *

My life story to this point:

The teacher looked at me like I was crazy.

The social-services worker looked at me like I was crazy.

The boy looked at me like I was crazy and then hit me.

The girl looked at me like I was crazy.

The woman looked at me like I was crazy.

The black homicide detective looked at me like I was crazy.

*   *   *

"I'm afraid you can't go, Julia," said the detective, shaking off his con-fusion at my utterances with a sigh and a grimace. He'd seen plenty in his day, could cope with a little more before needing to bust my chops over it—that was the feeling I got. "We're going to want to talk to you about Frank."

"You'll have to arrest me," said Julia.

"Why would you want to say that?" said the detective, pained.

"Just to keep things simple," said Julia. "Arrest me or I'm getting in the car. Lionel, please."

I humped the huge, unwieldy suitcase down the stoop and waved at the driver to pop the trunk. Julia followed, the detective close behind. The limo's speakers were oozing Mariah Carey, the driver still mellow on the headrest. When Julia slid into the backseat, the detective caught the door in his two meaty hands and leaned in over the top.

"Don't you care who killed your husband, Mrs. Minna?" He was plainly unnerved by Julia's blitheness.

"Let me know when you find out who killed him," she said. "Then I'll tell you if I care."

I pushed the suitcase in over the top of the spare tire. I briefly considered opening it up and confiscating Julia's pistol, then realized I probably didn't want to emerge with a gun in front of the homicide cop. He was liable to misunderstand. Instead I shut the trunk.

"That would involve us being in touch," the detective pointed out to Julia.

"I told you, I don't know where I'm going. Do you have a card?"

As he straightened to reach into his vest pocket she slammed the door, then rolled down her window to accept his card.

"We could have you stopped at the airport," he said severely, trying to remind her of his authority, or remind himself. But that *we* was weaker than he knew.

"Yes," said Julia. "But it sounds like you've decided to let me go. I appreciate it." She palmed his card into her purse.

"Where were you this afternoon when Frank was killed, Mrs. Minna?"

"Talk to Lionel," said Julia, looking back at me. "He's my alibi. We were together all day."

"Eat me alibailey," I breathed, as quietly as I could. The detective frowned at me. I held my hands open and made an Art Carney face, pleading for a common understanding between us—women, sus-

pects, widows, whattayagonnado? Can't live with 'em, can't live without 'em, eh?

Julia powered her tinted window back up into place and the Legacy Pool limousine took off, idiot radio trickling away to silence, leaving me and the detective standing in the dark of Baltic Street by ourselves.

"Lionel."

Alibi hullabaloo gullible bellyflop smellafish, sang my brain, obliterating speech. I waved a farewell at the detective and started toward Smith Street. If Julia could leave him flat-footed, why couldn't I?

He followed. "We better talk, Lionel." He'd blown it, let her go, and now he was going to compensate with me, exercise his deductive and bullying powers.

"Can't it wait?" I managed, without turning—it took a considerable effort not to swivel my neck. But I felt him right on my heels, like a pacing man and his shadow.

"What's your full name, Lionel?"

"Lullaby Gueststar—"

"Come again?"

"Alibyebye Essmob—"

"Sounds Arabic," said the detective as he pulled even with me. "You don't look Arabic, though. Where were you and the lady this afternoon, Alibi?"

"Lionel," I forced myself to say clearly, and then blurted *"Lionel Arrestme!"*

"That's not gonna work twice in the same night," said the cop. "I don't have to arrest you. We're just taking a walk, Alibi. Only I don't know where we're going. You want to tell me?"

"Home," I said, before I recalled that he'd been to the place I called home once already this evening, and that it wasn't in my best interests to lead him there again. "Except actually I'd like to get a sandwich first. I'm starving. You want to get a sandwich with me? There's a place on Smith, called Zeod's, if that's okay, we'll get a sandwich and then maybe part ways there, since I'm kind of shy about bringing people back to my place—" As I turned to deliver my speech my shoulder-lust was activated, and I began reaching for him again.

He knocked my hand away. "Slow down, Alibi. What's the matter with you?"

"Tourette's syndrome," I said, with a grim sense of inevitability. Tourette's was my other name, and, like my name, my brain could never leave the words unmolested. Sure enough, I produced my own echo: "Tourette is the shitman!" Nodding, gulping, flinching, I tried to silence myself, walk quickly toward the sandwich shop, and keep my eyes down, so that the detective would be out of range of my shoulder-scope. No good, I was juggling too much, and when I re-ticced, it came out a bellow: *"Tourette Is the Shitman!"*

"He's the shitman, huh?" The detective apparently thought we were exchanging up-to-the-minute street jargon. "Can you take me to him?"

"No, no, there's no Tourette," I said, catching my breath. I felt mad for food, desperate to shake the detective, and choked with imminent tics.

"Don't worry," said the detective, talking down to me. "I won't tell him who gave out his name."

He thought he was grooming a stool pigeon. I could only try not to laugh or shout. Let Tourette be the suspect and maybe I'd get off the hook.

On Smith Street we veered into Zeod's Twenty-Four-Hour Market, where the odors of baloney and bad coffee mingled with those of pistachio, dates, and St. John's bread. If the cop wanted an Arab, I'd give him an Arab. Zeod himself stood on the elevated ramp behind the Plexiglas-and-plywood counter. He saw me and said, "Crazyman! How are you my friend?"

"Not so good," I admitted. The detective hovered behind me, tempting me to turn my head again. I resisted.

"Where's Frank?" said Zeod. "How I never see Frank anymore?"

Here was my chance to deliver the news at last, and my heart wasn't up to it. "He's in the hospital," I said, unable now to keep from glancing nervously at the homicide detective. *"Doctorbyebye!"* recalled my Tourette's.

"Some crazyman you are," said Zeod, smiling and arching his hedge of eyebrows knowingly at my official shadow. "You tell Frank Zeod asks, okay, partner?"

"Okay," I said. "I'll do that. How about a sandwich for now? Turkey on a kaiser, plenty of mustard."

Zeod nodded at his second, an indolent Dominican kid, who moved to the slicer. Zeod never made sandwiches himself. But he'd taught his countermen well, to slice extraordinarily thin and drape the meat as it slid off the blade so it fell in bunches, rather than stacking airlessly, to make a sandwich with that fluffy compressibility I craved. I let myself be hypnotized by the whine of the slicer, the rhythm of the kid's arm as he received the slices and dripped them onto the kaiser roll. Zeod watched me. He knew I obsessed on his sandwiches, and it pleased him. "You and your friend?" he said magnanimously.

The detective shook his head. "Pack of Marlboro Lights," he said.

"Okay. You want a soda, Crazyman? Get yourself." I went and got a Coke out of the cooler while Zeod put my sandwich and the cop's cigarettes into a brown paper bag with a plastic fork and a sheaf of napkins.

"Charge it to Frank, yes, my friend?"

I couldn't speak. I took the bag and we stepped back out onto Smith Street.

"Sleeping with the dead man's wife," said the detective. "Now you're eating on his tab. That takes some gall."

"You misunderstand," I said.

"Then maybe you better set me straight," he said. "Gimme those cigarettes."

"I work for Frank—"

"Worked. He's dead. Why didn't you tell your friend the A-rab?"

"*Arab-eye!*—I don't know. No reason." I handed the cop his Marlboros. "*Eatmebailey, repeatmebailey, repeatmobile*—could we continue this maybe another time? Because—*retreatmobile!*—because now I really urgently have to go home and—*eatbail! beatmail!*—eat this sandwich."

"You work for him where? At the car service?"

Detective agency, I silently corrected. "Uh, yeah."

"So you and his wife were, what? Driving around? Where's the car?"

"She wanted to go shopping." This lie came out so blessedly smooth and un-tic-laden it felt like the truth. For that reason or some other, the detective didn't challenge it.

"So you'd describe yourself as, what? A friend of the deceased?"

"*Trend the decreased! Mend the retreats!*—sure, that's right."

He was learning to ignore my outbursts. "So where are we going now? Your house?" He lit a cigarette without breaking stride. "Looks like you're headed back to work."

I didn't want to tell him how little difference there was between the two.

"Let's go in here," I said, jerking my neck sideways as we crossed Bergen Street, letting my physical tic lead me—navigation by Tourette's—into the Casino.

*   *   *

The Casino was Minna's name for Smith Street's hole-in-the-wall newspaper shop, which had a single wall of magazines and a case of Pepsi and Snapple crammed into a space the size of a large closet. The Casino was named for the lines that stretched each morning to buy Lotto and Scratchers and Jumble 6 and Pickball, for the fortune being made on games of chance by the newsstand's immigrant Korean owners, for the hearts being quietly broken there round the clock. There was something tragic in the way they stood obediently waiting, many of them elderly, others new immigrants, illiterate except in the small language of their chosen game, deferring to anyone with real business, like the purchase of a magazine, a pack of double-A batteries, or a tube of lip gloss. That docility was heartbreaking. The games were over almost before they started, the foil scraped off tickets with a key or a dime, the contrived near-misses underneath bared. (New York is a Tourettic city, and this great communal scratching and counting and tearing is a definite symptom.) The sidewalk just outside the Casino was strewn with discarded tickets, the chaff of wasted hope.

But I was hardly in a position to criticize lost causes. I had no reason for visiting the Casino except that I associated it with Minna, with Minna alive. If I visited enough of his haunts before news of his death spread along Court and Smith Street, I might persuade myself against the evidence of my own eyes—and against the fact of the homicide cop on my heels—that nothing had happened.

"What're we doing?" said the detective.

"I, uh, need something to read with my sandwich."

The desultory magazines were shelved two deep in the rack—there weren't more than one or two customers for *GQ* or *Wired* or *Brooklyn Bridge* per month around here. Me, I was bluffing, didn't read magazines at all. Then I spotted a familiar face, on a magazine called *Vibe*: The Artist Formerly Known as Prince. Before a blurred cream background he posed resting his head against the neck of a pink guitar, his eyes demure. The unpronounceable typographical glyph with which he had replaced his name was shaved into the hair at his temple.

"Skrubble," I said.

"What?"

"Plavshk," I said. My brain had decided to try to pronounce that unpronounceable glyph, a linguistic foray into the lands *On Beyond Zebra*. I lifted up the magazine.

"You're telling me you're gonna read *Vibe*?"

"Sure."

"You trying to make fun of me here, Alibi?"

"No, no, I'm a big fan of *Skursvshe*."

"Who?"

"The Artist Formerly Known As *Plinvstk*." I couldn't quit tackling the glyph. I plopped the magazine on the counter and Jimmy, the Korean proprietor, said, "For Frank?"

"Yeah," I gulped.

He waved my money away. "Take it, Lionel."

Back outside, the cop waited until we'd turned the corner, into the relative gloom of Bergen Street, just past the F-train entrance and a few doors from L&L's storefront, then collared me, literally, two hands bunching my jacket at my neck, and pushed me up against the tile-mosaic wall. I gripped my magazine, which was curled into a baton, and the bag from Zeod's with sandwich and soda, held them protectively in front of me like an old lady with her purse. I knew better than to push back at the cop. Anyway, I was bigger, and he didn't really frighten me, not physically.

"Enough with the double-talk," he said. "Where's this going? Why are you pretending your man Minna's still with us, Alibi? What's the game?"

"Wow," I said. "This was unexpected. You're like good cop and bad cop rolled into one."

"Yeah, used to be they could afford two different guys. Now with all the budget cuts and shit they've got us doing double shifts."

"Can we go back to—*fuckmeblackcop*—back to talking nice now?"

"What you say?"

"Nothing. Let go of my collar." I'd kept the outburst down to a mumble—and I knew to be grateful my Tourette's brain hadn't dialed up *nigger*. Despite the detective's roughhousing, or because of it, our frenzy had peaked and abated, and we'd earned a quiet moment together. He was close enough to invite intimacy. If my hands hadn't been full I would have begun stroking his pebbly jaw or clapping him on the shoulders.

"Talk to me, Alibi. Tell me things."

"Don't treat me like a suspect."

"Tell me why not."

"I worked for Frank. I miss him. I want to catch his killer as much as you."

"So let's compare notes. The names Alphonso Matricardi and Leonardo Rockaforte mean anything to you?"

*   *   *

I was silenced.

Matricardi and Rockaforte: The homicide cop didn't know you weren't supposed to say those names aloud. Not anywhere, but especially not out on Smith Street.

I'd never even heard their first names, Alphonso and Leonardo. They seemed wrong, but what first names wouldn't? Wrongness surrounded those names and their once-in-a-blue-moon uttering. Don't say Matricardi and Rockaforte.

Say "The Clients" if you must.

Or say "Garden State Brickface and Stucco." But not those names.

*   *   *

"Never heard of them," I breathed.

"Why don't I believe you?"

"Believemeblackman."

"You're fucking sick."

"I am," I said. "I'm sorry."

"You should be sorry. Your man got killed and you're not giving me anything."

"I'll catch the killer," I said. "That's what I'll give you."

He eased off me. I barked twice. He made another face, but it was clear it all would get chalked up to harmless insanity now. I was smarter than I knew leading the cop into Zeod's and letting him hear the Arab call me Crazyman.

"You might want to leave that to me, Alibi. Just make sure you're telling me all you know."

"Absolutely." I made an honorable Boy Scout face. I didn't want to point out to *good cop* that *bad cop* hadn't learned anything from me, just got tired of asking.

"You're making me sad with your sandwich and your goddamn magazine. Get out of here."

I straightened my jacket. A strange peace had come over me. The cop had caused me to think about The Clients for a minute, but I pushed them out of view. I was good at doing that. My Tourette's brain chanted *Want to catch him as much as miss him as much as a sandwich* but I didn't need to tic now, could let it live inside me, a bubbling brook, a deep well of song. I went to the L&L storefront and let myself in with my key. Danny wasn't anywhere to be seen. The phone was ringing. I let it ring. The cop stood watching me and I waved at him once, then shut the door and went into the back.

*   *   *

Sometimes I had trouble admitting I lived upstairs in the apartment above the L&L storefront, but I did, and had since the day so long ago when I left St. Vincent's. The stairs ran down into the back of the storefront. Apart from that inconvenient fact, I tried to keep the two places separated in my mind, decorating the apartment conventionally with forties-style furniture from the decrepit discount showrooms far down Smith Street and never inviting the other Minna Men up if I could help it, and adhering to certain arbitrary rules: drinking beer downstairs and whiskey upstairs, playing cards downstairs but setting out a board with a chess problem upstairs, Touch-Tone phones downstairs, a Bakelite dial phone upstairs, et cetera. For a while I even had a cat, but that didn't work out.

The door at the top of the stair was acned with a thousand tiny dents, from my ritual rapping of my keys before opening the door. I added six more quick key-impressions—my counting nerve was stuck on six today, ever since the fatal bag of White Castles—and then let myself in. The phone downstairs went on ringing. I left my lights off, not wanting to signal to the detective, if he was still outside watching, the connection between upstairs and down. Then I crept to my front window and peered out. The corner was empty of cop. Still, why take a chance? Enough light leaked in from the streetlamps for me to make my way around. So I left the lamps dimmed, though I had to run my hands under the shades and fondle the switches, ritual contact just to make myself feel at home.

Understand: The possibility that I might at any time have to make the rounds and touch every visible item in my apartment dictated a sort of faux-Japanese simplicity in my surroundings. Beneath my reading lamp were five unread paperbacks, which I would return to the Salvation Army on Smith Street as soon as I'd finished them. The covers of the books were already scored with dozens of minute creases, made by sliding my fingernails sideways over their surfaces. I owned a black plastic boom box with detachable speakers, and a short row of Prince/Artist Formerly Known As CDs—I wasn't lying to the homicide cop about being a fan. Beside the CDs lay a single fork, the one I'd stolen from Matricardi and Rockaforte's table full of silverware fourteen years before. I placed the *Vibe* magazine and the bag with the sandwich on my table, which was otherwise clean. I wasn't so terribly hungry anymore. A drink was more urgent. Not that I really liked alcohol, but the ritual was essential.

The phone downstairs went on ringing. L&L didn't have a machine to pick it up—callers usually gave up after nine or ten rings and tried another car service. I tuned it out. I emptied my jacket pockets and rediscovered Minna's watch and beeper. I put them on the table, then poured myself a tumblerful of Walker Red and dropped in a couple of ice cubes and sat down there in the dark to try to let the day settle over me, to try to make some sense of it. The way my ice shimmered made me need to bat at it like a cat fishing in a goldfish bowl, but otherwise the scene was pretty calm. If only the phone downstairs would stop ringing. Where was Danny? For that matter, shouldn't Tony be back from the East Side by now? I didn't want to think he'd go into the Zendo without some backup, without letting us other Minna Men in on the score. I pushed the thought away, tried to forget about Tony and Danny and Gilbert for the moment, to pretend it was my case alone and weight the variables and put them into some kind of shape that made sense, that produced answers or at least a clear question. I thought of the giant Polish killer we'd watched drive our boss away to a Dumpster—he already seemed like something I'd imagined, an impossible figure, a silhouette from a dream. The phone downstairs went on ringing. I thought about Julia, how she'd toyed with the homicide detective and then flown, how she'd almost seemed too ready for the news from the hospital, and I considered the bitterness laced into her sorrow. I tried not to think of how she'd toyed with me, and how little I knew it meant. I thought about Minna himself, the mystery of his connection in the Zendo, his caustic familiarity with his betrayer, his disastrous preference for keeping his Men in the dark and how he'd paid for it. As I gazed past the streetlight to the flickering blue-lit curtains of the bedrooms in the apartments across Bergen Street, I lingered over my paltry clues: Ullman downtown, the girl with glasses and short hair, "the building" that the sardonic voice in the Yorkville Zendo had mentioned, and Irving—if Irving really was a clue.

While I thought about these things, another track in my brain intoned brainyoctomy brainyalimony bunnymonopoly baileyoctopus brainyanimal broccopotamus. And the phone downstairs kept on ringing. Sighing, I resigned myself to my fate, went back downstairs and picked up the phone.

"No cars!" I said forcefully.

"That you, Lionel?" said Gilbert's friend Loomis, the sanitation inspector—the garbage cop.

"What is it, Loomis?" I disliked the garbage cop intensely.

"Gotta problem over here."

"Where's here?"

"Sixth Precinct house, in Manhattan."

"*Dickweed!* What are you doing at the precinct house, Loomis?"

"Well, they're saying it's too late, no way they're gonna arraign him tonight, he's gonna have to spend the night in the bullpen."

"Who?"

"Who'd you think? Gilbert! They got him up on killing some guy name Ullman."

*   *   *

Have you ever felt, in the course of reading a detective novel, a guilty thrill of relief at having a character murdered before he can step onto the page and burden you with his actual existence? Detective stories always have too many characters anyway. And characters mentioned early on but never sighted, just lingering offstage, take on an awful portentous quality. Better to have them gone.

I felt some version of this thrill at the news that the garbage cop delivered, of Ullman's demise. But too, I felt its opposite: a panic that the world of the case was shrinking. Ullman had been an open door, a direction, a whiff of something. I couldn't spare any grief for the death of Ullman the human being—especially not on The Day Frank Minna Died—but I mourned nonetheless: My clue had been murdered.

A few other things I felt:

Annoyed—I would have to deal with Loomis tonight. My reverie was snapped. The ice would melt in my glass of Walker Red upstairs. My sandwich from Zeod's would go uneaten.

Confused—let Gilbert glower and lurch all he wanted, but he'd

never kill a man. And I'd watched him blink dumbly at the name Ullman. It had meant nothing to him. So no motive, unless it was self-
defense. Or else he'd been set up. Therefore:

Frightened. Someone was hunting Minna Men.

*   *   *

I took an agency car into Manhattan and tried to see Gilbert at the
precinct house, but didn't have any luck. He'd already been shifted
out of the front cage, to the back, where he'd been grouped with a
bunch of other fresh arrests for a night of what the cops euphemisti-
cally called "bullpen therapy"—eating baloney sandwiches, using the
toilet in the open if he had to go, shrugging off petty advances on his
watch and wallet, and trading cigarettes, if he had any, for a razor
blade to protect himself. Industrious Loomis had already exhausted
the cops' patience for Gilbert's rights and privileges: He'd had his
phone call, his moment's visitation at the cell bars, and nothing more
would be allowed to happen to him until the next morning at the
soonest. Then he could hope to be arraigned and sent out to the
Tombs to wait for someone to bail him out. So my effort was
rewarded by learning nothing yet being saddled with driving Loomis
back to Brooklyn. I took the opportunity to try to find out what the
garbage cop had heard from Gilbert.

"He didn't want to say much without a lawyer, and I don't blame
him. The walls have ears, you know? Just that Ullman was dead when
he got there. The homicides picked him up coming out the place like
they'd been tipped. Time I saw him, he'd mouthed a little and been
roughed around, asked for a lawyer, they told him he had to wait for
tomorrow. I guess he tried to call L&L but you weren't picking up,
fortunately I was around— Hey, sorry about Frank, by the way. It's a
shame a thing happens. Gilbert didn't look too good about it either I
can tell you. I don't know what he said or didn't but the guys weren't
too happy with him by the time I showed. I tried reasoning with the

guys, let them see my badge, but they treat me like I was lower than a fucking prison guard, you know? Like I couldn't make the fucking cut."

Gilbert had befriended Loomis somewhere near the end of high school, when they both were hanging around the Carroll Street park watching the old men play bocce. Loomis called to Gilbert's lazy, sloppy side, the nose-picker and cigarette-grubber, the part of him that didn't want to always have to keep up with Minna and us other Men. Loomis wasn't sharpened up the way even the most passive and recalcitrant of us orphans had to be—he was a sort of shapeless inadvertent extension of his parents' couch and television set and refrigerator, and he assumed independent life only grudgingly. At Gilbert's side he'd come slouching around L&L in the formative days and never show a glimmer of interest in either our cover-story car service or the detective agency lurking just underneath—we might have an open packet of Sno-Balls or Chocodiles sitting on the counter, though.

Loomis was nudged by his parents toward police work. He struck out twice at the civil-service qualification test to become a regular beat cop, and some kindhearted career counselor nudged him again, gently downward, to the easier test for the sanitation police, which he squeaked past. Before he was the Garbage Cop, though, Minna used to call him *Butt Trust*, a term he would apply with a measure of real tenderness.

Me and the other Boys let it go the first five or six times, thinking an explanation would be offered, before finally asking Minna what he meant.

"You got your brain trust, your most-valued," said Minna. "Then you got the rest of them. The ones you let hang around anyway. That would be the butt trust, right?"

I was never overfond of the butt trust. In fact, I hated Loomis—let me count the ways. His imprecision and laziness maddened my compulsive instincts—his patchiness, the way even his speech was riddled with drop-outs and glitches like a worn cassette, the way his leaden senses refused the world, his attention like a pinball rolling past unlit blinkers and frozen flippers into the hole again and again: *game over.* He was permanently impressed by the most irrelevant banalities and impossible to impress with real novelty, meaning, or conflict. And he was too moronic to be properly self-loathing—so it was my duty to loathe him instead.

Tonight, as we roared across the metal grating of the Brooklyn Bridge's roadway, he settled into his usual dull riff: The sanitation force gets no respect. "You think they'd know what it's like for a cop in this city, me and those guys are on the same team, but this one cop keeps saying, 'Hey, why don't you come around my block, somebody keeps stealing my garbage.' If it weren't for Gilbert I would of told him to stick it—"

"What time did Gilbert call you?" I interrupted.

"I don't know, around seven or eight, maybe nine almost," he said, succinctly demonstrating his unfitness for the force.

"It's—*Tourette is the stickman!*—only ten now, Loomis."

"Okay, it was just after eight."

"Did you find out where Ullman lived?"

"Downtown somewhere. I gave Gilbert the address."

"You don't remember where it was?"

"Nah."

Loomis wasn't going to be any help. He seemed to know this as well as I, and immediately launched into another digression, as if to say, *I'm useless, but no hard feelings, okay?* "So you heard the one about how many Catholics does it take to screw in a lightbulb?"

"I've heard that one, Loomis. No jokes, please."

"Ah, come on. What about why did the blonde stare at the carton of orange juice?"

I was silent. We came off the bridge, at Cadman Plaza. I'd be rid of him soon.

" 'Cause it said 'concentrate,' get it?"

This was another thing I hated about Loomis. Years ago he'd latched on to Minna's joke-telling contests, decided he could compete. But he favored idiot riddles, not jokes at all, no room for character or nuance. He didn't seem to know the difference.

"Got it," I admitted.

"What about how do you titillate an ocelot?"

"What?"

"Titillate an ocelot. You know, like a big cat. I think."

"It's a big cat. How do you titillate it, Loomis?"

"You *oscillate its tit a lot*, get it?"

"Eat me Ocelot!" I screamed as we turned onto Court Street. Loomis's crappy punning had slid right under the skin of my symptoms. "Lancelot ancillary oscillope! Octapot! Tittapocamus!"

The garbage cop laughed. "Jesus, Lionel, you crack me up. You never quit with that routine."

"It's not a—*root*—*ocelot*," I shrieked through my teeth. Here, finally, was what I hated most in Loomis: He'd always insisted, from the time we met as teenagers to this day, that I was elaborately feigning and could keep from ticcing if I wanted to. Nothing would dissuade him, no example or demonstration, no program of education. I'd once shown him the book Minna gave me; he glanced at it and laughed. I was making it up. As far as he was concerned, my Tourette's was just an odd joke, one going mostly over his head, stretched out over the course of fifteen years.

"Tossed salad!" he said. "Gotcha!" He liked to think he was playing along.

"Go touchalot!" I slapped him on the thickly padded shoulder of his coat, so suddenly the car swerved with my movement.

"Christ, look out!"

I tapped him five more times, my driving steady now.

"I can't get over you," he said. "Even at a time like this. I guess it's sentimental, like a way of saying, *if Frank were still here*. Since that routine always did keep him busted up."

We pulled up outside L&L. The lights in the storefront were on. Somebody had returned since my jaunt to the Sixth Precinct.

"I thought you were driving me home." Loomis lived on Nevins Street, near the projects.

"You can walk from here, *gofuckacop.*"

"C'mon, Lionel."

I parked in the open spot in across from the storefront. The sooner Loomis and I were out of each other's presence, the better.

"Walk," I said.

"At least lemme use the can," he whined. "Those jerks at the station wouldn't let me. I been holding it."

"If you'll do one thing for me."

"Whuzzat?"

"Ullman's address," I said. "You found it once. I need it, Loomis."

"I can get it tomorrow morning when I'm back at my desk. You want me to call you here?"

I took one of Minna's cards out of my pocket and handed it to him. "Call the beeper number. I'll be carrying it."

"Okay, all right, now will you lemme take a leak?"

I didn't speak, just clicked the car locks up and down automatically six times, then got out. Loomis followed me to the storefront, and inside.

Danny came out of the back, stubbing a cigarette in the countertop ashtray as he passed. He always dressed the prettiest of us Minna Men, but his lean black suit suddenly looked like it had been worn too many days in a row. He reminded me of an out-of-work mortician. He glanced at me and Loomis and pursed his lips but didn't speak, and I couldn't really get anything out of his eyes. I felt I didn't know him with Minna gone. Danny and I functioned as expressions of two opposed ends of Frank Minna's impulses: him a tall, silent body that attracted women and intimidated men, me a flapping inane mouth that covered the world in names and descriptions. Average us and you might have Frank Minna back, sort of. Now, without Minna for a conduit between us, Danny and I had to begin again grasping one another as entities, as though we were suddenly fourteen years old again and occupying our opposite niches at St. Vincent's Home for Boys.

In fact, I had a sudden yearning that Danny should be holding a basketball, so that I could say "Good shot!" or exhort him to dunk it. Instead we stared at one another.

" 'Scuse me," said Loomis, scooting past me and waving his hand at Danny. "Gotta use your toilet." He disappeared into the back.

"Where's Tony?" I said.

"I was hoping you could tell me."

"Well, I don't know. I hope he's doing better than Gilbert. I just left him in the lockup at the Sixth." I realized it sounded as if I'd actually seen him, but I let the implication stand. Loomis wouldn't call me on it, even if he heard from the bathroom.

Danny didn't look all that surprised. The shock of Minna's death made this new turn unimpressive by comparison, I supposed. "What's he in for?"

"*Ullmanslaughter!*—the guy Tony sent Gilbert to find, he turned up dead. They pinned it on Gilbert."

Danny only scratched at the end of his nose thoughtfully.

"So where were you?" I said. "I thought you were minding the store."

"Went for a bite."

"I was here for forty-five minutes." A lie—I doubted it was more than fifteen, but I felt like pushing him.

"Guess we missed each other."

"Any calls? See that *homosapien, homogenize, genocide, can'tdecide, candyeyes,* homicide cop?"

He shook his head. He was holding something back—but then it occurred to me that I was too.

Danny and I stood pensively regarding each other, waiting for the next question to form. I felt a vibration deep inside, profounder tics lurking in me, gathering strength. Or perhaps I was only feeling my hunger at last.

Loomis popped out of the back. "Jesus, you guys look bad. What a day, huh?"

We stared at him.

"Well, I think we owe Frank a moment of silence, don't you guys?"

I wanted to point out that what Loomis had interrupted *was* a moment of silence, but I let it go.

"Little something in the way of remembrance? Bow your heads, you turkeys. The guy was like your father. Don't end the day arguing with each other, for crying out loud."

Loomis had a point, or enough of one anyway, to shame me and Danny into letting him have his way. So we stood in silence, and when I saw that Danny and Loomis had each closed their eyes I closed mine too. Together we made up some lopped-off, inadequate version of the Agency—Danny standing for himself and Tony, I for myself, and Loomis, I suppose, for Gilbert. But I was moved anyway, for a second.

Then Loomis ruined it with a clearly audible fart, which he coughed to cover, unsuccessfully. "Okay," he said suddenly. "How's about that ride home, Lionel?"

"Walk," I said.

Humbled by his own body, the garbage cop didn't argue, but headed for the door.

*   *   *

Danny volunteered to sit by the L&L phone. He already had a pot of coffee brewing, he pointed out, and I could see he was in a pacing mood, that he wanted the space of the office to himself. It suited me well enough to leave him there. I went upstairs, without our exchanging more than a few sentences.

Upstairs I lit a candle and stuck it in the center of my table, beside Minna's beeper and watch. Loomis's clumsy pass at ritual haunted me. I needed one of my own. But I was also hungry. I poured out the diluted drink and made myself a fresh one, set it out on the table too. Then I unwrapped the sandwich from Zeod's. I considered for a moment, fighting the urge just to sink my teeth into it, then went to the cabinet and brought back a serrated knife and small plate. I cut the sandwich into six equal pieces, taking unexpectedly deep pleasure in the texture of the kaiser roll's resistance to the knife's dull teeth, and arranged the pieces so they were equidistant on the plate. I returned the knife to my counter, then centered plate, candle and drink on the table in a way that soothed my grieving Tourette's. If I didn't stem my syndrome's needs I would never clear a space in which my own sorrow could dwell.

Then I went to my boom box and put on the saddest song in my CD collection, Prince's "How Come U Don't Call Me Anymore."

*   *   *

I don't know whether The Artist Formerly Known as Prince is Tourettic or obsessive-compulsive in his human life, but I know for certain he is deeply so in the life of his work. Music had never made much of an impression on me until the day in 1986 when, sitting in the passenger seat of Minna's Cadillac, I first heard the single "Kiss" squirting its manic way out of the car radio. To that point in my life I might have once or twice heard music that toyed with feelings of claustrophobic discomfort and expulsive release, and which in so doing passingly charmed my Tourette's, gulled it with a sense of recognition, like Art Carney or Daffy Duck—but here was a song that lived entirely in that territory, guitar and voice twitching and throbbing within obsessively delineated bounds, alternately silent and plosive. It so pulsed with Tourettic energies that I could surrender to its tormented, squeaky beat and let my syndrome live outside my brain for once, live in the air instead.

"Turn that shit down," said Minna.

"I like it," I said.

"That's that crap Danny listens to," said Minna. *Danny* was code for *too black.*

I knew I had to own that song, and so the next day I sought it out at J&R Music World—I needed the word "funk" explained to me by the salesman. He sold me a cassette, and a Walkman to play it on. What I ended up with was a seven-minute "extended single" version—the song I'd heard on the radio, with a four-minute catastrophe of chopping, grunting, hissing and slapping sounds appended—a coda apparently designed as a private message of confirmation to my delighted Tourette's brain.

Prince's music calmed me as much as masturbation or a cheeseburger. When I listened to him I was exempt from my symptoms. So I began collecting his records, especially those elaborate and frenetic remixes tucked away on the CD singles. The way he worried forty-five minutes of variations out of a lone musical or verbal phrase is, as far as I know, the nearest thing in art to my condition.

"How Come U Don't Call Me Anymore" is a ballad, piano strolling beneath an aching falsetto vocal. Slow and melancholy, it still featured the Tourettic abruptness and compulsive precision, the sudden shrieks and silences, that made Prince's music my brain's balm.

*   *   *

I put the song on repeat and sat in the light of my candle and waited for the tears. Only after they came did I allow myself to eat the six turkey-sandwich portions, in a ritual for Minna, alternating them with sips of Walker Red. *The body and the blood,* I couldn't keep from thinking, though I was as distant from any religious feeling as a mourning man could be. *The turkey and the booze,* I substituted. A last meal for

Minna, who didn't get one. Prince moaned, finished his song, began it again. The candle guttered. I counted *three* as I finished a portion of sandwich, then *four.* That was the extent of my symptoms. I counted sandwiches and wept. At *six* I killed the music, blew out the candle and went to bed.

(TOURETTE DREAMS)

(in Tourette dreams you shed your tics)

(or your tics shed you)

(and you go with them, astonished to leave yourself behind)

BAD COOKIES

There are days when I get up in the morning and stagger into the bathroom and begin running water and then I look up and I don't even recognize my own toothbrush in the mirror. I mean, the object looks strange, oddly particular in its design, strange tapered handle and slotted, miter-cut bristles, and I wonder if I've ever looked at it closely before or whether someone snuck in overnight and substituted this new toothbrush for my old one. I have this relationship to objects in general—they will sometimes become uncontrollably new and vivid to me, and I don't know whether this is a symptom of Tourette's or not. I've never seen it described in the literature. Here's the strangeness of having a Tourette's brain, then: no control in my personal experiment of self. What might be only strangeness must always be auditioned for relegation to the domain of symptom, just as symptoms always push into other domains, demanding the chance to audition for their moment of acuity or relevance, their brief shot—coulda been a contender!—at centrality. Personalityness. There's a lot of traffic in my head, and it's two-way.

This morning's strangeness was refreshing, though. More than refreshing—revelatory. I woke early, having failed to draw my curtains, the wall above my bed and the table with melted candle, tumbler quarter full of melted ice, and sandwich crumbs from my ritual snack now caught in a blaze of white sunlight, like the glare of a projector's bulb before the film is threaded. It seemed possible I was the first awake in the world, possible the world was new. I dressed in my best suit, donned Minna's watch instead of my own, and clipped his beeper to my hip. Then I made myself coffee and toast, scooped the long-shadowed crumbs off the table, sat and savored breakfast, marveling at the richness of existence with each step. The radiator whined and sneezed and I imitated its sounds out of sheer joy, rather than helplessness. Perhaps I'd been expecting that Minna's absence would snuff the world, or at least Brooklyn, out of existence. That a sympathetic dimming would occur. Instead I'd woken into the realization that I was Minna's successor and avenger, that the city shone with clues.

It seemed possible I was a detective on a case.

I crept downstairs past Danny, who was sleeping on his arms on the countertop, black suit jacket shrugged up around his shoulders, small patch of drool on his sleeve. I switched off the coffee machine, which was roasting a quarter inch of coffee into sour perfume, and went outside. It was a quarter to seven. The Korean keeper of the Casino was just rolling up his gate, tossing his bundles of the *News* and the *Post* inside. The morning was clarifyingly cold.

I started the L&L Pontiac. Let Danny sleep, let Gilbert wait in his cell, let Tony be missing. I'd go to the Zendo. Let it be too early for the monks or mobsters hidden there—I'd have the advantage of surprise.

*   *   *

By the time I'd parked and made my way to the Zendo, the Upper East Side was warming into life, shopkeepers rolling fruit stands out of their shops, sidewalk vendors of stripped paperbacks unloading their boxes, women already dressed for business glancing at their watches as they hustled their dogs' waste into Baggies. The doorman at the entranceway next door was someone new, a kid with a mustache and uniform, not my harasser from yesterday. He was probably green, without tenure, stuck working the end of the overnight shift. I figured it was worth a shot anyway. I crooked a finger at him through the glass and he came out into the cold.

"What's your name?" I said.

"Walter, sir."

"Walter sir-what?" I broadcast a cop-or-employer vibe.

"Walter is, uh, my last name. Can I help you with something?" He looked concerned, for himself and his building.

"*Helpmewalter*—I need the name of the doorman working last night, about six-thirty, seven. Older gentleman than yourself, maybe thirty-five, with an accent."

"Dirk?"

"Maybe. You tell me."

"Dirk's the regular man." He wasn't sure he should be telling me this.

I averted my gaze from the his shoulder. "Good. Now tell me what you know about the Yorkville Zendo." I indicated the bronze plaque next door with a jerk of my thumb. "Dirkweed! Dirkman!"

"What?" He goggled his eyes at me.

"You see them come and go?"

"I guess."

"Walter Guessworth!" I cleared my throat deliberately. "Work with me here, Walter. You must see stuff. I want your impressions."

I could see him sorting through layers of exhaustion, boredom, and stupidity. "Are you a cop?"

"Why'd you think that?"

"You, uh, talk funny."

"I'm a guy who needs to know things, Walter, and I'm in a hurry. Anyone come and go from the Zendo lately? Anything catch your eye?"

He scanned the street to see if anyone saw us talking. I took the opportunity to cover my mouth with my hand and make a brief panting sound, like an excited dog.

"Uh, not much happens late at night," said Walter. "It's pretty quiet around here."

"A place like the Zendo must attract some weird traffic."

"You keep saying Zendo," he said.

"It's right there, etched in brass." *Itched in Ass.*

He stepped toward the street, craned his neck, and read the plaque. "Hmmm. It's like a religious school, right?"

"Right. You ever see anyone suspicious hanging around? Big Polish guy in particular?"

"How would I know he was Polish?"

"Just think about big. We're talking really, really big."

He shrugged again. "I don't think so." His numb gaze wouldn't have taken in a crane and wrecking ball going through next door, let alone an outsize human figure.

"Listen, would you keep an eye out? I'll give you a number to call." I had a stash of L&L cards in my wallet, and I fished one out for him.

"Thanks," he said absently, glancing at the card. He wasn't afraid of me anymore. But he didn't know what to think of me if I wasn't a threat. I was interesting, but he didn't know how to be interested.

"I'd appreciate hearing from you—*Doorjerk! Doorjam! Jerkdom!*—if you see anything odd."

"You're pretty odd," he said seriously.

"Something besides me."

"Okay, but I get off in half an hour."

"Well, just keep it in mind." I was running out of patience with Walter. I freed myself to tap his shoulder farewell. The dull young man looked down at my hand, then went back inside.

*   *   *

I paced the block to the corner and back, flirting with the Zendo, seeking my nerve. The site aroused reverence and a kind of magical fear in me already, as though I were approaching a shrine—*the martyrdom of Saint Minna*. I wanted to rewrite their plaque to tell the story. Instead I rang the doorbell once. No answer. Then four more times, for a total of *five*, and I stopped, startled by a sense of completeness.

I'd shrugged off my tired old friend *six*.

I wondered if it was in some way commemorative—my counting tic moving down a list, subtracting a digit for Frank.

Somebody is hunting Minna Men, I thought again. But I couldn't be afraid. I wasn't game but hunter this morning. Anyway, the count was off—four Minna Men plus Frank made five. So if I was counting heads, I should be at four. I had an extra aboard, but who? Maybe it was Bailey. Or Irving.

A long minute passed before the girl with the short black hair and glasses opened the door and squinted at me against the morning sun. She wore a T-shirt, jeans, had bare feet, and held a broom. Her smile was slight, involuntary, and crooked. And sweet.

"Yes?"

"Could I ask you a few questions?"

"Questions?" She didn't seem to recognize the word.

"If it's not too early," I said gently.

"No, no. I've been up. I've been sweeping." She showed me the broom.

"They make you clean?"

"It's a privilege. Cleaning is treasured in Zen practice. It's like the highest possible act. Usually Roshi wants to do the sweeping himself."

"No vacuum cleaner?" I said.

"Too noisy," she said, and frowned as if it should be obvious. A city bus roared past in the distance, damaging her point. I let it go.

Her eyes adjusted to the brightness, and she looked past me, to the street, examining it as though astonished to discover that the door opened onto a cityscape. I wondered if she'd been out of the building since I saw her enter the evening before. I wondered if she ate and slept there, whether she was the only one who did or whether there were dozens, foot soldiers of Zen.

"I'm sorry," she said. "What were you saying?"

"Questions."

"Oh, yes."

"About the Zendo, what you do here."

She looked me over now. "Do you want to come inside? It's cold."

"I'd like that very much."

It was the truth. I didn't feel unsafe following her into the dark temple, the Deathstar. I would gather information from within the Trojan Horse of her Zen grace. And I was conscious of my ticlessness, didn't want to break the rhythm of the conversation.

The foyer and stairwell were plain, with unadorned white walls and a wooden banister, looking as if it had been clean before she began sweeping, clean forever. We bypassed a door on the ground floor and went up the stairs, she carrying the broom ahead of her, turning her back to me trustingly. Her walk had a gentle jerkiness to it, a quickness like her replies.

"Here," she said, pointing to a rack with rows of shoes on it.

"I'm fine," I said, thinking I was supposed to select from among the motley footgear.

"No, take yours off," she whispered.

I did as she told me, removed my shoes and pushed them into an orderly place at the end of one of the racks. A chill went through me when I recalled that Minna had removed his shoes the evening before, presumably at this same landing.

Now in my socks, I followed her as the banister wrapped around through a corridor, past two sealed doors and one that opened onto a bare, dark room with rows of short cloth mats laid out across a parquet floor and a smell of candles or incense, not a morning smell at all. I wanted to peer inside but she hurried us along, up another flight.

On the third landing she led me to a small kitchen where a wooden table and three chairs were arranged around a thwarted back window, through which an emaciated shaft of sunlight negotiated a maze of brick. If the massive buildings on either side had existed when this room was built they might not have bothered with a window. The table, chairs and cabinets of the kitchen were as undistinguished and homely as a museum diorama of Cree or Shaker life, but the teapot she set out was Japanese, and its hand-painted calligraphic designs were the only stretch, the only note of ostentation.

I seated myself with my back to the wall, facing the door, thinking of Minna and the conversation I'd heard through the wire. She took water off a low flame and filled the pot, then put a tiny mug without a handle in front of me and filled it with an unstrained swirling confetti of tea. I warmed my chapped hands around it gratefully.

"I'm Kimmery."

"Lionel." I felt *Kissdog* rising in me and fought it back.

"You're interested in Buddhism?"

"You could say that."

"I'm not really who you should talk to but I can tell you what they'll say. It's not about getting centered, or, you know, *stress reduction*. A lot of people—Americans, I mean—have that idea. But it's really a religious discipline, and not easy at all. Do you know about zazen?"

"Tell me."

"It'll make your back hurt a *lot*. That's one thing." She rolled her eyes at me, already commiserating.

"You mean meditation."

"*Zazen,* it's called. Or *sitting*. It sounds like nothing, but it's the heart of Zen practice. I'm not very good at it."

I recalled the Quakers who'd adopted Tony, and their brick meetinghouse across eight lanes of traffic from St. Vincent's. Sunday mornings we could look through their tall windows and see them gathered in silence on hard benches.

"What's to be good at?" I said.

"You have no idea. Breathing, for starters. And thinking, except it's not supposed to *be* thinking."

"Thinking about not thinking?"

"*Not* thinking about it. One Mind, they call it. Like realizing that everything has Buddha nature, the flag and the wind are the same thing, that sort of stuff."

I wasn't exactly following her, but *One Mind* seemed an honorable goal, albeit positively chimerical. "Could we—could I sit with you sometime? Or is it done alone?"

"Both. But here at the Zendo there's regular sessions." She lifted her cup of tea with both hands, steaming her glasses instantly. "Anyone can come. And you're really lucky if you stick around today. Some important monks from Japan are in town to see the Zendo, and one of them is going to talk this evening, after zazen."

Important monks, imported rugs, unimportant ducks—jabber was building up in the ocean of my brain like flotsam, and soon a wave would toss it ashore. "So it's run out of Japan," I said. "And now they're checking up on you—like the Pope coming in from Rome."

"Not exactly. Roshi set the Zendo up on his own. Zen isn't centralized. There are different teachers, and sometimes they move around."

"But Roshi did come here from Japan." From the name I pictured a wizened old man, a little bigger than Yoda in *Return of the Jedi*.

"No, Roshi's American. He used to have an American name."

"Which was?"

"I don't know. *Roshi* just basically means teacher, but that's the only name he has anymore."

I sipped my scalding tea. "Does anyone else use this building for anything?"

"Anything like what?"

"*Killing me!*—sorry. Just anything besides sitting."

"You can't shout like that in here," she said.

"Well, if—*kissing me!*—something strange was going on, say if Roshi were in some kind of trouble, would you know about it?" I twisted my neck—if I could I would have tied it in a knot, like the top of a plastic garbage bag. *"Eating me!"*

"I guess I don't know what you're talking about." She was oddly blasé, sipping her tea and watching me over the top of the cup. I recalled the legends of Zen masters slapping and kicking students to induce sudden realizations. Perhaps that practice was common here in the Zendo, and so she'd inured herself to outbursts, abrupt outlandish gestures.

"Forget it," I said. "Listen: Have you had any visitors lately?" I was thinking of Tony, who'd ostensibly called on the Zendo after our conference at L&L. "Anyone come sniffing around here last night?"

She only looked puzzled, and faintly annoyed. "No."

I considered pushing it, describing Tony to her, then decided he must have visited unseen, at least by Kimmery. Instead I asked, "Is there anybody in the building right now?"

"Well, Roshi lives on the top floor."

"He's up there now?" I said, startled.

"Sure. He's in *sesshin*—it's like an extended retreat—because of these monks. He took a vow of silence, so it's been a little quiet around here."

"Do you live here?"

"No. I'm cleaning up for morning zazen. The other students will show up in an hour. They're out doing work service now. That's how the Zendo can afford to pay the rent here. Wallace is downstairs already, but that's basically it."

"Wallace?" I was distracted by the tea leaves in my cup settling gradually into a mound at the bottom, like astronauts on a planet with barely any gravity.

"He's like this old hippie who hardly ever does anything but sit. I think his legs must be made of plastic or something. We went past him on the way up."

"Where? In the room with the mats?"

"Uh-huh. He's like a piece of furniture, easy to miss."

"Biggish, you mean?"

"Not so big. I meant still, he sits still." She whispered, "I always wonder if he's dead."

"But he's not a really *big* person."

"You wouldn't say that."

I plunged two fingers into my cup, needing to unsettle the floating leaves again, force them to resume their dance. If the girl saw me do it she didn't say anything.

"You haven't seen any really big people lately, have you?" Though I'd not encountered them yet, Roshi and Wallace seemed both unpromising suspects to be the Polish giant. I wondered if instead one might be the sardonic conversationalist I'd heard taunting Minna over the wire.

"Mmmmm, no," she said.

"Pierogi monster," I said, then coughed five times for cover. Thoughts of Minna's killers had overwhelmed the girl's calming influence—my brain sizzled with language, my body with gestures.

In reply she only refilled my cup, then moved the pot to the countertop. While her back was turned I stroked her chair, ran my palm over the warmth where she'd been sitting, played the spokes of the chair's back like a noiseless harp.

"Lionel? Is that your name?"

"Yes."

"You don't seem very calm, Lionel." She'd pivoted, almost catching my chair-molestation, and now she leaned back against the counter instead of retaking her seat.

I didn't ordinarily hesitate to reveal my syndrome, but something in me fought it now. "Do you have something to eat?" I said. Perhaps calories would restore my equilibrium.

"Um, I don't know," she said. "You want some bread or something? There might be some yogurt left."

"Because this tea is corked with caffeine. It only looks harmless. Do you drink this stuff all the time?"

"Well, it's sort of traditional."

"Is that part of the Zen thing, getting punchy so you can see God? Isn't that cheating?"

"It's more just to stay awake. Because we don't really have God in Zen Buddhism." She turned away from me and began rifling through the cabinets, but didn't quit her musings. "We just sit and try not to fall asleep, so I guess in a way staying awake *is* seeing God, sort of. So you're right."

The little triumph didn't thrill me. I was feeling trapped, with the wizened teacher a floor above me and the plastic-legged hippie a floor below. I wanted to get out of the Zendo now, but I hadn't figured a next move.

And when I left I wanted to take Kimmery with me. I wanted to protect her—the impulse surged in me, looking to affix to a suitable target. Now that I'd failed Minna, who deserved my protection? Was it Tony? Was it Julia? I wished that Frank would whisper a clue in my ear from the beyond. In the meantime, Kimmery would do.

"Here, do you want some Oreos?"

"Sure," I said distractedly. "Buddhists eat Oreos?"

"We eat anything we want, Lionel. This isn't Japan." She took a blue carton of cookies and put it on the table.

I helped myself, craving the snack, glad we weren't in Japan.

"I used to know this guy who once worked for Nabisco," she said, musing as she bit into a cookie. "You know, the company that makes Oreos? He said they had two main plants for making Oreos, in different parts of the country. Two head bakers, you know, different quality control."

"Uh—" I took a cookie and dunked it in my tea.

"And he used to swear he could tell the difference just by tasting them. This guy, when we ate Oreos, he would just go through the pack sniffing them and tasting the chocolate part and then he'd put the bad ones in a pile. And like, a really good package was one where less than a third had to go in the bad pile, because they were from the wrong bakery, you know? But sometimes there wouldn't be more than five or six good ones in a whole package."

"Wait a minute. You're saying every package of Oreos has cookies from *both* bakeries?"

"Uh-huh."

I tried to keep from thinking about it, tried to keep it in the blind spot of my obsessiveness, the way I would flinch my eyes from a tempting shoulder. But it was impossible. "What motive could they possibly have for mixing batches in the same package?"

"Well, easy. If word got out that one bakery was better than the other, they wouldn't want people, you know, *shunning* whole cartons, or maybe even whole truckloads, whole deliveries of Oreos. They'd have to keep them mixed up, so you'd buy any package knowing you'd probably get some good ones."

"So you're saying they ship batches from the two bakeries to one central boxing location just to mix them together."

"I guess that's what it would entail, isn't it?" she said brightly.

"That's stupid," I said, but it was only the sound of my crumbling resistance.

She shrugged. "All I know is we'd eat them and he'd be frantically building this pile of rejected cookies. And he'd be pushing them at me saying, 'See, see?' I could never tell the difference."

No, no, no, no.

Eatmeoreo, I mouthed inaudibly. I crinkled in the cellophane sleeve for another cookie, then nibbled off the overhang of chocolate top. I let the pulverized crumbs saturate my tongue, then reached for another, performed the same operation. They were identical. I put both nibbled cookies in the same pile. I needed to find a good one, or a bad one, before I could tell the difference.

Maybe I'd only ever eaten bad ones.

"I thought you didn't believe me," said Kimmery.

"Mushytest," I mumbled, my lips pasty with cookie mud, my eyes wild as I considered the task my brain had set for my sorry tongue. There were three sleeves in the box of Oreos. We were into just the first of them.

She nodded at my pile of discards. "What are those, good ones or bad ones?"

"I don't know." I tried sniffing the next. "Was this guy your boyfriend or something?"

"For a little while."

"Was he a Zen Buddhist too?"

She snorted lightly. I nibbled another cookie and began to despair. I would have been happy now for an ordinary interruptive tic, something to throw my bloodhoundlike obsessions off the scent. The Minna Men were in shambles, yes, but I'd get to the bottom of the Oreo conundrum.

I jumped to my feet, rattling both our teacups. I had to get out of there, quell my panic, restart my investigation, put some distance between myself and the cookies.

"Barnamum Bakery!" I yelped, reassuring myself.

"What?"

"Nothing." I jerked my head sideways, then turned it slowly, as if to work out a kink. "We'd better go, Kimmery."

"Go where?" She leaned forward, her pupils big and trusting. I felt a thrill at being taken so seriously. This making the rounds without Gilbert could get to be a habit. For once I was playing lead detective instead of comic—or Tourettic—relief.

"Downstairs," I said, at a loss for a better answer.

"Okay," she said, whispering conspiratorially. "But be quiet."

We crept past the half-open door on the second landing, and I retrieved my shoes from the rack. This time I got a look at Wallace. He sat with his back to us, limp blond hair tucked behind his ears and giving way to a bald spot. He wore a sweater and sweatpants and sat still as advertised, inert, asleep, or, I suppose, dead—though death was not a still thing to me at the moment, more a matter of skid marks in blood and the Brooklyn-Queens Expressway. Wallace looked harmless anyway. Kimmery's idea of a hippie, apparently, was a white man over forty-five not in a business suit. In Brooklyn we would have just said *loser*.

She opened the front door of the Zendo. "I've got to finish cleaning," she said. "You know, for the monks."

"*Im*portantmonks," I said, ticcing gently.

"Yes."

"I don't think you should be alone here." I looked up and down the block to see if anyone was watching us. My neck prickled, alert to wind and fear. The Upper East Siders had retaken their streets, and walked obliviously crinkling doggie-doo bags and the *New York Times* and the wax paper around bagels. My feeling of advantage, of beginning my investigation while the world was still asleep, was gone.

"I'm *con-worried*," I said, Tourette's mangling my speech again. I wanted to get away from her before I shouted, barked, or ran my fingers around the neck of her T-shirt.

She smiled. "What's that—like confused and worried?"

I nodded. It was close enough.

"I'll be okay. Don't be conworried." She spoke calmly, and it calmed me. "You'll come back later, right? To sit?"

"Absolutely."

"Okay." She craned up on her toes and kissed my cheek. Startled, I couldn't move, stood instead feeling her kiss-print burning on my flesh in the cold morning air. Was it personal, or some sort of fuzzy Zen coercion? Were they that desperate to fill mats at the Zendo?

"Don't do that," I said. "You just met me. This is New York."

"Yes, but you're my friend now."

"I have to go."

"Okay," she said. "Zazen is at four o'clock."

"I'll be there."

She shut the door. I was alone on the street again, my investigation already at a standstill. Had I learned anything inside the Zendo? Now I felt dazed with loss—I'd penetrated the citadel and spent my whole time contemplating Kimmery and Oreos. My mouth was full of cocoa, my nostrils full of her scent from the unexpected kiss.

Two men took me by the elbows and hustled me into a car waiting at the curb.

*   *   *

The four of them wore identical blue suits with black piping on the legs, and identical black sunglasses. They looked like a band that plays at weddings. Four white guys, assortedly chunky, pinched in the face, with pimples, and indistinct. Their car was a rental. Chunky sat in the backseat waiting and when the two who'd picked me up crushed me into the back beside him, he immediately put his arm around my neck in a sort of brotherly choke hold. The two who'd picked me off the street—Pimples and Indistinct—jammed in beside me, to make four of us on the backseat. It was a bit crowded.

"Get in the front," said Chunky, the one holding my neck.

"Me?" I said.

"Shut up. Larry, get out. There's too many. Go in the front."

"Okay, okay," said the one on the end, Indistinct or Larry. He got out of the back and into the empty front passenger seat and the one driving—Pinched—took off. Chunky loosened his hold when we got into the downtown traffic on Second Avenue, but left his arm draped over my shoulders.

"Take the Drive," he said.

"What?"

"Tell him take the East Side Drive."

"Where are we going?"

"I want to be on the highway."

"Why not just drive in circles?"

"My car is parked up here," I said. "You could drop me off."

"Shut up. Why can't we just drive in circles?"

"You shut up. It should look like we're going somewhere, stupid. We're really scaring him going in circles."

"I'm listening to what you say no matter how you drive," I said, wanting to make them feel better. "There's four of you and one of me."

"We want more than listening," said Chunky. "We want you scared."

But I wasn't scared. It was eight-thirty in the morning, and we were fighting traffic on Second Avenue. There weren't even any circles to go in, just honking delivery trucks tied up by pedestrians. And the closer I looked at these guys the less I was impressed. For one thing, Chunky's hand on my neck was soft, his skin was soft, and his hold on me rather tender. And he was the toughest of the bunch. They weren't calm, they weren't good at what they were doing, and they weren't tough. None of them, as far as I could tell, was wearing a gun.

For another thing, all four of their sunglasses still bore price tags, dangling fluorescent orange ovals reading $6.99!

I reached out and batted at Pimples's price tag. He turned away, and my finger hooked the earpiece and jerked the shades off his face, into his lap. "Shit," said Pimples, and hurried the glasses back onto his face as if I might recognize him without them.

"Hey, none of that," said Chunky, and hugged me again. He reminded me of my long-ago kissing tic, the way he was crowding me close to him in the car.

"Okay," I said, though I knew it would be hard not to bat at the price tags if they came within reach. "But what's the game here, guys?"

"We're supposed to throw a scare into you," said Chunky, distracted, watching Pinched drive. "Stay away from the Zendo, that sort of thing. Hey, take the fucking Drive. Seventy-ninth Street there's an on-ramp."

"I can't get over," complained Pinched, eyeing lanes of traffic.

"What so great about the FDR?" said Indistinct. "Why can't we stay on the streets?"

"What, you want to pull over and rough him up on Park Avenue?" said Chunky.

"Maybe just a scare without the roughing-up will do," I suggested. "Get this over with, get on with the day."

"Stop him talking so much."

"Yeah, but he's got a point."

"Eatmepointman!"

Chunky clamped his hand over my mouth. At that moment I heard a high-pitched two-note signal. The four of them, and me, began looking around the car for the source of the noise. It was as if we were in a video game and had crossed up to the next level, were about to be destroyed by aliens we couldn't see coming. Then I realized that the beeping issued from my coat pocket: Minna's beeper going off.

"What's that?"

I twisted my head free. Chunky didn't fight me. "Barnamum Beeper," I said.

"What's that, some special kind? Get it out of his pocket. Didn't you chumps frisk him?"

"Screw you."

"Jesus."

They put their hands on me and quickly found the beeper. The digital readout showed a Brooklyn-Queens-Bronx prefix on the number. "Who's that?" said Pimples.

I frowned and shrugged: didn't know. Truly, I didn't recognize the number. Someone who thought Minna was still alive, I guessed, and shuddered a little. That scared me more than my abductors did.

"Make him call it," said Pinched from the front.

"You want to pull over to let him call?"

"Larry, you got the phone?"

Indistinct turned in his seat and offered me a cell phone.

"Call the number."

I dialed, they waited. We inched down Second Avenue. The airspace of the car hummed with tension. The cell phone rang, *dit-dit-dit*, a miniature, a toy that effortlessly commanded our focus, our complete attention. I might have popped it in my mouth and gulped it down instead of holding it to my ear. *Dit-dit-dit*, it rang again, then somebody picked up.

Garbage Cop.

"Lionel?" said Loomis.

"Mmmmhuh," I replied, squelching an outburst.

"Get this. What's the difference between three hundred sixty-five blow jobs and a radial tire?"

"Don'tcare!" I shouted. The four in the car all jumped.

"One's a Goodyear, the other's a *great* year," said Loomis proudly. He knew he'd nailed the riddle, no faltering this time, not a word out of place.

"Where are you calling from?" I asked.

"You called me."

"You beeped me, Loomis. Where are you?"

"I don't know"—his voice dimmed—"hey, what's the name of this place? Oh, yeah? Thanks. Bee-Bee-Que? Really, just like that, three letters? Go figure. Lionel, you there?"

"Here."

"It's a diner called B-B-Q, just like barbecue, only three letters. I eat here all the time, and I never even knew that!"

"Why'd you beep me, Loomis?" *Beep and Rebeep are sitting on a fence—*

"You told me to. You wanted that address, right? Ullman, the dead guy."

"Uh, that's right," I said, shrugging at Chunky, who still held my neck, but lightly, leaving me room to place the phone. He scowled at me, but it wasn't my fault if he was confused. I was confused, too. Confused and conworried.

"Well, I got it right here," said the Garbage Cop pridefully.

"What's the good of driving him around watching him make a phone call?" complained Pimples.

"Take it away from him," said Pinched from the driver's seat.

"Just punch him in the stomach," said Indistinct. "Make him scared."

"You got someone there with you?" said Loomis.

The four in the car had begun to chafe at seeing their faint authority slip away, devolve to the modern technology, the bit of plastic and wire in my palm. I had to find a way to calm them down. I nodded and widened my eyes to show my cooperation, and mouthed a just-wait signal to them, hoping they'd recall the protocol from crime movies: pretend they weren't there listening, and thus gather information on the sly.

I couldn't help it that they *weren't* actually listening.

"Tell me the address," I said.

"Okay, here goes," said Loomis. "Got a pen?"

"Whose address?" whispered Chunky in my other ear. He'd caught my hint. He was schooled enough in the clichés to be manipulable; his compatriots I wasn't so sure of.

"Tell me *Ullman's* address," I said for their sake. *Man-Salad-Dress* went my brain. I swallowed hard to keep it from crossing the threshold.

"Yeah, I got it," said the Garbage Cop sarcastically. "Whose else would you want?"

"Ullman?" said Chunky, not to me but to Pimples. "He's talking about *Ullman?*"

"Whose! A! Dress!" I shrieked.

"Aw, quit," said Loomis, jaded by now. My other audience wasn't so blasé. Pimples ripped the cell phone out of my hand, and Chunky wrestled my arm behind my back so I was wrenched forward nearly against the back of the driver's seat, and down. It was like he wanted me draped in his lap for a spanking. Meanwhile, up front, Pinched and Indistinct began arguing fiercely about parking, about whether they'd fit in some spot.

Pimples put the phone to his own ear and listened, but Loomis hung up, or maybe just got quiet and listened back, so they were silent together. Pinched managed to park, or double-park—I couldn't tell which from my strained vantage. The two up front were still muttering at one another, but Chunky was quiet, just turning my arm another degree or two, experimenting with actually hurting me, trying it on for size.

"You don't like hearing the name *Ullman*," I said, wincing.

"Ullman was a friend," said Chunky.

"Don't let him talk about Ullman," said Pinched.

"This is stupid," said Indistinct, with consummate disgust.

"You're stupid," said Chunky. "We're supposed to scare a guy, let's do it."

"I'm not so scared," I said. "You guys seem more scared to me. Scared of talking about Ullman."

"Yeah, well, if we're scared you don't know why," said Chunky. "And don't guess either. Don't open your trap."

"You're scared of a big Polish guy," I said.

"This is stupid," said Indistinct again. He sounded like he might cry. He got out of the car and slammed the door behind him.

Pimples finally quit listening to the silence Loomis had left behind on the cell phone, shut it down, and put it on the seat between us.

"What if we are scared of him?" said Chunky. "We ought to be, take it from us. We wouldn't be working for him if we weren't." He loosened his grip on my arm, so I was able to straighten up and look around. We were parked outside a popular coffee shop on Second.

The window was full of sullen kids flirting by working on tiny computers and reading magazines. They didn't notice us, carful of lugs, and why should they?

Indistinct was nowhere to be seen.

"I sympathize," I said, to keep them talking. "I'm scared of the big guy, too. It's just you can't throw a scare so good when you're scared."

I thought of Tony. If he'd come to the Zendo last night shouldn't he have triggered the same alarm I had? Shouldn't he have drawn these would-be toughs, this clown car loaded with fresh graduates from Clown College?

"What's so not scary about us?" said Pinched. He said to Chunky, "Hurt him already."

"You can hurt me but you still won't scare me," I said distractedly. One part of my brain was thinking, *Handle with scare, scandal with hair*, and so on. Another part was puzzling over the Tony question.

"Who was that on the phone?" said Pimples, still working on the problem he'd selected as his own.

"You wouldn't believe me," I said.

"Try us," said Chunky, twisting my arm.

"Just a guy doing research for me, that's all. I wanted Ullman's address. My partner got arrested for the murder."

"See, you shouldn't *have* a guy doing research," said Chunky. "That's the whole problem. Getting involved, visiting Ullman's apartment, that's the kind of thing we're supposed to scare you about."

Scare me, skullman, sang my disease. *Skullamum Bailey. Skinnyman Brainy.*

"Hurt him and scare him and let's get out of here," said Pinched. "I don't like this. Larry was right, it is stupid. I don't care about who's doing research."

"I still want to know who was on the phone," said Pimples.

"Listen," said Chunky, now trying to reason with me, as his gang's morale and focus—and actual numbers—were dwindling. "We're here on behalf of the big guy you're talking about, see? That's who sent us." He offered the morphic resonance theory: "So if he scares you you ought to be scared by us, without us having to hurt you."

"Guys like you could *kill* me and you still wouldn't scare me," I said.

"This was a bad idea," concluded Pinched, and he, too, got out of the car. The front seats were empty now, the steering wheel unmanned. "This isn't us," he said, leaning back in, addressing Pimples and Chunky. "We're no good at this." He raised his eyebrows at me. "You'll have to forgive us. This isn't what we do. We're men of peace." He shut the door. I turned my head enough to see him scooting down the block, his walk like a hectic bird's.

"Scaredycop!" I shouted.

"Where?" said Chunky, immediately releasing my arm. They both swiveled their heads in a panic, eyes wild behind the dark glasses, orange price tags dancing like fishing lures. Freed at last, I turned my head too, not searching for anything, of course, instead for the pleasure of aping their movements.

"Screw this," muttered Pimples.

He and Chunky both fled the rental car, hot on Pinched's heels, leaving me alone there.

*　　*　　*

Pinched had taken the car keys, but Indistinct's cell phone sat abandoned on the seat beside me. I put it in my pocket. Then I leaned over the seat, popped the glove compartment, and found the rental agency's registration card and receipt. The car was on a six-month lease to the Fujisaki Corporation, 1030 Park Avenue. The zip code, I was pretty sure, put it in the same zone as the Zendo. Which is where I was, as it happened. I rapped on the rental car's glove compartment door five times, but it wasn't particularly resonant or satisfying.

*　　*　　*

On my walk over to 1030 Park I flipped open the cell phone and rang L&L. I'd never made a street call before, and felt quite Captain Kirk–ish.

"L&L," said a voice, the one I'd hoped to hear.

"Tony, it's me," I said. "Essrog." That was how Minna always started a phone call: *Lionel, it's Minna.* You're the first name, I'm the last. In other words: You're the jerk and I'm the jerk's boss.

"Where are you?" said Tony.

Crossing Lexington at Seventy-sixth Street was the answer. But I didn't want to tell him.

Why? I wasn't sure. Anyway, I let a tic do my talking: "Kiss me, scareyman!"

"I got worried about you, Lionel. Danny said you went off with the Garbage Cop on some kind of a mission."

"Well, sort of."

"He with you now?"

"Garbage cookie," I said seriously.

"Why don't you head back here, Lionel? We ought to talk."

"I'm investigating a case," I said. *A guess tic eating a vest.*

"Oh, yeah? Where's it taking you?"

A well-coiffed man in a blue suit turned off Lexington ahead of me. He had a cell phone pressed to his right ear. I aligned myself behind him and imitated his walk.

"Various places," I said.

"Name one."

The harder Tony asked, the less I wanted to say. "I was hoping we could, you know, triangulate a little. Compare data."

"Give me an example, Lionel."

"Like did you—*Vesticulate! Guessticalot!*—did you get anything out of that, uh, Zendo place last night?"

"I'll tell you about it when I see you. Right now there's something important, you ought to get back here. What are you, at a pay phone?"

"Vestphone!" I said. "By any chance did a carful of guys try to warn you off?"

"Fuck you talking about?"

"What about the girl I saw go in before Minna? Did you find out about her?" Even as I asked I got the answer to the question I was asking, the real question.

I didn't trust Tony.

I felt the truth of it in the pause before he replied.

"I learned a few things," he said. "But at the moment we need to pool our resources, Lionel. You need to get back here. Because we got some problems coming up."

Now I could hear the bluff in his voice. It was casual, easy. He wasn't straining particularly. It was only Essrog on the line, after all.

"I know about problems," I said. "Gilbert's in jail on a murder charge."

"Well, that's just one."

"You weren't at the Zendo last night," I said. The man in the blue suit turned onto Park Avenue, still gabbing. I let him go, and stood in a crowd at the corner, waiting for the light to change.

"Maybe you ought to worry about your own fucking self and not me, Lionel," said Tony. "Where were *you* last night?"

"I did what I was supposed to do," I said, wanting to provoke him now. "I told Julia. Actually, she already knew." I left out the part about the homicide cop.

"That's interesting. I've been sort of wondering where Julia goes off to. I hope you found out."

Alarms went off. Tony was trying to make his voice casual, but it wasn't working. "Wondering when? You means she goes out of town a lot?"

"Maybe."

"Anyway, how'd you know she went anywhere?"

"Fuck you think we do around here, Lionel? We learn things."

"Yeah, we're a leading outfit. Gilbert's in jail, Tony." My eyes were suddenly full of tears. I knew I should be trying to focus on the Julia problem, but our betrayal of Gilbert felt more immediate.

"I know. He's safer there. Come in and talk, Lionel."

I crossed with the crowd but stopped halfway, at the traffic island in the middle of Park Avenue. The thumbnail of garden was marked with a sign that read VALIANT DAFFODIL (N. AMERICA), but the ground was chewed and pocked and vacant, as if someone had just dug up a plot of dead bulbs. I sat on the wooden embankment there and let the crowd pass by, until the light turned red again and the traffic began to whiz past me. A strip of sunshine laced the avenue and warmed me on the bench. Park Avenue's giant apartment buildings were ornate with shadow in the midmorning light. I was like a castaway on my island there, in a river of orange cabs.

"Where are you, Freakshow?"

"Don't call me Freakshow," I said.

"What should I call you—Buttercup?"

"Valiant Daffodil," I blurted. "Alibi Diffident."

"Where are you, Daffodil?" said Tony rather sweetly. "Should we come get you?"

"Goodcop, buttercup," I said, ticcing on through my tears. By calling me Freakshow—Minna's nickname—Tony had cued my Tourette's, had cut right through the layers of coping strategies and called out my giddy teenage voice. It should have been a relief to tic freely with one who knew me so well. But I didn't trust him. Minna was dead and I didn't trust Tony and I didn't know what it meant.

"Tell me where your little investigation led you," said Tony.

I looked up at Park Avenue, the monolithic walls of old money stretched out, a furrow of stone.

"I'm in Brooklyn," I lied. *"Eatmegreenpoint."*

"Oh, yeah? What's in Greenpoint?"

"I'm looking for the—*Greenpope!*—the guy who killed Minna, the Polish guy. What do you think?"

"Just wandering around looking for him, huh?"

"Eatmephone!"

"Hanging out in Polish bars, that sort of thing?"

I barked and clicked my tongue. My agitated jaw jerked against the redial button and a sequence of tones played on the line. The light changed and the cabs crossing Park blared their horns, working through gridlock. Another raft of pedestrians passed over my island and back into the river.

"Doesn't sound like Greenpoint," said Tony.

"They're filming a movie out here. You should see this. They've got Greenpoint—*Greenphone! Creepycone! Phonyman!*—Greenpoint Avenue set up to look like Manhattan. All these fake buildings and cabs and extras dressed up like they're on Park Avenue or something. So that's what you're hearing."

"Who's in it?"

"What?"

"Who's in the movie?"

"Somebody said Mel—*Gisspod, Gasspoint, Pissphone*—"

"Mel Gibson."

"Yeah. But I haven't seen him, just a lot of extras."

"And they really got fake buildings out there?"

"Did you sleep with Julia, Tony?"

"Why'd you want to go and say that?"

"Did you?"

"Who you trying to protect, Daffodil? Minna's dead."

"I want to know."

"I'll tell you in person when you get in here already."

"Dickety Daffodil! Dissident Crocophile! Laughable Chocodopolus!"

"Ah, I heard it all before."

"Likable lunchphone, veritable spongefist, teenage mutant Zendo lungfish, penis Milhaus Nixon tuning fork."

"You fucking Tugboat."

"Good-bye, Tonybailey."

*   *   *

Ten-thirty Park Avenue was another stone edifice, unremarkable among its neighbors. The oak doors split the difference between magnificence and military sturdiness, tiny windows barred with iron: French Colonial Bomb Shelter. The awning showed just the numerals, no gaudy, pretentious building name like you'd see on Central Park West or in Brooklyn Heights—here nothing remained to be proved, and anonymity was a value greater than charisma. The building had a private loading zone and a subtle curb cut, though, which sang of money, payoffs to city officials, and of women's-shoe heels too fragile to tangle with the usual four-inch step, too expensive to risk miring in dog shit. A special curb man stood patrolling the front, ready to open car doors or kick dogs or turn away unwanted visitors before they even tarnished the lobby. I came down the block at a good clip and swiveled to the door at the last minute, faking him out.

The lobby was wide and dark, designed to blind an unfamiliar visitor coming in from the sunlight. A crowd of doormen in white gloves and familiar blue suits with black piping on the legs surrounded me the minute I stumbled through the doors. It was the same uniform worn by the lugs in the rental car.

So they hadn't been lugs by training—that much was obvious. They were doormen, no shame in that. But *men of peace*?

"Help you with something?"

"Help you sir?"

"Name?"

"All visitors must be announced."

"Delivery?"

"Have you got a name?"

They encircled me, five or six them, not on special assignment but instead doing exactly what they were trained to do. Loom in the gloom. In their white gloves and their right context they were much scarier than they had been loaded into a rental car and fumbling as hoods. Their propriety was terrifying. I didn't see Pinched, Pimples, Chunky or Indistinct among them, but it was a big building. Instead I'd drawn Shadowface, Shadowface, Shadowface, Tallshadowface, and Shadowface.

"I'm here to see Fujisaki," I said. "Man, woman or corporation."

"There must be a mistake."

"Wrong building, surely."

"There is no Fujisaki."

"Name?"

"Fujisaki Management Corporation," I said.

"No."

"No. Not here. That isn't right."

"No."

"Name? Who's calling, sir?"

I took out one of Minna's cards. "Frank Minna," I said. The name came easily, and I didn't feel any need to distort it the way I would my own.

The band of doormen around me loosened at the sight of a business card. I'd shown a first glimmer of legitimacy. They were a top grade of doorman, finely tuned, factoring vigilance against hair-trigger sycophantic instincts.

"Expected?"

"Sorry?"

"Expected by the party in question? Appointment? Name? Contact?"

"Dropping in."

"Hmmm."

"No."

"No."

Another minute correction ensued. They bunched closer. Minna's card disappeared.

"There may be some confusion."

"Yes."

"Probably there is."

"Wrong building completely."

"Should there be a destination for a message, what would a message be?"

"On the chance that the destination in question is this one. You understand, sir."

"Yes."

"Yes."

"No message," I said. I tapped the nearest doorman's suit breast. He darted back, scowling. But they were penguins now. I had to touch them all. I reached for the next, the tallest, tried to high-five his shoulder and just grazed it. The circle loosened around me again as I spun. They might have thought I was staining them with invisible swatches of blacklight paint for future identification or planting electronic bugs or just plain old spreading cooties, from the way they jumped.

"No."

"Look out."

"Can't have this."

"Can't have this here."

"Out."

Then two of them had me by the elbows, and I was steered out onto the sidewalk.

*   *   *

I took a stroll around the block, just to glean what I could from the north face of the building. I was shadowed by the curb man, of course, but I didn't mind. The staff entrance smelled of a private dry-cleaning service, and the disposal bins showed signs of bulk food orders, perhaps an in-house grocery. I wondered if the building housed a private chef, too. I thought about poking my head in to see but the curb man was muttering tensely into a walkie-talkie, and I figured I'd probably better distance myself. I waved good-bye and he waved back involuntarily—everyone's a little ticcish that way sometimes.

*   *   *

Between bites of hot dog and gulps of papaya juice I dialed the Garbage Cop's office. The Papaya Czar on Eighty-sixth Street and Third Avenue is my kind of place—bright orange and yellow signs pasted on every available surface screaming, PAPAYA IS GOD'S GREATEST GIFT TO MAN'S HEALTH! OUR FRANKFURTERS ARE THE WORKING MAN'S FILET MIGNON! WE'RE POLITE NEW YORKERS, WE SUPPORT MAYOR GIULIANI! And so on. Papaya Czar's walls are so layered with language that I find myself immediately calmed inside their doors, as though I've stepped into a model interior of my own skull.

I washed down the tangy nubbin of the first dog while the phone rang. Papaya Czar's product did emulate an expensive steak's melting-in-your-mouthiness, frankfurters apparently skinless and neither bun nor dog crisped in the cooking, so they slid together into hot-dog cream on the tongue. These virtues could be taken in excess and leave one craving the greater surface tension of a Nathan's dog, but I was in the mood for the Czar's today. I had four more laid out in a neat row on the counter where I sat, each with a trim line of yellow mustard for an exclamation—*five* was still my angel.

As for papaya itself, I might as well be drinking truffula seed nectar or gryphon milk, for all I knew—I'd never encountered the fruit in any form except the Czar's chalky beverage.

"Sanitation Inspector Loomis," answered the Garbage Cop.

"Listen, Loomis. I'm working on this Gilbert thing." I knew I needed to tie it in to his friend's plight to keep him focused. In fact,

Gilbert was now the furthest thing from my mind. "I need you to pull up some information for me."

"That you, Lionel?"

"Yeah. Listen. Ten-three-oh Park Avenue. Write that down. I need some records on the building, management company, head of the board, whatever you can find out. See if any names you recognize pop up."

"Recognize from where?"

"From, uh, around the neighborhood." I was thinking *Frank Minna,* but I didn't want to say it. "Oh, one in particular. Fujisaki. It's Japanese."

"I don't know any Fujisaki from around the neighborhood."

"Just look up the records, Loomis. Call me back when you get something."

"Call you back where?"

I'd gotten the beeper and the cell phone mixed up. I was collecting other people's electronics. In fact, I didn't know the number of the phone I'd borrowed from the doorman in sunglasses. I wondered for the first time who I'd find myself talking to if I answered the incoming calls.

"Forget it," I said. "You've still got Minna's beeper number?"

"Sure."

"Use that. I'll call you."

"When do we bail out Gilbert?"

"I'm working on it. Listen, Loomis, I'd better go. Get back to me, all right?"

"Sure thing, Lionel. And, buddy?"

"What?"

"Good stature, man," said Loomis. "You're holding up great."

"Uh, thanks Loomis." I ended the call, put the cell phone back into my jacket pocket.

"Kee-rist," said a man sitting on my right. He was a guy in his forties. He wore a suit. As Minna said more than once, in New York any chucklehead can wear a suit. Satisfied he wasn't a doorman, I ignored him, worked on dog number three.

"I was in this restaurant in L.A.," he started. "Great place, million-dollar place. All the food is tall, you know what I mean? Tall food? There's this couple at a table, both of them talking on fucking cell phones, just like you got there. Two different conversations through the whole meal, yakking all over each other, what *Cindy* said, get away for the *weekend,* gotta work on my *game,* the whole nine yards. You couldn't hear yourself think over the racket."

I finished dog three in five evenly spaced bites, licked the mustard off my thumb tip, and picked up number four.

"I thought L.A., fair enough. Chalk it up. You can't expect any different. So couple months ago I'm trying to impress a client, take him to Balthazar, you know, downtown? Million-dollar place, take it from me. Tall food, *gangly* food. So what do I see but a couple of bozos at the bar talking on cell phones. My water's getting hot, but I figure, bar, fair enough, that's showing decent respect. Adjust my standards, whatever. So we get a table after waiting fifteen fucking minutes, sit down and my client's phone rings, he takes it out at the table! Guy I was with! Sits there yakking! Ten, fifteen minutes!"

I enjoyed dog four in Zen-like calm and silence, practicing for my coming *zazen.*

"Never thought I'd see it in here, though. Fucking California, Balthazar, whatever, all these guys with crap in their hair and million-dollar wristwatches like Dick Tracy I guess I gotta adjust my standards to the modern universe but I thought at the very least I could sit here eat a fucking hot dog without listening to yak yak yak."

I'd apportioned a fifth of my papaya juice for rinsing down the last dog. Suddenly impatient to leave, I stuffed a wad of napkins in my jacket pocket and took the dog and the drink in hand and headed back out into the bright cold day.

"Fucking people talking to themselves in a public place like they got some kind of illness!"

*   *   *

The beeper went off just as I got to the car. I drew it out for a look: another unfamiliar number in 718. I got into the car and called from the cell phone, ready to be irritated with Loomis.

"DickTracyphone," I said into the mouthpiece.

"This is Matricardi and Rockaforte," went a gravelly voice. Rockaforte. Though I'd heard them speak just two or three times in fifteen years, I would have known his voice anywhere.

Through the windshield I viewed Eighty-third Street, midday, November. A couple of women in expensive coats mimed a Manhattan conversation for my benefit, trying to persuade me of their reality. On the line, though, I heard an old man's breathing, and what I saw through the windshield wasn't real at all.

I considered that I was answering Minna's beeper. Did they know he was dead? Would I have to deliver the news to The Clients? I felt my throat constrict, instantly throbbing with fear and language.

"Speak to me," rasped Rockaforte.

"Larval Pushbug," I said softly, trying to offer my name. Did The Clients even know it? "Papaya Pissbag." I was tic-gripped, helpless. *"Not* Minna," I said at last. *"Not* Frank. Frank's *dead."*

"We know, Lionel," said Rockaforte.

"Who told you?" I whispered, controlling a bark.

"Things don't escape," he said. He paused, breathed, went on. "We're very sorry for you in this time."

"You found out from Tony?"

"We found out. We find out what we need. We learn."

But do you kill? I wanted to ask. *Do you command a Polish giant?*

"We're concerned for you," he said. "The information is that you are running, going here and there, unable to sit still. We hear this, and it concerns."

"What information?"

"And that Julia has left her home in this time of mourning. That nobody knows where she has gone unless it is you."

"Nojulia, nobody, nobodyknows."

"You still suffer. We see this and we suffer as well."

This was somewhat obscure to me, but I wasn't going to ask.

"We wish to speak with you, Lionel. Will you come and talk to us?"

"We're talking now," I breathed.

"We wish to see you standing before us. It's important in this time of pain. Come see us, Lionel."

"Where? New Jersey?" Heart racing, I allowed soothing permutations to course through my brain: *Garden state bricko and stuckface garbage face grippo and suckfast garter snake ticc-o and circus.* My lips rustled at the phone, nearly giving the words breath.

"We're in the Brooklyn house," he said. "Come."

"Scarface! Cigarfish!"

"What's got you running, Lionel?"

"Tony. You've been talking to Tony. He said I'm running. I'm not running."

"You sound running."

"I'm looking for the killer. Tony's trying to stop me, I think."

"You have a problem with Tony?"

"I don't trust him. He's acting—*Stuccotash!*—he's acting strangely."

"Let me speak," came a voice in the background of the call. Rockaforte's voice was replaced with Matricardi's: higher, more mellifluous, a single-malt whiskey instead of Dewar's.

"What's wrong with Tony?" said Matricardi. "You don't trust him in this matter?"

"I don't trust him," I repeated dumbly. I thought about ending the call. Again I consulted my other senses: I was in the sunshine in Manhattan in an L&L vehicle talking on a doorman's cell phone. I could discard Minna's beeper, forget about the call, go anywhere. The Clients were like players in a dream. They shouldn't have been able to touch me with their ancient, ethereal voices. But I couldn't bring myself to hang up on them.

"Come to us," said Matricardi. "We'll talk. Tony doesn't have to be there."

"Forgettaphone."

"You remember our place? Degraw Street. You know where?"

"Of course."

"Come. Honor us in this time of disappointment and regret. We'll talk without Tony. What's wrong we'll straighten."

*　　*　　*

While I considered what to do I used the doormen's phone again, called information and got the number of the *Daily News'* obituary page and bought a notice for Minna. I put in on a credit card of Minna's to which he'd added my name. He had to pay for his own notice, but I knew he'd have wanted it, considered it fifty bucks well spent. He was always an avid reader of the obituaries, studying them each morning in the L&L office like a tip sheet, a chance for him to pick up or work an angle. The woman on the line did it all by rote, and so did I: billing information, name of deceased, dates, survivors, until we got to the part where I gave out a line or two about who Minna was supposed to have been.

"Beloved something," said the woman, not unkindly. "It's usually Beloved something."

Beloved Father Figure?

"Or something about his contributions to the community," she suggested.

"Just say detective," I told her.

ONE MIND

There were only and always two things Frank Minna would not discuss in the years following his return from exile and founding of the Minna Agency. The first was the nature of that exile, the circumstances surrounding his disappearance that day in May when his brother Gerard hustled him out of town. We didn't know why he left, where he went or what he did while he was gone, or why he came back when he did. We didn't know how he met and married Julia. We didn't know what happened to Gerard. There was never again any sign or mention of Gerard. The sojourn "upstate" was covered in a haze so complete it was sometimes hard to believe it had lasted three years.

The other was The Clients, though they lurked like a pulse felt here or there in the body of the Agency.

L&L wasn't a moving company anymore, and we never again saw the inside of that hollowed-out brownstone on Degraw. But we were as much errand boys as detectives, and it wasn't hard, in the early days, to sense Matricardi and Rockaforte's shadow in some percent-

age of our errands. Their assignments were discernible for the deep
unease they provoked in Minna. Without explanation he'd alter his
patterns, stop dropping in at the barbershop or the arcade for a week
or so, close the L&L storefront and tell us to get lost for a few days.
Even his walk changed, his whole manner of being. He'd refuse to be
seated anywhere but in the corners of restaurants, his back to the
wall. He'd turn his head on the street for no reason, which I of course
cobbled into a lifelong tic. For cover he'd joke harder but also more
discontinuously, his stream of commentary and insult turned balky
and riddled with grim silences, his punch lines become non sequiturs.
And the jobs we did for The Clients were discontinuous too. They
were fractured stories, middles lacking a clear beginning or end.
When we Minna Men tracked a wife for a husband or watched an
employee suspected of pilferage or cooking the books we mastered
their pathetic dramas, encompassed their small lives with our worldli-
ness. What we gathered with our bugs and cameras and etched into
our reports was true and complete. Under Minna we were secret masters, writing a sort of social history of Cobble Hill and Carroll Gardens into our duplicate files. But when the hand of Matricardi and
Rockaforte moved the Minna Men we were only tools, glancing off
the sides of stories bigger than we understood, discarded and left
wondering at the end.

Once in the early days of the Agency we were dispatched to stand
guard in broad daylight around a car, a Volvo, and we picked up a
scent of The Clients in Minna's stilted, fragmentary instructions. The
car was empty as far as we could tell. It was parked on Remsen Street
near the Promenade, at a placid dead-end traffic circle overlooking
Manhattan. Gilbert and I sat on a park bench, trying to look casual
with our backs to the skyline, while Tony and Danny idled at the
mouth of Remsen and Hicks, glaring at anyone who turned onto the
block. We knew only that we were supposed to give way at five
o'clock, when a tow truck would come for the car.

Five o'clock stretched into six, then seven, with no truck. We took pee breaks in the children's park at Montague Street, ran through cigarettes, and paced. Evening strollers appeared on the Promenade, couples, teenagers with paper-bagged bottles of beer, gays mistaking us for cruisers. We shrugged them away from our end of the walk, muttered, glanced at our watches. The Volvo couldn't have been less conspicuous if it were invisible, but for us it glowed, screamed, ticked like a bomb. Every kid on a bike or stumbling wino seemed an assassin, a disguised ninja with aims on the car.

When the sun began to set Tony and Danny started arguing.

"This is stupid," said Danny. "Let's get out of here."

"We can't," said Tony.

"You know there's a body in the trunk," said Danny.

"How am I supposed to know that?" said Tony.

"Because what else would it be?" said Danny. "Those old guys had someone killed."

"That's stupid," said Tony.

"A body?" said Gilbert, plainly unnerved. "I thought the car was full of money."

Danny shrugged. "I don't care, but it's a body. I'll tell you what else: We're being set up for it."

"That's stupid," said Tony.

"What does Frank know? He just does what they tell him." Even in rebellion Danny obeyed Minna's stricture against speaking The Clients' names.

"You really think it's a body?" said Gilbert to Danny.

"Sure."

"I don't want to stay if it's a body, Tony."

"Gilbert, you fat fuck. What if it is? What do you think we're doing here? You think you're never gonna see a body working for Minna? Go join the garbage cops, for chrissakes."

"I'm cutting out," said Danny. "I'm hungry anyway. This is stupid."

"What should I tell Minna?" said Tony, daring Danny to go.

"Tell him what you want."

It was a startling defection. Tony and Gilbert and I were all problems in our various ways, while Danny in his silence and grace was Minna's pillar, his paragon.

Tony couldn't face this mutiny directly. He was accustomed to bullying Gilbert and me, not Danny. So he reverted to form. "What about you, Freakshow?"

I shrugged, then kissed my own hand. It was an impossible question. Devotion to Minna had boiled down to this trial of hours watching over the Volvo. Now we had to envision disaster, betrayal, rotting flesh.

But what would it mean to turn from Minna?

I hated The Clients then.

The tow truck came grinding down Remsen before I could speak. It was manned by a couple of fat lugs who laughed at our jumpiness and told us nothing about the car's importance, just shooed us off and began chaining the Volvo's bumper to their rig. Less Men than Boys in suits, we felt as though this had been designed as a test of our fresh-grown nerves. And we'd failed, even if Minna and The Clients didn't know about it.

*   *   *

We grew tougher, though, and Minna became unflappable, and we came to take the role of The Clients in the life of the Agency more in stride. Who had to make sense of everything? It wasn't always certain when we were acting for them anyway. Seize a given piece of equipment from a given office: Was that on The Clients' behalf or not? Collect this amount from such and such a person: When we passed the take to Minna did he pass it along to The Clients? Unseal this envelope, tap this phone: Clients? Minna kept us in the dark and turned us into professionals. Matricardi and Rockaforte's presence became mostly subliminal.

The last job I felt certain was for The Clients was more than a year before Minna's murder. It bore their trademark of total inexplicability.

A supermarket on Smith Street had burned and been razed earlier that summer, and the empty lot was filled with crushed brick and turned into an informal peddlers' market, where sellers of one fruit—oranges, say, or mangoes—would set up a few crates and do a summer afternoon's business, alongside the hot-dog and shaved-ice carts that began to gather there. After a month or so a Hispanic carnival took over the site, setting up a Tilt-a-Whirl and a miniature Ferris wheel, each a dollar a ride, along with a grilled-sausage stand and a couple of lame arcades: a water-gun balloon game and a grappling hook over a glass case full of pink and purple stuffed animals. The litter and smells of grease were a blight if you got too close, but the Ferris wheel was lined with white tubes of neon, and it was a glorious thing to see at night down Smith Street, a bright unexpected pinwheel almost three stories high.

We'd been so bored that summer that we'd fallen into working regularly as a car service, taking calls when they came, ferrying dates home from nightclubs, old ladies to and from hospitals, vacationers to La Guardia for the weekend flight to Miami Beach. Between rides we'd play poker in the air-conditioned storefront. It was after one-thirty on a Friday night when Minna came in. Loomis was sitting in on the game, losing hands and eating all the chips, and Minna told him to get lost, go home already.

"What's the matter, Frank?" said Tony.

"Nothing's the matter. Got something for us to do, that's all."

"Something what? For who?"

"Just a job. What do we have in here that's like a crowbar or something?" Minna smoked furiously to mask his unease.

"A crowbar?"

"Just something you can swing. Like a crowbar. I've got a bat and a lug wrench in my trunk. Stuff like that."

"Sounds like you want a gun," said Tony, raising his eyebrows.

"If I wanted a gun I'd get a gun, you diphthong. This doesn't take a gun."

"You want chains?" said Gilbert, meaning to be helpful. "There's a whole bunch of chains in the Pontiac."

"Crowbar, crowbar, crowbar. Why do I even bother with you mystic seers anymore? If I wanted my mind read I'd call Gladys Knight for chrissakes."

"Dionne Warwick," said Gilbert.

"What?"

"Psychic Hotline's Dionne Warwick, not Gladys Knight."

"Psychicwarlock!"

"Got some pipe downstairs," mused Danny, only now laying down the hand he'd been holding since Minna barged into the office. It was a full house, jacks and eights.

"It's gotta be swingable," said Minna. "Let's see."

The phone rang and I grabbed for it and said, "L&L."

"Tell them we don't have any cars," said Minna.

"This needs all four of us?" I said. I was courting fond notions of missing the crowbar-and-lug-wrench project, whatever it was, and driving someone out to Sheepshead Bay instead.

"Yes, Freakboy. We're all going."

I got rid of the call. Twenty minutes later we were loaded up with pipes, lug wrench, car jack and a souvenir Yankee bat from Bat Day in Minna's old Impala, the least distinguished of L&L's many cars, and another bad sign if I was trying to read signs. Minna drove us down Wyckoff, past the projects, then circled around, south on Fourth Avenue down to President Street, and back toward Court. He was stalling, checking his watch.

We turned on Smith, and Minna parked us a block below the empty supermarket lot. The carnival had shut down for the night, plywood boards up over the concessions, rides stilled, the evening's discarded beer cups and sausage wrappers glowing against the moon-lit rubblescape. We crept onto the lot with our implements, following Minna wordlessly now, no longer chafing at his leadership, instead lulled into our deep obedient rhythm as his Men. He pointed at the Ferris wheel.

"Take it out."

"Eh?"

"Destroy the wheel, you candied yams."

Gilbert understood soonest, perhaps because the task suited his skills and temperament so well. He took a swing at the nearest line of neon with his chunk of pipe, smashing it easily, bringing a rain of silver dust. Tony and Danny and I followed his lead. We attacked the body of the wheel, our first swings tentative, measuring our strength, then lashing out, unloading. It was easy to damage the neon, not easy at all to impress the frame of the wheel, but we set at it, attacked any joint or vulnerable weld, prying up the electrical cable and chopping at it with the sharpest edge of the wrench until insulation and wire were bare and mangled, then frayed. Minna himself wielded the Yankee bat, splintering its wood against the gates that held riders into their seats, not breaking them but changing their shape. Gilbert and I got inside the frame of the wheel and with all our weight dragged at one of the chairs until we ruptured the hinge. Then we found the brake and released the wheel to turn so that we could apply our malicious affection to the whole of it. A couple of Dominican teenagers stood watching us from across the street. We ignored them, bore down on the Ferris wheel, hurrying but not frantic, absolutely Minna's to direct but not even needing direction. We acted as one body to destroy the amusement. This was the Agency at its mature peak: unquestioning and thorough in carrying out an action even when it bordered on sheer Dada.

*   *   *

"Frank loved you, Lionel," said Rockaforte.

"I, uh, I know."

"For that reason we care for you, for that reason we are concerned."

"Though we have not seen you since you were a boy," said Matricardi.

"A boy who barked," said Rockaforte. "We remember. Frank brought and you stood before us in this very room and you barked."

"And Frank spoke of your sickness many times."

"He loved you though he considered you a freak."

"He used that very word."

"You helped him build, you were one of his boys, and now you are a man and you stand before us in this hour of pain and misunderstanding."

Matricardi and Rockaforte had looked sepulchral to me as a teenager and they looked no worse now, their skin mummified, their thin hair in a kind of spider-web sheen over their reflective pates, Matricardi's ears and scarred nose dwarfing his other features, Rockaforte's face puffier and more potatolike. They were dressed as twins in black suits, whether consciously in mourning or not I couldn't know. They sat together on the tightly upholstered couch and when I stepped through the door I thought I saw their hands first joined on the cushions in the space between them, then jerking to their laps. I stood far enough back that I wasn't tempted to reach out and play pattycake, to slap at their folded hands or the place their hands had been resting.

The Degraw Street brownstone was unchanged, outside and in, apart from a dense, even layer of dust on the furniture and carpet and picture frames in the parlor. The air in the room swam with stirred dust, as though Matricardi and Rockaforte had arrived just a few moments before. They visited their Brooklyn shrine less often than in the past, I supposed. I wondered who drove them in from Jersey and whether they took any pains not to be seen coming here or whether they cared. Perhaps no one alive in Carroll Gardens knew them by sight anymore.

A neighborhood's secret lords could also be Invisible Men.

"What is between you and Tony?" said Matricardi.

"I want to find Frank's killer." I'd already heard myself say this too many times, and meaning was leaking out of the phrase. It threatened to become a sort of moral tic: *findfrank'skiller.*

"Why don't you follow Tony in this? Shouldn't you act as one, as brothers?"

"I was there. When they took Frank. Tony—*Hospitabailey!*—Tony wasn't there."

"You're saying then that he should follow you."

"He shouldn't get in my way. *Essway! Wrongway!*" I winced, hating to tic now, in front of them.

"You're upset, Lionel."

"Sure I'm upset." Why should I confess my distrust to those I distrusted? The more Matricardi and Rockaforte spoke Tony's name, the more certain I was they were tangled together in this somehow, and that Tony was far more familiar with The Clients than I'd been in the years since our first visit to this crypt, this mausoleum. I'd come away with a fork, he with something more. Why should I accuse one half of a conspiracy to the other? Instead I squinted and turned my head and pursed my lips, trying to avoid the obvious, finally acceded to The Clients' power of suggestion and barked once, loudly.

"You are afflicted and we feel for you. A man shouldn't run, and he shouldn't woof like a dog. He should find peace."

"Why doesn't Tony want me looking into Frank's murder?"

"Tony wishes this thing to be done correctly and with care. Work with him, Lionel."

"Why do you speak for Tony?" I gritted my teeth as I spoke the words. It wasn't exactly ticcing, but I'd begun to echo The Clients' verbal rhythms, the cloistered Ping-Pong of their diction.

Matricardi sighed and looked at Rockaforte. Rockaforte raised his eyebrows.

"Do you like this house?" said Matricardi.

I considered the dust-covered parlor, the load of ancient furnishing between the carpet and the ceiling's scrollwork, how it all hung suspended inside the shell of the warehouse-brownstone. I felt the presence of the past, of mothers and sons, deals and understandings, one dead hand gripping another—dead hands were nested here on Degraw Street like a series of Chinese boxes. Including Frank Minna's. There were so many ways I didn't like it I didn't know where to begin, except that I knew I shouldn't allow myself to begin at all.

"It's not a house," I said, offering the very least of my objections. "It's a room."

"He says it's a room," said Matricardi. "Lionel, this is my mother's house where we sit. Where you stand so full of fury it makes you like a cornered dog."

"Somebody killed Frank."

"Are you accusing Tony?"

"Accusatony! Excusebaloney! Funnymonopoly!" I squeezed my eyes shut to interrupt the seizure of language.

"We wish you to understand, Lionel. We regret Frank's passing. We miss him sorely. It is a soreness in our hearts. Nothing could please us more than to see his killer torn by birds or picked apart by insects with claws. Tony should have your help in bringing that day closer. You should stand behind him."

"What if my search brings me to Tony?" I'd let The Clients lead me to this pass in the conversation, and now there wasn't any reason to pretend.

"The dead live in our hearts, Lionel. From there Frank will never be dislodged. But now Tony has replaced Frank in the world of the living."

"What does that mean? You've replaced Frank with Tony?"

"It means you shouldn't act against Tony. Because our wishes go with him."

I understood now. It was Tony's Italian apotheosis at last. I was thrilled for him.

Unless it had been this way for years without my knowing. Maybe

Tony Vermonte and The Clients ran deeper than Frank Minna and The Clients ever had.

I considered the word *replaced*. I decided it was time to go.

"I need your permission—" I began, then stopped. Who were The Clients, and what did their permission consist of? What was I thinking?

"Speak, Lionel."

"I'm going to keep looking," I said. "With or without Tony's help."

"Yes. We can see. And so we have an assignment for you. A suggestion."

"A place for you to apply your passion for justice."

"And your talent for detection. The training instilled."

"What?" Just a measure of the day's angled brightness penetrated the heavy curtains of the parlor. I glared back at a row of thuggish midcentury faces staring out from picture frames, wondering which was Matricardi's mom. The hot dogs I'd eaten were rumbling in my stomach. I longed to be outside, on the Brooklyn streets, anywhere but here.

"You spoke with Julia," said Matricardi. "You should find her. Bring her in as we brought you. Let us speak with her."

"She's afraid," I said. *A frayed knot.*

"Afraid of what?"

"She's like me. She doesn't trust Tony."

"Something is wrong between them."

This was exhausting. "Of course something's wrong. They slept together."

"Making love brings people closer, Lionel."

"Maybe they feel guilty about Frank."

"Guilty, yes. Julia knows something. We called her to see us. Instead she runs. Tony says he doesn't know where."

"You think Julia has something to do with Frank's murder?" I let my hand trace a vague line in the dust on the marble mantelpiece. A mistake. I tried to forget I'd done it.

"There's something on her mind, something weighing. You want to help us, Lionel, find her."

"Learn her secrets and share them with us. Do this without telling Tony."

Losing control somewhat, I inserted my finger into the grooved edge of the mantel and pushed, gathering a shaggy clot of dust.

"I don't get it," I said. "Now you want me to go behind Tony's back?"

"We listen, Lionel. We hear. We consider. Questions occur. If your suspicions are grounded the answers may lie with Julia. Tony has been less than clear in this one area. However strange and damaged, you'll be our hands and feet, our eyes and ears, you'll learn and return to us and share."

"Founded," I said. I reached the end of the mantel and thrust the accumulated dustball past the edge, following through like a one-fingered shot-putter.

"*If* they are," said Matricardi. "You don't know. That's what you'll find out."

"No, I mean founded, not grounded. Suspicions *founded.*"

"He's correcting," said Rockaforte to Matricardi, gritting his teeth.

"Find her, Essrog! Founder! Grounder! Confessrub!" I tried to wipe my finger clean on my jacket and made a gray stripe of clingy dust.

Then I belched, really, and tasted hot dogs.

"There's a little part of Frank in you," said Matricardi. "We speak to that part and it understands. The rest of you may be inhuman, a beast, a freak. Frank was right to use that word. You're a freak of nature. But the part of you that Frank Minna cared for and that cares so much for his memory is the part that will help us find Julia and bring her home."

"Go now, because you sicken us to see you playing with the dust that gathers in the home of his beloved mother, bless her sweet dishonored and tormented soul."

*　　*　　*

Conspiracies are a version of Tourette's syndrome, the making and tracing of unexpected connections a kind of touchiness, an expression of the yearning to touch the world, kiss it all over with theories, pull it close. Like Tourette's, all conspiracies are ultimately solipsistic, sufferer or conspirator or theorist overrating his centrality and forever rehearsing a traumatic delight in reaction, attachment and causality, in roads out from the Rome of self.

The second gunman on the grassy knoll wasn't part of a conspiracy—we Touretters know this to be true. He was ticcing, imitating the action that had startled and allured him, the shots fired. It was just his way of saying, Me too! I'm alive! Look here! Replay the film!

The second gunman was tugging the boat.

*   *   *

I'd parked in the shade of an elderly, crippled elm, trunk knotted and gnarled from surviving disease, with roots that had slowly nudged the slate sidewalk upward and apart. I didn't see Tony waiting in the Pontiac until I nearly had my key in the door. He was sitting in the driver's seat.

"Get in." He leaned over and opened the passenger door. The sidewalk was empty in both directions. I considered strolling away, ran into the usual problem of where to go.

"Get in, Freakshow."

I went to the passenger side and slid into the seat beside him, then reached out disconsolately and caressed his shoulder, leaving a smudge of dust. He raised his hand and slapped me on the side of the head.

"They lied to me," I said, flinching away.

"I'm shocked. Of course they lied. What are you, a newborn baby?"

"*Barnamum* baby," I mumbled.

"Which particular lie are you worrying about, Marlowe?"

"They warned you I was coming here, didn't they? They set me up. It was a trap."

"Fuck did you *think* was going to happen?"

"Never mind."

"You think you're smart," said Tony, his voice twangy with contempt. "You think you're Mike fucking Hammer. You're like the Hardy Boys' retarded kid brother, Lionel." He slapped my head again. "You're Hardly Boy."

My home borough had never felt so like a nightmare to me as it did on this bright sunlit day on Matricardi and Rockaforte's block of Degraw: a nightmare of repetition and enclosure. Ordinarily I savored Brooklyn's unchangeability, the bullying, Minna-like embrace of its long memory. At the moment I yearned to see this neighborhood razed, replaced by skyscrapers or multiplexes. I longed to disappear into Manhattan's amnesiac dance of renewal. Let Frank be dead, let the Men disperse. I only wanted Tony to leave me alone.

"You knew I had Frank's beeper," I said sheepishly, putting it together.

"No, the old guys have X-ray vision, like Superman. They don't know shit if I don't tell them, Lionel. You need to find a new line of work, McGruff. Shitlock Holmes."

I was familiar enough with Tony's belligerence to know it had to run awhile, play itself out. Me, I slid my hands along the top of the dashboard at the base of the windshield, smoothing away the crumbs and dust accumulated there, riffling my fingers over the plastic vents. Then I began buffing the corner of the windshield with my thumb tip. Visiting Matricardi's mother's parlor had triggered a dusting compulsion.

"You idiot freak."

"Beepmetwice."

"I'll beep you twice, all right."

He lifted his hand, and I flinched again, ducking underneath like a boxer. While I was near I licked the shoulder of his suit, trying to clean off the smudge of dust I'd left. He pushed me away disgustedly, an ancient echo of St. Vincent's hallway.

"Okay, Lionel. You're still half a fag. You got me convinced."

I didn't speak, no small achievement. Tony sighed and put both hands on the wheel. He appeared to be through buffeting me for the moment. I watched my saliva-stripe evaporate into the weave of his jacket.

"So what did they tell you?"

"The Clients?"

"Sure, The Clients," said Tony. "Matricardi and Rockaforte. Frank's dead, Lionel. I don't think he's gonna, like, spin in his grave if you say their names."

"Fork-it-hardly," I whispered, then glanced over my shoulder at their stoop. "Rocket-fuck-me."

"Good enough. So what did they tell you?"

"The same thing the—*Duckman! Dogboy! Confessdog!*—same thing the doormen told me: Stay off the case." I was mad with verbal tics now, making up for lost time, feeling at home. Tony was still a comfort to me in that way.

"What doorman?"

"Door*men*. A whole bunch of them."

"Where?"

But Tony's eyes said he knew perfectly well where, only needed to measure what I knew. He looked a little panicked, too.

"Ten-thirty Park Avenue," I said. *Energy pocket angle. Rectangle sauce!*

His hands tightened on the wheel. Instead of looking at me, he squinted into the distance. "You were there?"

"I was following a lead."

"Answer my question. *You were there?*"

"Sure."

"Who'd you see?"

"Just a lot of doormen."

"You discuss this with Matricardi and Rockaforte? Tell me you didn't, you goddamn motormouth."

"They talked, I listened."

"Oh yeah, that's likely. Fuck."

Oddly, I found myself wanting to reassure Tony. He and The Clients had drawn me back to Brooklyn and ambushed me in my car, but some old orphans' solidarity worked against my claustrophobia. Tony scared me, but The Clients scared me more. And now I knew they still scared Tony, too. Whatever deal he'd struck was incomplete.

It was cold in the car, but Tony was sweating.

"Be serious with me now, Lionel. Do they know about the building?"

"I'm always serious. That's the tragedy of my life."

"Talk to me, Freakshow."

"*Anybuilding! Nobuilding!* Nobody said anything about a building." I reached for his collar, wanting to straighten it, but he batted my hands away.

"You were in there awhile," he said. "Don't fuck with me, Lionel. What was said?"

"They want me to find Julia," I said, wondering if it was a good idea to mention her name. "They think she knows something."

Tony took a gun out from under his arm and pointed it at me.

*   *   *

I'd returned to Brooklyn suspecting Tony of colluding with The Clients, and now—sweet irony!—Tony suspected me of the same thing. It wasn't that much of a leap. Matricardi and Rockaforte didn't have any motive for humoring me. If they trusted Tony, they wouldn't have required him to wait and bag me outside in the car afterward. He would have been hidden inside, behind the proverbial curtain, soaking up the whole conversation.

I had to give The Clients credit. They'd played us like a Farfisa organ.

On the other hand, Tony had a secret from The Clients: the building on Park Avenue. And despite his fears his secret seemed intact. No point of this particular quadrangle had a monopoly on information. Tony knew something they didn't. I knew something Tony didn't, didn't I? I hoped so. And Julia knew something neither Tony nor The Clients knew, or else she knew something Tony didn't *want* The Clients to know. Julia, Julia, Julia, I needed to figure out the Julia angle, even if Matricardi and Rockaforte wanted me to.

Or was I outsmarting myself? I knew what Minna would have said. Wheels within wheels.

*   *   *

I'd never faced Tony at gunpoint before, but at some level I'd been preparing for this moment all my life. It didn't feel at all unnatural. Rather it was a sort of culmination, the rarefied end point of our long association. Now, if I'd had a gun on him, *that* would've freaked me out.

The gun also served splendidly to concentrate my attention. I felt my ticcishness ease, and a flood of excess language instantly evaporate, like cartoon blemishes in a television commercial. Gunplay: another perfectly useless cure.

Tony didn't seem all that impressed by the situation. His eyes and mouth were tired. It was only four in the afternoon and we'd been sitting in the parked car too long already. He had questions, urgent, particular, and the gun would help move things along.

"You talk to anyone else about the building?" he asked.

"Who would I talk to?"

"Danny, say. Or Gilbert."

"I was just up there. I haven't seen Danny. And Gilbert's in jail." I left out the part about the Garbage Cop, and prayed Minna's beeper didn't go off anytime soon.

Meanwhile, with his questions Tony was telling me more than I was telling him: Danny and Gilbert weren't with him in the Park Avenue caper. Yes, this Hardly Boy was still on the case.

"So it's just you," Tony said. "You're the jerk I've gotta deal with. You're Sam Spade."

"When someone kills your partner you're supposed to do something about it," I said.

"Minna wasn't your partner. He was your sponsor, Freakshow. He was Jerry Lewis, and you were the thing in the wheelchair."

"Then why'd he call for me instead of you when he was in trouble yesterday?"

"He was an idiot bringing you up there."

A shadow strolled past the car, indifferent to our curbside melodrama. This was my second time imperiled in a parked vehicle in the space of three hours. I wondered what goonish spectacles I'd overlooked in my own career as a pavement walker.

"Tell me about Julia, Tony—*Tulip Attorney!*" The magic curative of being at gunpoint was beginning to fade.

"Shut up a little. I'm thinking."

"What about Ullman?" I said. As long as he was allowing my questions I might as well ask. "Who was Ullman?—*Doofus Allplan!*" I wanted to ask about the Fujisaki Corporation, but I figured the extent of what I knew was one of the only things I knew and he didn't. I needed to preserve that advantage, however minuscule. Besides, I didn't want to hear what hay my syndrome would make of the word *Fujisaki*.

Tony made a particularly sour face. "Ullman's a guy who didn't figure numbers right. He's one of a little group of somebodies who tried to make themselves rich. Frank was another one."

"So you and the Polish killer took him out, huh?"

"That's so wrong it's funny."

"Tell me, Tony."

"Where would I start?" he said. I heard a note of bitterness, and wondered if I could play on it. Tony likely missed Minna in his way, and missed the Agency, no matter how he'd been corrupted or what poisonous information he knew that I didn't.

"Be sentimental for a change," I said. "Make me know you didn't kill him."

"Go fuck yourself."

"That was persuasive," I said. Then I made a sour face like an uptight British butler: *"Per-shwoosh-atively!"*

"The problem with you, Lionel, is you don't know anything about how the world really works. Everything you know comes from Frank Minna or a book. I don't know which is worse."

"Gangster movies." I fought to keep the butler-face from reappearing.

"What?"

"I watched a lot of gangster movies, like you. Everything we both know comes from Frank Minna or gangster movies."

"Frank Minna was two guys," said Tony. "The one I learned from and the chucklehead who thought you were funny and got himself killed. You only knew the chucklehead."

Tony held the gun floppily between us, using it to gesture, to signal punctuation. I only hoped he understood how literally it could punctuate. None of us had ever carried guns so far as I knew, apart from Minna. He'd rarely allowed us even to see his. Now I wondered what private teaching had gone on when I wasn't around, wondered how seriously I should take Tony's notion of the two Minnas.

"I suppose it was the smart Frank Minna who taught you to wave guns around," I said. It came out a bit more sarcastic than I'd intended, then I yelled, *"Frankensmart!"* which pretty much undercut my delivery. Tony really was waving the gun, though. The only thing it never pointed at was himself.

"I'm carrying this for protection. Like I'm protecting you with it right now, by convincing you to shut up and quit asking questions. And stay in Brooklyn."

"I hope you don't have to protect me—*Protectmebailey! Detectorbaby!*—by pulling the trigger."

"Let's both hope. Too bad you weren't clever like Gilbert, to get himself put under police protection for a week or so."

"Is that the current sentence for murder? A week?"

"Don't make me laugh. Gilbert didn't kill anybody."

"You sound disappointed."

"I'm long over my disappointment that Frank liked to surround himself with a cavalcade of clowns. It was a way of life. I won't be making the same mistake."

"No, you'll think up a whole bunch of new ones."

"Enough of this. Does every conversation with you have to be the director's cut? Get out of the car."

At that moment there came a tap on the window, driver's side. It was a gun muzzle that tapped. The arm holding the gun extended from behind the trunk of the elm tree. A head poked out too: the homicide detective.

"Gentlemen," he said. "Do step out of the car—slowly."

Ambushes within ambushes.

*   *   *

He still had that threadbare, jaded, coffee-isn't-working-anymore air about him, even in daylight. It didn't look like he'd gotten out of his suit since the night before. I believed him with a gun better than I did Tony, though. He waved us over to the front of the car and had us spread our legs, to the wonderment of a couple of old ladies, then took away Tony's gun. He had Tony open his jacket and show the open holster and lift his pant legs to prove there was nothing strapped to his ankles. Then he tried to pat me down and I began to pat him back.

"Goddamn it, Alibi, cut that out." He was still fond of that nickname he'd invented for me. It made me fond of him.

"I can't help it," I said.

"What's that? A phone? Take it out."

"It's a phone." I showed him.

Tony looked at me strangely, and I just shrugged.

"Get back in the car. Give me the keys first." Tony handed over the keys and we got back into the front seat. The homicide detective opened the back doors and eased into the seat behind us, training his gun on the backs of our heads.

"Hands on the wheel and the dash, that's good. Face forward, gentlemen. Don't look at me. Smile like they're taking your picture. They will be soon enough."

"What did we do?" said Tony. "A guy can't show another guy a gun anymore?"

"Shut up and listen. This is a murder investigation. I'm the investigating officer. I don't care about your goddamn gun."

"So give it back."

"I don't think so, Mr. Vermonte. You people make me nervous. I found out a few things about this neighborhood in the last twenty-four hours."

"Mister Gobbledy Gun."

"Shut up, Alibi."

Shut up shut up shut up! I kneaded the petrified foam of the Pontiac's dashboard like a nursing kitten, just trying to keep still and shut up. Someday I'd change my name to Shut Up and save everybody a lot of time.

"I got this case because you jokers brought Frank Minna into Brooklyn Hospital. That's where he died and that's in my jurisdiction. I don't get to work this side of Flatbush Avenue that often, you get me? I don't know all that much about your neighborhood, but I'm learning, I'm learning."

"Not so many murders over here, eh, Chief?" said Tony.

"Not so many *niggers* on this side of Flatbush, that what you're trying to say?"

"Whoa, slow down," said Tony. "You're leading the witness. Isn't that against the rules?" Tony kept his hands on the steering wheel and grinned into the windshield. I don't think the homicide cop had really meant to inspire such a smile.

"Okay, Tony," said the cop, his voice a little husky. I heard him breathing heavily through his nose. I suppose unsheathing his gun had gotten him a bit worked up. I imagined I could feel its muzzle centering first on my ear, then on Tony's. "Tell me what you meant," he said. "Set me straight."

"All I meant was not so many murders—am I right?"

"Yeah, you got the lid clamped down pretty tight around here. No murders and no niggers. Nice clean streets, nothing but old guys carrying around racing forms and tiny pencils. Makes me nervous."

It was honest of him to admit it. I wondered what Mafia horror stories he'd gathered in his day-old investigation.

"Around here people watch out for each other," said Tony.

"Yeah, right up until you off each other. What's the connection between Minna and Ullman, Tony?"

"Who's Ullman?" said Tony. "I never met the guy."

That was a Minna-ism: *never met the guy.*

"Ullman kept the books for a property-management firm in Manhattan," said the homicide detective. "Until your friend Coney shot him through the skull. Looks like tit for tat to me. I'm impressed with how quick you guys get to work."

"What's your name, Officer?" said Tony. "I get to ask that, don't I?"

"I'm not an officer, Tony. I'm a detective. My name is Lucius Seminole."

"Luscious? You gotta be kidding me."

"*Lu*cius. Call me Detective Seminole."

"What is that, like an Indian name?"

"It's a Southern name," said Seminole. "Slave name. Keep laughing, Tony."

"Detectahole!"

"Alibi, you are not making me happy."

"Inspectaholic!"

"Don't kill him, Superfly," said Tony, grinning broadly. "I know it's pitiful, but he can't help himself. Think of it as a free human freak show."

"Licorice Smellahole!" Not turning my head was driving me crazy: I had to rename what I couldn't see.

"You a car service or a comedy team?" said Seminole.

"Lionel's just jealous because you're asking me all the questions," said Tony. "He likes to talk."

"I already heard from Alibi last night. He near about drove me crazy with his talk. Now I'm looking for answers from you, straight man."

"We're not a car service," I said. "We're a detective agency." The assertion fought its way out of me, a tic disguised as a common statement.

"Turn around, Alibi. Let's talk about the lady who ran to Boston— Mrs. Deadguy."

"Boston?" said Tony.

"We'readetectiveagency," I ticced again.

"She booked the flight under her own name," said Seminole. "It's not the first time either. What's in Boston?"

"Beats me. She goes up there a lot?"

"Don't play stupid."

"It's news to me," said Tony. He scowled at me, and I made a dopey face back, stumped. Julia in Boston? I wondered if Seminole had his information straight.

"She was ready to fly," said Seminole. "Somebody tipped her."

"She got a call from the hospital," I said.

"Nope," said Seminole. "I checked that. Try another one. Maybe your boy Gilbert gave her a call. Maybe Gilbert took out Frank Minna before he took out Ullman. Maybe he and the lady are in this together."

"That's crazy," I said. "Gilbert didn't kill anybody. We're *detectives*."

I finally got Seminole's attention. "I looked into that rumor," he said. "None of you carry investigators' credentials, according to the computer. Just limousine operators' licenses."

"We work for Frank Minna," I said, and heard my own unconcealed nostalgia, my pining. "We assist a detective. We're, uh, operatives."

"You do stooge work for a penny-ante hood, according to what I can see. A *dead* penny-ante hood. You were in the pocket of a guy in the pocket of Alphonso Matricardi and Leonardo Rockaforte, two relatively deep old dudes. Only it appears the pocket got turned inside out."

Tony winced: These clichés hurt. "We work for the clients that come in," he said, oddly sincere. For a moment Minna again came alive in Tony's voice. "We don't ask questions we shouldn't, or we wouldn't have any clients at all. The cops do the same, don't try to tell me any different."

"Cops don't have *clients*," said the homicide detective stiffly. I would have liked to see the real Frank Minna handle Seminole.

"What are you, Abraham Jefferson Jackson?" said Tony. "You running for office with that speech? Give me a break."

I snorted. Despite everything, Tony was cracking me up. I threw in a flourish of my own:

"Abracadabra Jackson!"

*   *   *

The gun, and Seminole's status as a law-enforcement officer, didn't matter—he was losing control of this interview. What happened was this: Tony and I, so deeply estranged, had been drawn together by the point of the detective's gun. In this post-Minna era we Men were a little panicked and raw at facing one another head on. But triangulated by Seminole we'd rediscovered the kinship that lurked in our old routines. If we couldn't trust each other, Tony and I were at least reminded we were two of a kind, especially in the eyes of a cop. And Tony, seeing chinks in the detective's confidence, was turning on him with his old orphan's savagery. A bully knows the parameters and half-life of a brandished threat—the only thing weaker than a gun so long ignored was no gun at all. The cop had had to arrest us or hurt us or turn us against each other by now, and he hadn't. Tony would cut him apart with his tongue for the mistake.

In the meantime I considered what Seminole had been saying, and tried to sift the information from his dingbat theories. If Julia didn't get a call from the hospital how did she know about Minna's death?

Again I wondered: Was it Julia who missed her *Rama-lama-ding-dong*? Did she keep it in Boston?

*   *   *

"Listen, you scumbags," said Seminole. He was compensating desperately for his plummeting authority. "I'd rather tangle with *homies* doing *drive-bys* all day than wade into this Italianate mobster shit. Don't get big-headed, now—I can see you're just a couple of fools. It's the wiseguys pulling your strings I'm worried about."

"Great," said Tony. "A paranoid cop. *Wiseguys pulling strings*—you read too many comic books, Cleopatra Jones."

"Clapperdapper Bailey Johnson!"

"You think I'm stupid," continued Seminole, on a real tear now. "You think a dumb black cop is going to stumble into your little nest and take it on face value. Car service, detective agency, give me a break. I'm going to push this murder bag just far enough to turn it over to the Federal Bureau of Investigation, and then I'm going to get my ass out of here for good. Might even take a vacation, sit on the beach and read about you losers in the Metro section."

Stumble, wade: Seminole's choice of words betrayed him. He really and truly feared he'd already gotten in further than was good for him. I wanted to find a way to allay his fears, I really did. I sort of liked the homicide detective. But everything out of my mouth sounded vaguely like a racial slur.

"Federal Bureau of what?" said Tony. "I never met those guys."

"Let's go upstairs and see if Uncle Alphonso and Uncle Leonardo can explain it to you," said Seminole. "Something tells me they've got a working familiarity with the FBI."

"I don't think the old guys are home anymore," said Tony.

"Oh yeah? Where'd they go?"

"They went through a tunnel in the basement," said Tony. "They had to get back to their hideout, since they've got James Bond—or Batman, I can't remember which—roasting over a slow fire."

"What are you talking about?"

"Don't worry, though. Batman always gets away. These supervillains never learn."

"Uncle Batman!" I shouted. They couldn't know how much work it was for me to keep my hands on that dashboard, my neck straight. "Unclebailey Blackman! *Barnamum Bat-a-potamus!*"

"That's enough, Alibi," said Seminole. "Get out of the car."

"What?"

"Get lost, go home. You annoy me, man. Tony and me are going to have a little talk."

"C'mon, Blacula," complained Tony. "We've been talking for hours. I've got nothing to say to you."

"Every name you call me I think up a couple more questions," said Seminole. He waved at me with his gun. "Get lost."

I gaped at Seminole, incredulous.

"I mean it. Get."

I opened the door. Then I thought to find the Pontiac's keys and hand them to Tony.

Tony glared at me. "Go back to the office and wait for me."

"Oh, sure," I said, and stepped out onto the curb.

"Close the door," said Seminole, training gun and gaze on Tony.

"Thanks, *Count Chocula,*" I said, and skipped away, literally.

*   *   *

Have you noticed yet that I relate everything to my Tourette's? Yup, you guessed it, it's a tic. Counting is a symptom, but counting symptoms is also a symptom, a tic *plus ultra*. I've got meta-Tourette's. Thinking about ticcing, my mind racing, thoughts reaching to touch every possible symptom. Touching touching. Counting counting. Thinking thinking. Mentioning mentioning Tourette's. It's sort of like talking about telephones over the telephone, or mailing letters describing the location of various mailboxes. Or like a tugboater whose favorite anecdote concerns actual tugboats.

*   *   *

There is nothing Tourettic about the New York City subways.

Though at each step I felt the gaze of an army of invisible doormen on my neck, I was nevertheless exultant to be back on the Upper East Side. I hurried down Lexington from the Eighty-sixth Street station, with only ten minutes to spare before five o'clock: zazen. I didn't want to be late for my first. While I was still on the street, though, I took out the cell phone and called Loomis.

"Yeah, I was just about to call you." I could hear him chewing a sandwich or a chicken leg, and pictured his open mouth, smacking lips. Hadn't he been at lunch two hours before? "I got the goods on that building."

"Let's have it—quick."

"This guy in Records, he was going on and on about it. That's a sweet little building, Lionel. Way outta my class."

"It's Park Avenue, Loomis."

"Well, there's Park Avenue and then there's this. You gotta have a hundred million to get on the waiting list for this place, Lionel. This kind of people, their other house is an *island*."

I heard Loomis quoting someone smarter than himself. "Right, but what about Fujisaki?"

"Hold your horses, I'm getting there. This sort of place, there's a whole staff—it's like a bunch of mansions stacked together. They got secret passages, wine cellars, a laundry service, swimming pool, servants' quarters, private chef. Whole secret economy. There's only five or six buildings like this in the city—the place where Bob Dylan got killed, what's it, the *Nova Scotia*? That's a doghouse in comparison. This place is for the old-money people, they'll turn down Seinfeld, *Nixon*, doesn't matter. They don't even give a shit."

"Include me in that category," I said, unable to discern any useful information in the Garbage Cop's jabber. "I'm looking for names, Loomis."

"Your Fujisaki's the management corporation. Whole bunch of other Jap names in there—guess they own half of New York if you started digging. This is a serious money operation, Lionel. Ullman, far as I can tell, he was just Fujisaki's accountant. So clue me in: Why would Gilbert go after an accountant?"

"Ullman was the last guy Frank was supposed to see," I said. "He never got to him."

"Minna was supposed to kill Ullman?"

"I don't know."

"Or vice versa?"

"I don't know."

"Or did the same guy kill them both?"

"I don't know, Loomis."

"So you aren't learning much besides what I'm digging up for you, huh?"

"Eat me, Loomis."

*   *   *

"I'm so glad you're here," said Kimmery when she opened the door to me. "You're just in time. Mostly everybody's sitting already." She kissed me on the cheek again. "There's a lot of excitement about the monks."

"I'm feeling a lot of excitement myself." In fact, I felt an instant euphoria at Kimmery's alleviating presence. If this was the prospect of Zen I was ready to begin my training.

"You'll have to take a cushion right away. Just sit anywhere but up at the front of the line. We'll work on your posture some other time—for now you can sit and concentrate on your breathing."

"I'll do that." I followed her up the stairs.

"That's really everything anyway, breathing. You could work on just that for the rest of your life."

"I'll probably have to."

"Take off your shoes."

Kimmery pointed, and I added my shoes to a neat row in the hall-way. It was a bit disconcerting to surrender them and with them my street-readiness, but in fact my aching dogs were grateful for the chance to breathe and stretch.

The second-floor sitting room was gloomy now, overhead track lighting still dark, the fading November daylight insufficient. I spotted the source of the heavy smell this time, a pot of smoldering incense on a high shelf beside a jade Buddha. The walls of the room were covered with undecorated paper screens, the glossy parquet floor with thin cushions. Kimmery led me to a spot near the back of the room and sat beside me, folded her legs and straightened her back, then nodded wide-eyed to suggest I imitate her moves. If only she knew. I sat and worked my big legs into position, grabbing my shins with both hands, only once jostling the sitter ahead of me, who turned and quickly glared, then resumed his posture of grace. The rows of cushions around us were mostly full with Zen practitioners, twenty-two when I counted, some in black robes, others in beatniky street clothes, corduroy or sweatpants and turtlenecks, not one in a suit like me. In the dimness I couldn't make out any faces.

So I sat and waited and wondered exactly what I was there for, though it was tough to keep my back straight as those I saw around me. I glanced at Kimmery. Her eyes were already peacefully shut. In twenty-four hours—it was only slightly more than that since Gilbert and I had parked at the curb outside the day before—my confusion at the Zendo's significance had doubled and redoubled, become veiled in successive layers. The conversation I'd heard on the wire, those sneering insinuations, now seemed impossible to fix to this place. Kimmery's voice, ingenuous, unconspiring, was all I heard now. That, of course, against a background of my own interior babble. As I sat beside Kimmery, sheltered inside her tic-canceling field, I felt all the more keenly the uneasy, half-stoppered force of my own language-generator, my Multi-Mind, that tangle of responses and mimickings, of interruptions of interruptions.

I gazed at her again. She was *sitting* sincerely, not wondering about me. So I shut my eyes and, taking my own little crack at enlightenment, tried to unify my mind and get a fix on my Buddha nature.

*   *   *

The first thing I heard was Minna's voice: *I dare you to shut up for a whole twenty minutes sometime, you free human freakshow.*

I pushed it away, thought *One Mind* instead.

One Mind.

Tell me one, Freakshow. One I don't already know.

I vant to go to Tibet.

One Mind. I focused on my breathing.
Come home, Irving.
One Mind. Sick Mind. Dirty Mind. Bailey Mind.
One Mind.
Oreo Man.

*   *   *

When I opened my eyes again, I'd adjusted to the gloom. At the front of the room was a large bronze gong, and the cushions nearest the gong were empty as if readied for celebrity sitters, perhaps the *important monks.* The rows of heads had developed features, though mostly I was looking at ears and napes, the neckline of haircuts. The crowd was a mix of sexes, the women mostly skinny, with earrings and hairstyles that cost something, the men on average more lardish and scruffy, their haircuts overdue. I spotted Wallace's ponytail and bald spot and furniture-stiff posture up near the front. And a row ahead of me, closer to the entrance, sat Pinched and Indistinct, my would-be abductors. At last I understood: They *were* men of peace. Was there a severe shortage of human beings on the Upper East Side, so the same small cast of doormen was required to pose in costume, here as goons, there as seekers after serenity? At least they'd shed their blue suits, made a greater commitment to this new identity. Garbed in black robes, their postures were admirably erect, presumably earned by extensive training, years of sacrifice. They hadn't been working all that time on their strong-arm patter, that was for sure.

So much for my breathing. I managed to check my voice, though. Pinched and Indistinct both had their eyes shut, and I'd arrived last, so I had the drop on them. They weren't exactly my idea of big trouble anyway. But I was reminded that the stolen cell phone and borrowed beeper in my jacket might shatter this ancient Eastern silence at any moment. Moving quietly as possible, I drew them out and turned off the cell phone's ringer, set Minna's beeper to "vibrate." As I slipped them back into my jacket's inner pocket an open hand slapped the back of my head and neck, hard.

Stung, I whipped around. But my attacker was already past me, marching solemnly between the mats to the front of the room, the first in a file of six bald Japanese men, all draped in robes revealing glimpses of sagging brown skin and threads of white underarm hair. Important monks. The lead monk had swerved out of his way to deliver the blow. I'd been reprimanded or perhaps offered a jolt of enlightenment—did I now know the sound of one hand clapping? Either way, I felt the heat of blood rushing to my ears and scalp.

Kimmery hadn't noticed, just placidly Zenned right through the whole sequence. Maybe she was further along on her spiritual path than she realized.

The six moved to the front and took the unoccupied mats near the gong. And a seventh entered the room, a little behind the others, also robed, also with a polished bald skull. But he wasn't small and Japanese and his body hair wasn't white and it wasn't limited to his underarms. He had silky black plumes of back and shoulder hair, rising from all sides to circle his neck with a fringe. It wasn't a look the designer of the robe had likely had in mind. He moved to the front of the room and took the last of the VIP spots before I could see his face, but I thought of Kimmery's description and decided this must be the American teacher, founder of the Zendo, the Roshi.

Irving. When are you coming home, Irving? *Your family misses you.*

The joke nagged at me, but I couldn't put it to work. Was that Roshi's original name, his American name: Irving? Was Roshi-Irving the voice on the wire?

If so, why? What linked Minna to this place?

They settled into quietude up front. I stared at the row of bald heads, the six monks and Roshi, but discerned nothing. Even Pinched and Indistinct were meditating serenely. Minutes crept past and I was the only set of open eyes. Someone coughed and I faked a cough in imitation. If I kept one eye on Kimmery I was mostly calm, though. It

was like having a bag of White Castles beside me on the car seat. I
wondered how deep her influence over my syndrome could run if
given the chance, how much of that influence I could hope to import.
How close I could get. I shut my eyes, trusting Pinched and Indistinct
to stay planted obliviously on their cushions, and drifted into some
pleasant thoughts about bodies, about Kimmery's body, her nervous
elegant limbs. Perhaps this was the key to Zen, then. *We don't exactly
have God,* she'd said. *We just sit and try to stay awake.* Well, I wasn't
having any trouble staying awake. And as my penis stiffened it
occurred to me I'd found my One Mind.

I was jostled from my reverie by a sound at the door. I opened my
eyes and turned to see the Polish giant standing in the entrance to the
sitting room, filling the doorway with his square shoulders, holding in
his fist a plastic produce bag full of kumquats and gazing at the roomful of Zen practitioners with an expression of absolute and utter
serenity. He wasn't in a robe, but he might have been Buddha himself
for the benignity of his gaze.

*   *   *

Before I could figure a plan or response there came a commotion at
the front of the room. A commotion by the local standards anyway:
One of the Japanese monks stood and bowed to Roshi, then to the
other monks in his party, then to the room at large. You still would
have heard a pin drop, but the rustling of his robe was signal enough,
and eyes opened everywhere. The giant stepped into the room, still
clutching his kumquats like a bag of live goldfish, and took a mat—a
couple actually—on the other side of Kimmery, between us and the
door. I reminded myself that the giant hadn't seen me, at least not
yesterday. He certainly wasn't giving me any special notice—or anyone else for that matter. Instead he settled into his spot, looking ready
for the monk's lecture. Quite a gathering we made now, the various
mugs and lugs attending to the wise little men from the East. Pinched

and Indistinct might be real Zen students playing at thuggishness, but Pierogi Monster was undoubtedly the opposite. The kumquats, I was pretty sure, were a giveaway—weren't they a Chinese fruit, not Japanese at all? I wanted to hug Kimmery toward me, away from the killer's reach, but then I wanted to do a lot of things—I always do.

The monk bowed to us again, searched our faces briefly, then began speaking, so abruptly and casually it was as if he were resuming a talk he'd been having with himself.

"Daily life, I fly on an airplane, I take a taxicab to visit Yorkville Zendo"—this came out *Yolkville-ah*—"I feel excitement, thoughts, anticipations, what will my friend Jerry-Roshi show me? Will I go to a very good Manhattan restaurant, sleep on a very good bed in New York City hotel?" He stomped his sandaled foot as though testing out a mattress.

I vant to go to Tibet! The joke insisted itself upon me again. My calm was under pressure from all sides, the goons everywhere, my echolalia provoked by the monk's speech. But I couldn't turn and gaze and refresh my dose of Kimmery without also taking in Minna's titanic killer—he was so big that his outline framed her on all sides despite his being farther away, an optical trick I couldn't afford to find fascinating.

"All these moods, impulses, this daily life, nothing wrong with them. But daily life, island, dinner, airplane, cocktail, daily life is not Zen. In zazen practice all that matters is the sitting, the practice. American, Japan, doesn't matter. Only sitting."

I vant to speak to the Lama! The American monk, Roshi, had half turned in his spot to better contemplate the master from across the ocean. The profile below Roshi's gleaming dome stirred me unexpectedly. I recognized some terrible force of authority and charisma in his features.

Jerry-Roshi?

Meanwhile the giant sat disrespectfully pinching the skin of a kumquat, pressing it to his monstrous lips, sucking its juice.

"It is easy practice zazen in its external form, sit on the cushion and waste time on the cushion. So many forms of nothing-Zen, meaningless Zen, only one form of true Zen: actual making contact with own Buddha-self."

The High Lama will grant you an audience.

"There is *chikusho* Zen, Zen of domesticated animals who curl up on pillows like cats in homes, waiting to be fed. They sit to kill time between meals. Domesticated animal Zen useless! Those who practice chikusho should be beaten and thrown out of the zendo."

I obsessed on Jerry-Roshi's face while the monk sputtered on.

"There is *ningen* Zen, Zen practiced for self-improvement. Ego-Zen. Make skin better, make bowel movement better, think positive thoughts and influence people. Shit! Ningen Zen is shit Zen!"

Irving, come home, went my brain. *No soap, Zendo. Tibettapocamus. Chickenshack Zen. High Oscillama Talkalot.* The monk's wonky syllables, the recursions of the Tibet joke, my own fear of the giant—all were conspiring to bring me to a boil. I wanted to trace Roshi's enthralling profile with my fingertip—perhaps I'd recognize its significance by touch. Instead I practiced Essrog Zen, and stifled myself.

"Consider also *gaki* Zen: the Zen of insatiable ghosts. Those who study gaki Zen chase after enlightenment like spirits who crave food or vengeance with a hunger can never be satisfied. These ghosts never even enter the house of Zen they are so busy howling at the windows!"

Roshi looked like Minna.

Your brother misses you, Irving.

Irving equals Lama, Roshi equals Gerard.

Roshi was Gerard Minna.

Gerard Minna was the voice on the wire.

I couldn't say which got me there first, his profile in front of me or the joke's subliminal nagging. It felt like a dead heat. Of course, the joke had been designed to get me there sooner, spare me figuring it out while in the belly of the whale. Too bad.

I tried to quit staring, failed. Up front, the monk continued to enumerate false Zens, the various ways we could go wrong. I personally could think of a few he probably hadn't come across yet.

But why had Minna buried the information in a joke to begin with? I thought of a couple of reasons. One: He didn't want us to know about Gerard *unless* he died. If he survived the attack he wanted his secret to survive as well. Two: He didn't know who among his Men to trust, even down to Gilbert Coney. He could be certain I'd puzzle over the Irving clue while Gilbert would write it off as our mutual inanity.

And he felt, rightly, that no conspiracy around him could possibly include his pet Freakshow. The other Boys would never let me play. I could be flattered at the implied trust, or insulted by the dis. It didn't really matter now.

I stared at Gerard. Now I understood the charismatic force of his profile, but it inspired only bitterness. It was as though the world imagined it could take Minna away and offer this clumsy genetic substitution. A resemblance.

"California Roll Zen. This is the Zen of sushi so full of avocado and cream cheese might as well be a marshmallow for all you know. The pungent fish of zazen smothered in easy pleasures, picnics, get-togethers, Zendo becomes a dating service!"

"*Zengeance!*" I shouted.

Not every head turned. Gerard Minna's did, though. So did Pinched's, and Indistinct's. And so did the giant's. Kimmery was among those who practiced their calm by ignoring me.

"Ziggedy zendoodah," I said aloud. My erection dimmed, energy venting elsewhere. "*Pierogi Monster Zen master zealous neighbor. Zazen zaftig Zsa Zsa go-bare.*" I rapped the scalp of the sitter in front of me. "Zippity go figure."

The roomful of gurus and acolytes came to agitated life but not one of them spoke a word, so my burst of verbiage sang in the silence. The lecturing monk glared at me and shook his head. Another of his posse rose from his cushion and lifted a wooden paddle I hadn't previously noticed from a hook on the wall, then started through the rows of students in my direction. Only Wallace sat immobile, eyes shut, still meditating. I began to appreciate his reputation for imperturbability.

"Pierogi kumquat sushiphone! Domestic marshmallow ghost! Insatiable Mallomar! *Smothered pierogiphone!*" The flood came with such force, I twisted my neck and nearly barked the words.

"Silence!" commanded the lecturing monk. "Very bad to make disturbance in the Zendo! Time and place for everything!" Anger wasn't good for his English. "Shouting is for outside, New York City full of shouting! Not in Zendo."

"Knock knock Zendo!" I shouted. "Monk monk goose!"

The monk with the paddle approached. He gripped it cross-handed, like Hank Aaron. The giant stood, shoved his baggie of kumquats into the pocket of his Members Only jacket and rubbed his sticky hands together, readying them for use. Gerard turned and stared at me, but if he recognized in me the twitchy teenager he'd left behind at the St. Vincent's schoolyard fence nineteen years before, he didn't show any sign. His eyebrows were delicately knit, his mouth pursed, his expression bemused. Kimmery put her hand on my knee and I put my hand on hers, reciprocity-ticcing. Even in a shitstorm such as I was in at this moment, my syndrome knew that God was in the details.

"Keisaku is more than ceremonial implement," said the monk with the paddle. He applied it to my shoulder blades so gently it was like a caress. "Unruly student can do with a blow." Now he clouted my back with the same muscular Buddhist glee his colleague had applied to my scalp.

"Ouch!" I fished behind me for the paddle, snagged it, tugged. It came out of the monk's grasp and he staggered backward. By now the giant was headed in our direction. Those between us rolled or scuttled out of his path, according to their ability to unlock their elaborately folded legs. Kimmery darted away just as he loomed over us, not wanting to be crushed. Pierogi Man hadn't checked his shoes at the door.

That was when I saw the nod.

Gerard Minna nodded ever so slightly at the giant, and the giant nodded back. That was all it took. The same team that had doomed Frank Minna was back in the saddle. I would be the sequel.

The giant wrapped me in his arms and lifted, and the paddle clattered to the floor.

*   *   *

I weigh nearly two hundred pounds, but the giant didn't strain at all moving me down the stairs and out onto the street, and when he plumped me onto the sidewalk I was more shaken and winded than he by far. I straightened my suit and confirmed the alignment of my neck with a string of jerks while he unloaded his bag of kumquats and got back to sucking out their juice and pulp, reducing their bodies to husks that looked like orange raisins in his massive hands.

The narrow street was nearly dark now, and the dog-walkers were far enough away to give us privacy.

"Want one?" he said, holding out the bag. His voice was a dull thing where it began in his throat but it resonated to grandeur in the tremendous instrument of his torso, like a mediocre singer on the stage of a superb concert hall.

"No, thanks," I said. Here was where I should grow large with anger, facing Minna's killer right at the spot of the abduction. But I was diminished, ribs aching from his squeezing, confused and worried—conworried—by my discovery of Gerard Minna inside the Zendo, and unhappy to have left Kimmery and my shoes upstairs. The pavement was cold through my socks, and my feet tingled oddly as they flushed with the blood denied them by Zen posture.

"So what's the matter with you?" he said, discarding another of the withered kumquats.

"I've got Tourette's," I said.

"Yeah, well, threats don't work with me."

"Tourette's," I said.

"Eh? My hearing's not so good. Sorry." He put the bag of fruit away again, and when his hand reemerged it was holding a gun. "Go in there," he said. He pointed with his chin at the three steps leading to the narrow channel between the Zendo and the apartment building on the right, a lane filled with garbage cans and darkness. I frowned, and he reached out and with the hand not holding the gun shoved me backward toward the steps. "Go," he said again.

I considered the giant and myself as a tableau. Here was the man I'd been hunting and wishing to go up against, howling for a chance at vengeance like an insatiable ghost or marshmallow—yet had I planned a way to take advantage of him, a method or apparatus to give me any real edge, let alone narrow the immense gap in force his size presented? No. I'd come up pathetically empty. And now he had a gun to ice the cake. He shoved me again, straight-armed my shoulder, and when I tried, ticcishly, to shove his shoulder in return I found I was held at too great a distance, couldn't brush his shoulder even with long-stretched fingertips, and it conjured some old memory of Sylvester the Cat in a boxing ring with a kangaroo. My brain whispered, *He's just a big mouse, Daddy, a vigorous louse, big as a house, a couch, a man, a plan, a canal, apocalypse.*

"Apocamouse," I mumbled, language spilling out of me unrestrained. "Unplan-a-canal. Unpluggaphone."

"I said get in there, Squeaky." Had he caught my mouse reference, even with his impaired hearing? But then, who wouldn't be squeaky to him? He was so big he only had to shrug to loom. I took a step backward. I had Tourette's, he had threats. "Go," he said again.

It was the last thing I wanted to do and I did it.

The minute I stepped down into the darkness he swung the gun at my head.

* * *

So many detectives have been knocked out and fallen into such strange swirling darknesses, such manifold surrealist voids ("something red wriggled like a germ under a microscope"—Philip Marlowe, *The Big Sleep*), and yet I have nothing to contribute to this painful tradition. Instead my falling and rising through obscurity was distinguished only by nothingness, by blankness, by lack and my resentment of it. Except for grains. It was a grainy nothing. A desert of grains. How fond can you be of flavorless grains in a desert? How much better than nothing at all? I'm from Brooklyn and I don't like wide-open spaces, I guess. And I don't want to die. So sue me.

Then I remembered a joke, a riddle like one the Garbage Cop would tell, and it was my lifeline, it sang like a chorus of ethereal voices beckoning me from the brink of darkness:

Why don't you starve in the desert?

Because of the *sand which is* there.

Why didn't I want to die or leave New York?

The sandwiches. I concentrated on the sandwiches. For a while that's all there was, and I was happy. The sandwiches were so much better than the desert of grains.

"Lionel?"

It was Kimmery's voice.

* * *

"Mhrrggh."

"I brought your shoes."

"Oooh."

"I think we should go. Can you stand?"

"Rrrrssp."

"Lean against the wall. Careful. I'll get a cab."

"Cabbabbab."

I flickered awake again and we were slicing through the park, East Side to West, in that taxicab channel of tree-topped stone, my head on Kimmery's bony shoulder. She was putting my shoes back on, lifting my leaden feet one after the other, then tying the laces. Her small hands and my large shoes made this an operation rather like saddling a comatose horse. I could see the cabbie's license—his name was Omar Dahl, which invited tics I couldn't muster in my state—and a view upward through the side window. For a moment I thought it was snowing and everything seemed precious and distant—Central Park in a snow globe. Then I realized it was snowing inside the cab, too. The grains again. I closed my eyes.

*   *   *

Kimmery's apartment was on Seventy-eighth Street, in an old-lady apartment building, gloriously shabby and real after the gloss of the East Side, the chilling dystopian lobby of 1030 Park Avenue especially. I got upright and into the elevator on my own steam, with only Kimmery to hold the doors for me, which was how I liked it—no doormen. We rode to the twenty-eighth floor in an empty car, and Kimmery leaned against me as if we were still in the cab. I didn't need the support to stand anymore, but I didn't stop it from happening. My head throbbed—where Pierogi Man had clubbed me, it felt as though I were trying to grow a single horn, and failing—and the contact with Kimmery was a kind of compensation. At her floor she parted from my side with that nervous quick walk I already considered her trademark, her confession of some kernel of jerkiness I could cultivate and adore, and unlocked the door to her place so frantically I wondered if she thought we'd been followed.

"Did the giant see you?" I said when we were inside.

"What?"

"The giant. Are you afraid of the giant?" I felt a body-memory, and shuddered. I was still a little *unsteady on my pins,* as Minna would have said.

She looked at me strangely. "No, I just—I'm an illegal sublet here. There are people in this building who can't mind their own business. You should sit down. Do you want some water?"

"Sure." I looked around. "Sit where?"

Her apartment consisted of a brief foyer, a minuscule kitchen—really more an astronaut's cockpit full of cooking equipment—and a large central room whose polyurethaned floor mirrored the vast moonlit city nightscape featured in its long, uncurtained window. The reflected image was uninterrupted by carpet or furniture, just a few modest boxes tucked into the corners, a tiny boom box and a stack of tapes, and a large cat that stood in the center of the floor, regarding our entrance skeptically. The walls were bare. Kimmery's bedding was a flattened mattress on the floor of the foyer where we stood now, just inside the apartment's door. We were almost on top of it.

"Go ahead and sit on the bed," she said, with a nervous half smile.

Beside the bed was a candle, a box of tissues, and a small stack of paperbacks. It was a private space, a headquarters. I wondered if she hosted much—I felt I might be the first to see past her door.

"Why don't you sleep in there?" I said, pointing at the big empty room. My words came out thickened and stupid, like those of a defeated boxer in his dressing room, or a Method actor's, while playing a defeated boxer. My Tourette's brain preferred precision, sharper edges. I felt it waking.

"People look in," said Kimmery. "I'm not comfortable."

"You could have curtains." I gestured at the big window.

"It's too big. I don't really like that room. I don't know why." Now she looked like she regretted bringing me here. "Sit. I'll bring you some water."

The room she didn't like was the whole of the apartment. She lived instead in the foyer. But I decided not to say anything more about it.

There was something anyway that suited me in her use of the space, as though she'd planned to bring me here to hide, knew I'd have something to fear from the skyline, the big world of conspiracies and doormen that was Manhattan.

I took a seat on her bed, back against the wall, legs straightened to cross the mattress, so my shoes reached the floor. I felt my tailbone meet the floor through the pancake-thin mattress. Now I saw that Kimmery had double-knotted my laces. I lingered awkwardly over this detail, used it to measure my returning consciousness, allowing my obsessiveness to play over the intricacy of the knots and my stroboscopic memories of Kimmery tugging at my feet in the cab. I imagined I could feel the dented place in my skull and the damaged language flowing in a new direction through this altered inner topography and the words went *sandwiches sandwiches I scream for ice cream dust to dust* and so on.

I decided to distract myself with the books stacked near the bed. The first was called *The Wisdom of Insecurity,* by Alan Watts. Tucked into it as an oversize bookmark was a pamphlet, a glossy sheet folded in thirds. I pulled out the pamphlet. It was for Yoshii's, a Zen Buddhist retreat center and roadside Thai and Japanese restaurant on the southern coast of Maine. The phone number beneath the schematic road map on the back was circled with blue ballpoint. The heading on the front of the pamphlet said A PLACE OF PEACE.

Pleasure police.

Pressure peas.

The cat walked in from the main room and stood on my outstretched thighs and began kneading them with its front paws, half-retracted claws engaging the material to make a *pocka-pocka-pocka* sound. The cat was black and white with a Hitler mustache, and when it finally noticed I had a face it squeezed its eyes at me. I folded the pamphlet into my jacket pocket, then took off my jacket and put it on the corner of Kimmery's bed. The cat went back to working my thighs.

"You probably don't like cats," said Kimmery, returning with two glasses of water.

"*Chickencat,*" I said, ticcing stupidly. "*Cream of soup salad sandwich.*"

"Are you hungry?"

"No, no," I said, though maybe I was. "And I like cats fine." But I kept my hands away, not wanting to begin obsessing on its body—kneading back or mimicking its uneven, cackling purr.

*   *   *

I can't own a cat, because my behaviors drive them insane. I know because I tried. I had a cat, gray and slim, half the size of Kimmery's, named Hen for the chirping and cooing sounds she made, for the barnyard pecking motions her initial sniffing inspections of my apartment reminded me of. She enjoyed my attentions at first, my somewhat excessive fondling. She'd purr and push against my hand as I tapped her, taking her pleasure. I'd refine my impulses toward her as well as I could, stroking her neck smoothly, rubbing her cheeks sideways to stimulate her kittenish memories of being licked, or whatever it is that makes cats crave that sensation. But from the very first Hen was disconcerted by my head-jerks and utterances and especially by my barking. She'd turn her head to see what I'd jumped at, to see what I was fishing for in the air with my hand. Hen recognized those behaviors—they were supposed to be *hers.* She never felt free to relax. She'd cautiously advance to my lap, a long game of half measures and imaginary distractions before she'd settle. Then I'd issue a string of bitten-off shrieks and bat at the curtain.

Worse, her bouts of joy at my petting hands became a focal point for Tourettic games of disruption. Hen would purr and nudge at my hand, and I'd begin stroking her smooth, sharklike face. She'd lean into the pressure, and I'd push back, until she was arched into my hand and ready to topple. Then the tic—I'd withdraw my hand. Other times I'd be compelled to follow her around the apartment, reaching for her when she'd meant to be sly or invisible; I'd stalk her, though it was obvious that like any cat her preference was to come to me. Or I'd fixate on the limits of her pleasure at being touched—would she keep purring if I rubbed her fur backward? If I tickled her cheeks would I be allowed to simultaneously grasp her sacrosanct tail? Would she permit me to clean the sleep from her eyes? The answer was often yes, but there was a cost. As with a voodoo doll, I'd begun investing my own ticcishness in my smaller counterpart: Tourette's Cat. She'd been reduced to a distrustful, skittish bundle of reactions, anticipatory flinchings and lashings-out. After six months I had to find her a new home with a Dominican family in the next building. They were able to straighten her out, after some cooling-off time spent hidden behind their stove.

*   *   *

The big Nazi cat went on raking up thread-loops from my trousers, seemingly intent on single-handedly reinventing Velcro. Meanwhile Kimmery returned with water, in two glasses she placed on the floor near my feet. Though the room was dim—we were lit as much by the reflected skyline in the big room behind us as by the faint bulb there in the foyer—she'd removed her eyeglasses for the first time, and her eyes looked tender and small and searching. She slid down to seat herself against the wall, so we were arranged like clock hands on the face of the floor, our shoes at the center. According to the clock of us it was four o'clock. I tried not to root for midnight.

"Have you been living here long?" I asked.

"I know, it looks like I'm camping out," she said. "It's been about a month. I just broke up with this guy. It's pretty obvious, isn't it?"

"The Oreo Man?" I pictured a weather-beaten cowboy in front of a sunset, holding a cookie to his lips like a cigarette. Then, in frantic compensation, I conjured a tormented nerd in goggle-glasses, peering at cookie crumbs through a microscope, trying to discern their serial numbers.

"Uh-huh," said Kimmery. "A friend was moving out and she gave me this place. I don't even like it. I'm hardly ever here."

"Where instead—the Zendo?"

She nodded. "Or the movies."

*   *   *

I wasn't ticcing much, for a couple of reasons. The first was Kimmery herself, still an unprecedented balm to me this late in the day. The second was the day itself, the serial tumult of unsorted clues, the catastrophe of my visit to the Zendo; that extra track in my brain had plenty of work to do threading beads together, smoothing the sequence into order: Kimmery, doormen, Matricardi and Rockaforte, Tony and Seminole, Important Monks, Gerard Minna and the killer. Minna's killer.

"Did you lock your door?" I said.

"You're really afraid," said Kimmery, widening her eyes. "Of the, uh, giant."

"You didn't see him?" I said. "The big guy who took me outside?" I didn't mention what happened next. It was shameful enough that Kimmery had had to mop it up.

"He's a *giant?*"

"Well, what do you call it?"

"Isn't gigantism a genetic condition?"

"I'd say it is. He didn't *earn* that height." I touched the delicate spot on my head with one hand, kept the other calm at my side, ignoring every impulse to return the cat's pulsing and pawing at my legs. Instead I fingered the homely, hand-stitched coverlet on Kimmery's mattress, traced its inelegant, lumpy seams.

"I guess I didn't notice," she said. "I was, you know—sitting."

"You've never seen him before?"

She shook her head. "But I never met you before today either. I guess I should have told you not to bring anyone like that to the Zendo. And not to make noise. Now I missed practically the whole lecture."

"You're not saying the lecture went on?"

"Sure, why not? After you and your friend *the giant* were gone."

"Why didn't you stay?"

"Because my concentration isn't that good," she said, bitterly philosophical now. "If you're really Zen you sit right through distractions, like Roshi did. And *Wallace*." She rolled her eyes.

I was tempted to remind her that she'd moved to avoid being trampled, but it was just one objection among thousands.

"You don't understand," I said. "I didn't bring him to the Zendo. Nobody knew I was coming there."

"Well, I guess he followed you." She shrugged, not wanting to argue. To her it was self-evident that the giant and I were dual phenomena. I'd caused his presence at the Zendo, was likely responsible for his very existence.

"Listen," I said. "I know Roshi's American name. He's not who you think he is."

"I don't think he's anyone."

"What do you mean?"

"I didn't say, like, *Roshi's really Johnny Carson* or something. I just said I didn't know."

"Okay, but he's not a Zen teacher. He's involved in a murder."

"That's silly." She made it sound like a virtue, as though I'd meant to entertain her. "Besides, anyone who teaches Zen is a Zen teacher, I think. Probably even if they were a murderer. Just like anyone who sits is a student. Even you."

"What's wrong with me?"

"Nothing's wrong with you, at least according to a Zen outlook. That's my whole point."

"Taken."

"Don't be so sour, Lionel. I'm only joking. You sure you're happy with that cat?"

"Doesn't it have a name?" Feline Hitler had settled ponderously between my thighs, was purring in broken measures, and had begun to feature tiny bubbles of drool at the corners of its mouth.

"Shelf, but I never call him that."

"Shelf?"

"I know, it's completely stupid. I didn't name him. I'm just cat-sitting."

"So this isn't your apartment and this isn't your cat."

"It's sort of a period of crisis for me." She reached for her glass of water, and I immediately reached for mine, grateful: The mirroring scratched a tiny mental itch. Anyway, I was thirsty. Shelf didn't budge. "That's why I got involved with Zen," Kimmery went on. "For more *detachment*."

"You mean like no apartment and no cat? How detached can you get?" My voice was irrationally bitter. Disappointment had crept over me, impossible to justify or perfectly define. I suppose I'd imagined us sheltered in Kimmery's childlike foyer, her West Side tree house, three cats hiding. But now I understood that she was rootless, alienated in this space. The Oreo Man's house was her home, or possibly the Zendo, just as L&L was mine, just as Shelf's was elsewhere, too. None of us could go to those places, so we huddled here together, avoiding the big room and the forest of skyscrapers.

Now, before Kimmery could reply, I ticced loudly, *"Detach-me-not!"* I tried to block myself, interrupt my own ticcing with the glass of water, which I moved to my lips just in time to shout into the glass, fevering the surface of the water with my breath, *"Go-shelf-a-lot!"*

"Wow," said Kimmery.

I didn't speak. I gulped down water and fondled the stitching of her coverlet again, seeking to lose my Tourette's self in texture.

"You say really weird stuff when you get angry," she said.

"I'm not—" I turned my neck, put the glass of water down on the floor. This time I jostled Shelf, who looked up at me with jaded eyes. "I'm not angry."

"What's wrong with you, then?" The question was delivered evenly, without sarcasm or fear, as though she really wanted an answer. Her eyes no longer looked small to me without the black frames around them. They felt as round and inquisitive as the cat's.

"Nothing—at least from a Zen outlook. I just shout sometimes. And touch things. And count things. And think about them too much."

"I've heard of that, I think."

"You're the exception to the rule if you have."

She reached into my lap and patted Shelf's head, distracting the cat from its interrogative gaze. Instead it squeezed its eyes together and craned its neck to press back against her palm. I'd have craned as far.

"Don't you want to know Roshi's real name?" I said.

"Why should I?"

"What?"

"Unless you're really going to shock me and say he's, like, J. D. Salinger, what's the difference? I mean, it's just going to be Bob or Ed or something, right?"

"Gerard Minna," I said. I wanted it to mean as much to her as Salinger, wanted her to understand everything. "He's Frank Minna's brother."

"Okay, but who's Frank Minna?"

"He's the guy who got killed." Strangely, I had a name for him now, a name flat and terrible and true: *the guy who got killed*. When before I could never have answered that question, or if I started answering it I'd never have finished. Frank Minna is the secret king of Court Street. Frank Minna is a mover and a talker, a word and a gesture, a detective and a fool. *Frank Minna c'est moi.*

"Oh, that's terrible."

"Yes." I wondered if I could ever share with her how terrible it was.

"I mean, that's got to be one of the worst things I've ever heard, practically."

Kimmery leaned closer, comforting the cat, not me. But I felt comforted. She and I were drawn close within her dawning understanding. Perhaps this foyer had only waited for this moment, for me and my story, to become a real space instead of a provisional one. Here Minna would be properly mourned. Here I'd find surcease for my pain and the answer to the puzzle of Tony and The Clients and why Minna and Ullman had to die and where Julia was and who Bailey was, and here Kimmery's hand would move from Shelf's head to my thigh and I would never tic again.

"He sent his brother out to die," I said. "He set him up. I heard it happen. I just don't know why yet."

"I don't understand. How did you hear?"

"Frank Minna was wearing a bug when he went into the Zendo. I heard him and Gerard talking. You were there too, in the building." I recalled revising my surveillance note, trying to decide whether to declare Kimmery *girl* or *woman*, and my writing hand twitched, reenacting my crossing-out across the soft threads of her coverlet.

"When?"

"Yesterday," I said, though it seemed a long time ago now.

"Well, that's impossible. It must have been someone else."

"Tell me why."

"Roshi is under a vow of silence." She whispered, as if she were breaking such a vow at this moment. "He hasn't said a word for the last five days. So you couldn't have heard him talk."

I was tongue-tied for once. It was the logic of the Oreo Man, invading my moral puzzle. Or another Zen conundrum: What's the sound of a silent monk condemning his brother to death?

The quieter the monk, the gaudier the patter I thought, remembering the conversation on the wiretap.

"I can't believe you go around *bugging* people," she said, still whispering. Perhaps she imagined there was a bug in the room now. "Were you trying to frame this Frank person?"

"No, no, no. Frank wanted me to listen."

"He wanted to be caught?"

"He didn't *do* anything," I said. "Except get bumped off by his brother, the silent monk."

Though she regarded me skeptically, Kimmery went on rubbing the cat's neck and head while it nestled in my lap. I had more than the usual panicky reasons to ignore the captivating sensations, the fricative purring and chafing down there. I was suppressing two different kinds of response, two possible ways of poking back. I kept my eyes level on Kimmery's face.

"I think you've got a few things mixed up," she said gently. "Roshi's a very gentle man."

"Well, Gerard Minna's a punk from Brooklyn," I said. "And they're positively the same guy."

"Hmmm. I don't know, Lionel. Roshi once told me he'd never been to Brooklyn. He's from Vermont or Canada or something."

"Maine?" I asked, thinking of the pamphlet I'd secreted in my jacket, the retreat center by the water.

She shrugged. "I don't know. You should take my word for it, though, he isn't from *Brooklyn*. He's a very important man." She made it sound as if the two were mutually exclusive.

"Eat me Brooklyn Roshi!"

I was ticcing out of sheer frustration. In squaring her perceptions to mine I not only had a world of knowledge to build up but a preexisting one to tear down. Anyone faintly Zen was to her beyond reproach. And Gerard Minna, for the cheap act of shaving his likely-already-balding head, was secure in a pantheon of the holy.

And Gerard had a lot of damn gall to renounce the borough.

"Lionel?"

I grabbed for my glass, took another sip of water, averted my eyes from Kimmery's.

"How does it feel when you do that?" she said. "I mean, what are you thinking?"

She was close enough now, and I succumbed completely and reached for her shoulder, tapped it five times quickly with paired fingertips. Then I moved my water glass to the floor and leaned forward, forcing Shelf to make another bleary, pleasure-addled adjustment to his position in my lap, and straightened Kimmery's collar with both hands. The material was floppy, and I tried to prop it up as if it were starched, put the collar-tips on point like a ballerina's toes. And my brain went, *How are you feeling and how are you thinking and think how you're feeling,* and that became the chorus, the soundtrack to my adamant necessary collar-play.

"Lionel?" She didn't push my hands away.

"Liable," I said softly, my gaze lowered. "Think-a-mum Feely."

"What do the words mean?"

"They're just words. They don't mean anything." The question depressed me a little, took the wind out of my sails, and this was a good thing: I was able to release her collar, still my wriggling fingers.

Kimmery touched one hand, just briefly, as I withdrew it. I was numb to her now, though. She no longer soothed my tics, and the attention she'd begun to give them was humiliating. I needed to get this interview back on an official basis. Sitting here purring and being purred at wasn't going to accomplish anything. In the city on the other side of the door a giant killer lurched around unafraid, and it was my job to find him.

"What do you know about ten-thirty Park Avenue?" I said, resuming my investigation, the legitimate inquiry.

"Is that that big apartment building?" Her hand was back riffling Shelf's fur, her body ever closer to mine.

"Big building," I said. "Yes."

"A lot of Roshi's students do their work service there," she said lightly. "Working in the kitchen, cleaning up, that kind of thing. I was telling you about it, remember?"

"Doormen? Any—doormen?" My syndrome wanted to call them dogshirts, doorsnips, diphthongs. I gritted my teeth.

She shrugged. "I think so. I never went there myself. Lionel?"

"Yes?"

"You didn't really come to the Zendo because you were interested in Buddhism, did you?"

"I guess I thought that was obvious by now."

"It is obvious."

I wasn't sure what to say. I was narrowed to a fine point, thinking only of Frank and Gerard and the places I might have to go to finish my investigation. I'd shuttered myself against Kimmery's tenderness toward me, even shuttered away my own tenderness toward her. She was an incompetent witness, beyond that a distraction. And I was an investigator who supplied plenty of my own distractions, too many.

"You came to make trouble," she said.

"I came *because* of trouble, yes."

Kimmery rubbed the fur of Shelf's flank in the wrong direction, aggravating my senses. I put my hand on the cat for the first time, nudged Kimmery's fingers away from the chaos of up-sticking fur she'd caused, and smoothed the fur back into place.

"Well, I'm glad I met you anyway," she said.

I made a sound, half dog, half cat, something like *"Chaarff."*

Our hands collided in Shelf's fur, Kimmery's moving to rough up the area I'd just smoothed into sense, mine preemptively slipping underneath to preserve my work. It took a big indifferent loaf of a cat like Shelf to withstand it; Hen would have been across the room reordering herself with her own tongue by now.

"You're strange to me," said Kimmery.

"Don't feel bad about it," I said.

"No, but I mean strange in a good way, too."

"Uh." She was tugging on my fingers, and I tugged systematically back, so our hands were tangling, squirming, the cat a benign mattress underneath, one vibrating like a cheap hotel's.

"You can say whatever you want," Kimmery whispered.

"What do you mean?"

"The words."

"I don't really need to when you're touching my hand like that."

"I like to."

"Touch?" Touch shoulders, touch penguins, touch Kimmery—who didn't like to touch? Why shouldn't she? But this vaguest of questions was all I could manage. I wasn't only strange to her, I was strange to myself at that moment: tugging, lulled, resistant. Conworried.

"Yes," she said. "You. Here—"

She groped at the wall behind her head and switched off the light. We were still outlined in white, Manhattan's radiation leaking in from the big room. Then she moved closer: It was a minute after twelve. Somewhere as she fit herself in beside me the cat was jostled loose and wandered ungrudgingly away.

"That's better," I said lamely, like I was reading from a script. The distance between us had narrowed, but the distance between me and me was enormous. I blinked in the half-light, looking straight ahead. Now her hand was on my thigh where the cat had been. Mirroring, I let my fingers play lightly at the parallel spot on her leg.

"Yes," she said.

"I can't seem to interest you fully in my case," I said.

"Oh, I'm interested," she said. "It's just— It's hard to talk about things that are important to you. With a new person. Everyone is so strange, don't you think?"

"I think you're right."

"So you have to trust them at first. Because everything makes sense after a while."

"So that's what you're doing with me?"

She nodded, then leaned her head against my shoulder. "But you're not asking me anything about myself."

"I'm sorry," I said, surprised. "I guess—I guess I don't know where to start."

"Well, so you see what I mean, then."

"Yes."

I didn't have to turn her face to mine to kiss her. It was already there when I turned. Her lips were small and soft and a little chapped. I'd never before kissed a woman without having had a few drinks. And I'd never kissed a woman who hadn't had a few herself. While I tasted her Kimmery drew circles on my leg with her finger, and I did the same back.

"You do everything I do," she whispered into my mouth.

"I don't really need to," I said again. "Not if we're this close." It was the truth. I was never less ticcish than this: aroused, pressing toward another's body, moving out of my own. But just as Kimmery had some-how spared me ticcing aloud in conversation, now I felt free to incorpo-rate an element of Tourette's into our groping, as though she were negotiating a new understanding between my two disgruntled brains.

"It's okay," she said. "You need a shave, though."

We kissed then, so I couldn't reply, didn't want to. I felt her press her thumb very gently against the point of my Adam's apple, a touch I couldn't exactly return. I stroked her ear and jaw instead, urging her nearer. Then her hand fell lower, and mine too, and at that moment I felt my hand and mind lose their particularity, their pointiness, their countingness, instead become clouds of general awareness, dreamy and yielding with curiosity. My hand felt less a hand than a catcher's mitt, or Mickey Mouse's hand, something vast and blunt and soft. I didn't count her where I touched her. I conducted a general survey, took a tender sampling.

"You're excited," she breathed.

"Yes."

"It's okay."

"I know."

"I just wanted to mention it."

"Okay, yes."

She unbuttoned my pants. I fumbled with hers, with a thin sash knotted at her front for a belt. I couldn't undo it with one hand. We were breathing into one another's mouths, lips slipping together and apart, noses mashed. I found a way in around the knotted sash, untucked her shirt. I put my finger in her belly button, then found the crisp margin of her pubic hair, threaded it with a finger. She tremored and slid her knee between mine.

"You can touch me there," she said.

"I am," I said, wishing for accuracy.

"You're so excited," she said. "It's okay."

"Yes."

"It's okay. Oh, Lionel, that's okay. Don't stop, it's okay."

"Yes," I said. "It's okay." *Okay, okay:* Here was Kimmery's tic, in evidence at last. I couldn't begrudge it. I turned my whole hand, gathering her up, surrounding her. She spilled as I held her. Meanwhile she'd found the vent in my boxer shorts. I felt two fingertips contact a part of me through that window, the blind men and the elephant. I wanted and didn't want her to go on, terribly.

"You're so excited," she said again, incantatory.

"Uh." She jostled me, untangled me from my shorts and my self.

"Wow, God, Lionel you're sort of huge."

"And bent," I said, so she wouldn't have to say it.

"Is that normal?"

"I guess it's a little unusual-looking." I panted, hoping to be past this moment.

"More than a little, Lionel."

"Someone—a woman once told me it was like a beer can."

"I've heard of that," said Kimmery. "But yours is, I don't know, like a beer can that's been crushed, like for recycling."

So it was for me. In my paltry history I'd never been unveiled without hearing something about it—freak shows within freak shows. Whatever Kimmery thought, it didn't keep her from freeing me from my boxer shorts and palming me, so that I felt myself aching heavily in her cool grasp. We made a circuit: mouths, knees, hands and what they held. The sensation was okay. I tried to match the rhythm of her hand with mine, failed. Kimmery's tongue lapped my chin, found my mouth again. I made a whining sound, not a part of any word. Language was destroyed. Bailey, he left town.

"It's okay to talk," she whispered.

"Uh."

"I like, um, I like it when you talk. When you make sounds."

"Okay."

"Tell me something, Lionel."

"What?"

"I mean, say something. The way you do."

I looked at her open-mouthed. Her hand urged me toward an utterance that was anything but verbal. I tried to distract her the same way.

"Speak, Lionel."

"Ah." It really was all I could think to say.

She kissed me gaspingly and drew back, her look expectant.

"One Mind!" I said.

"Yes!" said Kimmery.

"Fonebone!" I shouted.

*   *   *

Another key contributor to my Tourette's lexicon was a cartoonist named Don Martin, first encountered in a pile of tattered *Mad* magazines in a box in the Ping-Pong room in the basement of St. Vincent's when I was eleven or twelve. I used to pore over his drawings, trying to find what it was about his characters, drawn with riotously bulging eyes, noses, chins, Adam's apples and knees, elongated tongues and fingers and feet that flapped like banners, named Professor Bleent, P. Carter Franit, Mrs. Freenbeen and Mr. Fonebone, that stirred such a deep chord in me. His image of life was garish and explosive, heads being stretched and shrunk, surgeons lopping off noses and dropping brains and sewing hands on backward, falling safes and metal presses squashing men flat or into boxlike packages, children swallowing coat hangers and pogo sticks and taking on their shapes. His agonized characters moved through their panels with a geeky physicality, seeming to strain toward their catastrophic contact with fire hoses, whirring blades, and drawbridges, and his sophomoric punch lines mostly hinged on reversals or literalizations—"The kids are upstairs with their ears glued to the radio"—or else on outright destruction. *Mad* often held the concluding panel of a Don Martin cartoon to the following page, and part of the pleasure of his work was never knowing whether the payoff would be a visual pun or verbal riff or merely the sight of a man in a full-body cast falling out a window into the path of a steamroller. Mostly, though, I recall the distortion, the torque in the bodies he drew: These characters had met disaster in being born onto the page, and their more extreme fates were only realizations of their essential nature. This made sense to me. And Fonebone made sense, too. He had a name I could get behind. For a while he almost supplanted Bailey, and he was lastingly traceable in my tendency to append *phone* or *bone* to the end of a phrase.

When I had sex with another person and my body began to convulse and move faster, my toes to curl, my eyes to roll, I felt like a Don Martin character, a Fonebone, all elbows and bowlegs and boomerang penis and gurgling throat in a halo of flung-off sweat drops and sound effects: *Fip, Thwat, Zwip, Sproing, Flabadab*. More than Daffy Duck, more than Art Carney, more than any other icon of my discomfort. Don Martin's drawings throbbed with the suggestion that disruptive feeling was all sexual. Though his venue denied him any overt reference his characters overflowed with lewd energies, which had to be manifested instead in tics and seizures, eruptions and deformations. His poor doomed Fonebones seemed to chart my path from twitch to orgasm, the way sex first smoothed away tics, then supplanted them with a violent double: little death, big tic. So perhaps it was Don Martin's fault that I always expected a punishment after sex, cringed in anticipation of the steamroller or plummeting anvil to follow.

Possibly Kimmery sensed it in me, this dread of a page about to be turned, revealing some ludicrous doom on the last panel of my cartoon. Another fact about Don Martin: He never used the same character twice—each was an innocent pawn with no carry-over from one episode to the next, no understanding of his role or fate. A Fonebone was a placeholder, a disposable clone or stooge. A member of the Butt Trust.

"Is something the matter?" she said, stopping what she was doing, what I was doing.

"Everything's fine. I mean, better than fine."

"You don't look fine."

"Just one thing, Kimmery. Promise me you won't go back to the Zendo. At least for a few days."

"Why?"

"Just trust me, okay?"

"Okay."

With that, her magic word, we were done talking.

*   *   *

Once Kimmery was asleep I dressed and tiptoed to her phone, which was on the floor in the big room. Shelf followed me in. I tapped his head five times, instantly reigniting his ragged purring, then pushed him away. The phone showed a number under its plastic window. I fed the number into the speed dial of the doormen's cell phone, wincing at the beeping tones, which echoed in the silent empty room like musical gunshots. Kimmery didn't stir on her mattress, though. She lay splayed like a child making a snow angel. I wanted to go and kneel and trace her shape with my fingertips or my breath. Instead I found her key ring and separated the five keys. The key to the apartment was easy to identify, and that was the only one I left behind—she'd have to deal with her suspicious neighbors to get into the lobby downstairs. I took the other four, figuring one would get me into the Zendo. The last two probably unlocked Oreo Man's place. Those I'd lose.

AUTO BODY

See me now, at one in the morning, stepping out of another cab in front of the Zendo, checking the street for cars that might have followed, for giveaway cigarette-tip glows through the windows of the cars parked on the deadened street, moving with my hands in my jacket pockets clutching might-be-guns-for-all-they-know, collar up against the cold like Minna, unshaven like Minna now, too, shoes clacking on sidewalk: think of a coloring-book image of the Green Hornet, say. That's who I was supposed to be, that black outline of a man in a coat, ready suspicious eyes above his collar, shoulders hunched, moving toward conflict.

Here's who I was instead: that same coloring-book outline of a man, but crayoned by the hand of a mad or carefree or retarded child, wild slashes of idiot color, a blizzard of marks violating the boundaries that made *man* distinct from *street*, from *world*. Some of those colors were my fresh images of Kimmery, flashing me back to the West Side an hour before, crayon stripes and arrows like flares over

Central Park in the night sky. Others weren't so pretty, roaring scrawls of mania, *find-a-man-kill-a-phone-fuck-a-plan* in sloppy ten-foot-high letters drawn like lightning bolts or Hot Wheels race-car flames through the space of my head. And the blackened steel-wool scribble of my guilt-deranged investigation: I pictured the voices of the two Minna brothers and Tony Vermonte and The Clients as gnarled above and around me, in a web of betrayal I had to penetrate and dissolve, an ostensible world I'd just discovered was really only a private cloud I carried everywhere, had never seen the outside of. So, crossing the street to the door of the Zendo, I might have appeared less a single Green Hornet than a whole inflamed nest of them.

*   *   *

My first act was to drop in next door. I found the original doorman, Dirk, asleep on his stool.

I lifted his head up with my hand and he jerked awake and away from my grasp. "Hello!" he shouted.

"You remember me, Dirk?" I said. "I was sitting in a car. You told me I had a message from my 'friend.'"

"Oh? Sure, I remember. Sorry, I was just doing what I was told."

"Sure you were. And I suppose you never saw the guy before, did you—*dirtyworker, dirketyname?*"

"I never saw the guy before." He breathed out, wide-eyed.

"He was a very big man, yes?"

"Yes!" He rolled his eyes upward to show it. Then he held his hands out, begging my patience. I backed off a little and he stood and neatened his coat. I helped him with it, especially around the collar. He was too sleepy or confused by my questions to object.

"He pay you or just scare you into giving me the bum steer?" I asked more gently. My anger was wasted on Dirk. Anyway, I felt vaguely grateful to him for confirming the giant's existence. My only other sure witness was Gilbert, in jail. Kimmery had begun to make me doubt my eyes.

"A man that big doesn't have to pay," said Dirk honestly.

*   *   *

One of the stolen keys got me inside. This time I held on to my shoes as I passed the sitting room and headed upstairs, past the floor where Kimmery and I had sat at tea, up to the Roshi's private quarters—a.k.a. Gerard Minna's hideout. The halls were darker the higher I climbed, until at the top I could only grope my way toward a thin margin of light squeezed out underneath a sealed door. I turned the handle and pushed the door open, impatient with my own fear.

His bedroom had the integrity of his self-reinvention. It was bare of furnishings except for a long low shelf against the wall, a board, really, propped on bricks and bearing a few candles and books, a glass of water and a small bowl of ashes, decorated with Japanese script, presumably some kind of tiny shrine. The spareness reminded me of Kimmery's empty studio apartment but I resented the echo, not wishing to see Kimmery as influenced by Gerard's Zen pretensions, not wishing to imagine her visiting his private floor, his lair, at all. Gerard sat propped on pillows on a flat mattress on the floor, his legs crossed, the book at his knees shut, his posture calm, as though he'd been waiting for me. I faced him head on for what might have been the first time—I don't know that I'd ever addressed him directly, stolen more than a glance as a teenager. In the candlelight I first made out his silhouette: He'd thickened around the jaw and neck, so that his bald head seemed to rise from his round shoulders like the line of a cobra's hood. I might have been overly influenced by that bald head but as my eyes adjusted I couldn't keep from understanding the difference between his features and Frank Minna's as the same as that between Brando's in *Apocalypse Now!* and *On the Waterfront*.

"Thehorrorthehorror," I ticced. *"Icouldabeenacontender!"* It was like a couplet.

"You're Lionel Essrog, aren't you?"

"Unreliable Chessgrub," I corrected. My throat pulsed with ticcishness. I was overly conscious of the open door behind me, so my neck twitched, too, with the urge to look over my shoulder. Doormen could come through open doors, anyone knew that. "Is there anyone else in the building?" I said.

"We're alone."

"Mind if I close this?"

"Go ahead." He didn't budge from his position on the mattress, just gazed at me evenly. I closed the door and moved just far enough into the room not to be tempted to grope behind me for the door's surface. We faced each other across the candlelit gloom, each a figure out of the other's past, each signifying to the other the lost man, the man killed the day before.

"You broke your vow of silence just now," I said.

"I'm finished with my sesshin," he said. "Anyway, you brought silence to a rather conclusive finish during today's sitting."

"I think your hired killer had something to do with that."

"You're speaking without thinking," he said. "I recall your difficulties in that area."

I took a deep breath. Gerard's serenity called out of me a storm of compensatory voices, a myriad possible shrieks and insults to stanch. A part of me wanted to cajole him out from behind his Zen front, expose the Lord of Court Street lurking, make him Frank's older brother again. What came out of my mouth was the beginning of a joke, one from the deepest part of the made-Frank-Minna-laugh-once archive:

"So there's this order of nuns, right?"

"An order of nuns," Gerard repeated.

"Ordinary nunphone!—an order of nuns. Like the Cloisters. You know, a monastery."

"A monastery is for monks."

"Okay, a nunastery. *A plannery, a nunnetarium!*—a nunnery. And they've all, these nuns, they've all taken a vow of silence, a lifetime vow of silence, right?" I was driven, tears at the edges of my eyes, wishing for Frank to be alive to rescue me, tell me he'd heard this one already. Instead I had to go on. "Except one day a year one of the nuns gets to say something. They take turns, one nun a year. Understand?"

"I think I understand."

"So the big day comes—*Barnamum-big-nun! Domesticated ghost-phone!*—the big day is here and the nuns are all sitting at the dinner table and the one who gets to talk this year opens her mouth and says 'The soup is terrible.' And the other nuns all look at each other but nobody says anything because of the vow of silence, and that's it, back to normal. Another year of silence."

"A very disciplined group," said Gerard, not without admiration.

"Right. So a year later the day comes and it's this other nun's turn. So they're sitting and the second nun turns to the first and says 'I don't know, maybe it's just me, but I don't think the soup's that bad'—and that's it, silence. Another year."

"Hmmm. Imagine the states of contemplation one could achieve in such a year."

"I never thought about it myself. Anyway, so the calendar pages flip, and the special day—*Flip-a-thon! Fuck-a-door! Flipweed! Fujisaki! Flitcraft!*—the special day comes around again. This third nun, it's her turn—*Nun-fuck-a-phone!*—so this third nun, she looks at the first nun and the second nun and she says 'Bicker, bicker, bicker.' "

There was silence, then Gerard nodded and said, "That would be the punch line."

"I know about the building," I said, working to catch my breath. "And the Fujisaki Corporation." *Unfuckafish* whispered under my palate.

"Ah. Then you know much."

"Yeah, I know a thing. And I've met your killing machine. But you saw that, when he dragged me out, downstairs. The kumquat-eater."

I was desperate to see him flinch, to impress him with the edge I had, the things I'd learned, but Gerard wasn't ruffled. He raised his eyebrows, which got a lot of play across the empty canvas of his forehead. "You and your friends, what are their names?"

"Who? The Minna Men?"

"Yes—Minna Men. That's a very good description. My brother was very important to the four of you, wasn't he?"

I nodded, or not, but anyway he went on.

"He really taught you everything, I suppose. You sound just like him when you speak. What an odd life, really. You realize that, don't you? That Frank was a very odd man, living in a strange and anachronistic way?"

"What's *cartoonistic* about it?"

"Anachronistic," said Gerard patiently. "From another time."

"I know what it means," I said. "I mean what's so *akakonistic* about it?" I was too wound up to go back and repair the tic-pocked surface of my speech. "Anyway, *enactoplasmic* as opposed to what? A million-year-old mystical Japanese cult?"

"You wear your ignorance as aggressively as Frank," said Gerard. "I suppose you're making my point for me."

"Point being what?"

"My brother taught you only what he knew, and not even all of that. He kept you charmed and flattered but also in the dark, so your sense of even his small world was diminished, two-dimensional. Cartoonistic, if you like. What's astonishing to me is that you didn't know about the Park Avenue building until just now. It really must come as a shock."

"Enlighten me."

"Surely you've got my brother's money in your pocket even as we speak, Lionel. Do you really believe that it came from detective work, from those scuffling little assignments he contrived to keep you children busy? Or perhaps you imagine he *crapped* money. That's just as likely."

Was *crapped* a chink in Gerard's Zen façade, a bit of Brooklyn showing through? I recalled the elder monk proclaiming the worthlessness of "Bowel Movement Zen."

"Frank consorted with dangerous people," Gerard went on. "And he stole from them. The remuneration and the risk were high. The odds that he would flourish in such a life forever, low."

"Talk to me about *fool-me-softly*—Fujisaki."

"They own the building. Minna had a hand in managing it. The money involved would dazzle your senses, Lionel." He gave me an expectant look, as though this assertion ought to dazzle me in the money's stead, ought to astonish me right out of my investigation, and his bedroom.

"These people, their other home is an island," I said, quoting the Garbage Cop—not that the phrase was likely to have originated with him.

Gerard smiled at me oddly. "For every Buddhist, Japan is his other home. And yes, it is an island."

"Who's a Buddhist?" I said. "I was talking about the money."

He sighed, without losing the smile. "You are so like Frank."

"What's your role, Gerard?" I wanted to sicken him the way I was sickened. "I mean, besides sending your brother out into the Polack's arms to die."

Now he beamed munificently. The worse I attacked him, the deeper his forgiveness and grace would be—that's what the smile said. "Frank was very careful never to expose me to any danger if he could help it. I was never introduced to anyone from Fujisaki. I believe I have yet to make their acquaintance, apart from the large hit man you led here yesterday."

"Who's Ullman?"

"A bookkeeper, another New Yorker. He was Frank's partner in fleecing the Japanese."

"But you *never met the guy.*"

I meant him to hear the sarcasm, or rather Frank Minna's sarcasm in quotation. But he went on obliviously. "No. I only supplied the labor, in return for consideration equal to my mortgage here on the Zendo. Buddhism is spread by what means it finds."

"Labor for what?" My brain tangled on *spread by means it finds, fed in springs by mimes, bled by mingy spies,* but I shook it off.

"My students performed the maintenance and service work for the building, as part of their training. Cleaning, cooking, the very sort of labor they'd perform in a monastery, only in a slightly different setting. The contract for those services in such a building is worth millions. My brother and Ullman tithed the difference mostly into their own pockets."

"Doormen," I said.

"Yes. Doormen, too."

"So Fujisaki sicced the giant on Frank and the bookkeeper."

"I suppose that's right."

"And he just happened to use the Zendo as his trap yesterday?" I aired out another Minna-ism: "Don't try to hand me no two-ton feather." I was dredging up Minna's usages on any excuse now, as though I could build a golem of his language, then bring it to life, a figure of vengeance to search out the killer or killers.

I was aware of myself standing in Gerard's room, planted on his floor, arms at my sides, never moving nearer to him where he sat beaming Zen pleasantness in my direction, ignoring my accusations and my tics. I was big but I was no golem or giant. I hadn't startled Gerard in deep sleep nor upended his calm with my griefy hostility. I wasn't holding a gun on him. He didn't have to answer my questions.

"I don't really believe in sophisticated killers," said Gerard. "Do you?"

"Go-fisticate-a-killphone," I ticced.

"The Fujisaki Corporation is ruthless and remorseless—in the manner of corporations. And yet in the manner of corporations their violence is also performed at a remove, by a force just nominally under their control. In the giant you speak of they seem to have located a sort of primal entity—one whose true nature is killing. And sicced him, as you say, on the men who they feel betrayed them. I'm not sure the killer's behavior is explicable in any real sense, Lionel. Any human sense."

Gerard's persuasiveness was a variant of the Minna style, I saw now. I felt the force of it, moving me authentically. Yet his foray against the notion of a sophisticated killer also made me think of Tony mocking Detective Seminole with jokes about Batman and James Bond supervillains. Was it a giveaway, a clue that Gerard and Tony were in league? And what about Julia? I wanted to quote Frank's conversation with Gerard the night he died: *She misses her Rama-lama-ding-dong,* find out what he meant. I wanted to ask about Boston, and I wanted to ask about Frank and Julia's marriage—had Gerard been at the ceremony? I wanted to ask him about whether he missed Brooklyn, and how he got his head so shiny. I searched for a single question that could stand for my thousands and what popped out was this:

"What's human sense?"

"In Buddhism, Lionel, we come to understand that everything on this earth is a vessel for Buddha-nature. Frank had Buddha-nature. You have Buddha-nature. I feel it."

Gerard allowed a long minute to pass while we contemplated his words. *Buddha nostril,* I nearly blurted. When he spoke again, it was with a confidence that sympathy flowed between us untrammeled by doubt or fear.

"There's another of your Minna Men, Lionel. He's pushing his way into this, and I fear he may have aroused the killer's ire. Tony, is that his name?"

"Tony Vermonte," I said, marveling—it was as if Gerard had read my mind.

"Yes. He'd like to walk in my brother's footsteps. But Fujisaki will be keeping a keener eye on their money from this point, I'd think. There's nothing to be gained and everything to be lost. Perhaps you'll have a word with him."

"Tony and I aren't exactly...communicating well, since yesterday."

"Ah."

I felt a surge of care in me, for Tony. He was only a heedless adventurer, with a poignant urge to imitate Frank Minna in all things. He was a member of my family—L&L, the Men. Now he was in above his head, threatened on all sides by the giant, by Detective Seminole, by The Clients. Only Gerard and I understood his danger.

I must have been silent for a minute or so—a veritable sesshin by my standards.

"You and Tony are together in your pain at the loss of my brother," said Gerard softly. "But you haven't come together in actuality. Be patient."

"There's another factor," I said, tentative now, lulled by his compassionate tones. "Someone else may be involved in this somehow. Two of them, actually—*Monstercookie and Antifriendly!*—uh, Matricardi and Rockaforte."

"You don't say."

"I do."

"You can't know how sorry I am to hear those names." *Never say those names!* warned Minna in the echo chamber of my memory. Gerard went on, "Those two are the prototype, aren't they, for my brother's tendency to dangerous associations—and his tendency to exploit those associations in dangerous ways."

"He stole from them?"

"Do you recall that he once had to leave New York for a while?"

Did I recall! Suddenly Gerard threatened to solve the deepest puzzles of my existence. I practically wanted to ask him, *So who's Bailey?*

"I'd hoped they were no longer in the picture," said Gerard reflectively. It was the nearest to thrown I'd seen him, the closest I'd come to pushing his buttons. Only now I wasn't sure I wanted to. "Avoid them, Lionel, if you can," he continued. "They're dangerous men."

He returned his gaze to my face, batted his lashes, moved his expressive eyebrows. If I'd been in striking distance I'd have tried to span his head with my hands and stroke his eyebrows with my thumb tips, just to soothe this one small worry I'd raised.

"Can I ask one more thing?" I nearly called him Roshi, so complete was my conversion. "Then I'll leave you alone."

Gerard nodded. *The High Lama will grant you an audience, Mrs. Gushman.*

"Is there anyone else—*Zonebone!*—anyone else at the Zendo who's involved in this thing? Anyone—*Kissmefaster! Killmesooner! Cookiemonster!*—anyone the killer might target? That old hippie, Wallace? Or the girl—*Kissingme!*—Kimmery?" I tried not to divulge the special freight of tenderness and hope behind this query. Whether the string of shrieks I issued in the course of its delivery made me appear more or less blasé, I couldn't say.

"No." Gerard spoke benevolently. "I compromised myself personally, but not my students or my practice as a teacher. Wallace and Kimmery should be safe. It's kind of you to be concerned."

I'm concerned about Pinched and Indistinct, too, I wanted to say. I doubted students could get any more compromised than that.

And then there was that nod of complicity I saw pass between Gerard and the giant.

The three of them—Pinched, Indistinct, and the nod—were three sour notes in a very pretty song. But I kept my tongue, feeling I'd learned what I could here, that it was time to go. I wanted to find Tony before the giant did. And I needed to step outside the candle glow of Gerard's persuasiveness to sort out the false and the real, the Zen and the chaff in our long discussion.

"I'm going now," I said awkwardly.

"Good night, Lionel." He was still watching me as I closed the door.

*   *   *

On second thought, there *is* a vaguely Tourettic aspect to the New York City subway, especially late at night—that dance of attention, of stray gazes, in which every rider must engage. And there's a lot of stuff you shouldn't touch in the subway, particularly in a certain order: this pole and then your lips, for instance. And the tunnel walls are layered, like those of my brain, with expulsive and incoherent language—

But I was in a terrible hurry, or rather two terrible hurries: to get back to Brooklyn, and to sort out my thinking about Gerard before I got there. I couldn't spare a minute to dwell in myself as a body riding the Lexington train to Nevins Street—I might as well have been teleported, or floated to Brooklyn on a magic carpet, for all that I was allured or distracted by the 4 train's sticky, graffitied immediacy.

*   *   *

The lights were burning in the L&L storefront. I approached from the opposite sidewalk, confident I was invisible on the darkened street to those in the office—I'd been on the other side of that plate of glass only two or three thousand nights in preparation for the act of spying on my fellow Men from the street. I didn't want to go waltzing into a trap. Detective Seminole might be there or, who knew, maybe Tony and a passel of doormen. If there was something to learn at a distance, I'd learn it.

It was almost two-thirty now, and Bergen Street was shut up tight, the night cold enough to chase the stoop-sitting drinkers indoors. Smith Street showed a bit more life, Zeod's Market lit up like a beacon, catering to the all-night cigarette cravings, to the squad-car cops in need of a bagel or LifeSaver or some other torus. Four L&L cars were scattered in parking spots near the storefront: the Minna death car, which hadn't moved since Gilbert and I returned from the hospital and parked it, the Pontiac in which Tony had shanghaied me in front of The Clients' brownstone, a Caddy that Minna had liked to drive himself, and a Tracer, an ugly modernistic bubble of a car that usually fell to me or Gilbert to pilot. I slowed my walk as I drew up even with the storefront, then turned my neck. It was pleasing to have a good solid reason behind turning my neck for once, retroactive validation for a billion tics. As I passed, I made out the shapes of two Men inside: Tony and Danny, both in a cloud of cigarette smoke, Danny seated behind the counter with a folded newspaper, radiating cool, Tony pacing, radiating cool's opposite. The television was on.

I walked past, to the corner of Smith, then swiveled and went back. This time I set up shop on the brief stoop of the big apartment building directly across from L&L. It was a safe outpost. I could duck my head and watch them through a parked car's windows if I thought they were in any danger of spotting me. Otherwise I'd sit back in the wings and study them in the limelight of the storefront until something happened or I'd decided what to do.

Danny—I gave Danny Fantl a moment of my time. He was sliding through this crisis as he'd slid through life to this point, so poised he was practically an ambient presence. Gilbert was in jail and I was hunted high and low and Danny sat in the storefront all day, refusing car calls and smoking cigarettes and reading sports. He wasn't exactly my candidate for any plot's criminal mastermind, but if Tony conspired with or even confided in anyone inside L&L's circle, it would be Danny. In the present atmosphere, I decided, there was no way I could take Danny for granted, trust him with my back.

Which meant I wasn't going inside to talk with either one of them until they were apart. If then—the image of Tony pulling his wobbly gun on me was fresh enough to give pause.

Anyway, something happened before I'd decided what to do—why was I not surprised? But it was a relatively banal something, reassuring, even. A tick of the clock of everyday life on Bergen Street, an everyday life that already felt nostalgic.

A block east, on the corner of Bergen and Hoyt, was an elegantly renovated tavern called the Boerum Hill Inn, with a gleaming antique inlaid-mirror bar, a CD jukebox weighted toward Blue Note and Stax, and a Manhattanized clientele of professional singles too good for bars with televisions, for subway rides home, or for the likes of the Men. Only Minna ever visited the Boerum Hill Inn, and he cracked that anyone who drank there was someone else's assistant: a district attorney's, an editor's, or a video artist's. The dressed-up crowd at the inn gabbled and flirted every night of the week until two in the morning, oblivious to the neighborhood's past or present reality, then slept it off in their overpriced apartments or on their desks the next day in Midtown. Typically a few parties would stagger down the block after last call and try to engage an L&L car for a ride home—sometimes it was a woman alone or a newly formed couple too drunk to throw to the fates, and we'd take the job. Mostly we claimed not to have any cars.

But the inn's bartenders were a couple of young women we adored, Siobhain and Welcome. Siobhain was properly named, while Welcome bore the stigma of her parents' hippie ideals, but both were from Brooklyn and Irish to their ancient souls—or so had declared Minna. They were roommates in Park Slope, possibly lovers (again according to Minna), and bartending their way through graduate school. Each night one or the other was stuck with closing—the owner of the inn was stingy and didn't let them double up after midnight. If we weren't actually busy on some surveillance job we'd always drive the closer home.

It was Welcome, at the door of L&L, now going inside. I saw Tony nod at Danny, then Danny stood and stubbed out a butt, checked in his pocket for the keys and nodded too. He and Welcome moved to the door and out. I lowered my head. Danny led her to the Caddy, which sat at the front of the row of parked cars, on the corner of Smith. She went around to the front passenger seat, not like the usual ride who'd sit in the back. Danny slammed his door and the interior light shut off, then he started the engine. I glanced back to see that Tony was now going through the drawers behind the L&L counter, searching for something, his desperado's energy suddenly lashed to a purpose. He used both hands, his cigarette stuck in his mouth, and unpacked papers onto the countertop hurriedly. I'd gathered a piece of vague information, I supposed: Tony didn't trust Danny with everything.

Then I saw a hulking shadow stir, in a parked car on L&L's side of the street, just a few yards from the storefront.

Unmistakable.

The Kumquat Sasquatch.

* * *

The car was an economy model, bright red, and he filled it like it had been cast around his body. I saw him lean sideways to watch the Cadillac with Danny and Welcome inside round the corner of Smith and disappear with a pulse of brakelights. Then he turned his attention back to the storefront; I read the movement in the disappearance of a nose from the silhouette, its replacement by an elephantine ear. The giant was doing what I was doing, staking out L&L.

He watched Tony, and I watched them both. Tony was a lot more interesting at the moment. I hadn't often seen him reading, and never this intently. He was searching for something in the sheaf of papers he'd pulled from Minna's drawers, his brow furrowed, cigarette in his lips, looking like Edward R. Murrow's punk brother. Now, unsatisfied, he dug in another drawer, and worked over a notebook I recognized even from across the street as the one containing my own stakeout jottings from the day before. I tried not to take it personally when he thrust this aside even more hastily and went back to tearing up the drawers.

The large shadow took it all in, complacent. His hand moved from somewhere below the line of the car window and briefly covered his mouth; he chewed, then leaned forward to dribble out some discarded seeds or pits. A bag of cherries or olives this time, something a giant would gobble in a handful. Or Cracker Jack, and he didn't like peanuts. He watched Tony like an operagoer who knew the libretto, was curious only to gather details of how the familiar plot would play out this time.

Tony exhausted the drawers, started in on the file cabinets.

The giant chewed. I blinked in time with his chewing, and counted chews and blinks, occupying my Tourette's brain with this nearly invisible agitation, tried to stay otherwise still as a lizard on the stoop. He had only to turn this way to spot me. My whole edge consisted of seeing without being seen; I had nothing more on the giant, had never had. If I wanted to preserve that wafer-thin edge I needed to find a better hiding place—and it wouldn't hurt to get in out of the stiff, cold wind.

The three remaining L&L cars were my best option. But the Pontiac, which I would have preferred, was up ahead of the giant's car, easily in his line of sight. I was sure I didn't want to face whatever ghosts or more tangibly olfactory traces of Minna might be trapped inside the sealed windows of the Death Car. Which left the Tracer. I felt in my pocket for my bunch of keys, found the three longest, one of which was the Tracer's door and ignition. I was preparing to duck-walk down the pavement and slip into the Tracer when the Cadillac reappeared, hurtling down Bergen, with Danny at the wheel.

He parked in the same spot at the front of the block and walked back toward L&L. I slumped on the stoop, played drunk. Danny didn't see me. He went inside, surprising Tony in his filework. They exchanged a word or two, then Tony slid the drawer closed and bummed another cigarette from Danny. The shadow in the little car went on watching, sublimely confident and peaceful. Neither Tony nor Danny had ever seen the giant, I suppose, so he had less to worry about in attracting attention than I did. But reason alone couldn't account for the giant's composure. If he wasn't a student of Gerard's, he should have been: He possessed true Buddha-nature, and would have surpassed his teacher. Three hundred and fifty-odd pounds instill a cosmic measure of gravity, I suppose. *What did the Buddhist say to the hot-dog vendor?* was the joke I remembered now, one of Loomis's measly riddles. *Make me one with everything.* I would have been happy to be one with everything at that moment.

Heck, make me one with anything.

I was pretty hungry, too, if I thought about it. A stakeout was customarily a gastronomic occasion, and I was beginning to get that itch for something between two slices of bread. Why shouldn't I be hungry? I'd missed dinner, had Kimmery instead.

With thoughts of food and sex my attention slipped, so that I was startled now to see Tony pop out of the storefront, his expression still as fierce as it had been when he was poring over the paperwork. For a moment I thought I'd been spotted. But he turned toward Smith Street, crossed Bergen, and disappeared around the corner.

The giant watched, unimpressed, unworried.

We waited.

Tony returned with a large plastic shopping bag, probably from Zeod's. The only thing I could discern was a carton of Marlboros sticking out of the top, but the bag was heavy with something. Tony opened the passenger door of the Pontiac and put the bag on the seat, glanced quickly up the street without spotting either me or the giant, then relocked the car and went back to L&L.

*   *   *

Figuring it was status quo for the time being, I made my way back down Bergen, up Hoyt Street, and around the block the long way, and checked into Zeod's myself.

Zeod liked to work the late hours, do the overnight, check in the newspaper deliveries at six and then sleep through the bright hours of the morning and early afternoon. He was like the Sheriff of Smith Street, eyes open while we all slept, seeing the drunks stagger home, keeping his eye on the crucial supplies, the Ding Dongs and Entenmann's cookies, the forty-ounce malt liquor and the cups of coffee "regular" with a picture of the Parthenon on the cup. Except now he had company down the street at L&L, Tony and Danny and the giant and myself enacting our strange vigil, our roundelay of surveillance. I wondered if Zeod knew about Minna yet. As I slipped up to the counter the groggy counter boy was punishing the slicer with a steaming white towel, replenishing the towel in a basin of hot suds, while Zeod stood exhorting him, telling him how he could be doing it better, squeezing some value out of him before he quit like all the others.

"Crazyman!"

"Shhh." I imagined that Tony or the giant could hear Zeod bellow through the shop window and around the corner of the block.

"You're working so late for Frank tonight? Something important, eh? Tony just came."

"Important Freaks! Important Franks!"

"Ho ho ho."

"Listen, Zeod. Can you tell me what Tony bought?"

Zeod screwed up his face, finding this question sensational. "You can't ask him yourself?"

"No, I can't."

He shrugged. "Six-pack of beer, four sandwiches, carton of cigarettes, Coca-Cola—whole picnic."

"Funny picnic."

"Wasn't funny to him," said Zeod. "Couldn't make him smile. Like you, Crazyman. On a very serious case, eh?"

"What—*becausewhich, besideswhich*—what sandwiches did he buy?" It was my suddenly ravenous appetite that steered this inquiry.

"Ah!" Zeod rubbed his hands together. He was always ready to savor his own product on someone else's behalf. "Turkey with Thousand, very nice on a kaiser roll, pepperoni-and-provolone hero with peppers inside, two roast beef with horseradish on rye bread."

I had to clutch the counter to keep from falling over, this storm of enticements was so heady.

"You like what you hear, I can see that," said Zeod.

I nodded, turned my head sideways, took in the fresh-gleaming slicer, the elegant curve of the fender that sheathed the blade.

Zeod said, "You want something, Crazyman, don't you?"

I saw the counter boy's eyes roll in weary anticipation. The slicer rarely saw this much action at two or three in the morning. They'd have to sluice it down with suds again before the night was done.

"Please—*ghostradish, pepperpony, kaiserphone*—please, uh, the same as Tony."

"You want the same? All four the same?"

"Yes," I gasped. I couldn't think past Tony's list of sandwiches. My hunger for them was absolute. I had to match Tony sandwich for sandwich, a gastronomic mirroring-tic—I'd understand him by the time I was through the fourth, I figured. We would achieve a Zeod's mind-meld, with Thousand Island dressing.

While Zeod rode his counter boy to complete the large order I hid in the back near the beverage cases, picked out a liter of Coke and a bag of chips, and reorganized and counted a disorderly shelf of cat-food cans.

"Okay, Lionel." Zeod was always most gentle with me when handing over his precious cargo—we shared that reverence for his product. "Put it on Frank's tab, right?" He gathered my soda and chips in a large bag with the paper-wrapped sandwiches.

"No, no—" I rustled in my pockets for a tight-folded twenty.

"What's the matter? Why not the boss man pick it up?"

"I want to pay you." I pushed the bill across the counter. Zeod took it and arched his eyebrows.

"Very funny business," he said, and made a *chuck-chuck-chuck* sound with his tongue in his cheek.

"What?"

"Same thing as Tony, before you," he said. "He says he wants to pay. Same thing."

"Listen, Zeod. If Tony comes back in here tonight"—I fought off a howling sound that wanted to come out of me, the cry of a sandwich predator over fresh kill he has yet to devour—"don't tell him you saw me, okay?"

Zeod winked. Somehow this made sense to him. I felt a thing that was either a nauseous wave of paranoia—perhaps Zeod was an agent of Tony's, absolutely in his pocket, and would be on the phone to him the minute I was out of the shop—or else my stomach spasming in anticipation of food. "Okay, Chief," said Zeod as I went out the door.

*   *   *

I came around the block the long way again, quickly confirmed that the giant and Tony were still in their places, then swerved across the street and slipped up beside the Tracer, key in hand. The giant's compact was six cars ahead, but I couldn't see his clifflike silhouette from where I stood as I unlocked the car. I only hoped that meant he couldn't see me. I plopped Zeod's bag on the passenger seat, jumped inside, and slammed the door shut as quickly as I could, praying that the brief flash of the interior light hadn't registered in the giant's rearview. Then I slumped down in my place so I'd be invisible, on the slight chance he did turn and could make anything out through a thickness of twelve darkened windshields. Meanwhile I got my hands busy unfurling the paper around one of Zeod's roast beef and horse-radish specials. Once I had it free, I gobbled the sandwich like a nature-film otter cracking an oyster on its stomach: knees up in the wiring under the dashboard, my elbows jammed against the steering wheel, my chest serving as a table, my shirt as a tablecloth.

Now it was a proper stakeout—if only I could figure what it was I was waiting to see happen. Not that I could see much from inside the Tracer. The giant's car was still in its place but I couldn't confirm his existence inside it. And at this extreme angle all I could see was a thin slice of bright L&L window. Twice Tony paced to the front of the store, just long enough for me to identify his form in shadow and a flash of an elbow, a left-behind plume of cigarette exhalation across the edge of Minna's destination map, the Queens airports at the left margin showing Minna's Magic Marker scrawl: $18. Bergen Street was a void in my rearview, Smith Street only marginally brighter ahead of me. It was a quarter to four. I felt the F train's rumble underneath Bergen, first as it slowed into the station and paused there, then a second tremor as it departed. A minute later the 67 bus rolled like a great battered appliance down Bergen, empty apart from the driver. Public transportation was the night's pulse, the beep on the monitor at the patient's bedside. In a few hours those same trains and buses would be jammed with jawing, caffeinated faces, littered with newspapers and fresh gum. Now they kept the faith. Me, I had the cold to keep me awake, that and the liter of Coca-Cola and my assignment, my will to influence the outcome of the night's strange stalemate. Those would have to slug it out with the soporific powers of the roast-beef sandwich, the dreamy pull of my fresh memories of Kimmery, the throb of my skull where the giant had clubbed me with his gun.

What was the giant waiting for?

What did Tony want to find in Minna's files?

Why were his sandwiches in the car?

Why had Julia flown to Boston?

Who was Bailey anyway?

I opened my bag of chips, took a slug of my cola, and put myself to work on those new and old questions and on staying awake.

*   *   *

Insomnia is a variant of Tourette's—the waking brain races, sampling the world after the world has turned away, touching it everywhere, refusing to settle, to join the collective nod. The insomniac brain is a sort of conspiracy theorist as well, believing too much in its own paranoiac importance—as though if it were to blink, then doze, the world might be overrun by some encroaching calamity, which its obsessive musings are somehow fending off.

I've spent long nights in that place. This night, though, consisted of summoning up that state I'd so often worked to banish. I was alone now, no Minna, no Men, my own boss on this stakeout with who-knew-what riding on its outcome. If I fell asleep the little world of my investigation would crumble. I needed to find my insomniac self, to agitate my problem-solving brain, if not to solve actual problems, then to worry at them for the purpose of keeping my dumb eyeballs propped open.

Avoiding becoming one with everything: that was my big challenge at the moment.

It was four-thirty. My consciousness was distended, the tics like islands in an ocean of fog.

Who needed sleep? I asked myself. *I'll sleep when I'm dead,* Minna had liked to say.

I guess he had his chance now.

I'll die when I'm dead, my brain recited in Minna's voice. Not a minute sooner, you kosher macaroons!

A diet of bread. A guy on a bed.

No, no bed. No car. No phone.

Phone.

The cell phone. I pulled it out, rang the L&L number. It rang three times before a hand picked it up.

"No cars," said Danny lazily. If I knew him, he'd been sleeping with his head on the counter, weary of pretending to listen to whatever Tony was ranting about.

I'd have given a lot, of course, to know what Tony was ranting about.

"It's me, Danny. Put Tony on."

"Yo," he said, unsurprisable. "Here you go."

"What?" said Tony.

"It's me," I said. *"Deskjob."*

"You fucking little freak," said Tony. "I'll kill you."

I outweighed Tony only by about fifty pounds. "You had your chance," I heard myself say. Tony still brought out the romantic in me. We'd be two Bogarts to the end. "Except if you'd pulled that trigger, you might have blown a hole in your foot, or in some far-off toddler on his bike."

"Oh, I'd of straightened it out," Tony said. "I wish I had put a coupla holes in you. Leaving me with that fucking cop."

"Remember it any way you like. I'm trying to help you at the moment."

"That's a good one."

"Eat me St. Vincent!" I held the phone away from my face until I was sure the tic was complete. "You're in danger, Tony. Right now."

"What do you know about it?"

I wanted to say, *Going out of town? What's in the files? Since when do you like horseradish?* But I couldn't let him know I was outside and have him rush into the giant's arms. "Trust me," I said. "I really wish you would."

"Oh, I trust you—to be Bozo the Clown," he said. "The point is, what can you tell me that's worth the time to listen?"

"That hurts, Tony."

"For chrissake!" Now he held his receiver away from his mouth and swore. "I got problems, Freakshow, and you're A-number one."

"If I were you, I'd worry more about Fujisaki."

"What do you know about Fujisaki?" He was hissing. "Where are you?"

"I know—*undress-a-phone, impress-a-clown*—I know a few things."

"You better hide," he said. "You better hope I don't catch you."

"Aw, Tony. We're in the same situation."

"That's a laugh, only I'm not laughing. I'm gonna kill you."

"We're a family, Tony. Minna brought us together—" I caught

myself wanting to quote the Garbage Cop, suggest another *moment of silence.*

"There's too long a tail on that kite, Freakshow. I don't have the time."

Before I could speak he hung up the phone.

It was after five, and bakery trucks had begun to roll. Soon a van would come and deliver Zeod's newspapers, with Minna's obituary notice in them.

*   *   *

I was in a comalike state when Tony came out of L&L and got into the Pontiac. A sentinel part of my brain had kept a watch on the storefront while the rest of me slept, and so I was startled to find that the sun was up, that traffic now filled Bergen Street. I glanced at Minna's watch: It was twenty minutes to seven. I was chilled through, my head throbbed, and my tongue felt as if it had been bound in horseradish-and-cola-soaked plaster and left out on the moon overnight. I shook my head and my neck crackled. I tried to keep my eyes on the scene even as I worked my jaw sideways to revive the mechanism of my face. Tony steered the Pontiac into Smith Street's morning flow. The giant poked his compact into the traffic a moment later, first allowing two cars to creep in behind Tony. I turned the Tracer's ignition key and the engine scuffed into life, and I followed, keeping my own safe distance behind.

Tony led us up Smith, onto Atlantic heading toward the water-front, into a stream of commuters and delivery trucks. In that stream I lost sight of Tony pretty quickly, but held on to the giant's pretty red compact.

Tony took the Brooklyn-Queens Expressway at the foot of Atlantic. The giant and I slid onto the ramp behind him in turn. Greenpoint, that was my first guess. I shuddered at recalling the

Dumpster behind Harry Brainum's, off McGuinness Boulevard, where Minna had met his finish. How had the giant contrived to lure Tony out to that spot?

But I was wrong. We passed the Greenpoint exit, heading north. I saw the black Pontiac in the distance ahead as we rounded the expressway's curve toward the airports and Long Island, but I kept dropped back, at least two cars behind the red compact. I had to trust the giant to track Tony, another exercise in Zen calm. We threaded the various exits and cloverleafs out of Brooklyn, through Queens toward the airport exits. When we turned momentarily toward JFK I generated a new theory: Someone from Fujisaki was disembarking at the Japan Air Lines terminal, some chief of executions, or a courier with a ticking package to deliver. Minna's death might be the first blow in an international wave of executions. And a flight to meet explained Tony's long, nervous overnight wait. Even as I settled on this explanation, I watched the red car peel away from the airport option, to the northbound ramp, marked for the White-stone Bridge. I barely made it across three lanes to stay on their vehicular heels.

*   *   *

Four sandwiches, of course. If I weren't prone to multiple sandwiches myself I might have made more of this clue. Four sandwiches and a six-pack. We were headed out of town. Fortunately I *had* rounded up my clone version of Tony's picnic, so I was outfitted too. I wondered if the giant had anything to eat besides the bag of cherries or olives I'd seen him gobbling. Our little highway formation reminded me of a sandwich, actually, a Minna Man on either side of the giant—we were a goon-on-orphan, with wheels. As we soared over the Whitestone I took another double shot of cola. It would have to stand in for morning coffee. I only had to solve the problem of needing to pee rather badly. Hence I hurried to finish the Coke, figuring I'd go in the bottle.

*   *   *

Half an hour later we'd passed options for the Pelhams, White Plains, Mount Kisco, a few other names I associated with the outer margins of New York City, on into Connecticut, first on the Hutchinson River Parkway, then on something called the Merritt Parkway. I kept the little red car in my sights. The cars were thick enough to keep me easily camouflaged. Every now and again the giant would creep near enough to Tony's Pontiac that I could see we were still three, bound like secret lovers through the indifferent miles of traffic.

Highway driving was maximally soothing. The steady flow of attention and effort, the nudging of gas pedal and checking of mirrors and blind spots with a twist of the neck subsumed my ticcishness completely. I was still bleary, needing sleep, but the novelty of this odd chase and of being farther out of New York City than I'd ever been worked to keep me awake. I'd seen trees before—so far Connecticut offered nothing I didn't know from suburban Long Island, or even Staten Island. But the *idea* of Connecticut was sort of interesting.

The traffic tightened as we skirted a small city called Hartford, and for a moment we were bricked into a five-lane traffic jam. It was just before nine, and we'd caught Hartford's endearing little version of a rush hour. Tony and the giant were both in view ahead of me, the giant in the lane to my right, and as I cinched forward a wheel-turn at a time, I nearly drew even with him. The red car was a Contour, I saw now. I was a Tracer following a Contour. As though I'd taken a pencil and followed the giant's route on a road map. My lane crept forward while his stood still, and soon I'd nearly pulled up even with him. He was chewing something, his jaw and neck pulsing, his hand now moving again to his mouth. I suppose to maintain that size he had to keep it coming. The car was probably brimful with snacks—perhaps Fujisaki paid him for his hits directly in food, so he wouldn't have to bother converting cash. They should have gotten him a bigger car, though.

I braked to keep him in front of me. Tony's lane began to slide ahead of the others and the giant merged into it without signaling, as though the Contour conveyed the authority of his brutish body. I was content to let some distance open between us, and before long Hartford's miniature jam eased. *Heartfood handfoot hoofdog horseradish* went the tinny song in my brain. I took a cue from the giant's chewing and rustled in the bag of sandwiches on the passenger seat. I groped for the hero, wanting to taste the wet crush of the Zeod's marinated peppers mixed with the spicy, leathery pepperoni.

I had the hero half devoured when I spotted Tony's black Pontiac slowing into a rest area, while the giant's Contour soared blithely past.

*   *   *

It could mean only one thing. Having reached this point behind Tony, the giant didn't need to trail him anymore. He knew where Tony was going and in fact preferred to arrive sooner, to be waiting when Tony arrived.

It wasn't Boston. Boston might be on the way, but it wasn't the destination. I'd finally put *men of peace* and *place of peace* together. I'm not so slow.

And appropriate to the manner of the evening's stakeout and the morning's chase, I still stood in relation to the giant as the giant stood to Tony. I knew where the giant was going—*a freakshow chasing a context*—I knew where they were both going. And I had reasons to want to get there soonest. I was still seeking my edge over the giant. Maybe I could poison his sushi.

*   *   *

I pulled into the next rest stop and gassed up the car, peed, and bought some ginger ale, a cup of coffee and a map of New England.

Sure enough, the diagonal across Connecticut pointed through Massachusetts and a nubbin of coastal New Hampshire to the entrance of the Maine Turnpike. I fished the "Place of Peace" brochure out of my jacket and found the place where the Turnpike left off and the brochure's rudimentary map took over, a coastal village called Musconguspoint Station. The name had a chewy, unfamiliar flavor that tantalized my syndrome. I spotted others like it on the map. Whether or not Maine's wilderness impressed me more than suburban Connecticut, the road signs would provide some nourishment.

Now I had only to take the lead in this secret interstate race. I was relying on the giant's overconfidence—he was so certain he was the pursuer he'd never stopped to wonder whether he might be pursued. Of course, I hadn't spent a lot of time looking over *my* shoulder either. I twitched the notion off with a few neck-jerks and got back in my car.

*   *   *

She answered on the second ring, her voice a little groggy.

"Kimmery."

"Lionel?"

"Yessrog."

"Where did you go?"

"I'm in—I'm almost in Massachusetts."

"What do you mean, almost? Is that like a state of mind or something, Massachusetts?"

"No, I mean almost there, literally. I'm on the highway, Kimmery. I've never been this far from New York."

She was quiet for a minute. "When you run you really run," she said.

"No, no, don't misunderstand. I had to go. This is my investigation. I'm—*invest-in-a-gun, connect-a-cop, inventachusetts—*" I mashed my tongue against the cage of my gritted teeth, trying to bottle up the flow.

Ticcing with Kimmery was especially abhorrent to me, now that I'd declared her my cure.

"You're what?"

"I'm on the giant's tail," I said, squeezing out the words. "Well, not *actually* on his tail, but I know where he's going."

"You're still looking for your giant," she said thoughtfully. "Because you feel bad about that guy Frank who got killed, is that right?"

"No. Yes."

"You make me sad, Lionel."

"Why?"

"You seem so, I don't know, guilty."

"Listen, Kimmery. I called because—*Missmebailey!*—because I missed you. I mean, I miss you."

"That's a funny thing to say. Um, Lionel?"

"Yes?"

"Did you take my keys?"

"It was part of my investigation. Forgive me."

"Okay, whatever, but I thought it was pretty creepy."

"I didn't mean anything creepy by it."

"You can't do that kind of thing. It freaks people out, you know?"

"I'm really sorry. I'll bring them back."

She was quiet again. I coursed in the fast lane with a band of other speeders, every so often slipping to the right to let an especially frantic one go by. The highway driving had begun to inspire a Tourettic fantasy, that the hoods and fenders of the cars were shoulders and collars I couldn't touch. I had to keep adequate distance so I wouldn't be tempted to try to brush up against those gleaming proxy bodies.

I hadn't seen any sign of either Tony or the giant, but I had reason to hope that Tony at least was already behind me. The giant would have to stop for gas if he hadn't, and that was when I would pass him.

"I'm going to a place you might know about," I said. "Yoshii's. A retreat."

"That's a good idea," she said grudgingly, curiosity winning over her anger. "I always wanted to go there. Roshi said it was really great."

"Maybe—"

"What?"

"Maybe sometime we'll go together."

"I should get off the phone, Lionel."

*   *   *

The call had made me anxious. I ate the second of the roast-beef sandwiches. Massachusetts looked the same as Connecticut.

I called her back.

"What did you mean by *guilty?*" I said. "I don't understand."

She sighed. "I don't know, Lionel. It's just, I'm not really sure about this *investigation*. It seems like you're just running around a lot trying to keep from feeling sad or guilty or whatever about this guy Frank."

"I want to catch the killer."

"Can't you hear yourself? That's like something O. J. Simpson would say. Regular people, when someone they know gets killed or something they don't go around trying to *catch the killer*. They go to a *funeral*."

"I'm a detective, Kimmery." I almost said, *I'm a telephone.*

"You keep saying that, but I don't know. I just can't really accept it."

"Why not?"

"I guess I thought detectives were more, uh, subtle."

"Maybe you're thinking of detectives in movies or on television." I was a fine one to be explaining this distinction. "On TV they're all the same. Real detectives are as unalike as fingerprints, or snowflakes."

"Very funny."

"I'm trying to make you laugh," I said. "I'm glad you noticed. Do you like jokes?"

"You know what *koans* are? They're like Zen jokes, except they don't really have punch lines."

"What are you waiting for? I've got all day here." In truth the highway had grown fat with extra lanes, and complicated by options and merges. But I wasn't going to interrupt Kimmery while things were going so well, ticless on my end, bubbly with digressions on hers.

"Oh, I can never remember them, they're too vague. Lots of monks hitting each other on the head and stuff."

"That sounds hilarious. The best jokes usually have animals in them, I think."

"There's plenty of animals. Here—" I heard a rustle as she braced the phone between her shoulder and chin and paged through a book. I'd had her in the middle of the big empty room—now I adjusted the picture, envisioned her with the phone stretched to reach the bed, perhaps with Shelf on her lap. "So these two monks are arguing over a cat and this other monk cuts the cat in half— Oh, that's not very nice."

"You're killing me. I'm busting a gut over here."

"Shut up. Oh, here, this is one I like. It's about death. So this young monk comes to visit this old monk to ask about this other, older monk who's just died. Tendo, that's the dead monk. So the young monk is asking about Tendo and the old monk says stuff like 'Look at that dog over there' and 'Do you want a bath?'—all this irrelevant stuff. It goes on like that until finally the young monk is enlightened."

"Enlightened by what?"

"I guess the point is you can't really say anything about death."

"Okay, I get it. It's just like in *Only Angels Have Wings,* when Cary Grant's best friend Joe crashes his plane and dies and then Rosalind Russell asks him 'What about Joe?' and "Aren't you going to do anything about Joe?' and Cary Grant just says, 'Who's Joe?'"

"Speaking of watching too much movies and television."

"Exactly." I liked the way the miles were flying past for me now, ticless, aloft on Kimmery's voice, the freeway traffic thinning.

The moment I observed the way our talk and my journey were racing along, though, we lapsed into silence.

"Roshi says this thing about guilt," she said after a minute. "That it's selfish, just a way to avoid taking care of yourself. Or thinking about yourself. I guess that's sort of two different things. I can't remember."

"Please don't quote Gerard Minna to me on the subject of guilt," I said. "That's a little hard to swallow under the present circumstances."

"You really think Roshi's guilty of something?"

"There's more I need to find out," I admitted. "That's what I'm doing. That's why I had to take your keys."

"And why you're going to Yoshii's?"

"Yes."

In the pause that followed I detected the sound of Kimmery believing me, believing in my case, for the first time.

"Be careful, Lionel."

"Sure. I'm always careful. Just keep your promise to me, okay?"

"What promise?"

"Don't go to the Zendo."

"Okay. I think I'm getting off the phone now, Lionel."

"You promise?"

"Sure, yeah, okay."

*　　*　　*

Suddenly I was surrounded by office buildings, carports, stacked overhead freeways clogged with cars. I realized too late I probably should have navigated around Boston instead of through it. I suffered through the slowdown, munched on chips and tried not to hold my breath, and before too long the city's grip loosened, gave way to suburban sprawl, to the undecorated endless interstate. I only hoped I hadn't let Tony and the giant get ahead of me, lost my lead, my edge. *Gotta have an edge.* I was beginning to obsess on *edge* too much: edge of car, edge of road, edge of vision and what hovered there, nagging and insubstantial. How strange it began to seem that cars have bodies that never are supposed to touch, a disaster if they do.

Don't hover in my blind spot, Fonebone!

I felt as though I would begin ticcing with the body of the car, would need to flirt with the textured shoulder of the highway or the darting, soaring bodies all around me unless I heard her voice again.

"Kimmery."

"Lionel."

"I called you again."

"Aren't these car-phone calls kind of expensive?"

"I'm not the one paying," I burbled. I was exhilarated by the recurrent technomagic, the cell phone reaching out across space and time to connect us again.

"Who is?"

"Some Zen doormat I met yesterday in a car."

"Doormat?"

"Doorman."

"Mmmm." She was eating something. "You call too much."

"I like talking to you. Driving is . . . boring." I undersold my angst, let the one word stand in for so many others.

"Yeah, mmmm—but I don't want anything, you know, crazy in my life right now."

"What do you mean by crazy?" Her tonal swerves had caught me by surprise again. I suppose it was this strange lurching dance, though, that kept my double brain enchanted.

"It's just— A lot of guys, you know, they tell you they understand about giving you space and stuff, they know how to talk about it and that you need to hear it. But they don't really have any idea what it means. I've been through a lot recently, Lionel."

"When did I say anything about giving you space?"

"I just mean this is a lot of calls in a pretty short period is all."

"Kimmery, listen. I'm not like other, ah, people you meet. My life is organized around certain compulsions. But it's different with you, I feel different."

"That's good, that's nice—"

"You have no idea."

"—but I'm just coming out of something pretty intense. I mean, you swept me off my feet, Lionel. You're kind of overwhelming, actually, if you don't already know. I mean, I like talking to you, too, but it isn't a good idea to call three times right after, you know, *spending the night.*"

I was silent, unsure how to decode this remarkable speech.

"What I mean is, this is exactly the kind of craziness I just got through with, Lionel."

"Which kind?"

"Like this," she said in a meek voice. "Like with you."

"Are you saying Oreo Man had *Tourette's syndrome?*" I felt a weird thrill of jealousy. She collected us freaks, I understood now. No wonder she took us in stride, no wonder she damped our symptoms. I was nothing special after all. Or rather my fistlike penis was my only claim.

"Who's Oreo Man?"

"Your old boyfriend."

"Oh. But what's the other thing you said?"

"Never mind."

We were silent for a while. My brain went, *Tourette's slipdrip stinkjet's blessdroop mutual-of-overwhelm's wild kissdoom—*

"All I mean is I'm not ready for anything too intense right now," said Kimmery. "I need space to figure out what I want. I can't be all overwhelmed and obsessed like the last time."

"I think I've heard enough about that for now."

"Okay."

"But—" I gathered myself, made a plunge into territory far stranger to me than Connecticut or Massachusetts. "I think I understand what you mean about space. About leaving it between things so you don't get too obsessed."

"Uh-huh."

"Or is that the kind of talk you don't want to hear? I guess I'm confused."

"No, it's okay. But we can talk about this later."

"Well, okay."

"Bye, Lionel."

*   *   *

Dial and redial were sitting on a fence. Dial fell off. Who was left?

Ring.

Ring.

Ring.

Click. "You've reached two-one-two, three-oh-four—"

"HellokimmeryIknowIshouldn'tbecallingbutIjust—"

Clunk. "Lionel?"

"Yes."

"Stop now."

"Uh—"

"Just stop calling now. It's way too much like some really bad things that have happened to me, can you understand? It's not romantic."

"Yes."

"Okay, bye, Lionel, for real now, okay?"

"Yes."

Redial.

"You've reached—"

"Kimmery? Kimmery? Kimmery? Are you there? Kimmery?"

*   *   *

I was my syndrome's dupe once again. Here I'd imagined I was enjoying a Touretteless morning, yet when the new manifestation appeared, it was hidden in plain sight, the Purloined Tic. Punching that redial I was exhibiting a calling-Kimmery-tic as compulsive as any rude syllable or swipe.

I wanted to hurl the doorman's cell phone out onto the grassy divider. Instead, in a haze of self-loathing, I dialed another number, one etched in memory though I hadn't called it in a while.

"Yes?" The voice was weary, encrusted with years, as I remembered it.

"Essrog?" I said.

"Yes." A pause. "This is the Essrog residence. This is Murray Essrog. Who's calling, please?"

I was a little while coming to my reply. "Eat me Bailey."

"Oh, Christ." The voice moved away from the phone. "Mother. Mother, come here. I want you to listen to this."

"Essrog Bailey," I said, almost whispering, but intent on being heard.

There was a shuffling in the background.

"It's him again, Mother," said Murray Essrog. "It's that goddamned Bailey kid. He's still out there. All these years."

I was still a kid to him, just as to me he'd been an old man since the first time I called him.

"I don't know why you care," came an older woman's voice, every word a sigh.

"Baileybailey," I said softly.

"Speak up, kid, do your thing," said the old man.

I heard the phone change hands, the old woman's breathing come onto the line.

"Essrog, Essrog, Essrog," I chanted, like a cricket trapped in a wall.

*   *   *

I'm tightly wound. I'm a loose cannon. Both—I'm a tightly wound loose cannon, a tight loose. My whole life exists in the space between those words, tight, loose, and there isn't any space there—they should be one word, tightloose. I'm an air bag in a dashboard, packed up layer upon layer in readiness for that moment when I get to explode, expand all over you, fill every available space. Unlike an airbag, though, I'm repacked the moment I've exploded, am tensed and ready again to explode—like some safety-film footage cut into a loop, all I do is compress and release, over and over, never saving or satisfying anyone, least myself. Yet the tape plays on pointlessly, obsessive air bag exploding again and again while life itself goes on elsewhere, outside the range of these antic expenditures.

*   *   *

The night before, in Kimmery's alcove, suddenly seemed very long ago, very far away.

How could phone calls—*cell-phone calls,* staticky, unlikely, free of charge—how could they alter what real bodies felt? How could ghosts touch the living?

I tried not to think about it.

*   *   *

I tossed the cell phone onto the seat beside me, into the wreckage of Zeod's sandwiches, the unfurled paper wrapping, the torn chip bag, the strewn chips and crumpled napkins gone translucent with grease stains in the midmorning sun. I wasn't eating neatly, wasn't getting anything exactly right, and now I knew it didn't matter, not today, not anymore. Having broken the disastrous flow of dialing tics, my mood had gotten hard, my attention narrow. I crossed the bridge at Portsmouth into Maine and focused everything I had left on the drive, on casting off unnecessary behaviors, thrusting exhaustion and bitterness aside and making myself into a vehicular arrow pointed at Musconguspoint Station, at the answers that lay waiting for me there. I heard Minna's voice now in place of my incessant Tourettic tongue, saying, *Floor it, Freakshow. You got something to do, do it already. Tell your story driving.*

*   *   *

Route 1 along the Maine coast was a series of touristy villages, some with boats, some with beaches, all with antiques and lobster. A large percentage of the hotels and restaurants were closed, with signs that read SEE YOU NEXT SUMMER! and HAVE A GREAT YEAR! I had trouble believing any of it was real—the turnpike had felt like a schematic, a road map, and I in my car a dot or a penpoint tracing a route. Now I felt as if I were driving through the pages of a calendar, or a collection of pictorial stamps. None of it struck me as particular or persuasive in any way. Maybe once I got out of the car.

Musconguspoint Station was one with boats. It wasn't the least of these towns, but it was close to it, a swelling on the coast distinguished more than anything by the big ferry landing, with signs for the Muscongus Island Ferry, which made the circuit twice a day. The "place of peace" wasn't hard to find. Yoshii's— MAINE'S ONLY THAI AND SUSHI OCEANFOOD EMPORIUM, according to the sign—was the largest of a neat triad of buildings on a hill just past the ferry landing and the fishing docks, all painted a queasy combination of toasted-marshmallow brown and seashell pink, smugly humble earth tones that directly violated Maine's barn-red and house-white scheme. This was one shot that wasn't making the calendar. The restaurant extended on stilts over a short cliff on the water, surf thundering below; the other two buildings, presumably the retreat center, were caged in a fussy, evenly spaced row of pine trees, all the same year and model. The sign was topped with a painted image of Yoshii, a smiling bald man with chopsticks and waves of pleasure or serenity emanating from his head like stink-lines in a Don Martin cartoon.

I put the Tracer in the restaurant lot, up on the hill overlooking the water, the fishing dock, and the ferry landing below. It was alone there except for two pickup trucks in staff spots. Yoshii's hours were painted on the door: seating for lunch began at twelve-thirty, which was twenty minutes from now. I didn't see any sign of Tony or the giant or anyone else, but I didn't want to sit in the lot and wait like a fool with a target painted on his back. An edge, that's what I was after.

Edgerog, 33, seeks Edge.

I got out of the car. First surprise: the cold. A wind that hurt my ears instantly. The air smelled like a thunderstorm but there wasn't a cloud in the sky. I went over the barrier of logs at the corner of the parking lot and clambered down the grade toward the water, under the shade of the jutting deck of the restaurant. Once I'd dipped out of sight of the road and buildings, I undid my fly and peed on the rocks, amusing my compulsiveness by staining one whole boulder a deeper gray, albeit only temporarily. It was as I zipped and turned to see the ocean that the vertigo hit me. I'd found an edge, all right. Waves, sky, trees, Essrog—I was off the page now, away from the grammar of skyscrapers and pavement. I experienced it precisely as a loss of language, a great sucking-away of the word-laden walls that I needed around me, that I touched everywhere, leaned on for support, cribbed from when I ticced aloud. Those walls of language had always been in place, I understood now, audible to me until the sky in Maine deafened them with a shout of silence. I staggered, put one hand on the rocks to steady myself. I needed to reply in some new tongue, to find a way to assert a self that had become tenuous, shrunk to a shred of Brooklyn stumbling on the coastal void: Orphan meets ocean. Jerk evaporates in salt mist.

"Freakshow!" I yelled into the swirling foam. It was lost.

"Bailey!" vanished too.

"Eat me! Dickweed!"

Nothing. What did I expect—Frank Minna to come rising from the sea?

"Essrog!" I screamed. I thought of Murray Essrog and his wife.

They were Brooklyn Essrogs, like me. Had they ever come to this edge to meet the sky? Or was I the first Essrog to put a footprint on the crust of Maine?

"I claim this big water for Essrog!" I shouted.

I was a *freak of nature*.

*   *   *

Back on the dry land of the parking lot, I straightened my jacket and peered around to see if anyone had overheard my outburst. The nearest activity was at the base of the fishing docks below, where a small boat had come in and tiny figures in Devo-style yellow jumpsuits stood handing blue plastic crates over the prow and onto a pallet on the dock. I locked the car and strolled across to the other end of the empty lot, then scooted down the scrubby hill toward the men and boats, half sliding on my pavement-walker's leather soles, wind biting at my nose and chin. The restaurant and retreat center were eclipsed by the swell of the hill as I reached the dock.

"Hey!"

I got the attention of one of the men on the dock. He turned with his crate and plopped it on the pile, then stood hands on hips waiting for me to reach him. As I got closer, I examined the boat. The blue cartons were sealed, but the boatmen hefted them as though they were heavy with something, and with enough care to make me know the something was valuable. The deck of the boat held racks covered with diving equipment—rubber suits, flippers, and masks, and a pile of tanks for breathing underwater.

"Boy, it's cold," I said, scuffing my hands together like a sports fan. "Tough day to go boating, huh?"

The boatman's eyebrows and two-day beard were bright red, but not brighter than his sun-scrubbed flesh, everywhere it showed: cheeks, nose, ears and the corroded knuckles he rubbed under his chin now as he tried to work out a response.

I heard and felt the boat's body clunking as it bobbed against the pier. My thoughts wandered to the underwater propellers, whirring silently in the water. If I were closer to the water I'd want to reach in and touch the propeller, it was so stimulating to my kinesthetic obsessions. *"Tugboat! Forgettaboat!"* I ticced, and jerked my neck, to hurl the syllables sideways into the wind.

"You're not from around here, are you?" he said carefully. I'd expected his voice to come out like Yosemite Sam's or Popeye's, scabrous and sputtering. Instead he was so stolid and patrimonial with his New England accent—*Ya nawt from around heah, ah you?*— that I was left with no doubt which of us resembled the cartoon character.

"No, actually." I affected a bright look—*Illuminate me, sir, for I am a stranger in these exotic parts!* It seemed as likely he'd shove me off the dock into the water or simply turn away as continue the conversation. I straightened my suit again, fingered my own collar so I wouldn't be tempted to finger his fluorescent hood, to crimp its Velcro edge like the rim of a piecrust.

He examined me carefully. "Urchin season runs October through March. It's cold work. Day like today is a walk in the park."

"Urchin?" I said, feeling as I said it that I'd ticced, that the word was itself a tic by definition, it was so innately twitchy. It would have made a good pronunciation for The Artist Formerly Known As Prince's glyph.

"These are urchin waters out around the island. That's the market, so that's what's fished."

"Right," I said. "Well, that's terrific. Keep it up. You know anything about the place up the hill—Yoshii's?"

"Probably you want to talk to Mr. Foible." He nodded his head at the fishing dock's small shack, from the smokestack of which piped a tiny plume of smoke. "He's the one does dealings with them Japanese. I'm just a bayman."

"Eatmebayman!"—thanks for your help." I smiled and tipped an

imaginary cap to him, and headed for the shack. He shrugged at me and received another carton off the boat.

*   *   *

"How can I help you, sir?"

Foible was red too, but in a different way. His cheeks and nose and even his brow were spiderwebbed with blossoming red veins, painful to look at. His eyes too showed veins through their yellow. As Minna used to say about the St. Mary's parish priest, Foible had *a thirsty face*. Right on the wooden counter where he sat in the shack was evidence of what the face was thirsty for: a cluster of empty long-neck beer bottles and a couple of gin quarts, one still with an inch or so to cover the bottom. A coil heater glowed under the countertop, and when I stepped inside, he nodded at the heater and the door to indicate I should shut the door behind me. Besides Foible and his heater and bottles the shack held a scarred wooden file cabinet and a few boxes of what I guessed might be hardware and fishing tackle beneath their layers of grease. In my two-day suit and stubble I was the freshest thing in the place by far.

I could see this called for the oldest investigatory technique of them all: I opened my wallet and took out a twenty. "I'd buy a guy a drink if he could tell me a few things about the Japanese," I said.

"What about 'em?" His milky eyes made intimate contact with the twenty, worked their way back up to meet mine.

"I'm interested in the restaurant up the hill. Who owns it, specifically."

"Why?"

"What if I said I wanted to buy it?" I winked and gritted through a barking tic, cut it down to a momentary "—*charp!*"

"Son, you'd never get that thing away from them. You better do your shopping elsewhere."

"What if I made them an offer they couldn't refuse?"

Foible squinted at me, suddenly suspicious. I thought of how Detective Seminole had gotten spooked by the Minna Men, our Court Street milieu. I had no idea whether such images would reverberate so far from Gotham City.

"Can I ask you something?" said Foible.

"Shoot."

"You're not one of them *Scientologists,* are you?"

"No," I said, surprised. It wasn't the impression I'd imagined I was making.

He winced deeply, as though recalling the trauma that had driven him to the bottle. "Good," he said. "Dang Scientologists bought the old hotel up the island, turned it into a funhouse for movie stars. Hell, I'll take the Japanese any day. Least they eat fish."

"*Muscongus* Island?" I'd only wanted to feel the word in my mouth at last.

"What other island would I be talking about?" He squinted at me again, then held out his hand for the twenty. "Give me that, son."

I turned it over. He laid it out on the counter and cleared his rheumy throat. "That money there says you're out of your depth here, son. Japanese yank out a roll, the smallest thing they got's a hundred. Hell, before they shut down the urchin market, this dock used to be littered with thousand-dollar bank bands from them Japanese paying off my baymen for a haul."

"Tell me about it."

"Humph."

"Eat me."

"Huh? What's that?"

"I said tell me about it. Explain about the Japanese to a guy who doesn't know."

"You know what *uni* is?"

"Forgive my ignorance."

"That's the national food of Japan, son. That's the whole story around Musconguspoint anymore, unless you count the Scientologists camped out in that damn hotel. Japanese family's got to eat uni least once a week just to maintain their self-respect. Like you'd want a steak, they want a plate of urchin eggs. Golden Week—that's like Christmas in Japan—uni's the only thing they eat. Except Japanese waters got fished out. You follow?"

"Maybe."

"The Japanese law says you can't dive for urchin anymore. All you can do is hand-rake. Means standing out on a rock at low tide with a rake in your hand. Try it sometime. Rake all day, won't get an urchin worth a damn."

If ever there was a guy who needed to *tell his story walking,* it was Foible. I stifled the urge to tell him so.

"Maine coast's got the choicest urchin on the globe, son. Clustered under the island thick as grapes. Mainers never had a taste for the stuff, lobstermen thought urchins was a pain in the ass. That Japanese law made a lot of boatmen rich up here, if they knew how to rig for a diving crew. Whole economy down Rockport way. Japanese set up processing plants, they got women down there shucking urchins day and night, fly it out the next morning. Japanese dealers come in limousines, wait for the boats to come in, bid on loads, pay in cash with wads like I said before—the money would scare you silly."

"What happened?" I gulped back tics. Foible's story was beginning to interest me.

"In Rockport? Nothing happened. Still like that. If you mean up here, we just got a couple of boats. The folks up the hill bought me out and that's that, no more cars with dark windows, no more Yakuza making deals on the dock—I don't miss it for a minute. I'm an exclusive supplier, son, and a happier man you'll never meet."

In the little shack I was surrounded by Foible's happiness, and I wasn't enthralled. I didn't mention it. "The folks up the hill," I said. "You mean Fujisaki." I figured he was deep enough in his story not to balk at my feeding him the name.

"That's correct, sir. They're a classy outfit. Got a bunch of homes on the island, redid themselves a whole restaurant, brought in a sushi cook so they could eat the way they like. Sure wish they'd outbid the Scientologists for that old hotel, though."

"Don't we all. So does Fujisaki—*Superduperist! Clientologist! Fujiopolis!*—does Fujisaki live here in Musconguspoint year-round?"

"What's that?"

"Fly-on-top-of-us!"

"You got a touch of Tourette's syndrome there, son."

"Yes," I gasped.

"You want a drink?"

"No, no. The classy outfit, do they all live up here?"

"Nope. They come and go in a bunch, always together, Tokyo, New York, London. Got a heliport on the island, go back and forth. They just rode in on the ferry this morning."

"Ah." I blinked madly in the wake of the outburst. "You run the ferry, too?"

"Nope, wouldn't want any part of that bathtub. Just a couple of boats, couple of crews. Keep my feet up, concentrate on my hobbies."

"Your other boat's out fishing?"

"Nope. Urchin-diving's an early-morning affair, son. Go out three, four in the morning, day's over by ten o'clock."

"Right, right. So where's the boat?"

"Funny you ask. Let a couple of guys take it out an hour ago, said they had to get to the island, couldn't wait for the ferry. Rented my boat and captain. They were a lot like you, thought I'd be real impressed with twenty-dollar bills."

"One of them big?"

"Biggest I ever saw."

*   *   *

My detour through the middle of Boston had cost me the lead in the race to Musconguspoint. Now it seemed silly that I'd imagined anything else. I found the red Contour and the black Pontiac in a small parking area just past the ferry landing, a tree-hidden cul-de-sac lot for day-trippers to the island, with an automated coin-fed gate and one-way exit with flexible spikes pointed at an angle and signs that warned, DON'T BACK UP! SEVERE TIRE DAMAGE! There was something I found poignant in Tony and the giant each paying to park here, fishing in their pockets for coins before enacting whatever queer struggle had led them to hire the urchin boat. I took a closer look and saw that the Contour was locked up tight, while the Pontiac's keys were in the ignition, the doors unlocked. Tony's gun, the one he'd pointed at me the day before, lay on the floor near the gas pedal. I pushed it under the seat. Maybe Tony would need it. I hoped so. I thought of how the giant had strong-armed Minna wherever he wanted him to go and felt sorry for Tony.

On my way up the hill I felt a buzz, like a bee or hornet trapped inside my pants. It was Minna's beeper. I'd set it to "vibrate" at the Zendo. I drew it out. It showed a New Jersey number. The Clients were home from Brooklyn.

In the parking lot I got into my car and found the cell phone on the seat with the sandwich wrappings, which were beginning to mature in the sun. I rang the number.

I was very tired.

"Yes?"

"It's Lionel, Mr. Matricardi. You beeped me."

"Yes. Lionel. Have you got for us what we want?"

"I'm working on it."

"Working is wonderful, honorable, admirable. Results—now those we truly cherish."

"I'll have something for you soon."

*   *   *

The interior was all inlaid burnished wood to match the exterior's toasted-marshmallow color; the carpet supplied the seashell pink.

The girl who met me just inside the door wore an elaborate Japanese robe and a dazed expression. I smoothed both sides of her collar with my hand and she seemed to take it well, perhaps as admiration for the silk. I nodded at the big windows overlooking the water and she led me to a small table there, then bowed and left me alone. I was the only customer for lunch, or the first anyway. I was starving. A sushi chef waved his broad knife at me and grinned from across the big, elegant dining room. The beveled-glass partition he worked behind made me think of the holdup-proof Plexiglas habitats for clerks in Smith Street liquor stores. I waved back, and he nodded, a sudden and ticcish bob, and I reciprocated happily. We had quite a thing going until he broke it off, to begin slicing with theatrical flair the whole skin off a slab of reddish fish.

The doors to the kitchen swung open, and Julia came out. She too wore a robe, and she wore it splendidly. It was her haircut that was a little jarring. She'd shaved her long blond hair down to military fuzz, exposing the black roots. Her face underneath the fuzz looked exposed and raw, her eyes a little wild to be without their veil. She picked up a menu and brought it to my table and halfway across the floor I saw her notice who she was bringing it to. She lost only a little something from her stride.

"Lionel."

"Pisspaw," I completed.

"I'm not going to ask you what you're doing here," she said. "I don't even want to know." She passed me the menu, the cover of which was thatched, a weave of bamboo.

"I followed Tony," I said, putting the menu gingerly aside, wary of splinters. "And the giant, the killer. We're all coming up here for a Frank Minna convention."

"That's not funny." She examined me, her mouth drawn. "You look like shit, Lionel."

"It was a long drive. I guess I should have flown into Boston and—

what's your trick, rental car? Or catch a bus? This is a regular vacation spot for you, I know that much."

"Very nice, Lionel, you're very smart. Now get lost."

"Muscongaphone! Minnabunkport!" I gritted back a whole series of Maine-geography tics that wished to follow these two through the gate of my teeth. "We really ought to talk, Julia."

"Why don't you just talk to yourself?"

"Now we're even, since that wasn't funny either."

"Where's Tony?"

"He's—*Tugboat! Tunaphone!*—he's on a boat ride." It sounded so pleasant, I didn't want to say who with. From the vantage of Yoshii's high window I could see Muscongus Island at last, wreathed in mist on the horizon.

"He should have come here," said Julia, without a trace of sentiment. She spoke as someone whose thinking had taken a very practical turn in the past day or so. "He told me to wait here for him, but I can't wait much longer. He should have come."

"Maybe he tried. I think he wants to get to Fujisaki before someone gets to him." I watched her as I dangled the theory, alert for any flinch or fire that might cross her expression.

It was flinch. She lowered her voice. "Don't say that name here, Lionel. Don't be an idiot." She looked around, but there was only the hostess and sushi chef. *Don't say that name*—the widow had inherited the dead man's superstitions.

"Who are you afraid of, Julia? Is it Fujisaki, really? Or Matricardi and Rockaforte?"

She looked at me and I saw her throat tighten and her nostrils flare.

"I'm not the one hiding from the Italians," she said. "I'm not the one who should be afraid."

"Who's hiding?"

It was one question too many. Her fury's crosshairs centered on me now, only because I was there and the person she wanted to kill was so very far away, working her by remote control.

"Screw you, Lionel. You fucking freak."

The ducks were on the pond, the monkeys were in a tree, the birds wired, the fish barreled, the pigs blanketed: However the players in this tragic fever dream ought to be typed zoologically, I had them placed together now. The problem wasn't one of tracing connections. I'd climbed into my Tracer and accomplished that. Now, though, I had to draw a single coherent line through the monkeys, ducks, fish, pigs, through monks and mooks—a line that accurately distinguished two opposed teams. I might be close.

"Will you take my order, Julia?"

"Why don't you go away, Lionel? Please." It was pitying and bitter and desperate at once. She wanted to spare us both. I had to know from what.

"I want to try some uni. Some—*orphan ocean ice cream!*—some urchin eggs. See what all the fuss is about."

"You wouldn't like it."

"Can it be done up as a sandwich of some kind? Like an uni-salad sandwich?"

"It's not a sandwich spread."

"Okay, well, then just bring me out a big bowl and a spoon. I'm really hungry, Julia."

She wasn't paying attention. The door had opened, pale sunlight flaring into the orange and pink cavern of the room. The hostess bowed, then led the Fujisaki Corporation to a long table in the middle of the room.

*   *   *

It all happened at once. There were six of them, a vision to break your heart. I was almost glad Minna was gone so he'd never have to face it, how perfectly the six middle-aged Japanese men of Fujisaki filled the image the Minna Men had always strained toward but had never reached and never would reach, in their impeccably fitted black suits and narrow ties and Wayfarer shades and upright postures, their keen, clicking shoes and shiny rings and bracelets and stoic, lipless smiles. They were all we could never be no matter how Minna pushed us: absolutely a team, a unit, their presence collective like a floating island of charisma and force. Like a floating island they nodded at the sushi chef and at Julia and even at me, then moved to their seats and folded their shades into their breast pockets and removed their beautifully creased felt hats and hooked them on the coatrack and I saw the shine of their bald heads in the orange light and I spotted the one who'd spoken of marshmallows and ghosts and bowel movements and picnics and vengeance and I knew, I knew it all, I understood everything at that moment except perhaps who Bailey was, and so of course I ticced loudly.

"I scream for ur-chin!"

*　　　*　　　*

Julia turned, startled. She'd been staring, like me, transfixed by Fujisaki's splendor. If I was right she'd never seen them before, not even in their guises as monks.

"I'll bring your order, sir," she said, recovering gracefully. I didn't bother to point out that I hadn't exactly placed an order. Her panicked eyes said she couldn't handle any banter right then. She collected the bamboo-covered menu, and I saw her hand trembling and had to restrain myself from reaching for it to comfort her and my syndrome both. She turned again and headed for the kitchen, and when she passed Fujisaki's table, she managed a brave little bow of her own.

A few members of the corporation turned and glanced at me again, ever so lightly and indifferently. I smiled and waved to embarrass them out of giving me the once-over. They went back to their conversation in Japanese, the sound of which, trickling over the carpet and polished wood in my direction, was a choral murmur, a purr.

I sat still as I could and watched as Julia reemerged to take their drink order and pass out menus. One of the suits ignored her, leaned back in his seat, and transacted directly with the sushi chef, who grunted to show comprehension. Others unfolded the spiny menu and began to grunt as well, to jabber and laugh and stab their manicured fingers at the laminated photographs of fish inside. I recalled the monks in the Zendo, the pale, saggy flesh, the scanty tufts of underarm hair that now hid behind the million-dollar tailoring. The Zendo seemed a distant and unlikely place from where I sat now. Julia went back through the kitchen doors and came out carrying a large steaming bowl and a small trivet with daubs of bright color on it. With these she threaded past Fujisaki, to my table.

"Uni," she said, nodding at the tiny block of wood. It held a thick smudge of green paste, a cluster of pink-hued shavings from a pickled beet or turnip, and a gobbet of glistening orange beads—the urchin eggs, I supposed. It wasn't three bites of food altogether. The bowl she set down was a touch more promising. The broth was milky white, its surface rippled from underneath by a thick tangle of vegetables and chunks of chicken, and decorated on top by sprigs of some sort of exotic parsley.

"I also brought you something you might actually like," she said quietly as she drew a small ceramic ladle and a pair of inlaid chopsticks out of a pouch in her robe and set them at my place. "It's Thai chicken soup. Eat it and go, Lionel. Please."

Tie-chicken-to-what? went my brain. *Tinker to Evers to Chicken.*

Julia returned to Fujisaki's table with her order pad, to contend with the corporation's contradictory barked commands, their staccato pidgin English. I sampled the uni, scraping it up in the ladle—chopsticks were not my game. The gelatinous orange beads ruptured in my mouth like capers, brackish and sharp but not impossible to like. I tried mixing the three bright colors on the wood, blobbing the tacky green paste and the shreds of pickled radish together with the eggs. The combination was something else entirely: An acrid claw of vapor sped up the back of my throat and filled my nasal cavity. Those elements were apparently not meant to be mixed. My ears popped, my eyes watered, and I made a sound like a cat with a hairball.

I'd garnered Fujisaki's attention once again, and the sushi chef's as well. I waved, face flushed bright red, and they nodded and waved back, bobbed their heads, returned to talking. I ladled up some of the soup, thinking at least to flush the poisons off the sensitive surface of my tongue. Another reverse: The broth was superb, a reply and rebuke to the toxic explosion that had preceded it. It transmitted warmth in the other direction, down into my gullet and through my chest and shoulders as it passed. Levels of flavor unfolded, onion, coconut, chicken, a piquancy I couldn't place. I scooped up another ladleful, with a strip of chicken this time, and let the nourishing fire flow through me again. Until placed in this soup's care I hadn't realized how chilled I was, how starved for comfort. It felt as if the soup were literally embracing my heart.

The trouble came with the third spoonful. I'd dredged low, come up with a tangle of unidentifiable vegetables. I drank down more of the broth, then gnawed on the mouthful of pungent roughage that was left in my mouth—only some of it was rougher than I might have liked. There was some resilient, bladelike leaf that wasn't losing the contest with my teeth, was instead beginning to triumph in an unexpected skirmish with my gums and the roof of my mouth. I chewed, waiting for it to disintegrate. It wouldn't. Julia appeared just as I'd reached in with my pinkie to clear it from my mouth.

"I think part of the menu got into the soup," I said as I ejected the bulrushes onto the table.

"That's lemongrass," said Julia. "You're not supposed to *eat* it."

"What's it doing in the soup, then?"

"Flavor. It flavors the soup."

"I can't argue with that," I said. "What's the name again?"

"Lemongrass," she hissed. She dropped a slip of paper onto the table by my hand. "Here's your check, Lionel."

I reached for her hand where it covered the slip but she pulled it away, like some version of a children's game, and all I got was the paper.

"*Lasagna ass,*" I said under my breath.

"What?"

"*Laughing Gassrog.*" This was more audible, but I hadn't disturbed Fujisaki, not yet. I looked up at her helplessly.

"Good-bye, Lionel." She hurried away from my table.

The check wasn't really a check. Julia's scrawl covered the underside:

THE FOOD IS ON THE HOUSE.

MEET ME AT FRIENDSHIP HEAD LIGHTHOUSE TWO-THIRTY.

GET OUT OF HERE!!!

*   *   *

I finished the soup, carefully putting the mysterious inedible lemongrass to one side. Then I rose from the table and went past Fujisaki toward the doors, hoping for Julia's sake to be invisible. One of them turned as I passed, though, and grabbed my elbow.

"You like the food?"

"Terrific," I said.

It was the one who as a monk had applied the paddle to my back. They'd been guzzling sake and his face was red, his eyes moist and merry.

"You Jerry-Roshi's unruly student," he said.

"I guess that's right."

"Retreat center a good idea," he said. "You need long sesshin. You got an *utterance* problem, I think."

"I know I do."

He clapped me on the shoulder, and I clapped his shoulder in return, feeling the shoulder pad in his suit, the tight seam at the sleeve. Then I tugged loose of his embrace, meaning to go, but it was too late. I had to make the rounds and touch the others. I started around the table, clapping each perfectly tailored shoulder. The men of Fujisaki seemed to take it as an encouragement to tap and poke me back while they joked with one another in Japanese. "Duck, duck, goose," I said, quietly at first. "Otter, otter, utterance."

"Otter-*duck*," said one of the men of Fujisaki, raising his eyebrows as though it were a significant correction, and elbowing me sharply.

"Monk, monk, stooge!" I said, circling the table faster, cavorting. "Weapongrass duckweed!"

"You go now," said the scowling paddle-wielder.

"Eat me Fujisaki!" I screamed, and whirled out the door.

*   *   *

The second boat had returned to the dock. I went back through Yoshii's parking lot and down the hill to have a closer look. Smoke still plumed from Foible's shack; otherwise the scene on the fishing pier was completely still. Perhaps the captain of the boat had joined Foible inside the shack for a drink from a new bottle of gin, on my twenty. Or maybe he'd just gone home to bed after a day's labor that had started at three in the morning, Urchin Daylight Savings time. I envied him if he had. I crept past the shack, to the other side of the pier. From what I could see the ferry landing was empty too, the boat itself out at the island, the ticket office closed until the late-afternoon landing. The wind was picking up off the ocean now and the whole coastal scene had a bleak, abandoned look, as though Maine in November really belonged to the ragged gulls who wheeled over the sun-worn pier, and the humans had just gotten the news and taken a powder.

It was farther on, in the tree-shrouded parking lot, that I saw something move, a sign of life. I went silently past the ferry landing to a place out of the harsh angled brightness so I could peer into the shadow and distinguish what the something was. The answer was the giant. He stood between his car and Tony's squinting in the wind and dappled sunlight and reading or at least staring at a bunch of papers in a manila folder, something out of the L&L files perhaps. In the minute that I watched he grew bored or dissatisfied with the papers and closed the file and ripped it in two, then two again, and walked across the lot to the edge where the pavement was divided from the sea by a wide margin of barnacled and beer-canned boulders. He hurled the torn quadrants of the folder in the direction of the rocks and water and the wind whipped them instantly back to flutter madly past him and disperse across the lot's gravel and into the trees. But he wasn't finished yet. There was something else in his hand, something black and small and shiny, and for a moment I thought he was making a call. Then I saw that it was a wallet. He rifled through it and moved some folding money into his own pants pocket and then he hurled the wallet, too, with more success than he'd had with the papers, so that it arced over the rocks and possibly reached the water—I couldn't tell from my perspective, and neither, I think, could the giant. He didn't appear particularly worried. Worry wasn't in his nature.

Then he turned and saw me: Laugh-or-cry Edgelost.

I ran the other way, across the ferry landing and the fishing dock, toward the hill, on top of which sat the restaurant, and my car.

*   *   *

The huff of my own exhausted breath, pounding of blood in my ears, squall of a gull and shush of the surf below—all were overtaken by the squeal of the giant's wheels: His Contour scraped into the restaurant lot just as I got my key into the ignition. His car barreled toward mine. The cliff was near enough that he might push me off. I revved into reverse and jerked my car backward out of his path and he skidded sideways to stop, nearly slamming into the nearest of the parked pickup trucks. I floored it and beat him back out of the lot, down onto Route 1, pointed south. The giant fell in right behind me. In my rearview I saw him bearing down, one hand on the wheel, the other gripping a gun.

* * *

Minna and Tony—I'd let them both be gently escorted to their quiet murderings. Mine looked to be a little noisier.

* * *

I screwed the steering wheel to the left, twitching myself off the highway toward the ferry dock. The giant wasn't fooled. He hung right on my bumper, as if the red compact were as correspondingly huge as his body and could climb over or engulf my Tracer. I veered right and left, contacting the ragged edges of the paved road to the dock in some half-symbolic finger-wagging or shooing maneuver, trying to dislodge the giant from my tail, but he matched my every vehicular gesture, Contour on Tracer now. Pavement gave way to gravel and I ground braking and sliding to the right to avoid riding straight up onto the dock and into the water. Instead I steered for the ferry's parking area, where Tony's Pontiac still sat, where the gun he hadn't gotten to use on the giant still waited under the driver's seat.

Gottagettagun, screamed my brain, and my lips moved trying to keep up with the chant: *Gottagettagun gottagettagun.*

Gun Gun Gun *Shoot!*

I'd never fired a gun.

I broke through the entrance, snapping the flimsy gate back on its post. The giant's car chewed on my bumper, the metal squeaking and sighing. Exactly how I would find breathing room enough to get out of my car and into Tony's to lay hands on the gun remained to be seen. I curled past Tony's car, to the left, opening a moment's gap

between me and my pursuer, and rode for the rock barrier. Shreds of
the torn file still fluttered here and there in the wind. Maybe the giant
would do me the favor of plummeting into the sea. Maybe he hadn't
gotten around to noticing it—since it was only the Atlantic it might
not have been big enough to make an impression.

He caught me again as I turned the other way to avoid a swim
myself, and veered with me around the outer perimeter of the lot.
DON'T BACK UP! SEVERE TIRE DAMAGE! shouted the signs at the exit,
warning of the one-way spikes meant to prevent free use of the lot.
Well, I'd gotten around that one. The giant's car made contact again,
rammed me so we both slid off to the left, toward the exit, away from
Tony's car.

Suddenly inspired, I darted for the exit.

I hit the brake as hard as I could as I passed over the flexible spikes,
came shrieking and skidding to a halt about a car's length past the
grate. The giant's car smashed against my rear end so that my car was
driven another couple of yards forward and I was slapped back
against the seat, hard. I felt something in my neck click and tasted
blood in my mouth.

The first blast was the giant's air bag inflating. In my rearview I saw
a white satin blob now filling the interior of the Contour.

The second blast was the giant's gun firing as he panicked or his
fingers clenched around the trigger in traumatic reflex. The glass of
his windshield splintered. I don't know where the shot went, but it
found some target other than my body. I shifted into reverse and
floored the gas pedal.

And plowed the giant's car backward toward the spikes.

I heard his rear tires pop, then hiss. The giant's rear end slumped,
his tires lanced on the spikes.

For a moment I heard only the hiss of escaping air, then a gull
screamed, and I made a sound to answer it, a scream of pain in the
form of a birdcall.

I shook my head, glanced in the mirror. The giant's air bag was sagging slowly, silently. Perhaps it had been pierced by the bullet. There wasn't any sign of motion underneath.

I shifted into first, swerved forward and left, then reversed into the giant's car again, crumpling the metal along the driver's-side door, deforming the contour of the Contour, wrinkling it like foil, hearing it creak and groan at being reshaped.

I might have stopped then. I believed the giant was unconscious under the air bag. He was at least silent and still, not firing his gun, not struggling to free himself.

But I felt the wild call of symmetry: His car ought to be crumpled on both sides. I needed to maul both of the Contour's shoulders. I rolled forward and into position, then backed and crashed against his car once more, wrecking it on the passenger side as I had on the driver's.

It's a Tourette's thing—you wouldn't understand.

*   *   *

I moved the map and cell phone to Tony's Pontiac. The keys were still in the ignition. I drove it out of the lot through the smashed entrance gate, and steered past the vacant ferry landing, up to Route 1. Apparently no one had heard the collisions or gunshot in the lot by the sea. Foible hadn't even poked out of his shack.

Friendship Head was an outcropping on the coast twelve miles north of Musconguspoint Station. The lighthouse was painted red and white, no atrocity of Buddhist earth tones like the restaurant. I trusted that the Scientologists hadn't gotten to it either. I parked the Pontiac as close to the water as I could and sat staring out for a while, feeling the place where I'd bitten my tongue slowly seal and testing out the damage to my neck. Free movement of my neck was crucial to my Tourettic career. I was like an athlete in that regard. But it felt like whiplash, nothing worse. I was chilled and tired, the replenishing effects of the lemongrass broth long since gone, and I could still feel my head throb in the place the giant had clubbed it twenty-four hours and a million years ago. But I was alive, and the water looked pretty good as the angle of the light grew steeper. I was half an hour early for my date with Julia.

I dialed the local police and told them about the sleeping giant they'd find back at the Muscongus Island ferry.

"He might be in bad shape but I think he's still alive," I told them. "You'll probably need the Jaws of Life to pull him out."

"Can you give us your name, sir?"

"No, I really can't," I said. They'd never know how true it was. "My name doesn't matter. You'll find the wallet of the man he killed in the water near the ferry. The body's more likely to wash up on the island."

*   *   *

Is guilt a species of Tourette's? Maybe. It has a touchy quality, I think, a hint of sweaty fingers. Guilt wants to cover all the bases, be everywhere at once, reach into the past to tweak, neaten, and repair. Guilt like Tourettic utterance flows uselessly, inelegantly from one helpless human to another, contemptuous of perimeters, doomed to be mistaken or refused on delivery.

Guilt, like Tourette's, tries again, learns nothing.

And the guilty soul, like the Tourettic, wears a kind of clown face—the Smokey Robinson kind, with tear tracks underneath.

*   *   *

I called the New Jersey number.

"Tony's dead," I told them.

"This is a terrible thing—" Matricardi started.

"Yeah, yeah, terrible," I said, interrupting. I was in no mood. Really no mood at all. The minute I heard Matricardi's voice, I was something worse or less than human, not simply sorrowful or angry or ticcish or lonely, certainly not moody at all, but raging with purpose. I was an arrow to pierce through years. "Listen carefully to me now," I said. "Frank and Tony are gone."

"Yes," said Matricardi, already seeming to understand.

"I've got something you want and then that's the end of it."

"Yes."

"That's the end of it, we're not bound to you any longer."

"Who is we? Who is speaking?"

"L and L."

"There's a meaning to saying L and L when Frank is departed, and now Tony? What is it to speak of L and L?"

"That's our business."

"So what is this thing you have we want?"

"Gerard Minna lives on East Eighty-fourth Street, in a Zendo. Under another name. He's responsible for Frank's death."

"Zendo?"

"A Japanese church."

There was a long silence.

"This is not what we expected from you, Lionel."

I didn't speak.

"But you are correct that it is of interest to us."

I didn't speak.

"We will respect your wishes."

* * *

Guilt I knew something about. Vengeance was another story entirely.

I'd have to think about vengeance.

FORMERLY KNOWN

There once was a girl from Nantucket.

No, really, that's where she was from.

Her mother and father were hippies and so she was a little hippie child. Her father wasn't always there on Nantucket with the family. When he was there he didn't stay long, and over time the visits grew both briefer and less frequent.

The girl used to listen to tapes her father would leave behind, the Alan Watts Lecture Series, an introduction to Eastern thought for Americans in the form of a series of rambling, humorous monologues. After the girl's father stopped coming at all, the girl would confuse her memories of her father with the charming man whose voice she heard on the tapes.

When the girl got older she sorted this out, but she'd listened to Alan Watts hundreds of times by then.

When the girl turned eighteen she went to college in Boston, to an art school that was part of a museum. She hated the school and the other students there, hated pretending she was an artist, and after two years she dropped out.

First she went back to Nantucket for a little while, but the girl's mother had moved in with a man the girl didn't like, and Nantucket is, after all, an island. So she went back to Boston. There she found a lousy job as a waitress in a student dive, where she had to fend off an endless series of advances from customers and co-workers. At night she'd take yoga classes and attend Zen meetings in the basement of a local YWCA, where she had to fend off an endless series of advances from instructors and other students. The girl decided she didn't hate only school, she hated Boston.

A year or so later she visited a Zen retreat center on the coast of Maine. It was a place of striking beauty and, apart from the frantic summer months when the town became a resort for wealthy Bostonians and New Yorkers, splendid isolation. It reminded her of Nantucket, the things she missed there. She quickly arranged to study at the center full-time, and to support herself she took a job waitressing at the seafood restaurant next door, which at that time was a traditional Maine lobster pound.

It was there the girl met the two brothers.

The older brother first, during a series of short visits to the retreat with his friend. The friend had some experience with Buddhism, the older brother none, but they were both a disconcerting presence there in placid Maine—vibrant with impatience and a hostile sort of urban humor, yet humble and sincere in their fledgling approach to Zen practice. The older brother was solicitous and flattering to the girl when they were introduced. He was a talker like none she'd never met, except perhaps on the Alan Watts lecture tapes, which still shaped her yearnings so powerfully—but the older brother was no Watts. His stories were of ethnic Brooklyn, of petty mobsters and comic scams, and some of them had a violent finish. With his talk he made this world seem as near and real to her as it was actually distant.

In some way Brooklyn, where she'd never been, became a romantic ideal, something truer and finer than the city life she'd glimpsed in Boston.

The girl and the older brother were lovers after a while.

The older brother's visits grew both briefer and less frequent.

Then one day the older brother returned, in an Impala filled with paper shopping bags stuffed full of his clothes and with his younger brother in tow. After a sizable donation to the Zen center's petty-cash fund the two men moved into rooms in the retreat center, rooms that were out of sight of the coastal highway. The next day the older brother drove the Impala off and returned with a pickup truck, with Maine plates.

Now whenever the girl tried to visit the older brother in his room, he turned her away. This persisted for a few weeks before she began to accept the change. The lovemaking and talk of Brooklyn were over between them. It was only then that the younger brother came into focus for the girl.

The younger brother wasn't a student of Zen. He'd also never been out of New York City until his arrival in Maine, and it was a destination as mysterious and absurd to him as he was mysterious and absurd to her. To the girl the younger brother seemed an embodiment of the stories of Brooklyn the older brother had entranced her with. He was a talker, too, but rootless, chaotic in the stories he told. His talk entirely lacked the posture of distance and bemusement, the gloss of Zen perspective that characterized the older brother's tales. Instead, though they sat together on the Maine beaches, huddling together in the wind, he seemed still to inhabit the streets he described.

The older brother read Krishnamurti and Watts and Trungpa, while the younger read Spillane and Chandler and Ross MacDonald, often aloud to the girl, and it was in the MacDonald especially that the girl heard something that taught her about a part of herself not covered by Nantucket or Zen or the bit she'd learned in college.

The younger brother and the girl became lovers after a while.

And the younger brother did what the older would never have done: He explained to the girl the situation that had driven the two brothers out of Brooklyn, to come and seek refuge in the Zen center. The brothers had been acting as liaisons between two aging Brooklyn mobsters and a group of suburban Westchester and New Jersey bandits who hijacked trucks on small highways into New York City. The aging mobsters were in the business of redistributing the goods seized by the truck pirates, and it was a business that was profitable for everyone associated with it. The brothers had made it more profitable for themselves than they should have, though. They found a place to warehouse a percentage of the goods, and a fence to take the goods off their hands. When the two mobsters discovered the betrayal, they decided to kill the brothers.

Hence, Maine.

The younger brother did another thing his older brother might never have done: He fell in love with the strange angry girl from Nantucket. And one day in the flush of this love he explained to her his great dream: He was going to open a detective agency.

The older brother in the meantime had grown distant from them both, and more deeply and sincerely involved in Zen practice. In the manner of so many spiritual practitioners past and present he seemed to draw away from the world of material concerns, to grow tolerant and wry but also a little chilly in his regard for the people and things he'd left behind.

When the younger brother and the girl were away from the retreat center they'd refer to the older brother as "Rama-lama-ding-dong." Before too long they even began to call him that to his face.

One day the younger brother tried to telephone his mother and found that she'd been taken to the hospital. He conferred with his older brother; the girl overheard some of their bitter, fearful conversations. The older brother was persuaded that their mother's hospitalization had been arranged as a trap to lure them back to Brooklyn for their punishment. The younger disagreed. The next day he bought a car and loaded it with his belongings, and announced he was going back to the city. He invited the girl to join him, though he warned her of the possible danger.

She considered her life at the retreat, which had grown as close and predictable around her as an island, and she considered the younger brother and the prospect of Brooklyn, his Brooklyn, of living there by his side. She agreed to leave Maine.

On the way they were married in Albany, by a justice of the peace at the state capital. The younger brother wanted to surprise and please his mother, and perhaps also wished to offer some excuse for his long disappearance. He took the girl shopping for clothes in Manhattan before they crossed the famous bridge into Brooklyn, and then, as an afterthought, he brought her to a salon on Montague Street, where they bleached her dark hair to platinum blond. It was as though she were the one who should be in disguise here.

The mother's sickness wasn't a trap. She was dead of a stroke by the time the younger brother and his new wife reached the hospital. But it was also true that the mobsters were aware of everything that happened in the neighborhood and were watching the hospital closely. When the younger brother was spotted there, it wasn't long before he was brought in to answer for his and his brother's misdeeds.

He begged for his life. He explained that he'd just gotten married.

He also blamed his brother for the crimes they'd both committed. He claimed to have lost touch with his brother completely.

He ended by promising to spend his life in service as the gangsters' errand boy.

On that condition his apology was accepted by the gangsters. They permitted him to live, though they swore again a vow of death against the older brother, and made the younger promise that he'd turn his brother in if and when he reappeared.

The younger brother moved his new wife into his mother's old apartment and the woman from Nantucket began her adjustment to life in Brooklyn. What she encountered was first intoxicating and frightening, then disenchanting. Her husband was a small-time operator, his "agents," as he called them, a motley gang of high-school-dropout orphans. For a while he installed her as a secretary in a friend's law office, where she worked as a notary public, humiliatingly on view in a shop window out on Court Street. When she protested, he allowed her to recede into privacy in the apartment. The old gangsters paid the couple's rent anyway, and most of the younger brother's detective work was on their behalf. The woman from Nantucket didn't like what passed for detective work in Brooklyn. She wished he genuinely ran a car service. Their married life was chilly and glancing, full of unexplained absences and omissions, no walk on the beach. In time she began to understand that there were other women, too, old high-school girlfriends and distant cousins who'd never left the neighborhood and never really been very far from the younger brother's bed either.

The woman from Nantucket survived, found occasional lovers herself, and spent most of her days in the movie theaters on Court and Henry streets, shopping in Brooklyn Heights, drinking in the hotel lobbies there and then taking slow walks on the Promenade, where she fended off an endless series of advances from college boys and lunch-hour husbands, spent her days any way except musing on the serene rural life she'd left behind in Maine, the faint uncontroversial satisfactions she'd known before she'd met the two brothers and been taken to Brooklyn.

One day the younger brother told his wife a dire secret, which she had to be sure to keep from leaking to anyone in Brooklyn, lest it reach the ears of the gangsters: The older brother had returned to New York City. He'd declared himself a roshi, an elder teacher of Zen, and started a Zendo on the Upper East Side of Manhattan, in Yorkville. This Yorkville Zendo was subsidized by a powerful group of Japanese businessmen he'd met in Maine, where they'd taken over and renovated top to bottom the homely Zen center and the lobster pound next door: the Fujisaki Corporation.

The men of Fujisaki were highly spiritual, but had found themselves in disrepute in their native country, where monkhood is reserved only for those born into certain esteemed bloodlines, and where capitalistic rapaciousness and spiritual devotion are viewed as mutually exclusive. Money and power, it seemed, couldn't buy Fujisaki the precise sort of respect its members craved at home. Here, first in Maine, now in New York City, they would make themselves credible as penitents and teachers, men of wisdom and peace. In the process, as the older brother explained to the younger, the younger then to his wife, the men of Fujisaki and the older brother hoped to do a little "business." New York City: land of opportunity for monks and crooks and mooks alike.

*   *   *

We stood at the rail at the sea edge of the lighthouse tower, looking out. The wind was still strong, but I was used to it now. I had my collar up, the way Frank Minna would. The sky out past the island was gray and uninspiring, but there was a nice line of light where it met the water, an edge I could work with my eyes like a seam of stitching between my fingers. The birds harassed the foam below, looking for urchin, perhaps, or discarded hot-dog ends among the rocks.

I had Tony's gun in my jacket, and from this vantage we could see for miles down Route 1 in both directions should anyone approach. I had a strong urge to protect Julia, to hold her or cover her with my presence, so as to feel that I'd helped someone safely through besides myself. But I doubted that the Fujisaki Corporation cared about me or Julia directly. She and I each had been part of Gerard Minna's problem, not Fujisaki's. And Julia showed no interest in my protective urges.

"I know what happened next," I told her. "Eventually the brothers dipped into the till again. Frank got involved in a scam to siphon money away from Fujisaki's management company." That part of what Gerard told me wasn't a lie, I understood now, just an artfully mangled version of the truth. Gerard had been leaving himself out of it, playing the Zen innocent, when in fact he was the wheel's hub. "With a bookkeeper named—*Dullbody, Allmoney, Alimony*—ah, a guy named Ullman."

"Yes," said Julia.

She'd been talking in a kind of trance, not needing me to prompt her more than once in a while. As the narrative got nearer the present day her eyes grew clearer, her gaze less transfixed on the distant island, and her voice grew heavier with resentment. I felt I was losing her to bitterness, and I wanted to draw her back. Protect her from herself if there was no other threat.

"So Frank was hiding the secret of his brother's existence from The Clients," I said. "Meanwhile the two of them are running a number on Gerard's Japanese partners. And then the deal goes—*lemongrass, sourball, fuckitall!*" I was unable to continue until I made a farting, fricative sound into the wind—"blew a raspberry," in the parlance—to satisfy the expulsive tic. Bits of saliva spattered back into my face. "Then Fujisaki figured out someone was taking their money," I said finally, wiping at myself with my sleeve.

She looked at me with disgust. I'd drawn her back, in a way. "Yes," she said.

"And Gerard fingered—*Mr. Fingerphone! Uncle Sourgrass!*—Gerard fingered Frank and Ullman to save himself."

"That's what Tony thought," she said, distant again.

"Fujisaki must have told Gerard to take care of it, as a show of good faith. So Gerard hired the killer."

Which was where I, innocent stooge, had walked into the story. Frank Minna had installed me and Gilbert there outside the Zendo two days before because he smelled a rat, didn't trust Gerard, and wanted some backup on the street. Warm bodies. If something went wrong he'd bring me and Gilbert up to speed, let us in on the scam, or so he must have thought. And if things went smoothly, it was better to keep us where we'd always been, were born to be—in the dark.

"You know more about it than me," said Julia. She grew agitated now, her storyteller's reverie dissipated, the talk turning to a killer's hiring and all that went with it unsaid. I had to turn away myself now, imitate her pensive searching of the horizon, though my fingers danced idiotically on the lighthouse tower rail, counting one-two-three-four-five, one-two-three-four-five. I'd grown more accustomed to her short new haircut, but those eyes of hers had blazed so long from behind a curtain of hair that without that curtain they blazed too hard. I was drawn and repelled at once, antic with ambivalence. Now I understood that when Frank showed her to us at the end of high school, she was only five or six years older than we were, though it seemed he'd plucked a woman off a fading movie poster. How Nantucket and Buddhism could have made her so old and fierce, I couldn't fathom. I suppose Frank himself had made her old in a hurry, in ways he'd intended, with panty hose and peroxide and sarcasm—and ways he hadn't.

"Let me work out the next part," I said. I felt as if I were trying to get through a joke without ticcing, but there wasn't a punch line in sight. "After Frank and Ullman were gone, Gerard had to make sure he eliminated any link between himself and Frank Minna. That meant you and Tony."

Gerard, I surmised, had been in a panic, afraid of Fujisaki and The Clients both. By having his brother killed he'd damaged a delicate system of controls, one that had kept him safe from Matricardi and Rockaforte for more than a decade. And Fujisaki had announced a visit to New York to inspect their holdings, to enact a little hands-on management (albeit disguised as monks), right as Gerard was frantically trying to mop up the mess. Perhaps they'd also wanted to see Gerard mop up the mess, wanted to feel him squirm a little.

Gerard had reasoned rightly that if Frank confided in anyone it would be his wife and his right-hand man, his groomed successor. Which was to say, Tony. This last part still came a little hard for me. That Tony had paid with his life for being Frank's intimate was a lousy excuse for consolation.

"It was Gerard who called to say that Frank was dead," I suggested. "Not the hospital."

She turned and looked at me with her teeth gritted, tears making glossy tracks on her face. "Very good, Lionel," she whispered. I reached for her cheeks to blot her tears with my sleeve, but she darted back, uninterested in my care.

"But you didn't trust him, so you ran."

"Don't be an idiot, Lionel," she said, her voice vibrant with hate. "Why would I come here if I were hiding from *Gerard*?"

"*Idiot Dressfork! Alphabet Tuningfreak!*" I cleared the tic with a jerk of my stiff neck. "I don't understand," I told her.

"He arranged for me to use this as a safe house. He said the people who killed Frank were looking for the rest of us. I trusted him."

I began to see. Lucius Seminole had said that Julia's records showed a series of visits to Boston. "This was your hideaway when you got angry at Frank," I suggested. "Your retreat into the past."

"I wasn't hiding."

"Did Frank know that you and Gerard were in touch?"

"He didn't care."

"Were you and Gerard still lovers?"

"Only when his . . . *spiritual path* allowed it." She spat the words. The tears had dried on her face.

"When did you figure out the truth?"

"I called Tony. We compared notes. Gerard underestimated what Tony knew."

What Tony knew was the least of it, I thought. Tony meant to take over Frank Minna's share of the Fujisaki scam, not knowing that nothing remained to take over. He wanted that and much more. As I ached always to be a virtuous detective, Tony ached to be a corrupt one, or even to be an out-and-out wiseguy. He'd been fitting himself for the darkest shoes in Frank Minna's wardrobe from the moment he learned they existed, perhaps on that day when we unloaded the guitars and amplifiers and were introduced to Matricardi and Rockaforte, perhaps even sooner, on some uglier errand only he and Frank knew about. Certainly he understood by the time Frank's van windows had been smashed. His special glee that day was at having his Mafioso fantasies confirmed, as well as at seeing Frank Minna's vulnerability for the first time. If Frank's fortunes could rise and fall, that episode said, then power was fluid, and so Tony might someday have a share of it himself. The moment Frank was dead Tony envisioned himself playing Frank on both stages, for The Clients in Brooklyn and for Gerard and the Fujisaki Corporation up in Yorkville, only playing the part with greater efficiency and brutality, without Frank Minna's goofy edges, those soft places that caused him to collect freaks like me or that finally led him astray.

Gerard's picture of Tony was another part of that convoluted after-hours story that hadn't been entirely a lie. I suppose Gerard couldn't be the many things he was without knowing how to x-ray a mind like Tony's at a single glance.

"You and Tony compared more than notes, Julia." I regretted it the minute I said it.

She looked at me with pity now.

"So I fucked him." She took out a cigarette and lighter from her purse. "I fucked a lot of guys, Lionel. I fucked Tony and Danny, even Gilbert once. Everyone except you. It's no big deal." She put the cigarette in her lips and cupped her hands against the wind.

"Maybe it was to Tony," I said, and regretted it even worse.

She only shrugged, worked the lighter uselessly again and again. Cars whirred past on the highway below, but nobody stopped at the lighthouse. We were alone in our torment and shame, and useless to each other.

It might not have been a big deal to Julia that she fucked the Minna Men, the Minna Boys, really, and maybe it was no big deal to Tony either—but I doubted it. *You were the original woman,* I wanted to tell her. When Minna brought you home to us we tried to learn what it meant for Frank to marry, we studied you to understand what a Minna Woman might be, and saw only rage—rage I now understood had concealed disappointment and fear, oceans of fear. We had watched women and letters soar past before, but you were the first that was addressed to us, and we tried to understand you. And we loved you.

I needed to rescue Julia now, retrieve her from this lighthouse and the bareness of her story against the Maine sky. I needed her to see that we were the same, disappointed lovers of Frank Minna, abandoned children.

"We're almost the same age, Julia," I said lamely. "I mean, you and me, we were teenagers at pretty much the same time."

She looked at me blankly.

"I met a woman, Julia. Because of this case. She's like you in certain ways. She studies Zen, just like you did when you met Frank."

"No woman will ever want you, Lionel."

"WantmeBailey!"

It was a classic tic, honest and clean. Nothing about Maine or Julia Minna or my profound exhaustion could get in the way of a good, clean, throat-wrenching tic. My maker in his infinite wisdom had provided me with that.

I tried not to listen to what Julia was saying, to focus on the far-off squalling of gulls and splash of surf instead.

"That's not really true," she went on. "They might want you. I've wanted you a little bit myself. But they'll never be fair to you, Lionel. Because you're such a freak."

"This person is different," I said. "She's different from anyone I've ever met." But now I was losing my point. If I made the distinction between Julia and Kimmery plain to Julia, to myself—*she's not as mean as you, could never be so mean*—I would only be sorry I'd spoken at all.

"Well, I bet you're different for her, too. I'm sure you'll be very happy together." In her mouth the words *happy together* came out twisted and harsh.

Crappy however.

Slappy forget her.

I wanted to call Kimmery now, wanted to so badly my fingers located the cell phone in my jacket pocket and began to fondle it.

"Why was Tony coming to Maine?" I asked, running for cover back to the plot we'd begun spinning together, which suddenly seemed to have little or nothing to do with our miserable fates, our miserable lives exposed out here in the wind. "Why didn't you just get away from here? You knew Gerard might kill you."

"I heard Fujisaki was flying up here today." Again she struck with the lighter against her cigarette, as if it were going to ignite like a flint against a rock. It wasn't just the wind she was fighting now. Her hands trembled, and the cigarette trembled where she held it in her lips. "Tony and I were going to tell them about Gerard. He was going to bring some proof. Then you got in the way."

"It wasn't me that stopped Tony from keeping the date." I was distracted by the phone in my pocket, the prospect of Kimmery's soothing voice, even if it were only the outgoing message on her machine. "Gerard sent his giant after Tony," I went on. "He followed Tony up here, maybe figuring to take out two birds with one flick of his big finger."

"Gerard didn't want me killed," she said quietly. Her hands had fallen to her sides. "He wanted me back." She was trying to make it so by saying it, but the words themselves were nearly lost in the wind. Julia threatened to recede into the distance again, and this time I knew I wouldn't bother trying to bring her back.

"Is that why he had his brother killed? Jealousy?"

"Does it have to be one thing? He probably figured it was him or Frank." The cigarette still dangled in her mouth. "Fujisaki required a sacrifice. They're great believers in that."

"Did you talk to Fujisaki just now?"

"Men like that don't cut deals with waitresses, Lionel."

"It's rotten for Tony the killer found him before he found Fujisaki," I said. "But it won't save Gerard. I made sure of that." I didn't want to elaborate.

"So you say." She paced away from the railing, gripping the lighter so tightly I expected her to crush it.

"What's that supposed to mean?"

"Just that I'm not acquainted with this giant killer you keep talking about. Are you sure you're not imagining things?" She turned and handed me the lighter, plucked the cigarette from her lips and held it out. "Would you light this for me, Lionel?" I heard a weird vibration in her voice, as though she were about to cry again, but without the anger this time, maybe begin to mourn Minna at last. I took them away from her, put the cigarette in my own lips, and turned my back to the wind.

By the time I had it lit she'd taken her gun from her purse.

*   *   *

I put up my hands instinctively, dropping the lighter, to make a pose of surrender but also of self-protection, as though I might deflect a bullet with Frank's watch like Wonder Woman with her magic wristbands. Julia held the gun easily, its muzzle directed at my navel, and now her eyes were as gray and hard to read as the farthest reaches of the Maine horizon.

I felt jets of acid fire in the pit of my stomach. I wondered if I would ever get used to facing gunpoint, and then I wondered if that was really anything to aspire to. I wanted to tic just for the hell of it, but at the moment I couldn't think of anything.

"I just remembered something Frank once said about you, Lionel."

"What's that?" I slowly lowered one hand and offered her the lit cigarette, but she shook her head. I dropped it on the lighthouse deck and ground it under my shoe instead.

"He said the reason you were useful to him was because you were crazy everyone thought you were stupid."

"I'm familiar with the theory."

"I think I made the same mistake," she said. "And so did Tony, and Frank before that. Everywhere you go, somebody who Gerard wants dead is made dead. I don't want to be next."

"You think I killed Frank?"

"You said we're the same age, Lionel. You ever watch *Sesame Street*?" she said.

"Sure."

"You remember the Snuffleupagus?"

"Big Bird's friend."

"Right, only nobody could see him except Big Bird. I think the giant's your Snuffleupagus, Lionel."

"*Shockadopalus! Fuckalotofus!* The giant is real, Julia. Put the gun away."

"I don't think so. Step back, Lionel."

I stepped back, but I pulled out Tony's gun as I did it. I saw Julia's fingers tighten as I raised it to her, but she didn't fire, and neither did I.

We faced one another on the lighthouse rail, the vast sky dimming everywhere and perfectly useless to us, the ocean's depths useless, too. The two guns drew us close together and rendered the rest irrelevant—we might as well have been in a dingy motel room, with an image of Maine playing on the television set. My moment had come at last. I had a gun in my hands. That it was trained not on Gerard or the giant or Tony or a doorman but on the girl from Nantucket who'd grown into Frank Minna's bruise-eyed widow, who'd chopped off her hair and tried to retreat to her waitress past and instead been cornered by that same past, by Gerard and the giant and Tony—I tried not to let it bother me. I'd been wrong, Julia and I had nothing in common. We were just any two people who happened to be pointing guns at one another now. And Tony's gun had object properties all its own, not a fork nor a toothbrush but something much weightier and more seductive. I slipped off the safety with my thumb.

"I understand your mistake, Julia, but I'm not the killer."

She had both hands on the gun, and it didn't waver. "Why should I trust you?"

"TRUST ME BAILEY!" I had to scream it into the sky. I turned my head, bargaining with my Tourette's that I could let the one phrase fly and then be done. I tasted salt air as I screamed.

"Don't scare me, Lionel. I might shoot you."

"We've both got that same problem, Julia." In fact my syndrome had just discovered the prospect of the gun, and I began to obsess on pulling the trigger. I suspected that if I fired a shot out into the sky in the manner of my verbal exclamation, I might not survive the experience. But I didn't want to shoot Julia. I flicked on the safety, hoped she didn't notice.

"Where do we go from here?" she said.

"We go home, Julia," I said. "I'm sorry about Frank and Tony, but the story's over. You and me, we made it through alive."

It was only a slight exaggeration. The story would be over at some secret moment in the next few hours or days when something found Gerard Minna, a bullet or blade that had been searching for him for almost twenty years.

Meanwhile, I flicked the safety back and forth, impelled, counting. At five I stopped, temporarily satisfied. That left the safety off, the gun ready to shoot. My fingers were unbearably curious about the trigger's action, its resistance and weight.

"Where's your home, Lionel? Upstairs from L and L?"

"Saint Vengeance Home for Bailey," I ticced.

"Is that what you call it?" said Julia.

Before my finger could pulse on the trigger the way it craved to I flung the gun out toward the ocean with all the force of my over-wound-watchspring body. It sailed out past the rocks, but the tiny splash of its disappearance into the sea was lost in the wind and the ambient crash of the surf.

One, I counted.

Before Julia could calculate the meaning of my action I darted as if for an elusive shoulder and grabbed the muzzle of her gun, then twisted it out of her hand and hurled with all the strength in my legs, like a center fielder deep at the wall straining for a distant cutoff man. Julia's gun went farther than Tony's, out to where the waves that would reach the rocks were just taking shape, the sea curling, discovering its form.

That made *two.*

"Don't hurt me, Lionel." She backed away, her shocked eyes framed by the bristly halo of her crew cut, her mouth crooked with fear and fury.

"It's over, Julia. Nobody's going to hurt you." I couldn't concentrate on her fully, needing something more to throw into the sea. I pulled Minna's beeper out of my pocket. It was a tool of The Clients, evidence of their hold on Frank, and it deserved to be interred with the guns. I threw it as far as I could, but it didn't have enough heft to keep from being knocked down by the wind, and so trickled down between two wet, mossy boulders.

Three.

Next I found the cell phone. The instant it came into my hand, Kimmery's number begged for dialing. I pushed the impulse aside, substituted the gratification of flinging it off the lighthouse deck, picturing the doormen in the rental car who I'd taken it from. It flew truer than the beeper, made it out to the water.

Four.

"Give me something to throw," I told Julia.

"What?"

"I need something, one more thing."

"You're crazy."

I considered Frank's watch. I was sentimental about the watch. It had no taint of doormen or Clients.

"Give me something," I said again. "Look in your purse."

"Go to hell, Lionel."

Julia had always been the hardest-boiled of us all, it struck me now. We who were from Brooklyn, we jerks from nowhere—or from somewhere, in the case of Frank and Gerard. We couldn't hold a candle to the girl from Nantucket and I thought I might finally understand why. She was the hardest-boiled because she was the unhappiest. She was maybe the unhappiest person I'd ever met.

I suppose losing Frank Minna, hard as it was, was easier for those of us who'd actually had him, actually felt his love. The thing Julia lost she'd never possessed in the first place.

But her pain was no longer my concern.

You choose your battles, Frank Minna used to say, though the term was hardly original to him.

You also distance yourself from cruelty, if you have any brains. I was developing a few.

I took off my right shoe, felt the polished leather that had served me well, the fine stitching and the fraying lace, kissed it good-bye on the top of the tongue, then threw it high and far and watched it splash silently into the waves.

Five, I thought.

But who's counting?

"Good-bye, Julia," I said.

"Screw you, you maniac." She knelt and picked up her lighter, and this time she got her cigarette lit on the first flick.

"Barnabaileyscrewjuliaminna."

It was my final word on the subject.

So I drove with my gas-pedal-and-brake foot clad only in a dress sock, back to Brooklyn.

GOOD SANDWICHES

Then somewhere, sometime, a circuit closed. It was a secret from me, but I knew the secret existed. A man—two men?—found another man. Lifted an instrument, gun, knife? Say gun. Did a job. Took care of a job. Collected a debt of life. This was the finishing of something between two brothers, a transaction of brotherly love-hate, something playing out, a dark, wobbly melody. The notes of the melody had been other people, boys–turned–Minna Men, mobsters, monks, doormen. And women, one woman especially. We'd all been notes in the melody, but the point of the song was the brothers, and the payoff, the last note struck—a scream? a bloody beat? a bare interrupted moan?—or not even a moan, perhaps. In my guilt I'd like to think so. Let it finish in silence. Let it be, then, that Rama-lama-ding-dong died in his sleep.

*　　*　　*

We sat together in the L&L storefront at two in the morning, playing poker on the counter, listening to Boyz 2 Men, courtesy of Danny.

Now that Frank and Tony were gone, Danny could play the sort of music he liked. It was one of a number of changes.

"One card," said Gilbert. I was the dealer, so I slid his discard toward me and offered him a fresh selection from the top of the deck.

"Jesus, Gil," said the ex–Garbage Cop. He was a driver now, a part of the new L&L. "You're always *one card* or *no cards*—why can't I get dealt anything but crap?"

"That's 'cause you're still in charge of garbage, Loomis," said Gilbert happily. "Even though you quit the force, doesn't matter. Someone's gotta handle it."

"Handle with garbagecrap!" I declared as I dealt myself three new cards.

Gilbert had been released two weeks before, after five nights in the lockup, for want of evidence in Ullman's killing. Detective Seminole had called us to apologize, excessively sheepish, I thought, as though he were still a little afraid. Gilbert's size and manner had carried him through the ordeal pretty well, though he came out short a wristwatch and had involuntarily given up smoking during his stay, having been connived out of every cigarette on his person. He was making up for it now in cigarettes, and in beer and coffee and Sno Balls and White Castles and Zeod's pastrami heroes, but no flow of indulgences could be constant enough to stem his complaints at how we'd abandoned him. Fortunately he was winning hands tonight.

Danny sat apart from the three of us, silent, eyebrows raised slightly between his poker hand and his new fedora. He sat a little farther apart and dressed a little sharper each passing night, or so it seemed to me. Leadership of L&L had fallen to him like an easy rebound, one he didn't even have to jump for, while the other players boxed and elbowed and sweated on the wrong part of the floor. What Danny knew or didn't know about Gerard and Fujisaki was never said. He took my account of the events in Maine and nodded once, and we were done speaking of it. It turned out it was that simple. Want to be the new Frank Minna? Dress the part, and shut up, and wait. Court Street will know you when it sees you. Zeod will put the tab in your name. Gilbert and Loomis and I couldn't have argued. We were Dapper and the Stooges, it was plain to the eye.

L&L was a detective agency, a clean one for the first time. So clean we didn't have any clients. So we were also a car service, a real one now, one that didn't turn away calls unless we truly were out of cars. Danny was even having flyers printed up, and new business cards, boasting of our economy and efficiency to points all over the boroughs. The Cadillac Minna had bled to death inside was clean now too, part of a small fleet of cars making regular runs between the Cobble Hill Nursing Home on Henry Street and the Promenade Diner at the end of Montague, between the Boerum Hill Inn and stylish apartment buildings along Prospect Park West and Joralemon Street.

As a matter of fact, the Boerum Hill Inn had just closed for the night, and Siobhain was at the door, her eyes dark-circled and her posture rather crushed from the effort of tossing out the tenacious flirting crowd. Gilbert put up a finger to say he'd take the job of driving her home, but first wished to lay his poker hand on the table—it appeared to be one he was particularly proud of. Seeing his recent enthusiasm for chaperoning Siobhain I suspected Gilbert had developed a little crush on her, or maybe it was an old crush he had just allowed to let show, now that Frank wasn't around to needle him constantly that she was playing for the other team.

"Come on, you suckers, I'm calling you," said Gilbert.

"Nothing," said Loomis, bugging his eyes at his hand, trying to embarrass the cards. "Load of crap."

Danny just frowned and shook his head, put his cards on the table. He didn't need poker triumphs just now, he had better things. For all we knew he was folding winning hands just to throw some glory Gilbert's way.

"Forks and spoons," I said, slapping my hand down to show the card faces.

"Jacks and twos?" Gilbert inspected my cards. "That won't do it, Freakshow." He tossed down aces and eights. "Read 'em and scream, like the maniac you are."

*   *   *

Assertions are common to me, and they're also common to detectives. ("About the only part of a California house you can't put your foot through is the front door"—Marlowe, *The Big Sleep*.) And in detective stories things are always *always,* the detective casting his exhausted, caustic gaze over the corrupted permanence of everything and thrilling you with his sweetly savage generalizations. This or that runs deep or true to form, is invariable, exemplary. Oh sure. Seen it before, will see it again. Trust me on this one.

Assertions and generalizations are, of course, a version of Tourette's. A way of touching the world, handling it, covering it with confirming language.

Here's one more. As a great man once said, the more things change, the harder they are to change back.

*   *   *

Within a few days of Gerard's disappearance most of the Yorkville Zendo's students had trickled away. There was a real Zendo on the Upper East Side, twenty blocks south, and its ranks were swelled by defectors from Yorkville seeking truer essences (though, as Kimmery had pointed out, anyone who teaches Zen is a Zen teacher). Those bewildered doormen had all originally been authentic students of Gerard's, it turned out, rudderless seekers, human clay. It was their absolute susceptibility to Gerard's charismatic teachings that made them available to be exploited, first in the Park Avenue building, then as a gang of inept drivers and strong-arms when Gerard needed bodies to fill ranks alongside the Polish giant. Frank Minna had Minna

Men while Gerard had only followers, Zen stooges, and that difference might have determined how the case worked out. That might have been my little edge. It pleased me to think so anyway.

The Yorkville Zendo didn't fold, though. Wallace, that stoic sitter, took over stewardship of what flock remained, though he declined to claim the title of Roshi for himself. Instead he asked to be called *sensei*, a lesser term denoting a sort of apprentice-instructor. So it was that each of the Minna organizations, Frank's and Gerard's, were gently and elegantly steered past the shoals of corruption by their quietest disciples. Of course Fujisaki and The Clients, those vast shadows, crept away unharmed, barely even ruffled. It would take more than the Minna brothers or Lionel Essrog to make a lasting impression.

I learned the fate of the Yorkville Zendo from Kimmery the only time I saw her, two weeks after my return from Maine. I'd been leaving messages on her machine, but she hadn't returned my calls until then. We arranged a rendezvous at a coffee shop on Seventy-second Street, our telephone conversation clipped and awkward. Before I left for the date I took the thoroughest shower I knew how to take, then dressed and re-dressed a dozen times, playing mirror games with myself, trying to see something that wasn't there, trying not to see the big twitchy Essrog that was. I suppose I still had a faint notion we could be together.

We talked about the Zendo for a while before she said anything to suggest she even recalled our night together. And when she did, it was "Do you have my keys?"

I met her eyes and saw she was afraid of me. I tried not to loom or jerk, though there was a Papaya Czar franchise across the street. I was pining for their hot dogs, and it was hard to keep from turning my head.

"Oh, sure," I said. I dropped the keys on the table, glad I hadn't chosen to hurl them into the Atlantic. Instead I'd been burnishing them in my pocket, as I had The Clients' fork once upon a time, each talisman of a world I wouldn't get to visit again. I said good-bye to the keys now.

"I have to tell you something, Lionel." She delivered it with that same hectic half smile that I'd been trying to conjure in my mind's eye for most of two weeks.

"Tellmebailey," I whispered.

"I'm moving back in with Stephen," she said. "So that thing that happened with us, it was just, you know—*a thing.*"

So Oreo Man was a cowboy after all, now striding back in from his sunset backdrop.

I opened my mouth and nothing came out.

"You understand, Lionel?"

"Ah." *Understand me, Bailey.*

"Okay?"

"*Okay,*" I said. She didn't need to know it was just a tic, just echolalia that made me say it. I reached across the table and smoothed the two ends of her collar toward her small, bony shoulders. "Okayokayokayokayokay," I said under my breath.

*   *   *

I had a dream about Minna. We were in a car. He was driving.

"Was I in the Butt Trust?" I asked him.

He smiled at me, liking to be quoted, but didn't reply.

"I guess everybody needs stooges," I said, not meaning to make him feel bad.

"I don't know if I'd put you exactly in the Butt Trust category," he said. "You're a little too strange for that."

"So what am I, then?" I asked.

"I don't know, kid. I guess I'd call you King Tugboat."

I must have laughed or at least smiled.

"That's nothing to be proud of, you radish rosette."

*   *   *

What about vengeance?

I gave it five or ten minutes of my time once. That's a lot, a lifetime, when it comes to vengeance. I had wanted to think vengeance wasn't me, wasn't Tourettic or Essroggian at all. Like the subway, say.

Then I took the V train. I did it with a cell phone and a number in Jersey, I did it standing by a lighthouse in Maine. I did it with a handful of names and other words, strung together into something more effective than a tic. That was me, Lionel, hurtling through those subterranean tunnels, visiting the labyrinth that runs under the world, which everyone pretends is not there.

You can go back to pretending if you like. I know I will, though the Minna brothers are a part of me, deep in my grain, deeper than mere behavior, deeper even than regret, Frank because he gave me my life and Gerard because, though I hardly knew him, I took his away.

I'll pretend I never rode that train, but I did.

*   *   *

The next call that came in that night was a pickup on Hoyt Street for a trip out to Kennedy Airport. It was Loomis who took the call, and he grimaced exaggeratedly when he offered it to the three of us, knowing that according to L&L lore JFK was an exasperating destination. I put up my hand and said I'd take it, just to deny him the point.

For another reason, too. There was a snack I had a hankering for. At the International Terminal at Kennedy, upstairs by the El Al gates, is a single kosher-food stand called Mushy's, run by a family of Israelis, with sauce-spattered metal tins full of stewing kasha and gravy and handmade knishes, a place utterly unlike the chain restaurants elsewhere in the terminal. Anytime I took a passenger out to the airport, night or day, I'd park the car and slip up to Mushy's for a bite. Their chicken shwarma, carved fresh off the roasting pin, stuffed into a pita and slathered in grilled peppers, onions and tahini is one of the great secret sandwiches of New York, redemption for a whole soulless airport. Permit me to recommend it if you're ever out that way.

Kimmery and lemongrass broth hadn't ruined my taste for the finer things.

*   *   *

The ghosts I felt sorriest for weren't the dead ones. I'd imagined Frank and Tony were mine to protect, but I'd been wrong. I knew it now.

It was Julia I couldn't shrug off, though she was hardly more mine than the others, though she'd barely recognized my human existence. Still, my tic of guilt took the form of her shape, standing in the wind on the lighthouse rail, standing still in a mist of bullets and shoes and salt air and my saliva, like the cursed icon from a black-and-white-movie poster she'd resembled when first glimpsed so long ago, or per-haps a figure of Zen contemplation, a mark of ink brushwork on a scroll. But I didn't try to find Julia—simple as it would have been, I knew better than that. Instead I let my obsessive instinct get to work tracing that figure, waiting for it to turn abstract and disappear. Sooner or later it would.

That left who? Only Ullman. I know he haunts this story, but he never came into view, did he? The world (my brain) is too full of dull men, dead men, Ullmen. Some ghosts never even get into your house they are so busy howling at the windows. Or as Minna would say, you pick your battles—and you do, whether you subscribe to that view or not, you really do. I can't feel guilty about every last body. Ull-man? Never met the guy. Just like Bailey. They were just guys I never happened to meet. To the both of them and to you I say: Put an egg in your shoe, and beat it. Make like a tree, and leave. Tell your story walking.

ACKNOWLEDGMENTS

I'm deeply indebted to the books of Lawrence Shainberg, Kosho Uchiyma, and Oliver Sacks, the words of Tuli Kupferberg, and to conversations with Blake Lethem, Cara O'Connor, David Bowman, Eliot Duhan, Matthew Burkhardt, Scott McCrossin, Janet Farrell, Diane Martel, Alice Ressner, and Maureen Linker and the Linker family.

Thanks also to Richard Parks, Bill Thomas, Walter Donohue, Zoe Rosenfeld, Tooley Cottage, the Zentrum für Kunst und Medientechnologie (ZKM) and the Corporation of Yaddo.